THE BIG DREAM

A Raymond Mackey Mystery

Book Three

Owen Thomas

For Marlo

ONE

"I can't breathe. That's the worst of it. Not having the one thing you need most. It's worse than the pain. The pain is what reminds me that I'm still alive. I'll take a lot of pain for a little more air.

"There are two of them. The guy behind me has my neck in a vice of muscle and bone. I'm not a small man, but he's bigger, this guy, a lot bigger. My feet are swinging in mid-air. There's a thick bag over my head that stinks like oily tobacco, motor oil, and death. I can't see anything but stars and I'm starting to see a lot of those. I try to pry the guy's arm loose but he's too strong and I'm too weak, so he keeps on crushing my larynx and I keep on dying. I've still got a grip on Sig, so I try to put a few bullets to good use. Both guys see that coming so they're trying to catch my wrist. I manage to blast a couple holes in my ceiling. It's the only thing I can possibly hit, but they still don't like the idea of me with a gun, so they loosen up my grip by smashing my head into the wall a couple times. Works like a charm. Now my walls and my ceiling have something to talk about. Sig hits the floor, and the stars all start coming together in a light at the end of a tunnel. I go limp and stop resisting, just trying to breathe. The big guy with the iron arm drags me by the neck to the living room and drops me. I fall like it's from two stories up. It takes forever. The edge of my coffee table tries to keep my face from hitting the floor. I can smell enough blood to make me worry and I feel like I'm going to be sick, but all I can do is cough and choke on the air. My lungs can't expand because of the boot-sized piano on my chest. They decide the piano fits better on the side of my face, like maybe the weight will stop the bleeding. It doesn't. And it's a lot more painful, but at least I can breathe. That's about when … when …"

There's the first bead of sweat. Right on cue. It emerges from the base of his graying hairline, above the scar along the nape of his neck. Carefully. Almost bashfully. Like it's ashamed of itself. As if the drop of sweat is an old man emerging naked from a forest. His collar provides full cover as the bead slips away down his back. Then another.

She can't see it, that fugitive bead. How could she? But *I* can see it.

"That's about when … what?" she asks. "Mr. Mackey?"

I see everything. And he hates that. Because then he sees what I see. And what I see is rarely a pretty sight. Doesn't help that I also know what it all means. That nearly invisible twitch of his left eye, for instance. There. And again. That's a referred irritation from the unreachable itch between his shoulder blades. He gets it whenever things get too personal. Too invasive. Like now.

She furrows her brow, just a little.

"Is this making you uncomfortable?"

"No," he lies, as if the tide of panic is not already rising in his chest. As if he has never experienced this tipping point before. As if it's not daily.

I've been up here with my back against the ceiling, waiting for it to happen. His breath is shallowing. His heart is quickening, wanting out of its cage, not keen to hang around for the next part of the story. He'll keep insisting it's just a dream. Like he has imagined the whole thing. He wants to sidestep the PTSD diagnosis on top of the Triple-D diagnosis. Too many letters to spell crazy.

"Keep going," she says.

Ray wants to be done. He needs to be done. The bit about the chainsaw is next. *Take off his legs.* He shakes his head. He keeps shaking it until the words come out.

"No," he says. "No, this is pointless. This is a waste of time. Yours and mine."

He swallows at nothing. He ventures a more direct look across the low table between them with its half-glass of water and its book on Claude Monet and its little, wooden clock. The table and chairs are perfectly framed on the faux Persian.

"Maybe not a waste of *your* time," he corrects. "I take that back. Your time drains down into little gold bars that the boys from Loomis come and haul away to the bank every night."

"Okay." She places the pad and pen on top of *The Artist's Garden at Giverny* and leans back in her cushion, crossing her legs. "So, are you saying you're concerned about the money?"

"No. No more than I am about oxygen. Mostly I'm just concerned about the entire conversation. Look. You do what you do and I'm fine with that. I am. I say good for you. As long as I'm not the person sitting in the chair across from those eyes of yours."

There it is. The beginning of the pivot. The octopus ink. *Let's talk about you,* says the pivot, *not me.*

"Do my eyes bother you?" she asks.

Ray oh-so-casually palms the back of his neck. It's wet with little, naked old men fleeing the forest. He repositions in the chair, drying his palm on his pant leg. He sends out the words, costumed in unconcern.

"I like hazel eyes as much as anyone. They might even be my favorite. But I like 'em best when they disappear every now and then. All that schooling should have included a course or two on blinking."

A rare smile.

"I'll keep that in mind. Maybe it's because I find your story interesting."

"Not a story, doc. It's just a dream."

"So you said. It seems real enough to me."

"Yeah? It's even better with your eyes closed."

"Given your occupational background, I'd normally like to explore the possibility of post-trau …"

"It's just a dream." Too sharp. He tries to soften it. "Okay? A simple dream. One of the annoying kind that never goes away. Like a commercial jingle that sticks in your head for weeks."

She reaches for the porcelain cup on the side table without looking away. Finishes her tea. She cradles the empty cup in her lap with both palms, clicking the rim with a manicured nail, appraising him like he's a forged abstract on the wall of the Louvre.

"So why do you think you don't want to talk about this simple, annoying dream? We've talked about several personal things. Why not that?"

He musters a fleeting amiability. Tries again.

"Look. Doris seems to think you hung the moon. And maybe you did. She was a mess when Buck died. She's okay now and maybe some of that is on you. I'll bet you can talk-therapy the spots right off the leopard. My mistake was unscrewing my head for Doris and giving her a peek inside. She hasn't shut up about it since."

"I suppose she's concerned about you. Tell me about your family."

"That's a short story. Doris and Phil are as close as it gets."

"Phil."

"My cat. Philomena. Point is I get concerned about Doris being concerned. I don't like it much because she doesn't let up. Me coming here to talk to you is my way of unconcerning her."

"So then let's continue with that."

"No. I came. We talked." Ray nods down at the table. "I've been looking at that clock for forty-five minutes and I don't feel a bit different. Now it's time to go tell Doris I'm cured so she can stop worrying."

"Do you think you need to be cured?"

"No more than the rest of humanity. We've all got a version of the same problem."

"Which is?"

"Mortality consciousness. I figure that keeps the pros like you in business eight days a week even if you only work four of them. But for all the talk and all the diplomas and dollars, there's only one real cure. It takes its own sweet time, but that cure is one hundred percent guaranteed."

"I see," she says. "Are you afraid of dying, Mr. Mackey?"

"No. I'm conscious of dying. I'm afraid of getting killed. Listen, doc. Can you call me Mack? Or Ray. Anything but Mr. Mackey. Makes me feel old. I know I'm old, but I like to pretend."

She cocks an eyebrow.

"You think my name is Doc?"

"Point taken. Dr. Warren? Samantha? What do your friends call you right before they leave and never see you again?"

"My friends?"

"Come on. That face? Those eyes? I'm guessing you've got thousands."

Look at him go. You'd think he was trying to make a play from a stool, holding down the bar with his elbows and five empty shot glasses. Devil may care bravado like a paper drink umbrella in a monsoon. Pathetic. He's losing a grip on himself, so he wants to turn the tables. Wants to make it all about her, like maybe she won't notice.

"Sam," she says. "My friends call me Sam."

"Okay, Sam. Swell meeting you. How much do you want me to contribute to your retirement fund?"

"Finish the dream."

"You can stop playing that song, Sam. I'm done."

"Maybe. But the dream is not done with you, Ray. You're working through some real trauma here. Your job, I'm guessing. Or something in your personal life. I don't know you well enough yet. This isn't just going away on its own. Can we talk about Marlo?"

"No."

She gives him a polite smile. She's good enough to know a brick wall when she hits one. And he's good enough to know that he was too emphatic in that answer. Shrinks actually like bumping into brick walls. They live for it. Helps them know what they need to tear down.

"Okay," she says. "But understand something, Ray: the dream you keep having – the dream you are now so afraid of that you don't want to go to sleep – is trying to express something important. You need to understand what it means. We all need to better understand what scares us."

Ray lifts his chin at the window over her shoulder, behind the clean, glass desk that looks like it has never been used. The window looks out over a collection of black iron benches placed, as if at random, around a small, grassy courtyard strewn with young maples. This, presumably, so that the clients of the various professional offices in the business park can sit and contemplate the variety of problems that brought them out here in the first place. The benches are empty now, beneath a slate, gunmetal sky emptying itself over greater Chicago.

"What scares me," he says, "is that it might never stop raining and I'm going to have to backstroke my way home from the bar tonight. Drinking and swimming don't mix."

He waits for a reaction. Anything will do. A laugh. A smile. There isn't one. She just looks at him.

"Because of the swallowing," he adds.

"Some people make jokes when they're frightened," she says at last. "It's a way of deflecting serious things that they don't know how to handle."

"I'm fine. I'll manage."

"Yeah? You'll manage? Okay. Well," Samantha Warren returns the teacup to the table so she can get her smooth, brown fingers involved. "We've established that you're frustrated in your work. You feel like you're surrounded by people who do not like you and would like to see bad things happen to you. You're falling asleep during the day because you're afraid of sleeping at night …"

"Didn't say I was afraid."

"… You're living in a near constant state of hypervigilance. You're depressed – *your* word, depressed – that your crime-writing hobby is not more successful. You're concerned that alcoholism …"

"No, no," he objects, "… that … I was talking about my cat."

"… that alcoholism is on the horizon. You feel like you're increasingly paranoid. You're angry that you can't kick your pack-a-day habit even though your doctor recently found a spot …"

"Shadow. He didn't say spot."

"… a *shadow* on your chest x-ray. And you have a diagnosed dissociative disorder that, by your own estimation, is only getting worse. By your own admission, you've got no friends except Doris and Phil. You're so lonely you've given pet names to your gun and your car. We don't have to start with the dream, Ray. Choose any one of those other threads and let's give it a tug. Pick one."

"Thank you. No."

"Is it that you don't trust me?"

"I trust you enough."

"Come on, Ray," she says with a half-cocked smile. "Meet me halfway here. You saying you didn't run every background check on me that you know how to run before even making this appointment? That why you staked out my parking lot for two hours before coming in here today? And yesterday too, outside my house?"

Ray pulls a face.

"You don't miss much, do you?"

"No. Stop following me."

"Okay. I'm sorry. I guess I trust you about as much as I trust anyone else that I don't know."

"Better."

Ray lets a long breath out of his nose and leans back in his chair. He's dead tired. He's living on four hours of sleep a day, most of that sitting up. He wants to close his eyes. He doesn't dare. He stares across the table. She doesn't flinch.

"Last guy I saw ..."

"Dr. Lindstrom."

He nods.

"I made that appointment at gunpoint. It was either that or get fired, but they did that anyway. Lindstrom dressed me up as crazy and then shared the pictures so they could kick me off the force and have a good laugh while doing it. So, no, I don't have a lot of trust for you people."

"You people?"

He's not choosing his words. He holds up his hands. No offense intended.

"Relax, Sam. It's not a black woman doctor thing. It's a shrink thing. Sorry. Mental health professional."

"And yet, here you are. Not at gunpoint."

"Like I said, you owe Doris a referral fee. I'm trying to put her mind at ease."

She thinks in silence, looking at him until she's ready. Then she tucks a soft, brown sheaf of hair behind her left ear.

"Is it possible, Ray, that Doris simply gave you permission? That she gave you the reason you needed to try to help yourself? Is it possible that the person who is most worried about what fate has in store for you is ..." She lets it hang. Then points. "... you?"

She leans forward in her chair, elbows to knees, interlacing her pampered fingers. Ray doesn't move.

"I'm guessing that with a bad case of Depersonalization-Derealization Disorder – triple D, as you call it – you can't get away from yourself. Not without enough booze to knock your lights out. That makes sleep your only escape. But sleep is where the dream is waiting. It's like escaping into a cage where some wild animal is waiting to tear you apart. The only thing worse than being awake is being asleep. And the triple D means you're keeping your own company in the worst of all possible ways."

I resent the implication. I'm the only friend Ray's got.

Where is she when the phone rings and there's no one on the other end? I'm right here. Where is she? When the bullets start flying. When the Camels are dead, and the bottle runs dry. I'm here, where is she? When every friend Ray's ever had wants to read his name in the obits. Where is she? Where?

I say *she*. Not Sam. I know where Sam is. Drinking her tea on the couch. I'm talking about Marlo. Where is she? Gone. Gone forever is where she is. Miserable company or not, I'm all the guy's got left. So excuse me if Madam Shrink here wants to brush me off the map as bad company.

"Is it possible, Ray, that *you're* the one who's worried and that it's *you*, not Doris, who won't shut up about it? You, talking to you?"

Outside the sky slips a shade darker. The rain comes harder, like the heavens are just beginning to tilt. Ray laughs a little and stands with something like a sideways smile. She gives him her best look of disappointment.

"Mr. Mackey. Ray. Come on now."

He turns and walks across the office for the coatrack. He puts on his coat and hat. The last look doesn't last long.

"Thanks, Sam," he says. "Time for a swim."

TWO

The streets are gray sea lanes, choked with submarines. Nobody knows how to drive under water any better than they do on dry land. The traffic lights are just as discretionary, maybe more so. All the sea captains need anger management. Nothing new, just wetter.

I hiss past the old Methodist church on 153rd. It hasn't been a church for ten years. It's a rehab joint now. The circle of junkies across the street, huddled together in the rain, gives it away. Someone in the circle wants one last hit of juice before going inside and trying to be someone else. For as long as that will last.

The roads on this side of town are about as level as a bowl of noodles. The nose of my Impala dips into a small lake. I lose the junkies and the church and the rest of the city in another wave across the windshield. The wipers only know one speed these days. Too slow to keep up. That feels familiar. I find the half-empty pack above the visor, knock out a Camel and pat myself down for a flame.

Dr. Feelgood is suddenly in my head with that look of his, yellow-stained eyeballs climbing over the top of his glasses for a higher perch from which to judge. His real name is Dr. Jha. First name, Dinesh. Short little Indian guy wearing a pair of John Lennon's specs, curry on his breath and an extra white office in one of the buildings behind Mercy General. I call him Feelgood because of the bouncy tone in his voice whenever he gives me bad news. His favorite word these days is *shadow*. Second and third places both go to the word *cancer*. I try to tell Feelgood that bullets are faster than shadows, but he's not big on listening.

I let the Camel dangle high and cold for a couple of wet miles, then I nose it down into my shirt pocket, tucking it away for later.

I pass a uniform on the side of the road standing next to a white Tundra, trying to write out a ticket under a waterfall. The driver is a muscle-pig in a wife-beater and a Cubs hat. He seems happy to be warm and dry. I change lanes to avoid a fantail but the guy behind me gets the cop anyway.

Poor wet hump. That wasn't on the academy brochure.

I check my mirrors again. I don't mind being followed by strangers, as long as they eventually hit the turn signal and go their own way; live their own miserab lives and show no special interest in mine. It's the people who know my name, driving cars I've seen before. They get under my skin. I haven't spotted anyone since leaving Sam the Shrink, but they're out there. I can feel them.

Who is the question. I don't know who. Somebody's goon. Or some cop earning a little extra scratch, or just out feeling the hate, looking for an opportunity to use me for target practice. Probably a few hundred of those who fit that bill. I also know a bad reporter who just can't seem to get enough of me. Could be him again. Could be any one of them back there someplace. It's somebody. Maybe all of them, cutting each other off, jockeying for the best view of my taillights.

Who they work for is another question, and it's anybody's guess at this point. Big Man. Or Frenchie Marie. Or maybe someone under cover for Chandler PD or Chicago PD or the OAG, working one of the investigations with my name on the folder. There's also a judge out there who hates me. Maybe she hired someone to keep tabs. Could be. All I know is that it's somebody. Somebody good enough to know how not to be seen.

And then there's me. I'm back there too, following myself like a balloon on a string, full of opinions. Like that doesn't get old.

I pull the wheel at the St. Vincent DePaul Distribution Center, hooking the Impala to the south on Clarendon. Laurel and Hardy are trying to wrestle a mattress out of a green van. In this rain, the thing is getting heavier by the second. Laurel shoots me a pained expression as I pass. I want to tell him that St. Vincent's charitable heart does not extend to mattresses. But then what do I know? Maybe St. Vinny's got a soft spot for waterbeds.

I stay on Clarendon, checking my mirrors the whole way. Still no one I recognize. Another ten minutes brings the Golden Arches into view over the hood. I pull into the drive-thru lane and wait my turn to order a cup of coffee. I'd ask for extra caffeine if there was such a thing, but there isn't. Not at McDonald's. At the window, I hand over Abe Lincoln along with the photo of Suri eating a Bic Mac.

"Ever seen her before?" I ask the greasy kid in the headset. He's got an ear full of shrapnel and some Sanskrit word tattooed on his neck. He gives me my change as he looks at the photo, then holds up a finger.

"That's two Double Quarter Pounders with cheese, one Big Mac, three large fries, one chocolate shake with extra whip, one strawberry shake with extra whip, and four apple fritters. Anything else?"

I hazard a glance in the rearview. Forrest green Volvo. A white-haired woman who looks to be early seventies has the wheel. I don't see anyone else in the car.

I'm guessing that either Pops is waiting at home with a couple of extra-large grandkids or she's trying to kill herself with food.

"That'll be $43.06 at the next window." He looks down at me for the first time. "Sorry. What now?"

I point at the sheet of paper in his hand.

"Ever seen that woman?"

"You a cop?"

"As a matter of fact."

I indulge the squinty eyed once-over that lasts far too long. Then I hold up a badge to speed things along.

"Not really," he says after a longer look at the photo.

"Does *not really* mean sort of?"

"It means I recognize the table." He taps the image. "That's our table. But her?" He shakes his head. "I don't know, man. I only work the window. You should ask someone who works the counter."

I don't tell him that I've already asked everybody that works the counter. He reaches out with the photo. I take it and tap my neck with my finger.

"What's the tat' say?" I ask. He touches his own neck like he's forgotten all about the ink.

"No excuses," he says. I must look dubious. "I was drunk," he adds. "Next window, man."

I collect the coffee and circle the Impala around the building. I slip into my usual parking spot and cut the engine. Someone turns the rain up a notch.

From here I get two good views for the price of one.

To my right, I can see all the tables inside the front windows of the Clarendon Street McDonald's, including the corner table where Suri got herself caught on camera, alive it turns out, going to town on a Big Mac while keeping both eyes peeled for whatever may be happening across the street.

Which is the other great view from this spot: straight ahead, through the front windshield and across two lanes of traffic, the parking lot for the Blue Lotus Dry Cleaners.

I'd been close to concluding that Suri was just one of those characters in a man's past he never sees or hears from again. Dead would have been my guess; a hole in the back of her head, covered in trash in some landfill between Chicago and Cape Cod, one shoe on and the other in the back of someone's trunk. If Big Man wants you dead, that's the way things tend to go.

But Suri's not dead. Not if Frenchie Marie's photo is real. Suri's in the pink, alive and well, eating poorly, and staking out Mayor Royce's dry cleaner. I keep hoping she shows up again so I can buy her a burger and catch up a little. If Frenchie's boys can get her into a viewfinder, maybe I can get her in the car and take her someplace for a long talk.

Although finding her, if that's possible, will be easier than talking to her, since Suri must hate me six ways from Sunday. After the bloodbath in Bloomington, who could blame her? I was the one who put her in the trunk and sent her to Bloomington in the first place. I thought I was saving her life, not saving her for Big Man.

But Suri doesn't know that. How could she?

So I keep coming back to the Clarendon McDonald's. Sitting and smoking and waiting and hoping. Three, four times a week. Sometimes more. It's turning into a habit. Sometimes I even order the food. The kids inside behind the counter are starting to recognize me. I'm the old cop with the picture. I figure if I keep this up the McDonald's corporation will eventually name another burger after me. I need to make a pitch for royalties.

I shouldn't be so surprised she's alive. Suri's always been a survivor. Dancer, hooker, snitch, addict, mob target, Suri has found a way to beat the odds and stay alive at every turn since she hit the streets at sixteen. She unofficially changed her name from Courtney Briggs to Ginger Turner so she could unofficially lose her clothes in strip dives all over Chicago without anyone in her former life catching wise. I don't know much of anything about the stepfather she left behind. I don't need to. That story is as old as the hills.

Stripping started all the wrong heads turning her way. Then she started turning tricks and robbing johns. Ginger was her stripper name. She wanted a new name for the new racket. Turns out that Suri is the Japanese word for pickpocket. Clever. She's about as Japanese as I am. Seems the Japanese guys touring the Chicago sex trade forget all about their pockets when Suri is in the room, doing her thing. As john demographics go, the Japanese aren't violent, they don't complain, and they cling to shame like grim death, which makes them perfect marks for an enterprising sex worker.

Suri made a bundle. For a street hustler? Please. A bundle. Better than most. Then she spent too much of it on heroin, along with every other drug on the street. Didn't take long for the addiction to take off the weight and add the mileage. She lost her curves and the shine in her eyes. She started looking like an old mop with a bad dye job that someone had leaned up against an alley wall. But then she beat the junk. Cleaned herself up on her own steam. No rehab clinic for Suri. Cold turkey all the way. She left the addiction at the curb and kept on moving. Not easy. That takes some iron.

In thirty years working homicide, Suri was the best informant I ever had. Hands down the best. Always delivered. Sure, I kept her off the books, unregistered, which was strictly against department policy. But those were her terms and I honored them. Honor for honor, promise for promise, strictly professional. We had a good thing going, me and Suri. I paid top dollar out of my own pocket, and she told me the secrets of the street so the homicide squad and I knew where to go fishing. The boys all wanted to know my source. But I stayed true to the deal. I kept her out of it.

That was another life. Things change in a hurry. Marlo gets murdered by her own pancreas. I get fingered as a mole for the mob and booted into early retirement. Suri ends up pulling the mayor's dry-cleaning ticket out of the pocket of a monster. I'm lucky to not be in prison and Suri's lucky to be eating Big Macs. And Marlo? Well, maybe she's just lucky not to be here.

The tables inside are full of people who will live their entire lives without ever being confused for a sex worker on the run from the cops and the mob. Same as always.

Across the street, the Blue Lotus parking lot is mostly empty. Two or three cars trading out every few minutes. People go in with bags and come out with flat boxes or with plastic over hangers. About what you'd expect for a dry cleaner. The building is low and flat, squatting beneath a large crabapple that will start showering pink blossoms in another month. That assumes it ever stops raining long enough to give photosynthesis a fighting chance.

The idea of another long wait in the rain for nothing makes my fingers restless. They know where to find the Camel and the lighter, so they busy about getting everyone in position. I open the window a crack and light the flame. That's when I see the folded piece of paper on the dash, tucked neatly beneath yesterday's *Trib*. I let the flame die and put the cigarette back to bed. I already know what the white square of paper is without having to reach for it. I reach anyway.

I open it to find my boss staring at me. The photo is enlarged and grainy, but clear enough. Orland Twill is sitting ramrod straight like a pool cue in the passenger seat of a white Hyundai Sonata. The driver's seat belongs to a woman half his age. Light skin. Dirty-blonde curls to the shoulder and a face for trouble. Twill is looking straight ahead, almost like he can see the zoom lens pointed at him fifty yards away. The woman is in profile, looking at him. No one said cheese.

I take a cursory look around the car, just to see if Frenchie Marie's boys left me anything else. If you're going to break into a guy's car while he's in fencing with a shrink, you need to make it worth his while. But I come up empty.

I drink my coffee and look again at the photo. The dirty blonde has something red around her neck. Not a necklace. It's wide and flat and cheap. Looks like a lanyard to me. Whatever is hanging from the other end is too low to be in the photo. I'm guessing it's a badge with a chip in it that gets her access to places other people can't go. That makes her either government or corporate. Or she's in town for a convention and the thing around her neck just identifies her as part of the gaggle. I have no idea.

But Twill does. He's full of ideas. Look at those eyes.

What's this about, boss? Sex? Business? Is she a source? Your handler? What exactly is she handling? Does she make you feel dirty or important? Both maybe.

Twill's not talking.

My phone suddenly wants attention. It counts to three before I can fish it out of my pocket and open it up.

"Where the hell are you?" Twill is talking. It's like the universe wants a voice to go with the photo.

"Hey, LT. Just leaving the dentist."

"You need a better lie, Mack. I've seen your teeth. The dentist thing isn't working."

"I was just leaving the proctologist."

"Better. You missed your OAG follow-up. They aren't happy."

"They're never happy. And I didn't miss it. I told them I needed to reschedule. Their left isn't talking to the right."

I set the folded sheet of paper on the dash above the steering wheel. The intensity of Twill's eyes boring out through the windshield of the white Sonata makes his voice feel telepathic.

"These are not people you want to piss off, Mack. A state-level corruption probe is as serious as it is rare. The politics are bad from every direction. That means you can bet everybody's ass is chapped and no one is playing around."

"I never suggested …"

"The whole Russian doll fiasco was yours. Okay? You own all of it. And either you help OAG make sense of it or the state of Illinois will hang the whole thing around your neck. We talked about this."

Twill's irritation comes through loud and clear. He's past wanting to cut me loose. He's fired me once already, and he doesn't like that he had to unfire me. He doesn't know why the Chief wants me to stay. I don't know why either. I doubt the Chief even knows why. Only Frenchie Marie knows, and she doesn't talk much. What she does better than anything, apparently, is pull strings attached to important puppets.

"It's nice to know you still care," I say.

"I don't. I've got too much to do to care. I'm done caring. But when you miss an interview, Mack, my phone rings."

My focus is still on the photo. The rain beats furiously against the glass like it wants to erase the ink. I want to ask Twill about the dirty blonde with a face for trouble and a neck for lanyards. I want to ask him about a lot of things. I want to ask him all over again about the bloodbath in Bloomington. I want to ask him about the Blue Lotus. But none of that's going to make him any happier.

"I'll call Brewster directly," I say. "His messengers aren't so good with messages. Sorry about the mix-up, LT."

"Good. Another thing."

"Yeah."

"Santiago tells me he heard from his sources that the forensics came back with nothing usable on any of those hotel rooms out in Aurora. Some prints but nothing in the system."

"All those prints belong to fingers born in other countries. Coming to Chicago for sex wasn't their idea."

"I haven't talked with the feds, but you can bet that there's no human trafficking investigation unless they find Nadia King and the other one, what's her name."

"Mila Kozlova."

"Mila. Thought you'd want to know."

"Everybody's in the wind. No one wants to be found. Me either, but I'm too old and slow to be in the wind, so I have to hang around and answer all the questions."

"I hope you're not looking for sympathy," he says.

"No. It's my mess. Like you said. And no surprise on the forensics. José Beggemon doesn't leave any trail he doesn't want you to follow."

"No, no. I'm not talking about Big Man. I'm done with that, Mack. Your obsession with that … that …"

"Threat to civilization?"

"… urban legend, is what put you, and everyone else, in this mess. Save it for Halloween. I don't want to hear it. What I want …"

"Is to see my wrinkled ass in my chair working my case load. I got that, LT."

"Then why is your chair empty? Never mind. I don't want to know. Just get here. Call Brewster first. Then get here."

I end the call and dial Dan Brewster's number. He's not in the answering mood. I leave a message apologizing for the miscommunication and offer myself up at the convenience of the OAG Special Investigations team. Bunch of jackals if you ask me, but they've got a job to do and I was, in fact, the guy who whacked the hornets' nest with his own head. So I do owe them as much cooperation as I can stomach.

Across the street, a perfectly normal looking woman exits the Blue Lotus, stepping out into the deluge. She holds her plastic-wrapped, newly dry-cleaned clothing over her head to keep from getting soaked as she bolts for her car. She drops her keys, and then everything comes undone. Now she's as angry as I am bored. I don't know what I'm looking for.

I fish the Camel out of my shirt pocket and put it where it belongs, again, feeling around in my coat for the lighter. My hand is in the wrong pocket, so I end up finding the thing I have taken to avoiding. I pull it out into the gloom of the car, looking at it like it might bite. Because it does.

It's a folded piece of paper, just like the one on the dash, also from Frenchie Marie, but this one has a different photo printed inside. I look at the perfect white square between my fingers. I don't unfold it. I don't need to. I see it in the sleep I never get any more. Marlo's in there. Sitting at the winner's table full of losers, champagne all around; graft, corruption and every kind of savage violence raising a glass to the future. The eventual mayor of Chicago looks so pleased his face might break open. But I never spend much time on that side of the table. Most of my focus is on the near side, closer to the camera. My wife's beautiful face in profile. Her hair. Her back. Her hand resting comfortably beneath that of a younger, but no less sinister, Victor Roby.

Whatever it is Frenchie Marie wants me to do – spy on my lieutenant, become the police department mole I have always insisted I am not, whatever it is – she knew this photo would get me to do it.

I lay my head back against the seat, Camel jagging between my lips with lack of purpose. The rain on the roof is loud and steady, registering in my chest more than my ears. It's got the feeling of something biblical. My eyes burn for sleep. I close them for a single second that stretches away from me like black bubblegum twirling around a finger.

The dream is waiting for me, like always, in complete blackness on the floor of my living room. I smell motor oil and stale cigarettes. I can taste my own blood.

There are two of them. One has a boot on my face. *Take off his legs*, he says, just before the chainsaw clears its throat.

I come awake with a jolt, Camel bent and in my lap. I'm breathing in quick, shallow gulps, heart rabbiting to keep pace with the fury of rain. The memory of a scream is all around me. My scream.

I straighten myself in the seat. Rub my hands over my face. They come back wet. I take a deep breath and let it go, reaching for the cup. The coffee is cold enough to make me wonder how long I was out. Too long and not long enough. The sky is now close to dark. I have that slightly queasy feeling in my gut that sometimes reminds me I'm hungry and other times reminds me that I'm mortal.

I check my mirrors and my perimeter. The rain ratchets up another notch, making it a curtain that brings down the last shreds of day in slick, gleaming streams, washing away all the color from a world now made of headlights.

A twist of the wrist and Paula roars back to life. I ease her out into the stream of anonymous traffic and head for the office.

THREE

The next day is as soggy, dark, and sleepless as the last dozen. The sun needs an antidepressant. It broods in its bed of grimy gray cumulus and the world glints back in wet streaks of borrowed light. All the streets hiss beneath my tires like a bed of angry snakes.

Fisher Freed meets me in the lobby of the building that the Department of Special Investigations for the Office of the Attorney General of the great state of Illinois calls home.

"Mr. Mackey," Fisher says from too far away, voice bounding off the marble walls. I get some looks from whatever the plural is for a group of lawyers. A suit of lawyers. A case. A bowel. That's it: a bowel movement of lawyers.

Fisher extends a hand like a pier attendant looking for me to throw him a bow line. We've spoken briefly on the phone. He doesn't look like he sounds. I'm pretty sure I look exactly like I sound. I cross the lobby and squeeze his hand.

"Good to meet you in person," he says.

He's younger than I imagined, and leaner than your average union rep. My dues have always bought me ex-cops, bruisers washed out of the service because of injury or excessive-force jackets or both, usually deep in the grips of a daily baker's-dozen habit that has left them doughy and bitter and full of back-in-the day bravado about the streets of Chicago, burning with apocryphal stories of near-death experience. I'm guessing Fisher here has never seen the inside of a squad car. He wouldn't know the street if he tripped over the curb. I'm guessing daddy wanted him to go to law school but working the grievance mill for the IFOP was as close as he could come.

"You ready for this?" Fisher asks, bumping the elevator button with his elbow.

"Sure," I say. "Can I bum a blindfold and a cigarette?"

"Oh, you'll do fine. Just don't lie about anything. Don't hand them an obstruction case. Easy-peasy."

"Says the guy not allowed to do anything except take notes."

We step on the elevator and Fisher lights up a button. I wait until the doors are closed.

"Look," I say, "I'm not nervous. I'm annoyed. Big difference, kid. I've been playing this game since you were a gleam in your mother's eye. I don't need a pep talk or a reminder of the rules."

"Okay."

"You IFOP boys always seem to come off as a few pancakes short of a full stack."

"The F is for fraternal, so …"

"The F is for flat and covered in syrup. The F is for fuck me if I can find someone to do the job. Because you boys always seem to come in one of two flavors: either hyper-aggressive or glib. So far, I figure you for the latter. Your predecessor was the other kind. Dan Brewster's an asshole but he's got a job to do. I respect that. His job is to decide whether he wants to eat me for lunch. My job is to come off as unappetizing."

"And my job?"

"Try not to stimulate his appetite. Take a good set of notes. Stay out of the way. I get that I'm entitled to have a rep in the room for anything that might be disciplinary. An OAG criminal corruption investigation probably qualifies. If I was a smart man with a lot of money, I'd have swapped you out for a barracuda with a JD and a three-piece suit. But I'm not especially smart and the last barracuda I hired swam off with a mouthful of my savings. Sure, I'll take what the IFOP owes me. Why not? But I don't want you in the way in there. If I want your advice, I'll lean over and ask you for it. If our shoulders aren't touching …"

"You don't want my advice."

"You catch on quick," I say with an encouraging nod. The distance between the seventh and ninth floors is awkwardly quiet. "I don't know why the union keeps swapping out my reps, but your predecessor was an ass. All big, swinging dick and no common sense. Couldn't shut up to save his life. He hurt more than he helped. I came down on him pretty hard, which maybe is why you're here pushing elevator buttons and not him. But when you see him at the watercooler, he'll tell you I have less than no tolerance for bullshit." I poke myself in the chest with my own thumb. "It's my ass in there. No offense."

"None taken," Fisher says with a shrug. "What else?"

"Brewster thinks like a prosecutor. He wants documents. They always think there's a piece of paper or a text or an email out there that'll make the case. Breadcrumbs that will connect me to some lowlife working the dark end of the street."

"Like Cosmo Green, you mean."

He says it without hint of malice and the elevator keeps climbing like it didn't just take on the extra weight of my entire career. I should be satisfied he's done his homework on my history. My name in Cecil Green's phone is required reading for anyone looking to understand why Dan Brewster is salivating on the twenty-third floor and why half the force thinks I was, and always will be, a traitor. I stop looking at the elevator buttons and turn to look at the dark button-eyes on either side of Fisher Freed's pert button nose.

"Yeah," I say, controlling my anger. "Like Cosmo Green. Only those were fake breadcrumbs and this time there aren't any. They've already dragged my phone and my email accounts. All of it. There isn't anything out there that they haven't seen. It's more likely, Fisher," I point to the ceiling, "it is more likely, that this elevator will shoot through the top of the building and go to the moon than it is that Dan Brewster will decide to not ask for more documents or data. So, when he does, I want him to get four convincing eyerolls, two of yours and two of mine. I'm done with the document requests. He's fishing, Fisher. Understand?"

"Got it."

Dan Brewster is reading a magazine in the small, holding cell inspired lobby that the OAG Special Investigations team uses to make people feel welcome. No windows. No art. Six chairs along two walls separated by a low table that holds a few coasters and several news magazines up off the industrial gray carpet. On the far wall is a scanner next to a steel security door. Two of the upper corners of the room sport small black security cameras, no doubt equipped with sensitive microphones, just in case people feel like getting the truth out of their system before trying to lie their way through an interview. Brewster turns the page and keeps reading before looking up.

"You're early," he says, finally lifting his face. He's got the kind of chin with more than a little cleft in it, like maybe he lost a hatchet throwing contest when he was a kid. But it goes nicely with the square jaw, and the piercing green eyes that he stole from a feral cat, and the stiff shelf of sandy brown hair you could crack an egg on. Dan Brewster always reeks of expensive cologne and cheap ambition. He thinks the guy in the mirror is AG material. Could be right about that. Brewster cocks an eyebrow.

"The office pool had six-to-one odds that you'd no-show us again."

"Did you win or lose?"

"I knew you'd show," he says, following up with a little smile. "But then, I won last time too."

I get out of my raincoat and leave it to drip on the floor from an ugly brass tree. Brewster leads us through the security door, down a warren of narrow white halls, to a conference room that looks out over the rain-soaked steel and glass of West Loop Chicago. The table comes complete with coffee, water and Dan's right-hand man, Connor Knobb, who is busy wrangling an intimidating stack of case files, full of irregularly protruding red adhesive flags. All for show, of course. *Look at all the things we know about you.*

Judging from our previous chats, Connor's mission is to make Dan Brewster look good, which maybe explains the low affect, the lower IQ, and the catcher's mitt face all wrapped up in the charm of leftover meatloaf.

"Connor," I say in greeting. "You're right where I left you. Don't they let you go home every now and then?"

He stays focused on leafing through one folder after another, not acknowledging us with anything more than a flick of his eyes and a head nod. Brewster is asking his first question before the door is closed and either of us have pulled out a chair.

"Here's what I still don't get," he says as Fisher pours me a cup of coffee and takes his seat. "This whole thing starts with an off-the-books investigation for your brother-in-law's fuck buddy. Nadia King."

"Late brother-in-law."

"Yeah? They find a body?"

"Matter of time," I say, thinking of Jimmy and wondering how it ended for him. How many trunk rides did it take before Jimmy Kline was delivered to the promised land? Well. Landfill. "Anyway, yeah. So?"

"So either you were moonlighting in blatant disregard of department policy, or you got approval from your chain of command. One of those possibilities looks a whole lot worse for you than the other."

"I told my LT I was looking into something for a friend of a friend. I didn't give him the rest. Not until much later."

"And he was okay with that? With not knowing?"

"He gave me some rope. Seemed okay."

I act like I don't see the point of the question. Truth is, Twill's willingness to let me off leash to help Nadia always struck me as odd. The Orland Twill I thought I knew is as by-the-book as it ever gets. And yet, he sticks his neck out to bring me into IAD – me, a guy everyone thinks is covered in the stink of corruption – only to let me wander around Chicago looking for a thing that may have looked like a Russian doll but that may as well have been a hand grenade dropped into the in-box of the Illinois justice system. None of it would have happened if Twill had refused to turn a blind eye.

"You sure about that?" Brewster asks.

"About what?"

"That you told him. That he shrugged you his approval for something contrary to policy that he never should have approved."

"My LT didn't know any details," I say. "Hell, I didn't either at that point. All I knew was that Nadia King needed help springing her mother's Russian doll from the Chicago evidence lock up. The fuller briefing came later."

"Later." Brewster cuts a glance across the table to Connor who shakes his ugly head. It's like they're watching a five-year-old lie about the crayon marks on the wall.

"Yeah," I say. "Later."

"Before or after you showed him fabricated evidence that a sitting judge and the Mayor of Chicago were on a mob payroll?"

"That was the fuller briefing."

Brewster flips back and forth through a notepad, snapping through the pages until he finds whatever it is he's looking for. Then he pushes the pad aside and leans back, crossing his arms so his suitcoat puckers at the shoulders.

"Okay," he says. "Let's just back up and review for a second. Nadia King, a woman you say you did not know and who just so happens to be banging your brother-in-law, shows up out of the blue and asks you to find her mother's antique Russian doll. She says it has been lost in the CPD evidence lock-up ever since Wayne Bishop was tried for the murder of her famous cop brother, Joe Novak. You find the doll, stolen from lock-up by a three-time loser named Casey Sweet to give to his girlfriend. You take the doll to Nadia King's mother, Ivah, who pulls a flash drive out of its ass ..."

"It just kinda fell out, actually."

"You download the data on the drive and rush the spreadsheet into HQ. And the spreadsheet shows ..." Brewster extends a finger spasm to Connor, who opens a file and hands over a sheet of paper with a red flag on it. "The spreadsheet data shows a whole long list of people who, apparently, or at least so it seems to you, are on the take, notably including Judge Jolie and Mayor Royce. And that marks the first occasion on which you advise your chain of command what you had been up to."

"Essentially. Yes."

"Essentially."

"Yes. Full stop."

"Okay. And as a result of that breathless conversation, word goes out to the powers that be and Judge Jolie, a very tough-on-crime sort of jurist, is immediately suspended from her entire criminal docket, resulting in all manner of case reassignments, delays and suspensions, and one," Dan Brewster holds up a manicured index finger, "one mistrial: the State of Illinois vs. Wrigley Menard, a murder case which just happened to involve late-developing allegations of Chandler Police Department corruption. A case in which, just coincidentally," the finger again, "*coincidentally*, according to a very angry Judge Jolie, you had been taking a rather daily devoted interest. Is all of that also true, Detective? *Essentially*, I mean?"

"I guess."

"You guess. Well, that's a whole lot of serendipity for an out-of-the-blue, off-the-books, contrary-to-policy investigation into the whereabouts of a Russian doll."

"Well jeez, Dan, the way you say it makes it sound suspicious."

"Doesn't it though?"

"Yeah. Makes it sound like I set out to shitcan what was going to be a lot of ugly testimony about police department corruption, and to make life-long enemies of a tough-on-crime judge and, also, just for fun, the Mayor of Chicago. And hey, the plan worked. Which I guess makes me brilliant."

"That the truth?" he asks, knowing better than to think I've just handed him a confession.

"I look brilliant to you, Dan? Connor here has a brain that runs circles around mine. He's got, like, the Usain Bolt of brains over there." I jerk my chin at the stack of files. "Just look at all those red flags sticking out. You help him with those or is that all him?"

"This is serious, Mack."

"Damn right it is. Any one of those flags stuck to something that suggests I can play this kind of three-dimensional chess?"

Dan Brewster looks pensively out the bank of windows. On a clear day even an old pair of eyes can make it over the river, across South Michigan to Grant Park. Butler Field. Millennium Park. Then drop right into the lake. Not today. Today it's like looking into the window of a washing machine at a low rent laundromat, dingy sheets tangling around Willis Tower, pillowing down into a sloppy, churning mess over the Chicago Board of Trade. The parks and the lake are just gloomy abstractions to be taken on faith without hard proof. Brewster clears his throat.

"What those little red flags suggest, rather emphatically, is that everyone who might be able to validate your story is conveniently dead or missing." He starts flicking fingers into the air like they're spring-loaded. "Nadia King, an illegal who it turns out is not actually the daughter of Ivah Novak, is missing. Mila Kozlova, missing. Ivah Novak, dead. Casey Sweet, dead. Your brother-in-law, Jimmy Kline …"

"Dead."

"Well. Missing for now. Burkhart Lang, the guy you claim was behind almost all of it, including the alleged trafficking of Nadia and Mila, dead."

"Burkhart. Yeah, Burkhart's *really* dead. His friends called him Hell. That was before they broke him in half and stuffed him in the back seat of an ugly champagne Malibu."

Brewster looks at his fingers like he's forgotten how to count. Connor snaps a file out of the stack, opens it, and slides it sideways across the table so Brewster can see. I steal a quick look over at Fisher. He's scribbling the names on a legal pad. He catches my glance and rolls his eyes dramatically with a little shake of his head. Quietly supportive, just like I asked.

"Right," says Brewster, flipping up another finger. "Steven King, Nadia's husband, the guy you claim was in league with Burkhart … sorry, in league with Hell … to manipulate Nadia into stringing you along, also dead. Then there's Garrett Hoosier, the guy you claim was an important cog in Hell's human trafficking machine, missing."

"Nah." I give Brewster a painful wince. "Garrett's certainly dead by now. You just haven't found the body yet. Not the smartest, Garrett. Addicted to frozen lasagna and bad decisions. Playing hide and seek was not his best move. The man had a lot to trade. Should have angled for witness protection. I'm guessing you'll find him one piece at a time."

Another finger.

"Donald Pleasants, the pornographer you claim as the reason you were so devotedly attending the Curtis Root murder trial …"

"Scooter. Yeah. He's dead."

"Right. Dead. With you as a suspect."

"Come on, Dan. That just makes you sound desperate. Chandler Homicide cleared me of Scooter and you know it."

"I look like Chandler Homicide to you?" he asks.

"No. You look like someone too busy to be rummaging through Stretch Martin's cleared suspect list just to shake me up. You don't need that, Dan." I nod at his hands frozen in the airspace above the table. "Look at all those fingers in the air. One more gets you ten."

It gets me a smile he doesn't want to give. The tenth finger joins the others. He shows all of them to me in case I want a recount.

"Billy Wise," he says. "The guy out in Aurora who you claim could have connected Burkhart Lang to the trafficking and drug operations, dead. Point is, there's no one around to sing your song, Mack. Your reputation is not your friend. Hell, your friends aren't even your friends. We've looked around for your actual friends but can't find many. Lot of people out there think you're in the tank, or crazy, or both. Mostly both. Paranoid, they say. Wrong in the head. Conspiracy minded. You see Big Man's shadow around every corner. That kinda thing. Your wife checked out and you sailed off the edge of the world inside a bottle. That's what they tell me."

I give him a shrug.

"Friends are overrated."

"Look. So you're not gonna be prom king. I know the shit people can say and I don't care if you're popular with the cool kids. But I'll be honest here, Mack. I'd be …"

"Honest," I say. "Good. We made it to the honest part."

"I'd be much more inclined to look skeptically at all the bad opinions if I knew why you chose to keep your chain of command out of the loop while you were doll hunting."

"This again."

"Yeah, Mack. This again."

"I don't know how many different ways I can say it. I told my LT what I knew."

"Sure you did. Right after it started raining shit. Right after it was too late to do anything about it."

"I'm gettin' old here, Dan. What do you want?"

"Same thing everybody has always wanted from you, Mack. I want to know who you're working for."

"The taxpayers."

"I have an apoplectic jurist and an upset mayor who think otherwise."

"I know you do. I get that. But they're wrong."

"Good to know. So I can put you down for *not* a puppet on a string."

"I got played, Dan. No question. I made it into the Patsy Hall of Fame. But I was as surprised as anyone else."

"Not the underworld mole everyone believes you are, then? Not an embedded rogue operator."

"Read a lot of fiction?"

"Me? No. I'm strictly a non-fiction guy. History. True crime. But I hear you write mysteries. Is that what you're spinning here? A potboiler about a hapless pawn of a detective? Stupid and unlucky? That you?" Brewster shakes his head, answering his own question. "Not buyin' it. Something tells me you always know what you're doing, Mack. Lots of people hate you; no one has ever made you for stupid or gullible."

"I got into law enforcement because the recruitment poster said I could make a difference. I'd say that's about as stupid and gullible as it ever gets."

"Chain of command. Who did you inform?"

"Christ. I've told you. Go talk to Twill."

"I have. At length. Twill says you disobeyed repeated direct orders to stand down. He says he knew next to nothing about your activities until you produced that fake spreadsheet and the whole department lost its collective shit." Brewster leans forward on his elbows, clasping his hands in front of him. "That makes you look a whole lot like a rogue operator serving someone other than your chain of command. So I'm here to ask you, one last time, for any document, record, recording, data, or anything else that might show your department chain of command was being kept apprised of your investigative activities."

I can feel Fisher's presence next to me grow nearer. Our shoulders are touching. His mouth is at my right lobe.

"I think it's time to play ball, Mack," he whispers. I turn slowly for a better look at the face making the sounds. I whisper back.

"What are you saying?"

"I'm saying give the man what he wants. Do you want to be done with this or not?"

"Of course …" There is more to say, but Fisher Freed, brimming now with an eerily new self-possession, doesn't give me a chance to say it.

"I agree," he says to me, loud enough for all to hear. Turning to Dan Brewster, he removes a sheet of paper from his notebook and slides it forward. Dan has to stand and reach for it across the table. He's reading even as he retakes his seat in a slow-motion descent, face puckering over some incomprehensibility.

"Here's your copy back," Fisher says handing me a sheet. The false implication that I had previously seen and discussed the document with him is not lost on me. It imputes prior knowledge and ownership of the document as well as my intention to disclose it, whatever it is, to the State. As immediately concerning as those implications are, they all take a back seat to me learning what the hell he just handed over to my inquisitors.

It appears to be a copy of an email from Warren Loudermilk, better known around the office as the Chandler Chief of Police.

LT. Twill:

Your briefing last week was much appreciated, as is your fidelity to the Code of Conduct of this department. As you noted in our last IAD Focus session, Detective Mackey seeks to make interagency inquiries into the whereabouts of a missing heirloom allegedly belonging to a Mrs. Ivah Novak. As I understand it, the citizen complainant is Mrs. Novak's daughter, Nadia King, an acquaintance of Det. Mackey's brother-in-law, James Kline.

As you are obviously aware, the proposed investigation is beyond the scope of Det. Mackey's assigned duties for IAD and, therefore, contrary to department policy absent express written permission. Notwithstanding, you have made special request that Det. Mackey be allowed to pursue the investigation. I have already conveyed my misgivings, which I will refrain from reiterating.

You have assured me that, per Det. Mackey, the proposed investigation will require minimal time and resources, will not require the involvement of other IAD or Chandler PD personnel, and that it is highly unlikely to require the surveillance or arrest of criminal suspects. Further, you have assured me that a thorough background review has been conducted into Nadia King and James Kline, that you have personally reviewed the findings of those background reports to your personal satisfaction.

Based on such assurances, and despite my considerable misgivings, you may consider this my approval for Det. Mackey to continue his work in the matter until such time as the investigation is concluded or you decide IAD workload necessitates that this approval be revoked. While Det. Mackey should obviously keep you well-briefed on his investigation, I expect you to keep me briefed with any significant developments.

Brewster is rattling the paper at me before I have finished reading. Connor stretches an arm over the table, but Brewster keeps the page out of reach, wanting to retain possession.

"Is this even real?" he asks. "Why would you sit on this?"

It's all I can do to keep my own confusion locked down.

"Never knew it existed," I say. "Until today."

"Where did you get this?"

"It was on my desk this morning," says Fisher. "Seemed relevant."

"Gee, you think? And no idea where it came from?"

Fisher shrugs. Connor still has his hand out. Brewster drops the page for him to read, refocusing on me.

"Looks like you've got a friend out there after all," he says. "And you had no idea Chief Loudermilk had approved the investigation? Assuming this is authentic."

"Come on, Dan. No."

"And you never briefed the Chief on the doll search?"

"No."

"Did Twill?"

"Did Twill what?"

"Brief Loudermilk."

"Apparently," I say, nodding at the paper in Connor's hands.

"I mean after that."

"No idea. Look, I've told you what I know three different times. Have you interviewed the Chief yet? Even once? Don't answer that. I'm guessing that's next on your list. While you're at it, maybe you should circle back around to Judge Jolie and ask her to pull another theory out of that big black sleeve of hers."

"Theory's the same, Mack. You kept your chain minimally informed, and you did not stand down as instructed. Then out of the blue you produce a bullshit spreadsheet falsely depicting Judge Jolie and Mayor Royce …"

"I presented my findings …"

"You delivered a trojan doll to the doorstep of the Illinois Department of Justice." Not a shout, but it's in the neighborhood.

"I presented my findings promptly to my lieutenant who, in turn, took them directly to Chief Loudermilk, both of whom, as it turns out, were well aware of my search for the doll from the beginning. I had nothing to do with what they decided to do with the spreadsheet data. Not to Monday morning quarterback, but they should have waited. Asked a few questions. Done some digging before they hit the panic button and suspended the good judge."

Brewster snaps the page out of Connor's hands and glowers his way through another silent reading. I spend the time looking sideways at Fisher Freed. I come up with just under a dozen different ways to kill him before he makes it out of the room. Dan Brewster clears his throat again. Something about the surprise is congesting his airway. He flicks the email sideways across the table.

"I think you're going to need another red flag," I say to Connor. He stretches for the email without looking up.

"You don't succeed in my job without developing a nose, Mack," says Dan. "Same is true in your job, I suspect."

"I got one of those. Yeah."

"So then are you smelling what I'm smelling?"

I play dumb. Six wisecracks come to mind, and I let two of them loose. The one about Brewster's aftershave gets a smirk out of Connor Knobb.

But yeah. I smell it. Sure I do. Hard to keep my gut from flipping over every time I take a breath. I used to be able to pin it down. Chase it. Like a dog for a bone. Now it's everywhere. The fix. The rig. The game. The tang of rot. The hollowing stink of decay. It's everywhere. Yeah, I can smell it. The email stinks to holy hell. I tell him I want a copy.

I have to wait until I've been dismissed by Dan Brewster to get some personal private time with Fisher Freed. He doesn't make it halfway down the hall to the elevator before I yank him into the nearest stairwell and back him up against the wall. I wait until the metal fire door clangs shut.

"Tell me why I shouldn't throw you down these goddamned stairs."

Fisher is much too calm. I'm either not as intimidating as I used to be, or he's got some skills I don't yet appreciate. He gives me a sad kind of smile.

"Because you're already in the hot seat, Mack. Killing your IFOP rep isn't going to help. Besides, I just made your life a little easier in there. Turns out the Chief approved your investigation. Who knew?"

"Why didn't you give me the email before?"

"Because you wouldn't have turned it over. Like I said, it's time to play ball. Withholding requested evidence is not a good move."

He starts to maneuver past me, but I shove him back against the wall.

"Who the fuck do you work for, Fisher? No bullshit this time."

"You, Mack. I work for you."

"Not anymore you don't."

"The question on everybody's lips is who do *you* work for," he says.

"Nobody, goddamnit. I'm obviously on my own here."

A sharp, loud clang rises up the stairwell from somewhere below us like a metal bubble. I jolt sideways in a half-turn, still holding Fisher against the wall with one arm and feeling for the gun I don't have.

Sam-the-shrink might call it paranoia. Or a chronic lack of sleep that keeps me hypervigilant. Doesn't really matter. I'm the only one who wants to start shooting.

"We all work for someone, Mack," says Fisher, placing a hand calmly on my shoulder. "Sounds like you're still trying to figure that one out. Good luck."

FOUR

Panic. Terror. Again.

I am in the chasm between light and dark. Life and death. The weight on my chest belongs to a boot. The sound in my head is a chainsaw, raw and savage and terrible, only I'm the one making the sound, screaming it, as though I could cut whole forests with my voice.

And yet, here I sit, panting behind the wheel of a quiet car, eyes wide with fear, flooded with the dingy, gray light that makes it through late afternoon rainwater and a smoke-grimed windshield.

The outside of the glass is clean. The grime, like the dream, is on the inside.

Outside the passenger window is the torso of a man. It's wearing Raphael Santiago's raincoat.

I can faintly remember the knock now, buried in the gore of my dream; something hard banging against my ribcage, trying to get out. *Knock, knock.* Trying to escape. *Knock, knock, knock.* I'd thought it was my heart. I rub my face with both hands and hit the unlock button. Raffi climbs in dripping.

"Starting to wonder," he says, water flying as he closes the door. "You require a secret code these days?"

"Sorry," I say, trying to get my breathing back under control. I lean my head back against the seat like that isn't what put me to sleep in the first place. "Dozed off, I guess."

"You okay?" Raffi asks. "You look like shit, Mack."

"Thanks. Never better. I'm working on my twenty-thousand steps a day. I find it's faster if I drive."

"Maybe you should settle for just twelve steps and call it a program."

"Twelve steps down into some dank church basement with tired aphorism posters on the wall? The folding chair will ruin my back, the stale donuts will clog my arteries, and the sad sack confessions will make me want to eat my gun. It's almost like you want me dead, Raffi."

"Hey, I've saved your sorry ass twice. I'm just going for the hat trick, man."

"How many times do we have to have this little talk?"

Raffi unwraps a stick of gum and pops it past his white Chicano teeth. Then he holds the pack out to me.

"Thanks, no. I'm trying to quit. Bad for the teeth."

"Sugar free, man."

"What happens if you roll one of those things into a tube and set it on fire? Just curious."

"Seriously, Mack," he says. He shakes his head and returns the pack to his pocket. "Pick one bad habit and kick it already. Your shit's gonna kill you one day."

"That's a long line, Raffi. You coming or going?"

"Headed out."

"Someplace fun?"

"You know the Griswold beating?" he asks.

"Yeah."

"Turns out the body cam shows a Camaro parked at the curb. Two women inside. Ran the plate. Got a name. She says she'll talk about what she saw if her husband is with her and if the coffee is on me. I was ready to close the file. Officer Cobb's in some kinda trouble."

"Good work."

"Thanks, man. Listen, I wanted to tell you ..."

"You wanted to tell me that forensics found a bunch of goose eggs in the Castle Hotel."

Raffi laughs a little.

"Should'a guessed. Twill?"

I nod. "We talked yesterday. That leaves us with exactly nothing on the human trafficking unless the feds pick up Nadia or Mila."

"Gee, Mack. Guess it's too bad you let 'em both go. I kept 'em in the car for you, just like you asked."

"Yeah, well, you need to get past that, Raf. They'd both be dead …"

"Maybe," he says.

"Maybe nothing, and you know it. A dead witness is no witness. And there was also an eight-year-old girl in the equation. Danika would've been ground down into a piece of raw meat, lost in the system. I can kill myself eight days a week, but I'm not doing that. Understand?"

Too strong. He's got his hands in the air, waving me off.

"Fuck, man. Calm down. Okay? Uncle. You made the call. I'm not arguing. It's done. Maybe they get picked up, and maybe they don't. That leaves nothing on the trafficking. Where'd you leave it with LT?"

I shrug. "I told him Big Man only leaves trails he wants you to follow."

Another wry laugh. "I'm sure he was receptive to that bit of wisdom."

"I've been banned from ever mentioning José Beggemon again in his presence." I look at him dripping in my passenger seat. "Sorry for the hair trigger, Raffi. I could use some sleep."

"Forget it. Between you and LT I'm getting used to hair triggers. The two of you need to hit the snooze button and roll over."

"Who? LT?"

"Yeah. He's off recently." Raffi looks at his watch. "I gotta go, man."

"Off how?" I try to sound mildly curious and miss.

"I gotta go."

"You got my front seat all wet, Raffi. Off how?"

"Just … I don't know. Aloof. Secretive. Edgy. Kinda like you, now that you mention it. No fuckin' patience to save the man's life. I mean, just look at him the wrong way and it's like … I don't know. Just … off. I gotta go do this interview."

"Jesus, Raf. You're the one buyin' the coffee. They'll wait. Tell me the thing you aren't telling me."

Raphael closes his eyes for a long blink and leans against the door. "He went off on me. Few days ago. Monday."

"About?"

"About, like, nothing. Seriously. I asked him about a file in the system that wasn't making sense. It was like he caught me fucking his sister."

"Back up. What file?"

"I'm behind on my stats. Stephanie keeps bugging me that she needs to update the scoreboard for the monthly report, but I've been too busy. And last week she took her leave and I thought I'd just, you know, I'd go into the system and input my own data my own fucking self like a big boy."

"And this has nothing to do with the way you look at Steph when she's loading the copier."

"Fuck you, man," he says with a laugh. "Spying on me like that. What if she loads that shit wrong? You know? Fucking paper jams. You ever think of that?"

"No. I haven't. Have you?"

"That's a delicate machine, man."

"Are you talking about Steph or the copier, Raffi? Don't answer. I don't care. So you're in the system."

"So I'm in the system. And I notice this one file that has no stats at all. Just a Concerned Officer name and an open date. At first, I'm thinking it must be one of mine, but then I check and see that LT is the assigned owner. The lack of any stats caught my attention, but it was the C-O name that really got me. Quentin Young."

The name is good for a few volts through my nervous system. I sit up a little straighter. Last time I saw Quentin Young's name it was on a list that dropped out of the backside of a Russian doll. By then it was the name of a dead man, blown to bits in a Bloomington hotel room by a terrified Suri holding a silver cannon twice the size of her own head. Quentin Young would not have been in that hotel room had he not been assigned by Twill to follow Suri the night I put her into the trunk of a car and sent her off to hide. Before the night was over, Quentin had managed to murder everyone else in sight, including his own partner, but failed to close the deal with Suri. She closed it for him. She hit the wind thinking I had set her up. Apparently, the very thought of me has driven her to fast food. Twill wears his shock and remorse about the whole thing on his sleeve. I eventually gave him a pass along with the benefit of the doubt. But now there's … whatever *this* is.

"What?" I ask.

"Yeah," says Raffi. "Quentin fucking Young, man. So I get curious. I start clicking around for uploaded docs. There aren't any. I go to the file room for the actual file. Not there. I go back to the file logs. The file is checked out to LT. Next day, Twill comes in and I ask him about it. He goes off like a Roman candle. Wants to know where I have the time to do Steph's job and reminds me of every case I'm behind on. I tell him I was just confused about why the file is in the system. He tells me that the case is just a hold-over from the Bloomington thing and that he has not gotten around to closing it out. Which doesn't make any sense because the open date on the file was only a few weeks ago. That and the system shows that not a single document has been logged into the file. Like, nothing. It's just a number and a C-O name. Where's the incident report? Where's the service record? Not even a complaint or a referral. How'd we even get the file? Where's it come from? IAD is purely complaint driven; so who complained? And since when does IAD ever open a file without an incident report, a service record, and a complaint?"

"You told him that?"

"Hell no. I said yessir, backed the fuck out of his office and closed the door."

"How's he been since then?"

"Weird. He apologized. Work stress blah, blah. We made nice. But ... I dunno, Mack. Something's off."

I want to commiserate. I want to tell Raffi my own concerns about the boss. Not just the part about him sending Quentin Young to Bloomington after Suri, but all the other things. Like how every lowlife this side of the Mississippi seemed to know about Twill's decision to fire me before I did. I want to show him Frenchie Marie's photos. Twill keeping company with the dirty-blonde lanyard lady in the white Sonata. Twill coming out of the Blue Lotus, a building Raffi spent hours watching at Twill's direction. I want to show him the email from this morning, evidence that Twill had actually pushed for the Chief's approval of my Russian doll investigation without ever breathing a word about it to me, letting me think he was going out on a limb when his ass was more than covered.

I want to, but I don't. I shrug instead.

"If I had LT's job for one day, I'd lose my mind. Whatever it is'll blow over soon enough. Don't worry about it. Cut a wide berth. Go buy some coffee."

"Roger that, man."

"What else is new? Anything?"

"Nah. Sounds like cancer finally took down Bob Kahn. You hear?"

"No," I say, wincing at the word. In my head, Dr. Jha shrugs and smiles. "Finally got him, did it?"

"Heard it on the news on the way in. Kicked it twice. Guess third time is the charm. Can't outrun the big C. Look, I gotta run. See you later, Mack. Get some sleep. Like, in a bed."

Raffi holds out his fist for a bump and I do the thing that I'm too old to credibly do. He opens the door and steps out into the rain like he's disembarking a submarine floating in high seas. Paula takes in another sheet of water before the door closes again and he's gone.

The Camel wants out of my pocket. I lay my head against the seat and listen to the water pounding the roof. My lids are taking on weight. I can feel the dream pulling me back into the dark. I resist, just like always. But it's not just the fear this time, rising again like a tide of anxiety in my chest. It's that my eyes won't close.

There's something in the way. A name. Quentin Young.

FIVE

My co-workers are goldfish, floating in place over their desks, cautious, expectant eyes, bulging at me like I'm coming to tap on the glass.

Twill has finally had some success in crowbarring the budget for some help, but it's still a small crew – only five plus me, Raffi, and the newly absent Steph. What they lack in numbers they more than make up for in awkward discomfort. They don't know what to make of me. They've all heard too much. Most of them have been with IAD less than a year, so the water cooler is still their best source of information. Sure, we share a mission to protect and serve and, more specifically, to enforce a code of conduct within the Chandler Police Department. But we share that mission like strangers sharing Bus 85A to North Central, and I'm the guy whose mug is on the front page of the newspaper everyone is reading.

They look up at me, one at a time, as I thread my way to my cubicle, raincoat over one shoulder like a swimmer's towel. I nod my greetings seriatim and keep moving.

The offices of the Chandler IAD lack the bullpen cubicle camaraderie that for thirty years of my life had defined my career on the fifth floor as a homicide detective. Homicide was a kind of locker room, a bunker, with the scent of war always in the air. A vibration. Ours was a bond of soldiers. Everyone was too close together. Like growing up in a family with too many kids, always up in each other's face, stepping on raw nerves right and left. I loved to hate my work family like I loved to hate my orphanage family. I wanted out from under the penguins of St. Evangeline's until getting out became a real possibility. Then I didn't want out. Three foster families in five years. All disasters. Each time I hated how much I wanted to go back. I missed wanting to be out.

Marlo broke the pattern. Whatever it was I got from my homicide family couldn't compete with what I got from Marlo. They all sensed it. I was still a part of the team, but something fundamental changed when I got married. Other guys on the squad were married. But not like I was married. And somehow, they all sensed it. My primary loyalty drifted. I drifted. They let me drift. Then I was on the outside even though I was still clearing cases and taking up a chair. Sometimes I think that was the real betrayal. Believing that I was in the pocket and trading secrets with Cosmo Green was just a convenient pretext to hate me. My real sin was loving Marlo more than I loved the war.

I don't make it to my desk before Twill is leaning up against his open doorway like a rake someone has forgotten to put away. He jerks his head and disappears inside. That's all it ever takes. I drop my coat over the back of my chair and squish my shoes his direction.

"You look like hell," he says, folding his limbs into the chair behind his desk. It's like watching a white praying mantis climb into a bumper car.

I close the door and pull up a chair opposite.

"People keep telling me I look like hell. I'm not sure what that means exactly, but one of these days I might start to believe it."

"You can go ahead and start believing. When was the last time you slept?"

"I sleep all the time, LT. It's getting hard to keep track."

Twill casually picks up a pen and gives it a few clicks. Of all his tells, this might just be the most reliable. If ever Orland Twill picks up a pen before changing the subject, it means he's about to reveal the top-of-mind purpose for calling you into his office. If you know how to read, people are billboards.

"How'd it go with Brewster?" he asks.

"We're not supposed to talk about that, remember? Your rules."

"I meant generally."

"Generally, Dan Brewster is still an ambitious asshole with a job to do. I told him what I know."

"Must have been something interesting," he says to the pen.

"Yeah? Why's that?"

"Because Brewster's people just called me to schedule a follow-up."

"With me?"

"No. With me. And I thought I was done. Brewster told me I was done. So whatever you told him now has him wanting more."

"I guess that is interesting."

Twill sets down the pen and interlaces his long fingers over the place his gut would be if he had one. "Anything I should know?"

The question comes across the desk with a little topspin. I can tell he's wondering whether I spent my afternoon evading responsibility for the Russian doll fiasco in a way that dumps it all on him. His hard brown eyes are doing most of the talking: *after all I've done for you* ....

I want to tell him that in my pocket is a copy of an email from the Chief I'd like him to read out loud, plus two photos that I'd love to watch him look at for the first time. After that, I've got a couple dozen questions for him to answer. But something in me is squeamish about putting all my cards on the table until I know who else is playing and what the stakes are. On the other hand, Brewster's about to walk him into a threshing machine over that email. And maybe that's okay. Maybe that's the way it should go.

"Wear your big boy pants, LT," I say. "Brewster's not in such a good mood."

"Meaning?"

"Meaning you'd better be sure you've turned over everything OAG has asked you for. If you haven't, now's the time."

"I get the feeling you're talking about something in particular."

"Your rules, boss. I'm not cooking any stories, and I don't want it to look like I'm helping you do that. First thing he's gonna ask you is what new information you've learned from me. That answer should be nothing."

"You think I'm cooking stories?" he asks.

"I know I'm sleepy, but I'm pretty sure I never said that. Just tell the man what he wants to know."

He glares at me for too long from across the desk, like he's trying to read some Sanskrit tattoo that I was dumb enough to put on my face. *No excuses*, I think back at him. *Just tell the truth.*

"Lot of work on your desk, Mack," he says finally, unlacing his fingers. "I expect you to get it done."

I make a good show of it for a couple of hours, working the stack of case files on my desk and making calls to people who aren't interested in talking. Marlo looks down at me from the shelf. The face I know so well now seems strangely alien, like the look of a word you've written down too many times. I can't look at her now without also seeing the version of her in Frenchie Marie's photo, sitting next to Victor Roby, watching the newly minted representative, Samuel Trenton Royce, celebrate the beginning of a political career that would take him straight to the mayor's office. That's why her face seems so different. There's a face inside that face that I'd never seen before. Now that I've seen it, I can't stop seeing it.

Twill's door opens. He emerges from his office at precisely five o'clock, raincoat on, briefcase in hand. We nod to each other across the office. He stops and bends himself in half for a brief word with Carolyn, a new recruit who looks younger than the lawful working age and who I have yet to observe without something in her mouth, a straw this time. She seems to agree emphatically with whatever he has said. A hand on her shoulder as he straightens, and then he's through IAD's sad excuse for a lobby, out the door and gone. The door slowly hisses closed behind him.

I stare at Steph's empty reception desk. That's when the idea shows up wagging its eyebrows.

I close the folder in front of me – Officer Decker's insubordination with a side of conduct unbecoming and alleged assault – and return it to the stack. Three clicks of the mouse and I'm looking at the IAD in-take screen. It takes a few minutes, but I manage to retrace Raffi's steps and find the current *Open Files* list. Quentin Young's name is right where Raffi left it, next to an open file date of six weeks prior and a standard five-digit IAD control number: *77145*. It's the control number I need. I write it down and close out of the in-take portal.

Next, I take a walk across the office to the lonely desk of Stephanie Nellis. I roll back the chair and have a seat. I wait until Carolyn and the others take their curious looks and get back to minding their own business, then I look around for what I need.

Steph's job includes opening the office mail, which she logs onto a computerized spreadsheet before distributing to the intended recipients. Once a month she prints out the spreadsheet and snaps it into a black binder. I have no idea where she keeps the binder, but her desk only has two drawers large enough to hold it. One of the drawers is full of equipment manuals and a day-glow orange thermos. The other drawer comes with a lock button that's busy keeping secrets. I have a quick look around for the key. A crowbar or a tire iron would work. Plastic explosives.

I have to wait until the office is empty. Carolyn is the last to leave, raising a hand to say goodnight as the other hand tugs on the red licorice whip between her teeth. I give it a good ten minutes just to be safe, then return to Steph's desk to finish what I started.

Turns out that defeating the locked drawer is as simple as completely removing the upper drawer. Once I find the correct angle, I can see three black binders inside the lower drawer. I have to maneuver all three binders up and out onto the desk before I find the one I need.

I isolate the spreadsheets for the last three months, scanning them as quickly as I can. Half of my attention is tuned into all the sounds in the hallway on the other side of the door. I imagine Twill returning for something he's forgotten. I try to think of a cover story that explains the dismantled desk. I can't.

In the past forty-five days, IAD has received three pieces of mail logged to control number 77145. All three pieces were addressed to Twill from a Sergeant

Kennedy of the Chicago Police Department, Homicide Division. The spreadsheet has a field for *Subject of Correspondence*. The two most recent entries leave that field blank. But the entry for the initial correspondence from Sgt. Kennedy includes a CPD control number and a couple of names: *Dennis/Carrie O'Toole.*

The names ring a bell, but I can't place them. I take a few notes but noises out in the hall refocus my priorities. Replacing the notebooks turns into a puzzle I don't have time to play. It takes the right order and just the right angle. I'm about ready to abort and leave the last notebook out when it finally drops back down into place next to the others. I replace the upper drawer and return Steph's desk to its pre-ransacked condition.

Dennis and Carrie O'Toole. The names want attention. My head is already too full of memory ghosts. People without names. Names without people. The dead and the living all packed in together on the Tokyo subway of my aging brain. Everyone makes room for a couple more anyway.

Safely back at my own cubicle, I get the internet involved. It doesn't take long. Dennis and Carrie O'Toole. Right there where I left them nearly five weeks ago, pressed like a couple of dead dried flowers in the pages of the *Tribune.*

I print out the article and grab it off the printer on my way out the door. I fold the pages and slip them in my coat pocket with all the other pieces of paper I want Twill to explain. Two surveillance photos, an email from the Chief he never disclosed, and now an off-the-books IAD file about a murder-suicide on the North Shore.

This keeps up, I'm going to need bigger pockets.

SIX

Shirley Horn has love for sale. She slips around the small room in syllables of lingering, silky declension as the rain pats its dark, wet fingertips against the window. The Old Forester sits almost empty on the oil-stained, battle-scarred desk, cozied up to the humming Smith-Corona. The page curling off the carriage is almost as empty as the bottle. It bends beneath the weight of six words, lonely and faded black: *The Russian Doll, by Raymond Mackey.*

Ray empties the bottle into the tumbler and then empties the tumbler into his mouth. The tumbler is functionally superfluous. A kind of chaperone for the sake of appearances. Ray wants to avoid the bottle-to-mouth vignette of the alcoholic. The tumbler, an intermediary of civility and restraint, changes everything.

Funny. It's not like there is anyone else in the room to see him. Just Phil, who is curled up on the desk, purring her response to the humming Smith-Corona in a soft contentment that cares nothing about alcoholism, except insofar as it results in an occasional drop of bourbon for her too, which she takes on the rasp of her tongue like a kind of warm fish oil, only better.

And me, of course. I'm here too, as always, up in the corner so I can take in the whole room. The tumbler is for me. I'm the one who will judge Ray for what he is. I'm the one who will feed him the late-night, bottle-to-mouth vignette on a loop. He knows that. And what I know is that after another six or seven shots of juice, he'll stop caring what I think. He figures the only way to shut me up is to drown me. It works eventually, but in the meantime, it only ends up giving me more to hold against him. More of what he hates. Six or seven more. Then that tumbler in his hand will tumble into irrelevancy and the old man will tumble over the border that divides the conscious from the unconscious. He'll sleep the sleep of the dead, right there in the chair.

Until the dream finds him. Then he'll wake up screaming. He'll struggle up and start the day with his heart in his throat, a pain in his neck, a hangover in his head, black coffee in his gut, and smoke in his lungs from the half a Camel between his lips that he will hate himself for smoking. The hair of the dog will howl his name. He'll consider dulling the serrated edges of the day with a drink. A shot. Half a shot, as the bargaining goes. It will all teeter in the balance for a second. Then he'll shake his head. He'll tell himself he is not that man. He does not want me to show him that man. He'll steel his nerves, and he'll travel the arc of the lit day like a man in no particular hurry to cross a burning bridge. And the earth will roll once more like a chipped marble into darkness, where the only one who can see him is me.

Repeat. Cheers.

Love for sale, she sings. Ray sets the tumbler on the desk. Phil lifts her head at the sound, showing the pink point of her tongue. Ray lifts the tumbler, tilting it so that the last amber drop of Old Forester slides to the very edge and bulges at the precipice. Phil rotates her face sideways and takes it in, then instantly resumes the uncomplicated sleep that Ray envies like almost nothing else on earth.

He turns off the typewriter, swiveling the chair so he can survey the room, disappointingly empty of bottles that are not disappointingly empty of bourbon. It will take a trip downstairs to the kitchen for a replacement, a trek for which he does not quite have the energy.

So, he sits and swivels in the old chair, timing the squeaks at ten degrees and one hundred seventy degrees like a metronome.

The box from the closet is still on the corner ottoman, contents already disgorged, examined, and returned. It's the third box this week, packed with Marlo's things. Like it's a hobby. But it's not a hobby. It's an obsession.

This box, like the others, does not happen to include any of Marlo's old files, which was the whole point of hauling it out of the closet in the first place. He could tell it was the wrong box immediately upon opening. That was back when the bottle was still mostly full.

But once the box is open, files or no files, there is no stopping him. Everything must come out. Everything. Every item must be felt. Smelled. Remembered. The blue wool mittens. The turquoise readers. The book of crosswords. Her father's threadbare Cubs cap. Buddy Guy's guitar pick. Her old, dead cell phone. The flannel shirt from Niagara Falls. The key ring with all the keys. The slippers. Boxes of stuff he doesn't know how to throw out.

If he ever finds them, the old files will likely be the least of her. They will lack the sentimentality of even her most pedestrian artifacts. The plastic, rose-colored hairbrush. Her white, coffee-stained mug declaring: *Capone – Best Audit Ever!*

The files, if he recalls correctly, are among the last holdovers from the life of Marlo Kline, a woman he once did not know except as a PI who happened to have some useful background on a homicide suspect. One thing had led to another. She'd traded out her long hair for something shorter. She'd traded in her freelance shingle for a steady meal ticket running fraud investigations for Rushmore American Insurance. Then she'd traded in her name for a ring and a homicide cop who never deserved her. Now she's in boxes.

Boxes, yes. But she's also in the old photograph from Frenchie Marie that Ray cannot comprehend, taken back when Marlo still had the maiden name and the longer hair and the freelance gumshoe gig. That's what has him up here in the middle of the night playing drunken archeologist. He wants to know why the woman who would become his wife, the woman on the pedestal of his battered and besotted heart, was keeping such cozy company with the likes of Victor Roby, Samuel Royce, and Anthony Rickens.

He doesn't know what the old files will show him. Nothing, he thinks. If he is forced to guess. Nothing useful. And the process of digging around in the memory of Marlo will cost him dearly at a time when he can usually count more empty bottles than reasons to get up in the morning.

But Ray is stubborn in ways difficult to fathom. I've seen the man refuse to die just because the idea of it irritated him. Just because dying would keep him from knowing something. He doesn't like not knowing the things he wants to know. He'll dig for answers until it kills him.

And it will, I think. If I am forced to guess. It will kill him.

Love for sale. She mews the words like she's letting them drop on a staircase, too silky for her lips to hold. There's a lonesome cop in the song and Ray wonders if that's him, watching her climb. He leans back in the chair with a squeak and craves the Camels that he purposefully left out in the car for the night. He doesn't crave just one. He craves them all. The whole mentholated herd. He'd smoke them all at once if he could.

He rubs his face in his hands, feeling the room slowly spin.

Outside in the dark, the rain wants in the upstairs window more than ever. From downstairs comes a pounding at the door. Three times hard. Ray pulls his hands from his face. Listens.

Look at those eyes. Feel that heart, panicking in its little cage. Poor guy. He thinks he's dreaming. He wants to wake up. He wants to escape the worst part for once. *Take off his legs.*

Again. Three times hard.

Phil stretches on the desk and sits up, sniffing at the tumbler.

Not a dream, he thinks, water lashing furiously at the pane behind him.

It would be just like Chicago to come up with a spring rain that can kick in a front door. It's either that or someone wants out of the weather.

SEVEN

The good thing is I'm still dressed. The last middle-of-the-night noise caught me in terrycloth. That's not how I want to be found at the end.

I look over the desk and out the window. I can't see anything for the light in the room. I head for the hall with Phil on my heels. She's hoping this might be about food. Me too.

I make it down the stairs and detour through the living room so I can grab Sig off the table and bring him along just in case. In case of what, exactly, I don't know, and Sig doesn't care. That makes him perfect for the job. I turn on the outside light and look through the narrow window next to my front door.

Two of them. Big fellas, dripping wet. Matching black raincoats over dark suits and ties. Square heads, matching scowls. I've seen them both before. Last time they abducted me everybody was cold and all the water was white. I open the door.

"Ever heard of a doorbell?" I ask, keeping Sig level and ready for anything. "All that pounding is hell on the wrist joint."

"She wants to meet," says the Asian.

"We all want a lot of things. I want to sleep. She has my number."

"Meet," he repeats. "Let's go."

They let me think it over for a second as we all stare at each other. Those raincoats either have pockets full of water or everybody came to my door prepared. That's a lot of bullets for one doorway. Long-haired Marlo is in my head, smoking a cigarette and finishing the bourbon. *Well? You want to know things, or don't you?*

"I'm not going anywhere without company," I say. The White guy eyes Sig in my hand and lets out something like a laugh. Then he shrugs.

"Bring two if it makes you feel better. Let's go, Ray. Get your coat."

It's the same shitty green Plymouth with the tinted windows, the broken side mirror, and the saggy tailpipe they made me ride in the last time. I take the back seat just like before.

A couple of breaths and I can tell she was here not long ago. The perfume and the smoke in the air keep her here even when she's not. That and the burn mark on the back of the passenger headrest. Makes me want a cigarette of my own. Just like everything else.

They both climb in front, giving me the back of the car to myself. Not a smart move if there's a chance of me blowing a couple of holes through the front seat while we're at a stoplight.

But she knows me better than I'd like her to, which means her boys aren't so worried about me either. Everything about them is government issue. They look like feds. The haircuts. The posture. The fingernails. I'm guessing they each know their way around Iraq and Afghanistan and that this latest gig is like falling backwards into clover. They get to stay clean and well-rested, dressed for success, and no one is shooting back for a change. Not even me, the guy in the back seat with two guns: Sig in one pocket, Barry in the other.

The man said I could bring two. I brought two.

They talk like feds too, which means they don't talk at all. I ask where we're going but I don't get the time of day. Fine by me. My head sloshes around for some ice. I settle in for the ride and try not to fall asleep.

We glide along the streets of Chandler like something darkly aquatic, road water suffused with headlights, spilling over sidewalks, flooding the gutters and drains. We keep to the old side of town, where the roads are broken, and the buildings are squat, stubborn piles of wet brick. The streetlights are hoary and tired, wrapping block after block with a dull, jaundice skin. People are pieces of shadow, hooded shades huddling in dry alcoves and flaring their single red dots. A man made of hair and rags pushes his three-wheeled shopping cart like a hand plow. He stops to adjust his load, shouting and pointing as we pass. The noodle place on 81st is yellow with steam. The liquor stores on Benning Street are both behind bars, leaving the Circle Liquor on Wilson as the only game on the block this time of night. Two black and whites are making all the water blue and red. One of the cops out in the rain looks my way as we pass. I give him a sympathetic, poor-bastard nod he can't possibly see. On 85th, two men roar at each other outside The Poling Place Strip Club, flailing their arms in the torrent. Hard to tell if they're joking or fighting. Twice as hard to care.

The wipers keep their calm, wax-on-wax-off rhythm. The water keeps falling by the soup ladle. Brake lights ahead flare the wet glass with red and we pick the other lane. In my head I can see Orland Twill's hard, dark eyes boring through the windshield of that white Hyundai, mystery woman at his side. Like he can see me.

Like he's daring me to take the first step.

On 107th we pull to the curb outside an all-night, hole-in-the-wall Chinese joint. The name of the place is on a red sign flickering in the window, but it's Greek to me. The Asian swings an elbow over the seat, turning around for a look.

"She's waiting," he says.

"What, not coming? How much to keep you idling?"

The elbow disappears and I don't get anything except the backs of their heads. I open the door and step out into the weather, eyeing the restaurant. The window flicks its neon tongue.

It's a small place that feels smaller for being mostly empty. The walls are lined with plastic bamboo. Hanging plants hide the corners. I count four people at three tables. All older, bent-cigarette Asian men who don't seem to care about me being in the room. There's a hiss coming from the kitchen that smells of peanut oil and ginger. Almond. Seared chicken. Suddenly I'm starving.

The hostess appears from out of a hole in the air next to a plastic fountain. Long black hair, red and black silk pajama uniform. She gestures at my coat. I shake my head.

"I'll hang on to it," I say. "Just in case your sprinklers go off."

She genuflects like a pro, then gestures for me to follow, so I do. We cross the main floor to a narrow hall accessible from the kitchen. In the space of a doorway, I see a teenager in a dirty white apron pull a banded bunch of scallions from a bucket. An older man pours oil into a hissing wok.

At the end of the hall is an unadorned room. Four dingy white walls around an assortment of carboard boxes, wooden chairs, a large rolled-up carpet, and an old wooden podium, all beneath a yellowish-white popcorn ceiling. In the middle of the room, a square card table holds up a plate of Kung Poa something, a cup of tea, and a couple chopsticks. Frenchie Marie doesn't look up.

"*Bonsoir*, Detective," she says to her plate. "I started without you. Got to keep my blood sugar up or I get cranky. We don't want that."

Quaffed mahogany hair. Fuchsia lipstick. Gold loop earrings. Black dress with patent leather buckled shoes. The black purse hangs from the top of the chair. If I didn't know better, I'd say an old Black woman got lost on her way to the Baptist church social and found a way to make the best of it. But I do know better.

"The phone is faster, Marie. And drier."

"Don't like phones much," she says, frowning as she chews. "Faces say a lot of things that words don't." She pinches a piece of meat with the chopsticks and sends it home. "Pull up a chair, Raymond. Let's get you a menu."

She lets fly with a barrage of Chinese directed over my shoulder at the hostess, who responds with something encouraging and starts to leave before I stop her.

"I'm not hungry," I lie. "And I'm not staying."

Marie sniffs out a laugh. She dismisses the hostess with a wave of chopsticks and keeps eating.

"Suit yourself," she says. "You can also keep standing in the doorway like a fool if you want, but the chairs work fine."

I walk over to the wall and unstack a chair, dragging it back to the table. I keep the raincoat on and sit across from her.

"Why am I not surprised you speak fluent Chinese?"

"Language is a hobby. Some people like model trains. Stamps. I like to communicate. Makes me feel connected."

"Any language you can't order people around in?"

Marie shrugs.

"Not so fluent in stupid. I know it when I hear it, but I can't understand it."

"That doesn't leave many people to communicate with. In my experience, stupid is the universal language."

"You don't get out enough, Detective. Lots of universal languages out there. Self-interest. Fear. Hate. Love. Loyalty. Stupid is just a muddy dialect that makes everything more difficult." Marie looks up at me for the first time. The whites of her old, chocolate brown eyes are veined with yellowish-pink threads. She sets down the sticks and takes a drink of tea. "What about you, Ray? I gettin' through to you yet?"

"I get your messages. I'm just not sure what you're trying to tell me."

Marie nods, as if in some silent approval.

"You have questions."

"A list longer than my arm. Let's start with why I'm here, Marie. Or whatever your real name is."

"You're here because you have questions. Questions you hope I can answer."

"Who are you? Who do you work for?"

"Come on, Detective. Not those questions. We've been through that. You can do better. Try again."

I want to stand up and walk out. Show her I'm not in the mood. I don't.

"Lieutenant Twill," I say instead. "The Blue Lotus. The woman in the car."

"There we go."

"Who is she?"

"Amanda Tate. Employed as an assistant for a brokerage firm once called Byrd, Smythe and Dellahar. That proved to be a mouthful, so they changed it to BSD Investments. She was married once to a Russell Tate of Skokie. That lasted fifteen minutes. She kicked Russell to the curb, sold the ring and kept his name, probably because she liked it better than Ramada."

"Amanda Ramada? Could've been worse. Travelodge. Motel 6."

Marie gives me an obligatory smile.

"You make jokes when you're uncomfortable. Are you uncomfortable, Detective? Take off your coat. You can air out your gun on the table if you like. Guns, I should say."

There's nothing this woman doesn't know.

"Amanda Tate," I say.

"Yes. Well, we know most of the things about her that we know about everyone else. She owns a little place out in Edison Park. She's under water on her mortgage. She has a peanut allergy. She votes Democratic. Her credit score is in the mid-600's, higher than yours."

"What's her connection to Twill?"

"That's one of the things we don't really know. Not yet, anyway. We think you might be able to help with that."

"We."

"You think I'm out here on my own?" she asks. "We all work for someone, Detective."

"What agency?"

"Not at liberty to say."

"What country?"

"Raymond."

"Lot of languages under that tongue of yours, Marie. You told me yourself that international problems require international solutions. What country?"

Marie takes another drink of tea.

"I can assure you that I am as American as you and Abe Lincoln."

"Dodge much? That's not an answer."

"No," she says. "It isn't."

"I ought to run you up the flagpole, Marie. See what comes back down."

She seems to think this is funny.

"And I'd like to see you try, Detective. If I work for some other country, the people you ask will not know me from Eve. If I work for this country, the people you ask will deny knowing anything about me. Either way …" She lets the rest go with a shrug.

"What makes you think I know anything about Twill and this Ramada woman? Tate."

"Oh, I'm sure you know nothing about them," she says. "But we think you're in a position to learn something. Or could be."

"That why I'm still drawing a paycheck?"

Marie lifts the cup again and smiles.

"Whatever do you mean, Detective?"

"Chief Loudermilk."

"Yes."

"You convinced him to override Twill and keep me employed at IAD. How?"

"Warren Loudermilk speaks one of those universal languages I mentioned."

"Yeah? Which one?"

"Hard to tell. Maybe it's love. Or loyalty. Doesn't matter. As to the why, let's just say we both thought it important that you stay on board."

"So that I can help you bring down Twill."

"Interesting supposition. Do you think he needs bringing down?"

"I'm not the one that has him under surveillance."

She nods a little, poking the last of her food with a chopstick.

"Your lieutenant's actions are … concerning."

"Concerning to whom?"

"Law enforcement."

"What law enforcement?"

"Nice try."

"What actions are concerning? Why?"

Marie sets down the chopstick and rotates in her chair for her purse. She extracts a cigarette and lights it, offering me the pack. Turkish from the look of the logo, but I can't be sure. French maybe.

"Trying to quit," I tell her.

"Good for you," she says, blowing out a cloud. "I gave up quitting a long time ago. It was killing me." She returns the pack and the lighter and hands me a folded sheet of paper. I open it up to find Dennis O'Toole looking back.

"Know him?" she asks.

"Should I?"

"Dennis O'Toole. Securities trader at BSD. Amanda Tate's boss. He was anyway. Now he's a red stain on a slab of concrete. Your colleagues over at Chicago PD think Dennis shot himself on his driveway after beating his almost ex-wife to death out by the pool. Matching text messages show that Carrie messaged Dennis that she was home and wanted to talk. He showed up, maybe expecting a change of heart only to be disappointed. He didn't take it well. Case closed."

"You say that like you don't believe it."

"We think it's a double homicide. Text message came from Carrie's phone, but not from Carrie, who was probably already dead. Dennis took the bait."

"Then who?"

"We have a list of possibles. Nothing very solid yet. But we think it was arranged by Amanda Tate."

I can feel her reading my face as she smokes, sizing up my reaction. I'm still woozy from the bourbon. And hungry. I'd kill for a noodle and plate of cigarettes. I should have said yes to both. All I've got are a couple of guns and a list of questions Frenchie Marie won't answer. And now there's this new thing. Amanda Ramada and the O'Tooles, like some bad doo-wop experiment from the fifties with, I'm guessing, Orland Twill on drums. I give her as close to nothing as I can.

"Okay."

"Dennis and Carrie O'Toole were in mid-divorce. Nasty from the depositions I've read. No kids or pets but lots of money and lawyers to play with. Carrie caught him dipping his wick in the company ink."

"Amanda," I say. Marie nods.

"For years. Looks like Carrie waited in the weeds. Collected evidence. By the time she was ready to play, she was holding all the cards. She went after his share of the BSD brokerage along with all the other marital assets. Second house in the Grand Caymans with a boat and a Bentley. Loaded."

"What did Dennis have to say for himself?"

"He copped to the affair but said it was over years earlier. Said Amanda was aggressive at a time that he was weak." Marie tisks as she takes another drag, cocking her head as if at an exotic animal in a zoo. "You poor men. How awful it must be for you. Beset by weakness like that."

I can't tell if she's taking a shot at my own infidelity. She seems to know everything else. Not a stretch to imagine that she knows about that too. I'd like to put a bullet or two in her judgment but that judgment tracks with my own. One murder-suicide is enough for now. If I was in the bait-taking mood I'd have ordered the Kung Pao.

"So Dennis ended it then?" I ask. "With Amanda?"

Marie shrugs.

"Claimed in his deposition that he came to his senses because he wanted the marriage instead."

"You believe that?"

"I look stupid to you? Our source at BSD says Dennis and Amanda were like a couple of bunnies to the end."

"So why does Amanda have them killed?"

"We don't know everything. Best guess? Carrie was coming hard for Dennis. Most of their pile of money came from her family up in Greenwich. She was going to leave Dennis hollowed out on the curb like a jack-o-lantern in December. So Dennis wants her dead. Just so happens that his assistant Amanda knows a guy who knows a guy."

"Twill?" I manage a disbelieving laugh. "Forget it. What else are you selling?"

"You're too old to be so naïve about a man you barely know. We think Amanda reached out to Twill with a fat envelope and whatever body part she thought would be the most persuasive. We know the money had to have come from Dennis. Amanda doesn't have that kind of money. You look confused."

"Why do you care about all of this, Marie? You working on some amateur sleuth podcast I'm not aware of?"

Her eyes harden in a flash.

"What about me says amateur to you, Detective?"

"Why am I listening to this story, Marie?"

She considers the smoldering cigarette, watching the smoke curl and weighing whether she should tell me the thing that's queued up next.

"We've been watching the Blue Lotus for some time. We think it's a front."

"For what?"

"Lots of things. Drugs. Sex. Human smuggling. Bribery. Contract killings."

"Come on."

Marie takes a long drag and blows it out with a self-amused laugh.

"Surprised?"

"Drugs? Sure. Sex trafficking? Maybe. Assassinations? You don't buy that kind of thing at the store."

"This is America, Raymond. Everything and everyone has a price. Everything and everyone is for sale. The rest is only a matter of convenience. Why not a corner store for all of that? Someone has found a way to open up the market to non-professionals and to monetize the lay criminal impulse. Wholesale, retail.

One-stop shopping for busy people with ugly intent but no expertise, tools, or connections."

All I can do is laugh and shake my head and not rip the cigarette out of her mouth. Her penciled eyebrows shrug some indifference.

"I'm not here to convince you, Detective. We know what we know. We suspect what we suspect. There's a system for anonymously placing the order for whatever illegal thing or service you want, a system for collecting payment in advance, and a system for delivering on the contract without the customer ever knowing who ultimately provides the goods or service. We think all of that is coded somehow into the dry-cleaning tickets."

I feel myself flinch at that one. It gets a sly smile from across the table. She doesn't miss a thing. She can read my bourbon-soaked brain like a book in the pool.

"Starting to come together?" she asks.

"The photo of Twill coming out of the Blue Lotus."

"We were as surprised to see him as you were. So we gave him a tail. Turns out he was spending a lot of time with Amanda Tate on a tour of cheap hotels. We didn't know who she was, and we didn't care much, but we went through the motions of getting the basics on her anyway. Then a month later, Dennis and Carrie O'Toole end up in the newspapers."

"Coincidence."

"You don't believe in coincidences, Detective. Why are you resisting? We catch a police lieutenant coming out of a dry cleaner that is, to us, and to you, a known front for criminal activity. We follow him. We catch him playing with the tonsils of a woman who just happens to be the lover of a man who murders his wife and kills himself. Allegedly."

"And you think Twill shows up to this party already dirty."

"And you don't? After all you've been through? Come on, Ray. You're a smart man. Wake up and smell the fix. Twill tried to cut you loose right before you went off to die in an auto-salvage lot. But you didn't die, did you? The triggerman in the tree had other instructions; lets you walk out of Hell on your own steam. That leaves Twill feeling more than just a little insecure, like maybe someone out there has your back and not his. Like maybe he never knew the bigger plan. So now Twill is trying to hang you out to dry with OAG."

"What do you know about OAG?"

Marie smokes and thinks at me for a few beats.

"Our line into OAG is not the best," she concedes. "That's a pretty tight ship. But we know Twill is spinning the story that you deliberately kept him in the dark. And we know he hasn't been entirely forthcoming. We know your little Russian doll fiasco had advance approval."

The words punch me in the chest.

"Christ. Fisher Freed is working for you. I should have guessed. Where'd that missing email come from?"

"Back-up cloud server. Your boss doesn't know much about deleting electronic documents. Funny thing is that the Chief's approval in that email gives Twill cover. That's why he sought the approval in the first place. All Twill had to do was turn the email over to OAG. But he didn't." She narrows her eyes and pulls in another lung full. "Why do you think that is?"

"You tell me."

"Because he wants the scandal to take you out. For good this time. That means making it look like you were all on your own, no approval, keeping company with bad people and dreaming up phony spreadsheets."

"Orland Twill was the guy who fought to bring me into IAD."

"He brought you in to do a job, Detective. You did that job. You went out and found a poison apple and then brought it back for everyone to eat. Now the entire justice system has the shits. Well done. Mission accomplished. Now Twill thinks it's time for you to go."

The boss secretly having it in for me is not a new idea. But it's the first time I've heard it outside my own head. I must have skipped a blink because Marie reacts to my reaction.

"Oh, don't act so surprised. You've worked that much out for yourself already. Why else does the lieutenant of an over-worked IAD department let a new recruit spend his time violating policy to chase down some Russian relic for a friend?"

"I didn't know where it was all headed."

"Sure, but you can bet he did. The other thing you didn't know was that your lieutenant convinced the Chief of Police to come on board for the ride. A little insurance just in case someone decided to pin everything on him for letting you wander around playing detective. Twill figured he'd never have to use that email. He figured you'd end up dead."

"And if I didn't die?"

"If you didn't die, worst case was that the shit starts flying and everyone ducks for cover, so you look like some rogue cop on the take keeping no one in the loop about anything. Twill figured under those circumstances the Chief would not want his approval to see the light of day."

"So you stepped in with the missing email."

"Let's just say we saw a miscarriage of justice in the making."

"Thought you didn't speak stupid," I tell her. "I'm not an idiot. You didn't see a miscarriage of justice. You saw a chance to keep a trained rat inside IAD."

Marie gives me a fake pout.

"You make it sound so dirty. You've used informants every day in a thirty-year career."

"What do you want from me?"

"We think Twill is tied into the Blue Lotus and the organization behind it, which is likely the same organization that used you to soil the good judge and suspend all her cases."

"Big Man." The words bust out into the room on their own. Marie shrugs.

"If that name works for you. My people aren't big on ghosts and fairy tales. We have our suspicions, all based on hard evidence. We think Twill is tied in."

"Tied in how?"

"Dennis O'Toole decides he wants to take a short cut out of the divorce proceedings. He gets the hit-money together and gives it to his errand girl. Amanda gives Twill his cut and he gives her whatever credentials she needs to open up an account at the Blue Lotus. Or maybe Twill puts the order in for her on his own account. We don't know that part. But one way or the other, the order goes in. Payment is made, however that works. Time passes. And then one day the job is done: the mean, litigious wife with east coast money is dead. Only problem is that whoever beat Carrie O'Toole to death decided that a fake murder-suicide was the way to get the job done." Marie lets out a wry laugh and shakes her head. "Hard not to find a certain justice in Dennis getting killed by his own hitman. I don't think Amanda expected that part. Dennis certainly didn't."

"But why? You're saying it was a mistake?"

"Could have been." Marie shrugs. "Whole point of this business model is anonymity. Contractor and client don't know each other. Or maybe it was planned. Could be that Twill wanted to be sure Dennis was out of the picture. Or Amanda did. Still lots of questions. Obviously."

"So go arrest them. Get some warrants. Turn the dry cleaner upside down. Shake in some extra starch and get yourself some answers."

I get a hard look from her grandmotherly face.

"You like people telling you how to do your job, Detective?"

"Almost never."

"Then don't make that mistake with me. We've got too much into this to have everything blown away in a fit of impatience. You're closer to Twill than we can reasonably get."

"I guess I could buy him lunch and ask him if he had a hand in a double homicide. Something tells me he's not going to open up."

"You're going to have to be more creative."

"You just said he's trying to sabotage me."

"He most certainly is. But those plans are failing. You're going to stay at IAD and Twill's going to start feeling the heat of OAG's attention. He's got a lot of *what did you know and when did you know it* questions in his future. You're the last person he wants as an enemy. He's going to need you as an ally. Use that."

"Use it how?"

"You'll think of something. We're looking for anything that …"

"You're looking for a dry-cleaning ticket."

A big smile, the kind all grandmothers have tucked away for the kids of their kids. Marie stabs what's left of her cigarette into the small pile of uneaten food.

"Exactly. Anything connecting him with Amanda Tate or connecting either of them to the Blue Lotus. I don't know what form it will take. Anything transactional will be coded. It will look like nonsense."

"That describes most of my life. You're going to need to be more specific."

"Wish I could. I can't tell you more than that because we don't know more than that. We just need you to keep your eyes open."

"That's getting harder and harder," I say. "Look, if you think I'm going to be ransacking the boss's desk and bringing you boxes of files …"

"Don't be so dramatic. What good is inadmissible evidence? If you see something, or hear something," she shrugs, "then say something. That's all we're asking, Detective. All we need is enough for a warrant."

"You're saying you want the 4th Amendment in the room."

"Absolutely. We do this by the numbers or not at all. If we find something, and if Twill goes down, then you get credit for the assist, which should go a long way towards clearing your name with the good judge and everyone else who seems to think you're playing for the wrong team." Marie reaches a hand into her purse and extracts a white card with ten numbers on it. She hands it over. "Like I said, Detective; you see something, you say something."

"You're going to take my calls personally, are you?"

"I don't take anything personally. It's all business." She points at the card in my hand. "No one answers that phone. But I'll know you reached out. And I always know how to find you. So what do you say?"

I push myself back from the table and stand, chair legs scraping the floor. Frenchie Marie folds her hands in her lap as she watches me get taller.

"I think you shouldn't hold your breath, Marie. This whole thing stinks to high heaven. You want me to stick my neck out for a well-dressed, multilingual stranger handing out photos and phone numbers for an unnamed agency hopped up on some mystery mission, all on the hope of polishing up my reputation? I'll pass, thanks. You don't trust me enough to tell me your name or who signs your paycheck, why should I trust you?"

"I don't expect you to trust me, Detective. You don't trust anyone and neither do I. We're alike in that way. I never thought you'd stick an oar in the water because you trusted me. I figured you'd help because you have questions and," she pauses so her face can take on a little extra meaning, "because maybe we have some answers."

Our eyes lock for a rubber second or two. I stick my hand down into the left pocket of my raincoat, the one with the Baretta and the folded-up photos. I drop the card with her number, nudge Barry aside and pull out the paper. I unfold the photo of Suri eating a Big Mac and slap it down on the table. Marie takes it in without moving.

"Courtney Briggs on a bad diet," she says. "What about her?"

"Where is she?"

"How should I know?"

"Because you know her name. Because you caught her staking out the Blue Lotus just like you. That means you followed her just like you followed Twill. Where is she?"

"Safe. Living her life. Eating bad food. That stuff will kill her faster than the heroin habit she kicked."

"Why is she looking at the Lotus?"

"Beats me. And I don't really care."

"We have no deal unless and until I talk with her."

Marie makes a face as she mulls it over. Behind her fuchsia lips her tongue patrols her teeth, looking for food.

"Okay," she says eventually. "I'll work on that. What else?"

I pocket the photo of Suri and slap down the other one.

"What do you know about this photo?"

Marie takes it in from a distance. Then she sends her eyes back up to me.

"I'd ask you the same thing," she says. "What do *you* know about that photo?"

I mash the face of Chicago's popular mayor beneath my index finger.

"Samuel Trenton Royce, way back in the day, keeping company with psychopaths and conmen." My finger hops one face to the right, to the slab of beef mugging for the camera just over Royce's shoulder. "Tony Rickens: a fixer for the mob with muscle and a badge; a woman-beating killer giving landfill-stink a bad name ever since one of the women in his trunk came out swinging." Next, across the table strewn with plates of half-eaten banquet food and three bottles of Dom Pérignon, to the face of the man with his hand on my wife. "Victor Roby, king of swindlers and cheats; the goblin of high finance for low rent housing."

"You missed one," says Marie. I let her find the bullseye. "What's she doing there, Ray?"

"You tell me," I say. There's almost enough anger buried beneath those words to flip the table over.

"What makes you think I know anything?"

"Because you seem to know everything, Marie. At least you think you do. You gave me the photo."

"Do we have a deal?"

I pick up the photo and shake it at her. "How did you get this?"

"Public domain, Detective. The nineties were a long time ago, but we did have newspapers back then."

"Why did you have it in the first place?"

"I'm a history buff. Funny how people are never who we need them to be. Sometimes we never really know them at all. Isn't that right?"

I don't play. I keep looking at her in the way a hammer looks at a nail.

"Look," she says. "Help us out with Twill. Do your country this service. Do that and I'll open the book on what we know about Marlo Kline. Do we have a deal, Detective Mackey?"

My jaw muscles won't unclench my teeth. The words make it out anyway.

"First, I connect with Suri ... Courtney. Meantime I'll think about the rest."

"That's a lopsided deal. I'll take it because I like you. We're both disaffected analog relics, you and I, trying to make it in the digital age. We don't much like the way things ended up and we're too old and stubborn to evolve. We miss the newsprint rubbing off on our fingertips in the mornings. Landline telephones. Three or four television networks. Smoking in restaurants. We find the internet ..."

"Exhausting," I say.

Marie laughs, uncomplicatedly, like we're a couple of old classmates sharing Chinese food in storage room at one in the morning.

"Yes," she says. "Exhausting. I like knowing you're out there, Ray. I like the company. But understand this." Marie unclasps her hands and leans into the table, leaving the smile behind. "The minute you become useless or irrelevant to us is the minute you lose your job and all the access that comes with it. What is done can be instantly undone. At that point we're done, and we work this case without you. Understood?"

"You do whatever you have to do, Marie."

"Alright then." She leans back against the chair. "Anything else?"

"Can I assume your goons are good for a ride back home?"

A shrug.

"You can assume anything your heart desires. You can even assume that I'm running a shuttle service for people caught out in the rain."

EIGHT

The cab pulls up outside the restaurant in a spray of gutter water like a boat to a dock. Rajnish Malik is at the wheel inside a cloud of patchouli with his Pakistani charm, a full set of white teeth and a smoldering Camel.

"Mack," he says with a smile as I close the door. "I can think of ten better Chinese joints a lot closer to where you live and with no chance of getting shot or stabbed or mugged."

I tell Raj I like to try new things.

"You?" he asks like he doesn't believe me. "I don't think so. And you're lucky I'm driving nights. Where's Paula?"

"Asleep in the garage," I say, "dreaming about handsome convertibles."

"You're working a new case," he says, pulling the Camel free so he can show me a smile with all the enthusiasm he intends. "You're on the hunt. Almost two in the morning in the rain on the shitty side of town? You're working. Who'd you meet? Who gave you the ride?"

"Settle down, kid. Just a late-night yen for some MSG and a game of twenty questions."

"What can I do, Mack? How can I help? Give me an assignment."

"Last assignment nearly turned you into a fond memory, Raj. Cleo too. Your assignment days are over."

Raj swats me in the bicep with the back of his hand.

"Don't be that way, Mack. Share the load. I won't tell Cleo. Just you and me, man. Give a brother someone to follow."

Red neon flickers inside a thousand drops of water, flaring through the glass against the side of my face. If I'd had my own car, I might have followed Frenchie and the boys when they left. Unsettling how well she knows me and how little I know her. Makes me wonder if they just drove around the block and parked so they could see who picks me up. I use the rearview to survey the street behind me. It just lays there in the rain like it's been run over.

"You want an assignment? Here's an assignment. Act like a cabbie. Hit the meter and take me home. You can follow whoever you want as long as they're going to my place."

He laughs good naturedly and pulls into the street. His right hand finds the pack of Camels and holds it my direction.

"No," I say without an ounce of sincerity. "I'm full up."

"You? Since when?"

I want to tell him since Dr. Jha started looking at me over his glasses and tossing around dog names like spot and shadow. Since Senator Kahn finally lost the race to cancer. Poor bastard kicked it three times but it just kept coming for him. I should grab the whole pack and drop it out the window. I nudge his hand away.

"Since this headache," I say. "You can smoke for both of us tonight."

He lets me ride in silence for most of the way. He's dialed back the youthful enthusiasm. He thinks I'm not myself. Joke's on him. I'm more myself than ever. That's the whole problem. I'd turn over a lot of money to not be myself for a few minutes, but I left my wallet at home. Not much in it anyway.

The cab dispatcher mumbles through the static as the city slides past in staccato-lit shades of wet gray and black. I spend my time looking for tails in the mirror and thinking about Orland Twill and the messy O'Tooles; about Amanda Ramada Tate somehow knowing guys who know guys in the dry-cleaning business. I think about the proposition of becoming a rat to help convince people I'm not a mole.

"You doing okay, Mack?" Raj asks as he pulls in the driveway. I can hear the worry in his tone.

"Nothing a big drink and a little sleep won't fix. Let me swim inside and get my wallet."

"Forget that, man," he says. "This one's on me. Call me when you've got someone to follow. I'll tell Cleopatra you asked about her."

I watch Raj hiss away into the night as I open the door to the house and then step inside. Phil is on the back of the recliner waiting like the concerned mother I never had. Doesn't take long for me to shed the wet coat and join her with a couple of ice cubes floating in a bath of Old Forester. I put Carmen McRae on the spindle and Sig and Barry on the coffee table and I collapse backward into the chair. Phil relocates to my lap, waiting patiently for the obligatory drop, so I wet my finger and deliver the goods. She takes the taste and rattles her head rapidly.

"I know," I tell her. "It'll clear your sinuses. But in a good way. You want a cigarette? I bet people would pay a lot of money to see a cat smoking a Camel. I should sell tickets. Retire. Buy that boat we've been talking about."

Phil curls up in a ball and hits the purr switch somewhere in that tiny white head. I should take the hint and go upstairs where there's a bed and a pillow and room to stretch out for some real sleep. I could do that. Or I could stay right here and bob my head until the sun comes up, taking my sleep in tiny sips. Just so I don't drown in the dreaming.

I wake up just like always, breathing hard and feeling for my legs. They're both still where I left them, attached but aching from the strain of dreaming about hungry chainsaws.

The lamplight is still pushing up against my dark windows like it wants out of the room, but it saves a glint or two for the empty tumbler on the floor. The clock on the shelf is too blurry to read, like maybe the sound of the rain is smearing the numbers. I try to get my breathing under control, blinking until the white numbers on the clock come into better focus. It's almost four. I groan and shift in the chair. Phil meows at me from the fireplace. I'm guessing something about the thrashing and the screaming made her feel safer across the room.

I collapse the leg rest and stand. It takes a minute to reacquaint myself with gravity. I bend down to pick up the glass. That doesn't help any and it gets my legs complaining about the exercise.

Back in the day these legs could move. They could carry me across a gridiron in nothing flat. *Just get the ball to Mackey*, coach would tell them. Same on the street. These legs could chase perps down dark alleys, even in the bitter cold, closing the distance around blind corners, the closed liquor stores and open dumpsters flying by like fence posts on a midnight country road. These days I'm lucky the legs are still attached and holding me high enough above the floor for my arms to reach the liquor shelf.

I collect Barry and Sig from the table and shuffle toward the kitchen with the glass trying to think of what to do with myself. That's when I hear the bottle.

I'm not that kind of crazy or that kind of alcoholic. Liquor bottles don't talk to me. But I can hear them when they fall over behind my house, just like anybody else.

I set the glass on the counter and take both guns with me to the back door. I flatten my face against the wall and try to get an angle out the window. I can see dark water streaming off the eaves, but not much else. I slip the Baretta into my waistband and open the back door to the rain, keeping Sig out and ready for anything.

The wind has the trees in a frenzy. There's a white plastic bag trying to climb my back fence. I step out into the weather and move quietly to the corner. I hold up at the edge of the house, breathing and listening, trying to ignore the rain soaking my clothes. I step and turn in a single motion, aiming Sig at the chest of whoever is waiting.

But no one is waiting. Just the rain falling on a half-submerged, dirty strip of concrete between a wooden fence on one side and a wall of dirty siding on the other. The gate at the front of the house is closed. Along the wall next to me are my two garbage cans, one for trash and one for recycling. My pissing match with Chicago Green Recycling means the recycling can has been full for two months. Ten bottles of Old Forester have been arranged on the pavement next to the can like bowling pins. One of those pins is now on its side, rolling around in the wind.

That should be explanation enough. And maybe it is. The wind. A cat. Maybe.

Except that the wind hasn't tipped any of the other bottles and cats aren't crazy about being out in the rain. I'm realizing that paranoia means never making a final decision about these kinds of things. I stand the bottle back up and have another look around, covering the full perimeter of my home, before going back inside.

Phil is up on the back of the recliner looking at me drip all over the floor like maybe I really have lost my mind. I want to tell her that it's not paranoia if there really is someone following you. She leaps soundlessly to the floor and walks off to the kitchen. I think I see her shake her little white head. Maybe I am paranoid.

An hour later I'm cleaned up and shaved, sitting in a back booth at *Over Easy* on West 93rd. I'm one of six in the place, all of us sitting alone and eating eggs and drinking coffee and looking out the window at the dark, wet world. The server is a kid with less mileage than any pair of shoes I own. He gives me the ticket and says I remind him of someone, but he can't place it. I try to be sympathetic.

"Happens to me every time I look in a mirror. Drives me crazy. If you ever figure it out let me know."

I leave him scratching his head and make the drive downtown. The IAD office is still empty. I snap on the fluorescents. My cubicle sits indifferently in the corner against the windows, knowing better than to ask why I'm back so soon. I hang up the raincoat and hat and take my seat. Marlo looks down at me from the shelf. She knows why I'm here. She knows everything. More than I do.

I fire up the computer and poke out Samuel Trenton Royce's name. The search brings up oceans of information about Chicago's most popular mayor in decades. All of it is way too recent. I want the old stuff. I want the beginning. I want the photo of the beginning. I don't find what I'm looking for until I start working in the names of print newspapers. A headline from an old *Tribune* article catches my attention.

His for the Taking: Royce Trounces Jones in Uphill Melee for the 42nd Ward.

Had I not scrolled, I'd have missed it. Mid-article is the now familiar photo of Royce toasting victory with a table of miscreants. The photo is cropped to slightly smaller dimensions than the one in my coat pocket, but most of Marlo's profile is still visible. Her hand is still on the table, beneath Victor Roby's. There is no photo credit but at least now I know what paper to call so I can get a lead on the photographer. The odds are low that the staff shutter bug is going to remember anything about who was doing what that night. But I live and breathe low odds. Always have. It's a place to start.

I print the article for safe keeping, look up the *Tribune* number and punch in the numbers. It takes three transfers before I'm talking to someone with any capacity to know what I'm asking.

"You want the photographer," she asks in her two-packs-a-day voice. I can smell the smoke on her breath over the phone. She's part of the machinery over there; I can tell that too. Buried in the records bureaucracy where she's been for a couple billion years. She can tell stories about the microfiche days. Vellum scrolls. Stone tablets. Cave drawings. She was there in the beginning. Someone showed up and gave her a stool and built the building around her. She's seen and heard it all.

"Yeah," I say, like we're sitting next to each other on a bus. "I'm working on an investigation. I think whoever snapped the photo might be able to help."

"You sound like a nice boy," she says.

"Depends on who you ask."

"I can't help you."

"Can't or won't?"

"Both. I don't know who it was that took the picture."

"I thought maybe …"

"Even if I did, that's non-public information. We got more rules than ink over here, Detective. We're drowning in rules. You'll need to contact our legal department."

"Think I stand a snowball's chance?"

"Without a subpoena?" She gives me a phlegmy laugh. "I'd cut those odds in a hundred pieces and throw out the first ninety-nine."

I hang up and read the article. It's a longish piece that starts at the beginning. Royce growing up on the Hanson Park side of Belmont Cragin, an only child to a criminal defense attorney and a hospital administrator. A devoted Cubs fan since forever. He loves to tell the story of the bluebird day in 1975 when he caught a home run ball off Jose Cardenal's bat, a present on his 11th birthday that literally dropped out of the sky. Royce says that's about as good as omens ever get. He still has the ball sitting on a shelf in his Gold Coast home. Says he knew at that moment, eleven-year-old palms still stinging from the catch, that he'd never leave the place he was born; that Chicago's destiny would be his own.

After giving the valedictorian address at Kelvyn Park High, Royce takes a trip through the Ivy Leagues and stuffs his pockets with diplomas. He brings them back and hangs them on the wall of his father's practice, a small, five-person firm tucked away in a stately two-story, Logan Square Greystone on Milwaukee Avenue. That gig lasts for another ten years, then one day dear old dad forgets to look both ways crossing the street to the courthouse and turns his briefcase into a Frisbee. That's when Royce quits the law, gets hitched to a former high school sweetheart, and flings himself into the cesspool of Chicago politics, the only profession that makes criminal defense work look like a Cotillion soirée.

Royce sets his sights on becoming the 42nd Ward's next alderman. The odds were never good. The incumbent, Dominic "Lucky" Lucas, a career prosecutor with deep pockets and a tough-on-crime face, had run unopposed in the 42nd for three consecutive terms. Word was he had it all sewn up for a fourth. Then, thirteen months before the primary, Lucky downs a few too many and pitches sideways off his 62-foot cabin cruiser. He ends up cracking his melon on the side of the pier, dropping into Belmont Harbor like a bag of cement.

The accident leaves Royce feeling a lot luckier than Lucky, taking the news as sad, but encouraging. Only problem was every other politically minded yahoo living between East Bellview and West Van Buren was also encouraged, including a couple of career candidates who knew a thing or two about campaigning. In the article, Royce quips that there were more candidates than voters. The columnist calls out the exaggeration and supplies the facts: forty thousand voters, eight candidates. Royce finishes in second place behind Fredrick "Bubba" Jones, native of River North and owner of a couple of Lincoln dealerships in Gold Coast and Streeterville. Nobody breaks fifty percent of the vote, so the contest goes a second round. Campaigning is Chicago-style-ugly, and the final count comes down to twelve hundred votes. Royce credits his ground game, his volunteers, his wife

Connie, who he claims is the smartest person he's ever met, and God. I'm guessing it was God who produced the radio ad about the 1988 conviction of Bubba's half-brother for sexually assaulting a postal employee in the back of a mail truck.

The rest of the article meanders through the new alderman's agenda for the 42nd. Crime. Education. Business development. Streets. Casinos. Not much has changed in two decades.

I make a note of the reporter and call the *Tribune* back. I get a guy who sounds like he's in a hurry. I identify myself and tell him I need to speak with a reporter named Mattia Lewis. The line goes quiet until someone in personnel picks up. This one sounds like she's got all the time in the world. I give her the name. Twice. Then I spell it. I listen to her peck the name out on her keyboard like Big Bird on valium.

"Nope," she says. "Don't think there's anybody here by that name. You sure she's one of ours? Oh. Hold on. Lewis, Mattia R. Got her. Yeah, she doesn't work here now."

I look up to see Twill walking into the office with Carolyn. Once they clear the reception foyer, they both doubletake me on the phone at my desk. Twill looks at his watch.

"Do you have contact information for her?" I ask. "Some way I can reach her?" I already know the answer. More rules than ink. But I wait for her to break the bad news anyway. I thank her for nothing and hang up.

Twill towers over me, wet coat draped over his arm. Briefcase in his hand. He looks at me like he cares.

"You look like the opposite of a well-rested man," he says.

"It's my sleepy woman disguise. Works every time."

I wasn't looking for a laughs and Twill isn't giving any. He shakes his head to himself and turns away.

"My office," he says.

I do as I'm told, following him across the office to the corner cube he calls home. I close the door behind me. Twill snaps on the light, hangs his coat on the rack and folds himself into the chair behind the desk.

"Why so early?" he asks.

"I could ask you the same, LT."

"I'm always in this chair by eight-thirty, Mack. That's when the workday starts around here. Not that you would know."

Twill closes his eyes like maybe he doesn't mind if they stay that way for a while. They open again soon enough.

"Never mind," he says. "You look terrible. If I was your mother, I'd take you to a doctor."

"No, if you were my mother, you'd take a runaway taxi to the morgue and leave me behind for the nuns."

"I'm sorry I said anything. New case came in yesterday. Kid named Coopersmith. Ryan A. Coopersmith. Working downstairs in Property Crimes for ten years. Just got himself busted for slinging heroin on the side. Chicago PD was working a sting up in Wicker Park. They reeled in their nets and there he was. His locker search came up clean, but then they found a hundred grams of smak in the trunk of his cruiser. He's lawyered up and not talking."

"Okay. What do you want me to do?"

"Interview the cops down in Property. See if anyone had a sense of what Coopersmith was doing. Meanwhile, try to keep tabs on CPD's investigation to the extent they will let you. The point man over there on this case is a guy named … hold on."

Twill fishes around on his desk until he finds a file he likes. He opens it, reads, then hands it across the desk.

"Sergeant Zimmerman," he says. "Play nice, tell him you'd just like to stay updated on CPD's progress. Coopersmith is Chandler PD's cop, but if Chicago PD will let you shadow its investigation, then we won't need to be in their way, talking to all the witnesses that they want first crack at. If Zimmerman is agreeable, he'll need our open and active IAD file number before he gives you anything. IAD's confidentiality mandate contains an exception for interagency cooperation but it only extends to the file number, the initials of the accused, and the general subject of the allegation. Nothing else."

"So they give to us, but we don't give anything back. Hardly seems fair."

"It isn't. But Chicago's IAD confidentiality rules are just as strict. They won't expect reciprocity, but it's still a delicate ask."

I want to ask him if that's why he and Sergeant Kennedy are new pen pals. Makes me think Twill is shadowing CPD's investigation into the O'Toole murder-suicide, or maybe the O'Toole murder-murder if you take Frenchie Marie's view of things. The IAD file with Quentin Young's name on it suddenly makes some kind of sense. Twill had to dummy up a Chandler IAD file just to have a conversation with CPD about the O'Tooles. Question is why.

"That ever work for you, LT?" I ask.

"Once or twice. It's rare. CPD is funny. Depends on who you get over there. Usually they want you to conduct your own investigation and also to stay the hell out of their way. I don't have any experience with Zimmerman. The brass these days are banging the interagency cooperation drum, so it's worth a shot."

"Okay. I'll reach out to him this morning. What else?"

Twill looks at his watch.

"That's all for now. I'm out of pocket for the next couple of hours, maybe longer if Dan Brewster is fully caffeinated."

"That's this morning?" I ask.

"Twenty minutes. He's coming here. The man is champing at the bit." Twill and I look at each other over the desk. I could guess what he's thinking, but I don't have to. "Anything you want to tell me, Mack?"

"Lots of things, LT. Better that I don't. A wise, bald man once told me that OAG investigators are not people you want to piss off. Like you said, everybody's ass is chapped, and no one is playing around. I'd tell Brewster everything you know."

I know suspicion when it's sizing me up. Twill's eyes don't blink.

"Yeah," he says. "I thought I already did that."

NINE

I take the new case file back to my desk and give it a quick read.

Ryan Coopersmith, ten years carrying a badge for Chandler PD. Two A.M. on a wet Saturday morning, he gets himself popped doing the fifty-yard dash across a Wicker Park soccer field. He's not as fast as he needs to be. CPD takes him down on North Damon Avenue, pockets empty. His two pursuers say they saw him launch a baggie full of horse for a storm drain and miss. The file is still bare-bones thin, but it looks like a successful sting to me: one undercover man with a wad of bait, five cops in the bushes, junkies and dealers running every which way, resulting in three arrests including Ryan Coopersmith.

I poke Sergeant Zimmerman's number into the phone and wait. He picks up and gets right to the point.

"Zimmerman. Go."

Not a talker, Zimmerman. I can tell he doesn't have time for me, so I keep things short. I give him my name and tell him Chandler IAD needs to investigate one of his perps. I tell him I can stay out of his way if he'll include me on the mailing list. I'll make sure CPD has first crack at Coopersmith and any other witness not currently employed by Chandler PD. It doesn't take him long to think it over.

"Yeah. I don't care. Sure. What's your name again?"

"Ray Mackey."

"You have an open and active Chandler IAD case file, Ray Mackey?"

I give him the case file number and he reads it back to me. Then I ask him how it works.

"How it works is I give the okay to CPD Records that you're cleared for distribution on interview and report docs that I approve. Reach out to Records with our case number and your case number. They'll hook you up with whatever I have authorized to release. You need something, deal with them. You have questions, deal with them. You're unhappy about some fucking thing, deal with them. No offense, but coordinating with Chandler IAD is not on my list of things to accomplish. Interagency cooperation and all that bullshit. I get it, but I don't have time for it. You read me?"

I thank Sergeant Zimmerman and hang up, staring at the phone. Ryan Coopersmith and Sergeant Zimmerman are suddenly the last people on my mind. Dennis O'Toole and Sergeant Kennedy are my new favorites.

I take a quick look over my shoulder at Twill's office. I'm just in time to see him leaving for the conference room where Dan Brewster and Connor Knobb must be waiting with a couple hundred questions about undisclosed emails from the Chief of Police.

When he's safely around the corner I find the notes I had scribbled from the correspondence log in Stephanie Nellis' disassembled desk. Then I call Chicago PD and ask for the Records Department. The gal on the other end has a smile to her voice. Abby, she says. Abby wants to know all about names and numbers. I do my best to sound like this is the last thing I want to be doing, not the first.

"The name on your end is Sergeant Kennedy," I say. "Your victims are Dennis and Carrie O'Toole. CPD control number is CPD-23-992031. Our open and active IAD number is 23-77145."

"Your suspect?" she asks. I almost blurt out Orland Twill before Quentin Young comes to the rescue.

"Sorry," I say. "Our IAD confidentiality rules say I can only give you initials."

"Q.Y.?" she asks.

"Correct."

"That explains it. I thought QY was an odd name. What is Q.Y. accused of doing?"

It's a question without an answer. Thanks to Suri and her silver cannon, half of Quentin Young is still between the floorboards of a motel in Bloomington. Whatever lie Twill has used to get past the gatekeepers at CPD is a mystery to me. All I can do is come up with a lie of my own.

"Violation of Chandler PD Code of Conduct 6.15.103 for starters; followed by COC 8.19.505. Insubordination. Failure to report."

"Okay, let's see." I can tell she's too busy reading to listen. "My screen says we already sent this stuff over."

"Your screen is correct. You sent them to my LT. He got busy and tossed the Q.Y. case on my desk because that's what lieutenants do best. I'd get the stuff from him but he's out of pocket for the next two days and I need to get started now or he's going to do the other thing lieutenant's do best."

"I hear that," she laughs. "How about I just email you everything we sent to Lieutenant Twill so you're all up to date."

"That works," I say and then recite my address. "Let me ask you something, Abby. How do you keep that smile in your voice this early in the morning? Must be some kinda breakfast."

"I don't eat breakfast."

"Yeah? What's your secret?"

"My secret is being thirteen days into my two-week notice. I'm outta this god-forsaken shithole after tomorrow."

"Congratulations."

"Thanks. Anything else I can help with?"

"Could you make it stop raining?"

"Sure, but you're going to have to move with me to Nevada."

"I know a couple dozen casinos that would second that motion. I'll look you up next time I have a pocket full of money I don't want. Meantime, have a nice life, Abby. Don't look back."

I hang up and open my email and wait for Abby to do her thing with the electrons. The speed of light takes too long, so I get up for some coffee. The email is waiting for me when I return. It has a dozen attachments. I start reading and don't stop until the coffee is cold.

The O'Toole marriage checked the box on 'til death do us part with some gusto. A call from a UPS driver sent CPD to the couple's home tucked away in a posh corner of Glencoe. I know the area. It's the kind of place where borrowing a cup of sugar from a neighbor requires a car and a half a tank of gas.

They found Dennis' body in the driveway and Carrie's body out back next to the concrete pit where they put the pool in the summer. His body was cleaner than hers, except for his head which was mostly gone from the .357 to the temple. Carrie's body was a mess, having lost an argument with the business end of the Louisville Slugger that they found under a tarp in the back of Dennis' Tesla. Based on the trail of wreckage through the house, she'd made him work for it. His prints and her blood are on the bat. His prints are on the gun. The photos show that Dennis' clothes caught a little bit of everything, like he'd wandered between Jackson Pollok and a canvas.

One of the attached files is Carrie O'Toole's six-hundred-page transcript in her divorce action. Ten minutes of spot reading connects me with enough anger to last a few lifetimes. Amanda Ramada Tate figures prominently. Carrie wasn't buying the part about the affair between Amanda and Dennis being a short-lived mistake. Her plan was to make Dennis pay with all the money that was never really his in the first place. The house in the Grand Caymans. His precious boat. She traces it all back to her side of the family. For dessert she wants a chunk of his BSD brokerage shares. Page 392 is a keeper.

MR. ADAMS: Mrs. O'Toole, I will ask you again. Direct your response to me, not …
WITNESS: I'm coming for you, Dennis …
MR. ADAMS: I would instruct the witness to answer the questions I ask and to refrain from …
WITNESS: I know what you've been doing. Does BSD know? They're going to, Dennis. Everybody's going to know. Did CME know? You left CME because you got caught, didn't you? You knew it was over and left.
MS. COLLETTE: Carrie, now isn't the time for this. Let's just answer the …
WITNESS: You'd better fuck her while you can, Dennis. Because where you're going …
<CROSSTALK>
MR. ADAMS: Mrs. O'Toole, I will direct you once more to stop threatening my client and answer …
MS. COLLETTE: Carrie …
<CROSSTALK>
WITNESS: Because where you're going your whore can't follow.

I leave the rest for later and skim the attachment list for CPD's interview with Amanda Ramada Tate. It reads just about like Frenchie Marie represented. She's in shock about the shooting. Devastated. Clueless. She knew about the divorce. She knew Dennis was angry and depressed, but she had no idea he was *that* angry and depressed. She first started working with him as a brokerage assistant when Dennis was a trader with the Chicago Mercantile Exchange. Dennis left CME a few years back after some dust-up with management that Amanda knows nothing about except that there was a lot of bad feelings and Dennis could not take the hostile environment. He had an in with some of the traders at BSD and jumped ship. Ten months later, she jumped too.

OFF. GANN: Were you and Dennis romantically involved prior to you joining him at BSD?
WITNESS: Yes. For … oh, I think it was for about a year before I left CME to join him at BSD. It kind of continued from one place to the other.
OFF. GANN: He asked you to join him at BSD?
WITNESS: Yes. It took him awhile to convince me. I liked CME. I'm a cautious person.
OFF. GANN: Were you involved with Dennis up until the time of his death?

WITNESS: Romantically? No. I mean, I still work at BSD, but Dennis and I ended the relationship like, oh, two years or so ago.

OFF. GANN: Why did you end it?

WITNESS: Carrie. His wife. Dennis' marriage had been awful for as long as I had known him, but he decided that he really wanted to work on it. He said that wasn't possible as long as he and I were, you know. Involved. I respected the decision. We were just friends and colleagues after that. He was a good boss. He looked after me. I still can't believe …

Seems there's a lot she can't believe, including that Dennis O'Toole was anything but a good man with a mean wife and the best of intentions. She'd met Carrie O'Toole several times, all at BSD or CME social functions. *Frosty. Harsh. Brittle.* She gives credit to Dennis for wanting to save the marriage, but she never understood the attraction. She disliked Carrie for the pain she caused Dennis.

But I didn't, like, kill her or anything if that's what you're suggesting. Jesus.

I move on to the reports from Peter Chow, Lead Forensics Tech at the Cook County Medical Examiner's Office. Pete and I go back twenty years to the Cicero Four case: three brothers and a cousin conspire to drop a pineapple into the back seat of their boss' Pontiac when he's behind the wheel in a Cicero parking lot. But the bomb is a home-made kind that doesn't detonate until the boss scoops it up, figures out what it is, and in a panic throws it into the bed of a passing pickup. The thing does what it was made to do, the pickup driver turns into spaghetti, and his truck plows into a park bench on which two of the brothers had been sitting. They'd wanted front row seats for the explosion. A dozen witnesses to the Hail Mary pass means the boss got a free ticket to a triple homicide trial. He was headed for life in prison until Pete Chow untangled the forensics.

Pete and I have crossed paths at least a dozen times since then, not all of them friendly. Pete's got an annoying habit of being right about most things and not caring who knows it. Every time I shake the man's hand, he likes to remind me: *It was the brothers, not the boss.* Just so I never forget. So far that's worked like a charm.

This time around, Pete's reports paint a clear picture of murder-suicide at the home of Dennis and Carrie O'Toole. Carrie was already wounded and bleeding by the time she made it through the house to the pool, the Louisville Slugger connecting with the side of her face just past the kitchen. Dennis finished her off in short order, then walked around the outside of the house to the driveway where he had parked his Tesla. He stuffed the bat under a tarp on the floor of the back seat and then put a .357 to his right temple and flexed his index finger. Pete Chow can read bloody fingerprints and spatter patterns with the best of them. Makes me wonder if Frenchie Marie's double-homicide theory is all wet or if she knows something Pete Chow doesn't.

But then there's another thing that makes me wonder. On the last page of the forensics report on Dennis O'Toole is a control number. That number ends with letter V and the number 2. Maybe Frenchie is on to something.

I lean back and look around the fluorescent world outside my cubicle. Everybody is here in their seats talking on the phone or poking at a keyboard. Raffi's got both elbows involved holding open a file as he dials. Carolyn gnaws on a red rope of licorice as she types. Outside the windows a cottony, gunmetal sky squats over Chicago like a wet hen on a nest.

I need to think things through. That's not going to happen here. I need a thinking stick and a lighter and someplace private I can put them together. I save all the attachments to a folder in my hard drive and forward Abby's email to my personal email account just in case. I shut down the computer, grab my coat and head for the door, swatting Raffi on the shoulder as I pass.

"You coming back?" he asks, hanging up the phone.

"I never really know, Raffi."

I pass the conference room on my way out the door. I can't make out the words, but Dan Brewster is shouting. So is Twill. I swing my coat into place and keep moving.

TEN

Look at him. Standing out in the rain. Like his battery died right before he could get in the car.

Ray holds the front door of the Impala open, staring at the white, folded sheet of paper sitting on the front seat. He takes a quick look around the parking lot and climbs in, closing the door. He holds the paper square by the corner, away from his body to keep it dry. Opens it.

This one is like all the others: one photo, no words. Orland Twill – hat, open raincoat – stands in front of a closed garage under a dripping eave, index finger extended in furtherance of whatever words have just left his mouth. At the other end of the finger is Peter Chow, no hat, no coat, and a face that doesn't seem to like the smell of the exchange.

"How do you do that?" Ray mutters. Not to Twill. To her. To Frenchie Marie. It's not about getting into a locked car. That's easy enough for someone with a Slim Jim and the stones to jerk the lock in a police parking lot. No, he can't figure out how she manages to break into his head at precisely the right time.

He finds a cigarette and puts it where it belongs, studying the photo as he fumbles around for a flame. He finds the lighter but then immediately stops thinking about the photo. Now he's thinking about Dr. Jha and that shadow on his x-ray. Smoking used to help him put two and two together. It used to lubricate the machinery. Not anymore.

Ray drops the lighter into the cupholder, leaving the Camel between his lips.

He folds up the photo and stares out the window into the rain. He wonders if it was one of Frenchie's G-men out behind his house this morning. He wonders what business Twill has with Peter Chow. He wonders why a man would bother to conceal a murder weapon under a tarp before he kills himself. He wonders if it's possible to never really know the love of your life.

And that could be the whole day, right there. Once Ray starts thinking about Marlo, he usually doesn't stop until the bottle is empty. He pulls out his phone and looks at the call log for her signature. *Unknown Caller. Number Blocked.* It has been over five weeks since the last one of those; a call from a dead woman. Just long enough for him to worry all over again that those calls were never from Marlo in the first place; just digital hiccups from an antiquated phone held to the ear of an old man just desperate enough to imagine the impossible and just crazy enough to believe it.

A man crosses his field of vision. He's a dead ringer for Orland Twill in a bad mood. There's a good reason for that.

The lieutenant moves fast, putting on his coat as he goes, like it might be possible to beat the rain. He makes it to the black Navigator in the front row of reserved spaces and climbs in, slamming the door. The beast roars to life, backs out and lurches forward with a short, sharp screech.

Ray doesn't have to think this one over for long. He pockets the phone and drops the cold Camel in the cupholder with the lighter.

Then he starts the car.

ELEVEN

The rain comes in sullen, wind-driven torrents, confounding the traffic and slowing everything down. That helps keep Twill from getting too far ahead and making turns I can't see. It also helps that his Navigator is higher off the pavement than almost everyone else on the road. It's about as tough as following a small aircraft carrier.

I give the boss plenty of room, as much distance as I can and still call myself a tail. Roughly halfway between us is a silver Nissan that seems to like all the same turns we do. By the time Twill makes it to the freeway, I'm fairly convinced he has two tails. It's enough to make me check my own mirror to see if anyone is following me. Lots of people, it turns out. Hard to tell if that's on purpose.

We all keep our positions up I-294. We head north for so long I start to wonder if Twill is aiming for Wisconsin. He exits the freeway near Rivers Casino. The Nissan does the same. I'm certain now that I'm not the only one curious to find out where he's going. The question is who. Best guess is that it's one of Frenchie Marie's boys keeping tabs on him like she's been doing for however long.

We all exit the 294 and work our way west, away from Rosemont toward Edison Park. Eventually, Twill's Navigator finds a little brick townhouse it likes better than all the others. The silver Nissan keeps driving past the house and I detour up a street before I reach the driveway. I give it half a block and turn around, parking a good three hundred feet from the corner so I can keep an eye on things without being seen. My guess is that whoever is in the Nissan is somewhere two corners away doing the same thing.

I try to turn up the wipers. They're going as fast as they want to go. Twill is standing beneath a black umbrella at a ground floor window of the narrow, two-story house. He runs his hand along the sides of the glass and then moves on to the next window, working his way counterclockwise around the building. He disappears around the back just as the front door opens. A woman sticks her head out into the weather, looking both directions. Dirty-blonde curls to the shoulder and a face for trouble. Amanda Ramada Tate looks just like her surveillance photo. She steps back inside and closes the door.

I wait another fifteen minutes without any developments. I put Paula in gear and take a short tour of the neighborhood. I spot the Nissan right where I expected it, at the curb a block over and three houses back from the corner, wipers working at time and a half like I wish mine would. I keep driving, making one lefthand turn after another until I'm approaching him from behind. I go slow enough to see his license plate, then accelerate, passing him like I'm worried about the ice cream melting before I can make it home.

I venture a sideways glance as I pass. One man behind the wheel, fiftyish, brown hair, looking at his phone. No one else in the car. I take a right at the corner and reclaim my old spot on the next block. I've got my phone out and poking at it before I put the Impala back in park.

"Mack," Raphael Santiago answers.

"You know, Raffi, in my day you never knew who was calling you until you actually answered the phone."

"You mean telegram."

"Good one. I need a favor."

"You always need a favor."

"This one's easy. I just need you to run a plate."

"Last time I ran a plate for you half a dozen people fell over dead. Dispatch can run plates, Mack. It's on their list of things to do. But you already know that, just like you know that they keep a record of the call, which means you're calling me because you don't want anyone to know anything about whatever it is you're doing."

"Boy, can't get anything past you, can I?"

"What are you doing?"

"Reading you a plate number. Silver Nissan Sentra. Illinois plate Echo Mayday Romeo seven two nine."

"Seriously," he says over the sound of his keyboard clicking. "Can I ask what you're doing?"

"Sure you can."

"What are you doing?"

"I can't tell you. Not yet."

"Of course not. Hey, how about I keep all of this under my hat and lie to everyone about what I know until you decide it's okay for me to have additional information? That work for you?"

"Good plan, Raffi. Boy, you've got all the best ideas. You sound exercised about something."

"Seen Twill today?" he asks.

"This morning. Why?"

"He came out of whatever meeting he was in like an angry bull. Nearly ran me over on his way out. I made the mistake of asking if he could spare five minutes for a few questions on the Blakely case. He answered by crawling up my ass and asking if I knew where you were. Not his words. I've cleaned it up a lot. I'd stay clear."

"Thanks for the heads up."

"Okay, your plate is registered to a Darin McDonald. Five-eleven. Brown and blue. One hundred ninety pounds. Lives at 1515 King Street. No warrants or priors. That's … hold on. He's law enforcement, Mack. His profile is coded to the State Troopers."

"OAG." I mean to say it to myself. I forget my mouth has the volume on.

"OAG?" asks Raffi. "Mack, whatever you're up to, please stop. We have to let them finish up the last rat-fuck investigation before they start on another one. You're going to break the machine."

Through the rain I see the garage door lifting. Twill emerges clutching his collapsed umbrella. The car inside the garage is the white Hyundai Sonata I recognize from Frenchie's photograph of Twill and Amanda Tate. The Sonata taillights flare as Twill steps from the garage out onto the driveway. He opens the door to the Navigator and climbs up inside.

"You're right as always, Raffi. Forget I called. Thanks for the help."

Twill reverses out into the street and holds his position, letting Amanda back the Hyundai out, close the garage door and surge forward. I can see him look my way as he waits. For a second or two I worry that he can see me. When Raffi suggested that I steer clear of the boss, I don't think this is what he had in mind. I try thinking of explanations that might pass muster but come up empty. Twill faces forward again and follows Amanda up the street and out of view.

I wait another twenty seconds. A black Subaru comes and goes, then Darin McDonald hisses past in his little silver Nissan, right on cue. I let him go, give him a little room, then I ease out and follow along.

Always loved parades, even in the rain.

There's a red light on Kempton Steet at the edge of the neighborhood. We all line up and wait. Amanda is blinking left. Twill is blinking right. I can only follow one of them at a time. Darin McDonald signals that he wants to go wherever Twill is headed, maybe back to IAD. I weigh my options. I figure if Twill is looking for me in his rearview, I'd rather not be there waiting. Besides, I've been to work already today. I'll keep Amanda from getting lonely.

The parade splits in two and we go our separate ways. Twill and McDonald get smaller in the mirror as Amanda leads me downtown toward West Loop. She's harder to follow. She drives faster and her car is smaller, but I manage. It helps that the Subaru seems to want to go everywhere she goes. Every time I lose the white Hyundai, the black Subaru is there to point the way. Every turn and lane change makes that Subaru less and less a coincidence. Makes me think again about whoever is back there in the wet traffic following me. And maybe there's someone following him. Or her. We're a nation of followers. Life is one big conga line in the rain.

Amanda pulls the Hyundai Sonata up to the entrance of a secure parking garage connected to a large white edifice in the heart of the financial district. If I still had my old football arm, I could throw a silver dollar and hit both the Chicago Board of Trade and the Federal Reserve. There are several corporate logos displayed on the building connected to the parking garage. One of them is for BSD Financial.

I slow to a crawl. Amanda lowers her window and holds a pass connected to a dangling red lanyard under the electronic reader. The gate to the garage lifts to let her in. The black Subaru is cued up two cars behind her. Whoever is driving the Subaru seems confident he has the credentials to lift that security gate.

The guy behind me thinks I should be moving forward. He gets his horn involved just to make his point. I make him ask again then hit the gas.

There's no place to park so I circle the block hoping for something to happen that I can't really identify. Instinct is funny that way. Never ask why. Just do as it says. Obeying my gut has saved my bacon more times than I can count. So I keep circling. I'm starting to get dizzy on tour number three when I spot the Subaru leaving the garage and merging back into traffic. I switch lanes and fall in behind. Why? I have no idea why. Only thing I know about the black Subaru is that it likes following the white Sonata. So we have something in common.

We play follow the leader for twenty minutes, moving back in the general direction of where all of this started. I use my time to call Raphael again.

"I'm gonna start charging for these calls, Mack."

"Sure thing, Raffi. Put it on my tab. Black Subaru. Illinois plates. Charlie Echo Charlie three one seven."

Thirty seconds and I have an answer.

"Kevin Canady. Five-nine. Hazel and brown. 3219 West Blackshire Loop. No warrants. Prior misdemeanor conviction in 2014 for unlawful computer access and tampering. Also stalking, same year. Domestic restraining order."

"Okay," I say. "My guess?"

"Yeah."

"Marriage on the rocks. The guy, Kevin, can't take no for an answer. He's convinced his woman got help in ruining a beautiful relationship. He wants a name, but she's not talking. He gets pushy. Then he gets tossed out on his ass with his Subaru and a restraining order to keep him warm. He finds his way back into the house to look for vindication on her computer. Nanny Cam inside the nose of a teddy bear sitting up on the shelf catches the whole thing. Teddy drops a dime."

"Don't know, Mack," says Raphael. "That's some Nanny Cam."

"Technology, Raffi. It's coming for all of us eventually."

"Talk to me, Mack. Seriously. What are you into?"

"A big bowl of questions, Raffi. Thanks, man."

I follow the Subaru to South Marker Street. It signals and pulls abruptly up against the curb. I keep moving on past, pulling into a parking lot up the street. I back into an open space near the front so I can see back to where the Subaru is parked, but the car is just out of view. I almost pull out to look for a better spot but then I suddenly lose all interest in the Subaru.

Across the street from where I sit Orland Twill is holding his open umbrella above the door of a midnight blue Mercedes. The door opens and out steps Amanda Ramada Tate.

I read once that a shocking percentage of live magic performances involve the use of twins. I'm tempted to reach that conclusion here. More likely, Amanda switched cars in the BSD parking garage and her Subaru tail stayed attached anyway.

I crane my head around all directions, looking for Trooper Darin McDonald. I spot the silver Nissan in a loading zone across the street outside the Marker Westpoint Suites. I can't see him through the rain, but he's in there. Darin and Kevin and I are all watching the same show.

Twill helps Amanda out of the car, taking her hand and pulling her against him under his umbrella. She bends back in, pulls a rolling carry-on from the passenger seat, locks up and they quickly make their way Trooper Darin's direction. They stop at the front entrance of the Marker Westpoint. Twill collapses the umbrella and gives it two quick shakes. Then they disappear into the hotel.

We all sit and wait, listening to the rain. Ten minutes turns into twenty. I can't see Kevin Canady in his Subaru, but unless he made a U-turn in the middle of the street and went the other way, he's still sitting at the curb waiting for someone to follow. Darin McDonald is self-conscious about occupying a loading zone. He's got his hazards on. I'm guessing he's got his badge in his lap ready for anyone who has ideas about evicting him.

Me, I spend my time thinking about Twill's wife, Wendy. I've met her a couple of times in passing. Seems like a perfectly nice, attractive cop's wife. Loyal to a fault. Part Korean. Her head stops below Twill's shoulders. Little, tiny thing. But she teaches self-defense, MMA and Tae Kwon Do to most of the women and a decent percentage of the men on the Chandler police force.

You never know what goes on inside a marriage. I don't judge. I can't judge. But I sure wouldn't want to piss off Wendy Twill for some afternoon delight with Amanda Tate. I think of the photo of Twill and Amanda sitting in her car and I wonder how long this has been going on. And why? That's the real question. Why? Whatever is going on up in that hotel room, it's about much more than sex.

Movement. Kevin Canady's Subaru splashes through a puddle as it passes. I put Paula in gear and follow. Why? I don't know. I do it anyway. I fish my phone out of my pocket and dial.

"Mack!" Says Raj, his voice in the shape of a smile. "What's up, man?"

"You still want to follow someone?"

"Always! Who, where and when?"

"Head for the Marker Westpoint Suites on South Marker. You know the place?"

"Who do you think you're talking to?"

"Okay. Good. Tall, bald white guy. Suit and tie under a black raincoat. He's with a blonde that has stopped a clock or two in her day. Navy raincoat. He drives a black Navigator. She's in a blue Mercedes, Illinois plate Kimo Lima Echo seven one three. They're both in the hotel now."

"Now we're talking. You want some pictures?"

"Get out of the gutter, kid. It's not that kind of case. They've been in there twenty minutes. I need you to follow her. Maybe they go someplace together, but if they split up, stay on her, not him. No contact. Just let me know where she goes."

"On my way. Hey, either of these people kill other people?"

"I don't know yet."

"Because last time ... Last two times ..."

"This isn't like last time. There's an undercover Trooper in the loading zone. Silver Nissan. Stay clear of him. Understood?"

"Roger that."

"Don't say Roger that, Raj."

"Roger that."

TWELVE

Kevin Canady leads me directly back to where we started, parking at the curb three houses down from the house Amanda Tate seems to own. The house looks the same as it did an hour ago, only wetter.

I pull up another street and double back for a spot with a good view. I swing around in time to see Kevin step out into the weather, pull up his collar and speed walk to Amanda's house. He crosses the driveway and then disappears through the wooden gate that leads around back.

I reach over the seat for the umbrella in the back. It's a collapsible, half-sized number with a broken spoke, but it does the job okay if the wind isn't blowing. I climb out into the rain and make my way to the Subaru at the curb, careful to keep one eye on Amanda's house for any sign that Kevin is coming back.

It's all locked up except the driver's door. Fine by me. I only need one way in. I climb inside and close the door and fish around in the glove compartment. On top is a BSD temporary security access pass inside a plastic sleeve attached to a red lanyard. At the bottom of the card is a blank filled in with a red pen: *Keven Canady, Whitehorse I.T. Solutions.* WITS. Well, that's clever. I put it back and double check the registration and insurance card. The names match. It's him alright.

I close up the glove compartment and give the car a once over. There's nothing much to catch my eye except a bag of tools on the floor of the back seat that gives me an idea. I unlock all the doors with the push of a button, yank the hood release, grab a socket wrench and climb out of the car.

THIRTEEN

Ray likes the rain about as much as Phil does. Look at him. Trying to narrow his shoulders so he can fit inside that broken, collapsible thing he calls an umbrella. He tries to shorten up his strides, but he doesn't fit, plain and simple. It's emasculating.

He makes it up the driveway of Amanda Tate's house and casually slips in through the gate to the back yard. He stops halfway, shifting the umbrella to his left hand so he can pull Sig out of the holster. Then he moves forward again slowly, pausing at each of two windows for a look inside. All the blinds are pulled, but some of the fat wooden slats allow for sliver-sized views into the house. Nothing much to see. He keeps moving.

The back door is closed and locked. No sign of forced entry. It's a good lock. Either Amanda left it unlocked, or Kevin's got himself a key. As for the man himself, there's no sign of him until Ray gets to the last window on the back wall of the house. He has to stoop and put his face up against the glass to see through the slats, but it's enough.

Kevin is still in his wet grey raincoat. He sits in the dark at a desk, hunched in the glow of a computer screen. He's nervous. Twitchy. His head jerks back around over his shoulders every few seconds as his hand pushes a mouse around the desk. He's wearing black cotton gloves to keep his fingerprints to himself. He is not particularly large or muscular for a B&E criminal, if that's what he is. Shark fin nose on a pallid face with dark, deep-set eyes. Allergic to shampoo, apparently. Ray opens his coat enough to nose Sig back into bed.

Inside, Kevin keeps it up for another ten minutes, his face glaucous in the wash of computer light. Then he trades the mouse for a cellphone. It's a short call with a lot of headshaking but not many words, none of which Ray can make out. Kevin slips the phone back in his pocket, turns off the monitor and then, after a quick search of the desk drawers, he stands and exits the room. Ray takes a position around the corner and waits. Ten minutes. Fifteen. He leans his back up against the house and watches the rain stream off the roof. He tries to materialize a Camel between his lips just by wanting it badly enough. He thinks of Marlo. Wonders who she really was. He can see that sideways enigmatic smile of hers, glowing out of the dark of his memory. *Come and get me,* she says. *If you can.*

That's when he hears the back door open and close. Kevin Canady rounds the corner on a head of steam, stopping short like Ray has punched him in the chest.

"Hey, Kev," says Ray. "What's the haps?"

Could have gone a lot of ways. No telling how a man is going to react hearing his name from a stranger in the rain, especially as he's leaving a crime scene. Kevin Canady plays it like he's at the line of scrimmage, plowing through Ray in a mad dash for the gate, shoving him against the side of the house hard enough that the momentum takes Ray all the way down to the pavement. He's through the fence and racing down the driveway before Ray is back on his feet.

Ray stoops to reclaim the umbrella. Then he turns and walks out through the gate. Now he's dirty and wet. He may as well have left the umbrella in the car.

But you gotta hand it to the guy. He does know how to think ahead.

FOURTEEN

Kevin's behind the wheel when I get there, frantically cranking the key to a car that may as well be a block of cheese. I can't read his lips through the windshield, but I don't need to. He's making up brand new words at this point. He looks at me through the glass, seized with panic, punching the door lock button like it's a detonator. I ease open the passenger door and climb in.

"Power locks won't work without a battery, Kev."

I pull the socket wrench out of my pocket and drop it over the seatback to the floor. Panting just short of hysteria, he looks at me dripping in the passenger seat like you might look at a big, strange dog in your bedroom.

"Who the fuck are you? Get the fuck out of my car!"

"Who the fuck am I? I'll tell you who I am, Kevin Canady of 3219 West Blackshire Loop. I'm the guy who will add resisting arrest to your indictment for breaking and entering if you don't put both hands on that steering wheel. You get three seconds to think about it. Then it gets ugly."

Kevin closes his eyes. He grips the wheel with both hands. I tell him all about the Constitution as I slip a zip tie out of my pocket and bind his wrists. I don't need to pat him down, but I do it anyway. No weapons. When I'm done, I lean back against the door and size him up.

"That your house back there?"

Kevin makes his lips tight and thin so nothing can get out. Now his nose is doing all the panting.

"I'll take that as a no. You want to tell me what you were doing inside a house that doesn't belong to you?"

"Fuck you," he says. "I'm not saying shit to you."

"Good call, Kev. Why help yourself at this point? You just added breaking and entering to the stalking and computer crimes already on your sheet and you're headed for prison. Maybe your ex-wife will come visit you just to rub it in."

He stares at me like this is the first time he's really thought about the future. I keep at it.

"Maybe the D.A. throws in a count or two for burglary. Or maybe another computer crimes charge just to show the judge you haven't changed a bit. Doesn't really matter, does it? Those are just details. You're going away for a while. That what you want? Or do you want to try to break your fall?"

We look at each other and listen to the rain. The windows of the Subaru are coated with steam. I can see him thinking. Teetering maybe. I give him a push.

"You see, Kev, I'm the only guy who knows you're here. Give me what I need and maybe this goes any way you want it to. Why were you inside that house? Who sent you? What were you looking for?"

"Fuck you."

I lean in and stick my hand into his coat pocket. I pull out his cell and wake it up. The home screen features a teenage girl with Kevin's hazel eyes and mousy brown hair and a soccer ball all her own. I'm guessing she went with mom in the divorce.

The phone doesn't like strangers, so I hold it up to his face. Works like a charm. Kevin makes a lot of noise as I navigate to his recent calls list. I look at him and wag the phone.

"Here's your last chance to see her score a goal before she clears high school and her mom packs her off to college. I guess you can go to prison if you want, but she's not going to be here when you get out."

Kevin looks away, shame now wrestling with anger.

"Look at me," I say, holding a finger over the number of whoever it was he called while he was snooping his way through Amanda Tate's computer. He looks. "I'm going to tap this number. When you hear a voice on the other end, I want you to say four small words. Four and only four. I want you to say *I'm out. What's next?* Got that, Kev? *I'm out. What's next?* Go ahead, give it a dry run."

It takes a beat or two, but then he mumbles it.

"I'm out. What's next?"

"Perfect," I tell him. "Should have been an actor, Kev. You're a natural."

I tap the number on the phone and wait. Three rings. Then a baritone, black as night.

"Damn, Blue Shoe! I just said don't call my ass again from a job. This fuckin' opposite day or some shit? What da' fuck, man?"

I hold the phone up to Kevin's ashen face along with four fingers, one for each word I want him to say.

"I'm busted," says Kevin. "There's a cop listen …"

I pull the phone back.

"Who am I talking to?" I ask. But whoever he is, he's already gone. I'm talking to an empty phone. I can feel the guy ripping the sim card out of his phone and dropping it into a garbage disposal. I slip the phone in my pocket and give Kevin Canady a raised eyebrow.

"Interesting choice. Blue Shoe, was it? Didn't figure you for a dancer."

"Fuck off."

I clap him on the shoulder.

"Cheer up, Kev. Maybe she'll play soccer at the Olympics. You can watch Team USA on the Stateville TV. Let's go get your fingers dirty and your picture taken. We can take my car. It's hooked up to a battery and everything."

FIFTEEN

Been a while since I've booked someone. And it's the first time since joining IAD. The paperwork hasn't changed since my homicide days. I cross my t's and the boys at the desk take Kevin into custody without a hitch. I do get a lot of looks. They don't like IAD much. But it's more than that. It's me they don't like. Ray the rat, the mole, back in the house, playing detective.

I wish Kevin luck. I'm already missing the way he says fuck you. It feels better than the looks I'm getting from everyone else. My phone rings as I'm pushing through the outside doors. I hold up under the eave to take the call dry.

"Raj," I say, patting myself down for the Camel I don't have. "What's the word, brother? Where are you?"

"A loading zone on West Jackson. Kind of at a dead end, man."

"Let me guess, she took you to a secure parking garage that won't let you in unless you happen to get a paycheck from one of six different brokerage firms."

"Good guess."

"I played that game already this morning. Keep your eyes open for a white Hyundai Sonata. She's using the garage to switch cars where nobody can see."

"Got it. Who is she? What's her game?"

"Too early to tell." Two cops want into processing. I'm in the way. I move over with a nod and get a couple of dirty looks anyway. I don't know them, but they obviously know me. "So did they come out of the hotel together or separate?"

"I never saw a tall bald guy. The Trooper you warned me about was nowhere around that I could see. I found the blue Mercedes and sat on it. A nice-looking woman showed up alone and got inside. Only she had black hair, not blonde."

"What? You sure?"

"I know my hair colors, Mack. I followed her to a Blondie's out on West Lake in Addison."

"Wait. Where?"

"West Lake. Addison."

"No. The other thing."

"Blondie's."

"What's that?"

"You know. *Blondie's?* The restaurant? Surfboard fries? Triple stack steak? Home of the Big Dream? How can you not know Blondie's? There's like six of them. Carpet-bomb TV ads?"

"I don't watch TV. It rots your brain. Does Blondie's serve a Dagwood sandwich?"

"What?"

"Never mind. So, a black-haired woman goes to Blondie's. Then what?"

"I figured she wanted lunch, but she just sat there in the parking lot forever. Like forty minutes. Then this guy in a black Lexus pulls in. Blondie's is not really a Lexus kind of joint, Mack. Mercedes either. They both stood out."

"Describe him."

"Medium everything. Maybe late forties. Whiteish hair. Short beard. Doesn't like the rain. Black briefcase."

"Whiteish?"

"Yeah. Blond going gray, no yellow. Told you I know my hair colors. Nice suit. Shiny shoes."

"He meets with her, this Whitey guy?"

"Whiteish. No, but she's all eyes. The guy gets out, goes inside. Ten minutes later he's back inside the Lexus driving off."

"Take out?"

"Nope. Nothing in his hands but the briefcase he walked in with."

"They never meet? Talk. Wave. Nod. Nothing like that?"

"Nope. She watches him drive off and then she goes inside. Like I said, she sat there for at least forty minutes, and this is when she decides it's time to go inside. She's in and out in less than thirty seconds. She's got a takeout bag with her. Large. Like she's catering the playoffs. No way she placed an order that big that fast. Besides, Blondie's has a drive thru." Raj drops his voice a little, like the words suddenly weigh heavier. "I think this was a drop, Mack. He put whatever it was in the briefcase inside a jumbo Blondie's bag, and he leaves it for her someplace. She goes inside to get it. Would have been easier to just do a hand off in the parking lot, so I'm thinking she didn't want him to know who she is."

"Okay, Detective Malik, settle down. Then what?"

"She left. I followed. She didn't make it easy. The woman likes to speed. She drove straight to the financial district and pulled into the garage. Here I sit."

"For how long?"

"Twenty minutes. What now?"

"Nothing. She works at one of those firms. She could be there for the rest of the day. But my guess is that somewhere far away from you is a blonde woman in a white Sonata. Either way, there's no use wasting your time. Go do your thing, Raj. Make some money. Speaking of which …"

"No charge, man. This shit's fun when no one is trying to kill you. You want the plate number?"

"I have the plate number, dummy. I'm the one that gave it to you."

"Not the Mercedes, Mack. I'm talking about the Lexus. Whitey-Whiteish. Dummy."

I have to go back inside Central Booking to bum a pen and a scrap of paper. A younger version of me could be certain that the plate number would stay safe in my memory until I got up to IAD. The current version of me knows better. I take dictation and then send Raj on his way, still asking for more.

I repark Paula and walk across the lot to the main building for the Chandler PD. The elevator takes me and about a bucket of water up to IAD. It's too early to quit for the day but too late to actually accomplish anything substantive. I figure I can at least run Whitey's plate. Whiteish. I can also check in and see if Twill made it back and what kind of mood he's in.

That doesn't take long. The elevator doors slide open to reveal the man himself. He's dressed like he wants more of the weather. I try to make it sound like I haven't been following him all day.

"Hey, LT," I say, stepping into the hall.

Twill plants all five fingers of his right hand on my chest and pushes me back into the elevator. He's angry, that much is clear. Clean shaven and bald gives the blood pressure no place to hide. It's like being pushed around by a thermometer in a raincoat. My best guess is that he saw me in his rearview mirror and has spent the whole day trying to figure out who I'm working for. I wish I knew. The elevator doors close behind us. Nobody pushes any buttons.

"I want to know what you're up to," he growls. "I'm so sick of your bullshit, Mack."

"Tough day?" I ask.

"You kept me in the dark about the Russian doll." He points to me and then himself so I can follow along. "You know it and I know it. I turned you loose and you played everything close to the vest until you show up with a list of names that I was supposed to do something with."

"So?"

"So why am I reading emails from the Chief of Police suggesting that I was fully informed of your operation in advance? That I actually got the Chief to sign off on your bullshit with a promise to keep him informed? None of that ever happened."

"We shouldn't be talking about the investigation, LT."

"Fuck that. The email is a plant and you planted it. Don't try to deny it. What I can't figure out is whether you did it on your own to save your own ass from the jaws of OAG, or whether you and Chief Loudermilk are working together to kick me out of the department." His eyes narrow into little black drills. "Is this about my job, Detective? Is he looking to put you in my chair? You couldn't do what I do in a million fucking years."

"You got that right. Your job would kill me faster than any bullet. I don't have the people skills. Or the emotional control."

I mean it as something of a concession, trying to confirm that I would never be interested in running IAD. But he's not listening. He's too busy losing control of his emotion.

"You can barely do the job you have. The job I fucking gave to you, contrary to the strong advice of absolutely every last person in the building, including the Chief."

"Look, LT, if you're going to fire me, just …"

"Fire you? I wish I could, Mack. I can't fire you. I tried that already. The Chief, after insisting I was a fool for asking to bring you on board, now wants you to stay in IAD. Go fucking figure."

I raise my hands in surrender to get him to shut up for five seconds.

"LT. Take a breath. Listen. I knew nothing about the email. Okay? My IFOP rep dropped it on the table during the interview. First time I'd ever seen it."

"Bullshit, Mack. You wrote that fucking thing and gave it to Brewster so OAG could shove it up my ass. That sure puts me in the hotseat, doesn't it? Now they're looking to me for answers. Answers I don't have. Because I never knew fucking … fucking *anything*, because you kept me in the dark. Brewster is making noises like maybe I was pulling your strings the whole time. I brought you, a once suspected mole, into a job you shouldn't have. I let you ignore your IAD work so you can follow a trail to a doll with a list of names up her skirt that you bring back to the department like a dirty bomb and then detonate. He's wondering if I orchestrated the whole fucking thing. He's wondering if I hired you as the perfect patsy."

I think to myself that the same theory has crossed my mind more than once. Then my mouth opens, and the words tumble out into the elevator.

"I have to admit it has crossed my mind, LT."

Rage follows the incomprehension, pushing up against the top of the thermometer. This could all end in an aneurism. The elevator jolts to life, starting to descend. Twill's temperature heads the opposite direction.

"It's crossed your … Fuck you, Mack. Fuck you for ever thinking that. I knew nothing but what you told me and only when you decided it was okay for me to know something … when you *decided* to give me a scrap of information. I hired you and gave you a mile of leash and now you're trying to hang me with it. So fuck you and whatever you and the Chief are telling Dan Brewster and OAG."

Maybe it's lack of sleep, or maybe it's the pounding in my head, but something about Twill's aggression flips a switch inside.

"Where were you today, Orland?" I ask.

"What?"

I straighten my shoulders, lifting myself to my full height so I can look him in the eyes. He doesn't look away. But he wants to. I can feel it. He wants to look for a place to hide. Maybe he shouldn't have pushed me into an elevator.

"Where you been, boss?"

"Working," he says. "What are you insinuating?"

I want to answer his question. I want to tell him everything. I want to pin him up against the elevator buttons and show him the photographs in my pocket. Him and Amanda Tate. Him in a Cubs cap coming out of the Blue Lotus. Him giving what for to the chief forensics investigator in the O'Toole murder-suicide. I want to ask him what it is about Peter Chow that makes the veins in Twill's neck stick out. I want to ask him what he's doing taking a dead man's mistress to a hotel before she wigs up and heads out to Blondie's for a bag of take-out she never ordered. There's a long list of questions I never get to ask because Twill's not done being outraged and because the soft touchdown bounce of the elevator tells me the conversation is over anyway.

"Where have I been?" he asks. "Fuck you, Mack."

"People keep telling me that today."

The doors separate with a ding and start to slide open. Twill pokes my breastbone with his index finger, now whispering harshly.

"Where have I been? Where have *you* been? Your ass hasn't been at your desk all goddamned day."

I give him a polite nod and a quizzical look.

"How would you know that?"

SIXTEEN

Fully dark now; almost two hours. Ray is oblivious. He's outside time.

Phil pushes her white plushness up into a sitting position, looking at Ray from across the desk. She grooms a paw, then resumes her uncompromising gaze. Lesser cats would swipe the tumbler from the desk to the floor just to make the point. Phil never goes for such low brow drama. A look will do. She has trained him well.

Ray looks up at her from the cardboard box at his feet, pricked by hypnotic suggestion. He sits up in the chair.

"You're starting to worry me," he says.

He dips his forefinger into the tumbler and pulls up an amber drop, swelling with the pull of gravity.

"One, it's addictive and you'd never last ten minutes in a support group. Cats don't acknowledge a higher power. And you'd hate the coffee." Phil leans in and takes the drop. He dips again. "Two, it's getting expensive with both of us hitting the sauce. Three, Marlo'd box my ears if she saw this. Just don't let me catch you smoking."

Phil takes the second drop and lowers herself back down to the desk, laying her head up against the keys of the Smith-Corona.

"Maybe she *has* seen this," he mutters to himself, bending down again to the box. "You up there, Marlo?"

He wonders if she is here. In the room. He wonders that a lot these days. It's that feeling of being watched. Of being under constant surveillance. He knows it's me up here. And by that, I mean he knows I'm a fragment of himself. But then everything gets a little slippery and he starts to confuse himself with me and me with her. Like maybe she's the one condemned to follow his sad-sack ass around Chicago. That's what he wants to believe.

He remembers sitting with her parked outside Victor Roby's gargantuan home, watching her watch Roby through a telephoto lens the size of an elephant gun. Victor had sat in his living room, calmly talking on the phone, ensconced in his bubble of golden light, no idea they were sitting out there in the dark. Marlo had been close to making her employer's case for insurance fraud. Ray had just been along for company.

"He's busy watching his own reflection," Marlo had said, not looking up from the camera. "Meanwhile, the rest of creation is loitering outside in the midnight black universe, busy watching him. Not watching Victor Roby the window-reflection, watching Victor Roby the over-leveraged crook. The Victor Roby who files fraudulent, hundred-million-dollar insurance claims for overvalued discount fur warehouses that he arranged for someone to burn down. Get what I'm saying?"

Ray had shifted in his seat.

"You're saying that Victor here doesn't know he's mugging for a camera owned by Rushmore American Insurance."

Marlo had turned away from the viewfinder and looked at him.

"What I'm saying, honey, is that we all live in little bubbles of light. I'm saying we never know who's out in the dark universe looking in. And I'm saying it's always someone."

And now here he is, pawing through Marlo's old boxes, wondering if that feeling at his back is just me floating around the ceiling like normal, or if it's Marlo out in the dark universe looking in, watching him in his bubble of light as he plies her cat with Old Forester.

The box at his feet is full of old files, most of which are now in a stack on the floor, all bits of investigations Marlo felt like keeping for reasons that remain unclear. Probably just because some aspect of these investigations had been unresolved at the time, and then the world had kept turning and life had moved on and she had never gone back to throw them out.

It's the last file in the box that gets his attention. It's empty except for a stack of business cards. They're all the same. He pulls one off the top and holds it under the lamp on the desk.

Chicago Tribune. Mattia Lewis. Staff Reporter.

Not one card. A stack of them. All the same. *Mattia Lewis.* He picks up the tumbler. *Mattia Lewis.*

Questions. A lot of them. He washes them down one by one. When the glass is empty, he sets it down on the desk and cradles Phil's chin in the tips of his fingers.

"Saddle up, Philippa. Let's go see Doris."

SEVENTEEN

I haven't taken her out on the town in a while. She rides stretched out on the little space between the backseat and the rear window, head on a swivel, her complicated green eyes following the wet lights behind us like she's looking for tails. Who better for that than a cat?

Last time Phil left the house in a car she was in the trunk of a Champagne-colored Malibu with a bunch of duct tape that was wrapped around the face of Marlo's kid brother, Jimmy. At the wheel was one of Big Man's monsters, a brick wall of a German named Burkhart Lang, aka Hell. It was the beginning of the end for Jimmy. Hell too, actually. He ended up in the back seat broken in half like a used popsicle stick.

Phil's the one who should have PTSD. Jimmy had to know he was going to die. I can't imagine he took any of it well. That'd be enough for any cat to never want near a car again.

I glance up in the mirror. She seems okay. She's the only one who came through the Russian doll fiasco in one piece. Everyone else is either dead or headed to prison or on the run or under investigation. I'm guessing I'm the only one who came through it paranoid and unable to sleep more than ten minutes without shrieking nightmares.

José Beggemon seemed to come out okay. Big Man always does. Bet *he's* not seeing a shrink. Bet *he* doesn't dream about losing his legs. No shadow on *his* lungs.

The silver Tacoma in front of me doesn't like green lights. I honk out some encouragement, pushing it forward so I can make a left on Driscoll Street.

I imagine Big Man reading one of the two books currently on my laptop in various stages of completion: *Message in a Bullet*, maybe eighty percent done, and *The Russian Doll*, barely started. I wonder what he'd think. Maybe he'd like them. Maybe he's got his meaty fingers into the publishing industry.

Now there's a moral dilemma to chew on. Would I finally cozy up to the dark side in exchange for some Barnes & Noble bookshelf real estate? Confirm everybody's suspicions just so I can get my pulp published? That's the question that takes me all the way to the parking lot on the corner of 73rd and Warner. I turn off the engine and look at Phil in the rearview. She turns her head like she's telepathic.

"Wonder what kind of royalty advance you'd get from a guy like that?" I ask.

She looks away again, like it's something only a crazy person would ask. I guess that shoe fits.

I sit in the dark for ten minutes, taking note of every car coming and going, looking for anyone who may be playing follow the leader. Mostly I look for stillness in the dark. Almost still. Idling engines. Burning cigarette taillights. Wipers set to lazy. The more I look for them, the more I'm sure they're out there. I hope so. It's the only way I'm not paranoid.

There's a herd of Camels calling my name from the glovebox, begging for air. As much as I want to help, and I do, I reach for the half-broken umbrella instead. Phil likes the rain about as much as any cat. Even with the umbrella, I have to carry her inside my raincoat to get her from the parking lot to the front door.

Doris is behind the bar with a rag. She looks up just in time to see Phil pop her head up through the opening above the buttons.

"Phil!" Doris could make anyone want to be a cat. "You've come for a visit."

Slow night. Maybe ten patrons in the bar. All of them now think my name is Phil. Doris drops the rag and comes around the bar for a proper greeting. I hand over Phil, draping her leash over Doris' shoulder, and get down to the business of collapsing the umbrella and taking off my coat. Doris coos in breathy whispers, pulling Phil against her chest, swaying her dishwater curls like a curtain over Phil's face.

"She wanted the good stuff for a change," I say. "And by that, I mean both the booze and the company."

"No alcohol," says Doris, still nuzzling. "But I can swing some tuna. How about that?"

"We're talking about Phil, right?"

She doesn't answer. I look to Kyle Aubrey who has appeared suddenly behind the bar with his youthful athleticism and his genial good looks like he grew out of the floorboards.

"I'm not here for the tuna, kid. Everybody needs to understand that up front."

Kyle smiles and flips a rag over his shoulder. We shake hands as Doris wanders away toward the back with Phil.

"One glass of something not tuna fish coming up," he says. "Maybe Old Forester will work."

"Maybe a double will work twice as good." On the shelf behind him, a bottle of blue sapphire gin gets my attention and knocks out a theory. "Let me ask you something, Kyle. You ever heard of a blue shoe?"

Kyle fishes a bottle of Forester from under the counter, slaps down a clean glass and gets it wet. He slides me the glass and holds the bottle by the neck like he's just planted a flag in the middle of the bar.

"Blue shoe," he says. "You mean like Elvis?"

I take a drink and close my eyes as it melts into my tissue. I shake my head as much to answer his question as to keep from falling asleep.

"No. Leave the suede out of it."

"If someone said the words blue shoe to me, I'd make up a batch of blue Hawaiian Punch, stir in some white cranberry juice, add in some Seven-Up, pour it in a martini glass and then take it outside to wash the puke off the sidewalk."

"That bad."

"It puts the glass of tuna in perspective. There are better mocktails out there, Mack, if you're looking to …"

"Perish the thought, Kyle. Is there an alcoholic version of a blue shoe?"

"Not that I know of. You getting tired of the bourbon?"

"You can perish that thought too. I was just chasing a hunch. How's Doris? She dating anyone these days?"

Kyle stoops to return the bottle beneath the bar. He comes back up with a grin I don't like much.

"You asked me that the last time you were in," he says. "Like, what, three days ago."

"Things can change."

"That's true. But some things never change, Mack. Like me not gossiping about the boss. Even to you."

"Only a test, Kyle. Congratulations, you passed. Let's pretend I never asked."

"I can do that," he says with a sharp nod.

"Great. How's Doris? She dating anyone these days?"

Five minutes later I'm in a booth across the table from Doris and Phil. She took the side with her back to the bathrooms before I could object. That leaves me with my back to the rest of the bar and the front door, an arrangement my new nervous system doesn't like much. No reason to think I'm in danger. Not in Bucks. That's what worries me.

Phil is mostly out of sight, curled up on the seat eating fish chunks out of a bowl as Doris strokes the back of her head. Up above, Ella works her way through *Ill Wind*, blowing the song like a hot breeze through the grassland of dollar bills tacked to the ceiling. I take another sip and close my eyes.

It's blowing no good, she sings. Like she knows it's coming. Something ugly and rank and painful. Maybe something you don't survive. I don't have Ella's perfect pitch, God knows. But it seems we've both got the same gut. Something's coming.

I open my lids and find a pair of eyes looking back. Most people don't look so good when they're worried. Most people aren't Doris Welling.

"You look like hell," she says. "When was the last time you had a decent night's sleep? Have you gone to see Samantha Warren?"

I pinch my tired eyes and lean back against the booth.

"Which one of those do you want me to answer?"

"Pick one," she says.

"Did you know her friends call her Sam?"

"Yes. What'd you talk about? What'd she tell you?" She shakes her head at herself. "Never mind. You don't have to ... just tell me if she was helpful."

"She was very helpful," I tell her.

"Good."

"My wallet was way too heavy. She helped with that like a pro."

"Oh, Ray. Are you going back?"

"No."

"Ray."

"I'm fine, Doris. We talked about some issues. Marlo. The job. The dreams. I'm better."

Surprise in those blue eyes. Hope.

"You opened up about Marlo? Really?"

I take a drink and set down the glass, rolling it in my palms. Phil's face appears over the table. She looks at me as she chews, like maybe she knows a lie when she hears one. Then she disappears again.

"No," I say. "Not really. That would have made it all worse. Look, the therapy thing isn't for me, Doris. Thanks for trying. You're all I need. You're better than any shrink. You've got the dreamy eyes and the endless supply of booze that I think are integral to the psychotherapeutic arts."

"Yeah? That all I am to you? A full glass and dreamy eyes?"

"You know better."

Doris reaches across the table and grabs hold of my wrist.

"I'm worried about you, Ray. Marlo would want me to look after you. Talk sense to you. I don't feel like I'm doing such a good job."

Dr. Jha is in my head tapping my x-ray film with the tip of his pen. Another few drinks and I'd probably open up about the shadow. I'm a long way from that kind of drunk. I can't do that to Doris.

"How do you know?" I ask.

"Know what?"

"Know that she'd want you to look after me. Talk sense to me. How do you really know what she'd want?"

Doris looks at me like I've sprouted a couple of antennae.

"Because Marlo was one of my dearest friends. Because I know who she was and what she wanted, and I know how much she loved you."

I can feel my heart hardening.

"Do you? Because I'm starting to feel like I never really knew her at all, Doris."

"What on earth …"

"And maybe that's only fair. She had to wonder the same about me after seeing the photos of me and Ronni Lodge. She had to wonder if she ever knew her own husband. Difference is she checked out and I'm still down here in the swamp wondering."

"Ray." She waits for me to look. "Of course you knew her. Why are …"

I can see where we're headed. I don't have it in me. I try to steer around the feelings.

"She ever talk to you about Victor Roby?" I ask. "Or Samuel Royce?"

"Like, as in Mayor Royce?"

"Yeah, but long before he was mayor."

"Before? No. I don't think so."

"What about Roby?"

"Here and there, yeah. That fraud case. She didn't talk shop with me, but she was kind of obsessed with winning that case so, yeah, it came up. But I don't remember anything, like, in particular. It was just … Something about fur warehouses that burned down. He filed a claim … Rushmore American suspected arson, or … well you know it better than I do, Ray."

"I'm talking about long before the fraud case. Before Marlo worked the insurance beat. Back when she was a P.I."

"That's before I knew her."

"Me too," I say over my glass. "Neither of us knew her back then. She could have been anybody as far as we know. She could have been anybody."

"What are you saying, Ray? Marlo was never anybody but Marlo. I mean … right?"

I ignore the question and pull the business card out of my pocket. I put in on the table.

"Ever heard of her?"

"Mattia Lewis?" she says, picking up the card. "No. *Trib* reporter, I'm guessing?"

"Not for a while now. Marlo ever mention her?"

"You're asking me? That's some kind of desperate, Ray."

"Think."

Doris thinks in silence, staring at the card intently with a slow shake of her head. Above, Ella has handed things over to Ruth Brown. *Rain is a Bringdown*. Ruth moans it out like she might be across the bar at a window seat, looking at all the night water through the slats and thinking about things that will never change.

"No," says Doris. "Mattia Lewis … Mattia Lewis. There's something familiar there but, no … I can't. I mean, if Marlo did mention her, then I have no memory of it." She hands the card back with a little attitude. "You going to tell me what this is all about?"

"No." I give her the courtesy of a direct look. "Because I don't know what this is all about, Doris. I don't know anything anymore. Anything or anyone. It's down to you and Phil. That's it. By the way, thanks for blabbing to Sam the Shrink about Sig, Barry and Paula. She thinks I'm lonely."

"Who names their guns and their car, Ray? You are lonely."

"I don't like anyone enough to want more. Present company excepted. I include myself on that list. I'd feel better if I wasn't always hanging around."

"Hang in there with Sam, Ray. Keep trying. She can help you if you let her."

I don't acknowledge the advice or the pleading look, pushing the empty glass across the table instead.

"I've got an errand to run. You mind watching Phil for a couple hours? She's the one who needs more company."

"You're working? At this hour? You're half drunk."

"Yeah, but it's the other half who's going to work. Stop worrying."

"Can't you go home and go to sleep?"

"Sure. Right after this thing. I'll swing by for Phil and then it's off to la-la land. Scout's honor."

I grab my coat and umbrella next to me and stand. They both watch me get taller. Phil licks her lips. Doris reaches for my hand.

"Wait."

"Stop worrying," I say. "I'm fine."

"Teelew," she says.

"What?"

"Mattia Lewis. She could be Teelew."

"More," I say. I stand there, watching Doris clutch my wrist and trying to remember.

"She had this story. College. Marlo and one of her classmates put together a piece for the school newspaper."

"*The Daily Northwestern,*" I say, sitting again. "I forgot about that."

"Right. Journalism majors feeling their oats, that kind of thing. They outed a provost for … for something. Nepotism or conflict of interest or … shady financial dealings … something."

"Okay."

"Admissions. Or tuition. Or alumni donations. I don't remember. It was just the two of us after a movie. You and Buck were fishing, I think. Marlo was laughing about how they convinced the editor to print the story, which I think was the whole point, but I don't remember that part either. But the friend was named Teelew. I remember that. She was a focus. Teelew this, Teelew that. Could be a nickname, maybe?"

I stand again and kiss Doris on the top of her beautiful head.

"It's a place to start," I say. "I'll be back for Phil. Couple hours. Don't let her smoke."

EIGHTEEN

IAD is empty and dark. I leave the lights off and make a straight line for my cubicle. When Phil and I left the house, I had three items on my agenda for tonight. Now I have four.

I poke Mattia Lewis' name into the database. She's led a clean life. No warrants or priors, which means I come up empty. I try the motor vehicles database, which produces a list of possibles as long as my arm. I decide to wander into the internet wasteland and the social media sinkhole. Forty-five minutes vaporize in an instant, leaving me with nothing but the kind of tension headache that comes from being bludgeoned by selfies and narcissistic angst.

I'm one cat video away from surrender when I finally find her. It's a video of a woman testifying two years ago in front of the Chicago City Council about the homelessness problem. Tia Lewis, president of Housing First Chicago, LLC, is an early-fifties Latina with short dark hair and a penchant for pointing up to God when she gets worked up about the inhumanity foaming up off the streets of Chicago. Her remarks reference a previous career with the *Chicago Tribune*. Bingo. A quick search of the Illinois Corporations database gets me the details on Housing First Chicago, LLC, the non-profit founded by Mattia R. Lewis, which gets me the phone number and address of its registered agent, one Mattia R. Lewis. I verify the address with the motor vehicles list. Still there.

Item number two on the agenda is to run the plate on the blue Mercedes that Amanda Tate likes to drive when she's wearing a wig and hanging out in burger joint parking lots. The car comes back to a Saul Margolis who owns a comfortable collection of house numbers out in Winnetka. I make a note of Saul's name, address and phone number and move on.

Item number three is to run the license plates for Whitey-Whiteish. Turns out his real name is Constantine Papadopoulos. No warrants or priors, but he did once file a police report about his car being stolen. A 2015 Mountaineer taken from a loading zone outside his place of employment, the Chicago Mercantile Exchange. They never found the car, so I guess Constantine bought himself a Lexus and moved on with his life which, apparently, includes very quick lunches at Blondie's. I make a note of his number and address right under the details for Tia Lewis and Saul Margolis. Three for three. I don't remember when I've been so productive. I should work the nightshift more often.

Item number four on the agenda is the one I don't want to do. It's the one that gets me fired and maybe sent to jail if I mess it up. Even if I don't mess it up, I'm not going to like what I look like in the mirror.

But that's nothing new. Doesn't matter anyway. I can't help myself.

I stand up and survey the parking lot from the window. I walk to the front door and check the outside hall just for good measure. Then I head for Twill's office.

NINETEEN

For a man who insists he isn't a mole, Ray's got a funny way of proving it. Skulking around the boss' office in the dark. Hunched over the lieutenant's desk, pulling open drawers, opening files to read in the spectral glow of the computer monitor. Drops of water on the window carry the sodium-vapor charge of the parking lot lamps like a hundred tiny searchlights. He feels each of them burning at his back.

Just listen to that heart, adrenaline laced with guilt, beating like the fist of a traitor against the door to his own soul.

He tells himself a different story. Of course he does. He has to. It's the story of a man who's in it only for the answers. The story of a man who owes Frenchie Marie exactly zero and who has every intention of delivering less. It's the story of a man on a mission of exoneration, bent on disproving the thing he most fears is true.

He'll even believe that story for a while. Until he finds what she expects him to find. Then what, Ray? Do you give her what she wants? Or do you keep Twill's dirty secrets? Who will you choose to betray and to what end?

TWENTY

It might help if I knew something more about what I'm looking for. I don't. *Anything transactional will be coded*, she'd said. *It will look like nonsense.* So I'm looking for nonsense.

I open folders and notebooks. None of them come with the title: *Blue Lotus Order for Double Homicide*. None of them have Amanda Ramada Tate's name on them. No receipts for hit man coordination. I learn plenty about Twill's IAD caseload, but nothing about his extracurricular activities.

Doesn't take me long to give up on the various sheets of paper that document the life of a police lieutenant and focus on the computer. The screen saver is a photo of Orland and Wendy on a small bridge strewn with cherry blossoms. In the background, a Japanese pagoda rises up into a pinkening sky. It's a better picture than the one of Twill in the front seat of a white Sonata with a woman who is not Wendy; one who likes lanyards and wigs and take-out from Blondie's. Any picture at all is better than a black screen. It means Twill left without signing off. That gets me in the front door without any password.

But it's the smile on Twill's mug that gets my attention. Who knew the man could smile? Twill's face has always been as serious as faces ever get, so it's hard not to read the smile as a big fuck you. The smile says he sees what I'm doing. That I'll never figure it out. That I'll never survive the effort. He's not worried in the least. He's amused.

Maybe he's smiling because he knows I'm not going to get far on the computer without a password to access any file I might find interesting. I'm not in a guessing mood. I have a hard enough time guessing my own passwords. I start clicking anyway.

I keep one eye on the outer office for any sign of movement and scroll the directory. None of the document titles hold any interest until I find the folder entitled *Quentin Young*. A double click gets me two subfolders: *CPD Documents* and another titled *Forensics*. I open the first subfolder and find all the same titles of the documents relating to the O'Toole investigation that I received earlier from Abby. I open the *Forensics* subfolder to find three more subfolders:

O'Toole, Carrie – Forensics (58397)

O'Toole, Dennis – Forensics (58403v.1)

O'Toole, Dennis – Forensics (58403v.2)

Two forensics reports for Dennis. I only got one. Now I'm interested.

I double click on each of the subfolders, not just once but several times with varying degrees of urgency, like maybe the computer will sense the depth of my interest and let me in without a password. It dares me to guess. I make several stabs at it. Variations of Wendy's name. Twill's birthday. His badge number. It ends just like I expect. I curse at the screen and move on.

Twill's internet browser is the only program that's not off-limits to people without a secret code. I open it up, click on the search history tab and start crawling back in time. Nothing particularly interesting. The weather. The Cubs' season dates. Coffee makers on Amazon. Chicago theater. News channels.

From out in the hall comes the faintest tinging sound, like the tine of a silver fork against the side of a wine glass. But I know better. That's the sound of risk exceeding reward. The sound of an elevator delivering the realization that the contents of the boss' Amazon shopping cart cannot possibly be worth the consequences of getting caught. If anyone opens that front door, there is no way I can leave this office without being seen. My last seconds to leave are rapidly running out.

I wait. Listen. Hope. All is still. I keep clicking.

On the screen in front of me is a page from the *Chicago Sun-Times* that Twill had dialed up almost a month ago. But the headline isn't a month old; it's nearly ten years ago: *Chow Sentenced to 20 Years for Deaths*.

I remember the basics about Pete's brother well enough, but the rest comes back as I read. Three teenaged girls dead at a West Ridge intersection, their Kia all but flattened by Andy Chow's F-150 moving at nearly eighty miles per hour. Two previous DUI convictions had made number three the charm for Andy. That night he'd been under the influence of every unlawful substance known to humankind. His body had sailed through the windshield and landed nearly three hundred feet away on top of an elderly homeless woman sitting on the other side of the intersection in a fortress of cardboard. The woman ended up with a broken arm. Andy Chow had brushed himself off and walked away. And kept walking. They found him in a nearby drugstore, still seeing triple and trying to purchase medical supplies for the lacerations on his face and arms. It had taken the jury just under ninety minutes to return a verdict, roughly thirty minutes for each dead cheerleader.

At the time, Pete Chow and I were entangled in the Irving Park murders and were not on especially friendly terms. Unlike the Cicero Four case, I'd been right about the Irving Park murders and Pete knew it. But Pete had been unwilling to give up the ghost and I was too cocky for my own good. We'd had some hot exchanges. I'd tried to put the acrimony aside long enough to tell him I was sorry about Andy. Turned out Pete was touchy about his brother. Maybe he thought I was gloating. The effort got me an abrupt dial tone. I never raised it again. The question is why Orland Twill is taking an interest in Pete's brother ten years later. The even better question …

A solid thump comes from out in the office, jerking my attention up over Twill's computer monitor. The front door half opens with an explosion of light as the Internal Affairs Division of the Chandler Police Department floods with fluorescent panic.

It's all instinct now. I close the browser and turn off the monitor as I stand and return the chair to where it belongs, grappling for any plausible explanation. Wanting to put insomnia to some productive use is easy enough; maybe someone believes that. But how do I explain working with all the lights off, not to mention skulking in the boss' office? Not good.

Worst thing I could do is leave Twill's office like a perp fleeing a crime scene. I plant myself resolutely at the bookcase and pull volume four of the Illinois Revised Criminal Code off the shelf. *It will look like nonsense*, Marie had said. Well, it's not what I had imagined, but mission accomplished anyway. Because this does look like nonsense. Five seconds ago the entire office was dark. I wish I'd thought to turn on the desk lamp. That might have helped. Too late now. Whoever it is …

I turn, rotating casually toward the door, as if curious at the new presence in the quiet office, bracing for some harsh questions about why I was reading the criminal code in the dark.

He's more than just a little surprised to see me. Those eyes betray shock. Even some fear. He freezes where he stands in the doorway. But the surprise resolves quickly to apology rather than accusation. I can see from his expression that, whatever I am doing, he has disrupted me, and he is sorry.

I smile and nod. My Vietnamese is rusty, so I dispense with any pleasantries. I return to Twill's desk and hand over the trashcan.

TWENTY-ONE

Hard to say whether she's glad to see me. Dripping in the doorway, I get a luxuriously languid look from the back room of the bar, lids heavy, limbs leaden and splayed. She doesn't exactly leap into my arms.

Doris isn't leaping into my arms either. At least Phil is good for a soft meow from her makeshift bed of towels piled up against the thrumming wine cooler. Doris merely pivots from her tiny desk, turning her back to the spreadsheet on her computer, and lowers her readers to look at Phil.

"I know, sweetie," she coos. "Looks like the mean man is back and wants to take you out in the rain."

Behind me, I can hear Kyle telling his bear-on-a-Ferris-Wheel joke to a couple of regulars as Miles Davis works his way through "Blue in Green" like he's got all night to do it.

"Thanks for that," I say, pulling the leash off the doorknob as I kneel. "She's already thinking of replacing me." I pat the floor in front of me. "Let's go for a swim, tiger."

Phil just looks at me, not moving. Doris laughs. She stands and scoops Phil up in her arms, then delivers her.

"Successful night?" she asks, transferring possession.

"Nobody died, if that's what you're asking. I'll take that."

"Me too," she says, stepping back and catching my eye. "I've been thinking, Ray."

"I did that once. It wasn't for me. Wait, did you say thinking or drinking?"

"I was thinking about you wondering if we ever really knew Marlo."

"I should have kept my mouth shut. Don't pay any attention, Doris."

"I was remembering that when Buck finally came clean about stepping out on me, I wondered the same thing. Did I ever really know the man I married. Because that sort of betrayal ..." She sighs and looks at the floor. "I just ... it was impossible. It was something only someone else could have done. Not my Buck. Not him." Her eyes climb their way back up to mine. "But it *was* him, because here he was on the bed crying and trying to explain himself. And I remember thinking, what else don't I know about you? Who the hell are you to be able to do such a thing to me? If I didn't know that about you, then maybe I don't know you at all. Maybe I never knew you."

I tuck Phil inside my coat and button her up. Doris clips the leash on the collar and wraps the other end around her fingers, trying to find the words. I wait.

"It didn't matter what he had done or what he was capable of doing," she says. "I loved Buck. I simply couldn't imagine my life without him. That was the only thing that mattered."

"Doris …"

"Maybe Marlo had her secrets, just like you had yours. Okay. So what? Maybe you didn't know everything about her. So what? Maybe she kept things from you like you kept things from her. So what, Ray? In the end, none of that matters. I loved Buck, faults and all. Secrets and all. I'm sure Marlo was shocked when she found out about Ronni. Disappointed. Angry. Hurt. But I know none of that touched her love for you. Just like I know that whatever it is you never knew about Marlo, just doesn't matter. Not in the big picture. It doesn't come close to mattering."

"I appreciate what you're saying, Doris. I do. But this could be different."

"It's not different, Ray. Look. I don't know what you're onto. What case you're working or how Marlo is mixed up in it. I don't want to know. I already know everything I need to know about Marlo, and so do you. My advice is that you let go of the little stuff, Ray. Everything but the love is just little stuff. Let it go."

TWENTY-TWO

The very idea of Chicago proper, the visceral sense of it, looms behind me like a midnight tidal wave, holding its immensity aloft as it slides inexorably forward. In the foreground, I navigate the dark, wet streets of Chandler thinking about whether it's possible to take Doris' advice. Just let it all go. Keep what feels the best, pour another drink, and let the rest dissolve away in the rain.

Phil stays curled up in the passenger seat like maybe she's as tired as I am of looking backward, watching the world shrink and slip away down storm drains of pain and regret until all the light goes out like a lit match into the gutter. She purrs beneath my free hand. It's the only thing that keeps me from waking up a Camel and putting it to good use.

The house is right where I left it. I slip Paula into the garage, cut the engine and push the button on the visor. The door seals us in. We sit in the quiet blackness, neither of us caring to move. I pet, Phil purrs. I think some more about whether I can let it all go like Doris wants me to. The photo of Marlo at the table with Victor Roby and Tony Rickens and Mayor Royce burns in my pocket as the memory of my wife burns in my head.

Marlo. The woman I thought I knew.

It's not possible to let it go. I know better. So does Doris.

I open up the car and follow Phil inside. I shed my coat and head for the closet. She pads off for the kitchen like she's hungry. Like maybe I don't know she's been eating all night.

"Keep it up," I call after her. "You'll end up like Garfield. Not the cat, either. I'm talking about the president. You want that? Fat won't look good on you."

I open the closet and reach in for a hanger. The guy inside has other plans. I try to see his face, but his fist keeps getting in the way. I take all five knuckles to the bridge of my nose as the man explodes out into the room after me. He keeps it coming until I topple backward over the chair. I can feel Sig in his harness at my chest ready to jump in, but it's all happening too fast. I roll off the chair, bloody face first to the floor, reaching under me for the gun, but before I can find the grip, my new friend is on top of me, pulling my arms behind my back. He rams his knee into the small of my back to settle me down, then binds my wrists behind me.

"Listen," I say, trying to slow things down. But the man from the closet isn't in the mood. He yanks Sig from the holster and smashes the butt against my head several times until the room wobbles into a spin and I can smell the blood. I can taste it in the back of my throat. I want to vomit. So, I do. I cough violently, then feel myself slip beneath the pain and go limp. I close my eyes and watch the stars circling the black hole drain in the center of the universe.

True darkness comes with a bag over my head, sinched tightly with a cord. I've been here before. Face down in my living room with a knee in my back and my head in a bag. Suddenly I know that this is just another dream. I've dozed off in the car with Phil. I'm still sitting in the dark garage, legs twitching. All that's left is to wake up screaming.

But then the stench of blood and vomit and the acid burn in my throat tell me otherwise. It's all really happening. This is my life. I figure the boys are back to finish the job they threatened to finish if I didn't turn over the Russian doll. I listen through the bag for the sound of that chainsaw. I feel for the little metal teeth at my leg.

Nothing comes. I wriggle and get a new dose of pain from the knee in my spine. I wait. So does the guy with the knee. We both wait, but I'm the only one who doesn't know what for. I take as deep a breath as I can manage.

Now there's a new smell in the mix. Or maybe it was there all the time.

Perfume.

TWENTY-THREE

All Phil and I can do is watch history repeat itself, Phil from the back of the couch, and me up here against the ceiling over the front door.

Funny. History is not interested in revisiting the good stuff. It's got a fondness for mistakes. Pain. Fear. Humiliation. It sticks to the things we hope we never experience again; the lessons we were supposed to learn but didn't. It's the abusive father we dare not cross: *don't make me tell you again.* When history repeats itself, it's going to hurt.

Just ask Ray, face down on his living room floor next to a puddle of sick, with blood in his mouth, a bag over his head, and a knee in his back. Again.

The fear of death is here again too. It's like an odor; a stench with top notes of sweat and blood and some hormone the body emits whenever the brain reaches out in the blackness and feels the edge of the abyss. Ray's down there in the dark listening for that chainsaw. Smelling for it. Motor oil or gasoline. But he's getting a whiff of something floral instead. Maybe they're going to kill him with tuberose.

He wants me to tell him what I see. He wants to know who's in the room with him. Wish I could help. Triple D doesn't work that way. I show him what it looks like to be him. I'm a product of his sensory experience filtered through a fractured psyche. In the room with him is a cat, a big bag of muscle and flesh with body odor and bloody knuckles, and a woman who steps lightly in rubber-soled shoes and who smells like the opposite of death. That's what I see. If you can call it seeing. He knows all of that already.

Mostly what I see is a once-great homicide detective face down on his own floor trying not to wet himself this time. I see a man who wants to go out with a little dignity and who knows he's going to miss that train by a country mile.

TWENTY-FOUR

The guy rolls me on my back so he can punch me twice more in the face through the bag. He's a lefty, this guy. A southpaw allergic to soap and deodorant. I'm bracing for the third punch when he grabs me by the shoulders and pulls against gravity, standing me up like I'm a rolled-up carpet with a body inside. He moves me around the room and then gives me a push in the chest. I fall backward just like he wants me to.

I'm not used to sitting in my recliner with my hands behind my back. It's better than the floor so I don't complain. Not much I can do but sit here in the dark and bleed. A lucky kick might find his crotch. I'm set to give that a try, but then I get another whiff of perfume.

"Maybe you should give your knuckles a rest," I say. "Let the lady tell me why you're here. Go take a shower. Don't spare the soap."

It gets me another two shots to the right side of my head. My ears are ringing. The room around me wants to take my brain for another spin.

"Enough," she says. "Let him be."

The voice is in front of me to the left, from the general direction of the couch. And from what feels like a long time ago. It's not hard to speak her name. It comes out all by itself.

"Suri."

"Hello, Mack."

"Jesus, kid."

"I know. Take a breath. While you still can."

"Your boy here knows how to punch."

"Doesn't he though?" I can hear her light a cigarette. The smoke comes through the bag two seconds later. "Pinky spent a lot of time in the ring. Didn't you, Pink? I'd offer you a drag for old time's sake, but I don't really see how that would work."

"Guess you could take this bag off my head."

"Not interested in doing that."

"Because?"

"Because I don't look like I used to look, Mack."

"None of us do. You should see the guy in my mirror. What makes you so special?"

She takes another drag, like she's considering her answer.

"If you somehow manage to get out of this house alive, I don't want to make it so easy this time for you to hunt me down, stuff me in a trunk and pack me off to some Bloomington shithole where your monkeys are waiting to tear my head off."

"Suri." I want to see through the bag. I want to look her in the eyes. "They weren't my monkeys. I had no idea. I was trying to keep you …"

"No." The next word is calm and not for me. "Again," she says.

The fist to my jaw is like some kind of iron piston jabbing out of a clockwork machine that Charlie Chaplin types always manage to duck just in time. Let's see Charlie try it with his head in a bag.

"Safe?" Her voice cuts through the pain in my head. "You weren't trying to keep me safe, Mack. You were trying to kill me. I'd pissed off Big Man by calling up his piece of shit pimp, Royce. I was tired of being beaten. Used. And I was drunk as hell to help with the pain. I wanted to scare him into leaving me the fuck alone. So I called him up and left a message that you, the one and only Raymond fucking Mackey … my knight in shining armor … my private policeman, was coming to take the whole organization down. Royce, Big Man, everybody."

I listen to her smoke. She laughs to herself.

"Silly me, right? Silly because that was a stupid phone call to make, sure. But even sillier because you were already on the payroll. You *are* the organization, just like the word on the street. Ray Mackey is a dirty cop. In the pocket. As corrupt as they come. I refused to believe it. Looks like I should have."

I know better than to interrupt. Interrupting hurts too much. I wait.

"I shouldn't have made that call. That one's on me. Never drink and dial. I've done a lot of stupid things in my life. More than most. I don't have to tell you. But making that call was right up at the top of the list of stupid things. I couldn't count to three before Sluggo Royce picks me up, nearly beats me to death, then tosses me in his trunk for a ride out to the DeKalb landfill. Who'd have guessed I'd find a way to kill Sluggo Royce before he killed me? Not him. Not Big Man. Not me, that's for damn sure. Not you."

Her words fall away for a moment into an uneasy silence. She's remembering. Rickens was her first. You never forget your first. His one-eyed corpse will twitch and gurgle through her every dream, every quiet waking moment she has from here on out. She doesn't have any choice. It's going to keep coming back to be remembered.

"But I did it anyway, Mack," she says. "I put the motherfucker down. And then I disappeared. Tried to, anyway. I hit Carl up for a place to hide. God bless that man, Mack. He's dead because of me. *Me.*" I can tell her emotion over Carl is still right there on the surface, like gasoline coloring a puddle. "He tried to help me and now he's a fucking ghost. He should've slammed the door in my face. He didn't. He stepped up and took me in and stood by me until the end, Mack. Unlike you."

"Suri, you don't under …"

"Again," she says quietly. Almost sadly.

The punch comes from the other side this time, direct to the left temple. I say something that I'm not in control of and that I don't understand. A curse. A plea. I don't know. My neck goes soft, and my head bounces off my right shoulder. I must black out for a second because my world is no longer black. I can see Marlo sitting at that white-linen banquet table with Royce and Rickens and all the others, drinking champagne and celebrating Royce's election as new alderman of the 42nd ward. Marlo leans over and plants a kiss on Victor Roby's cheek. Then she looks back at me. Sees me. I'm not even there, but she looks back and sees me anyway.

When I wake up, my arms are still losing their circulation behind my back and my aching head is still in a bag of blackness. Suri is talking.

"Because what I didn't know was that Big Man had reached out to the one man who could find me. Raymond fucking Mackey. Big Man is extra pissed because his boy Sluggo Royce is now dead at the dump. So he reaches out to you with instructions to rub me out. You do your duty like a good soldier. You find me as only you could. You get me and Carl to trust you; to put our lives in your hands. Stupid us. We made it easy. You stuff me in that fucking trunk, and you have Carl drive me out to Bloomington so your monkeys can do their business, and you can keep your fucking clothes clean."

Her words are worse than Pinky's punches. I want to speak. I want to defend myself. I don't.

"There were two of them at the motel. Carl saw them first and started shooting. I didn't know what was happening until Carl disintegrated all over the bedroom wall. I've added that to the list of things I can't unsee. Carl as wallpaper."

Silence. She can't talk and remember at the same time. It's too awful. I've seen the photos of Wallpaper Carl. I know it's not the same as being there. I want to tell her that. I want to tell her that my own *can't unsee* list is five times as long as hers. I keep it to myself.

"Then one of the guys dropped dead in front of me, although I still don't know how 'cause I didn't shoot him. And I don't care how, because it gave me the second that I needed to save my own life. I grabbed the gun out of Carl's dead hand and then put the second guy down. I had to empty the fucking thing, but I got him. And then I got the fuck out. I didn't look back. I drove until I nearly ran out of road. Then I turned the car around and I came back to Chicago. You know why, Mack?"

Yeah. I know why. Hard not to know at this point. It hurts. It feels like a fist to the face. But I also know better than to open my mouth.

"I came back for you," she says. "I came back to talk to you. I came back to hurt you. Maybe kill you. Because I'm getting good at killing bad people, Mack. First Royce in DeKalb, and then whoever that was in Bloomington. So why not you too? I figured when I didn't turn up in one of the Bloomington body bags, you'd keep looking until you found me. So why not beat you to the punch? Pinky here is the best puncher I know. So I reach out to Pinky and we start looking."

The fog inside the bag clears enough for me to place the man with the fists of iron. Pinky was a bouncer at one of the strip clubs Suri used to work, back when she was still working a pole as Ginger Turner. I can see him sitting like a white toad on his stool, filling most of that ugly red entrance, checking ID's. Only four fingers on his right hand. Guess which one is missing. I'm betting he's carried a torch for Suri ever since. He'll do anything for her. He'd kill himself if she asked him. He'd make it hurt. In the meantime, there's me.

"Problem is," she says, "I didn't know how to find you. I didn't know where you lived. You're not police anymore because your corrupt ass got fired, which makes the Chandler Police station a dead end not worth my time. So I figured sooner or later you'd turn up at Big Man's dry cleaners. The Blue Lotus. That's where Royce went. That's where all you gangster fucks go to get clean."

"Permission to speak," I say.

"Denied. So Pinky and I mark some time watching the dry cleaner, waiting for you to turn up. You never do. So I try some of our old haunts, because, you know, where the hell else am I going to look? I get Pinky to take me on a history tour of you and me drinking bad coffee and trading information about bad people doing bad things. Made me miss you, Mack. Well, not *you*-you. The good guy, you. The you I thought you were. Turns out you're a good guy only when you need something that I have. Like information to help you put the competition away and to grease your career as a cop. But if I don't have the something you need, or if someone needs me dead, then you're not such a good guy anymore. Are you?"

She lets that sit for a minute, smoking and listening to me breathe. Maybe she wants me to speak. Plead my innocence. I keep my mouth shut.

"Anyway, Pinky here always said I was wasting my time and his gas looking for you. He put the word out and nothing much came back. Someone thought you were dead. Someone else thought you were doing time in Stateville. I was about ready to give up until a couple of days ago someone puts a plastic baggie on Pinky's windshield. Inside the baggie is a photo of you pulling into your garage. House number as plain as day. Whoever it was wrote the word Maltese on the back. Pinky figured out that was a street name. The rest was easy."

I can feel her lean closer. The smoke and the perfume get more intense.

"So. Thing is, Mack, someone out there obviously wants me to find you. And that bothers me a little. Who? Who wants me to find you? Why? And what's really keeping me awake at night is how they knew where to find *me*. And what's going to happen to me after I'm done with you? Well, fuck that. I'm not hanging around to find out. I'm in the wind all over again, this time with a whole new look. I thought I'd drop by for some answers and to even things up. And then say goodbye, Mack. For-fucking-ever."

Silence. Just the breathing and smoking and bleeding.

"You can speak, asshole."

I clear my throat. I need to spit. I can't.

"There's a lot you've got wrong," I croak.

"Such as."

"The guy pimping you out and beating you to a pulp every other week was not named Royce. His name was Anthony Rickens. He was a cop for Chicago PD. As dirty and violent as they come. He was into everything except policing."

"Yeah? Well, the dry-cleaning ticket I pinched from his pocket said S. Royce."

"Ever heard the name Samuel Trenton Royce?"

"No, wait … The fucking… The fucking *mayor*?"

"The same. Sam Royce and Tony Rickens go way back. I'm guessing Rickens and Big Man go back even further. Rickens turned you out on the street because he wanted to use you as a courier, delivering decoy information about the operations of a criminal task force."

"The empty bullets?" she asks.

"Casings," I say.

"Casings. And those little scraps of paper?"

I don't know if she can see me nod inside the bag. I do it anyway.

"It's a game Big Man likes to play. Distract. Confuse. Get everybody chasing their own tails. They'd have killed you eventually, Suri. Just because you knew too much. But that phone call of yours. That moved things along. Rickens tunes you up for old time's sake and drives you out to the DeKalb landfill, just like you said. You gave him what he had coming, Suri. A nail to the eye and six bullets to the chest. He got off easy if you ask me."

"I didn't ask you. Where do you come in?"

"Minding my own business until a guy I thought I knew told me everyone was out looking for you. That gave me a bad feeling. I wanted to find you first. So I did. I got lucky and there you were, hiding out above Carl's liquor store. I shuffled you and Carl off to Bloomington because I was trying to hide you. I had no idea … Shit. They weren't my monkeys, Suri. I don't have any monkeys."

"Who does?"

"Big Man. José Beggemon. The Boogie Man. A lot of people have died since I put you in that trunk. More than you know. I was set up to set you up. I've been looking for answers ever since. Turns out these are the rattlesnake kind of answers that you don't see until you step on them. If you and Pinky want to hold off on the homicide, I'll tell you a story about a little Russian doll that'll curl your hair."

Suri laughs to herself. I can feel her shaking her head. Then the sound stops abruptly. It's like a bird hitting a window.

"Who knows how to find me, Mack? Who knows I'm here?"

"A woman I call Frenchie Marie, and her merry band of G-men. I don't know her real name. Law enforcement she says, but she's shy about the details. I don't know much about her at all except that she likes late-night *lo mein* and jerking me around to get information she wants and that I don't have."

"What kind of information?"

"Dry cleaner information."

I can feel that bit of news land home.

"Dry cleaner information? No shit?"

"According to Frenchie. If I can trust her. She says the Blue Lotus is some kind of Big Man front. She thinks there's a Chandler police tie-in. She wants to use me to help her figure that out."

"But you're not police."

"Yeah, well, Frenchie Marie pulled some strings and fixed that for me. They brought me out of retirement so they'd have someone on the inside."

"And you're good with that?"

"I told her what she could do with her chopsticks. Told her I wasn't going to be in a helping mood until she put me in contact with you. She said she'd work on it. Guess she wasn't kidding."

"Why'd you want to find me, Mack? You looking to finish the job?"

"Come on, Suri. I wanted to confirm you were alive. To tell you I'm sorry. To help you any way I could. It's still me inside this bag. I'm telling you nothing has changed. I've never worked for Big Man, and I never would."

"Yeah? Well he wanted me found, Mack. You did that for him."

"That just makes me a clueless chump off his game, not an accomplice. Big Man needed my help to find you, not to kill you. He knows how to do the killing thing all by himself."

Silence. Pinky's stench beside me makes its own noise, but Suri is quiet. I can hear her stub out her cigarette in the ashtray. Eventually she speaks.

"How'd you know this Frenchie bitch would have any idea where to find me?"

"Because she once handed me a photo of you eating a burger at the McDonald's across the street from the Blue Lotus. She was trying to get my attention. It worked."

"And so now she's delivered me. Like you asked. You working for her now?"

It's the question of the hour. I answer her with a certitude I wish I had.

"I don't work for people I don't know. And I don't know who she is. I don't know who anybody is any more, Suri. Everyone I thought I knew is turning to dust. Except the cat somewhere in this room and you. I still know who you are."

"Yeah? Who's that, Mack?"

"A survivor. When this city finally incinerates, you're the one who walks out brushing ash from your shoulders."

"Me and Big Man."

"Yeah," I say. "Him too."

"What about you?"

"Me? I'm the old guy with an old bag on his head, a wife in the ground, and a new shadow on his lung. I'm lucky to make tomorrow. I've got one foot on the ladder, kid."

"The ladder. What ladder?"

"The one propped up against the cloud. The one that leaves all this behind and disappears up into the big dream."

"The big dream," she says in a kind of soft amazement. "I told you about the big dream?"

"Yeah. When we were up above Carl's liquor store."

"I have no memory of telling you …"

"You were just this side of hysterical. You were having a tough time telling me what you did to Tony Rickens. Your brain took a little detour. You wanted to talk about your john …"

"Delaney."

"That's the one. Crazy Delaney. You told me about the time Delaney told you he had started seeing himself from up inside the big dream. Looking down on himself. Watching himself like a bug under a glass. Delaney told you that when you see yourself from up inside the big dream, that's when you know you're about to die."

"And then he did," she says, remembering.

"And then he did."

"Like … a just a few days after that. He fucking died, Mack."

"So you said."

"And that's happening to you?" she asks. "You see yourself like that? Like a bug under a glass?"

"All the time, Suri."

I suddenly feel the tips of her fingers on my knee.

"Tell me," she says.

"The shrinks have a name for it. I call it Triple D. I'm looking down on myself 24-7."

"What's the D stand for?"

"I think it might stand for Delaney. Looking for you got me a long ride in a small trunk out to the railyards. Big Man's crew. Turns out they were looking for you too. My job was to give you up and then take a bullet to the head. I watched it all from above. Just like Delaney said. Just like you saw Rickens from above, pulling you out of his trunk by the hair, back when he had two eyes and a chest without any holes. Same thing for me. I felt like I was on that ladder, Suri. Climbing my way up into the big dream."

"Jesus," she whispers. "But you didn't die, Mack."

"Neither did you."

"Are you afraid?"

I want to tell her that I'm not afraid of death; that it's getting killed that concerns me. But I know she wants the truth. I know she needs it. I know I owe it to her.

"Yes," I say in the dark. "Always."

"Afraid that you're going to die?"

"Yes. And that my ladder is too short to reach."

Silence.

"What's up there you think, Mack?" she asks.

"Don't know, Suri. Wish I did."

"What do you *want* to be up there?"

It's suddenly not a conversation I want to have. I'd rather start up again with Pinky. The word, the answer, comes out anyway.

"Forgiveness."

Another empty beat. Then I feel her hands at my throat, fingers fumbling at the cord around my neck. She removes the bag from my head. The sudden light feels like a fist. I close my eyes in the flash of pain.

Suri places a soft palm on each side of my face and kisses me on the lips, pillowing my senses with perfume and smokey breath. When she pulls away, my eyes are open. The woman in front of me is bald, with multi-colored tattoos, green vines and pink flowers, covering her scalp. A man's clothing – a soaking, stained denim shirt and khaki cargo pants – not Pinky's, but still much too big, hangs on her frame. They make her seem like a child in daddy's clothes. She sits back on the couch next to Phil and a wet, pink baseball cap I do not recognize. Phil makes eye contact but doesn't move except to push herself closer into Suri's leg.

"Courtney," I say, using the forbidden name. Because this is not Suri sitting in front of me. Not Ginger Turner. Not a hooker or hustler or vamp. This is the runaway girl who escaped her stepfather to the streets so many years ago. The survivor. Now running all over again. She holds up a hand.

"No," she says. "This is not the beginning of something new, Mack. This is the end of something old. Maybe I am a survivor. But the only way I survive is by trusting no one. Not even you. Maybe especially not you. I came back to Chicago to even the score. For Carl. And for me. But I don't like that your Frenchie friend knows I'm here. And I don't like that maybe you're telling me the truth about things. And I don't like liking you so goddamned much. So I'm going to trust you one last time. I'm going to trust you not to follow me. Not to look for me. Not to help me. If you violate that trust, Mack …"

Behind me I can hear Pinky shift his considerable weight. My muscles tense for another beating that doesn't come. She finishes her sentence like she means it.

"I will do … whatever I have to do."

"Don't disappear on me," I say. "Not again. Let's go have a burger someplace. You can get yours cooked and eat it and I can get mine raw and put it on my face. We can catch up. Compare notes. Figure all of this out. Like old times."

Suri gives Phil a final stroke on the top of her head, stands and tosses the bag and rope across the room to Pinky. She scoops the cap off the couch and pulls it over her head, walking up even with my chair. She lets her hand linger on my bruised and bloody cheek before she pulls her fingertips away and then disappears behind me. I hear the front door open to the sound of a hard, steady rain.

"See you up in the dream, Mack," she says. "Let's catch up there. We can drink whatever we want. Look down on whoever's left."

TWENTY-FIVE

He stays right where she leaves him. Face swelling up. Losing circulation in his arms. Plastic restraints cutting into his wrists. Blood trickling off his left lobe and down his neck.

Listening to the rain outside.

Listening to the dry quiet resettling inside his home like volcanic ash.

Phil stretches and stands, padding her way in his direction across the cushions. The couch only has two of its original legs, the other two having been amputated with a chainsaw during his last living room assault. He's releveled the thing with wooden blocks so that his future assailants have a comfortable place to sit as they watch him bleed.

It's all the same to Phil. She leaps onto the recliner, circling his lap once before lowering herself into position. She wants her drop of Old Forester and to be petted to sleep.

Sure she does. Who doesn't want that?

"Sorry," he says. "My hands are tied."

His head feels like a ripe, punctured melon. He leans it back in the chair. The blood finds a different place on his neck to drip.

He listens. Swells. Bleeds. Thinks.

Sleeps.

TWENTY-SIX

In the dream, Marlo has taken my arms. Turns out you can twist them off my shoulders like grapes from a vine. She hands one of them over to Tony Rickens, who looks pretty good for a slab of meat with one eye and a chest full of holes. He uses my arm as a bat to my head. I come awake with a full-body jolt just as Rickens connects like Sammy Sosa unloading on a ninth-inning swing against the Cardinals.

Phil is on the table, looking at me like she wants to keep her distance. The clock on the shelf says I've been out two hours and change. Feels more like a couple of years. Outside it's raining harder than ever. I can hear it through the walls. A billion little fists, pounding to come in and drown me where I sit.

I manage to stand. Not pretty, but I get there. I make my way to the garage where I know there's a saw blade I can reach. I have to back up against the garage door and reeducate my fingers on how to turn a knob, but they get the job done. The saw is where I remember and soon enough my arms are dangling at my sides again like a couple of sausage links. The blood returns like water through a ruptured dam. I liked it better when I couldn't feel them.

Everything hurts. All of it. Even the parts Pinky never punched, hiding in places I've never seen before.

I pour myself a drink. Phil is at my heels meowing so I give her a drop of bourbon from my finger and open a can of fish into a bowl on the floor. I clean up the puke in the living room and then take my glass upstairs so it can wait for me while I shower the dried blood off my face and neck. I lean back against the tile and let the water come. I snake my hand out of the shower and grab the glass from the vanity. I drink and rattle the cubes in their bath. I pull one out and hold it against my face. If there were a chair in here, I'd stay all day.

The guy in the mirror looks like some kind of pumpkin patch mutant. My left eye is a cocktail onion looking back from the inside of a Bloody Mary. Both ears are swollen and cut and seeping. My nose and lips are bleeding. My front teeth are limned in scarlet. The skin over my cheekbones has split like overripe fruit and the sides of my face are brooding into a dark, purplish red.

Something to dampen the pain would be nice. I search for any Vicodin left over from the last assault in my living room but come up empty as I knew I would. I settle for something over the counter, then I double it and throw them back with another glass of Old Forester. I return to the recliner and bury my face beneath bags of frozen raspberries and peas that have been in the freezer since before Marlo died. I can feel Phil find my lap again. She curls up to sleep.

Me, I hurt too much to sleep. So I try to use the time to think things through. I can't do that in this much pain without a cigarette. I feel around in the pocket of the lounger and find a pack and a lighter in easy reach, right where they aren't supposed to be. I knock a Camel out of the corral and make a hole between the frozen raspberries and the frozen peas. I insert the thing where it belongs.

Dr. Dinesh Jha is in my head with a little smile on his lips that part just enough to let out the word *shadow*. I think two big words back in his direction – *extenuating … circumstances* – and then I throw in three small ones for free: *fuck you, doc*. He smiles and holds up a photo of Senator Kahn.

I can light a cigarette with my eyes closed. I cannot, apparently, light a cigarette from beneath bags of frozen fruits and vegetables. The lighter fumbles, leaving my fingers for a bump off my foot and skitters across the floor. It hurts too much to move. So I don't.

I keep the Camel in position. It'll last longer this way. The guy up against the ceiling with all the opinions thinks I look like a ridiculous version of my former self. He might be right, but I hurt too much to care. Question is whether I can think through any of this mess without nicotine. It feels like a ten-thousand-piece puzzle with all but a handful of those pieces upside down. The ones I can see don't exactly connect.

Frenchie Marie has now delivered on what she thinks was a bargain. She's delivered Suri to my doorstep. So Marie is going to expect me to deliver something on Twill. All I can deliver are unanswered questions. A second forensics report from Peter Chow that I can't open. A photo of a hot exchange between Twill and Chow that is anything but news to Frenchie Marie since she's the one who gave me the photo in the first place. Twill's new girlfriend, Amanda Ramada Tate, wearing a wig and driving Saul Margolis' car to Blondie's so she can watch Constantine Papadopoulos come and go without so much as a hello or goodbye.

I don't know what any of it means. All of it hurts to think about. So I switch channels and think of Marlo. And why not? May as well. That's where all the real pain hangs out anyway. Ground zero for everything.

Why does Marlo have a stack of Tia Lewis' old business cards tucked away for safe keeping? Is Tia Teelew? If so, what's she got to do with any of this?

I think of Marlo sitting at the banquet table. That tendril of hair along the slope of her back. Victor Roby's hand on hers. She doesn't know I'm looking at her from decades into her future. Makes me wonder who's looking at me from the future. Makes me wonder if I'm dead too.

Another five hours in the chair brings a gray, underwater daylight through the shades. Phil is a fluffy white bowling ball on my legs and the pain of sitting now rivals the pain of standing. I relocate her to the couch, leaving a trail of raspberry juice from the bag that never seemed punctured when it was frozen. I clean things up as best I can and then go outside for another shower on my way to breakfast.

I park on the curb and walk the half block like every step doesn't hurt. I shake the rain off outside Sonny's, holding the door for a couple of guys on their way out. They're all set to use their briefcases as umbrellas.

"Don't wet your briefs," I tell them.

They give me a frightened sort of look and move a little faster out into the weather. I step inside a fragrant cloud of dough and sugar and sizzling meat and let the door close behind me. Above my head, Tinkerbell lets everyone know I'm here. No one cares.

Seven-thirty has Cleopatra slinging hash and eggs and black coffee for a cross-section of working-class Chicago. They're all watching her come and go, wondering what the Queen of Egypt is doing taking orders and pouring refills. It's the poised, chin-up posture and the dark skin and sleek, black mane, and the way her high cheekbones hold up those deep-velvet, chocolate eyes. Someone took her scepter and gave her a ball point pen, but they let her keep the gold pyramids hanging from her lobes. She's twenty-nine going on immortal.

Poor Cleopatra. She didn't get to choose her name. I don't want her to feel self-conscious. So I usually call her Isis. She usually answers.

There's a booth in the back with my name on it. I head that way, shedding my coat as I go. I sit and wait. It doesn't take her long to show up and be offended.

"Jesus Christ, Mack. Your … your *face*."

"Yeah, it's mine. I take it everywhere I go. Morning, Isis."

She slips in across from me, pitcher of coffee in one hand and a tray of someone else's drinks in the other. She sets her load on the table and focuses with an intensity that hurts.

"What happened to you?" she asks. I wave off her concern.

"Playing Marco Polo with some friends. They like to use horses and mallets."

Cleo grabs my napkin and leans over the table, dabbing it beneath my ear. It comes back scarlet.

"You're bleeding, Mack," she says.

"That's raspberry juice, Cleo. They *really* didn't know the rules of Marco Polo."

"You need attention."

"Thanks, but I've had enough attention for one day. Instead, I'll have a black coffee, two over-easy eggs with bacon, and a buckwheat pancake on the side. Hold the raspberry sauce. I brought my own."

Her lips tighten.

"You know, *this* is why I tell Raj he needs to focus on a real job."

"I thought Raj had a real job. Best cabbie in the city."

"Not talking about driving a cab. I'll take him as a cab driver any day. But he's bent on getting a detective license, Mack."

"What?" I ask, genuinely surprised. "Since when?"

"Since day one. And whose fault do you guess that is?"

"Charlie Chan," I say. "Miss Marple. Nancy Drew."

I get a look that feels like a slap. "You done?"

"Sorry."

"He told me you've got him following criminals all over town. Again."

"Suspects, Cleo. Innocent until proven …"

"You want a mirror, Mack? You want another look at what your innocent little suspects can do?"

"Different people, Cleo. They weren't …"

"Raj could have been killed the last time. Me too, for that matter. Or have you forgotten?"

"No, I haven't forgotten. But he wasn't killed. Neither were you. You both kept your cool under pressure. He …"

"I love you, Mack. I do. But I don't want Raj to end up looking like you. Living like you. No offense."

I show her my palms.

"None taken, kid. I'll talk to him. I will. I'll talk to him."

"You do that. Try it without a cigarette in your mouth and a gun strapped to your chest. He wants to be you, Mack. That frightens me." She gives me a coffee and an orange juice meant for someone else. "I'll be back."

The food arrives faster than it should in the morning rush, which is good because I'm hungrier than I should be after a thorough beating from a guy with nine fingers. It hurts to chew, but I do it anyway. When I'm done, I leave a healthy tip and stand to go. Isis intercepts me, grabs me by the elbow and escorts me to the employees-only rest room. I pause at the threshold, one foot in, one foot out.

"Who needs the help in here, Isis, you or me? People are gonna talk. I've got a reputation to worry about."

"Shut up, Mack. Just stay here. I'll be back."

I do as I'm told. She's back in two minutes with a bag full of makeup she doesn't need.

"You can't walk around in public like this," she says. "You'll scare people."

She pulls out a brush and a tin of powder. My masculinity clears its throat.

"Cleo, look …"

"Shut up and stand still."

I pull up outside the Robert J. Stein Institute of Forensic Medicine feeling like a new man: less hungry, less raspberry drizzle behind my ear, and more pancake on my face than in my gut. Everything else feels about the same. It still hurts to have a head.

The building is a large, imposing block of gray concrete with sharply chiseled, cavernous windows and modern exterior angles to justify what the Cook County taxpayers forked over to the architects. The good Dr. Stein has long since left the building, but the edifice with his name on the wall carries on as a concrete bunker for those who investigate deaths that occur under suspicious circumstances. When the bombs finally come, the people working for the Cook County Medical Examiner are going to be just fine.

I park in front beneath three flags hanging on their poles like wet, patriotic dishrags. The rain keeps at it. I walk faster than I want to for the front door, pushing through the pain, because I'm afraid my makeup will run. I shake off at reception and ask for Peter Chow.

"Is he expecting you?" The young woman seems mesmerized at my face.

"No one has ever expected me. That includes my mother. Tell him it was the brothers, not the boss."

"Excuse me?"

"Ever hear about the case of the Cicero Four?"

"No," she says.

"Look it up sometime; I just gave you the spoiler. Tell Pete there's a guy in the lobby saying the brothers did it, not the boss."

The kid is game. She picks up the phone and pushes a couple of buttons, then follows instructions like a pro. It's a short conversation.

The Lead Forensics Tech for the Cook County ME is just standing up from his desk as I enter. Pete Chow hasn't changed a bit. Same bifocals. Same doughiness in the cheeks. He's still shorter than I am and I'm guessing he's still smarter. He should look ten years older than the last time I saw him. He doesn't. Maybe it's the Asian features. He just doesn't need the makeup like I do. He's got his hand out, so I cross the office and give it a wag.

"Hey Pete," I say.

"Mack. Been a while. What the hell happened to you?"

"Angry makeup artist packing foundation and concealer."

He shakes his head and moves his finger in a small, pointing circle.

"No, I mean all the color underneath. And the swelling. The left eye. You really took a beating."

"Boy, can't hide anything from forensics geeks."

"I've seen prettier corpses. Sit."

I sit. So does he.

"Heard you were back working for Chandler PD," he says. "Internal Affairs of all places. You must be making lots of friends. Don't tell me cops did this."

"Okay, I won't. It's a long story you don't want to hear, and that I don't want to relive."

"Okay. Well." Pete gives me his time-is-money look. "Are you here to remind me I was right about the Cicero four?"

"No, no. I just wanted to get your attention. I don't have an appointment and everybody likes being right. Guess it worked."

It gets me a small smile and a slow shake of the head.

"That qualifies as shameless manipulation. But I guess I can't quibble with success. What's on your mind?"

"Couple of stiffs."

"Isn't it always? Want to narrow it down?"

"Dennis and Carrie O'Toole."

The sound of those names in the air is like a foul, bitter wind that makes Pete Chow pull in all his extremities. He leans back in his chair and crosses his arms. His eyes narrow. His lips tighten. He knows corpses. I know people.

"What about them?" he asks.

"We have a piece of that action. My LT is working it himself."

"Odd for Chandler IAD to have an angle on a Chicago homicide, but okay."

"So then this is the first you're hearing about Chandler IAD's interest?"

"News to me," he says with a couple of unnecessary blinks.

"Homicide or double homicide?"

Pete wrinkles up his face.

"Excuse me?"

"You just called it a Chicago homicide. Was it one lump or two?"

"Uh … you subscribe to any newspapers? I wrote that one up as a murder-suicide."

"How many reports did it take you to get there, Pete?"

"How many reports?"

"Yeah, how many reports?"

"I do a couple of preliminary drafts as the different forensics tests start to roll in. Then I …"

"No, no. How many *final* reports?"

"There's only one final forensics report. Well, two total in that case. One for Dennis O'Toole and one for Carrie O'Toole. What's this about?"

"Only one report for Dennis?"

"Yeah. One."

"And does that final report come in different flavors, Pete?"

Pete looks at me like I'm not making sense. It's a look I get a lot, so I recognize it immediately. He scratches his eyebrow.

"What are you asking, Mack? Two bodies, two final forensics reports. The forensics analysis is an appendix to the MER, the Medical Examiner Report, which is like the global …"

"I know what an MER is. What I don't get is why on the last page of the forensics report for Dennis there is a document control number followed by v2."

"A v2?"

"Yeah, Victor-two, as in version two. Small print but plain as day. In my limited experience, version two usually follows version one."

Pete's features harden a little.

"Look, Mack. I'm not really sure what this is here. Is there some kind of problem?"

"I'm just trying to understand what you think happened to these people."

"What happ … Dennis O'Toole beat his wife to death and then he shot himself in the head. Not complicated. I wrote it up as a murder-suicide. I don't know what else I can …"

"I know how you wrote it up, Pete. I'd like to know what you found."

The color in Pete's face starts to change.

"What are you insinuating?"

"I'm a long way from insinuating, Pete. I'm still way back at the wondering stage."

Pete takes a quiet breath, like he's trying to keep some emotion locked down. He wants me to think it's anger. Could be. Could also be fear.

"Then what the hell are you wondering?" he asks under new control.

"I'm wondering if there was an earlier forensics report calling Dennis a homicide, not a suicide. I'm wondering if you've been persuaded to rethink what happened to Dennis in light of … other considerations."

"What other considerations?"

I give it a couple of empty beats as I decide whether it's time to talk about his brother Andy.

"You tell me, Pete."

"I can't tell you because none of what you're saying makes any sense. Look, I don't know what you're trying to get out of me, Mack, but I've got full plate today so …"

Pete picks up a nearby pen just so he can point it at the door. I pretend I don't see it.

"What's with the v-2?" I ask.

"I don't know. I never noticed it. I'm not the last person to touch a final forensics report before it goes out. Someone probably saved it wrong. One single change after final and our system automatically saves it as a new version. Seriously, Mack, time to go."

"So you're telling me you never wrote this case up as a double."

"That's what I'm telling you."

"And no one has been around showing an interest."

"No one but you, unfortunately. Time to go, Mack."

I'm not ready to leave. I turn up the temperature a little.

"How's Andy doing, Pete?"

That gets his attention. He sets the pen down and slowly recrosses his arms. Reminds me of a man on a plane ride fastening a seatbelt. Question is why he feels nervous about the ride.

"As well as can be expected," he says. "What's Andrew got to do with this?"

"You tell me. Coming up for parole in another year, right?"

Pete smiles. Then he laughs in a not-so-funny kind of way.

"What … you think my brother's parole is some kind of pressure point for me? No one thinks that's happening. Not me. Not him. He'll serve the full sentence."

"Too many dead cheerleaders?"

It's an unnecessary poke in the eye that Pete doesn't deserve. He wasn't even in the car. But he stops smiling and gives me some stone-cold credit for being right.

"Yeah," he says. "Too many dead cheerleaders. Anything else, Officer Mackey?"

I've had lots of practice in knowing when I'm not wanted. I scoot forward to the edge of my chair.

"Just this." I reach in my pocket for the photo. I pull it out and open it up. "You want to tell me what this was all about?"

I watch him take it in. Orland Twill pointing his finger, giving Pete what-for on the other side of a curtain of rain streaming off the roof of Pete's garage. The back end of Twill's Escalade is in the foreground.

"Where'd you get this? Are you fucking surveilling me?"

"No. But somebody is. What's the story, Pete?"

He pulls the glasses down his nose and looks at the photo like I've handed him the fine print of a car rental contract.

"I don't … I don't …"

"Listen to me, Pete. We've had our differences, sure. I'm not on your Christmas card list and you're not on mine and maybe that's too bad. But I know you as a straight shooter. Buckets of integrity and professional credibility to spare. You're a guy with a lot to lose. You always have to work the same side of the corpse. Sometimes I have the benefit of working things before there is a corpse, so let me tell you something that maybe isn't so obvious: if someone out there is running you down, then trying to run faster isn't going to work. You've got to get off the road, brother. Understand? You've got to get out of the way. Let me help you with that. Tell me what's going on."

I can't see his face. I'm talking to the back of the photo. But maybe the silence is telling.

"This is bogus," he says, finally.

"What is?"

"This photo." He hands it back across the desk and points at it as I take it. "That discussion, or whatever it is pretending to be, never happened. Not with Orland Twill. Whoever gave this to you has swapped Twill in."

I look at the photo, then back at Pete.

"You sure?"

"I'm a forensics scientist. I know a fake photo when I see one. And this is a photo of me and my neighbor, Fritz Holland. They … I don't know who, someone, hell, maybe you, I don't know, but someone has digitally substituted in Twill for Fritz. Good job too. Hard to tell. And printing on cheap copy paper helps cover the tracks. But I remember that conversation with Fritz. This is a fake."

Pinky did a number on the little muscles around my eyes. It hurts to squint. I hold the photo up to my face and squint anyway.

"Why do you remember the conversation with Fritz?" I ask.

"His movers backed a van into my mailbox and cracked the post. He came up to the house to apologize and offer to repair it. He didn't point a finger in my face, not that I remember, and he wasn't angry. And he didn't lose all his hair and grow twelve inches either."

"When did that conversation happen?"

Pete winces, screwing up his face.

"Well, Fritz and Gayle moved out the last week in May so it would have been earlier that month."

"Last year. Last May."

"Yes. I wasn't aware I was on candid camera. Why were you surveilling me?"

"I wasn't. I'm not. Like I said."

"Where'd the photo come from?"

"I can't tell you that."

"Well look, Mack, whoever gave you this photo either doesn't know it's a fake or is taking you for a ride. The idea that there was someone in the bushes by my house with a camera makes me want to start packing."

"Packing to move?"

"Packing a gun."

"Oh. Thought you were thinking of leaving, Pete."

"No, Mack. That's you."

I fold up the paper and return it to my coat pocket. I don't bother shaking the man's hand.

"Thanks for the time," I say. "Sorry for the intrusion."

"Let's make it a long time before we do this again, Mack."

I nod and head for the door, stopping myself before stepping into the hall.

"Where'd he move to?" I ask.

"Who?"

"Your neighbor. Fritz whatshisname. Holland."

Pete cocks his head, squinting.

"Europe. Germany, I think. I don't know the town."

I nod at the cruel inconvenience and close the door behind me.

Outside I sit in the parking lot and listen to the rain beat out an homage to Buddy Rich on Paula's dented hood. I try to think my way to whatever is next. Guess I could check his story. Fly to Germany and ask if anybody knows a guy named

Fritz. I replay Pete cocking his head, squinting, trying to remember where Fritz Holland ended up. Like the very act of remembering all the way back to last May hurts Pete's brain.

Remembering hurts my brain too. But the pain never seems to stop the memories from coming full bore anyway. If pain was an effective shield against memory, I'd have forgotten Marlo a long time ago.

But it isn't, so I haven't. I remember her like she's still here. Like I last saw her twenty minutes ago, back at the house bent over the paper at the kitchen table, working the crossword in pen as the coffee maker gurgles and wheezes into the pot.

Little things. Her fingers in her hair, absently twirling as she reads. Or working her garden in the spring, turquoise gloves, wearing her father's Cubs hat, smelling of citronella and tomato vine.

I remember her at the farmers' market. A bag of romaine under one arm as she examines the handmade stain glass hummingbird rain gauge. Marlo liked measuring. Quantification. She once showed me the toxicology report on a man who left behind a grieving widow, a top-shelf life insurance policy, and trace amounts of thallium.

"Not all truth can be measured, Ray," she'd said, "but everything you can measure is true."

Marlo had asked me to put the rain gauge in the back yard where we could see it from the kitchen window. She's five years gone. Five and some change. I see that stained-glass bird every day, beak open and drowning in the rain, and I can remember the day she bought it like it just happened. Like she's behind me, bent into the refrigerator, putting away the romaine as I'm pulling the glass bird out of its box.

Just like I can remember that May of last year was the driest May in Chicago history. All the headlines complained of drought and all the articles connected the dots to global warming and all the stain glass hummingbirds in all of Chicago thirsted for rain.

But there was nary a drop to fall in May. Not one. Not at my house.

Maybe all the rain that month happened above Pete Chow's garage.

Or maybe not.

TWENTY-SEVEN

He goes to work. The noun, not the verb. The *place* he calls work. Maybe because everything about that place is so unpleasant it takes effort just to be there. Just walking in the front door makes him want to curl up in a bottle and rest.

He leaves most of the water in the elevator and keeps his head down, hoping to get to the cubicle he calls home without catching anyone's attention. That's never going to happen.

"Jesus, Mack." Stephanie Nellis is at her desk, back from leave with all her powers of observation intact. "What the hell happened to you?"

"Happy Halloween, Steph. Not sure I really get your costume."

"Office Assistant. And you're a crash test dummy?"

She's young and adorable. Full of energy. She belongs in a toothpaste commercial, this kid. She owes her job to a ten-thousand-watt smile and an uncle in administration, but she keeps that secret by being irreplaceably competent. Ray should feel worse than he does about ransacking her desk.

"Close," he says. "I was going for the after-photo in a public service ad." He keeps walking to avoid anything protracted. "And don't call me a dummy."

They all watch him cross the office. Steph from behind. Carolyn leans back in her chair and takes another pull on her rope of licorice, chewing, secretly opining. She tosses a look to Raffi who swivels in his chair like a satellite dish tracking a slow UFO. No one says anything.

Twill is standing in the doorway of his office. Ray gives him a nothing-to-see-here nod. Twill shakes his head in a *not-this-again* sort of way and with a look that agrees: Nothing to see here. Nothing to care about here. Then he turns and closes his door.

TWENTY-EIGHT

My chair catches me like a foul ball into the stands, sending up a judgmental groan. The light from the window next to me is wet and moody. It belongs in a glass with a splash of amber in a room full of smoke and maybe someone who knows how to hold a microphone singing about being locked out in the rain. But the overhead fluorescents kill everything. Everything except the job and the stacks of files on my desk, growing in colonies of rectangles, breeding headaches and new enemies.

Marlo looks down at me from her perch on the shelf. That look doesn't ask what happened to my face. That look already knows. It knows a lot more than I do. Always did.

My first order of business is to figure out who Saul Margolis is and why Amanda Ramada Tate is dressing up in a wig to drive his car around Chicago. Since she likes switching cars in a members-only parking garage attached to her place of employment, I make an educated leap that Saul also works for BSD Financial. Turns out I'm right.

"Mr. Margolis is out of the office." The woman on the phone knows how to deliver bad news so you almost don't mind the rejection. She purrs out a bonus question. "Can someone else assist you?"

"When do you expect him in?"

"I'm sorry, Mr. Margolis is in Israel on indefinite leave. But he does check in for messages. Can I have him call you?"

I tell her all about my badge and give her my number. I hang up in time to see Santiago making his way to my corner of the room.

"Looking a little worse for wear, Mack," he says, draping an arm over the cubicle wall. "Should I ask you what the hell happened or is this the part where you laugh it off because you're not ready to tell me what kind of shit you're into now and just how deep it's getting?"

I give him a whiplash smile that hurts me to make.

"Ask me no questions, Raffi, I'll tell you no lies."

"That's going on your headstone, Mack. I'll make sure of it."

"And what if *I* bury *you*? What do you want me to chisel on yours?"

"Let's go with: 'I never should have asked.'"

"So it's going to be my fault, is it?"

"The odds are good," he says. "Can we talk?"

"Aren't we?"

"Conference room in fifteen."

I nod and watch him saunter back to his desk. I don't know what's on his mind, but it's something he doesn't want to talk about in the open.

I take a look at my watch and mark the time, then I riffle through my notes for the scribbles about Whitey Whitish, the fastest, fast food consumer in the west. I don't know what kind of game Amanda is playing with this guy, but I know from experience that the direct approach from me will only push it underground. I'm not in the mood to dig.

The odds that the number in the motor vehicle database actually connects to the phone in the correct man's pocket are about thirty-seventy in favor of needing to do a lot more research. This time I beat the odds. An educated baritone tells me I've reached the phone of Constantine Papadopoulos and that I should leave a message. I know how to follow instructions. Just like I know how to bait a hook.

"Mr. Papadopoulos. You left something at Blondie's yesterday. We need to have a conversation about that. I like telephones about as much as you or your family like the police. I'll see you there at 3:30. I'll be the guy in the booth looking at his watch. It's not in your interest to waste my time. See you then."

I disconnect and drop the phone back in my pocket. Let's see if that gets him hungry for some fast food.

One more bit of business before I go find out what's got Raffi twisted into knots. I do a quick internet search for Housing First Chicago. The website is loaded with photos of Windy City homeless looking relieved to be out of the wind and every other kind of weather. I click over to the Staff page and find the face I'm looking for. She's the one in front of everybody else, right above the phone number. I pick up the desk phone and dial.

"I'd like to speak to Tia Lewis, please."

"Ms. Lewis is out of the office at a fundraiser. Can I leave a message?"

It's a good question for a receptionist to ask, but harder for me to answer. I want to ask about the wife I never knew and why I've got a stack of Tia's old business cards, but that's jumping the gun.

"Tell her Ray Mackey called. Marlo's husband. I need to schedule some time."

Santiago is already in the conference room when I show up and close the door. He's at the far end of the table unwrapping a stick of gum. He holds out the pack as I take a chair.

"Trying to quit," I say.

"Chewing?"

"Yeah. If I can't drink it, I don't want it. What's this about, Raffi?"

Raphael's face darkens a little. Either his gum is fish-flavored or he doesn't like what he needs to say.

"OAG," he says. "I don't like the questions they're asking, man."

"Stop." I show him my palms. "Whatever they're asking you isn't for me to hear about. Don't back yourself into something that's not your problem. You don't owe me anything, Raffi. Be smart about this."

"I appreciate that, Mack. I do. I'm not going to tell you something I shouldn't. Brewster's not asking about you. Not as much anyway. Understand?"

I do understand. So I give him a soft nod. He's got more to say. He's like a man who's not through being sick. Nothing to do but let it come.

"Yesterday LT called me in. Said he wants me to keep an eye on you. Said he wanted me to take the day and see how you were spending your time."

"Christ." The news hits hard, but I try my best to shrug it off. "Assignment like that could kill you with boredom, Raffi."

"I doubt that. From the way you look today? You're into something, Mack. Maybe something bad. I don't know what's going on. But between Brewster and LT, I'm getting pulled into the middle of something ugly. And I don't like it, man."

"Understood, Raffi. I'm not asking."

"You're the only one who's not asking. Probably why I'm coming to you. Which probably gets me fired for six different reasons."

"What'd you tell him?"

"I asked him what this was all about. He said he couldn't tell me and that I was better off not knowing anyway. He said he just needed some eyes on you for a day or two. Like that's no big deal."

"Where'd you leave it?"

"I told him no. I told him I can't surveil someone on my own team."

"How'd he take it?"

"I don't know. I'm guessing disappointed. Until I added the thing I shouldn't have."

"Which was?"

Raffi sighs and throws his head back so he can keep an eye on the ceiling.

"I told him that I wouldn't surveil him either." He lets the ceiling go and looks back at me. "What I meant was …"

"I know what you meant. You meant he's part of the team."

"Yeah. But it came out like I think maybe there's good reason to keep an extra set of eyes on him."

"Didn't put a smile on his face, I take it."

"I don't know why I said it. I think I had Brewster's voice still banging around in my head. They're asking a lot of questions, Mack."

"Look, Brewster asks questions. That's what he does best. Maybe those questions mean something and maybe that's just Brewster looking to shake you up like a warm can of beer. It was no different when I was working homicide. Turn up the heat. Make everyone uncomfortable. See what happens."

"LT asked me to do something, Mack. I said no. That's insubordination. That's …"

"He's not going to can you, Raffi. He doesn't have enough bodies up here as it is. IAD can't afford another empty chair. Keep your head down. Do your work. Stay clear of this shitstorm as best you can. You're going to come through it. Hell, you'll probably be the only one left standing."

Raffi nods with another heavy sigh.

"This thing between you and LT, Mack …"

I give him a polite headshake.

"Ask me no questions, Raffi."

TWENTY-NINE

I work my cases like a good boy, shuffling files and scaling the mountain of paper like I'm bucking for a promotion.

I make a modicum of progress in the Ryan Coopersmith case. I pull up the list of people Chicago PD has already interviewed and let my fingers do the walking. I call down to the second floor and make initial contact with three of Coopersmith's fellow officers. *Former* fellow officers. Two of them play hard to get with flimsy excuses about the time. One of those pretends his LT is trying to get his attention, like his mother is calling him to supper.

The third guy is more accommodating. He's got a name he can swing around: Alphonse K. Jarr. The K stands for Kingston. Turns out Jarr's lid isn't screwed on as tight as the others, at least not when he's alone in his squad room. According to him, everybody knew Coopersmith was slinging on the side. He's been at it so long he got tired of the risks. Tired of avoiding them. Worrying about them. He started to act invincible. Just a matter of time before he got caught in someone's net.

Jarr says he's good for more, but I have to make a production of bringing him in kicking and screaming with a formal request. I tell him I can do that and thank him for his time.

I put together three draft interview requests and ask Steph if she can work up the pink sheets and send them out.

She's staring and squinting more than she's listening.

"Who does your makeup?"

I leave early for my date with Constantine Papadopoulos at Blondie's, thinking I've got even odds that he shows at all. If he doesn't show, then I'll call him up and tell him I'm parked outside his house. That usually focuses the attention. He'll suggest meeting someplace other than where his wife and kids sleep. I'll offer up that, hey, maybe Blondie's would be a good place.

I point Paula through the curtains of rain to the 294, keeping an eye on the mirror just in case I have company. Lots of cars back there. Trick is figuring out which ones are interested in going the distance. Best way to spot a tail on a freeway is to cut your speed in the right lane as you approach an offramp and see who doesn't care about slowing down. So I do. Turns out lots of people care. They all blow past me with a hissing spray and matching scowls that recommend the bus. Behind me, a new slate of cars takes their place.

I don't know any of them. I suspect all of them.

Sam the Shrink is in my head. She thinks it's the paranoia talking.

Maybe.

Or maybe that's just what she wants me to think.

So I keep moving forward while looking backward.

I find Blondie's tucked away off West Lake Street in Addison, just like Raj said. I signal early and take my time pulling into the lot just to give whoever's following me a chance to adapt. Then I square Paula to the building and take a good look.

Blondie's.

The lit red, cursive letters along the top of the facade gleam in the rain like they've been dipped in nail polish and buffed to a high shine. The front windows are big, clean rectangles with rounded corners, all framed in chrome. Reminds me more of the windshield and the spit-shine grillwork of a vintage Ford than it does the front of a restaurant. The dozen or so cars in the lot are all huddled up against the building like boats docked at the shoreline. Mostly employees, I'm guessing, since it looks like only a few tables have people at them. Most of the action seems to be in the drive-thru lane curving around back. I count seven cars in line. Number eight, a silver Volt, is on its way across the parking lot.

Behind number eight is a slow-rolling, moss-green Tacoma that seems uncomfortably familiar from the drive over. It acts uncertain about the drive-thru, like maybe it wants to park off by itself and think about things. So it does. Lights off. Idling.

Okay. Not paranoid, then.

I park near the front and splash my way inside. I shake myself from wet to damp and cross the gleaming checkerboard tiles to take a seat in a red leather booth at one of the front windows. I don't know what the food is like, but you could eat it off the floor. Cleanest fast-food joint I've ever seen. Every surface shines like it's new, which is something for a business pretending to be seventy years old.

Framed black and whites cover the walls: Chubby and Elvis and Grace and Humphrey and Sophia. Marlon. Liz. The Platters are singing about smoke getting in your eyes. I have a sudden urge to pat myself down for a Camel. Buddy Holly is looking down at me like he wants to know what happened to my face.

A pimply kid in a starched white uniform with red piping and a paper hat stops by with an armload of red plastic trays. He jerks his head toward the front counter.

"You have to order up front," he says. "No table service."

He's missing the roller skates and the pencil behind his ear and the squeaky-clean manners.

"I'm waiting on the The Big Bopper and Little Richard," I say. "We'll all order together."

He pretends to understand and keeps moving.

Three tables other than mine are occupied. Two singles and a triple. They've all spent their time at the front counter before I got here. Everyone seems too into their food to care much about me.

My table comes with all the requisite squeeze bottle condiments arranged around a napkin dispenser made to look like a miniature jukebox. Next to that is a silver card holder full of lottery tickets and tiny wooden pencils. I pull one out for a closer look.

Blondie's Big Dream Lottery. The lettering is arched over the top of the card in rainbow colors emerging in and out of a fluffy white cloud. Below that are twelve rows of bubbles, ten bubbles in each row, numbered zero through nine. Four rows per game makes three games per card. Fill in one bubble in each row, put your email on the line at the bottom and give it to someone in a paper hat.

The back of the card is all business. In-person submissions only. One lottery card per customer per day per visit. No purchase necessary. No refunds or substitutions on awarded food and drink. Not redeemable for cash. Exclusive prize options: (1) one *Big Dream Malted Milkshake*, any flavor as available; (2) one large fountain beverage (no refills); (3) one *La Bamba Burger* (any toppings); (4) one *Please, Please, Please Burger* (any toppings); (5) one large *Yakety Yak Surfboard Fries*, or (6) one *Tutt Frutti Pie* (apple, cherry, peach, or as available). There's another paragraph in painfully small print about trademarks and legal remedies that is less appetizing.

I put the card back in the holder in time to notice a charcoal tweed business suit in the entry. It's hiding under a wet, black overcoat wrapped around a short-bearded, white-haired guy looking for something other than a *La Bamba Burger.* Pretty sure that something is me. I hitch my chin his direction just to confirm.

Constantine Papadopoulos freezes in the moment of connection, sizing me up, his face wrestling between fear and anger and unconvincing cool. The new customer coming in behind him is hungry, eager to get his backpack and his cowboy hat and his pet mustache out of the rain. Constantine looks over his shoulder at the man in irritation for getting pushy. He gets back an attitude as good as he gives. Constantine turns and starts my direction as the wet cowboy slips behind him and heads for the counter.

"Constantine Papadopoulos," I say when he is close enough to hear. "That's a mouthful. I'd bet a lot of money the people in your life have shortened that up a bit. Connie? Papa-Dop? C-Pap?"

He stares down at me, dripping and glowering.

"Oh, don't get offended," I say. "I'll call you whatever you want. I'm just breaking the ice. Take a load off. Sit, sit. You're hurtin' my neck down here."

He keeps his coat on, sliding in uncertainly across from me. His beard is giving up the white for gray. A thin trail of hair from the left corner of his mouth down to his chin is a little darker than the rest. Like he's got some kind of oil leak.

"Who are you," he asks.

"Call me Mack. Hungry?"

"No. What do you want with me?"

Fear in those eyes. This is a man waiting in the dark for the drop of a shoe. He's all ears and heartbeat.

"I'm here about that payoff yesterday. You left like you weren't having any fun."

The man's face tightens in anger. He doesn't play this game much. Twenty seconds and he's ready to pop. Then he does.

"I'm not doing this again," he growls, leaning in and gripping the table with both hands. He keeps his voice on a leash as his eyes dart around the restaurant, but the leash is tight. His teeth are as white as his hair, but not as straight. "Twice is more than fucking enough. Got that? Mack? Whoever the fuck you are? I'm done. I'm more than done with your bullshit."

"Getting all worked up isn't going to solve your problem, Connie."

"I think you're the one with a problem."

I'm ready to tell him that I don't really see things his way, but then I do see things his way. The Samoan hunched over the corner table making love to a *La Bamba Burger* is a lot faster and quieter than I'd have assumed. He's standing on my side of the booth in no time, dabbing the corner of his mouth with a napkin. Between his black t-shirt and his mostly open Chicago Bears bomber is a leather shoulder harness that's about as empty as his stomach. He bends over the table a little because he wants me to see it.

So I do. Glock 19.

Then he wants in. He doesn't ask permission.

"No table service," I say as his shoulder slides me all the way to the window. He's got an erect middle finger tattooed on his neck. "They make you go to the counter here. Maybe you already knew that."

He rotates his head to look at me. His face is frying-pan-flat with a couple of sausage links for lips. His nose is used to being broken and his eyes are already bored with the unpleasantness they expect. His baseball cap is on backward, but I recognize Detroit's colors.

"Your hat and your coat like different teams," I say. "When the Lions come over to play the Bears, what part of you gets left out in the cold?"

He pretends like he's thinking about the question. He looks to Papa-Dop and back to me.

"Your face looks like someone's already told you to shut up once today," he says. "Want me to tell you again?"

I look back across the table at Constantine.

"I get the impression you have something you want to say."

Having a friend in the booth hasn't relaxed Papa-Dop one bit. But he does seem more confident. His words hit the table like chunks of ice.

"The shakedown stops now," he says. "Understand? You don't look like a man who takes a lesson once and moves on."

He seems to want a reaction to the insult. I toss him a shrug like I'm guilty of epic stupidity. I sell it just fine. Epic stupidity and I are old friends.

"You assured me it was a one-time thing," he says. "Remember that? I pay and I never hear from you again? Remember? But then you came at me again, and this time ..." He swallows hard, like he has to get a hold of himself, glancing first at the restaurant around us and then briefly at my new big friend. "This time with a threat to my family." His index finger stabs the table like it wants to make a hole. "My ... *family*."

A young couple approaches with plastic trays full of food, looking for a place to sit. They've got an eye for the window booth abutting ours. The Samoan next to me gives them a slow shake of his head. He points a fat finger to the other side of the restaurant as Patsy Cline shambles into *Walkin' After Midnight*. The couple doesn't know what the hell's going on, but they know how to follow instructions. They keep walking. Constantine keeps talking.

"And so I pay over a second time. That makes me an asshole who believes I can make this stop by cooperating. Stupid move. Your stupidity is contagious, Mack, because now you obviously think I'm a fucking ATM. You reach out a third time, the next fucking day, this time by telephone to set up an in-person sit-down, which tells me you're desperate. Tells me you're in over your head. You owe someone a lot of money and now they're making it hurt, judging from your fucked-up face. You decide that I'm the guy who saves your life. Well, fuck you, Mack. Whatever your fucking name is. We are done with this game. We're gonna play a new game. New rules. You're going to return everything I've paid you in the past nine months or I'll make sure you look a lot uglier than you do now. Okay?"

"No offense," I say, "but you don't look the type."

He leans back in the booth and lets that one roll over him.

"I'm not the type," he says with a little more calm. "I'm a securities trader, as you fucking know, not a violent criminal. But I know people who are the type." He gives the big guy a nod. "My friend here, for example. He's going to do some damage unless you cooperate. Whoever you owe money to is not going to have anything left of your face to work with. Okay? So let's start with some ID. I want to know who's been fucking me over. Wallet on the table. Now."

Constantine and I stare at each other over the table as Patsy hands things off to The Five Satins singing *In the Still of the Night.*

"Look," I say, "if you want money for a burger …"

Constantine brings back all of the old intensity, the angry finger drilling down onto the tabletop again.

"Wallet. Now. Or he shakes it out of you."

The big guy turns his large head my way, leaning his shoulder into mine for emphasis.

I nod. My left hand goes in my pocket for the wallet and comes out with the thing that looks like a wallet. Constantine holds out his hand, but I toss it on the table instead. By the time he flips the thing over and is staring at my Chandler Police shield, Sig is out of his holster and sniffing Samoan crotch. Constantine's beard has hole in it, no sound coming out.

"Palms flat on the table," I tell them. I kick Constantine hard under the table. "Don't test me."

It's happening too fast for them to get ahead of it. They do as they're told. I get the Glock out of my seatmate's holster. He doesn't like that much. I can feel his body tense. I ram Sig in a little deeper just to loosen him up again. Works like a charm. His beefy fingers flex like they want to dig into the table. Eight out of ten have a tattooed letter: HARD TIME.

I put the Glock on the seat next to me up against the wall, out of sight and out of reach.

"You got a name?" I ask him. He glowers back in silence. I nod sideways at Constantine. "Come on. Connie over there has enough name for six people. He got your name too?"

His mouth barely moves.

"Momo."

"A real name."

"That is a real name, motherfucker."

"Okay, Momo. You have any other weapons on you?"

"No."

Across the table, Constantine is getting twitchy.

"Hands, Connie," I say, keeping my focus on Momo. "Flat on the table. Your immediate future depends on that. How about a wallet, Momo? Got one of those?"

He doesn't answer because he doesn't have to. His wallet is in the pocket closest to me. I fish it out and open it up. His face smiles up at me through the little plastic window. I'm betting he was a cute kid.

"Montague O. Moliga. Really?"

"Hey, fuck you, man."

"Hands on the table, Monte. This is the part where you dial it way down because you've got a loaded gun at your ball sack. It's also the part where I ask you to show me your concealed carry permit."

Momo stares at his hands in silence.

"Big surprise. Okay, Montague Moliga of 1533 East Champion Court, Unit 2, here is how this is going to work. I tell you to take your wallet and what's left of your burger over there and go directly home. An officer will be waiting to take down some information and get you processed for carrying a concealed weapon in a public place without a permit. But you won't go home. You know why? Sure you do. So do I. Because you know you've already been in the system. You're a man who likes to play rough and the state of Illinois won't give you a carry permit because you shouldn't be carrying any kind of gun anywhere. So while the officer at your house interviews whoever is over there, you're not going to show. You're going to be trying to get a jump on the warrant for your arrest for violating the conditions of your parole. And you're already thinking that one through, aren't you, Monte? Sure you are. Because you really don't want to go back to the joint, where they've got a whole lot of nicknames and alphabet tattoo artists, but not one *La Bamba Burger* to save your life. So, you're thinking maybe Michigan. Wisconsin. Indiana. You've got some choices, Monte, but not a lot of time."

I ease Sig out of Momo's crotch. He doesn't look at me or at Constantine. We watch him breath in and out for a couple of beats. Then he slides out of the booth and heads for the door. Stops. Doubles back for the rest of his burger. Then he's gone.

THIRTY

Ray likes being right. It might be his favorite non-drinkable thing.

Momo was a guess. Educated, sure, but still a guess. He could have been wrong. Hard to know how things would have played if Momo had been just a little less afraid of prison. Arms like that? One elbow puts Ray's head through the window.

But he wasn't wrong. He was dead on.

He likes that. It makes his face hurt just a little bit less.

He slips Sig back into bed and drops Momo's Glock into his coat pocket. Then he looks across the table at Constantine Papadopoulos.

"And then there were two again," he says. "All of that gave you a couple of minutes to work on your story. What'd you come up with?"

"I thought you were someone else," Constantine says contritely. He keeps his hands on the table like he's afraid it will float away. "I'm sorry."

"I'll bet."

A new wave of suspicion crosses the table.

"Unless … Unless it *is* you. A badge doesn't prove anything."

"It proves that unless you start talking, we're going to trade this booth for a small room with a metal table."

"I haven't done anything," he says, voice climbing an octave. "I'm the victim."

"Two minutes ago you threatened to use a large ex-con with an unlicensed firearm to rearrange my face. Something about you wanting me to pay you a lot of money. But hey, you want to go with the victim thing? Let's take it downtown and make it official."

Ray waits. It doesn't take long.

"I had an affair," Constantine says quietly to his hands. "Someone found out. I'm being blackmailed. I thought you were the guy. First demand was about nine months ago."

"How much?"

"Fifty."

"Must love your wife. I mean marriage."

"Three kids."

"Devoted family man who likes to pretend he's single. I know the type."

He does too. Ray knows that type all too well.

So did Marlo, at the end.

"It was a mistake," says Constantine.

"You think? How'd this person contact you?"

"Email. My work address."

"Chicago Mercantile Exchange," says Ray.

Constantine looks up sharply. Swallows. Nods.

"If you're not my blackmailer, how do you know where I work? Am I a suspect or something?"

"You're something. Let's go with that for now. So you get an email. From whom?"

"My address."

"To you and from you? Same address?"

"Yes."

"That's fun. You blackmailing yourself?"

"No. I'm sure that's a standard hack."

"What made you take it seriously?"

"There was a photo. Photos. Me and … this other person. I'm not getting her involved."

"Yeah? Little late for that. Maybe she sent the email."

"No."

"Happens all the time, Connie."

"No."

"Still have that email?"

"No."

"And the money drop was here?"

"Yes." Constantine nods past Ray's shoulder. "Corner booth, under the bench. All in hundreds. I leave it in a big Blondie's bag. I had to make a special trip before the drop and order a shit ton of food just to get the large bag."

"So you're out the fifty large plus the cost of enough food to fill a large bag."

"Yes. No. I've done this twice now. I'm out a hundred so far plus the cost of two bags of food."

"Maybe Blondie's is behind it. They're making a killing off this scam."

"Plus the two thousand I paid useless fucking Momo." He catches Ray's smile. "It's not funny."

"Didn't say it was," says Ray. "So you leave and don't hang around to see who collects."

"The drop doesn't count until I'm back on the freeway. He said they're watching. Attached photos of my car. And my house. I didn't take any chances. I wanted it done. I made the drop and left."

"Tell me about the second time. Yesterday. Another fifty?"

"Yeah, yesterday. After nine months of nothing, then suddenly, boom. Again. The email showed up the day before yesterday. It was nearly identical. Another fifty. Same drill. I thought I was done. Fucker said it was a one-time deal. One and done, he said."

"In the first email?"

"Yeah."

"No other communication with this guy until the second email?"

"No. One and fucking done, he said."

Ray shakes his head in disbelief.

"You really that naïve, Connie? I figured commodities traders as smart and sophisticated."

"What choice did I have?"

"Renew your vows and keep your dick in your pants. There's a choice. Or divorce your wife and buy your girlfriend a ring. Buy her a couple of rings. You'd still be money ahead. Where'd you pick up Momo?"

"Friend of a friend of a friend. I got your call and I thought … I thought *here we go again*. I just needed it to end. I didn't want anybody to get hurt. I just wanted to send a message."

"Right. As I recall that message was give me all my money back or Momo will rearrange your face."

"I was frustrated."

"Your frustration is what started all of this in the first place, Connie. How long have you worked at the Merc?"

"Seventeen, eighteen years."

"That's a stretch."

He wants to itch his beard. His hands are busy. He tries to use his shoulder.

"Yeah. I was there before we merged with the Chicago Board of Trade. Before CME Group gathered up the New York Exchanges and made us all stepchildren. Can I take my hands off the table?"

"Sure, if you want to put them behind your head."

"Are you arresting me?"

"Don't know yet. Would you like to be arrested? What do you do for CME?"

"Commodities trading. Futures. Agriculture mostly. Some precious metals."

"You know a guy named Dennis O'Toole?"

Ray calls this kind of question the slap. Out of nowhere. Unconnected. It's good for authentic reactions. Constantine's reaction comes with popping eyes and a jittery heart.

"Dennis? O'Toole? You mean …"

"Yeah. The futures trader at BSD who ran out of future. He used to work at the Merc, right?"

Constantine clears his throat of authenticity.

"What's Dennis got to do with any of this?"

"He's got everything to do with the question I just asked."

A shrug.

"Yeah. I knew Dennis. First rate prick. I was glad to see him go."

"Yeah?" Ray asks, lifting his eyebrows.

"Not as in kill himself. Jesus. I was glad to see him leave the Merc. He was a pain in the ass. Lots of swagger. Always selling himself. He landed on his feet getting a desk over at BSD. Good for him, I guess. Didn't end well though, did it?"

"Why'd he leave the Merc?"

"He was … shown the door, as they say."

"Why?"

Constantine's mouth opens, but the words are late. It takes a couple of tries.

"Do I look like HR to you?" he asks.

"Do I look like I'm in the mood for official bullshit? Long time trader gets shit canned, people talk. What did you hear?"

Constantine falters, looking out at the parking lot. Ray has to try again.

"What did you …"

"Look, the Merc is big on rules. Okay? There're a billion of them. Dennis broke some. I don't know which ones. But they must have been the important kind. They didn't hand him any second chances."

"Did Dennis have a specialty?"

"Dennis was big into cheese and bitcoins. Some Euro currencies, I think when he left. There were three of them that got the boot."

"Other traders?"

"Yeah."

"Names."

Surprise leads to a laugh of amazement.

"Names? Fuck. It's been …"

"Names."

Constantine closes his eyes. He spreads his fingers like he's getting a psychic reading from the table.

"Simon someone. And Gene. I don't remember, wait …" He opens his eyes. "Fisk. Feeks. Simon Feeks. Gene somebody and Simon Feeks. Or Fesk. Something like that. They all three hit the sidewalk about the same time."

"Where did they land, Simon and Gene? They go over to BSD Financial too?"

"What, you think I'm bored? I don't keep track of those guys. We were never friends to start with. BSD? No way. That's a prestige shop. I'd have heard about them landing at BSD. Simon was pushing retirement anyway. Wherever he is, he's not working. And Gene? Fuck if I know. Watching volleyball, maybe."

"Volleyball? Is that a thing?"

"Probably for Gene. His son made the US Olympic Team for the games in Rio. I forget the kid's name. Gene took a leave of absence to be there. I hate volleyball. Look, what's the call here, officer? I've ignored a busy afternoon to be here for nothing, apparently."

Ray gives him a slow, sad smile.

"You seem disappointed. You were happier when you thought I was here to blackmail you."

"I need it to stop," he says. "Can you help?"

"Maybe. You have those emails?"

"I told you I don't."

"Then maybe not." Ray extracts a business card from a leather pocket behind his shield and slides it under Constantine's fingers. "If you get another contact, I'm your first call. Understand?"

Constantine lets go of the table and picks up the card.

"Yes. Thank you."

"And you're now in the business of taking my phone calls. Right?"

"Yes."

A pair of headlights sweep wet silver against the window. Constantine looks. Ray does not.

"If you don't pick up the phone, Connie, you and I are going to pick up where we left off. We're going to talk about your future in futures."

Constantine Papadopoulos looks back across the table. His eyes have lost their anger. They're heavy and tired now. They know there is only one answer that works.

"I understand."

THIRTY-ONE

Ray watches Constantine go. He sits, staring at the door. Thinking. Trying to put it all together. The rain lashes at the glass like it wants his shoulder. Outside, Constantine makes a run for the black Lexus. He gets in and drives away into the settling gloom.

Ray closes his eyes to focus. That's a mistake. They want to stay closed. He's too tired. He needs sleep. He wants to fold himself into the booth and not wake up for a day.

Overhead, the Everly Brothers conspire about dreaming.

But that's not happening. The dream won't let him sleep. The dream is a vicious animal, biding its time. Waiting. It snarls from the other side of the veil.

Ray opens his eyes. Shakes his head.

He eases out of the booth and heads for the front counter. The girl in the paper hat and the spotless apron has a long brown ponytail and limpid blue eyes that have not yet seen the world as it really is. She watches him read the big board behind her. She's trying not to look at the bruising.

He orders one vanilla *Big Dream* malted milkshake with a fat, red plastic straw and a picture-perfect cherry. He pays cash and walks it back to the table where the cowboy who had come in just after Constantine Papadopoulos is eating his way through a small stack of *Yakety Yak Surfboard Fries*.

Ray takes a seat opposite and sets down the glass. He slides it across the table next to the man's fries. Then he takes one of the *Yakety Yaks* for himself. As if in some bargained exchange. The cowboy sighs.

"What gave me away?"

"A good disguise is supposed to make you blend in, kid. How many other Pakistani cowboys you see in this place? And what kind of self-respecting cowboy comes in to eat a small order of fries?"

"I'm not hungry," says Raj. "And I didn't know how long you'd be here."

"You've got ketchup on your caterpillar."

Raj takes off his hat and sets it on the backpack in the seat next to him. Then he peels off the mustache and wipes it off with a napkin. He drops it in the hat.

"It's all I could find on short notice," he says dejectedly. "God, you look like shit. Who did this to you?"

"Cattle rustlers. Seen the sheriff around?"

"Funny. It was either cowboy or hot nurse."

"You should have gone with the other one."

"Next time." Raj jerks his head toward the window booth. "Who were those guys?"

"Those guys are none of your business, Raj. You're in the transportation-for-hire business. Where'd you get the green Tacoma and why are you tailing me all over Chicago?

Raj's mouth unhinges.

"You saw me? Where? How? I thought I was next to perfect."

"Tricks of the trade. Not your trade, Raj. My trade." He takes another fry. "Start talking."

Raj leans back and takes a long pull on the *Big Dream* milkshake.

"Friend of mine needed a favor. His cab is in the shop and he needs the fares. I loaned him my cab. He let me drive his cousin's Tacoma for the day."

"Where'd you start with me?"

"Your house. This morning. I thought I'd ..." Raj shakes his head sheepishly. "I don't know ..."

"You thought you'd see if you could get away with being my shadow. A little something extra to add to your private investigator license application."

Raj Malik is a vision of stupefaction.

"How ..."

"Cleo. She's ready to beat some sense into you by beating it out of me."

"I told her not to tell you."

"Cut her some slack. She's worried about you. Then I showed up looking like I do and scared it out of her. Besides, she's right. You really need to think this through."

"I have," he says. "I've thought about it a lot. My father drove a cab his whole life. New York, Philly, then here. He died in his cab. They found him in the cab line at the fucking airport. He just ... I don't want to be that guy."

Ray looks at him for a beat or two.

"You have the cooties?"

"The *cooties*? No."

Ray pulls the milkshake across the table and lowers the *Big Dream* in the parfait glass by a third. It's like drinking from a cloud, he thinks. White and cold and sweeter than Heaven. He imagines St. Peter polishing the counter of a malt shop.

"Good. Neither do I."

He slides the cup back across the table.

"Twenty, twenty-five years ago I chased down this guy. Lenny. Lenny Rizzo. Lenny had run over this woman and her kid crossing the street." Ray points blindly like it happened right outside in the parking lot. "You know the Walgreen's on South Abrams? Across from that piece of shit parking garage that they won't tear down?"

Raj nods.

"That's the intersection. It was before Walgreen's showed up. Lenny was driving a stolen black Gran Torino built for speed and he was using every last horse in that engine. He caught the mom on her left hip. Spun her like a top out into the intersection where she met the front end of a moving van. The kid, ten years old, well he sees it coming and tries to run. He gets it in the dead center of his back. The Torino just mows over him like a weed.

"Wasn't on purpose. They were crossing with the light, and Lenny was the wheel man in a pawnshop heist gone bad. So Lenny was spending most of his time in the rearview mirror and wasn't caring much about the color of the stoplights.

"So he runs 'em down, sight unseen. Kills them both. Keeps going. Nearly takes down half a dozen other people. Keeps going. Gone. Poof.

"Takes us four days to put the puzzle together. We get a break on one of the other two guys in the robbery and give him a crash course education on the felony-murder rule. He spills the beans on his partner and the wheel man, Lenny.

"So, long story short, Stretch Martin and I go looking for Lenny. Takes some doing, because Lenny doesn't want to be found. But we get there. He's holed up in the back of that rattrap trailer park that used to be out there between Marsh and 125th. Stretch takes up a position on the far side of the trailer and I knock on the door, you know, sideways like you're supposed to do. Before I can say the word *police*, a hole the size of my head opens up in the middle of that trailer door. Lenny must have been standing right on the other side with his sawed-off. I don't wait around for an invitation. I take advantage of the hole. I drop, aim and squeeze off two rounds. I can hear him hit the floor. In we go.

"Turns out I got him in the leg and the chest. Blood everywhere. The trailer stinks like a slaughterhouse in July. Smell of blood always makes me woozy, so

I'm trying to hang on to my lunch. We tie off the leg and I'm applying pressure to the chest wound while Stretch calls it in and radios for an ambulance.

"And Lenny, well Lenny's in shock. His eyes are like white dessert plates. They're the only part of him that's clean. Anyway, he looks up at me as I'm trying to keep the pressure on his chest and he says, *You don't know.* And he keeps saying it. *You don't know. You don't know.* And so I ask him what it is I don't know, figuring he's gonna try to tell me that we don't have what it takes to put him away for the hit and run. Figuring he's gonna tell me that I don't know it was him. Turns out that's not what was on his mind."

Ray pulls the glass towards him again. Takes another pull of cloud. Slides it back.

"What are you telling me, Mack?" asks Raj.

"I'm telling you that we always think we know where things are going to lead, but we don't. We get these ideas about the future. We think we know how things are connected and that if we do this thing over here, we get that thing over there. So we take a first step in a direction, following that vision, thinking we know where we're going. But we're always stepping into the woods, kid. And we don't know where that path goes. We think we know, but we don't."

"So…"

"Lenny Rizzo married for love. Put a ring on the finger of his high school wet dream. He knew her family was bad news. Everybody did. Didn't bother Lenny. The girl was sweeter than a basket of peaches and Lenny knew for fucking certain that his proximity to the family would have no particular consequence to him. He knew who he was. The plan was to get her – I don't remember what her name was, let's call her Peaches – the plan was to get Peaches away from the family – the brothers and the father and the uncles – live in a nice house all their own, couple of kids. The good life, you know? To pay for that good life, Lenny's plan is to open up his own auto shop. Fix cars for a living. He has a talent under the hood. That's an honest living he can get behind. It's not a secret plan. Everybody knows about it. They all want to help make it happen. So Lenny and Peaches get a couple dozen envelopes at the wedding.

"And suddenly he's in the auto repair business. Boom. Rizzo's Rims, out in Near West Side, right on Roosevelt. Guess where the extended family starts bringing their cars?"

"Rizzo's," says Raj.

"Pretty smart for a cowboy. Rizzo's. They're all looking for the family discount. And Lenny's a stand-up guy, so he gives it to them. Every time. What else is he gonna do? Problem is his new family starts bringing in cars that they don't actually own. Cars that don't actually need fixing. Before you know it, Lenny is in the auto storage business. Then he's in the auto stripping business. Then he's in the lying-to-police-when-they-show-up-asking-questions business. Then he's in the auto-driving-just-a-quick-errand business. Then he's in the wait-in-Uncle-Bruce's-stolen-Grand-Torino-outside-the-pawnshop business. You know where this is going?"

"Yeah, Mack. I know where it's going."

"No, you know where it *went,* Raj. You're playing pin the tail on the donkey without a blindfold. Hindsight is good that way. Harder to see where it's going before any of it happens. One minute you're turning a wrench under the hood of some old lady's Caddy trying to keep the grease off your new wedding ring and the next minute you're bleeding out in a trailer with a cop on your chest taking confession.

"Lenny tells me he had no idea they were knocking over the pawnshop. First time he saw the gun was when his brother-in-law and the other guy were getting out of the car. Once they disappear inside Lenny knows that he can't keep going down this road. He had no idea how *his* life had put him outside *that* pawnshop. That's what he was trying to tell me. *You don't know. You don't know. You never fucking know.*

"So Lenny hears the first gunshot from inside the pawnshop and takes off like he heard a starter pistol. Four days and two dead pedestrians later, Lenny is hiding out in a shitty trailer waiting for fate to lay down the next card. His phone rings. It's Peaches. Their coming for you, she tells him. She's not talking about me and Stretch. She's talking about her own family. She'd let it slip about the trailer park. She wasn't thinking. Or maybe blood is thicker than ink and Peaches was calling to say goodbye. Anyway, Lenny is ready to take the sawed-off he'd found in the trunk of the Grand Torino and go hide someplace else. That's when I knocked on the door."

Raj shakes his head with a disbelieving kind of laugh.

"You're saying that if I go out and get a PI license …"

"I'm saying there's no such thing as adjacent to rot, Raj. Maybe at first, while your energy is up. But not over the long haul. When it comes to organic matter like you and me, the rot is naturally corrupting. That's what it does. It assimilates everything it touches. It rubs off on you. Then it takes over. And here you are looking for a license to swim in the rot for a living; all for a few bucks and a story or two to tell the bartender as he helps you drown your sorrows."

"Your wife was a PI, you said. Didn't rub off on her. Right? Didn't corrupt her."

The kid's eyes are uncertain. He doesn't know how to read the eyes looking back at him. He's wary at having invoked the dead, revered wife. He's worried he's been reckless.

"Marlo was different," says Ray.

But look at him. He's thinking about that photograph. Sam Royce. Tony Rickens. Victor Roby. All at the same table. With Marlo. He's wondering if Marlo is really the exception, or if she proves his point.

"What about you," says Raj. "You're out there … *swimming in it.*"

"Yeah? Look at me, Raj. Take a good long look."

"You're beat up, Mack, not corrupt."

Ray flinches. He's seeing himself as I did, rummaging through locked IAD filing cabinets, nosing through his own lieutenant's computer, looking for information he's supposed to hand over to Frenchie Marie, a woman who could be anybody camped out in the rain on the same slippery slope.

"Depends on who you ask," he says.

"I don't care what anyone else thinks," Raj objects. "The truth has to count, Mack. Whatever they think about you, you know better. I know better. The truth has to count."

He wants to tell him that the truth is an old, paranoid, washed up drunk, disappointed in all the mirrors in his life, as afraid of dreaming as he is of the new lung shadow on his mortality, and with no juice left to get him through a full day. He wants to slap that truth down on the table and make Raj take a good long look at it.

But he doesn't. He can't.

"I appreciate that, Raj. I do. I'm not saying don't do this thing if that's what you really want. I'm just saying don't let your guard drop just because you think you're incorruptible, or because you think you know how one thing leads to another. Because you're not incorruptible and you don't know how one thing leads to another. You don't know. And thinking you do know is what gets you killed. That's what gets Cleo a life changing phone call in the middle of the night."

Ray grimaces and reaches for what's left of the glass full of Heaven. He pulls it close.

"Then she'll come looking for me."

THIRTY-TWO

The remains of the day put me back in my seat at IAD, pretending to love my work. I make a good show of shuffling the stack of files for everyone who's looking, including Boss Twill who leaves his office two or three times to consult with Raffi and then Carolyn before they punch out. He returns with a pair of eyes that know how to find the side of my head.

I wait until Twill is back in his office, then I set about trying to run down a couple commodities traders that know a thing or two about losing a desk at the Merc.

There are thirteen Simon Feeks living in the state of Illinois. Putting some birth year parameters on the search narrows the field to nine, which is seven people more than my headache and energy level will allow this late in the day. I switch the focus to a guy named Gene.

There is a truckload of lanky muscle that played men's Olympic volleyball for the United States in Rio. Only two of those guys hale from Chicago. One of those two is Asian. The other is whiter than I am: Corey G. Wilke. Good looking kid. Toothsome might be the word I'm looking for. His official Olympic photo looks like he's a model for the American Dental Association. In another shot, Corey and his teammates are all biting bronze. I'm guessing Corey got his middle name and his good looks from his old man, Gene, who paid for the early orthodontics with CME pork belly commissions.

I dig a little deeper. Since Rio, Corey Wilke has joined the ranks of the Olympic coaching staff. A brief bio makes him a current resident of Los Angeles. It includes a quote by Corey crediting his success to the lifelong support of his old man, Gene. There's a photo of the two of them together. Gene's in a wheelchair. Someone has disconnected him from the oxygen for the sake of the photo, but the tank is still in the frame, right next to a woman who is almost as tall as Corey. Cassandra Wilke-Barnsmith. How many Wilke-Barnsmiths could there be in the world? I have no idea, but there's only one in Chicago. Five minutes of poking the keys gets me a phone number.

"Is this Cassandra Wilke-Barnsmith?"

"Yes? Who is this?"

"My name is Detective Raymond Mackey with the Chandler Police Department. I'm looking to connect with a Mr. Gene Wilke, I believe he is your father?"

"Yes." Her tone is cautious. Protective. "What is this about?"

"I'm conducting an investigation and I think your father may have some helpful information. The investigation does not concern him. He's not in any kind of trouble. I'd just like to talk with him for a few minutes. Do you know how I can reach him?"

"My father is not well, Detective. He does not have the energy for an interrogation."

"Interrogations are long conversations in small, windowless, uncomfortable rooms. That's not what this is. The room can be as big as you like and full of windows. I'll come to you. You can be present if that helps. Just a few questions."

It takes another few minutes of assurances, but Cassandra Wilke-Barnsmith finally coughs up an address and time for me to be there. I thank her and end the call just in time to answer another one.

"Detective Mackey?"

"Speaking."

"This is Tia Lewis returning your call."

"Ms. Lewis. Thanks for getting back to me. We haven't met, but …"

"I know who you are, Ray. I'll meet with you for curiosity's sake if nothing else. But I don't have time to talk now. I'm between handshakes and air kisses at a Housing First Chicago fundraiser. It's my party so I have to play hostess."

"Sounds fun," I lie.

"Hardly. But it's what I do. It's at the Ritz on Pearson. The mayor will have come and gone by nine so I should be able to wrap up by ten if you want to get a drink after. I suspect I'll need one by then, along with an excuse to leave. I know that's late notice for an even later meet-up, but I'm pretty busy tomorrow, so if not tonight, then it'll have to wait until probably next week."

I'm almost too tired to finish the call, let alone attend a fundraiser. But the part about the mayor and the promise of a drink gets my attention.

"Maybe I'll show up early and make a donation."

"Every little bit helps. I'll put your name on the guest list so they'll let you in and give you a name sticker."

"I don't do name stickers, Ms. Lewis."

"Tia," she corrects. "How will I know you?"

"I'll be the one without a name sticker. I'll find you. Or you can look for the walking bruise in a wet trench coat circling the bar. I'll see if I can find a carnation."

I end things with Tia Lewis in time to see Raphael Santiago headed for the door. Steph Nellis, coat and purse slung over one shoulder, is propping it open with the toe of a black pump. Waiting.

Raffi casts a backward glance my way. I give him a quiet salute that turns into a cautionary wagging finger, warning him against an ill-advised office romance. He tosses me a wink and the two of them are gone behind the closing door.

When I look around, Twill is in his doorway looking at me. It's all the invitation I'm going to get.

"LT," I say when I make the doorway.

Twill is back behind his desk putting papers into files and files into drawers that he closes with his big boney knees. Seems like only yesterday that I was sitting in that chair poking at his keyboard and playing guess the password. It *was* only yesterday.

"Coopersmith," he says pulling a briefcase from under the desk, not looking up. "Status report."

Terse and strictly business. He thinks it'll paper over his anger. It doesn't but I play along anyway.

"I've got one guy ready to give him up. Two more are playing shy. Three pink sheets are in the pipeline. Chicago PD is cooperating. Witnesses on our payroll are free game for me to interview. Anyone else I need CPD's blessing. Cop downstairs by the name of Alphonse K. Jarr says Coopersmith has been slinging so long without getting caught he thought he'd turned invisible."

"Okay. Next. Holstein. Status report."

"Bossy, but full of milk. All I need is a bucket and a stool."

Twill looks up from the open briefcase. Getting a smile was a longshot. I can tell I missed by a mile.

"Does it look like I'm in the mood for your bullshit, Mack?"

"No, sir. It looks like you've got enough of your own. Maybe you should unconstipate yourself and let it out. Sir."

Twill glares. I brace myself for the speech about unprofessional demeanor. Instead, I get words that hit the desk like frozen rocks.

"Holstein. Status. Report."

"I've got three unreturned calls to the taxpayer who says Holstein wrote her up for speeding after she refused an invitation for drinks. I figure we're two calls away from her telling me the anger has boiled off and she's lost interest."

"Doesn't mean the case goes away," he snaps.

"I know that. You want to stop making love to your briefcase long enough to tell me what your problem is?"

Twill looks up. Nothing like insubordinate bluntness to get your lieutenant's attention. He stands, rising above the desk like a timelapse beanstalk. He closes the briefcase.

"You think you can do my job?"

"Not in a million years," I say. "Hard enough doing my own."

"Then why don't you quit, Mack? Go do something else. Go back to patrolling the mall for shoplifters."

"Because a certain lieutenant brought me on board with a promise of reading me into certain on-going investigations. I'm still waiting."

Twill laughs to himself and shakes his head.

"Mack, those investigations dried up and blew away when you ass-fucked the entire Illinois justice system with a Trojan doll and a list of names that Dan Brewster and his OAG goons are now trying to tattoo on my goddamned forehead. There is no investigation. Got it? Not into the dry cleaner or the mayor or any of the paranoid, Big Man fever dream fantasies that you seem to live off of. Okay?" Twill points past my shoulder. "That desk out there is all you get, Mack. That's all there is for you here. So why don't you quit and save us both the headache."

"Problem, LT, is that I get stubborn when I feel pushed. As much as I hate IAD, your fingerprints on my back make me want to hang around."

"No, the problem is you and the Chief are plotting to put your ass in my chair. And, for the life of me, I honestly don't know why either of you want that. I know he thinks you were a bad hire because I had to fight with him to get you in. And I believe you when you say you hate IAD. So that just makes me wonder who you're really working for. Someone wants you in my chair. Who?"

"I'm not conspiring with the Chief. You're starting to sound like me, LT. Careful or people will start to call you paranoid and think you're crazy."

"Crazy like a fox maybe."

"Stop it. Nobody wants me for your job, starting with me."

"Nice try. Who's pulling your strings, Mack?"

"Mr. Innuendo and I are old friends, LT. He'll be your friend too if you're not careful."

"That a threat?"

"No, it's a fact. I'm going to give you some free advice."

"Advice. From you? No thanks."

I step forward until the edge of the desk won't let me take another one.

"Leave Raffi out of this … this, whatever it is between us. He's a good cop, Orland. Don't ask him to keep tabs on me. Give that job to someone outside this office. Brewster. Or do it yourself. *You* follow me around the city. I'll give you a route and my itinerary so you can keep up. You don't trust me and I don't trust you and that's that state of things and that's too bad. But leave the kid out of it. Raffi doesn't deserve carrying that kind of weight. It was beneath you to ask him."

The look on Twill's face tells me I hadn't told him something he hadn't already told himself. There's still some shame left in the man after all. But the anger is back in record time, elbowing the shame aside. I can tell his next word starts with an 'F'. But then suddenly Stephanie Nellis is in the doorway making apologies with her face. Twill swallows the *F*.

"What," he snaps.

"Sorry. I forgot something in my desk and had to come back. The Chief just called. He wants to see you upstairs."

"Fine," says Twill. "Thank you, Steph. I'll go up in a minute."

Steph is confused. Then embarrassed. She glances at me and then back at Twill.

"Oh. No, sir. Sorry. He's looking for Mack."

THIRTY-THREE

Thirty years working in a shit-flows-downhill world and Ray's been up to the seventh floor of the Chandler Police Department maybe a dozen times. The toilets up here have a reputation.

Chief Loudermilk has a demigod's corner perch, two walls nothing but glass, looking down over greater Chandler. In the wet, darkening distance, Chicago looms out of the north like a phosphorescent tidal wave frozen in time, lights glittering in the rain. The Chief sits ensconced in an over-stuffed leather catcher's mitt, nursing a scotch. Legs crossed. Waiting.

"Officer Mackey." He pats the arm of the neighboring chair with a liver-spotted bearpaw.

"Chief." Ray crosses the room, coat draped over his arm. He stops at the small round, knee-high table, just large enough for a stack of coasters and a couple of highballs. "I like your desk better than mine."

Chief Loudermilk stands, extending a hand. He seems to keep rising for a full minute. The man could go outside and look back into his seventh-floor window without a ladder. They shake and the Chief retakes his seat.

"Good to see you, Mack. Amazing how long you can go without bumping into a guy who works in the same building. How's life treating you?"

"Like a soccer ball. You?"

"Complaining never got me anywhere. I'm not starting now."

He's seventy-something but the last ten of those years figured out how to be mostly invisible. He's got a pair of shoulders you expect in a guy people call *Chief.* A large head full of wavey white hair. A couple of glassy blue marbles on either side of a sniffer so broad it could double as a church bell on Sundays. He fills the real estate between his nose and upper lip with a white, snowplow mustache that likes the taste of anything the Chief is drinking.

The Chief takes in Ray's sorry face, then points with his tumbler hand.

"Liquor is that way. The cabinet next to my *actual* desk. Help yourself. Make it a double. You look like you need it."

Ray looks. It's a handsome oak cabinet with sliding doors and burnt bronze hardware. On top is a bronze sculpture of some Chicago Cub swinging for the cheap seats.

But look at him. Poor lush. It's the inside of that cabinet Ray cares most about. He sees the world through amber-colored glasses. Shot glasses.

"Thanks, no," he says with a swallow. "There's a rule or two about taking a drink in this building. I think that rule might be my best friend."

The Chief nods and sips.

"Suit yourself. Sit." He gestures at the neighboring chair and then upward, toward Ray, in a way to encompass everything above Ray's shoulders. "You get all of that in the line of duty?"

"Strictly extracurricular," says Ray, sitting. The chair is comfortable. He wants to sleep.

"Bar fight?"

"I don't know what the guy was swinging. Felt like a bar. What can I help you with, Chief?"

Loudermilk conducts a silent appraisal for another beat or two, as if confirming a decision already made, covering with another sip of scotch.

"You can help me through some changes that are coming to IAD."

Ray lets it sit there before he picks it up.

"Changes," he says at last.

"Yeah. Twill is on his way out." The Chief points a meaty finger. "That's not for you to talk about. This is between us. Understand?"

"Okay. When? Why?"

"The when is tomorrow. After the briefing. The why is above your paygrade, which you already knew. Let's just say the department needs a change."

"And I come in how, Chief. You don't want me for that job."

Loudermilk laughs and drinks.

"Don't flatter yourself. You and desks aren't a great match, Mack. For that matter, you aren't so great with people either. Leading IAD requires people skills that I think might be a little beyond your grasp. No offense."

"None taken. Why are we talking?"

"I need you to be the temporary department head as we recruit a replacement. There's a whole HR process to that. I'll spare you the details and the headache. It'll take a couple of months. At least."

"You just made the case that I'm unqualified."

"You are. For the permanent job. But you'll do in a pinch. I need someone who has been around the block a couple times and who has the stones not to be pushed around by people looking to take advantage of a headless department. You're new over there, but with Sandra gone so is everybody else, more or less, and you've logged more hours in this police department than all of them combined."

"And everybody already hates me. Is that it?"

The Chief smiles. *Now, now*, it says. He's the kindly uncle everyone likes to remember.

"Look. The biggest threat to any internal affairs department is the cozy relationship. Favors owed and favors granted. Looking the other way for old times' sake. I don't sense that you have any of those friendships here. Not anymore. Distrust helps maintain boundaries. That makes you perfect."

"So your strategy is maintaining departmental integrity."

"Something like that. I don't want the wheels coming off while we're looking for Mr. Right. Or Ms. Right."

"Delay the announcement," says Ray. "Recruit first, fire second."

"Can't do that." The Chief can see the question forming on Ray's face. We both can. "You want to know why. Of course you do. But I can't tell you why. Don't ask me questions you know I'm not going to answer."

"Okay, no questions. This isn't you talking out of school, this is just me talking out loud. Take a sip of that drink if federal law enforcement has been around playing follow-the-leader."

Ray might have mentioned Frenchie Marie, the pushy old black woman in the back seat of a green, beat-up Plymouth Breeze with a sagging tailpipe and tinted windows that keep a cloud of smoke and a gaggle of well-strapped G-men inside. Maybe Frenchie has taken the Chief out for Chinese too. He might have mentioned her just for the reaction. But he doesn't. Loudermilk trades one-quarter of a smile for a sip of his scotch.

"Right," says Ray. "Let's say the feds like Twill for something that's above both of our paygrades. They send out a team to see how LT spends his time when he's not sitting at his desk. Eventually they reach out to you with a courtesy heads-up that they're getting close to decapitating Chandler's IAD. They think maybe you'll want to take care of that yourself. Quietly. Discretely. Performance based. Something boring. Lack of confidence. Time for a change in department management. Better that you do it now before they do whatever it is they have to do and the newspapers get involved. Maybe they're just being courteous, maybe not. Doesn't matter; you don't like it. You ask for a little information but being Feds means they hold on to information like squirrels hold onto their nuts. You've never met a Fed who isn't squirrelly, so you give up. Your instinct is to protect your own. But you run it up the flagpole anyway like a good soldier. My flagpole stops in this office, but your flagpole goes all the way up to Chandler City Hall. And the Honorable Frank Houston, Mayor of our fair city, tells you that whatever loyalty you feel for your IAD lieutenant isn't worth a federal-sized headache. He tells you to play ball and to cut Twill loose. You like that idea about as much as you ever did. But you'll do it anyway because that's not the hill you want to die on, just like defending me against the torches and pitchforks in Lieutenant Nutsack's mole hunt wasn't the hill you wanted to die on. How'm I doing?"

Loudermilk takes another sip. "Maybe."

"Maybe nothing, Chief. If I get any more right, you'll be out of scotch and too drunk to drive home. In fact, being so right is starting to make me thirsty."

The Chief keeps his gaze, getting heavier with time. Then he blinks it away.

"Help yourself, Mack. Like I said."

Ray stands and makes the trip over to the liquor cabinet against the wall. The first drink of the day is coming earlier than scheduled after all.

Not scheduled. Permitted. Allowed. Earlier than allowed. Because Ray is breaking a rule here.

Not a rule. A vow.

He had wanted to prove his resolve. His strength. But this is the opposite of that. He's proving the opposite. He's proving his weakness. He fumbles the latch as the Chief fumbles with history.

"You understand that I never believed a word of what Lieutenant Nosek was selling, Mack. Your number in Cosmo Green's phone doesn't prove anything. Never did."

Ray picks a glass then fingers his way through the bottles to find the right color. He finds what he wants. It's not Forester, but, as the Chief would say, it'll do in a pinch. He straightens, puts the glass on the cabinet next to the swinging Cub and unscrews the bottle. Behind him and far away, the Chief keeps at it.

"I'd've gone the distance. Had it come to that. I'd've backed you. I'd've had some tough discussions with Nosek. And others. He wasn't the only one, obviously. I'd've talked with whoever. But next thing I knew you'd thrown in the towel. You took the papers without so much as a knock on my door. You could have come to me, Mack. You should have. I'd've put my thumb on the scale to give a good cop the benefit of the doubt. Besides, Nosek was a first-rate prick. Best day of my life was when he moved on."

Ray pours. Returns the bottle. Straightens. Sips, keeping his back turned. He wants to be unobserved in this moment of weakness. Surrender. It's not so much the Chief that bothers him. It's me he doesn't like watching. He wants to savor the sensation of that first drink of the day, like a man dying of thirst suddenly in the presence of a gutter puddle. He's down on all fours, lapping it up. He wants to do that alone. He feels me judging from up here in the corner. He doesn't like that.

So he takes a moment to himself with his back turned, admiring the silver-framed black and whites on the wall above the credenza.

"This you and Richard M.," he asks. "Back in the day?"

Two men, arms akimbo, laughing into the flash. The Chief is young, dark hair, no mustache, Adam's apple like a neck nose. Richard M. Daley, the future six-term Mayor of Chicago, is slick and dapper and full of teeth.

"He was still State's Attorney," says the Chief. "I was dripping wet out of the Academy. My dad was a Chicago murder cop, may he rest in purgatory. He worked with Richard M. on the Andrew Wilson trial. My dad was actually in on that arrest."

"No shit?"

"No shots fired," says Chief. "If my pop told you to give it up, with or without a gun, then brother, you got to your knees."

"Sounds like maybe you learned that lesson the hard way."

"A couple of times. Anyway, after Andrew Wilson's conviction, Dad went to the afterparty and brought me along. Richard M. knew how to throw a party. Probably how he stayed mayor for twenty-two fucking years. He just kept pouring."

Ray takes another drink and nods, leaning in over the credenza for a closer look at the photo.

Andrew Wilson. It's an ugly story that Ray knows cold, like every other Chicago cop. 1975. Andrew and his kid brother Jackie are driving around the city after an armed robbery. They get pulled over by a couple of Chicago PD gang crimes officers. The brothers both have outstanding warrants, so Andrew knows where the story is headed before either cop gets out of the car. In mid-arrest, Andrew manages to strip one cop of his gun and put a bullet in his head. He puts the other five bullets into the second cop and the two brothers disappear into the night.

Every cop with a badge volunteers for the dragnet to find these guys. They end up shaking Southside like a dark-skinned ragdoll. One detective decided *Kristallnacht* was about the best metaphor he could think of to describe the effort.

They find the guys. Jon Burge, the gang crime lieutenant in charge, puts Andrew Wilson in a small room with a few angry cops, a hot radiator, an electric cattle prod, and a couple of plastic garbage bags. They torture out a quick confession in what had become an old, common and, by the time they got around to Andrew Wilson, a highly efficient routine to grease the wheels of justice.

So the medical director of the prison hospital decides that he doesn't like the radiator burns and electrocution wounds. He complains to the Chicago Police Superintendent, who forwards the matter to the politically ambitious States Attorney, one Richard M., who decides to ignore the torture and go for the win anyway. The mayor-to-be moves forward with the murder prosecution, winning a conviction and the death penalty. The Illinois Supreme Court, not liking the idea of tortured confessions, overturns the conviction five years later. And then the world kept turning, including retrials, new convictions, a scandal that revealed a legacy of similar post-arrest torture, and six consecutive terms of the Richard M. Daley administration.

"What do you think of the current mayor?" Ray asks, turning and making his way back.

"Frank Houston? He's …"

"Not ours. Chicago's. Sam Royce."

"I think I've made it this far by not sharing my opinion about any person whose nameplate includes the word *Honorable*. And you're stalling, Mack."

Ray purses his lips. Nods.

"Your right, Chief. I am."

"Because."

"Because I wanted to get most of this drink in me before I decline your offer for a temporary promotion. I'm grateful for the vote of no-confidence, but I don't want to die on the same hill that you don't want to die on. Maybe Twill's execution is coming from on high, and maybe you don't want to throw your body in front of the bullet, but I don't want to be the one keeping his chair warm."

Another long, appraising look, as if from a man weighing options.

"Loyalty is an admirable quality, Mack. But you should know a couple of things before you take up for Lieutenant Twill. The first thing you should know is that he's not exactly standing up for *you*. I know you've gone a few rounds with Brewster and OAG. So have I. So has Twill. He's … well." A drink. A slight shake of his large snowy head. "We shouldn't talk about it. Suffice it to say, Twill is feeling unconstrained by history. He's hanging you out to dry, my friend. You would do well not to stand too close."

"That's the problem with the modern workplace. Trying not to stand too close to one guy means standing too close to someone else. A planet this populated makes watching your own back almost impossible."

"I see you take a dim view of humanity," he says. "An old cop's view."

"Humanity is fine. It's the people I can do without. What's the second reason?"

"The second reason is that I'm not giving you a choice, Mack. This is the job I have for you, for as long as it lasts. Couple of months. Four maybe. Depends on how motivated my HR Director finds herself these days. The job is yours until we have a replacement vetted, approved, and installed. You know what? Don't think of it as a job. Think of it as an assignment."

"And if I don't take the assignment?"

The Chief raises his glass in a mock toast.

"Then I will thank you for your service and wish you luck among the civilians. I'm sorry to be a hard ass, Mack, but my options are limited."

A smile stretches out beneath the white, cow-catcher mustache.

"That, and you're drinking some very expensive bourbon. Against the rules, by the way."

THIRTY-FOUR

Last time I pushed a Ritz-Carlton elevator button was as a plus-one. Eleven years ago. Like it was yesterday.

Rushmore American Insurance had made a snack out of some regional casualty underwriter, and everybody was in the mood for cucumber-prosciutto canapés and a glass full of bubbles. Marlo got a be-there-or-else invitation, so she reminded me of the misery-loves-company rider to our wedding vows. It was a predictably stuffy, hand-shaking affair that made my smile muscles hurt and kicked my small talk intolerance into overdrive. *Well, you must be the homicide detective we've heard so much about.*

It's not hard to figure out where to go. I follow the murmur of mingling that rumbles and bumbles through the well-appointed 12th floor of the Ritz like too many tennis balls in a dryer. Somewhere behind that is a Julie London sound-alike leading a jazz trio through the middle of Ellington's *I Got It Bad (And That Ain't Good)*. Whoever she is, she sounds sincere about helping the homeless.

I give my name to the woman sitting at the table in front of the ballroom door. Auburn hair and a couple of sharp green eyes that don't believe a thing her smile is saying. They give me the once-over a couple of times.

The house-shaped sticker on her chest wants me to call her Hope. She hopes I'm going to wear one of those things too. I hope she's not too disappointed.

Her red fingernails get busy chasing down the name. It takes a minute. Then she does her best to smile past my colorful face and give me a name tag. *Raymond Mackey.* I slip it into a pocket so my car keys will know who I am. Then I step around the table and into the fray.

The Housing First Chicago fundraiser looks to me to be about the same sort of affair as the Rushmore American merger party. People in small clots of twos and fours and sixes, men in black or navy and the women in punches of color, everyone vibrating in a noisy buzz around tablecloth hives. My Triple D chips in a birds-eye perspective from the chandelier. From above, the room looks like a slide of something under a microscope, lots of blobs and bubbles associating and unassociating, squishing around each other, elongating toward more important, better looking, wealthier blobs and bubbles. Highballs at the ready. I look for myself down there among the blobs. It isn't difficult. I'm the blob in the long brown coat cutting through all the rest of it, in a razor-straight line for the bar.

I Got it Bad hands off to that other homeless anthem, *They Can't Take That Away from Me.* Julie London's sound-alike was hired out of central casting; a sultry, two-legged giraffe with pouty lips, raven-black hair to her shoulders and a couple of eyes that, for all the glittery blue moondust on her lids, know how to follow a guy through a crowd. I give her a respectful nod as I approach the trio. She enunciates the word *away.* I don't take it personally and keep moving for the bar.

I order three fingers of Forester and pick up where I left off in Chief Loudermilk's office. I look around for Tia Lewis, hoping she resembles her internet photo.

There are other short-haired Latinas in the room but only one without a drink in her hand. Only one that everybody seems to know or want to talk to. Her cocktail dress can't decide whether it's blue or green. That makes her easy to track as she makes her way from one conversation to the next like a blue-green bee pollinating a field of flowers.

Tia comes to a longer stop in the far corner of the room where she takes to explaining something to a couple of silk-suited wallets. She turns to the window behind her, pointing through the reflection. Both men look out into the rain dumping back into Lake Michigan. Maybe she's making a point about the weather. *How'd you like not having a roof on a night like this?*

I look at my watch. Still too early.

I leave Tia to her work and head off to claim a lonely, out-of-the-way two-top by the window. Same thing I did at the Rushmore American party as soon as I could give Marlo the slip. In fact, this just might be the exact same table looking out at the same collection of glass and steel spires glinting back then in the snow-speckled darkness. The Chicago Water Tower. The Wrigley Building. Aqua Tower. Aon Center. Willis Tower in the distance like a giant spear made of deep blue glass, lit from within. Marlo hadn't had any difficulty finding me.

"Wallflower." She'd slipped into the chair and taken a dip into my bourbon in a single move. I'd pretended offense.

"Get your own drink, lady. Who do you think you are?"

"Your wife. For whom you took a vow of not parting 'til death, if I recall."

"I took no vow regarding insurance merger parties and other *fêtes* worse than death. You're on your own, kid."

She'd pouted adorably. A mocking affectation she knew always worked to make me laugh at myself.

"It's not so bad," she'd said.

"You're right. It's worse."

"Come on. You're charming as hell. They're eating you up out there."

"Sure. That's because your friends think I'm a turkey drumstick."

"They're not my friends, Ray. They're my colleagues. This is work."

"I'll say."

She'd returned my drink with a sad smile that said I was hopeless.

"You sound like Jimmy," she'd said.

"Jimmy? Your Jimmy? Them's fightin' words, Marlo."

"I mean in high school. He was always brooding about how other kids were looking down on him. He had a whole complex over it. My dad liked to tell him to be more like his big sister. That didn't help. Only made him hate me."

"Yeah, well, he seems to have gotten over that."

"Whatever remark you're about to make, don't. He's my brother, faults and all."

"Faults and all. You two couldn't have come from the same gene pool. How did your mother and the mailman get along?"

"I'll ignore that one. And if Dad were sitting here, he'd smack you a good one."

"For insulting your mother or just because I'm me?"

"For suggesting nature is more important than nurture. It was all about the parenting with them, not the genes."

"You telling me Jimmy was adopted?"

"Don't be ridiculous. Jimmy was not adopted. I'm just telling you that I know an inferiority complex when I see it. You spent your whole childhood in the company of orphans and nuns, rejected every other week by would-be parents who decided you weren't the one." Marlo had jerked her head to the party roiling behind her. "Polite, well-to-do society where everyone wears success on a sleeve is alien. Rejectful. It's not the place you belong. But all of that is a learned reaction, Ray. You can unlearn it. If you want to. If you try. You don't have to like it. God knows I don't. But you also don't have to let it push your buttons. Maybe do the work on deactivating those buttons."

"Now I'm confused. Am I a turkey drumstick or a bomb?"

"Neither. Would you rather be with Stretch Martin, out there in the snow and the cold chasing psychopaths?" The toe of her shoe had found my leg. "Or would you rather be nice and warm having a drink up here in the clouds with me?"

"I think you meant *alone*."

Her hand had found mine.

"Are we not alone?"

"For now," I'd said. "You can wear that dress, lady."

Marlo had stood, a prelude to disappearing, smoothing the black fabric against her body, tugging in all the right places.

"This old thing?"

"It's what's inside that counts. What say we give everyone the slip and go get a room. If anyone asks you can say it's about a pending merger."

I remember the smile before the kiss. It had come with a look that was full of mystery and secret understanding. Marlo was always a dozen steps ahead. Just out of reach. Here I am sitting at the same table, still waiting for her to come back.

I finish the drink, watching people like fish in a bowl. I think about Twill being invited to a closed-door sit-down with the Chief after tomorrow morning's briefing has adjourned. He's no dummy. He'll know what's coming. He'll think I had something to do with it. He'll think I'm enjoying myself. The Chief will escort Twill out with a bear paw on his shoulder and a banker's box full of essentials in his arms. Twill's chair will be empty by 9:30. That's when I should probably say a few words to the IAD squad room. Let them know that I'm just a placeholder. That I don't know anything about anything and maybe some other things they'll never believe.

I make another trip to the bar for a refill. The trio has slipped into a bossa nova groove with a sultry cover of *Agua de Beber*. I don't know the lyrics, but I know a good drinking song when I hear one.

The bartender hasn't forgotten me. I put my glass on the bar and do a thing with my finger that she seems to understand. She's back in a flash trading me a half-glass with a couple of cubes for a big smile and handful of presidents. I tell her to keep the change and she winks like we're best friends. Okay by me. Everyone should be so lucky as to have a good-looking bartender for a best friend. Now I've got two. Makes me wonder if Doris is out on another date. Which makes me wish I hadn't wondered.

I'm good and ready to go back to my table when I recognize a guy at the bar talking to three other guys that I don't know from Adam. I linger until the three strangers disappear in a flurry of handshakes and shoulder slaps. Then I make my move. I know what I'm going to say about as much as I know the lyrics to *Agua de Beber*, but it's not an opportunity I can just let melt away with the ice. I walk over and stick out the hand that isn't holding a drink.

"I guess nothing says save the homeless like a cash bar at the Ritz," I say.

The Honorable Samuel T. Royce, mayor of the city of Chicago, shakes my hand, looking at my chest with a casual intensity for the name that's stuffed down in my pocket. My new best friend hands him a glass of Chardonnay. He thanks her and sips with a wince as he takes in my colorful face.

"Booze is the secret ingredient to any fundraiser," he says with a chuckle. "Lubricates the wallet hinges. You look like you can use that drink."

"I can and I will."

He points vaguely at my chest.

"And you seem to have lost your name."

"Boy, ain't that the truth. But you can call me Mack."

"Good to meet you, Mack. Thanks for your support tonight. This is a good cause. We've just got to do better as a city. Well, as a nation. And Chicago can help lead the way. This has to be a priority. Who are you with?"

"Tia Lewis," I say. It gets me a salute from both eyebrows.

"Ah. Tia's a force of nature. HFC might just be the best-run nonprofit in the city. When Tia calls, I pick up the phone. I'll bet she's worked the whole team ragged putting this thing together tonight. Great job."

His eyes and his smile are ready to wrap things up and his hand emerges for a good-bye shake. It's the politician two-step. Make some educated assumptions to stick a pin in your demographic. Calculate the best angle on your interest. Give you a couple of strokes. Say something that fits on a bumper sticker. Deflect any pointy questions. Then disappear into the fog. Royce is as good at it as any of them. And he's handsome to boot. Onyx-black hair and a strong, chiseled chin. He might just have the most symmetrical face I've ever seen. Like it was made to be on a poster. Maybe in the Post Office.

"It is curious, though," I say as Royce grudgingly retracts his hand.

"What's that?"

"What's a man like Tony Rickens doing with the Mayor of Chicago's dry-cleaning ticket in his pocket?"

The slap. And at a fundraiser cocktail party. The slap works best when they can't see it coming. Keeps the reaction pure and easy to read. The reaction I get back from Royce is not *what are you talking about?* Instead, it's *who are you and how would you know such a thing?*

"Excuse me?"

"I think you probably heard me. But I can ask again if you want."

"What is your name again?"

"Mackey. Ray Mackey. Chandler PD."

I wait for the lights to come on. Doesn't take long.

"Ah. Detective Mackey. Yes. Your reputation precedes you, I'm afraid. Quite a mess you made. You and your made-up list."

"I am sorry about the mess, Mr. Mayor. I trust you have a good dry cleaner. The question I'm asking is why you would ever entrust a corrupt, murderous psychopath like Tony Rickens with the ticket for your nice, clean suits."

"I don't have any idea what you're talking about, Detective. And I don't know any Tony Rickens."

My free hand has a mind of its own. I've got the photo out of my pocket and up in front of his face without any warning to either of us. I tap the head of the late Anthony Rickens with my finger.

"There's Tony. Standing right behind you. Pushing that ugly goatee right up to your ear so you can hear him over all the champagne corks."

Royce narrows his eyes and bends at the waist to get closer without touching the unclean thing. He restraightens and smiles.

"Long time ago, Detective. I don't remember all my babysitters and teachers either."

I move my finger to the opposite side of the banquet table.

"What about these two? Remember them?"

It gets me a disbelieving laugh.

"Are you really interrogating the Mayor of Chicago at a Ritz-hosted homelessness fundraiser?"

"You're right. It's absurd. My apologies, Mr. Mayor. Let's go get a room."

"I think not."

"So then the answer to my question is that you don't know them?"

He glances again at the photo.

"My campaign manager. Victor Roby. And she was a reporter, if I recall. I forget her name. Maggie? Maddy? Victor was her access to the campaign."

"You're saying she was sleeping with Victor for access?"

He brushes the question off with a polite smile.

"I'm saying Victor was a good campaign manager."

"Yeah, Victor's good at a lot of things. He can burn down his own buildings like nobody's business."

If Royce is rattled, he doesn't show it.

"Nice chat, Detective. Thanks again for supporting the cause."

"No, thank *you*, Mr. Mayor. See you soon. And tell Alexi Novak I said hi."

It's the first spider-vein crack in his composure. A barely detectible hitch in the man's breath. He covers well.

"Friend of Alex, are you?"

"His family called him Alexi, back when they were alive. On the streets of Big Man's city, he goes by Stoli. I met him in my living room one night for some radical redecorating."

"Sorry." Royce gives up a little laugh. "I don't know what that means."

"Better that you don't. That was before Alexi killed his mother for knowing too much. But you tell him that Ivah was a proud mother to the end. Her baby workin' for the Mayor of Chicago. Quite the feather in the cap when you think about it. The life span of most Big Man stooges is too short for them to climb all the way up into the mayor's office. Maybe Alexi's the one picking up your laundry now that Tony Rickens is in the dirt. I say good for him. Kid's going places. Small, dark places. Probably sooner than he thinks."

Royce looks at me like the gears behind his eyes are having some trouble grinding.

"Heard you're a fiction writer," he says.

"I couldn't make this up if I drank my dinner for a solid week. Which is the other thing you heard about me."

"Oh, I've heard a lot of things, Detective. Thanks for the chat."

Royce turns to leave but gets pulled up short by none other than Tia Lewis, placing a hand on his shoulder.

"Mr. Mayor," she says. "I think it's time for you to make the pitch."

Royce smiles. Hard to tell if the extra wattage is coming from a special reserve of garden variety insincerity or if it's just relief.

"Lead the way, Tia. I was just hydrating. I'm ready."

Tia looks my way, noticing me for the first time as I'm folding up the photo and tucking it away.

"Are you …?"

I cut her off with a nod.

"I am."

Royce takes his leave for the podium, a hand on Tia's shoulder like he is escorting a child through a carnival. She looks back at me and points to the ceiling. Then she thrusts her index finger my way and I nod just as the crowd fills in the space between us.

She wants to meet upstairs for a drink. She'll be there in an hour. My plan is to be there immediately. Find a quiet table and start enjoying not being here. I finish my drink and then make my way across the room, listening to an amplified Mayor of Chicago hold forth on behalf of the homeless. He's a gifted public speaker. Makes me wonder who's giving him the gifts.

He's still at it by the time I'm out of the room missing the glass in my hand and waiting for the elevator. The sound of him fills the space. Maybe it's the tone. Maybe some part of me is still paying attention to his words echoing off the walls. Whatever it is, it makes me want to amble slowly back toward the ballroom so I can hear him a little better.

"… so I have no illusions that this is news for many of you in this room who are so plugged into the heartbeat of this city that you know more about my life than I do. You laugh, but it's true. I'm always the last to know what I'm doing next. Ask my wife. She'll tell you.

"Seriously, though, it has been my life's greatest honor to serve this greatest of all cities. And make no mistake, I will be serving the remainder of my term with vigor and purpose, with an eye toward making a difference in some key challenges – crime, economic expansion, health care, the latest Covid variant, education, labor – none of them more important that the homelessness problem. I'm not giving up. As mayor and as a citizen, I'm not giving up. We've just got to do better as a city. We've got to do better as a nation. And Chicago can help lead the way. This has to be a priority. The initiative we are discussing tonight is key. It is a rallying point. But we all know that the fight to protect our most vulnerable citizens will continue into the future and it must remain a priority. Whoever my successor may be, you can be sure that I will be urging him or her to keep this initiative on the front burner.

"Connie and I will start planning the next chapter of our lives, which I'm sure will involve the kind of leisure travel that is not possible while serving as mayor. She is promising to confiscate my phone at the airport."

He gets a hearty laugh at that one. I can't see him, but I can hear him laughing with them. The nametag lady is sure laughing with a few vigorous head nods thrown in. Like she confiscates her man's phone all the time.

"You think I'm kidding. I'll be lucky to get it back. I plan to smuggle a burner in with my luggage. Because, while I can step away from the office of mayor, I can never quit Chicago. Wherever we go and whatever we do, my heart will always be here with you and the triumphs and continued struggles of this amazing city."

THIRTY-FIVE

Look at him. Tucked into a booth, back wedged into a corner, cradling a crystal tumbler of Forester. Sad. Pathetic. The heavy lids. Head bobbing. He's the child at the adult dinner party, up past his bedtime. He's taken the day too far.

He wants to be home in his lounger, Phil on his lap, trying to hold the nightmares at bay on his own turf, in private, where no one will hear him scream.

Torali gets as much attention for its attached, amber-lit bar and its open-air, rooftop dining as it does its Italian steakhouse menu. Eventually the Chicago water levels will rise high enough to allow gondolas to dock along the Ritz rooftop. For now, the rain has closed the open-air lounge, keeping Ray inside where it's too easy to fall asleep. Everyone who was here when he first shambled in, looking sideways at him over raised drinks and forks, is now gone, replaced by a fresh supply of new people, all perky and unbeaten, blissfully unaware of the tired heap in the booth.

The windows in three directions are coated in a clear, glycerin-like ooze that smears the city lights and shape-shifts the monuments of Chicago in the rainy gloom. Overhead, *Torali* favors an ivory-tickling mix of Elian Elias and Bill Evans. It's enough to rock a crib over the cliff.

He gives his head a rapid shake to wake himself up. The rattling pain in his skull helps. He looks at his watch. Mattia Lewis' hour has stretched another twenty minutes. The server has stopped checking in. He wonders if he should go back down and get her. Interrupt her conversation. Confiscate her phone.

"Sorry that took so long."

Tia's voice clears the back of the booth before the woman herself is visible. For an instant he wonders if he has slipped back into dream. Wonders if Tia Lewis will have the chainsaw this time.

"I had to fight my way to the door." She is as she was when he last saw her only now carrying a coat, umbrella, and purse, all of which she dumps unceremoniously into the booth and slides in. She nods at his face. "Looks like you did too."

Ray scoffs.

"This? No. This happened trying to get in. The nametag lady wasn't convinced I belonged."

"Oh?"

"She thought I was homeless, there to collect my money."

Tia's face is too weary from smiling and making polite conversation to register the humor. She answers as if to defend her strategy.

"Big doners give more if they're ensconced in their element. The soup kitchen guilt setting doesn't work. I've tried."

Ray shrugs.

"I guess the engine of compassion needs lubrication."

"Forget compassion. Forget municipal policy initiatives. This is all about competitive ego gratification. Publicity. The fundraisers need to be swanky and social and dick-swinging. See and be seen. Whatever works. I'll take it any way I can get it."

The server stops by with a question on her face. Tia orders a Chenin Blanc. Ray holds up his empty with instructions for another.

"Success?" he asks. It's Tia's turn to shrug.

"We moved the ball. Never far enough, but that's the game. The mayor helped."

"I'll bet," says Ray. "Interesting speech. Didn't know he isn't signing up for another term."

Tia nods.

"Yeah, that bit of buzz has been out there for a few weeks. He's burned out. He seems tired. Man, I get it. At some point you just have to turn the page. Start something new."

Ray nods like he knows what she means. He does. They could just as easily be talking about his own tired-burned-out-needs-something-new urge to turn the page.

The conversation meanders, looking for a purpose. They talk to be polite, avoiding the dead woman in the room until the drinks arrive. It's awkward, not saying her name.

"I'm sorry," Tia says eventually, not bothering with a segue. "I know it must have hurt to lose her so early. I lost her too, only a lot sooner than you."

Looks to me like Ray is the one who's lost, confusion tugging at the skin between his eyes. Tia sees it just like I do. She doesn't follow up.

"What can I help you with, Ray?"

Ray digs into his shirt pocket. He puts the business card on the table.

"I found a stack of these in an old case file. I'm trying to make sense of it."

Tia picks up the card. Laughs. Her face is pretty in a clean, plain way. Her expressions, all of them, even this laugh, are efficient, suffused with self-sufficiency. She's figured out how not to need other people.

"Another life," she says. "Got to a point that I just couldn't muscle another story through a gauntlet of editors who knew less than half what I did."

"About what?"

"About everything. About this confounding city and how it works. How it doesn't work. Like I said, sometimes it's just time to make a change. But that's probably not why you're asking."

"I'm trying to figure out why she had a dozen of these cards all to herself."

Ray measures her reaction for confusion. He waits for a shoulder shrug. He doesn't get either. If she is surprised that Marlo was hoarding her business cards, she doesn't let on.

"What do you know about me, Mack?"

He tips his glass, like it's the burn in his throat that helps him think.

"I know you worked for the *Trib*. I know you've built a non-profit from the ground up. That you've made a name for being effective. I know the mayor wishes you were working for him. I know you share an alma mater with my late wife and that the two of you majored in journalism. I know you like Chenin Blanc when you're beat. I know that once upon a time you answered to the name of Teelew."

Tia laughs again.

"Teelew. Christ. Been awhile."

Tia disappears behind a long blink. It looks like she needs a moment, so Ray gives her two. When she speaks, it's to the business card in her hand, turning it end over end.

"She was the only one who ever called me Teelew. It was Marlo's name for me. I called her Makline. We were like some bad *Cagney and Lacey* knock-off. Woodward and Bernstein go to college. Teelew and Makline. We got into some real shit back in the day. We were lucky to graduate." Tia shakes her head and looks back up at Ray. "Marlo Kline. Man, she was something else."

"Yeah," says Ray after a pause that almost doesn't end. "She was."

"Tell me something, Ray. How much of that stuff about me did you learn from her? From Marlo."

He doesn't have to think long to sort it out.

"None of it."

"Did she ever mention me?"

Ray shakes his head.

"Not that I remember. Sorry."

Tia gives a slow, knowing nod and drinks her wine. Doesn't take a great detective to see the pain.

"Our last year in school. Writing for the *Daily Northwestern*. The DN we called it. Marlo locked onto this tip about a provost selling admissions. I didn't believe her at first. I made her prove it to me. She did. She had the guy cold. She had two highly reluctant but corroborating sources. I don't know how she found them. She wouldn't tell me. The woman had a nose. Anyway, it wasn't just once or twice. It was an annual thing for this guy to take special interest in one or two applicants. He had a couple of confederates in the admissions office. We nailed down the story together, worked it up, and took it to the editor of the *DN*. Joel Bergman. Gutless little shit from Boston. Always had that little rope of spit between his lips when he condescended to you across his desk. Bergman wanted to sleep on the story for a night. So he did. Then he woke up the next morning and spiked it. Said it wasn't the hill he wanted to die on. He had the final say. Nothing we could do. Or so I thought. Marlo wouldn't let it go."

"Took it to a real paper?"

Tia shakes her head. "Then it wouldn't be our story. She was too stubborn."

"What'd she do?"

"She worked the problem. Went to school on Bergman. He was an English major. His dissertation was all about how the literary modernist movement started closer to Dostoyevsky's *Crime and Punishment* than Conrad's *Heart of Darkness*."

Ray yawns on cue.

"Sorry. Come again?"

"Hey, that's a forty-year gap in the annals of formative literature. Might have made for a good dissertation if Bergman hadn't cribbed most of it from other sources."

"He plagiarized his dissertation?"

"Like seventy percent."

"Okay." Ray is confused. Then he gets it. "Wait. Marlo blackmailed him?"

"Well." Tia rolls her eyes. "Blackmail. Marlo wrote up the story like any good journalist. Headline: *Editor in Chief Loses Way Somewhere Between 'Darkness' and 'Crime.'* Then she submitted it to Bergman for publication like it was any other story. She showed it to me after it was too late to pull it back. I think she knew I'd try to talk her out of it. She was right. Marlo had all the guts in those days. My guts didn't show up until much later."

"And?"

"Bergman was dishonestly unoriginal, not stupid. He got the picture. He spiked the story that was all about his plagiarism and approved the story about the provost selling access."

"I'll bet that went down smooth."

"All hell broke loose. Bergman had more than a few detractors in the administration. He defended the story like he was the one who'd written it. That's what plagiarists do best, I guess. He defended us, his reporters, like his own children. The provost and two guys in Admissions were invited to leave. The lawyers got involved. Bergman resigned. Marlo and I made it to graduation."

Ray is quiet. He drinks, brow furrowed. Tia gives a soft laugh.

"Never heard that one, I'm guessing."

Ray shakes his head. Tia shrugs.

"Not surprised," she says. "It would be just like her to keep that little episode to herself. I'd be one to blab about it at every cocktail party, but she'd just … she'd just let it sink to the bottom, down there with all the stuff you'd never know about her unless you knew enough to ask."

Ray can tell there's more. He waits.

"Marlo was always a mystery to me. I loved that about her. She never got old. There was always something deeper to her. Something I didn't know. Something I couldn't know. It made everything about her … I don't know … magnetic."

Ray looks at her, silently fighting with himself. It's the look in her eyes as she remembers Marlo. He's seen it before in the mirror.

"Were you … were the two of you …"

He gets back a sad smile.

"You *can* say it out loud, you know," she says.

Ray doesn't say anything, despite the invitation. Doesn't need to. He already knows without really knowing. It's just the understanding that's missing. Tia relents.

"Okay. Maybe you can't say it. Yes, Mack. Yes, we were."

All he can do is stare and blink. Tia reaches. Taps his hand.

"But before you go rewriting history too thoroughly, I will add that there was only one lesbian in that relationship, and it wasn't Marlo. Took me a long time to figure that out."

"Then …" *Torali* threatens to become a revolving restaurant. Ray grips his tumbler. "Then why?"

Tia tips her glass and shrugs.

"I kept coming back to the idea that she had not known her own essence. A fundamental confusion about who she was, leading to some experimental sexual fluidity or even ambivalence, which she hid from me out of insecurity. Completely alien to me because I've known which team I play for since I was twelve, but I thought, maybe she was just lost." Tia laughs as if at something ridiculous. "That sound like Marlo to you?"

"No," says Ray.

"No," she confirms. "Marlo was never lost. Marlo always knew everything."

"Then …"

"I think she didn't like being fully known by people. She didn't like being understood. To be understood was like giving away parts of herself to others. I think it translated as a kind of loss of essential integrity. She didn't like being figured out. Too much existential risk. It was better for her … easier … safer … if I believed we were the same. Simple. Clean. It was a pill for me to swallow. Kept me away from more complicated explanations."

"Such as?"

"I've stopped trying to figure that one out. You were married to her, Mack. You have to know some of what I'm saying."

Ray doesn't answer. He keeps his reaction to himself. But inside that battered head, where only the two of us have access, Tia's words are ringing like a bell up on a hill. He remembers her, he can't help it, Marlo, his wife, his beloved, not as a person, but as an idea of a person, stripped to her essence. She is vaporous. Ungraspable, just out of reach, part of her always merging with shadow.

Had she done the same to him? Let him believe whatever he wanted; deduce whatever he could and leave the rest uncorrected? Is his cherished understanding of her nothing but a pocketful of loose dimes he'd picked up here and there? How many of those dimes had been planted for his benefit? How many of those dimes were Canadian? Couple months ago, he'd have bet that number was zero. Now all he feels is a pocket full of tin foil circles. Across the table, Tia is still making sounds.

"She managed her emotional entanglements by allowing this … this *other person* to be known instead. To be understood. To be devalued … to be devoured by devotion and affection and companionship. She gave me the parts of herself that I had fabricated for my own satisfaction, mostly out of unchecked assumptions. I've concluded that the Marlo I loved was a generous blend of what she showed me and what I wanted to believe about her. But I won't lie, Mack, she deliberately obscured herself. The longer she was gone, the more I realized how little I had actually known her."

Ray nearly winces. He wants to tell her that she has just stuck her finger into the bullet hole of his life. That oozing, emptying sense of knowing Marlo less and less with each passing day. He drowns the impulse in bourbon. He betrays nothing.

"Look," she says, "I've had years to think about Marlo. Who she was and was not. These days I love her and hate her all at the same time and in roughly equal proportions. I call that progress. I'll spare you all that. I am curious about her childhood, though. I'm betting whatever broke in her, broke early."

"I'm not conceding that anything in Marlo was broken," he says.

"Okay. No offense intended. It's my perspective."

"Her parents were good midwestern stock. I didn't know either of them well, but well enough. They didn't molest her or beat her or neglect her if that's what you're looking for."

Tia's eyes flash anger, telling him she doesn't need to be here.

"I'm not the one here looking for something, Ray."

Ray takes a breath, then he surrenders a contrite nod.

"Sorry. Maybe I'm a little defensive."

"Look. I get it. I'm not trying to be disrespectful."

"She had a kid brother. Jimmy. A real piece of work."

"I met Jimmy," she says. "He was a riot. He spent a weekend or two with us at Northwestern. We had to sneak him in. He was on a mission to bag a coed. More charm than sense. Seemed to know his big sister was good for date money."

"That's Jimmy."

"Marlo loved him to death. Where is he these days?"

"Several places, I'm guessing. That's a story for another bottle. What'd she tell you about me?"

It's a needy question and I let him know it. He hates himself instantly for asking, but I pile on anyway. Tia pops her eyebrows.

"You? She never told me about you until … Until it was too late to convince her she was making a mistake." Tia sticks out a hand. "Let me rephrase. I'm not saying you were a mistake. I'm saying I desperately wanted you to be a mistake."

"Okay."

"I tried convincing her, but it was done. Arguing was pointless. We had stopped being together, for a number of years by then, so it's not like you broke up a relationship. But I think I always hoped we could … you know. Rekindle. We had been off and on enough before. It was possible. So I kind of hated you from the beginning, Ray. Sorry to say. I made you into a charismatic tornado that spun into her life and carried her away. That was the story that hurt the least."

Ray sits. Waits. The couple two tables away can't eat and hold hands at the same time, so they let the food get cold and let their eyes do all the eating instead.

Outside the glass cage, the drizzle has returned to pounding on all sides. Elian Elias wants someone to cry her a river. Maybe that's Ray.

"She said you were a Chandler Homicide detective. Handsome. Funny. Humble. Smart. Going places. Big shoulders. Bigger heart. Loyal to a fault. She said you two had been at it for eighteen months." Tia shakes her head in an old disbelief. "Eighteen goddamned months. We'd seen each other casually a few times during those eighteen months and that was the first time I knew you even existed."

"You said her mystery was magnetic."

"Yeah, well, that's not how you treat people you love. And I didn't take it well. Everything I had bottled up inside came out all at once. I said a lot of hurtful things. About her. About you. I've got some harsh opinions about most cops. I said you'd cheat on her before the marriage blew apart. I told her she'd deserve it. I'm not proud of it. It was infantile. She kept her cool through all my snot and tears and I hated her for that too. Her steely composure. I couldn't reach her. It was like I was suddenly irrelevant. She was already safely gone." She shakes her head at her wine. "So like her to put everything in place – quietly, secretly – and then show up out of the blue and pull the pin. It was the last time I saw her."

Tia takes a deep breath and lets it go. Eventually she looks up from her glass. She weighs the silence and sizes him up.

"It's a lot," she says eventually. "All this. I'm sorry. You okay?"

Turns out Tia Lewis' compassion needs no lubrication. Ray feels all the worse for it. He leans back in the booth. His eyes catch the passing server like a couple of drowning kids flailing for the lifeguard. He holds up the glass.

"I'm fine," he says. "Tired. I'm in a building full of beds and none of them are mine. What can you tell me about the stack of business cards?"

She drinks with a look of grudging admiration. Here she's offered him the rabbit hole full of ghosts that she can't resist, and he wants to talk about business cards.

"She must have just … taken them," she says.

"Business cards?"

"I'd remember if I'd given her a stack of cards. Why would I do that? I didn't."

"And you don't know why she would take them?"

"I can guess," she says with a wistful smile.

"Let's hear it."

"This was still years before she met you. We'd been off-and-on for a while. Infrequent contact. I was slugging it out at the *Trib* and Marlo was doing her private-eye thing. She shows up one day out of the blue and asks me to lunch. I probably should have said no. I was a good reporter. I had good instincts. I knew the odds. But I said yes for all the wrong reasons. We believe what we want to believe." Tia looks. "Don't we, Ray?"

The new glass of Forester shows up. Ray drowns the answer.

"So we go to lunch. It instantly feels like old times. We relived all the old adventures. We toasted Joel Bergman. We caught each other up. I wasn't seeing anyone at the time. Stressed out. Lonely. I was a sitting duck. She wasn't involved either, so …"

"I get it, Tia. You started up again. What'd she want?"

Her expression reflects the interruption.

"Lunch," she says. "With me. She missed me. That's what she said. She missed me. No agenda other than that."

"Okay."

"Lunch led to dinner. It became a nightly thing."

"Did she talk about her cases? Was she working on something that …"

"Marlo didn't talk about her cases with me. Not ever. Maybe that's the kind of thing you do for husbands. I didn't have the right security clearance I guess."

"It wasn't you," he says. "She was tight lipped about her work. With me too."

He gets back a wan smile.

"Okay. Thanks for that. She said her work was down. Like, way down. She said she didn't have much to do. The money was drying up. She said she was toying with getting back into journalism. I wanted to remind her that I had tried to talk her out of chasing a PI license in the first place. But I didn't. Marlo Kline was back in my orbit drinking and sharing. I didn't want to say anything … you know. I was on my best behavior."

"Was she looking for a leg up? A referral to the *Trib*?"

"It didn't really come off that way, no. I wanted to believe it was all about me, not about a new career for her. But we did have this conversation one night. She insisted she could ghostwrite a column for me and that no one would know the difference."

"Did that ever happen?"

"Of course not," she says. "Well. Not really. Sort of."

"I always liked multiple choice. Can I pick the one I like?"

"We got onto politics one night. It was a thing with us. Any time we got high, we argued about politics."

"Got high. You mean pot?"

"Yeah. Frequently. Not with you?"

Ray shakes his head. Marlo had never even hinted an interest.

"I stopped years ago," she says. "It was making me stupid and dull. I couldn't keep up. I miss it. Cigarettes too. I was working a pack a day during the depth of my reporting career. Decided I wanted to live past fifty. You look like a Joe Camel man to me."

"The hump and the nose always give me away."

"Still at it?"

"I quit."

"Good for you. How long?"

"Yesterday. Also the day before. I could go on, but I'm getting bored and that always makes me want a cigarette."

"Right. Well, Marlo always had a good weed source. We had a spirited discussion that night about different ballot races. I probably started it by letting on that I had been assigned to cover as many of the city council elections as possible. You know, background pieces. Ward-by-ward, who are the candidates and where did they come from kind of thing."

Ray is still trying to reconcile Marlo with a joint. He nods.

"Couple of days ago I read your column on Royce winning the 42nd Ward."

Tia's face comes alive with fresh interest.

"A couple of days ago? That piece is, like …"

"Research. I was trying to track you down. Good bit of writing. Thorough."

"Research. Wow." She laughs. "Not sure I've ever been researched before."

"Congratulations."

"That column published shortly after the election. I can't take much credit."

"Why's that?"

"Because I only wrote about three percent of that article."

"Who gets credit for the other ninety-seven?"

"Your late wife."

It's Ray's turn to react.

"Marlo?"

"How many late wives do you have?"

"Just the one. Care to fill me in a little?"

"I'm trying."

"Sorry."

"We talked about all of the council races, but kept coming back to the 42nd Ward just because it was so … I don't know … bizarre. The thing with Dominic Lucas."

"Lucky Lucas," says Ray, lifting his glass. "May he have better luck in the afterlife. Who drinks himself over the side of his own boat and misses the water?"

"Right? He had that election sewn up for a fourth term before campaign season even started and then, suddenly, he's dead and everybody is jumping into the race. Like five, six characters out of nowhere. Royce had no political experience, but he was kind of the normal one in that group. But, what's his name, Jonathan King? The mattress titan of Fulton River? Give me a break. He had no business in polite society, let alone the city council."

"Funny you think the Chicago City Council belongs in polite society."

Tia is too lost in reverie to respond. She laughs instead.

"God, and Fredrick Bubba Jones? Marlo was all over Bubba. She knew all about the half-brother doing time for sexually assaulting the postal carrier in the back of the mail truck. She wanted me to work that into my pre-election spray. I laughed her off, but she thought the voters had a right to know. That's when she offered to write the piece for me. She said she could interview the candidate as my assistant. I laughed that off too. She said she could just pretend she was me because no one knew what I looked like. She said she could write it in my voice and no one would know the difference. I *really* laughed that one off. I didn't want that to be true."

"Did she convince you?"

"We tussled. She let it go. We were too stoned to care."

Tia cradles her glass, looking into the Chenin Blanc like she's holding liquid memory. She drinks like maybe Marlo is inside.

"What happened?" he asks.

"Everything. Nothing. She was wonderful for a few days and then she was gone, suddenly too busy to get together. Big case, she said. Suddenly swamped. Longer and longer to return my calls. I came to my senses and stopped trying. I can be a love-struck dunce, but it's usually temporary. Less temporary whenever it was Marlo."

"And the article?"

"Articles. There were two. Shortly before the election I received a hand-delivery at the *Tribune*. A manilla envelope with a bunch of hand-written interview notes and a flash drive. The flash drive was rubber banded inside a handwritten note that said *Teelew and Makline ride again* and a winky smiley face. The drive had one article about Royce and one about Fredrick Bubba Jones. The notes showed that she had interviewed the candidates and their respective campaign managers."

"The business cards," says Ray. Tia nods.

"Until you showed up tonight, I'd assumed she had posed as my assistant gathering background data. Now it's pretty clear she just flat out impersonated me."

"You never asked?"

"Is that a serious question?" Tia's eyes have sharpened. "You think I didn't want to know? She basically vanished. I didn't see her again until … well, not for a long time."

"You're rubbing shoulders a lot with Royce these days. Most recently tonight. Has he ever said anything about you interviewing him but you not really looking like you?"

"Too many reporters over too many years. He knows my name is on the piece we're talking about, but I wrote others subsequently. I think it's all a blur. I had long hair back then too, so …"

"The interview notes Marlo gave you. You still have those?"

"Long gone. Sorry. There have been several great purges to get rid of Marlo."

"So you published the articles?"

"No. The series agenda at the *Trib* had changed in the meantime. Lots of stuff was going on at that time and we no longer had the column space for a pre-election spray. That, and covering all of the candidates for all wards just became a ridiculously heavy lift. Our team's marching orders were to focus only on the council winners. So, I couldn't have published both pieces even if I wanted to. I had to wait to see who actually won the hearts of the 42nd Ward."

"Royce."

"Right."

"Would you have gone with the article about Bubba Jones if he had won?"

Tia makes a face like she's bitten into something sour.

"No. Marlo's draft was really lacking an objective voice. And it was way too focused on the half-brother sexual assault thing. It was pretty negative. These weren't supposed to be puff pieces exactly, but they were expected to be generally spin-free. If Bubba had won, I'd have had to do a lot of cleaning up."

"And you think Marlo was expecting pre-election publication?"

"Yeah. She would have had no way to know the paper had changed its election coverage strategy. To the best of her knowledge, the pieces would run pre-election."

"What'd you think of the Royce article?"

"Beautiful. And it sounded like me, just like she said. Thorough. Fact-forward. Very well written."

"Okay, so the election happens. Royce and Jones are on top of the heap, but they each stop short of fifty percent and go into a runoff election. Royce wins. You publish Marlo's piece on Royce."

"Essentially, but not exactly. It felt wrong to publish it at all, because I didn't write it. But I was suddenly in a box. I had to write a piece on Royce, but he and his campaign manager, I forget the guy's name …"

"Victor Roby."

"Roby. That's him. Royce and Roby had already been interviewed. By her *as me,* apparently, or as my assistant, as I thought at the time. Marlo is not answering her phone. So what am I going to do? Ask them to do it all over again? I also had more deadlines than I could manage and was more stressed out than I had ever been in my life and suddenly here was this great article right in front of me. Exactly what I needed. All I had to do was publish it and hope Marlo had been accurate."

"So you did?"

"No. I tore the piece apart and basically reorganized it, rewriting bits here and there, just so I could feel more like it was mine. Then I emailed a draft of the article to Sam Royce and Victor Roby and said to let me know if they thought anything was inaccurate. They both gave it a thumbs up. They thought it was great. I submitted it to my editor. He loved it too." Tia shrugs. "Out it went."

"And absolutely no contact with Marlo?"

"Briefly. She called me from Venezuela shortly after the Royce article landed."

"Venezuela?"

"Some rich client looking for a nephew sent her to Caracas to find him. She'd been living there for a month."

Memory, suddenly, unbidden. Early in the marriage. A dark restaurant. Marlo in an off-the-shoulder number that accentuated the slope of her neck. The server had turned up with two drinks they hadn't ordered, pointing to another table.

"Ah, yeah," says Ray. "I actually know about that one. The way Marlo told it the nephew was hiding out in the mountains after seducing the daughter of a mobbed-up banana magnate. Marlo smuggled him back in a bag of coffee beans."

"Apparently she did talk about her cases," says Tia.

"Not really. The rich client bumped into us out to dinner one night. He bought us drinks and did all the talking about the nephew he still has. He seemed convinced Marlo had magical powers."

"She did," sighs Tia. "She could have returned my calls, Mack. Even from Caracas. That doesn't take magic."

"It might if you're on a donkey in the mountains. Sounds like she did call eventually. How'd that go?"

"Not pleasant. I wanted a pound of flesh for the position she put me in. I also wanted answers. She claimed she had hoped to relieve my workload stress. She said she thought it would be a hoot, just like the old days. I made it clear I was not amused. She apologized for the stunt and for being unavailable. She dodged a lot of questions. I figured the real answers would wait until a face-to-face. Like an idiot, I proposed that we get together over drinks when she got back to the States. She said she'd be in touch. That was never going to happen. I know that now."

"Did you believe her?" He feels like a heretic for asking. "About just wanting to save you time and stress?"

"I don't know what to believe. Never have."

Ray nods. He doesn't know what to believe either. They're both working hard to keep the universe from unraveling.

"I'm not proud of what I did, Ray. I'd have been fired on the spot if anyone had found out. That's a career-ender for a journalist. As it turned out, it actually helped my career. My stock at the *Trib* rose after that piece on Royce. I had to work twice as hard after that to feel like I deserved it. They started calling me *tireless Tia*."

"I'm not in the habit of apologizing for my wife," says Ray. "But it sounds like you're due."

"I put it all to bed a long time ago," she says, waving him off. "I think what I hated the most was that, if I'm really honest with myself, I ran the piece on Royce because it felt like Marlo and I were doing something together again. Teelew and Makline. I wanted that old partnership. I had hoped it would somehow bring her back." She doesn't need to add the rest. She does anyway. "To me."

Tia Lewis slides her half-empty glass to the side and pulls her coat and purse into her lap. She looks at Ray with an exhaustion that rivals his own.

"Because I loved her, Ray. Desperately. There has never been anyone like Marlo. I still don't know who she was. Not really. Maybe that's for a spouse to know. I'll never understand her. I hope you have better luck."

THIRTY-SIX

It's a careless backhanded sweep to clear the counter. The two mostly empty cans clank down into the sink where they will stay for at least a day, maybe two, until the stink of cat food fills the kitchen and starts to explore the front hall.

He bends at the waist, wanting to place the bowl on the floor. It freefalls the final two feet. Phil flinches at the sound, then sniffs indifferently at the mound of fish and saunters away, tail in the air.

"You don't mean that," says Ray, trying to re-erect himself against the sink. "Phil." He closes his eyes. "Phil."

Gravity. He slides his back against the counter, pushing down on the bottle in his left hand to slow his descent, using the Old Forester like a brown glass cane, until he is sitting on the floor next to the stainless-steel bowl. He leans his head back against the counter and broadcasts out into the dark house.

"You don't mean that. C'mere, Phil. C'mere. Eat goddamnit. Want me to eat it? Because I will. I will eat it."

He won't.

"Here I go. Eating. This is delicious. Phil. Phil."

He's already on the verge of sick. Cold, wet cat food will empty his stomach, and he knows it. The smell alone might do it, which is why he normally feeds her straight tuna. He's out of tuna. There is no tuna.

He drinks from the bottle. Closes his eyes again. Leans his head back. Listens to the rain in the gutters.

Marlo, he thinks.

He sees her now, as if through a waterfall beyond his reach. *Marlo*.

He might have gone to bed. There was a moment, briefly, just inside the front door. Tia Lewis still in his head with Marlo in a sex-saturated cloud of cannabis. Or someone pretending to be Marlo as she pretends to be Tia Lewis in some smokey, makeshift campaign headquarters for Fredrick Bubba Jones, asking the candidate about his family. Asking about the U.S. Postal Service. A buck or two in her pocket from Victor Roby, disbursement from the dirty trick campaign fund for Samuel Trenton Royce. Marlo, working for Roby and Royce. Jesus H.

There was a moment just inside the front door when what he wanted most was to escape the mystery of Marlo and burrow into the great, black unconscious.

He might have gone to bed right then. Dropped his coat on the floor, called it a night, and gone upstairs to sleep.

But no. Couldn't do that. That's where the dream was waiting; inside the great, black unconscious. Waiting with hot, serrated terror.

Take off his legs.

So. A drink then. And another. Ella does Ellington on the turntable. Rain at the windows and Phil at his heels, meowing for him to sit. So he'd sat, heavily, like a front-end loader off a bridge, collapsing into his chair with the weight of everything that he does not understand pushing him down into the cushion. And he had, for an hour, contemplated the hole in his chest the shape of a woman he no longer knows. Marlo.

He had dozed twice while in the chair, Sig still strapped to his chest just in case whoever is following him around the city – for he is convinced it is someone – decided to come in for a nightcap and a quick beating. He had not been asleep long enough to dream. He was still too vigilant to let that happen. Not yet drunk enough.

Close. But not yet.

He had shaken it off. Stood and turned up the lights. Retrieved his laptop and retaken the chair with renewed purpose. He had booted up the latest unfinished project and searched for the place he had left off, pretending at being a writer instead of who he actually is. Pretending he has some control by manipulating a shallow characterization of himself.

And I had called him on it.

Clever, Ray, I told him. *Abstract yourself out of your own head and try to save that guy, that entirely make-believe person, from mortal danger. Funny though*, I said, *how the character in your book doesn't have a shadow on his lung. You <u>do</u> have a shadow on your lung. The character isn't a paranoid alcoholic with PTSD; you <u>are</u>. The character hasn't lost the truth of Marlo; you <u>have</u>.* I told him I call that cheating. I told him he was a coward for not facing his own life head on. For hiding inside a collection of bottles. For sanitizing himself in the pages of a book written for an audience of one.

I didn't hide my disgust. I laid it on thick. It felt good.

He knew I was right. But he kept looking for his place in the story anyway. Stubborn to the end, this guy. All the words on the screen were losing their focus, sloughing their integrity, and bleeding into each other like a true massacre of literature.

He'd finally found the part where Detective <u>McMannis</u> meets the comely Russian woman for the first time. Polina, he's named her. Her eleven-year-old daughter, Sasha, coloring dragons at the table. It's an unscheduled meeting in the IAD office of a fictional Illinois city that brings them together. Polina wants McMannis to help her find her mother's Russian doll. She has McMannis in her pocket with the first smile.

It hadn't lasted long. Ray had contributed one new sentence before the words on the screen became a senseless pile of tiny black sticks. He had stared at the screen until it turned black. He'd kept staring. *Marlo*, he'd thought, trying to remember her, flailing for something substantial. Something immutable. Something true.

He'd remembered. She, in bed, propped up on an elbow, stroking his forehead with a finger, sweat cooling on her skin. Her face had seemed to find his question amusing.

Why on earth would you want to do that, Ray?

Because I love you.

Yeah? So. What's marriage got to do with it?

Ask your parents. They'll tell you.

Sure they would. Doesn't mean the answer will make any sense.

You've taken their stability for granted.

You don't know the first thing about my family, Ray.

So tell me.

Pass. Maybe you're reacting to the instability of no family except orphanages.

Maybe.

Marriage isn't about love or being happy.

Okay. Then what's it about, Marlo?

Being less afraid. It's religion with benefits.

Maybe.

I'd have to put my PI license in a drawer.

Why?

Ray. Come on. Can't be a married PI. That doesn't work.

I'm afraid to ask why.

Sexual tension. Obviously. It's in all the books, Ray. You need to read more. Beautiful dame walks in the door with a pair of gams that go all the way to the floor, a purse full of presidents and a problem she can't solve by herself.

Only you're the beautiful dame.

Sweet. I've never carried a purse in my life. Point is I'd need to do something else.

Do something else like what?

I don't know. Journalism. Insurance work. Trade my gun for a camera. Start pulling in regular money and stop with all the casual client sex.

Kind of hoping you've already made that transition.

You'll never know.

Wait, is it the clients that are casual or the sex?

The clients, dear. Sex is never casual.

I can't see you working for an insurance company.

Me either. But I'd do it. Probably.

You would?

Probably.

Why?

Because ...

He had not been able to remember her answer. Because she loved him? Because marriage meant something to him and he meant that much to her?

He had not even been certain how much of the memory was fraudulent, made from scraps of longing pasted together in a brain soggy with grief and Old Forester.

He'd wondered. Couldn't help it. Had Victor Roby been a casual client? Had Tia Lewis been her beautiful dame? Marlo had never carried a purse. That much was true.

Phil had then leapt to the chair, padding across the keyboard and made more progress on *The Russian Doll* in three seconds than Ray had managed in a month. She'd sat and meowed insistently up into his face, making herself clear.

Ray had lowered the footrest, dispossessing Phil of her perch, trading the computer for the bottle. He'd stood swaying in the spinning room for a full minute, listening for the sound of someone, anyone, a shadow, standing outside in the dark, ready to drop everything and yank Sig from his holster at the slightest break in the unrelenting patterns of the rain.

Had that been necessary, he'd have been lucky not to shoot himself.

But it had not been necessary. The rain had kept its unrelenting pattern. Sig had stayed in his leather bed. Ray had wobbled for the kitchen.

"Tuna," he'd said. "Let's get you some tuna."

There is no tuna.

THIRTY-SEVEN

He is straining to see through the oily burlap threads, the bag tightened around his carotid with something elastic. Her head is turned away, looking behind her. Hair short, swishing when she moves like black seaweed in the current. She turns back, gripping his ankles even harder. Then he sees. Tia Lewis. It is Tia holding his legs, joint in her mouth, as the other one steps slowly into view. Saddle shoes appearing and disappearing beneath the hem of gaberdine slacks, belted under the folds of a white linen blouse. Garments he knows well, garments his mind can smell, from her own closet. He tries to say her name. *Marlo. Marlo.* It is a thought, her name, not a sound. Victor Roby is on the couch. He makes the only sound. *Take off his legs.* Tia Lewis smiles. Then, from behind her, the chainsaw. It sounds like a telephone.

Ray's body jerks, mouth and eyes open wide simultaneously, as if by some powerful electric shock.

And I, too, come back to life in that moment. Sleep, unconsciousness, is where I lose him, like he has passed into some mountain tunnel and my reception winks out until his consciousness comes through the other side and reconnects. In these first moments after waking, before his muscles have unclenched, the dreams are still with him, powerful and vivid and real, and I can look backwards in time, through the veil, through the burlap bag over his head. I can see what he has seen. I can see what he has been through. That is how I know his dreams.

Ray sputters and coughs. Phil looks up from the nook she has made for herself in the fetal space between his legs and his chest, muscles tensed, ready to leap from the floor to the counter if necessary. It is not necessary. Ray groans and drops his head back to edge of the empty silver bowl on the floor. Phil yawns and nestles back into the softness of Ray's belly. The phone in his pocket rings a second time, a stiletto-shaped sound that finds his temple. Twice more. Then it is silent.

Ray groans. His hand finds Phil's back. He pets her gently and she purrs. This is how he returns to the world.

Eventually he has strength enough to push himself upright, propping his once powerful shoulders up against the kitchen cabinets. A knob digs into his spine. He doesn't care. Too far down his list of sensations. He blinks slowly at the long lake of bourbon covering the kitchen floor, the edges now lit like kerosine in the early morning light seeping in through the rain-streaked glass of the kitchen window.

I give him a good look at himself. I lay it on thick. If a picture is worth a thousand words, this picture comes with an over-abundance of words like *disgusting* and *pathetic* and *loser. Alcoholic. Bum. Waste of oxygen.* I give him my worst. He takes it like a drunk. He's seen this picture full of words before.

He breathes in and out. Pets Phil. Rights the Old Forester next to him. Breathes. Slips the phone from his pocket and looks at the call log.

Unknown Caller. Number Blocked.

That clears away some of the fog. He sits up straight against the cabinet, squeezing the phone like it might try to escape. Phil senses the change in focus and, licking the puddle once, pads away. Ray stares at the phone.

Unknown Caller. Number Blocked.

First time in what, five weeks? Six? He scrolls the call history. He finds another one at 3:33 in the morning. *Unknown Caller. Number Blocked.* He says the word he could not say in the dream as Tia Lewis held his ankles in a vice and the gaberdine slacks had swished into view.

"Marlo."

There is no one to answer that word. That name. That sound in his kitchen. No one to confirm or deny. It is simply the sound of what, against all logic, reason, and science, he wants to be true. *Marlo.*

The phone rings in his hand as he is looking at it. It jolts his entire body. He answers without any benefit of comprehension.

"Marlo."

"Mr. Mackey?"

"Yes."

"This is Christina from Dr. Jha's office confirming your appointment this afternoon."

Coherence is slow and grudging, but it shows up eventually. Dinesh Jha wants to point at shadows.

"I have to cancel," he says. "Something's come up."

"Oh. When can we reschedule?"

"I'll have to call you later."

Standing is an undignified ordeal. He leans against the kitchen counter, panting, both hands clutching the phone like some religious relic he has brought to help him pray. I show him the spectacle, live and uncensored. He hates me for it. I send all of it right back with extra loathing.

The man can make coffee with his eyes closed. Good thing. The sound and the smell bring him gradually back to life. He drops a roll of paper towels into the lake of bourbon and pushes it around with his foot. Two more rolls later and the lake is mostly gone. He soaks a dishrag for the final mop-up, drops it on the floor and moves it around as best he can. He pushes it all into a pile next to Phil's empty bowl for when he feels it is safe to bend over and use his hands.

I show him what all of this looks like from my perch up against the ceiling. He hates me for that too. *Back at you, champ.*

Ray pours himself a cup and heads upstairs for a hot shower. I follow along behind with more opinions. He wonders who came by and made the staircase longer when he was asleep.

THIRTY-EIGHT

I prop myself up against the tile and let the water run over me until it goes cold. Some might call that wasteful. I call it my only incentive to get out of the shower and start a new day. The man in the mirror looks like he wants a quiet drawer in the morgue. He'll settle for a bed as long as there is an actual mattress involved. I'm ready to take him up on that, but then the phone rings.

"Mack?"

"Who is this?"

"This is your personal wake-up call from the Chief of the goddamned Chandler Police Department."

"Shit. I mean … Chief. Sorry. I'm not … I'm not …"

"You're not here, Mack. That's really all I care about. I need you to be here. *Now*."

"What's …"

"My hope was to intercept your lieutenant at his usual report for duty; break the bad news before the day starts. He hasn't shown and the lights are coming on around here. I need you in place to address the troops, just like we talked."

"Troops? I don't have troops, Chief."

"You do now, Mack. IAD is yours. There's a memo. On the double."

The Chief is gone. The man in the mirror slowly puts down the phone and rescinds his offer for some mattress time. The morgue is his final offer.

The troops, all six of them, are in their usual places doing their usual things. Half of them are on the phone. The other three are all about paperwork. The only thing different about today as far as they are concerned is that I'm standing in the doorway to Twill's office trying to get their attention. It takes an awkward minute for the calls to end. Then I start to say things that don't make any sense to anyone, especially me.

"If you check your in-boxes, you'll find a memo from Chief Loudermilk. That memo will explain a personnel change coming to IAD leadership. Everything there is to know about that personnel change is contained within the four corners of that memo. I don't know any more about it than you do, so don't ask."

I have lost the attention of every last one of them as they log into their email and read. I wait until, one-by-one, their eyes find the eyes of their neighbors and then return to mine. Carolyn has stopped chewing her morning licorice. She has turned backward in her seat, coaxing reactions from Mark Forge and then Glen Sugarman. Stephanie Nellis leans a shoulder against the door to the conference room and crosses her arms. She lifts an eyebrow at Raffi Santiago who shrugs and swivels his chair back around so that he is facing me.

"I've been asked to walk in LT's shoes as the department runs the recruitment process. I'm sure you all have your opinions about that. So do I. LT's shoes are too big for me to fill. So I'll make you a deal. I won't pretend I know what I'm doing if you don't. Work your cases. Do your job. I'll be whatever help to you that I can be. I'll spitball whatever needs spitballing, and I'll run whatever kind of interference the brass balls upstairs will tolerate. We'll muddle through as best we can until they fill the chair with someone who wants to be your boss. That's not me. And this," I close Twill's door behind me, "is not my office."

I leave it there and, just to make the point, head for the cubicle I call home. I can feel the eyeballs on me, but I pretend I don't. Eventually, the men and women of the Chandler IAD resume work at a confused half-speed. I pull a file from the top of the stack and open it up. I pretend to care about what's inside and wait for the inevitable. It takes about three minutes.

"Hey boss," says Raffi, arm draped over the wall of my cubicle. I don't want to see the smile, so I keep my eyes on the page in front of me.

"Call me that again and I'll dock your pay and make you work Saturdays."

"Okay," he says. "I get that. When was the last time you saw LT?"

"Yesterday. Close of business. You?"

"This morning."

If he's trying to get my attention, it works. I look up at him.

"This morning? Doing what?"

"Running for his car as I was pulling in. I don't think he saw me."

"What time?"

"Maybe five."

"Five? What in the hell …"

Santiago jerks his head back in the direction of his desk.

"My backlog is killing me. I'm trying to dig out. I get more done when no one is here. LT was in a hurry. Or maybe it was just the rain. He was moving fast. And limping."

"Limping?"

"Yeah. Something's not right, man." He gestures down at me like I'm a raccoon at a computer. "Now this. No offense."

"None taken."

"You look like hell."

"Thanks, Raffi. It's nice to be noticed."

"You seriously know nothing?"

It's another chance to clue Raffi in on the federal sharks in the water sizing Twill up for lunch. I still don't know any of the whys, but the more I imagine Frenchie Marie working my chain of command to separate Twill from his job, the more that seems about right. I look up at Santiago, considering anew whether to read him in. He sees me thinking.

"Jesus," he says. "You're holding out, aren't you? What do you know, Mack?"

I can't do it. He wants a better look at the lions and tigers from inside the cage. He's better off on the outside.

"You're better off if you know less than I do, and I know nothing. I got the assignment last night. Chief just wants me to keep the seat warm."

"Why you?"

"Isn't that the question of the hour. He made it sound like it has to do with the number of years I've been in the building."

"But?"

"Could be true. I've got the seniority if you ignore the break in service from being booted out as a mole for organized crime."

"You're too paranoid to think it's about seniority, Mack. What do you think is going on?"

I try to harden my face.

"What's going on? I'm being grilled by an underling. That's what's going on."

"That didn't take long," says Raffi.

"I might like this gig after all. Drop and give me twenty."

"Maybe it's a test. Maybe they like you for the permanent post."

"The only permanent post they have for me is a spike out front where everybody can see how it ended."

"Yeah," he concedes with a long, slow nod. "I guess that would surprise me. So how'd all this go down with LT?"

"I don't think he knows yet. Still waiting for him to show up."

"I hate this, Mack. I should've taken a sick day."

"Wanna trade?"

"Thanks, no. Too much to do. I'm about a half-hour from bringing you two reports to approve. They're already late so, maybe …"

"You want me to hurry them along."

"Thanks, boss."

I spend the morning dividing my time between my own caseload and pretending to manage the department caseload from my over-taxed cubicle. The office-wide skittishness for thinking of me in a management role evaporates more quickly than I'd like. I engage with everyone in the office at least once and some, like Steph Nellis, keep coming back for more. I have a new-found respect for Twill's ability to keep the place running.

The interruptions come in two flavors: questions relating to investigative protocol and requests for supervisory approval to do all manner of things I care infinitely less about than the number of hours left before I can have a drink. I'm batting five hundred at best on the questions. My shoulder muscles are sore from all the shrugging. The approvals are my favorite; I haven't said no once. I'm a dead-beat dad trying to suck up to the kids.

I look up in time to notice Steph making another trip from reception. I put down my pen and rub my eyes while I wait. She starts talking before she arrives.

"Just got another call from Matt Wendig." She can see my confusion and doesn't wait. "New LT down in property crimes?"

"Right. Wendig."

"It's his second call in two days. He's not happy about our pink sheet for Alphonse K. Jarr in the Ryan Coopersmith investigation. That's your file, right?"

"Yeah," I say with a sigh heavier than I intend. "Coopersmith got busted by CPD for slinging skag and so we fired him. His buddy Alphonse agreed to talk to me but wants to keep his interview quiet."

"Don't think that's going to happen. Wendig doesn't like your name on the pink sheet. He's pretty free with his opinions. I'll spare you."

"Thanks."

"He called yesterday wanting something in writing from LT personally verifying the interview request. I put something together and gave it to the boss yesterday, but I never got it back. It's probably still on his desk. Question is whether he signed it."

"Okay. Go have a look. If Twill already signed it, send it out. If not, bring it to me and I'll sign it as temporary department head. That'll be fun. Maybe Wendig'll have an aneurism and go home so we can do our job."

Steph laughs. Hard not to see Raffi's attraction. The white teeth and the green eyes and the swishy, glossy brown hair. She's got that kind of radiant youthful wattage that make men Raffi's age want to take up jogging and men my age wish she came with a dimmer switch. Her eyes are still laughing, but her lips have moved on.

"Yeah, no. I'm not going into LT's office and rooting around without a witness. This place is getting weird."

We go together, Steph in the lead, a room full of eyeballs at our backs. I leave the door open and we circle the desk like a couple of vultures looking for carrion, picking here and there at stacks of documents.

"I don't see it," she says. "Check the drawer. Top left. That's his to-do stack."

I open the top drawer to find what looks to be the same stack of documents that had been there the night I was digging around Twill's office unsupervised. I pull up his chair and sit and begin flipping through the stack.

"Oh …" says Steph.

"Oh what?" I ask, not looking. I keep flipping, caring less about the approval we are looking for than something that might help explain the behavior of the man I thought I knew.

"Oh shit, is the phrase I think she's looking for," says Orland Twill.

And not in a nice way.

THIRTY-NINE

Twill's eyes nail me to the back of his chair. Somehow, I manage to stand anyway. His face is bruised and swollen around his mouth and eyes, a faint crust of blood rims one nostril. Still outside the door behind him, Nancy Horn-Feldman stands uncomfortably like an HR Director pretending to be a mop. It's the two empty banker's boxes, one in each hand, that give her away.

"LT," I say. "You know how to make an entrance."

Steph swallows and points to the desk. She sounds like a teenager caught in the liquor cabinet.

"We're just looking for the signed approval for Wendig in the Coopersmith case. I put it …"

Twill answers me like she's not in the room.

"This isn't an entrance, Mack. This is an exit. But you knew that already."

"Your face looks like maybe we have the same exterior decorator. You okay?"

"My face is fine. Hurts a lot less than the knife in my back. And I'm not your boss anymore, Mack. That might make all of this bearable. This may be the last time I say these words, so I want to enjoy them. Get the fuck out of my office."

It takes Twill twenty minutes to fill two boxes as Nancy Horn-Feldman stands in the doorway and keeps an eye on her shoes. As he leaves, Twill looks at no one. Says nothing. He carries both boxes himself. Nancy gets the door and then they are both gone. The entire office looks at me in Twill's doorway. I make a rolling gesture with my finger. Everybody gets back to work.

"What now?" asks Steph.

"Print out a new approval for Wendig. Make it for my signature as Acting Department Head." I glance at my watch. "I've got a two o'clock out of the office. I'll sign it before I leave. Send it to Wendig so his head can explode before the day is out."

"Got it." She says it like she might salute. She doesn't.

I close Twill's door and head back to my cubicle where I pick up the phone and call Nancy Horn-Feldman. I leave her a message to call me when she's done escorting Twill from the building. He must have gone willingly because the phone rings ten minutes later.

"That was some great timing, Nancy. We need to put a bell on you."

"Do you really think I'm in control of any of this, Mack?"

"No, I don't. What's he saying?"

"I'm not saying anything about anything. You know better. Is that why you called?"

"Worth a shot but, no, that's not why I called. Twill's computer is password protected. I can't get to any of the files I need to run this place. I know better than to call any of your I.T. goons myself. It needs to come from you, Nancy."

"They're not goons."

"I was trying not to be vulgar."

"Tell me something, Mack."

"What?"

"I was dialed in forty-five minutes ago. Did you see this coming?"

"You think this is my idea of a good time?"

"That's not an answer."

"No. It isn't."

"I'll tell I.T. to make it a priority. They'll get to it when they can."

"Maybe don't tell them I called them goons. Thanks, Nancy."

At 12:30 I head for the exit, swatting Santiago on the shoulder and stopping by Steph's desk to sign the Department Head approval that Lt. Wendig thinks will make him feel better.

"What should I tell him when he calls?" she asks. "Because he *will* call, Mack. And he won't be happy. He'll want to know what's going on."

"He doesn't get any details. Not from you. Tell him I said he has an obligation to make his officers available to IAD requests and not to impede IAD process. There's a Code of Conduct rule about that. Look it up and have it ready. If he has a problem with that, tell him my suggestion is that he take it up with Chief Loudermilk. How's that?"

"Can do, boss," she says smartly.

"Save that, kid. I'm just a temp."

I've left myself plenty of time to make my way across the city for a two-o'clock sit-down with Gene Wilke and his over-protective daughter. I'm soaked by the time I make it to the Impala. The steam rises from my body and coats the windows so completely that I can't see much of the outside world. Ordinarily, that might be just fine. The ensconcement would feel great. But my spiking paranoia has rewired my brain. I don't much like being a bug under a smoke-filled glass with no way to see who's coming. I start the engine and run the blower and clear the windows with the back of my hand.

The rain sounds like an avalanche on the roof. I dig around in the glove compartment for the pack of Camels and knock one free. The taste and the smell are almost enough to improve the day. There's a lighter in the door pocket. It's like my fingers have eyes.

But Dinesh Jha has his own eyes. Dr. Feelgood. The shadow pointer. His eyes are behind John Lennon's glasses, and from fifteen miles away they look right into my brain. I can see his little smile. I can hear his bouncy Indian cadence whenever he talks about cancer. I try to decide whether cancelling my appointment with Dr. Jha so I can meet with Gene Wilke makes me more or less entitled to light up a Camel. It's a mindbender of a conundrum I can't resolve without a drink. I leave the lighter in the door pocket and the Camel between my lips and put Paula in drive.

The traffic out to Buffalo Grove is slow, snarled, wet and angry; a gray constipated python writhing its way north past Chicago proper, like maybe Wisconsin will be better. I-294 is a mistake I can't take back. Paula keeps trading the lead with an ambulance in the next lane. The EMT riding shotgun rolls his eyes in commiseration. I want to roll down my window and ask if I can buy some painkillers for my face and maybe get some lights and sirens just to loosen up the traffic. I decide to keep the window up and the Camel dry. It hasn't shortened even a centimeter. The lighter within reach is like an itch in the center of my brain.

My pocket sounds like a telephone. My first thought is a familiar blind hope. *Marlo.* I can't help it. I'm back on the kitchen floor next to Phil's empty bowl looking at my call log. *It's Marlo calling.* But willing the impossible only makes my head hurt and by the time I hear that second ring, I know it's not her. I check my mirrors and answer, not really caring who it is.

"Is this officer Mackey?"

"It is. Who's calling?"

"This is Saul Margolis, returning your call."

The voice sounds like old newsprint, soft and dry and wrinkled into tissue. The traffic eases a little and I leave the ambulance behind.

"Mr. Margolis. Thanks for getting back to me. Are you back in town or are you calling from the promised land?"

"Israel. This is home now. I still have a house in Winnetka. My nephew and his little monsters live there in the summer. It will likely be some time before I return. I check my messages at BSD every week or so. Our receptionist left me a voicemail about your call. She didn't know much."

"Yes, sir. She doesn't know much because I didn't tell her much. I was calling about your car."

"My car?"

"Yeah. A slick blue Mercedes CL. Plate KLE713. Routine traffic stop on a failure to signal while merging. The woman driving the vehicle could not produce evidence that the car was hers or that she was authorized to drive it. Our research shows the car is registered to you. I'm just following up to make sure the vehicle isn't stolen, Chicago being what it is."

"A woman?"

"Yes, sir. An Amanda R. Tate."

"Amanda. Amanda. No, I … Oh! Yes. Amanda Tate. She's Dennis' assistant. *Was* Dennis' assistant."

"Dennis."

"Dennis O'Toole. He was an associate of BSD before he died. I asked him to look after the car; drive it around every so often, just to keep it in shape. I keep it parked in the company garage. Dennis loved that car. It was a win-win solution. Amanda was his assistant. I don't know her well. She must have taken on the car as her responsibility when Dennis … when Dennis left us. Sweet of her."

I weigh the odds that lying to this guy will get me in some kind of trouble. Then I remember that he's in Israel. And that I'm now the acting head of IAD. Let him file a complaint. I relax and give the lie some gas.

"I guess that tracks with what Amanda told me, more or less. She said she had your permission."

"Well. Dennis had my permission. Again, I don't really know this Miranda person."

"Amanda."

"Right. She showed up at BSD just before I retired."

"How long had Dennis been there before you retired?"

"Dennis? Well, let's see, I took him in, oh, it'd have been a good two years earlier. He was pretty desperate for the work. Almost turned him away. My stable was full and the last thing I needed was another trader to keep track of. Turned out to be a good decision though. He was pretty sharp on the job. Until he died. Sorry, that's more than you want to know. My wife says I ramble in my old age. Snore when I'm asleep and ramble when I'm awake."

"Count your blessings, Mr. Margolis. Could be worse. How'd he die?"

"Who, Dennis? Took his own life. Sad thing. Marital problems. Killed his wife first and then shot himself. Surprised you didn't hear about that."

I've got enough space on the freeway to pick a better lane, so I do. The rain comes harder. I try to move the wipers into a higher gear. There isn't one. I keep playing dumb.

"O'Toole, you say?"

"Yeah," says Saul.

"Okay. Yeah, it's snapping into place now. Dennis O'Toole."

"Right."

"I thought he was a Chicago Mercantile trader."

"He was with the Merc before he came knocking on my door. CME kicked him out. Some tough personalities over there. I called for a reference check, but they shined me on. Dennis seemed like a nice enough kid. Earnest as hell. So I took a chance and put him to work. Like I say, turned out to be a good call until he died, which was like four months after …" Saul falls into a fit of hacking and returns a little short of breath. "… after I retired and moved over here. Sorry. We've got dust today. None of which has anything to do with his assistant, what's her name?"

"Amanda."

"Amanda. Driving my car."

"Does she have your consent to continue driving your car?"

"Was she driving recklessly?"

"No. Just needs to use her turn signal when she merges."

"How's the car look?"

"Beautiful. Wish I had that car." I pat Paula on the dashboard and shake my head in reassurance.

"Then I'm okay," says Saul. "Yeah, sure. What the hell. She can drive it."

"Okay, Mr. Margolis. I'll close the book on this. I appreciate the call back. Happy retirement. Enjoy the dry weather."

"Raining where you are, is it?"

"Ugly. I'm buying lumber by the cubit."

FORTY

Cassandra Wilke-Barnsmith lives in a yellowish, middle-class home with shallow eaves and a long, narrow driveway that widens just in time for the garage. Normally I'd park on the street and walk up the driveway. Today I'm too tired to swim, so I pull in like my name is on the mortgage.

I slip Paula in park and keep an eye on the street behind me for any passing cars that seem familiar. Three cars hiss past, one right behind the other. All of them seem familiar, but that's just my paranoia working overtime. Unlikely that I'm being followed by a convoy, but maybe between OAG and Frenchie Marie's people and whoever wants a chance to ruin my day, they all have to share the same road, so they're all bound to end up bumper-to-bumper at some point. Either way, there's nothing much I can do about it. I climb out and hustle through the rain, shaking off the water as I go.

I figure Buffalo Grove can lay claim to eight or nine major neighborhoods and somewhere between forty and fifty thousand people. I'd bet a lot of money that the Wilke-Barnsmith residence is the only one with two peepholes in the front door, one to see my face and one to make sure my pants are zipped. The shallow eaves force me to crowd the door to stay out of the rain. I poke the house in the button and wait.

The door opens to reveal a handsome woman in her late fifties dressed in house slippers, black slacks and a turquoise cashmere sweater. Her hair is a coarse salt and pepper bouffant headed for iron gray. Her face is made up just so, especially the smile.

"Cassandra?" I say. "Good afternoon. I'm Raymond Mackey. I trust this visit is still okay with you."

"Officer Mackey," she says stiffly, stepping back inside to pull open the door. "You are welcome as long as we can keep this short and no one gets excited."

"Scout's honor," I say, holding up three fingers.

"Please come in and take off your shoes."

I skip a joke about Japanese dining and do as I'm told, trying to keep the conversation from freezing while I'm unlacing.

"Never seen two peepholes in a door before," I say.

"My father has been confined to a wheelchair for a few years. He wanted the ability to see who is at the door when my husband and I aren't home."

"Makes sense," I say. "He's lucky to have you to look after him."

"He's a good man. He raised his kids right. Our turn to take care of him."

I position my shoes neatly by the door and straiten myself.

"Am I right that your brother is the Olympic medalist Corey Wilke?"

The question gets me something like a smile.

"You don't strike me as a volleyball enthusiast," she says suspiciously, but then corrects her tone. "Yes. Corey is my younger brother. Pride of the family. My father is in his den. Please follow me."

The path to the den traverses a spacious living room and a short hallway hung with awkwardly posed family portraits, each locked into identical dark, lacquered frames. Gives me the willies. Too many teeth and too much hair arranged around expressions trying too hard to make a good impression. Reminds me of photo day back at the orphanage. Or a prisoner exchange line-up.

Cassandra stops at a doorway, extending a hand into a small but comfortable room dressed in shades of chocolate and buckskin. One wall is mostly windows looking out into a wet, rectangular yard bordered by fencing and a hedge of green. On the opposite wall hangs a large flat television. Ordinarily I'd guess that this is the most watched wall in the room, but I'd be wrong. A third wall is devoted entirely to shelving that supports a multi-level shrine to Corey Wilke's athletic career and, in particular, to the United States Olympic Volleyball team for which he played. Trophies, ribbons, medals, and photos. At the heart of the arrangement are two volleyballs, each scribbled with autographs.

"You don't look like a cop," says Gene Wilke, not unfriendly. He points with a large, black remote control.

He's in a wheelchair backed up against the windows under a fringed reading lamp. He's a small man with thin, gray hair and silver glasses, hunched slightly forward in a pair of black pajamas with brown bedroom slippers on his feet. A plastic nosepiece trails a stretch of clear tubing that coils over the top of a blue oxygen tank at his side.

"Good," I say, pausing in the doorway. "Keeps the bad guys guessing."

"Oh, so you think I'm a bad guy, do you?" The smile is real enough. All the teeth inside are fake.

"Your daughter says you're a good man, Mr. Wilke. That's good enough for me. Thank you for agreeing to talk to me."

"Sit, sit." He gestures with the remote to an overstuffed couch that runs along the fourth wall, crouching beneath an abstract of the moon glowing cold bone through the Chicago skyline. I do as I'm told, nodding at the shrine as I lower myself onto the cushion.

"That's some legacy you've got yourself there, Mr. Wilke."

The man beams. He doesn't look at the wall. He doesn't need to. It's all in his head.

"You like volleyball? You don't look like a volleyball guy to me."

"I also don't look like a cop, remember?"

Gene points a crooked finger at the festival of violence between my ears.

"You been in a fight? You've had a rough go of it."

"What can I say? Volleyball is a rough sport if you play it right."

It gets me a phlegmy but sincere laugh.

"You want a drink? Cassie," Gene, no longer laughing, looks up sharply at his daughter in the doorway. "Get the man a drink. What's your poison?"

"No, thanks," I say. "I'm good. If you water me, I'll grow roots and never leave. I promised to keep this short."

"Suit yourself. I'll have a scotch."

"You're not having a scotch at two in the afternoon," says Cassandra wearily.

"Okay, then." Gene takes the oxygen hose off his face and drops it over the tank.

"Dad."

"I'm fine, Cassie. I'm fine. Good Christ. You'd think that once the bastards in the white coats tell you that you're not going to see another Christmas, everybody would finally relax a little and let you live." Gene removes his glasses and rubs his eyes, pink with exhaustion, languishing in the holes of a sallow, stubbled face. He catches me looking. He returns the glasses with authority. "We've both had a rough go. Let's get on with it. What's this all about?"

"Right. I'm conducting an investigation that involves a man you used to work with. Dennis O'Toole."

Gene registers the name with a blink and a slow, somber nod.

"Dennis. Okay. Yeah, I worked with him. I knew him. Quite an exit. Bet a lot of people never saw that coming."

"Did *you* see that coming?"

Gene shrugs. He sets the remote on the table beneath the lamp.

"I dunno. Maybe not. We're all so much smarter looking backward."

"You two worked together at the Merc."

"Yes."

"How long?"

"Oh, let's see. Eight, ten years maybe."

"What kind of man was he?"

"Smart. Ambitious. Lots of energy. Kind of full of himself. He liked giving advice. Always thought he had a better way of doing things. Sometimes he was right. Not always."

"Okay, how about emotionally?"

"Never spent much time in the middle. He was either high or low or moving rapidly from one to the other. A bad mood lasted for days, during which you couldn't pry a smile or two words out of the guy. Then, suddenly, he was your best friend, and you'd think he'd won the lottery. That's not me. I'm pretty right down the middle. I don't show those cards."

"How'd he get along?"

Gene leans his head back and closes his eyes like maybe he needs to download the answer. Then he looks at me again.

"CME was a weird place sometimes. Lots of little, you know, cliques. Fiefdoms. I kind of kept more to myself. Which I was used to. I was diagnosed with cystic fibrosis in college so I guess I've never been the most social guy. I had friends at CME, you know, it was friendly, there was a group of us. But I kinda liked to do my thing and go home. Dennis was more of a social climber. He was always networking. Always kissing the ass of someone higher up. You know the type."

"Sure."

"He had a thing going with his assistant. She was a looker. Hard to tell if they thought none of us had eyeballs or if they just didn't care. Everyone knew."

"What was her name?"

"Amanda Taft. Tate. Amanda Tate. She was something. Hell, maybe it was true love. When Dennis left, she eventually followed him to BSD Financial. That's another brokerage. About six blocks south of the Merc. Dennis left and got snapped up by BSD and then I guess she jumped ship and joined him several months later." Gene holds up his hands. "Hearsay. Hearsay. I wasn't there. I was long gone by then."

"My understanding is that CME terminated several traders all around the same time, including Dennis and you. Is that accurate?"

Gene looks at me for too long without answering. I figure it's the first time my questions have felt personal. He's deciding whether and how to take the next step. I lean back and cross my legs and give him some room to think.

"Yeah," he says eventually. "That's right. All within about a month. Dennis, me, and Simon."

"Simon Feeks?"

"Yeah."

"You still in touch with Simon?"

"No. But I might be soon."

"Yeah? How's that?"

"Cancer dropped Simon last year. I figure maybe I'll be seeing him around Christmas. Maybe sooner. Senator Kahn too. I'll finally get to give that son of bitch a piece of my mind. Not sure what kind of cancer dropped him, but I hope it was ass cancer. Politicians are a cancer, far as I'm concerned. Every last one."

"Dad ..." Cassandra, still holding up the doorway, shakes her head in exasperation like he's violating some pact they have about staying positive. Father and daughter look at each other across the room. Gene shrugs his shoulders and lifts his eyebrows up above the rim of his glasses as if to challenge her to prove him wrong. There's nothing else she can say to him. She turns to me instead.

"Are you getting close, Detective?"

I smile and refocus on Gene. I'm ready with another question but Cassandra's resistance has put Gene in the mood to elaborate. I let him run.

"Dennis was the last of us to get the boot. I was first, then Simon, then Dennis. Dennis looked me up the day after he was canned. We went over to Finnegan's and closed the place down. Dennis drank his weight in scotch and got sick outside by a mailbox. He took it harder than I did. I was a lot older and nearly ready to quit anyway. Docs were telling me the CF had found another gear and that it was going to start kicking my ass. It had stayed fairly mild and manageable since my twenties." Gene shrugs. "Something changed. I took the pink slip from CME as a sign that I needed to turn the page. So I did. But Dennis ..." Gene finishes with an eyeroll.

"Not so ready to turn the page, I take it."

"Well, that's the thing. Like I said, he was extreme in both directions. That first night at Finnegan's it seemed like Dennis was ready to take a dive off Willis Tower. Two days later he's back on his feet with a solid job at BSD and we were back at Finnegan's, only this time he's slapping me on the back to cheer me up, buying me drinks and trying to recruit me."

"Recruit you. To work at BSD?"

"Yeah. He said he'd gotten a call from a partner over there. He said ..."

"What partner?"

"Saul Margolis. He said Saul had heard the news and was looking for a couple of good traders. Saul hired Dennis in three goddamned minutes over the phone and asked him to reel me in too. He'd made a run at Simon Feeks too, but Simon was a hard no. And Dennis wanted my help poaching another CME guy, but that didn't work out either."

"What other CME guy?"

"Stan."

"Stan who?"

"Papadopoulos. First name is Constantine. Everyone calls him Stan."

"And Dennis wanted your help poaching Stan to go work for Saul Margolis at BSD."

"Right. I wasn't interested in twisting Stan's arm. I'm not that kind of guy. Didn't make sense for me to make the pitch to Stan anyway since I wasn't going over to BSD. I think Dennis probably gave it a shot on his own. But Stan was comfortable at CME. No reason for him to jump ship. Dennis kept working on me to join him, but it was pretty clear that my next task master was going to be cystic fibrosis. So I was a hard no too. Far as I know, Saul got Dennis over there but no one else. Well, except Amanda. She went over later. Not that Saul cared anything about Amanda. That was all Dennis."

"And you're saying Saul reached out to Dennis, not the other way around."

"Yeah. That first night at Finnegan's, Dennis was talking about selling the house and moving the family back to Boston. Said his wife always wanted to go back east to live closer to her family. He'd never wanted to do that because he hated Carrie's family, and they hated him. But without a career at CME, Dennis thought Carrie would probably win that fight. He had some contacts at some accounting firm out there. He figured that was his best play. Until Saul called him and offered him a six-month fast track to a BSD partnership."

"How did Saul know to reach out?"

You don't spend thirty years in this business without learning to recognize hesitation hiding inside silence. Gene purses his lips and swallows before he answers.

"Turned out they had a mutual friend. Turned out we all did."

"What mutual friend?"

Gene stares past me, not answering. Like he's weighing alternatives. I start to worry that one of those alternatives might be to stop talking completely so I try a different question.

"Why were you fired, Mr. Wilke?"

Gene starts to cough. Cassandra takes a step into the room, but he extends his right hand while his left grabs the nosepiece from the oxygen tank and puts it in place. He takes a deep, calming breath.

"I'm fine. Settle down, Cass. I'm fine."

"I think it's time to end this," she says sternly to both of us. I start to stand, but Gene gestures for me to keep my place. I do. He looks up at his daughter.

"I think it's time you left us alone to talk," he says.

"Dad …" The alarm on her face sharpens to anger.

"I promise to keep the O2 attached, Cassie. This is gonna go faster without you. Go do something."

Cassandra flexes her jaw, looking at each of us in turn. Then she retreats, slamming the door behind her.

"She means well," says Gene. "I'm not an easy border. I'd've done better with Corey, but he's not set up for someone like me. I take a lot of tending. He's travelling all the time with the team. His life is already too demanding. Between the regional qualifiers and the world tour, he's stretched too thin as it is. Coaches have it as bad as the players. Worse. So I'm here in Buffalo Grove to the end." Gene nods his head at the closed door. "And she's gonna kill me before I can die, just by trying to keep me alive."

"I'm sorry," I say. He nods. Outside, the back lawn is under water. The rain falls in fresh torrents.

"Seeing the end of things changes a person, Detective. You start to look down on yourself, like you're up above, watching this guy that looks like you, living his little life. Brushing his teeth so he doesn't get tooth decay. Taking his little pills. Making his bed. Looking for the sports page. Bargaining with his daughter. And you're up there looking down and wondering what it's all about and why you should care at all about what that little guy down there is doing." Gene looks at me. "And then one day you don't care. The show is old and predictable and pathetic, and you don't care to watch any more of it. Like it's not you down there and you're just wasting your time paying any more attention. Seeing the end of things changes a person."

I suddenly want the drink he offered me more than ever. I want to stand up and walk out and put on my shoes and stand outside in the rain and smoke one Camel after another.

"Had an informant once," I say. "She told me about this guy she knew. Delaney. Crazy Delaney. He was a junkie who died on a sidewalk with someone else's bullet in his head. Delaney was with her before he died. Before he had any reason to think it was his last day. He told her he felt like he was climbing up into what he called the big dream. Looking down on himself and thinking that, from up there, this life was like a puppet show for little kids. Simple and silly. Nothing to be scared or sad about. Keep climbing. Let it end."

Gene stares at me a bit. Then he nods.

"Yeah," he says, pointing a little. "That's dead on. Your guy Delaney could see the end. Or he could feel it. Something in him knew it was coming. That changes everything." A few seconds of quiet. He nods to himself. "The big dream. I like that."

"You said the three of you had a mutual friend."

Gene breathes deeply through the tubing. Then he takes it off again and drops the hose back over the tank. He interlaces his fingers and sets his hands in his lap.

"Detective, what do you know about spoofing?"

"Spoofing?"

"Spoofing."

"I don't know. Pretending? Deceiving?"

"It's a term of art in the commodities trading business."

"Okay. What's it mean?"

"It means Dennis was playing with fire and didn't know when to drop the match."

FORTY-ONE

By the time I'm backing down Gene Wilke's long driveway, the rain has eased to a steady drizzle; the wet, gunmetal sky is darkening; and my brain is doing that thing it does on those rare occasions when the world starts to make some sense.

I throw Paula into drive and poke some numbers into my phone. Constantine Papadopoulos doesn't sound pleased to hear from me. He's busy and doesn't want to meet. Calling him Stan doesn't help much so I tell him that my next visit will be to his wife to ask what she thinks about him being blackmailed for infidelity. That seems to do the trick.

An hour later I'm in my favorite booth at Blondie's with a straw in my mouth, sucking down a *Big Dream* milkshake and wondering if he's actually going to show. My phone pipes up with an idea about how to pass the time.

"Mack."

"Raffi. Give me a headline."

"Shit meets fan."

"That's familiar. What's going on?"

"Where are you?"

"Having a drink with a friend." The silence on the phone is deafening. "Not that kind of drink, Raffi. The kind with a straw and a lot of whipped ice cream."

"Whatever. You need to come back here, man."

"You want to tell me …"

"A friend of mine at CPD just sent me a copy of the incident report on a response to 1515 Philips Way out in Albany Park last night."

"Okay. Is that supposed to …"

"That's Peter Chow's home. He's the …"

"I know who Pete Chow is," I say, sitting up just a little straighter. "What happened? Why are you in that loop?"

"CPD got a call late last night from LT."

"Our LT?"

"Orland Twill. That's why my friend slipped me the report. Twill met them at Chow's front door. Report says the place was all busted up and so was Twill.

Chow was nowhere to be found. Twill told them he was out there at Chow's request to follow up on a case. He said the door was open and he went in and found someone inside going through a desk. LT got the jump on him, finds a gun on the pat down, then the guy kind of explodes and beats the crap out of LT and splits. The report says the fight basically destroyed a couple of rooms. I don't know where the family was, but …"

"No family there. It's just Pete."

"You two are tight?"

"No. But we go way back. Any description of the assailant?"

"Medium height. Shorter than Twill …"

"That narrows it down."

"Caucasian, he thinks. The guy was wearing a mask and gloves. Not much else to go on. Twill got a boot in the gut and lost all his air but managed to keep after the guy. Until he couldn't. Whoever it was took off through the house and left through a back door. Twill called it in."

"What time?"

"CPD responded a little after eleven. Guess that explains how LT looked today when he came in to clean out his office."

My brain is like a cat with a new ball of yarn, so I stop talking and stare out the window into the rain trying to put things together. A pair of headlights sweep Blondie's parking lot. It's Stan Papadopoulos' black Lexus doing the sweeping. Raffi keeps at it.

"What I can't figure is what case Twill is working that crosses paths with the Chicago Medical Examiner's Office? Last I checked, Chandler IAD doesn't have any Chicago homicides on the board. Any ideas?"

"Yeah. One or two."

"Why am I not surprised? You're holding out as usual. What do you know?"

"Just enough to make my head hurt. It's going to have to wait, Raffi. I have to take this meeting."

"Thought you were getting a drink with a friend."

"That too. Any sign of Pete Chow?"

"None that I know of."

"Blood?"

"Yeah. Hard to say whose."

"Make me a copy of that report, will you? Put it on my desk."

"Which desk? You have two of them, boss."

Constantine Papadopoulos stands for a moment in the doorway, dripping. I raise my *Big Dream* glass with a smile, doing my best to put Pete Chow and Orland Twill in a take-out bag for later. Constantine swings out of his coat and drops it wetly in the booth. He looks down at me like he's not so happy to see me.

"I cancelled a teacher conference to be here," he says.

"Went back to school, did you? Good for you, Stan."

"Not for me. My twelve-year-old. What do you want?"

"For starters," I hold up the parfait glass, "I want one of these things once a day for the rest of my life. You ever tried one? I'll get you a straw."

"I don't want a goddamned milkshake. I've told you what I know. What the fuck do you want?"

I give him a smile that isn't going to help his mood.

"You're worked up. You're scared. I would be too if I were you. Take a breath. Settle down."

"I'm not scared. What do you ..."

"I want to know why you lied to me, Stan. Can I call you Stan?"

"What do you mean? I didn't lie."

"Oh, sure you did. And you're still at it, apparently. Let me shorten this up and tell you what I believe."

Constantine swallows, fidgeting with his watch. He's scared alright.

"Whatever. What the fuck do you believe?"

"I believe that maybe you *are* a family man after all. I don't think you're being blackmailed over an affair. I don't think you ever had an affair. Or, maybe you have, but not one that I or anyone else except your wife and mistress would care anything about."

"So you don't think I'm being blackmailed? Then why ..."

"Didn't say that. You are being blackmailed. But you made up the part about having an affair." I take another pull on the straw, trying not to close my eyes. I swallow and give him my full attention. "You're being blackmailed for spoofing."

Constantine looks at me, stroking his beard with his palm like he's petting a face ferret. Like he's trying to calm it down.

"Cat got your tongue, Stan?"

"What are you talking about?"

"You know what spoofing is?"

"Of course I know what spoofing is."

"Good. So do I. And so does the person asking you to make cash deposits at Blondie's, literally under the table."

"Whatever you think I've done ..."

"Stop talking, Stan. You're just digging yourself deeper here. Shut up for a second and let me tell you why you're lucky. Want to know why you're lucky?"

"Why am I lucky?"

"You're lucky because I don't really give a shit about you. As far as I'm concerned, the less paperwork I have with your name on it the better. That includes arrest paperwork. Do I look like the SEC would give me a badge and a paycheck? That's not my beat. If you want to stick to the blackmailed-for-infidelity story, then I'm going to want you to prove it. That means, at the very least, talking to the mistress, and I can't promise that investigation doesn't slop over onto the home front. You get what I'm saying?"

Constantine stares at me, unmoving.

"Nod your head if you understand. Paw the ground with a hoof. Something."

"I understand that now *you* are blackmailing me," he says.

"No. Pretty sure I didn't ask you for any money or anything of marketable value. I'm just investigating the story you gave to me. The story to explain why you and your pal Momo sat in this very booth and threatened me, a police officer, with bodily harm unless I gave *you* money. You with me?"

Constantine sighs. Then he nods.

"Good. Now, if you're ready to start telling the truth, all I want is some information so that I can conduct my investigation into things that don't really concern you. Other people, not you. Understand?"

"You want me to be a snitch."

I take a long pull on the straw and swallow, leaning back in the booth.

"You watch too much television, Stan. I need information. You want to keep me from investigating you, then help me investigate someone else."

"Who?"

"What are we, partners now? Doesn't work that way."

"Why should I? If I'm not actually having an affair, what do I have to worry about on the home front, as you put it?"

"Come on, Stan. Keep up here. You're not playing to save your marriage. You never were. You're playing to stay out of prison. You think whoever it is will decide you've paid enough money and just go away? You think that dime doesn't get dropped when you stop paying? Tell me you're smarter than that. You need to get out of the spoofing business, like *yesterday*, and tell me what you know. Get ahead of this thing. Get on the record as a cooperator before the subpoenas start dropping."

Constantine thinks for a second then wrinkles his nose like he doesn't like the way I smell. He shakes his head.

"No thanks," he says. "I'll take my chances." He tries to smile like the guy who is in love with the cards he's holding. In the entire history of gambling, that smile has never not been a bad bluff. He pushes against the tabletop like he's about to stand.

"Your chances?" I ask it like I'm amused.

"Yeah."

I reach over to the little silver caddy on the table beneath the window and take a *Blondie's Big Dream Lottery* card from the top of the stack. I flick it across the table. Constantine picks it up by the rainbow and looks at me.

"Yeah? So?"

"Three games on each card. Four chances to win in each game. You're looking at what, a hundred and twenty little bubbles there? What do you think your odds are?"

"How the fuck should I know? Shitty."

"No. You're way off. I'm guessing about eighty to a hundred percent, Stan. Know why? Because it's good for business. They want you to come in and collect your free soda. Or your free order of fries. Must redeem in person. So then there you are up at the counter holding a free drink in your hand and looking up at the big board. How many people aren't going to accessorize with a burger and a *Big Dream* shake? I'll tell you how many, Stan. Zero. Every last winner is going to pay for the rest of a meal, buy a wagon full of food for their kids, and fill out another lottery card while they wait."

"What's your point?"

"My point is you're playing a losing game that makes you feel like a winner. And that winning feeling keeps you coming back for more. You've got a blackmailer on your doorstep and a cop willing to give you a chance and you still want to come back for more. And when the music finally stops, what do you really have for all the trouble?"

He stares at me like he doesn't understand. But he understands. He just doesn't want to.

"I'm sure it seems like a lot of money. It helps with the college fund. Your Lexus out there isn't even a year old. I'm guessing you swap it out every couple of years from something better. So, yeah, that's nice. But at the end of the day, what do you really get? It may as well be some fries and a soda. That's what you get. That enough for you, Stan? 'Cause that's what he's really giving you to hang out there in the wind and the rain for all the cops and blackmailers to see."

"Who?"

"Who. Come on. The big man at the top of your food chain, and I'm not talking about your boss at the Merc. I'm talking about the man who can snuff you out between his fingertips. How long you think he's going to put up with your kind of problems?"

"I don't … I don't even know what you're …"

"Yeah? You really think Dennis O'Toole killed himself?"

I let him sit there in silence with the ghost of commodity traders past. I look out the window at sheets of rain flashing in a new pair of headlights. I wonder if whoever is following me has used the drive-thru to beat back the hunger while they wait.

I turn back to Constantine. He's almost as pale as my *Big Dream* shake. I suck it down until it makes a slurping sound. I push the glass aside.

"Now. How long have you been spoofing?"

FORTY-TWO

By the time I finish with Stan Papadopoulos, my head is twice as full as my stomach and still ready for more. Stan pretends he's all tapped out and I pretend he hasn't been helpful. He knows more than he's saying but he wants me to make promises about how all of this shakes out in the end. I tell him we're all gonna die in the end. He wants to bounce that off a lawyer and get back to me.

"You might need a good priest more than a lawyer, Stan. I'd keep looking over your shoulder and answering your phone."

I leave Blondie's to Stan and the dinner crowd, making a run for the car. I can feel his eyes at my back through the booth window. Of all the eyes watching me get wet in the Blondie's parking lot, Stan's are the ones I don't care much about. At least I know who owns those eyes, which is more than I can say about all the others. I jam the key in the door and twist, yanking it open into the rain.

The folded sheet of paper laying white and dry in the driver's seat takes my breath. I stand in the deluge and look at it like it might bite. Then I come to my senses.

I grab the paper, climb in, and slam the door. I unfold the single page and stare at the image. Not a photo, this time. A symbol. It is as simple and as elegant a representation of my soul and its prospects for redemption as I will ever find. It is, in Bookman Old Style font, an enormous, solitary question mark.

I close up the sheet and toss it on the dash, looking in all directions through rain-streaked glass for any sign of who might have left it. Not that there is any particular mystery about that. The question mark is Frenchie Marie's way of saying she wants an update. She delivered Suri to my doorstep like I asked and now she wants to collect. Fair enough, I suppose, but I'd like to tell her that Suri showed up with a big friend named after a missing finger and that he used the other nine fingers to beat me senseless. I want to tell her that Pinky was never part of the deal and that should warrant a little more time for me to deliver. But I already know that pitch is dead on arrival. I'm guessing it's the rare excuse that cuts any ice with Marie.

I put the key in the ignition and light up the rain. The wipers pick up where they left off. I slip Paula into gear and roll forward, out into the gloom.

The office of the Chandler Police Department Internal Affairs Division is as empty as a church on Mardi Gras. The last one out forgot to turn off the lights, or maybe that's their protest against the new administration. I walk a crooked line, navigating desks to my cubicle, hang my sopping coat on a peg and sit.

Santiago has left the Chicago police report about Twill upside-down on top of a stack of files that has grown eight inches since this morning and that now sports a multi-colored stubble of sticky notes directing my attention to empty signature lines where I might express my approval. I have newfound respect for the burdens of command and what it took Twill to get through an ordinary day.

I grab up the report and read all about Twill's late-night adventure at Pete Chow's house. Raffi hadn't left much out in the retelling. "Significant" bloodstains in a downstairs hallway. Evidence of forced entry through a front window. Broken and upended furniture. Okay. But sometimes it takes a bad fiction writer to spot the bad fiction. The author of the report, one CPD Officer Roderick Slattery, keeps the eyerolls out of the narrative, just like they teach you at the academy.

> LT. TWILL states that he was unarmed at the time of the initial confrontation because he had left his service weapon in the glove compartment of his vehicle, which CPD confirmed at the scene. LT. TWILL is certain that he identified himself as a police officer. He states that he conducted a standard pat down of the suspect and recovered a handgun from the suspect's belt. LT. TWILL is unable to verify the make or caliber of the handgun. LT. TWILL states that he instructed the suspect to remove his mask as LT. TWILL was attempting to secure the weapon. LT. TWILL states that the suspect "suddenly kind of exploded" "kicking and punching me until I lost my balance and fell backward into the table." LT. TWILL states a belief that the suspect may have had martial arts training. LT. TWILL states that as he was falling, he aimed the weapon at the suspect and pulled the trigger, but the weapon did not discharge. LT. TWILL states that he was unable to maintain control of the gun which was knocked away during the fight. LT. TWILL states that the suspect hit him very hard in the head and kicked him in the stomach, leaving him momentarily incapacitated, during which time the suspect retreated through

the house and escaped out a back door. LT. TWILL states that he was too weak from the fight to give effective pursuit. He states that he searched the area of the altercation for the weapon but was unable to locate it prior to CPD's response. LT. TWILL stated his assumption that the suspect had recovered the weapon and taken it with him. Inspection of the scene by CPD Officers SLATTERY, CANE and ABRHAMS failed to discover any weapon.

It goes on. I glance up to see Marlo in her frame looking down at me over the stack of files. She doesn't buy it either. Mighty convenient, this masked man carrying a gun that doesn't fire. That's the inconvenient thing about most guns: they leave evidence behind to be analyzed. Slugs to be dug out of the wall. Not the gun in Twill's story.

Ten gets you twenty that the missing gun had been fired recently and that someone is hiding a couple of the bullets inside Pete Chow. If I'd've caught this case, back in the day, I'd probably suspect Twill of killing Pete, getting rid of the body, and then calling up CPD to come out and give him a merit badge. Why does a smart man do that? A smart man doesn't. This has desperate man written all over it.

If it were my case, I'd probably conclude that this whole shaggy dog story is all about the gun. A gun Twill no longer has control of. He's lost it somehow. Or someone took it from him. Maybe whoever put him up to killing Pete now wants to make sure he goes down for the crime. So now he's worried the gun is going to turn up as an exhibit, lousy with the memory of his fingers. What's a desperate man to do? He scrubs his hands of any power residue, for starters. Then he beats himself up a little. Maybe gets a friend to do it for him. Or maybe that work on his face had already been done. Maybe Pete had some fight in him before Twill could pull the trigger. Doesn't matter. He goes back to Pete's place. He stages a fight. Breaks a lot of furniture. Throws some lamps around. Then he does the stupid, desperate thing. He calls CPD. He wants to get ahead of a story he can't control. He spins a yarn about walking in on an unidentifiable killer rummaging through a desk and cleaning up a crime scene. A fight. A gun. Conveniently, the gun in this story is a special gun that takes fingerprints just fine but doesn't fire any bullets. No slugs in the wall. Just Pete's blood all over the hallway and a murder weapon, yet to be found, with Twill's perfectly explainable prints.

That's what I'd have concluded, back when I solved dead people for a living. That'd be the story in my head just to get me going. But, then, I'm cynical. I'd have taken a sample of the blood on Twill's face. Might have been his. Might have been Pete's. No indication that CPD did that in this case.

But it's not my case. Not officially. I slap the report back down on top of the stack and look around over my shoulder at Twill's darkened office.

My office.

I turn back to my computer and fire it up, clicking my way to my email folder, hoping that Nancy has done what she promised. Hard to tell given the dozens of emails that have landed in the past three hours. It takes me a minute to stop looking for an email from Nancy Horn-Feldman and to look instead for something directly from the IT Department. I find it right where it should be. Two clicks gets me a long administrative password and a new mission.

FORTY-THREE

I've got all the lights on this time. No more snooping around in the dark like I'm someplace I shouldn't be. It is my office after all. Twill's half-Korean wife, Wendy, looks down at me from the bookcase, smiling like she's delighted to see me. I resist the urge to turn the photo around.

The computer is off this time, screen black. I'm guessing the last thing Twill did before he walked out and left his office to me was sign out. I push the button and wait for the empty rectangle I'm supposed to fill. Nine letters, four numbers and a question mark in between opens it up like a key in a lock.

I pull up the directory and pick a file at random just to see if the internal passwords have been removed as promised. The file opens without a problem. I close it and begin looking for things I actually care about. First stop is the subfolders I couldn't open the last time I was crawling around in Twill's hard drive:

O'Toole, Dennis – Forensics (58403v.1)
O'Toole, Dennis – Forensics (58403v.2)

I double click the first folder. Empty.

The second folder has the same report that I already have: suicide.

I backtrack to the main directory and start a folder-by-folder, file-by-file search for anything Marie might consider interesting. I'm at it for fifteen minutes before my shovel hits something solid.

He's buried it someplace boring: in a subfolder labeled 'ART' which is inside a main folder labeled 'ADMIN SEMINARS' sharing space with a dozen or more files full of seminar agendas and curricula pertaining to every mandatory law enforcement and internal affairs seminar Orland Twill has ever attended or presented in his career. I'm not sure what persuades me to click on 'ART'. Maybe I'm wondering what the Mona Lisa is doing at a police seminar. Or maybe something about Amanda Ramada Tate's initials makes me curious.

The ART folder only contains two files, each with gibberish names. I double click on the first file. The photo that fills the screen comes with a punch in the face: a dry-cleaning ticket from the Blue Lotus Dry Cleaners. My heart rattles its cage a little. *Bingo.*

Beneath the name of the business is an eleven-digit account number, followed by an inventory of clothing items: *3 dress shirt, 2 pant, 2 tie.* Next is an available for pick-up date: May 29 of last year. Under that is a small paragraph of tiny print disclaiming liability for damaged items, followed by a paragraph of nonsense, an unbroken stream of letters and numbers documenting what can only be a kind of digital computer sludge that gets spit out with each ticket.

I double click the next file. Another dry-cleaning ticket fills the screen. Different account number. Different clothing inventory: *2 dress shirt, 1 pant, 1 vest, 1 suitcoat, 3 tie.* Pick-up date: April 2 of last year. Same disclaimer followed by a different paragraph of nonsense.

I arrange the tickets so that they are next to each other on the screen and study them. The account numbers consist of ten numbers followed by a capital letter: C on the first ticket and L on the second ticket. If I ignore the letters, I'm left with ten numbers. Anytime I see ten numbers in a line it makes me want to make a phone call.

I almost reach for my cell phone, but then think better of it. I yank the receiver off of Twill's desk phone and poke in the numbers from the first ticket. Four rings gets me an automated invitation to leave a message. I don't. Instead, I disconnect and call the number on the second ticket. I nearly disconnect at the end of the fourth ring, but then I let the impulse pass. I'm glad I do.

This is Dennis. Please leave a message. Thanks.

I pass up the invitation. Instead, I hang up and stare at the wall for a while. I cue both tickets to the printer. Two copies: one for me and one for Frenchie Marie just in case I decide to play ball. I stand to head out for the printer room when a whirring to my left reminds me that Twill has his own printer. Well, now there's a perk.

I exit the directory and switch over to Twill's email. The effort gets me nothing until I search specifically for the word *Chow.* A second bingo in one night makes me feel like I'm yanking slots at Horseshoe Hammond. Not that I've ever left the double-H with money in my pocket, but this is what I dream it'd feel like. I open it up. It's an email that doesn't waste any letters.

Don't do this. Push again and I'll report it.

Short and sweet. Pete Chow to Orland Twill. Dated May of last year. Busy month, May. Someone is picking up dry cleaning at the Blue Lotus on May 29. I'm guessing that's when Twill put on a Cubs cap and wandered into Frenchie's photo. Same month that Twill is conducting internet research on Pete's brother,

Andy, still cooling his heels in Statesville for plowing into a car full of cheerleaders. Same month that Pete Chow's neighbor backs a moving van over a mailbox and ends up in a photo full of rain during a rainless month apologizing to Pete on his driveway; a photo Pete claims was altered to substitute in Twill. I didn't believe that story the first time. This email almost makes Pete's lie laughable.

But the questions are too many for laughing. *Don't do this. Push again and I'll report it.* What is Twill pushing and why? And why is Pete lying?

I keep looking. I get a second hit on my email search. Chow's name shows up in an email from a Janice Kingfisher with the Illinois Prisoner Review Board.

> *Dear Lieutenant Twill: Thank you for your inquiry. Inmate Chow's next hearing has not yet been scheduled. You have requested information regarding any individuals who may have requested or opposed the inmate's early release. That information is confidential by statute. Accordingly, the IPRB requires a judicial order to comply with your request. Thank you for your inquiry.*

Dated mid-May of last year.

I make another fruitless pass through the emails. The trick to holding onto that winning feeling from a good night on the tables is knowing when to quit. So I do. I grab up the copies from the printer and head back to my lowly cubicle, snapping off Twill's lights and clicking the door closed behind me.

I sit down in my own chair hard and heavy, thinking things through. Dark water lashes at my face from the other side of the window. The knuckle prints on my orbital bone throb at the idea of being touched. My screen glows back to life, scolding me all over again for the number of unopened emails. It – the computer, or maybe my nosey alter ego floating up near the ceiling – thinks my unopened mail is a sign of neglect, unbecoming a temporary department head. It's a solid argument.

I take a closer look at the list. Most of them seem to be from Carolyn and Mark pinging me for approvals to open new cases or to close out old cases. Reminders that the towering stack in front of me contains things I need to read, sign and get back to them. I consider whether now might be as good a time as any to be productive; to actually step up and help the department as I have been ordered to do.

It's the thought of Doris pouring me a shot of Bucks' Old Forester that wins the moment. I never asked for the top job and Chief Loudermilk knows what he's getting. No sense going thirsty.

I grab the mouse to shut everything down. That's when I see the email from *Chow, Peter,* sent 3:14 a.m. yesterday morning. Comprehension takes a full three seconds. My trigger-happy index finger clicks in the wrong spot. I have to close the mistake before I can open the right message. But I get there eventually. There's only one line in a sea of empty white space.

It's not the brothers; it's the boss. Let's talk.

I read it a dozen times before I see that there's an attachment. I click with extra precision this time. I have to wait a short eternity for the digital bureaucracy inside my computer to pump up my blood pressure. The virus program needs to give the attachment a clean bill of health before the PDF program is allowed to open it up. Eventually, a white rectangle unfolds from the inner space on my screen.

It's the final forensics report that tells the end of Dennis O'Toole. The *initial* final report. Version 1.

I read it from top to bottom and look at all of the pictures. Not that I need to. I know the end of the thing before I start the beginning.

Homicide. Not suicide, homicide.

FORTY-FOUR

Look at him. Pushing his way into Bucks like a man on a mission. The mission is to keep his outside dry and get his inside wet. Beyond that is anybody's guess; even his.

There are some birds that catch their sleep on the wing. Ray doesn't have the excuse of a long migration. Look at those lids, slow blinking as he moves, adjusting his bearings. It's worse on the inside of those eyelids. His brain is an old drawer full of tangled fishing line, packed with rusty hooks, broken rubber bands, and pens that don't write. He needs to dump it all out on a table and figure out the beginning and the end of what he knows. Separate out the useful and throw away the useless. But he doesn't know how to do that. Not when he's this tired. Not when there's a shot glass somewhere with his name on it.

"Hey, Mack."

"Mr. Aubry." Ray slides out of his coat and drops it over a barstool. He looks away from Kyle to assess the room. Only two tables are occupied. Ruth Brown is spilling from the speakers, complaining again about how rain is a bringdown, just like her man. The cash on the ceiling flutters in the circulating air. "Slow tonight."

"Still early. Give it an hour." Kyle grabs a glass and pours. He knows better than to ask. Ray jiggers his finger to keep the pour coming. Kyle nods. "Long day?"

Ray closes his eyes and sips.

"Five years and counting."

Kyle tips the bottle of Forester toward Ray's battered face.

"Looks like maybe you took a couple for the team."

"Wrong team. Wrong sport. Where's the boss?"

"Just missed her. She said to give you a kiss if you came in. I'm not going to do that."

"I'll tell her you didn't disappoint. Don't tell me she's on another date?"

"Okay. I won't. Because I know you would not want to put me in that position, Mack. It's called a private life for a reason."

Ray drinks like he's hard of hearing.

"Is it the same guy? Tallish? Handsome in an ugly, disgusting sort of way? Looks like a bag of bad breath in a nice suit?"

Kyle smiles.

"Sure be a shame if we suddenly ran out of Forester."

"All right, all right. Christ. Relax, kid. I'm just making conversation. Doris knows how to take care of herself."

Kyle smirks.

"I don't think she's in any danger."

"No one thinks they're in any danger until they're wrong."

The banter lightens as Ray's edge softens in the booze. He tells the one about the three nuns and the Jewish armadillo. Always good for a laugh and Kyle doesn't disappoint. He pours Ray a second and then leaves him alone to tend to a threesome in from the rain. Ray rolls the glass between his palms, staring at a chink in the top of the mahogany bar. It's been refinished, but you can still see the discolored wood. Ray traces it with a fingernail. He can't stop thinking about Pete Chow.

It's not the brothers; it's the boss.

He tries to keep an open mind. Maybe the bourbon warming in his gut helps with that. Still. Hard for Ray not to read those words as a dead man pointing a finger at Orland Twill.

He has his third drink at home with Phil, sitting by the fire with his computer in his lap and Lena Horne stirring the air above his head, singing about how she gets the blues when it rains. On the screen, Jack McMannis is staring out his second-story office window, watching his new Russian client cross an icy parking lot to pack her daughter and a stuffed dragon into the car.

It's like looking through the wrong end of a twisted telescope: me looking down at Ray, as he looks down at Jack, as Jack looks down at Polina and little Sasha. If Ray can't solve his own problems, he'd at least like to solve some of Jack's. Shouldn't be difficult since Ray has already lived Jack's story and survived, if only to churn that story into a growing stack of pulp that no one will ever read.

But solving Jack's problems, or his own, means staying awake. Staying awake, apparently, is not possible for more than five or six minutes separated by twenty-minute nods during which Ray rests his chin on his chest and breathes in great wheezing gulps before jerking back to consciousness. He might go upstairs to bed and make a night of it. But that's not happening. Not tonight. Maybe not ever again.

Phil meows next to him. He blinks and closes the laptop, stretching for the glass. He dips in a finger and gives her a drop of amber.

"Let me ask you something," he says.

I know he's not talking to me. That leaves Phil or Marlo. Phil rolls onto her side, pawing the air.

"Let's say the boss has a hand in offing Dennis O'Toole. Carrie too. Maybe not himself, but say he had it done. Forget the motive for now. He'd like a murder-suicide headline to put it all on Dennis and his ugly divorce, so he pressures Pete Chow to make that happen. Pete needs convincing so the boss puts Andy Chow in the crosshairs. No parole. Shiv in the shower. Something." Ray drinks. Closes his eyes like he needs to concentrate. "Pete pushes back but Twill wins the argument and gets a fresh forensics report. Murder-suicide. Done. But then Pete gets squirrely. Maybe his conscience gets a new set of batteries and Twill gets nervous. Or maybe Twill figures nothing good will happen if Pete continues walking around breathing in and out. So Twill decides that's enough of Pete."

Ray opens his eyes and looks down at Phil.

"Why kill the guy in his own home and remove the body, only to then call the cops so you can tell them it was somebody else who did the deed?"

Phil meows. She has no earthly idea. Another drop would help her think. Ray obliges, then takes another sip of his own.

"Risky way to clear yourself if you ask me. Why do that? Maybe you're worried about the prints, hair and fibers. You need a way to explain the forensics trail. Explain away the evidence of you in Pete Chow's house. Nerves got the better of you. You don't do this kind of thing every day. You're an IAD cop, for Christ's sake. That makes this a desperate act by a desperate man. It was going to be either Twill or Pete, so he did what he had to do. The shock set in. He came unraveled over the invisible forensics. He knows his prints are on the gun and the gun is, for some reason, lost or out of his control. He needed a story. Could be." Ray swirls the cubes in their bath. "Could be."

Phil stretches, hunching her back into a hillock of fresh snow, then pads off for places unknown.

Ray thinks about the bottle in the kitchen and about drink numbers four and five. Six. But he's too tired to make the trip. He needs to train Phil to bring him a bottle. Figure out some sort of body harness. Or a little wagon. He needs to buy a bourbon monkey.

He leans his head back against the chair. Closes his eyes. He holds the almost empty tumbler atop the closed computer on his lap like he's in an airline seat twenty thousand feet above the drowning city he loves and that he can't wait to leave. He wonders where he's going. We both do.

FORTY-FIVE

Seven o'clock in the morning finds me easing Paula up to the foot of Pete Chow's driveway. I look across the cul-de-sac at his neighbors, wondering which house used to belong to the Fritz Holland family, now living conveniently out of reach someplace in Germany. I scribble down the house numbers for the property research that will answer the question. Then I roll my way up the steep, arching drive to Pete's place.

The house is secluded from view and larger than I had imagined. It's a one-story stucco number tucked beneath tall trees on either side. Hexagonal stone pavers lead from the driveway to a large carved front door. On the other side, a concrete path leads around to the back. Nothing about the exterior of the house says anything about murder or abduction except the yellow tape across the door.

In front of me is the white garage door I recognize from Frenchie Marie's supposedly altered photo, complete with water cascading over the top. The only thing that's missing is a finger-pointing conversation between Twill and Pete under the two-foot eave. I think about how much I want to climb out and have a look around the perimeter of the house. My curiosity wants a look around back, but the rain also has a say.

So does the CPD cruiser that pulls up alongside. The cop inside looks like he was in diapers when I was making my first arrest. He slides down his passenger window. I lower mine.

"Who are you and what are you doing here?" he asks.

The car number is 0705, Marlo's birthday. I take it as a sign that she's everywhere. She saturates everything. I can't *not* see her, even if I try. She's become the rain over a wasteland world made of cardboard. That, or my obsession is finally devouring my brain. My wipers don't care much. I flash the kid my badge.

"Ray Mackey. Chandler IAD. It's my LT that called in the six-fifty a couple of nights ago. I'm a friend of Pete Chow. Little worried about him."

"This is a crime scene," he says. "Not sure how they do it in Chandler, but …"

"Yeah," I say. "Okay. Bad idea. I'm leaving. You heard whether there's any sign of him? Pete Chow?"

"Not my case, man. I'm just patrol."

"Got it." I put Paula in reverse. "Have a better one."

As I roll backward, I try to figure where an ambitious photographer might hide if he wants a good shot of Pete's garage door. The house itself is secluded up there on its perch; a guy could get away with murder up there. But there's not enough space anywhere up there for the telephoto shot Frenchie's people left in my front seat. And the foliage here along the driveway between the house and the cul-de-sac doesn't offer much cover.

Maybe. Awfully gutsy, though.

Once I'm back down at the bottom of the driveway I spot the unfinished two-stories of wet plywood one street to the west. I crack the window and listen for the sound of builders doing their thing. Nothing. Just the weather. Whoever is putting that house up either likes to sleep in, doesn't like swinging hammers in the rain, or hasn't been paid to finish the job. I can't tell if it has a clean angle on Pete's place. But it's possible.

A well-dressed man wrapped inside a gray coat is rolling his trash can out to the curb beneath a black umbrella. I keep moving backwards and slide my window down a little more.

"Morning. Looking for Pete Chow. Don't suppose you've seen him."

"You police?"

Close-cut silver hair. Nice shave. He looks like a guy who gets to decide whether you get the loan or don't. I nod and flash him the shield.

"You boys need to talk to each other," he says.

"Different department, same questions."

"Last time I saw Pete was two days ago. Passed each other right here in the cul-de-sac. About seven-thirty in the evening. I was coming home, he was headed out. I don't know where he was headed. He was alone in the car. We waved but did not speak."

"How'd he seem?"

"Normal, I guess, from what you can tell from a wave. He smiled. Good guy. I always liked Pete. Hope he's okay."

"Me too. See or hear anything out of the ordinary two nights ago?"

"All I hear anymore is the sound of water."

I nod, satisfied the guy is on the level and knows nothing.

"Okay. Thanks for your time. What's your name?"

"Fritz. Fritz Holland."

The name gets Fritz an invitation to sit in the front seat out of the rain and talk some more. He looks at his watch in the way people do when they don't want to tell you how much they don't want to keep talking. I play dumb and act like he's just curious about the time. He parks the garbage can, folds up the umbrella and climbs in just as the cruiser sporting Marlo's birthday glides down into the cul-de-sac. I give the cop a wave. He pauses but then moves on. My guess is he circles back in ten minutes to see if I'm back up at the house.

Turns out Fritz isn't living in Germany after all. That was never the plan. Germany was just a three-week summer vacation. The move was to Lansing. They'd put the house on the market and watched it sit there underperforming for three months. Then Fritz's wife got an unexpected promotion. So they yanked the sign out of the lawn and decided to stay. I ask him about running over Pete's mailbox.

"Oh, yeah." He pauses long enough to replay the question in his head and screw up his face. "You know about the mailbox?"

"I do. What happened?"

"About a year ago." He jerks his head in the direction of the house. "Getting the place ready to list we completely gutted the garage, which was packed with stuff going back twenty years. You know how that is. All this crap. I rented a moving van. All they had was this huge dump truck sized thing. I was trying to back it into my driveway. I swung wide. Took out Pete's mailbox."

"How'd that go over?"

"Oh, Pete was fine. He laughed it off. I replaced it in like two days."

"You tell him about it in person?"

"Uh, no. I called him on the phone. He came down and met me at the bottom of his driveway." Fritz points at Pete's mailbox. "We looked at the broken post."

"So you never went up to see him? Up to his place?"

Fritz shakes his head.

"You remember the day and time?"

"Day and time. Uh. Late afternoon. My kid was shooting hoops with his friends. So it must have been a Saturday or Sunday."

"Weather?"

"Sunny. Hot. I can't blame it on the weather. I don't think we even got a drop last year this time. What happened with that? Feels like we're being punished."

I leave Fritz Holland on his driveway with a lot of questions and an umbrella that doesn't open as fast as he'd like it to. I roll back through the neighborhood, circling around to the west past houses that all look pretty close to the one before until I finally find the one that doesn't.

The house under construction is tall and narrow, wedged into the last vacant lot on the street. The framing is up. Subflooring is down. Roofing is over. But that's it. No sheetrock. No glass. It's just a tall sluice box of wet lumber at the top of a new driveway, maybe until the builder clears his indictment, or the owner finds another box of money.

I cut the engine, climb out and head inside like it's my job to get the construction back on track. I take the flight of stairs and head to the back of the house into an area that wants to be a bedroom. I keep walking until I'm at the empty rectangle in the plywood. It's got dreams of glass.

The view is dead east, where the sun should be working its way up a bluebird spring sky. Instead, all I can see are dark, blackish-gray clouds of spun steel hanging over the adjacent block, where a river of rain pours over the edge of Pete Chow's garage.

FORTY-SIX

Turns out to be a decent place to think things through, alone and out of the rain. I walk the empty structure, hands in my pockets, listening to my wooden footfalls as I rummage for a Camel and something to set it on fire. I maybe could have skipped the craving until later this afternoon, but the cigarette butt on the floor beneath the window flipped a switch in my head. So now I'm searching my pockets for what I know isn't there.

Could belong to anyone, that cigarette. Construction workers have been known to smoke. But so do photographers. My guess is somebody lit up a Winston to pass the time, waiting for something interesting to happen on Pete's driveway. Could mean the guy was just staking out Pete's place, making note of who comes and goes. I've spent a lot of time in my life with those orders. Or it could mean someone was waiting specifically for Twill to show up. Like he knew that the man was coming.

I know what I need to do. I just don't want to do it. I pull out my phone and poke in the number to Orland Twill's front pocket. It rings through to voicemail. I almost disconnect, but I don't.

"LT. It's Mack. We need to talk. I don't like making this call any more than you're gonna like returning it, but you need to do that anyway. Sooner is better."

I end the call and stare down at the phone in my hand, uneasiness growing in my gut like something feral and hungry. There's a snowball's chance of Twill returning that call. That doesn't change my need to find him. I put my thumbs back to work.

"Raffi."

"Mack. Calling in sick?"

"Been on the job a good hour already, waiting on your lazy ass."

"Yeah? I'm in my chair, Mack. Where are you?"

"Thought I'd take a look at Pete Chow's place. I need a favor."

"Shoot."

"I need LT's home number."

"You mean like his house?"

"You really want me to answer that?"

"Who still has land lines?"

"Just me and Orland Twill."

"Hang on, I'll find it. What's going on?"

"What's going on is too many questions and not enough answers. I've got a feeling Pete Chow is never coming back."

"I've got the same feeling," says Raffi darkly.

"Right. That means LT's life is about to change forever."

Raffi spits out a sound of disbelief. "You like LT for Pete Chow?"

"Still trying to figure that out, but I know how CPD will see it. How is your source over there?"

"Solid. She owes me big."

"I don't want the details."

"It's not like that."

"Send her some chocolate and roses anyway. We need to stay informed."

"Got something to write this down?"

"No."

"Text or email?"

"My phone doesn't do that."

"You need a new phone. How's your memory?"

"What's your name again?"

Santiago gives me the number and I repeat it over and over until I can disconnect and dial. Wendy Twill picks up on the second ring and repeats my name with a smile in her voice that makes it sound like she's glad I called. I'd have guessed that my name was like a clod of dirt in the mouth of everyone in the house, including the dog.

"How you been, Mack? Haven't seen you in a while. Orland says he's keeping you busy. How's IAD treating you?"

"Never a dull moment, Wendy. I'm going to need you to give me some karate pointers so I can defend my right to take a lunch break."

She laughs again, just like someone who has no reason to hate me. That makes her either a mushroom or Meryl Streep.

"Any time, Mack," she says. "What's up?"

"Is the man in? I need a word."

"In? Like, here? No. He's still in New Orleans."

"New Orleans?"

"National IAD conference?" Wendy laughs. "Don't tell me you haven't noticed him missing for the last week. You *have* been busy."

"Oh, the conference. Yeah, yeah. I thought it was in Vegas."

"That was last year. These are not productive venues if you ask me."

"I thought he was back today," I say, scrambling to keep up.

"Next week. He called last night and said he might extend a couple of days. He's got family in Shreveport."

"How'd he sound? Let me guess: like he'd been up 'til two drinking mint juleps and listening to the best of Bourbon Street."

"He sounded pretty ragged, yeah." That should have been a laugh line, but suddenly there's no smile in her tone, only the worry she doesn't want to betray. "He doesn't sleep well on the road. He'll be okay."

"I'll catch him when he's back," I say. "Thanks, Wendy."

"Wait. You saying he's not returning your calls or something? Orland is always on the job."

"I left a message. He'll call when he's free. Just thought I'd catch him at home before he came in."

"Want me to have him call you if he checks in?"

"No, that's …" I'm so busy lying and back-paddling I've stopped thinking. "Yeah. Sure. That'd be great."

I disconnect with Wendy, clomping my way back down the stairs of the half-finished house and step out into the rain. I sit in the car trying to figure my next move to find Orland Twill. He doesn't have an office and he's staying away from home. Makes a man hard to find. I consider staking out Amanda Tate's place or maybe finding a parking spot outside the Marker Westpoint Suites where I saw them together last. Maybe that's their nest, the place they go when they don't want to be found and the rest of the world is full of eyes. Or I could hang outside the Blue Lotus and see if he drops by to pick up his laundry. All long shot ideas and I know it.

The folded sheet of paper on the dash has a better idea. I open it up and stare at the question mark, instantly in secret conversation with my paranoia. It's like a crowbar, this thing, clawing out of my chest everything I don't yet know.

Frenchie Marie wants some answers, does she? Well so do I.

I dig around in my coat pocket until I find the white card with ten black numbers that she handed to me over a plate of Kung Pao and cigarette ash. She predicted that no one would answer, but that she'd always know where to find me.

Okay. Let's put that to the test.

FORTY-SEVEN

I leave Albany Park and point Paula south on North Cicero, keeping half of my attention behind me. The traffic is fairly light and slow this direction, making it easy to spot the tails. I don't have any. Not yet. Every intersection is a small lake. If you catch a green light and have any speed at all, your first hundred feet on the other side is blind. It's like driving a flying fish.

I make it almost all the way to West Roosevelt in Cicero before a beat-up, muddy-green Pontiac lights up the rain from behind. It's been with me for maybe five miles after joining the parade from the intersection at Irving Park Road. Car by car, it's been working its way closer to my back bumper. It confirms what I suspected: Paula's got a bug on her belly. Marie really *can* find me whenever she wants.

I exit just past 31st Street, less than a mile from the Sanitary and Ship Canal, and pull into a mostly empty Wendy's parking lot. I cut the engine and wait, yanking Sig out of bed to double-check the clip. I know it's full. I check it because I can, like I double check the stove top I know I haven't used and the liquor cabinet I know is fully stocked. What's a little OCD to add to my list of crazy? I'm going for the whole alphabet before I check out.

I nose Sig back into the holster just as the Pontiac pulls up alongside. The driver is big and white, six-five if he's an inch, and he isn't afraid of the rain. He gets out and opens the back door of the GTO. He bends so he can look at me through my passenger window. A dark blue baseball cap is pulled low over his jarhead. The jar is made of rock. I think I recognize him from pictures of Easter Island. I'll take it on faith that his mouth works when he wants it to.

I look past him into the back seat of the GTO. The soft brown suede of Frenchie Marie's face glows warm in the flame.

FORTY-EIGHT

"I'd offer you a cigarette," says Marie, taking her time. "But I seem to recall you quit. How's the abstinence wearing?"

"Like a suit of wasps." I hand her the folded question mark as the driver climbs back in and closes the door. The car smells like wet smoke and French perfume or maybe it's French smoke and wet perfume. "You wanted to see me?"

Marie drops the paper on the seat next to her without looking. She takes a drag and then nods as she blows a blue stream into the front seat.

"I'd like to know where we are, Detective."

"Wendy's. This a breakfast meeting, Marie?"

It gets me a smile so flat it doesn't count.

"Where are we in your efforts to deliver on our deal? I delivered your informant, Courtney Briggs, as promised. I'd like to know what you have for me."

I like being made to feel a lackey about as much as the next guy, but I like it even less from strangers.

"What you delivered, Marie, was a beating that still hurts whenever I use my face, which is whenever I'm awake. Which, these days, is always."

"Interesting friends," says Marie. "I had nothing to do with who Ms. Briggs decided to bring with her to your house, or what they did to you while they were there." She shows me that she can smile when she wants to. Her teeth are whiter and younger than she is. "But you already knew that. I did what you asked, Detective. It's your turn."

"I told you it would take Courtney to keep this conversation going. So here I am. I didn't promise anything else."

"And yet here you are."

"I was summoned."

Her eyes are deep brown and dubious.

"Something tells me you've got an agenda all your own."

"You said if I helped you out on Twill, you'd open the book on what you know about Marlo."

"So you *have* found something," she says with a sideways look. "You just want to haggle the exchange. You want to learn about your late wife. Is that our bargain, Raymond? Our tit for tat?"

"The price has gone up."

"You disappoint me," she says, looking away.

"That's a big club. I disappoint a lot of people."

"Still. I'd have thought you'd have a greater fidelity to your word than you did to your wife."

A reminder she knows that my greatest pain is not in my face. It's hard to respond while I'm grinding my teeth, but I try anyway.

"Yeah? What do you know about it?"

"Cops talk. We have rather excellent sources. We know a lot about you. Your poorly timed infidelity with the dishy brunette in the records department. Your novelist aspirations. Your feline affections. You're a man of quirky contradictions. Greedy opportunist was not specifically on my list for you, but I suppose it is now. What else do you want from me, Raymond?"

"I want to know where I can find Orland Twill."

"I have no idea," she says.

"Bullshit."

The Wendy's drive-thru line is up to four cars with two more trundling their way across the lot like a couple of trawlers headed for the marina. Marie shrugs her eyebrows and smokes.

"If you say so."

"You want me to believe you haven't been on Twill for weeks like a bad smell?"

"He's a person of interest in our investigation. *The* person, actually. Of course we've been following him. Wouldn't you?"

"Yes. I would. So where is he?"

"I can't honestly say. I can tell you that his Escalade is in long-term parking at O'Hare." Marie flicks her ashes onto the floor and slots her old, bloodshot eyes my direction. "He ditched us two days ago somewhere on the other side of a convention ticketing clusterfuck at United Airlines."

"Embarrassing."

"We're dedicated, not perfect," she says. "We'll find him. If it's any consolation, my office isn't too happy about it either."

"I'll bet. Which office is that again?"

"The one that wants a quick conviction and Twill out of circulation."

"Right. For what, exactly?"

"That's information you have to earn, Detective. Which you haven't. But let's start with conspiracy to murder the O'Tooles."

"You saying Twill got on a plane?"

"Certainly not. We're not perfect, but we're also not stupid. It was a competent ruse. *Un mignon petit acte de disparition.*" Another drag. I wait until she can talk again, craving a Camel. She exhales. "He's here. We just don't know where. We were hoping you could help. Sounds like you don't know where he is either. Or maybe that's just what you want me to believe."

"This is a small back seat for more than one hyper-suspicious paranoid, Marie."

"Then tell me something I can trust. What have you learned about your lieutenant? I know why *I* want to find him. Why do *you* want to find him?"

I recognize the fork in the road. I stare out at the drive-thru lane and give the question a couple of beats to breathe, just so she can see me thinking. The guy in the front seat is filling up the mirror with eyes that seem to care about my answer.

"Okay," I say. "I'll pay a little into the pot. I'll do that. But then it's going to be your turn, Marie. And whether you get any more from me depends on what I learn from you."

Marie shrugs, sucking her stick. She lets out another stream of exhaust. "Let's see what you've got."

"Two nights ago, Twill calls CPD from Peter Chow's house. Same house in the photo you gave me of Twill and Pete having a finger-pointing heart-to-heart on the driveway. Twill tells CPD that he was coming to talk to Pete about a case. He said the door was open and someone was inside sporting a mask and gloves. Twill and whoever it was broke up a bunch of furniture and the guy escaped out the back. Pete was nowhere to be found. The blood in the hallway makes it a pretty good bet he didn't go out for coffee."

"And the lieutenant is innocent because he notified the police. Do I have that right?"

She's a teacher transparently suggesting a wrong answer just to test my mettle as she condescends. I ignore the attitude and press on.

"Twill calling it in to CPD was just bad theater. Soon as someone finds Pete's body, Twill's name will be on everybody's lips. Not good for you, because that party is way too crowded for the kind of questions you want to ask, and it leaves you on the outside looking in. If your team lost Twill at the airport two days ago, that tells me he gave you the slip just so he could meet with Pete in private and take care of business."

Marie purses her lips as she stares out at the rain.

"Plausible," she says. "What business?"

"My guess is Twill likes that murder-suicide finding just the way it is. He doesn't want it to change. Doesn't want Pete to start talking."

Marie nods, just once.

"We knew that was a risk," she says. "We just didn't think it was so … imminent."

"Guess you were wrong."

"Guess so."

"If you knew the O'Toole forensics report was cooked under pressure, why not just turn up the heat on Pete Chow? Get him to flip on Twill and then go scoop him up."

Marie gives me a wry, regretful smile like it's a gift.

"You think we didn't?"

"And?"

Marie wants to smoke and think before she answers. That takes too long, so I keep at it.

"Let me guess. Pete stood by his report. You spooked him with all of this cloak-and-dagger-in-the-back-seat-of-an-unmarked-car bullshit. You couldn't show him a badge he could trust because after Twill he doesn't trust any badges. So he stuck to the story. Murder-suicide. That left you with no evidence against Twill. What's an enterprising foreign agent outside of her jurisdiction to do?"

The fuchsia lips stretch out into their languid, enigmatic pose.

"You tell me."

"Okay. You used Pete to bait a trap. Sure, you could have grabbed Twill up any time, but you don't want Twill as much as you want what Twill knows. You want him to talk, and there's nothing quite like a credible case of attempted murder to get a guy to start sharing. You figured Pete would reach out to Twill about your little visit and that Twill would start to feel insecure about Pete losing sleep at night. Maybe that was the whole plan anyway: rattle Pete so he would rattle Twill, who would eventually show up to fix the rattle problem for good."

"Seems … *rash*, for an experienced police officer."

"Maybe Twill's not so experienced on the other side of the law. Maybe the promise to keep Pete's brother in Stateville forever, or to get him released from the joint inside a box, was starting to wear thin."

Marie makes a face.

"So you know about the brother."

"Everybody knows about the brother. Andrew Chow is the opposite of Pete in every way, but he's the only family Pete has, which makes Andy's future pretty decent leverage. Good enough to get Pete to cook the forensics report. But then a little pressure from you and Pete starts to come to his senses. And that makes Twill so nervous maybe he decides there's only one option left."

"It was always a risk," she says. I almost laugh.

"Just stop, Marie. You're going to embarrass yourself."

"I doubt that, Detective."

"Twill going for Pete Chow wasn't a risk, it was the plan. You and your boys cool your heels until Twill pulls the trigger. That's when you were set to hit the floodlights so everybody could come out of the bushes to give Twill a ride downtown. Then you could start negotiating with CPD and the State Department over custody. Twill's a big guy. Maybe there's enough of him to go around and no one will care much about jurisdiction. Or maybe you just stuff him in a car and take him someplace private so you can get what you need before the American jackals get their turn. Hell, maybe if he really sings you offer to let him go and to forget all about Pete Chow. How'm I doing?"

Marie smiles a little, tossing an eyebrow. I can't tell if she's impressed or amused. I keep at it.

"Problem is Twill was onto your tail and he took you on a tour of the airport. So now Twill is in the wind and poor Pete is somewhere under water feeding the fish and you're left taking your frustrations out on a pack of French cancer sticks and asking me for help finding your own target."

"You do have an active imagination."

"Don't I though? What I can't figure is why you didn't have someone permanently camped out in the half-built house over-looking Pete's driveway. The same place your people snapped that photo. You could have invested in a chair and a cooler full of snacks to make the wait more comfortable. You know, just in case Twill showed up to do the thing you wanted to catch him doing. Killing Pete Chow."

Marie picks a fleck of something from the corner of her lip with a red nail and flicks it away.

"Like I said, we're not perfect."

"That's a long way from perfect, Marie. That's rank incompetence. Maybe you're stretched thin on personnel. Too many guys following the tiger and not enough watching the bait. I don't know what language the taxpayers who fund your agency speak, but they deserve a refund."

"I'm not so worried about our taxpayers."

"That's pretty clear. You don't worry about much of anything. I don't even think you're particularly worried about poor Pete, or even Dennis and Carrie

O'Toole. I don't think blood is really your thing, Marie. None of this is really about murder, is it?"

She rotates to look at me. It's the first time I've grabbed her attention in this conversation. She's aiming for nonplussed. She misses by a mile.

"It's not? Then please enlighten me, Detective. What's it all about?"

"Money."

"Money?"

"Money trumps blood every day of the week for some people. I'm thinking that's you and whatever foreign minister signs your paycheck."

"I'm sure you have a theory," she laughs. "I can't wait to hear it."

"I'm guessing that someone in your chain of command gets a boat load of campaign funds from someone who happens to be losing his shorts in the commodities game. Maybe that's a lot of people. Your bosses have dressed you up and sent you across the pond to turn up the heat on a spoofing syndicate that's finally gotten too big for its britches."

"Spoofing?"

"Don't play dumb, Marie. You're too smart to pull that off and it only makes you look stupid. Spoofing. I'm not going to give you a definition because you don't need it and I'm tired of playing games with you."

Marie looks at me through squinted eyes, crow's feet scratching for her old leathery temples, like she's trying to identify a bug before she steps on it.

"You obviously have something to say." She takes a draw and blows. "Why don't you just say it."

"Dennis O'Toole got paid to play a kind of blindfolded poker. His job was to sit at a trading desk and keep upping the ante and to not ask questions about who else was playing. He forgot that second part and got curious. Maybe he figured it out for himself or maybe someone like Saul Margolis gave him some help. Doesn't matter much because just knowing the other players set him on the path that got him killed. Somebody heard the keys to the kingdom jangling around in Dennis' pocket and killed him to keep him quiet. The same someone killed the soon-to-be ex-wife too, just to make it look like a murder-suicide."

"Someone. Well, that *is* a help."

"Oh, come on, Marie. You know who did it and so do I."

She smiles like you do at ridiculous people who don't know they're ridiculous. She raises one of her black, grandmotherly hands to stir the smoke with a royal flourish.

"*Le Grande Homme?*"

"*Oui.* Not personally, of course. He used Twill or Amanda Ramada Tate or some number of Blue Lotus dry-cleaning assassins to punch Dennis' ticket, but it all comes down to Big Man in the end, doesn't it?"

"You need to see someone about this obsession of yours, Raymond."

"Maybe he's not so big where you're from. Maybe your people call him something else. Maybe he's got a different name for every language you speak. Here on the streets of Chicago, he's Big Man. José Beggemon. Joe Boogieman."

I let the name do a couple of laps around the inside of the car, thickening the smoke and poisoning the air before I continue.

"But I don't need to explain any of this, do I? He's no stranger to you. Our first meeting you confirmed it was Big Man who put Wrigley Menard up a tree to kill everyone in Deke's Salvage Yard except me. You confirmed he was behind everything."

"Only because you seemed so desperate to believe it. A helpful narrative to get your attention. Sorry for the deception, but it's how this game is played, I'm afraid."

"Nice try. You even said he was obsessed with me."

"You say that like maybe you want it to be true, Detective. Have you fallen in love with the monster you've created to explain your … your pathetic downfall?"

"Stop being coy. Twill's just an appetizer. You're in Chicago hunting big game. You started at the dry cleaner, and you've had your nose to the ground ever since, following blood-soaked breadcrumbs. Dennis, Carrie, now Pete. Twill's a means to an end. Big Man has broken into the global commodities game and pissed off everyone on your side of the world. The people who pull your strings have started yanking hard. So now you've got orders to put Big Man in your sights. And nothing else matters, does it? You're as obsessed with him as I am."

I intend it as a challenge that I don't expect her to answer. She's full of surprises.

"I suppose we all need something to get us up in the mornings, don't we. A little obsession is better than the next drink."

"So you admit …"

"I don't care what people call him."

"He's why you're here. He's who you're hunting."

"If that pleases you."

"And you're flying below our radar because you want to kill him, not arrest him. A man like that loves the system. He owns the system. Stopping his heart is the only way to take him out of the game. You don't give two shakes for Twill or Pete Chow or the O'Tooles. They're all means to an end. Bloody breadcrumbs."

Frenchie Marie looks at me with a hard glare beneath her coiffed mahogany bouffant, her pearl drop earrings swinging ever-so-slightly in the smoke. She pulls hard on the last of her cigarette, stubs it out on the back of the passenger seat headrest and drops it on the floor. She exhales a gray-blue cloud. She doesn't answer.

"Come on, Marie. That puts us on the same side. I get that it's all top secret. Who am I going to tell and who would believe me if I did? I talk about Big Man until I'm blue in the face and can't get the time of day."

Marie folds her hands over her lap and looks at me indulgently.

"Your fever dream is getting tiresome, Raymond. How about some facts? I'll give you three questions and no promises. What is it you want to know?"

"Is Mayor Royce involved with the Blue Lotus Dry Cleaners?"

"Yes. But only as a customer with bad taste in suits and normal dry-cleaning needs. Medium starch, on hangers. We've cleared him of anything else. We're still watching, but he's dropped off the list of people we care much about."

"What do you mean you've cleared him?"

"Investigated thoroughly. We went back to the early days. Back to that photo you love so much. Evaluated all of his connections and associations. We found . . ."

"Associations like Tony Rickens? And Victor Roby?"

"You know a lot of bad people too, Raymond. Does that make you a criminal? I think not. Politicians attract all kinds, good and bad. We found Royce lacking a criminal disposition with no unlawful connections to the Blue Lotus Dry Cleaners. So we cleared him and moved on. Just like we did with you."

My face gets tired of the poker. Marie doesn't miss the slip.

"Don't look so surprised. Do you think we'd be talking if you hadn't checked out? You're clean enough. You saying we got that wrong?"

"No. But that's not the talk at the office."

"Talk is cheap. Whether we're talking about you, or the mayor, or anyone else, I don't care about the talk. I care about the facts. The fact is, you're not a criminal. Maybe you're a bad man. Maybe you're lucky that cheating on your wife isn't a crime. Maybe you're headed for Hell. Lots of bad men out there who aren't criminals. My father was a criminal. I had two brothers who were criminals."

"And you took the road less travelled?"

"I've got a nose for crime. I put it to productive use. My father used to tell me that the Devil would come get me if I told anyone about what they were up to. Half my family was doing some kinda time before I was seventeen."

"And you were the one who put them away?"

"Devil was busy I guess."

"Any husbands in the mix?"

Marie doesn't like the question. She pulls a black purse from between her body and the door, opens it and extracts a new cigarette. She finds a lighter and puts it to work. Then she replaces the purse and looks at me.

"Why? Are you proposing?"

"Not if I'm ever going to quit smoking. I'm trying to decide whether you have any business judging my marriage."

"I couldn't care less about your marriage, Detective. Except that it helps me get your attention. I'm married to my work."

"Nice way of not answering my question."

She takes a drag and contemplates the cigarette out in front of her like maybe it has a better memory. She nods.

"Once. I married him and then I buried him. And I moved on."

"A good man, this husband?"

"To the core. And as dull as a sack of dust. I married him for his shoulders and the way could pound a fence post into a hole. Now he's in a hole and I do this every day. Sit in the shadows and watch. Several decades now. Because it turns out my fascination has always leaned toward the bad men. Criminals especially. Good men who turn bad most of all."

"Daddy's girl to the end."

"Satisfied?"

"Not about the mayor."

"Wanting it doesn't make it true, Raymond."

"Maybe."

"Royce is about as corrupt as any other garden variety politician. More corrupt, certainly, than Judge Jolie. But not enough to pique our interest."

"So then Royce's name on that list …"

"You were played, Detective. Your Russian doll list was a ruse. You need to accept that."

"A ruse by whom?"

"Best guess?" She takes another drag and looks at me. "Orland Twill and his handler."

"What handler?"

She lets out a sigh, either of boredom or resentment at having to explain.

"We call them *La Pourriture*. Or, if you're Italian and don't care about the kind of sounds that come out of your mouth, *Il Marciume*."

"What if you're an American and speak a perversion of the King's English?"

"Then you call them *The Rot*. Not sure what they call themselves, if anything."

"The Rot?"

"Yes. They emulate organic decomposition. Crime by infiltration and eventual, unavoidable decay. Water in the wood. All they ever need is a way in."

"A way in where?"

"Anywhere. Everywhere. A corporation. A police department. A city. A man. Once they're in, all they need is time. Human nature supplies the bacteria that does the rest. The organization is decentralized and loosely structured, but there is still accountability. People at Twill's level have handlers."

"Okay. So Twill and his handler stick a list up the ass of a Russian doll. Toward what end?"

"Discrediting you and the Chandler PD, for starters. Gumming up Judge Jolie's docket. Springing their assassin. Beyond that it's hard to say. Pretty clear whatever they had planned blew up in Twill's face. Now you've got his job and he's on the run. Good thing Chief Loudermilk's email to Twill surfaced in time for the OAG investigation. You're welcome, by the way."

"Thanks, but I didn't need the help."

"You're a bad liar when your pride is wounded. You needed all the help you could get. So did OAG. All we did was get them looking in the right direction. Twill was hiding the ball. We unhid it. Now …" Marie looks at me with a resolve to wrap things up. "That was a lot of questions for someone who was only allowed to ask three. I think we're done."

"Did my wife ever work for Samuel Royce or Victor Roby?"

I get a long look, holding me in suspense.

"We believe so. Yes."

"Why? For what purpose?"

"We don't know."

"Prove it. And that's not a question."

"You want me to prove it? What are you prepared to do for us?"

"What needs doing?"

"You've searched Twill's office. What have you found?"

The two dry-cleaning tickets are burning a hole in my pocket. They want to come out and smell the smoke. I also think about Pete's email – *it's not the brothers; it's the boss* – along with his original double-homicide forensics report on the

O'Tooles tucked safely away in my trunk. I could cooperate now, open the kimono, but then I might not have anything to trade later.

"Yeah," I say, "I've looked. And I've found exactly squat. A bunch of expense reports that need approving and three dozen case files that are suddenly my responsibility to work. I haven't found anything you'd care about. But then again, I have no idea what you're looking for."

"We believe Twill is likely to have information, digital information, that will prove his connection to *La Pourriture* and, if we are lucky, will point to the dry cleaner order that resulted in the murders of *la famille* O'Toole."

"Information."

"Data."

"And you want me to bring it to you."

"Your powers of deduction are superb."

"A few big problems with that plan, Marie. For starters, I have the man's office, and his desk, but not his computer. I've tried snooping, but it's all password locked. Our IT Department needs to disable all of the security."

"Seems like a reasonable request for the head of IAD."

"Yeah. I can make that request. I'm only temporary head of IAD but I'm guessing they'll allow it after some head-scratching. How else can I run the department without access to the files on Twill's computer, right? Something tells me that's why I've got the job."

"Then can we assume access is not really much of a problem?"

"I can make that case."

"But?"

"But that leads to the second problem."

"I'm listening."

"I'm an old-school luddite. I don't know the first thing about how to go about crawling through a hard drive looking for whatever it is you need me to find. Give me a dead body and I can tell you everything about him including his favorite song and his deepest regret. But computers? That was always for the geeks in forensics. Once I get access, I can bumble my way around Twill's directory, but just because I can't find anything doesn't mean it's not there."

"We have someone who can help." Marie reclaims her purse and opens it. She extracts a folded slip of paper and hands it to me. "He can drop by any time that's convenient."

I open the scrap to find a phone number and the name John Murray.

"Computer savvy, is he?" I ask.

"He knows what to do."

"Right," I say, stuffing the paper in my pocket. "Well this brings us right to the doorstep of problem number three: The United States Constitution. You promised the 4th Amendment gets invited to any parties."

Marie clamps the cigarette in her lips and leans forward to stretch a hand over the front seat. The driver seems to know what she wants, handing back a manilla envelope. She opens it and extracts three sheets of paper. Then she hands them to me.

"I trust this will help alleviate your concern."

The search warrant is just like the ten thousand others I've seen over the years. I read as Marie smokes and the rain lashes against the roof of the car. The warrant authorizes agents of the Federal Bureau of Investigation to conduct a search of any and all computers, computer systems, and electronic devices including cellular telephones capable of storing or retrieving computerized data to which one Orland Twill currently has access or the right to access, or to which he has had access or the right to access in the past two years. The warrant identifies two specific locations – Twill's work and home – but is clear that the warrant extends to anywhere the subject computers and devices may be located.

I flip to the back page. The warrant is signed by Federal District Court Judge Timothy W. Selkirk and stamped by the clerk of the Central District of Illinois.

I look up. Marie is waiting.

"FBI?" I ask.

"They owe us a back scratch or two. We're cashing in."

"You're telling me the FBI has been read in on all of this?"

"Have you ever known your FBI to do anything without being fully informed?"

"So then they've got an oar in the water?"

"They're helping us cross the t's. They'd rather not be involved."

"Because?"

She puckers and shakes her head a little.

"*Pas de mon ressort.* Above my paygrade. It's complicated. They've got a conflicting investigation. If our investigation blows up, they want to keep their suits clean."

"Going to be difficult with their name on the warrant, don't you think?"

"Not really my problem."

"Well, Hell's bells, Marie, you've got your warrant. Go search already. Why do you need me?"

"We'd like to avoid a big splash. When it comes to searching Twill's home computers, or his phones, the wife gets involved, the personal lawyers get involved. Leaks to the media. There's no turning back." She cocks an eyebrow. "But the office ..."

The smoke clears just enough for me to see the game.

"Ah. The office computer is not technically Twill's computer. All the contents belong to the department and the city of Chandler. And, conveniently, he's no longer around. I'm the department head and I can let you in to execute the warrant."

"Correct." Marie shrugs. "Why make it harder than it needs to be?"

"But Chief Loudermilk could give you the same access that I can. *Better* access. You seem to be on good terms. Why not him?"

"Chief Loudermilk is a good man. The best of men. A good egg, as they say. But he's a political animal. That makes him a coward when it comes to things that he is not specifically ordered to do."

"Oh, I get it. You're worried you can't get the Mayor of Chandler on board. So he can't give the order to his Chief of Police because you haven't told him anything about any of this. My whole chain of command is in the dark."

"Your chain of command is not my chain of command. Your chain of command poses an operational liability. Your chain of command is superseded by federal law enforcement. The FBI has its warrant. All we need is you."

"I'm not an FBI agent."

"But John Murray *is* an FBI agent. And he's on loan. All you need to do is make the call."

"And when my chain of command learns that I have kept them in the dark during a federal search of highly confidential IAD files? Is that another thing that's not your problem?"

Marie shrugs with that insouciance I'm beginning to hate.

"Depends on how things go, doesn't it? If we get our man ..."

"Bullshit, Marie. If you don't get your man, I'm left looking like the traitor everyone already believes me to be. And even if you do get your man, that won't make up for the deception. Letting the feds in the back door will never be forgiven. I'm trying to rehabilitate a career here, not drown it in the tub."

"When the time comes, Chief Loudermilk will play ball."

"You just called him a coward. You can't deliver the Chief and you know it. That's no assurance at all. This leaves me hanging out there."

"This is not the kind of thing Chief Loudermilk cares to know about in advance. Not officially."

"You mean if it all goes sideways, he wants the room to say I was the one to let in the feds and it was all a surprise to him."

"It's almost like you've done this before," Marie says with a smile.

"That's how you convinced him to give me Twill's job. Temporarily."

"Like I said, your Chief a political animal."

"I need more. If I'm going to do this …"

"More? You've already leap-frogged into the boss' office. How about making that permanent?"

That one does make me laugh.

"If you really think I like this IAD gig, I'm going to subtract some IQ points. After I leave this parking lot, I'll be spending the rest of my day in that office pissing on tiny fires and pretending to care. I don't care. I want out."

"I'm open to suggestions."

We look at each other for an extra couple of beats. The bargaining is now overt. We've been maneuvering each other to yes. She's waiting for me to commit. To name my price.

"Homicide. I want to go back to my office being in the front seat of my car and me doing what I'm good at. Reading bodies."

"A few words to the Chief after all the dust has settled … maybe that works. But if I'm honest, Raymond … If your chain of command *does* decide you're a traitor and hates you for letting in the feds, then there's not much I can do."

"I'm not talking about Chandler PD," I say. "I'll never get Chandler's boot print off my ass. There's not a uniform in that building that doesn't hate me and suspect me of treachery. Even if I liked IAD, I can't do the job. I want a ticket to Chicago PD Homicide in my back pocket before I call up this John Murray guy and do this thing for you."

Marie closes her eyes. I know the expression. The day that will never end. The obstacles that will never cease. I don't care. I keep pushing.

"You're going to tell me that you don't have that kind of pull over at Chicago PD and I'm not going to believe a word of it, Marie. You've got Chief Loudermilk on speed dial and you and the goddamned FBI are in the middle of a mutual back-scratching party. Something tells me you can help find me an extra chair at Chicago Homicide."

"My clock is ticking, Detective," she says, opening her eyes. "I've got thirty days to execute on that warrant. Twenty-eight actually, including today."

"Then you'd better get started. And something else, just to hedge my bets. If you find Twill, I want a heads up so I can be there when you put the cuffs on."

"You want credit for the assist."

"Damn right I do. I'm tired of being on the wrong side of the equation."

"And you're prepared to simply trust that I'll give you that heads up on an arrest if and when the time comes?"

"No. I don't trust you any more than I can speak French. But I'm starting to trust that maybe we both want the same things. I'll accept a down payment to prove that you're acting in good faith."

"And what is this down payment?"

"Proof that Marlo was working for Sam Royce and Victor Roby."

"How can that possibly matter now?" she asks.

"It matters to me."

Marie stubs out the second cigarette and lets it drop. She looks at me with something like grandmotherly concern.

"This obsession will end you, Detective. The water is always rising. You'll drown trying to carry that weight. You need to move on. Loving her does not mean you have to die for her memory. You need to keep the memories you have and cut her loose."

I open the door out into the deluge.

"You should start an advice column. I need to know more about who I'm cutting loose. I always thought the French would die for love eight days a week, even drown."

"How and why you die, Raymond, is not my concern. And I never said I was French."

I step out in the rain and turn back, bending in for one last look at Marie before closing the door.

"You want me to play ball, that's what it's going to take. And next time I call your number I want to hear you on the other end. I'm tired of this game. Thanks for breakfast. I'm late for a job I hate."

FORTY-NINE

He's got that look on his face. Jaw set. Eyes hard. Creases deepening across his brow. It's how he looks when he's starting to understand things that don't want to be understood. This is how he looks whenever he wants to make up for lost time and he thinks that just might be possible.

The rain is falling harder, like it knows the same thing he knows and wants to stop him, or at least slow him down. Nothing doing. He gives Paula some speed and works his phone. Raj Malik answers like he's been waiting. Maybe he has.

"Mack!"

"Raj. You free?"

"Always, man. What's doin'?"

"Coppa Joe's in an hour?"

"On my way to the airport, but I can fix that. Where are you?"

"Cicero. Headed for Chandler PD."

"Hmm. Your car obviously works. You're headed for the office. And you want me to pick you up across the street. I'm getting the feeling this is about more than transportation. Wait, let me guess. You've got someone following you and you want them to think you're at work not off chasing bad guys."

"Or I was just going to treat you to lunch and a cup of coffee."

"Really?"

"We need to work on your gullibility. But there's nothing wrong with your deductive reasoning, Sherlock. Hope you haven't traded in the Camels for an opium pipe."

"Huh?"

"Never mind. See you in an hour. Motor running, Raj."

"Got it."

FIFTY

I turn the knob and push open the door. The room catches its breath, grinding slower by the second, seizing to a stop.

I was always about as popular as the plague when I was a kid. The attention I got whenever I walked into a room full of people was usually the kind of attention that made you want to steer clear of rooms altogether; made you want to spend the rest of your life under an open sky, sailing or camping or farming. Except for a few good seasons of football, not much changed until I started working homicide. That made me part of a team. Having your partner's back because you could bet your life that he had yours. Feeling like you could enter any room you wanted because you walked into that room together, maybe guns drawn. Doing something good every day as a member of a family, or something like it. That was okay. For a guy who never had a family? That was all right.

Not like marriage. Marlo was the brass ring that turned out to be solid gold. I could have let the world burn to chunks of cinder and lakes of boiling acid as long as I had Marlo. The only room that ever mattered during those years was the room she was in. But then Marlo found an exit and the homicide squad room was the only room left on planet earth with any oxygen. My brothers in arms kept me alive. For a while.

Then my number showed up in the cell phone of a mid-level heroin pusher and all that good-feeling camaraderie turned to shit in the space of a weekend. Suddenly, the only person who had my back was my lawyer. I hated that guy and his relentless devotion to bad news. I had to pay him by the hour to be my friend. Walking into rooms full of people became the same experience it always had been, only worse because the people in most of the rooms of my life felt justified in hating me. That kind of hatred counts double for feeling righteous and popular.

So here I stand in the doorway of the Chandler Internal Affairs Division and the reception I get is disconcerting. Let's just say it's not what I'm used to. Everyone sees me push my way through the front door. Mouths open, eyes keen. They all care intensely that I am here. They each want a moment of my time for a favor. Hate, suspicion will not serve their interests in this particular room. Not now. Not as long as I'm in charge.

Stephanie Nellis is the closest. So she's the first.

"Morning, boss," says Steph. "Glad you're here. Bunch of people want a word with you, starting with Lieutenant Wendig. The man is pissed. He got the pink sheet and called the Chief just like you said he would. Not sure what the Chief told him but whatever it was didn't do anything to cool Wendig's jets. He wants you to come see him ASAP about this request to interview his guy, Alphonse Jarr. He doesn't want a phone call. He said …"

I hold up a hand and keep walking.

"It'll have to wait, Steph."

"But …"

"I know. It'll still have to wait."

Carolyn is next, intercepting me as I pass Santiago's desk and turn for Twill's office. She hands me a stack of three files.

"The top two just need stage-one approvals. The third file is the Beaumont investigation which is about to jump the tracks. You need to read that one."

I keep moving. She falls away as I make it to Twill's office. Glen Sugarman is leaning up against the jamb. He's a round, saggy-eyed black man with an asymmetrical face that makes it look like his lower lip and his nose are working through a divorce. Best dresser in the office, this guy. Different tie clips and cufflinks every day. Like he's killing time before ascending the pulpit and waking up the congregation.

"LT," he says.

"I'm not a lieutenant, Glen."

"May as well be. You're a temporary lieutenant. You're a TLT. Or maybe an acting lieutenant. An ALT."

"Glen." I push past him into Twill's office and turn, one hand on the door like I'm ready to close it on his feuding face. If I let him in, he'll sit down and start telling stories.

"I need to take a couple of personal days next week. I'm trying to schedule a procedure. Couple of months ago I was in my basement hunched over this old …"

"HR, Glen. That's what they do; approve and disapprove."

"I did. I'm out of leave time. They said it requires *your* approval."

"You mean they disapproved unless I grant special dispensation."

"Correct."

"And you're all prepared to tell me the nasty details of this procedure and make the case that you have to have it now, and not after you accrue some more leave."

"Correct."

"Somewhere you've got a doctor's note I won't be able to decipher, just in case I resist."

"I can get one if …"

"Request granted. Good luck." I start to close the door. He stops it with a hand, holding a pen and a sheet of paper.

"I need a signature."

"Turn around and bend over," I say, taking the paper and pen. He doesn't ask. He just does it as the rest of the room looks on. For all the times I have wanted to kick Glen Sugarman in the ass, this is my chance. I resist for the sake of office morale. I use Glen's back as a pinstriped desk and sign above where it says Commanding Officer.

As I look up, I catch Santiago's face from across the room. Perfectly symmetrical, that mug. A little sad, a little amused, slowly moving from side to side. I close the door.

The phone is ringing before I hit the chair behind the desk. I let it ring.

I wake up Twill's now defenseless, unprotected computer and access the directory I need for the number to the Chandler Pretrial Detention Center. The Ceepeedeecee, as we all call it. I poke a few numbers into the phone and fight my way to a clerk who can answer some questions about my old B&E, computer crimes pal Kevin Canady. Questions like who posted his bail and the terms of his pretrial release.

Turns out Kevin's mother bailed him out. She has also agreed to act as his third-party custodian. He's allowed to spend time at her place in Tinley Park or at the Chandler Public Defender's Office, which is right across the parking lot from where I sit, or at his place of employment, Whitehorse I.T. Solutions, *WITS*, assuming he has been lucky enough to keep his job. They also gave him an ankle bracelet just in case he gets a case of wanderlust.

I hang up and call Kevin's employer hoping to check two items off my list at the same time. The kid who answers the phone chirps out a glossy professionalism.

"Whitehorse I.T. Solutions, this is Sherrie, may I help you?"

"Yeah, this is Ray over at BSD Financial. I'm reviewing our I.T. service accounts and I wanted to confirm whether Whitehorse I.T. has scheduled any maintenance visits or upgrades for us this quarter."

"Well, let me just look that up here. One second. BSD Financial?"

"Correct."

"Uh, says here that you are still on just the regular quarterly maintenance plan. One per quarter, plus necessary patches, upgrades and troubleshoots. No upgrades are currently scheduled."

"Great. And can you remind me of the name of the tech you sent out the last time?"

"Sure. Let's see. Kevin Cana … Oh, he no longer works here. Sorry. The new tech assigned to BSDF is Kamal. Kamal Chopra."

I thank her and hang up, grab my notes and head for the door which I fling open only after a deep breath. I move through the office with enough pace and purpose to keep from collecting questions. Steph still manages a look before I'm gone.

"I'll be back," I say. "Don't let them run with scissors."

In the hallway I turn left instead of right and take the back stairs all the way to the bottom. I point myself for the exit in the rear of the building. Along the way I encounter not a single person except one guy on the short list of people I want to see the least.

"Mack," says Dan Brewster with a smile.

"Brewster. Sneaking in the back way, I see. Guess you and OAG are about as popular as I am these days."

He's just coming in, popping the water off his black umbrella. He juts out his wrist like he wants me to see his watch.

"I'm a slave to my Fit Bit. I only take the stairs."

"Got it," I say, holding out my wrist and its department store timepiece. "I don't go anywhere without my Fat Bit. It counts shots and cigarettes."

"Used to work out every other day," he says. "Not recently. Not since your Russian doll landed on my desk. I'm spending all of my time asking questions and scratching my head. Got to try to stay in shape any way I can."

"I guess that figures. State of Illinois likes to keep its employees lean and fit. Keeps you off the medical benefits. City of Chandler has a different strategy."

"Which is?"

"Permissive over-indulgence leading to early death. Free donuts and cocktails with every elevator ride."

Brewster squints, focusing on my face.

"You look like someone's been asking you harder questions than I have."

"At least you wait for me to answer." I turn to go, but he's not quite done.

"I heard about Twill," he says.

"That didn't take long. What part?"

"Him getting the boot. Is there another part?"

"Guess we'll find out."

"And I guess you're moving up in the world."

"Funny. Doesn't feel like it. Feels like I'm running up the down escalator. I'm guessing you're here to see the Chief."

"My interview schedule is …"

"Confidential. Yeah, I know. How many extra steps does your Fit Bit give you for clenching your ass while you make small talk?"

"Funny. Your boss, your old boss, still owes me a follow-up. You know where I can find him?"

I shrug. "New Orleans?"

"That's what his wife told me thirty minutes ago. She seemed surprised at the word suspension. She stuck to the story, but I don't think she was a believer when I hung up. So where is he, Mack?"

"Beats me, Brewster. But if you find him, tell him he can have his job back any time."

"I don't think you have that authority."

"Never stopped me before."

I leave Brewster to his exercise and push through the exit out into the rain. I pull up the collar of my coat and wish mightily I'd stolen his umbrella.

A whistle cuts through the wet air. Raj is right across the street where he's supposed to be, window cracked so he can let out the smoke. I hustle through the downpour dodging traffic and climb in through the passenger door, slamming it behind me. Raj looks at me with a detached bemusement; like a stray dog has climbed onto the front seat looking for a ride.

"You look like hell, Mack," he says, cigarette dangling.

"Yeah? Thanks. What are you gonna do about it?"

Raj reaches into his front pocket and holds out a half-full pack of Camels. I want to grab the whole thing and eat it. I pull one free and place it between my lips. Raj holds out a lighter and gives it a flame. I gently push it away.

"Seriously?" he asks.

"What, you still setting them on fire? Grow up, kid." I lay my head back against the headrest. "Let's go."

Raj puts the cab in gear and angles out into the street.

"Where are we going?" he asks.

"To bail a man out of purgatory."

FIFTY-ONE

Kevin Canady's mother works from home. Convenient when your divorced kid, father to your grandchild, needs a third-party custodian to make sure he behaves before his felony charges can be adjudicated and to keep his ankle bracelet from chafing. I show her the badge. She's not impressed. Maybe it's the cab idling in the driveway.

"He's not going anywhere," she says. She adjusts the black headset over her head and rests the heel of her hand on the cellphone bracketed to her hip. Like it's a gun.

She's in a bathrobe and slippers, gray hair pulled back with a black elastic band. She's early seventies with an unmade face and a couple of dull, steel-hard eyes. I'm guessing they used to be a dewy blue looking through a wispy-blonde tangle when she was younger, putting it out there and making baby felons. Not anymore. She's all about survival now. I can tell she's won more battles in her day than she's lost but the score is still closer than she'd like, so she hasn't relaxed her guard for years now. Decades. Doesn't trust anybody, most especially Kevin, who I'm guessing reminds her a little too much of his old man, may God save his no-good, miserable cheating, loafing soul. He may or may not be living, but I can tell he hasn't been in the picture frame for a long time. It was him or her and she finally won. Kicked him to the curb and kept on making the ends meet, day in and day out, because life is always one thing after another until it all stops for good. So Evelyn Canady here is vigilant; always on edge, looking to intercept and defeat the next thing to threaten her or hers. Today, that's me. I'm the next thing.

"He's my responsibility," she says. "I promised the judge. He's not going anywhere."

She rolls her eyes and taps her phone. "Fit for Life Beauticeuticals. Can you hold please? Thank you." She taps her phone again. "He's not going anywhere."

"I didn't say he's going anywhere, Mrs. Canady. I said I'd like to speak with him. May I come in?"

"No. You may not come in. You may not come in and he cannot leave. If you have to speak with him, you can do it right here. You … Fit for Life Beauticeuticals. Can you hold please? Thank you." She inclines her chin and then tips her head backward and shouts. "Kevin!"

I wait, grateful for the generous eave keeping the stoop dry. The man himself shows up behind his mother in the doorway after a slow avalanche of footfalls down a wooden staircase I can't see. Then his face rises like a pale sun over Evelyn's shoulder. Same shark fin nose on a pallid face with dark, deep-set eyes. His hair is clean this time. Living with mom is good for something.

It takes him a second to place me. I can tell the memory registers in his gut like a slab of spoiled meat. I play it formal, gambling that as bad as I am, I'm still a shade better than Evelyn.

"Kevin Canady? I'm Officer Mackey from the Chandler Police Department, just checking in with you to make sure you are satisfying the terms of your pretrial release. Do you have a few minutes to talk?"

Confusion grips his face. He doesn't know how to respond. It reads like apprehension, which is fine by me. I fill the silence.

"Your mother thinks it is better if I don't come in, which is fine. Maybe we can chat for a few minutes out here."

"Uh … I guess."

"Good. Can you step out here so I can inspect the ankle monitor for signs of tampering?"

"He hasn't done any tampering," says Evelyn with a little extra disgust. "I check it every night before he goes to bed."

"Christ," breathes Kevin, pushing past his mother out onto the stoop. He holds out his left leg as I kneel.

"Looks good to me," I say, standing. "I need to confirm your whereabouts since your release from Ceepeedeecee."

"Where?" asks Evelyn.

"Sorry. Chandler Pretrial Detention Center."

"He's only been … damnit. Fit for Life Beauticeuticals. Can you hold please? Oh. Mr. Woodhouse. Yes. I'm so sorry." Kevin and I look at each other as she listens. "No. Yes. The volume today has … Yes, sir. Let me get to my computer."

Evelyn looks at each of us hard, first me, then Kevin. Then she disappears into the house and ascends the stairs. Kevin has suddenly found his voice, but it comes out in a dry whisper.

"What the fuck is this, man?"

"How'd you like to get out of here?" I ask.

"Duh." He gestures angrily down at his left ankle. "I can't go anywhere, man."

"Not even back to Ceepeedeecee to get these charges dropped?"

His mistrust is Nigerian Prince email grade. "What?"

"Your lucky day, Kev. You've got something I need and I'm willing to trade. You want your ankle back and to get out from under mom's thumb, now is your chance. But I'm in a hurry and you're useless to me in a couple of hours. Actually, I'm guessing you're useless to me as soon as Evelyn gets off that call. So what do you say?"

He looks over his shoulder inside the house. When his face comes back, I can see he's biting his lip.

"I should talk to my lawyer," he says.

"You've got this backwards, Kevin. Lawyer up when you get arrested. I'm trying to unarrest you. You going to let your public defender make this decision? How long do you think it will take for him to check his voicemail and get back to you? I'll be out of your life in the next thirty seconds. You're the easiest way to solve my problem, but I've got other options."

Kevin looks past me at Raj idling in the driveway.

"Why should I trust you?" he asks. "Why are you in a cab?"

"Suddenly you've got some high standards for who gets your trust. That's funny, Blue Shoe, because it seems to me you've been trusting anyone who gives you a cocktail nickname and a few felony assignments. Now you've lost the best job you've ever had, you're looking at a slam dunk for a lot of years with a cell mate, and, in the meantime, as the wheels of justice grind you into a fine powder, you've got warden-mom to contend with. Maybe you'd like to be free of all this. Trade the cellmate for some time with your daughter before she goes to college."

I let that sit for a second and watch him think. Three seconds and I can feel him rolling backwards. I give him another push to get him over the hill.

"Gotta tell you, Kev, I didn't think I'd have to sell you on not going to prison. Sure, I'm in a cab. Maybe you don't trust taxis. We're all afraid of something. I've got a thing for chainsaws. But you're in an ankle bracelet looking at a decade of government housing and group showers. And mom is winding up that phone call. Come with me now, and I mean right now, or take your chances with the shitty cards you're already holding. What's it gonna be?"

FIFTY-TWO

It's a risk. No doubt. But Ray lets Kevin Canady slip into Raj's back seat without cuffing him. Solidly against department protocol. Kevin could get violent. Take over the car. Make a run for it at the intersection of *What Were You Thinking* and *Better Safe Than Sorry.*

But Ray wants the idea of freedom to sink into Kevin's bones. He knows he'll need to trade on that hopeful future, that taste of freedom, if he wants Kevin to do what he needs him to do. So he treats him like a citizen. Just two guys climbing into a cab like a couple of regular Joes.

Besides, if Kevin was going to run, he'd have done that already. Where's the man going to run with an ankle bracelet?

Raj checks them in the rearview mirror every few seconds, but he keeps his mouth shut just like Ray asked him to. Ray keeps to himself, looking out at the rain and thinking things through until Kevin's knee-bouncing agitation gets in the way.

"Relax," says Ray. "Once you're a free man you can go back and apologize to the warden. Show her your ankle. She'll forgive you."

"I'm not worried about her," he says.

"If you say so."

"I want to know …"

"You want to know what I need. You want to know the tit for tat."

"Yes."

"First stop is Ceepeedeecee. We check in. I show them that I've got you in custody and that you haven't gone joyriding. I'm going to need to cuff you for that part, but that will be temporary. While I'm there I'll pick up the paperwork I'm going to need to fill out in order to amend my arrest report and drop the charges against you."

"Okay …"

"Then we're going across the parking lot to my office. While we're there, I'm going to fill out the paperwork for your release. I'll also need to call the DA's office and your public defender just to let them know what's happening. And while I'm busy with all of that, you're going to provide me with a little tech support."

That gets his attention. Raj too. Ray looks out at the rain like he might be done talking. No chance of that. Talking is the only way Ray is staying awake. He's just building some interest. He wants Kevin to lean in.

"What kind of tech support?" asks Kevin when the silence shows no sign of stopping. "What do you want me to do?"

"All in good time, Kev."

"I'm not doing anything criminal for you," he says defiantly, like maybe this is some kind of test.

"And I wouldn't ask it of you. But, for the record, you've already done something criminal. And I don't mean your old computer crimes conviction either. I'm talking about the new stuff. The breaking and entering in order to unlawfully access a computer. Did you know her?"

"Did I know who?"

"The homeowner."

"I'm not answering your questions. I'm not here to be interrogated."

"Fair enough. Let me tell you what I think happened, Kev. I think you fell on hard times ten years ago, give or take. On the outs with your wife. She's moving on to someone else and you get put outside with the trash. You don't like that much so you break back into the house that used to be yours to hack into her computer and find out whatever it is that you want to know. That little stunt got you a shoving match with your ex, a restraining order and a misdemeanor computer crimes conviction. You also lost whatever chance you had for shared custody. You get stuck with strictly supervised visitation. But you managed to keep your job at Whitehorse I.T. Services. Good for you. That's because you're good at what you do, which is to keep other people's computers working. You're good at getting in and finding things that aren't supposed to be in there. Glitches. Malware. Viruses. That kind of thing."

"It's more than that."

"I'm sure it is. Point is your skills keep your job and your job keeps you out of trouble. For a while. You keep your head down and do what you're supposed to do. Mom chips in to help you get a little place out on West Blackshire Loop and you do your job and live your life and look forward to seeing your kid's soccer games. So far so good on the road to redemption. But you're lonely. A nine-to-five only gets a man so far. You've got some itches to scratch. You go out looking. And somewhere out there you find someone. A woman maybe. A real looker. Things are looking up. She comes with a bunch of her own friends and before you know it, you're enjoying yourself. You're out on the town most nights, hitting the clubs and ordering blue shoe cocktails like it's nobody's business. Suddenly, that's your new name. Blue Shoe. Hilarious. Everyone thinks so. Even you."

"That's not, like …"

"Then, one night, one of your new friends lays out a chance for you to make some serious money. Easy money for someone with your skill set. The kind of money where no one gets hurt and everyone thinks you hung the moon. Righteous and just money, too. That helped. Your new friends give you an address and a long story about a woman who stole some information that wasn't hers to take. They think she's got it stashed away on her hard drive. They don't know computers, but you sure do, don't you, Kev? You know how to get inside a computer like some people know how to get inside a bottle of booze or a pack of cigarettes. You make it look easy."

Kevin leans his head back and places a hand over his eyes, squeezing at the temples. Whatever is inside that head of his is starting to hurt.

"Anyway, they've got a key to her place, and you've got a chance to be a hero. You balk at first. Of course you do. But they keep working on you. *She* keeps working on you. A man is only so strong. Am I right, Kev? A man needs money. A man needs company. Friends. A little tongue in the ear. They wore you down. They paid you something up front just to get your eyes spinning. Then they gave you a key and a list of search terms and sent you in to do the job."

Ray slips Kevin a sideways look, just checking in. Kevin doesn't acknowledge him. Ray keeps going.

"Right. So you stake the place out first. You catch a good-looking blonde and a tall bald guy leaving the house. You call that in and get instructions to follow her just to make sure she's going to be gone for a while. So you do. She leads you out to a restricted parking garage in the financial district. She's got a security pass, but you've got your own pass, so that works out nicely. She switches cars, trading a white Hyundai for a blue Mercedes. Then she leads you to the Marker Westpoint Suites. You call it in. Whoever's on the other end of your phone tells you it's safe to go back to her place, let yourself in, and poke around with her computers. So you do. You use the key. You find the computer. You hack your way in. You run your searches and you come up empty. Then you try to leave in a car with a disconnected battery." Ray swats him in the leg with the back of his hand. "The rest is history. And now here we are in the back of a taxi trying to roll back time and make it all right again."

Kevin has been taking most of the story looking out at the dirty gray Chicago outskirts that will never get clean no matter how much it rains. The streets, the weather-stained buildings, the people shuffling between dry portals with varying degrees of urgency. It all looks so much the dirtier for being wet. But now Kevin turns to look at Ray sitting next to him with an expression of bemused sympathy.

"Is your point to, like, talk me to death, or ..."

"What you don't understand, Kevin, is that you didn't find new friends. They aren't friends and you didn't find them. They're criminals. And they found you. They were waiting for you. The job they gave you wasn't just a job. It was a test. Pass the test and you get the real job. The job that comes with a lot of risk and a lot of money. The job they'd marked you for from the beginning. Not just because you're you, Kevin, as special and talented as you are. Mostly because you work for Whitehorse I.T. Services, which has a particular corporate account that matters a whole lot to these people. The real job is for you to dig into *those* computers. Run your searches. Copy what you find. Delete. Sabotage. Who knows. Now I'm guessing. Point is, Kev, you were selected because you already have a servicing relationship with the company they want to hack."

"BSD," he says in a breath, more to himself than to Ray. But then he turns his head Ray's direction. "The woman, Amanda Tate, her house. She works for BSD. There was a BSD Financial notepad on the counter. I thought it was a coincidence. Fuck. There are no coincidences."

"And people say you're not so smart."

"Yeah, like you," he says, jerking his chin at Ray. "*You* said I'm not so smart."

"*Mea culpa*. But that's just because you were dumb enough to get caught searching a computer that didn't belong to you. Twice."

"Why are you telling me all of this? I'm not saying you're right about everything."

"You're not saying I'm all wrong, either. I'm telling you all this, Kevin, because I need you to search a computer that doesn't belong to you."

FIFTY-THREE

I get Raj to park along the back of the police station near where he picked me up. I slip the unused Camel back in his pocket and push open the door, telling tell him to stay put and to keep the meter running.

"On the house," he says. "On the job training."

"No, it isn't. You drove me around in a cab."

"You bought me a milkshake."

"You gave me a Camel."

"You never smoked the Camel."

"I don't have time to argue, Raj."

"Well then you better get going, Mack."

Kevin and I climb out into the rain and stand outside the back entrance as I fumble with my mag-card to open the door.

"You always come this way?" Kevin asks.

"Today I do. Head down, mouth shut."

We walk through a couple of long halls, up a small flight of stairs to the ground floor level and then right back out into the rain pounding the front staircase of the police station. Paula's parked a hundred yards away in her reserved spot, right where I left her.

Kevin's confused. He points across the lot at the Ceepeedeecee.

"He could have dropped us right there. Why …"

"Arm down, Kev. In fact …" I spin him around and cuff his wrists behind his back. "This is the part where you keep every thought in your head to yourself."

We descend the stairs and cross the parking lot. I march Kevin into the opening of the cinderblock that is the Chandler Pretrial Detention Center, hanging onto him arm like I'm taking a dog with an ankle monitor to the vet. We wait in line for a few minutes before I can explain to the duty sergeant that Kevin is in my custody and, despite what his ankle monitor might be saying, that he has not been violating the conditions of his release.

The duty sergeant is a couple of biceps growing out of a stack of bricks. The baggiest part about him are his eyes, which are red and swollen, like he's allergic to something in the air. Maybe me. He's not so busy filling out his uniform that he doesn't recognize me from the last time he saw me, back when I was pulling Kevin Canady in by the arm to book him. He didn't like me much then because my reputation precedes me and he thinks of me as a traitor to the mission of law and order. Unbooking Kevin is not going to warm his affections any, but maybe he'll do his job anyway.

I start to say something else, but he puts a buff finger in the air as he looks at his screen. That's my cue to shut up and wait. So I do. Then he cuts his saggy eyes my way.

"Canady?" he asks.

"Yes."

"An *Evelyn* Canady called in about twenty minutes ago."

"His mother," I say. "Third party custodian."

"Not so happy, Detective. Something about a cop in a cab stealing her kid. Wants us to tell the judge it wasn't her fault. Wants an APB. Wants the National Guard. The Marines. The President. You get the picture."

"Yeah, I get it. Empty nest. They never like to see their babies leave home. She'd made up his old room into Guantanamo."

I ask for a copy of the initial arrest paperwork and the forms I need to amend it. Keven keeps his mouth shut and stares down at his shoes. I get another long, hard look from across the counter, loaded with everything he thinks he knows about me.

"Problem?" I ask, still gripping Kevin's arm.

"With you?" He hands me the forms with something like a smile. "Never."

I hustle Kevin back across the parking lot, up the steps and into the Chandler HQ lobby. We get some looks but we also get to take the elevator alone, which is a plus. I shake off the rain and light up the right button. Once the doors are closed, I uncuff Kevin and give him a few pointers.

"Almost free, Kev. I'm working my end of things, now it's time for you to work your end."

"Where are we going?"

"To another room full of cops, only these cops think of me as a boss. And in that room, you are not a criminal or a suspect. Got that? You're just a guy helping me with a case."

"What case?"

"What case? The case of the guy who can still blow it and go back to mommy-jail, that's what case. The case of the guy who doesn't have the power of speech unless I ask him a direct question. Don't worry about the details, Kev. Just follow."

I use the hallway to get up a head of steam, open the door to IAD and keep moving with Kevin close behind. Stephanie Nellis is at her desk, right where I expect her. In an instant, she's walking next to me with a mouthful of questions. I don't answer except to say I'll get to them later and that right now I need to *deal with this witness interview.*

"What case?" she asks, looking back briefly at Kevin.

"Coopersmith," I say, like it's the truth. "This shouldn't take long, but I don't want to be disturbed."

"So does this mean you connected with Lieutenant Wendig?"

"No. No one tells me how to run my cases."

"The conference room is open," says Steph, trying to be helpful. I open the door to Twill's office, gesturing for Kevin to enter. Then I give Steph, and the rest of the room, the most relaxed smile I can muster.

"This will do fine," I tell her. "Hold my calls."

Steph nods smartly and turns away like a good soldier. The last thing I see before closing the door is Raphael shaking his disbelieving head.

Kevin is sitting in one of the chairs meant for guests of the Director of the Chandler PD Internal Affairs Division. Same chair I always sit in when I'm being yelled at for misbehaving. I pull him up by his arm and march him around the desk to the big chair.

"This is your seat for now," I say. "Don't let it go to your head."

"What am I doing?"

"I want you to search this computer just like you did Amanda Tate's computer."

"For what?"

"Whatever you were looking for at Amanda's. What was that?"

Kevin looks up at me warily, mistrust filling his eyes. It's the same question I asked when I arrested him. He refused to answer then and now the *déjà vu* has got him spooked. He's afraid his next words will be as good as a confession.

"Think about it, Kev. You really think any of this would be admissible in court? You think this is some sort of con I'm playing to get you to talk? Pretty long way for me to go just to get laughed out of the courtroom and thrown off the force."

The look hasn't changed much. Kevin chews at the inside of his lip.

"Look, Einstein, we've got you cold for breaking and entering and resisting arrest. Doesn't matter one little bit what you were looking for. Let me know if you want to go back and try your luck. I can have you back to the warden in no time. It would save me the job of unarresting you."

Kevin sighs and rubs his face. He points at what I'm holding.

"You really going to fill out that paperwork?"

"Yeah. And call your lawyer. And the DA's office." I point at Twill's dark screen. "Once we get through this part."

"What if I don't find anything?" he asks.

"Let's hope you do. Now what the hell were you looking for?"

Kevin leans back in Twill's chair and taps the keyboard with a forefinger. The screen lights up with the great seal of the City of Chandler Illinois.

"Numbers," he says.

"What numbers?"

"IP addresses. They never told me that, like, specifically or anything. It was just a list of numbers, but I know IP addresses when I see them. I had a list of five sets of numbers. And then a sixth number that had, like, fifteen digits to it."

"And where is that list of numbers?"

"I got it by text."

"Let's see your phone?"

He shows me his palms.

"I don't have my phone. Left in kind of a hurry if you recall." Whatever Kevin sees in my eyes, he doesn't like it. Maybe it's the death of any hope of escaping prison. "But if I can use this computer to access my account ..."

He doesn't need to finish. I bend over the keyboard and unlock Twill's computer with the new administrative password.

"Get to it."

I take a seat across the desk, splitting my attention between watching Kevin work and working on amending my own arrest report.

"Okay," he says eventually. "Got it."

"Print it."

I stand and wait for Twill's bookshelf printer to whir to life, grabbing the page when it's free. I'm looking at six lines of numbers. The first five each have between eight and twelve digits. The last one has fifteen, just like he said.

"And you're saying these top five lines are IP addresses."

"No doubt," says Kevin.

"No dots. I thought IP addresses come with dots."

"Beats me, man. But look at all the 255's and 192's. They're IP addresses. Doesn't really matter. I was just supposed to find the numbers."

"And the last line?"

"No idea. Whatever they're looking for has one, some or all of these sequences."

"How long does it take you to search a hard drive for these numbers?"

"How long does it take you to call my lawyer?"

"A lot longer than it takes me to rip up these forms."

Kevin shakes his head and sighs. "Can't believe I'm doing this," he mutters as he sits up and gets his fingers busy. "If I get busted and do time for this shit … you're going with me."

"You need this?" I ask holding out the sheet. Kevin shakes his head.

"Cutting and pasting, man. Cutting and pasting."

I fold up the sheet and slip it in a pocket, ready to finish undoing Kevin's arrest. Two sharp knocks on the door stop me in my tracks. Behind me, the clicking stops and I can feel Kevin look up in a panic. I want to tell him to relax and keep working as I send whoever it is away. But then again, I want a lot of things I never get. The door opens before my mouth gets the chance. Raphael sticks his head in the room.

"Mack …"

"Not now, Raffi," I say, moving to block his line of sight. I can tell I'm too slow, Raffi's eyes feasting on Kevin Canady, my supposed witness, behind the desk, working Twill's computer. His expression constricts into a worried confusion.

"I'll be out in …"

Santiago pushes his way in and closes the door behind him. He gestures at Kevin.

"Mack, what in the …"

"Raffi …"

"Never mind. I don't want to know, man. I mean, I *do*, but …" Santiago pulls his eyes away from Kevin and looks at me. "Whatever in the hell you're doing, you need to know something."

There's a squishy feeling in my gut. No stranger, this feeling. It shows up anytime I realize that the game I'm playing has just changed, usually for the worse. Raffi approaches me, one eye on Kevin across the desk, and puts his lips to my ear.

"CPD's got a body. A farmland ditch five miles outside of Manhattan. Near Jackson Creek. Two bullets, chest and face."

"Pete Chow," I say.

"Yeah. Unofficial, but yeah. Search warrants are out for the boss' rig and house. Shit just got real, Mack. Where the fuck is he?"

I close my eyes long enough to feel the edge of sleep I'm never going to get.

"I'm working on it."

FIFTY-FOUR

It's Ray's turn for the big chair. Kevin is across the desk where the underlings are supposed to sit, just in case they get interrupted again. They've stopped talking. Nothing to do now but let the printer finish the job. Thirty-one pages and still counting.

Ray has made his calls. First to the DA, then the PD. Mistaken identity he'd told them; he had not seen what he thought he'd seen. He needs to walk back the arrest. Plenty of confusion to go around, but they'd both let it go without a lot of questions. No one fights a chance at less work. Kevin had listened from across the room with an expression of relief that looked like it might hang around for a while. If nothing else, Ray here is good for his word.

Now they're waiting on the printer. Not that Ray can make any sense of what the thing spits out. Nothing but numbers. Row upon row of numbers. Thirty-two pages of them. Thirty-three. Still going.

Kevin had found the file hiding in the operating system suburbs of Twill's hard drive. That file contained two documents. One document included the number sequences that Kevin continues to insist are IP addresses, buried within a sea of undifferentiated numbers that goes on for five pages. Turns out the search terms on his list were only samples. He was able to pick out and highlight nearly three dozen other number sequences that he insists are IP addresses.

The second document, now thirty-four pages long, includes a single occurrence of the last number sequence on Kevin's search list. It appears on the seventh page. Kevin had highlighted the fifteen-digit number when page seven had emerged from the printer and handed it to Ray.

"I don't know what that is," Kevin had said.

"But not an IP address."

"No."

Ray had stared at the highlighted sequence for a few minutes and then returned the page to its proper order on the printer. He emailed both files to his private email account and had then leaned back with a focused expression on his face.

He hasn't moved since.

Maybe Kevin reads the expression as Ray juggling the numbers in the quiet of his head: sifting for patterns or working some kind of special forensic long division that would break the brains of mere mortals.

Wrong. Ray's not much of a math guy. He can't balance his own checkbook. Truth is Ray stopped thinking about the numbers twenty pages ago. The only thing in his head now is a Manhattan, Illinois ditch full of farmland runoff, mud, and Pete Chow. Pete's last email is running on a loop in his brain: *It's not the brothers; it's the boss. Let's talk.* Ray missed that boat by a mile. The couple of extra holes in Pete's head aren't connected to any vocal cords. Pete's all done talking.

But that email, Ray thinks. *It's the boss.* That's a dead man pointing a finger. Ironic, and more than just a little disappointing, that sitting in the boss' chair and hacking the boss' computer doesn't give a guy any better idea of where the boss is or how to find him.

"When does this thing come off?" asks Kevin, lifting his ankle above the desk.

"It's the new fashion, Kev," he says, coming back into the present. "Everybody's got one."

"You don't."

"I'm not even remotely cool enough."

"Seriously, man."

"It's with you for a few days. Keep following the rules unless you want to get arrested for violating the terms of your release. Once they process the paperwork, they'll call you to come in and get it removed."

"Aw, man!" Kevin thumps his foot to the floor. "Can't they just … can't we just go over there and …"

"You're right. This is really unfair, Kevin. Let's scrap the whole plan and go back to the way things were."

The printer stops. Forty-one pages. Ray stands, grabs the sheaf of paper and clips it with a binder. He folds the amended arrest paperwork into an envelope and seals it. Then he shuts down Twill's desktop and grabs his raincoat. He folds the sheaf in thirds and stuffs it into the inner pocket of his coat.

"On your feet, Kev. Let's go. Same rules. No talking out there."

"Where to?"

"There's a mother and child reunion at a local bed and breakfast prison I know. You'll love it. Let's go."

They move through the office quicky, Kevin first, head down with Ray close behind and me up above, bumping along the ceiling. Everyone looks, marking their exit, but they all seem to know better this time than to risk interfering. Raphael Santiago is the only exception. He's out of his chair and following them into the hall like he's part of the group.

"Mack," he says once the door has closed. Ray leaves Kevin in the hall halfway to the elevator and doubles back. He hands Santiago the envelope.

"Get this filed with Ceepeedeecee. Don't open it unless you want to know more than is good for you and you like answering lots of questions. Just drop it in the in-box on the counter."

Santiago turns the envelope over in his hands.

"Okay. This have anything to do with LT?"

"Maybe. Keep your ear to the ground, Raffi. If you hear anything, call me."

He's already walking away again. Santiago takes another step or two forward.

"Because you're going to do the same for me," he says, frustration warming to anger. "Right, Mack? Because this right here feels a whole lot like a one-way street."

Ray turns, but he keeps walking backward toward Kevin, who is now making new progress to the elevator.

"It is, Raffi," says Ray. "It is a one-way street. A busy one. Don't get caught going the wrong direction."

Ray turns his back on Santiago and hustles Kevin into the elevator. He punches the key for the lower level, crosses his arms and leans back hard against the wall as the doors close. I know that expression. The set jaw. The unfocused eyes. He's trying to see what he can't. Trying to figure out what comes next.

He's thinking about the name on the scrap of paper in his pocket, the one Frenchie Marie gave him not three hours ago.

John Murray. FBI.

He's wondering what Agent Murray and Frenchie Marie would make of the pile of numbers that he and Kevin just found inside the boss' computer. He's wondering why both Big Man and whatever agency employs Frenchie Marie would want those numbers. He's wondering what it means that Twill had tucked those numbers away for safekeeping inside his computer. He's wondering what CPD will find when they execute on the warrants for Twill's house and car. He's wondering where Twill is and just how to shake him out of the nearly nine million people who live in and around Chicago.

He's wondering what Marlo would do. Of course he does. Just like always. But now, wait for it. There it is, right on schedule. Look at the eyes, like a couple of hazel balloons slowly losing their helium. He's wondering – because he can't help himself, because he's a sad-sack glutton for gut-wrenching misery – he's wondering who Marlo ever was in the first place. He can feel Tia Lewis' heartache and anger burning through time – *There has never been anyone like Marlo, Mack; I still don't know who she was* – burning through the walls of a city that eats heartache for breakfast.

He's beating himself, again, with the same unanswerable question: *who was Marlo Kline?* He wants to ask her. He wants to demand some answers. Some accountability. But Marlo's not talking. Santiago can complain about one-way streets, but Ray has got one of his own.

He tries to tell himself that the sinking feeling in his gut is just the elevator dropping.

Sure it is, Ray. Except we both know better.

FIFTY-FIVE

Raj works the traffic like a pro. We leave Kevin Canady in the rain at the foot of his mother's driveway. He's in better shape than we found him, but his expression is much the same. I crack the window to leave him with something to think about.

"What is undone can be redone, Kev. The slightest whiff of you back in this game and I won't hesitate. Understand?"

"What if someone asks me … asks me …"

"If someone puts you under oath, then tell the whole truth and nothing but. Otherwise, you took a ride to Ceepeedeecee, we did a bunch of paperwork to unarrest your guilty ass, and I brought you back home. All of which is true. Can you live with that?"

Kevin nods, water running off his face, just as the front door to the house behind him is opening. The voice cuts through the deluge like a shiv in the shower.

"Kevin!"

Raj works his way through the afternoon snarls to get me into the financial district. He knows better than to fall for the Dan Ryan Expressway this time of day. He puts together a combination of side streets and parkways that leaves Englewood a blur and gets us past Fuller Park, Armour Square, and Chinatown like so many telephone poles on a country road.

Raj talks as he drives. Eager beaver as always. He's wide-eyed and full of questions. He wants to know more about *the case*, like it's a leather box full of riddles, mysteries and danger that you can carry around by a handle. He wants to know all the answers. Me too, but I'm still working on the questions. I keep to myself, trying to think things through. Raj tries to pry me open with a Camel. I wave it off.

"I know this Indian in a white coat who thinks that's a bad idea."

"You're serious, huh? You're like quitting for real?"

"We'll see. Guy I work with is big into gum. Maybe I'll switch to gum."

"Gum? I don't know, man." Raj puts the Camel between his lips and lights up. He takes a drag and lets it loose as he whips the cab around a woman with a wet carpet on her back heaving a grocery cart full of cans over a curb. He shakes his head. "I don't see you and gum."

"Never know, Raj. Maybe someone makes a bourbon-flavored gum."

Raj throws his head back and laughs.

"You serious?"

"As a heart attack, Raj. Bourbon-flavored gum. Let it age in big wooden casks. Glop it out onto a table. Pound it flat into a pancake. Drag it through a pile of toasted tobacco. Dust it generously with nicotine. Roll it into a stick. Let it dry and then light that sucker on fire. I should patent that. I'd be rich in two seconds."

Raj laughs again. It's an uncomplicated sound that makes me nostalgic.

"Don't forget your friends, man," says Raj. "When you make it big in the gum-smoking business you won't be taking cabs anymore. You'll have your own helicopter. I'll build a heliport on top of my agency so you can come visit."

I'm not the smartest fish in this lake, but I know when to take the bait.

"Your agency, huh?" I give him a look. "That still happening?"

"Oh, it's happening, man. Some day. It's happening."

"How's Cleopatra with that?"

"Cleo? Oh, Cleo loves the idea. She just doesn't know it yet. Hey," Raj looks at me, white teeth gleaming, "if the gum idea doesn't work out you should drop by. Fill out an application. We could go into business together."

"An application? I have to fill out an application?"

"That's how it works, Mack. Got to apply. I'd hire you. Don't worry." He backhands me in the shoulder. "I like the cut of your jib, man. You're going places."

Raj pulls over near the corner of South Wells and West Van Buren, where the rain falls harder than anywhere, but only because it's made of silver. I hand him some cash and push open the door. He tells me he wants an assignment. He'll take anything, he says. I tell him to stop playing detective and do his job. He leans across the passenger seat so I'll be sure to hear him.

"I'm training, Mack."

"No, you're dreaming, kid. Big difference. You want to train, go to Union Station."

"How are you getting back?"

"Private transportation."

I close the door on whatever comeback he had planned and hustle my way across the street. I duck into the parking garage that just happens to be where a small sliver of the Chicago financial services industry keeps its cars dry.

The spaces reserved for BSD Financial are five levels off the ground. Once I figure that part out, it doesn't take me long to find the two cars I care about most: the white Hyundai Sonata Amanda Tate drives to work and Saul Margolis' midnight blue Mercedes, the car that Amanda Tate drives when she wants to be alone, wear a black wig and shake people down for extra cash. The reserved parking signs come with a phone number.

"BSD Financial Services, can I help you?"

"I hope so. I'm in the parking garage and I just accidentally backed into a car in one of your reserved spots. It's a white Hyundai Sonata, with a small crystal tear drop hanging from the mirror. I guess I could give you the plate number, couldn't I? Let me see here."

I give her the number and then have to listen to two minutes of some easy listening ensemble laying waste to *Here Comes the Sun*. It's a small price to pay, all things considered. I make out better than The Beatles.

"Sir?"

"Yes, ma'am. Still here."

"I found the owner. She said she'd be there in five minutes. She's leaving now."

Five minutes turns out to be optimistic, but she doesn't miss it by much. I can hear her before I can see her, high heels echoing against the concrete walls like maybe a horse is looking for its buggy. But then Amanda Tate rounds the corner. This is no horse. A clothes horse, maybe. She's dressed like she works for a top shelf financial services firm; shades of cream and beige from her cashmere shoulders down to the pointy leather pumps peeking out from beneath the flare of her pant legs. She's left her coat at the office, but she's brought her purse. I'm guessing somewhere in there is a wallet with her insurance information. And maybe a wig.

"So sorry about this," I say as she approaches.

She gives me a quick once-over. It's an irritated, sour glance for such an attractive face. She's younger than I thought she'd be. Mid-thirties and mid-beautiful, drunk on her own power to feed a world full of hungry eyes. She's still too young to know that she's not as young as she thinks she is. She doesn't spend much time on me. Mostly she's surveying the Sonata for damage.

"What happened?" she asks. "Where'd you hit it? I don't even ..."

"Relax, Amanda," I say. My badge is out to collect her sudden and full attention. "The car is fine. You need to be more worried about you."

"What ... what is this?"

"I thought we might have this conversation in private rather than in the lobby of your employer."

"Are you arresting me?"

"Have you done something worthy of arrest?"

"No."

"Good. I'm guessing Constantine Papadopoulos has a different opinion on that issue, but maybe you can convince me why he's wrong and why arresting you is unnecessary."

It's too much all at once. All she can do is stare, mouth half ajar, blinking at me. A black Nissan comes around the corner with a slow rubbery screech. It's enough to pull Amanda back to her senses. She turns and looks, returning the driver's knowing wave as he pulls in several spaces away.

"You've got some choices, Amanda. We can have this conversation standing here in the parking garage. Or we can go back to your office and get a bunch of eyeballs involved. Or we can go to the police station. Or maybe we can just sit in your car and chat. What do you think?"

She's smart enough to find the only real option in the choices I have given her, but not smart enough to come up with one her own. Lawyering up right here and now would have been her best bet, but she's too busy working on the idea that her eyelashes can talk her way out this mess. She swallows once and smiles, gesturing at the car.

She digs in her purse and pulls out a set of keys, unlocking the doors with beep and a flash of parking lights.

"Any weapons in the car, Amanda?" I ask once I'm in the passenger seat.

"No."

I point at the bag in her lap.

"Any weapons in that purse?"

"No."

"Mind if I double-check, just in case you've forgotten?"

She holds it open, so I can see. No guns. I wasn't expecting any. I'm looking for a cell phone. She's got two of those. I reach in and pull them out. She doesn't like that much.

"Hey!"

"You'll get them back. If you cooperate." I hold the burner phone up in the light. "Otherwise, I'm guessing this one will become Exhibit A. I'm just going to hold onto them for now while we're talking."

Amanda slumps hard into her seat, crossing her arms as she sputters bewilderment to God.

"This is ... this is just ..."

"Isn't it though?" I ask. "Constantine thinks so too. He thinks it's so unfair that you're still walking around a free woman. Did you know people at work call him Stan? I figured it would be Connie. Or Papa. It's Stan. Go figure. But you know that already. Of course, you do. You used to work with Stan at the Merc. He never figured you for a shakedown artist."

I can almost read her mind. She's trying to figure out whether I'm telling her the truth. She's trying to fathom any way that Stan could have known who was squeezing him. Eventually she'll realize that it doesn't really matter whether Stan knows it was her or not. Because I clearly do.

"I don't know what the hell you're talking about," she says.

"You want me to believe you don't know Constantine Papa ..."

"Yes, I know him. *Stan*. Okay? I know him. I worked with him. He's a huge jerk. And a liar. He hates me. I don't know what he's saying about me, but I haven't ..."

"So you're saying you haven't been driving Saul Margolis' slick blue Mercedes around town, pretending you have black hair and that you're hungry for *La Bamba Burgers*."

She's not in much control of her startle reflex. Her head snaps my direction involuntarily. She makes the best of it by flexing the lines in her forehead and pretending to be painfully confused.

"What? No."

"You ever had a *Blondie's Big Dream*?" I ask. "One of those shakes will make your day, especially if it comes with a big bag full of cash."

"Mr. Margolis is out of town. I'm supposed to ..."

"Oh, you can save all of that. Don't embarrass yourself, Amanda. Taking care of Saul's car was Dennis O'Toole's job. You stepped into Dennis' shoes when Dennis stopped needing shoes. Saul Margolis barely knows you exist."

"You want to arrest me for driving Saul's car without his like, *explicit, written* permission?" She lapses back into shrugs and sputters. "I just ... I mean I can't even ..."

"Settle down. Saul seems pretty forgiving about the car."

"Okay. So you want to arrest me because *Stan* says I, what, stole his money or something? He's lying. I don't know what his problem is, but ..."

I hold up a hand.

"Stop. Okay? You're not helping yourself here. And, just an observation if I might: you seem overly concerned about being arrested for someone lucky to still be alive."

"Alive? What do you mean?"

"I mean having Dennis out of the way might have opened up some opportunities for you, but it also bought you some attention, didn't it?"

"Attention? I don't …"

"*Didn't it*, Amanda?" I look at her like I'm her father with her purse in one hand and a bag of weed in the other. She breaks eye contact, but I keep pushing. "How long do you think two cars, a couple of phones and a good wig are going to keep you breathing in and out? I know you're not living at home, but so do they. Not two hours after you locked the door, they had someone inside your house going through your desktop computer."

Her eyes come back to me in a hurry, like they've been someplace terrifying. "What? You don't …"

"I do. I know because I watched it happen and then arrested the guy myself."

"Who?"

"Guy named Kevin, but he's the least of your worries. It's the people who gave him the job you need to be concerned about. You can sleep wherever you want; you think they don't know how to find you? They do. You're easy to find. That's going to make for a short life, Amanda, and the last part of it is going to hurt. You've got something they want. Or maybe you had it and then hid it. Or gave it to someone else for safe keeping. They've been careful so far, but that's not going to last. They're coming for you, sooner or later. Don't take my word for it. Ask Dennis."

Anger now, tapping into secret terror. I'm getting somewhere, finally. She stabs herself in the cashmere with a finger.

"Look. I've already talked to the police about Dennis. A couple of times. Okay? You think I wanted him to die? You think I *ever* saw that coming? I loved Dennis. I don't have to explain myself to you." She flicks her eyes at me disapprovingly, as if seeing me for the first time. "Who are you? What is your name?"

"Detective Mackey. Ray Mackey."

"I don't have to explain myself to you, Detective Mackey."

"No, you don't have to explain yourself to anyone. Constitution gives you a right to remain silent. You won't even have to testify in your own defense."

"So, then you *are* arresting me."

"That's how this works. You can either start telling the truth or you can get arrested. You don't seem interested in talking."

"Well, I'm not talking to you, if that's what you think. I want to talk to my lawyer."

"There it is. Good for you. But you get to make that call after you're booked. See, your lawyer doesn't prevent you from being arrested. He only starts draining your bank account after we get your thumbs dirty and you start making new friends in lock-up. You ready for that?"

She looks at me like she's actually considering the question, weighing it against unarticulated alternatives. Her eyes go away for a long blink. When they come back, they're narrower, slinging the hint of a smile and a slightly softer voice.

"Any other options we can … consider?"

Hard to separate out how much of that is stupidity and how much is desperation. I don't try to sort it out. I play dumb.

"Not many, Amanda. Sorry to say, at this point, based on your answers and your attitude, I'd have to be specifically instructed *not* to arrest you. The only person who can do that is my boss."

"Your boss? Who is that?"

"My lieutenant. Orland Twill."

Stillness fills the small car like a kind of dense foam. Her eyes are now delicate blue-gray saucers, as still as porcelain. She knows it's too much of a coincidence for that name to drop into this conversation. But who hasn't gambled on the wildly improbable at some time or another? Desperation never plays the odds.

"Well then maybe I should talk to *him*," she says, working her way back to angry. "Maybe you should call him. I'll talk to your stupid boss. I'll tell him that this is all horseshit."

I nod, but slowly, uncertainly, like I've got some unformed suspicions of my own.

"Okay," I say. "You'll talk to him?"

"Yeah. Sure. I'll do that. If it'll get you off my back, I'll talk to him. What's his name again?"

"Twill. Lieutenant Twill." I point at the ignition. "Let's go."

She doesn't understand. Poor thing.

"Go? Go where? Where are we going?"

"To talk to my lieutenant. He's waiting."

FIFTY-SIX

They play the left, right, turn here, turn there, game for a while until the dirty blonde in cashmere recognizes the route and figures out where they're headed. That's when she sends all hopeful coincidences off to live with the tooth fairy and threatens to turn the car around. Ray is wishing he'd found a way to do the driving. He gives self-interested reason another shot.

"If you want to find your way out of this mess alive, Amanda, I'm your best play."

"You said we were meeting Orland."

"We are."

"How do I know you're not working for … for …"

"For who? You can say it. Who are you afraid of, Amanda? Who were you really working for? Who was Dennis working for?"

"You're not a cop."

"Sure I am," he says.

"Who do *you* work for?"

"Orland Twill. Just like I said."

"Right. How do I know you're not taking me someplace to kill me?"

Ray points through the windshield at the tallest building on the block.

"You think I'm going to kill you at the Marker Westpoint Suites? You're not so smart, are you? Take a left here. Park it in the lot."

Amanda gets one of those last-chance impulses that squeezes the accelerator and rockets them up 125th Street. Ray has to grab the wheel and turn it himself to get them on to South Marker.

"Goddamnit!"

Nearly hitting a parked Tahoe brings her own mortality into focus and convinces her to cooperate, at least while they're moving. He keeps a hand on the wheel, just in case.

"Killing us both on the road still leaves you dead, Amanda. Look, I get that you're scared. But if I wanted to kill you, I'd have done it back in the parking garage. Better yet, I'd have wired a surprise into Saul's ignition switch. But I don't want to kill you. It's a real badge. I'm a real cop. I just want some answers. Is that so hard for you to understand? If I have to arrest you, I will. I'm trying something different here."

They pull into the lot across the street and find a space facing the Marker Westpoint. Ray reaches over and puts the car in park. Turns off the engine. Takes the keys.

"Home sweet home away from home," he says. "Let's go."

"He's not here," she says, sounding defeated. "Is he?"

Ray opens the door into the rain.

"Let's go see."

FIFTY-SEVEN

We make our way through the hotel without talking. I keep her in front of me where I can see her, which leaves a whole world behind us to be concerned about. I make the most of every mirror and other reflective surface we pass. Nothing gives me any confidence that we didn't pick up a tail as soon as we hit the lobby.

I'm ready for her to make a break for it, gambling that I'm too old to keep up and too smart to shoot her in the back in a hotel hallway. She'd be right on both counts. I'm guessing it's Twill up in the room waiting for us that keeps her moving forward. I wonder where she got that idea.

Home away from home turns out to be tucked into the northwest corner of the ninth floor. I let her work the card key and push open the door. I pull Sig out of bed and keep him ready just in case there really is someone waiting inside. I step in slowly and quietly behind her and let the door close behind me.

The room looks and sounds empty. Bedroom ensuite on the right, tiny living room on the left. I give the place a quick tour, looking in the closet, the shower, and under the bed. Nobody but us paranoid chickens. Amanda soaks it all in, especially Sig, nosing into every place in the room large enough to hold an ugly surprise.

"That gun for Orland?" she asks.

"No. The gun's for me."

"You said he'd be here," she says accusingly. The rain has had its way with the dirty blonde hair, not to mention the creamy cashmere. The bed suddenly has my full attention. I want to tie her up and put her in the closet and go to sleep for a few days.

"You're right. I did. He'll be here. With any luck."

"How are you so sure?"

"Because I sent him a text asking him to drop whatever he's doing." I point at the loveseat in the living room. "Have a seat."

She sits. I take the chair next to her, putting one foot on the small table in front of us. There's an empty, uncomfortable looking chair on the other side of the table just like mine. Beyond the empty chair is the alcove that belongs to the front door. It's a straight shot from where I'm sitting. I keep Sig out and ready.

"A text?" she asks. "When did you do that?"

"On the elevator. You were busy sulking."

"So that's how it is with your boss? You text and he comes running?"

The very idea makes me laugh a little.

"No. No, that literally never happens. That's why I sent it from your phone. I'm guessing you know how to get his attention better than I ever could."

She manages to find some fresh indignation.

"*My* phone? You used *my* phone?"

"Yeah. I had a couple to choose from. I used the one without a security code. Next time you get a burner, you should think about that. You two already had quite a thread going. I just added another bubble."

"Fuck you. You can't do that."

"I think you mean I *shouldn't* do that. Which is true, but entirely different. You should be glad I did. I probably just killed any chance of using anything on that phone as evidence against you in court. Prosecutors have nightmares about trying to sell fruit from poisoned trees."

"The only reason you'd do that is if you know I haven't actually done anything wrong."

"Oh, sure you have. You're up to your neck in wrong, lady."

"So then why did you?"

Her voice has got some steel in it. There's a toughness here. I roll my head sideways, then look away again.

"Ever been fishing, Amanda?"

"Been awhile," she says.

"I'm going home with the biggest fish I can catch tonight. I'm betting that's not you."

"I'm the bait," she says with an unfriendly laugh.

"In cashmere, no less. You're not so dumb after all."

"Did he respond?"

I fish around in my coat pocket and pull out the phone for a look.

"Not yet."

I put the phone away and we sit in silence. Across the room, out the corner windows, the rain smears the world into disconsolate shades of gray and longing. Distant sirens wail, rising above the traffic, then fading away and rising again, like a long, deep wound that won't heal. The exhaustion behind my eyes is suffocating. My attention is threadbare, taking orders from an overtaxed nervous system. I'd walk a mile for a Camel on my knees if I had the chance. But I don't. Every part of me wants a drink. I point my gun across the room.

"What's in the mini fridge?"

"Water," she says. "Fruit. You can't have any."

Marlo liked to say that women want to be understood more than just about anything else in the world. More than they want to be loved and adored. Sometimes more than they want to live another day of not being understood. She liked to say that a little empathy will open doors in women that all the muscle and charm in the world cannot. That's some real cheek coming from a woman who refused – *refuses* – to be understood. I feel like I might understand Marlo less now than when I married her. But that doesn't make her wrong.

"Must be tough," I say. Amanda looks sideways.

"What."

"Working in a man's world, like you do. Taking shit all day from guys like Stan Papadopoulos. I don't pretend to know what goes on in financial firms like BSD, but I can't imagine it's a bastion of equality."

"Big feminist, are you?"

"I have an equally low opinion of both genders. I'm just saying you strike me as someone who has had to fight for it every step of the way. Forced to endure lugs like Stan just to keep your head above water."

Amanda Ramada Tate takes a long look.

"What happened to your stupid feminist face? A woman do that to you?"

She's aiming for savage sarcasm. The bullseye is a surprise.

"Kind of," I say with a nod, touching the bruise. It still hurts. "She had some help."

"Did you deserve it?"

"Kind of. Yeah. She was right to think so."

"Then good for her."

I lean back with a sigh that sounds like a dying wheeze. All I can do now is feel the acid building in my gut. I don't know the face of what comes next, even if I know the face of the man who does. Sitting and waiting for him doesn't help anything.

We pass the time like a couple of strangers on a bench, not talking as they wait for a bus. At the one-hour mark I'm starting to consider my next move. I need something that keeps Amanda close and useful without flirting with false imprisonment. I have ten minutes of bad ideas when I hear a card key beep from the other side of the door. We both do. We both tense instantly, muscles tightening like Spanish guitar strings.

But she's the only one who shouts.

"Orland!"

One stride is all it takes for the former head of the Chandler IAD to make it through the door and into view. My arm is up. Sig is ready for the finger twitch that puts a bullet into Twill's chest. But the boss is no dummy. He's come just as prepared to do the same.

FIFTY-EIGHT

His right arm is rigid, angling in and then ramming forward into the tiny living room like a tree branch. The Glock in his hand is no smaller or less deadly than Sig, but Twill's height makes the thing look like a toy. That helps a little. It shouldn't, but it does anyway. I try to keep the temperature down.

"Say we kill each other, LT. Then what?" I tilt my head sideways. "Who's gonna take care of Princess Charming over here?"

Twill's eyes tell the story of a man who is ready for almost anything, but who is not expecting me. He's still in the suit he was wearing when I saw him last. The hair on his face has gotten a little longer, but not enough to hide the swollen bruising, which is coming along nicely. We've got that in common at least. His coat is still dripping.

"You alright?" he asks her, not taking his eyes off mine. I can feel Amanda next to me nodding, too frightened now to speak.

"How about this," I say. "Let's talk first. Bring each other up to speed. Then trade bullets." I jerk my chin across the table. "We saved you a chair. Keep the gun if that helps."

Twill considers his options, looking over at Amanda for the first time. I give the telepathy experiment a few seconds and then interrupt.

"Okay, what is it with you two thinking that hotel rooms are good for shooting people? Fifty sets of eyeballs in that lobby saw me walk in here. I'm here to talk, boss, not mess up the carpet. Have a seat already."

Twill's muscles relax, just a little. He moves sideways toward the chair, his Glock still looking me in the eye. Then he sits.

"How's the office?" he asks. It comes out bitter and angry.

"In need of management," I say. "I can barely manage my own nap time."

"Then why don't you get back to that?"

"I'd like to. Believe me. I'm spending all my time looking for you. Keeping up with your girlfriend partner in crime over here. Convenient that you've got the card key to her hotel room. You two don't need to knock for each other I guess."

"I'm tired of this already. What do you want, Mack?"

"Let's start with a headline for you to chew on. Pete's dead. CPD found him in a runoff ditch outside Manhattan with two extra holes in his head. You're at the top of their list, LT. They've got warrants out for your house and your horse."

I watch him absorb the blow. His shoulders sag a little. That Glock is getting heavy.

"And you're here to bring me in. Is that it?"

"Might go that way, yeah. Pete was a stubborn pain in the ass, but he was also a good forensics tech and a good man who deserved better than a ride in a trunk out to Manhattan, Illinois."

"And you've decided I did that, have you?"

"Not my decision to make. That's why we give people their day in court. All I've decided is that you're in way over your head, Orland. And you're tall enough to make that alarming. Pretty clear at this point that CPD doesn't buy your story about what went down at Pete's house the other night."

"Guess not," he says. "Do you?"

"Let's just say the biggest thing in your favor is that the story seems too stupid for a smart person like you to make up."

"So then you believe I'm innocent."

"I didn't say that either. You're spending too much time doing shady things in the company of shady people to be innocent."

"What shady people? And how would you know anyway?"

"Well, your girlfriend here for starters. And I know because I've got eyes and because I've been in the guilt and innocence business for more than a minute or two. I've got a photo of you two looking pretty serious in Amanda's Sonata. I've also got a nice one of you standing in front of Pete's garage trying to poke a hole in his chest with your finger. No one looks very happy in that picture. It's not as good as the one of you coming out of the Blue Lotus."

"So." He nods slowly, repositioning the Glock. "You've been following me."

"Did you think I picked this hotel at random? Yeah, I've followed you once or twice. But I'm not the only one, LT. Other people are paying attention. The only one who doesn't know about you and Amanda here might be Wendy. She said you're in New Orleans rubbing shoulders with other Internal Affairs geeks." I give a nod toward Amanda. "I'll bet none of those boys can wear cashmere like she can. So either Wendy's in the dark or she's gunning for an Oscar. Either way, the closest you've been to New Orleans recently is O'Hare, which is where you stashed your Escalade."

That one catches him off guard. Twill tries to keep from reacting. He's too tired to pull that off.

"CPD doesn't know that yet," I add. "But they're gonna find it eventually. They're gonna look for Manhattan mud in those tire treads. They're gonna bring their UV flashlights, looking for drops of Pete. It'll happen sooner or later, boss. That might depend on me. So this might be the part where you try to convince me it should be later. Start talking."

"To you?" He tries to laugh. "I don't know who you're working for anymore."

"Funny, neither do I."

"I don't fucking trust you, Mack."

"Far as I'm concerned, LT, that makes this a level playing field. But you let me know if you want me to drop a dime to CPD. We can all sort it out together over bad coffee."

"Fuck you, Mack." He makes the point by pushing the Glock a little closer. "Don't work your tired routine on me. I'm not a fucking perp."

"Tell it to CPD. Think shooting me is going to help convince them?"

Twill leans back in the chair and closes his eyes. Hard to tell if he's thinking or sleeping. Next to me, Amanda is still gripping the arm of her chair hard enough to keep the blood out of her knuckles. Twill opens his eyes and leans forward, setting the Glock on the table.

"Orland ..." Amanda whispers his name. Twill holds up his hand.

"She's not my girlfriend, Mack."

I nose Sig down into his holster.

"No promises," I say. "But I'm listening."

FIFTY-NINE

"Amanda's my niece," he says. "My younger brother, half-brother, Walter …"

"Orland …" Amanda leans forward in her chair, like she wants to reach for him across the table. Twill shakes his head.

"I know. Not a lot of choice here, Mandy. We have to play this as it comes." Amanda takes in a lung full and lets it out slowly like she needs it to last. Twill looks back at me. "Walter died in his twenties. I made some promises. She's like a daughter." I can see the blood rising in his face in a tide of anger. "And, by the way, for your fucking information, Wendy knows everything. Okay? So fuck you for thinking otherwise."

"Okay," I say. "I'll take that for now."

We have to wait for the tide to recede again. Twill rubs his face in his hands.

"Mandy works at BSD Financial. She was an assistant to Dennis O'Toole. They were … *involved*, for a number of years. I didn't know that until … you know about Dennis, right? I mean …"

"I read the paper. I'm up to speed on Dennis."

"Right. So when Dennis and Carrie O'Toole hit the newspapers last year, I reached out to Mandy just to, you know, touch base. She gives me the basics. Tragedy. Never saw it coming. The whole firm is reeling in shock. That kind of thing. Couple of weeks pass and Mandy reaches out to me. She needs to talk. So we meet up for a drink."

"Okay."

"She's afraid and confused. CPD has put her through a couple of interviews. They weren't gentle. They want to do it a third time. She tells me that she and Dennis had been involved at some point for a few years, starting when they worked together at the Chicago Mercantile Exchange. Dennis was married. Obviously. The affair …"

"I'm sitting right here," says Amanda, irritated. "How about I tell my own story?"

Twill wheels on her. Maybe he's angry she helped him into this trap. Maybe it's something else. But Uncle Orland is pissed.

"How about you not say anything? Lest it be used against you. Understand?"

Amanda rolls her eyes and nods. Twill turns back to me. He's trying to find the place he left off. I give him some help.

"So the affair followed them both over to BSD Financial. That's when the boyfriend and his wife die in spectacular fashion. Then CPD shows up to work the jealous mistress angle to see if any of it sticks. That's how this business works."

"Right," says Twill. "Mandy's concerned they're going to try to pin it on her. I tell her they're just working on theories. I tell her I'll keep an eye on the investigation and let her know if we need to get her a lawyer."

Twill closes his eyes, knitting his eyebrows like he's trying hard to keep all the events in the right order. Same expression liars make when they're making up history on the fly.

"But there was a problem ..." he starts.

"Yeah. Problem is you can't keep an eye on an investigation that's being run by a different police department. So you close your office door and open a dummy IAD file. You use Quentin Young's name because he's dead enough not to need it anymore. You call up Sargent Kennedy at CPD Homicide and tell him that Chandler has a non-disclosable internal affairs angle on the O'Toole investigation. You ask if CPD will keep you in the loop as an interdepartmental courtesy. You know they're gonna give you scraps. They're not turning over their murder book. But at least it's something. Yeah, I got all that."

Twill is simmering.

"You want me to tell you what I know, or do you want to show off?"

"Both, if possible. If I've got something wrong, I want to know about it. What's next?"

He regathers himself. Picks up the thread.

"What's next is that Mandy seemed in serious trouble. She needed help."

"What kind of trouble?"

"She was being followed. Threatened."

"By whom?"

"I don't know. Caucasian, we think. Five-elevenish."

"Black boots," says Amanda.

"Black boots. Sitting outside her house three nights in a row."

"Four," Amanda corrects with a little attitude. She doesn't take quietly to being silenced.

"Four. Three one week, then one the next week. That she saw. Could have been more."

"Sitting outside."

"Yeah."

"On the curb? In his car?"

"Motorcycle."

"What, in the rain?"

"In the rain. We've been through them all. She thinks it's a Suzuki or a Mitsubishi."

"I don't know motorcycles," says Amanda.

"Face? Hair?"

"Helmet," says Twill. "Solid black."

"Plates?"

"None that I could see," says Amanda.

"Okay. Threatened how?"

"Phone call," says Twill. "Middle of the night. Male voice. Tells her he knows what she has …"

"*I know what he gave you,*" Amanda corrects again.

Twill points her back into silence.

"I know what he gave to you. You're going to die for what you have. Give the numbers to anyone, and I'll make it hurt."

"You saw the guy on the bike talking on the phone?"

"No," says Amanda. "But I could hear a siren outside my window and also through the phone at the same time. After he ended the call, I went to the window and looked. He was out there. He saw me looking. Then he took off."

"Okay. One call and nothing since?"

"Just the once," says Twill. "That was enough. She got herself this hotel room and hasn't been back to the house, except in the middle of the day to get things. I try to be there when that happens."

Amanda tilts forward in her chair.

"Yeah, I also bought a black wig and started driving Saul's Mercedes around," she says angrily. "Because I don't appreciate being followed. And because I'm fucking scared shitless. Okay?"

"Mandy," says Twill. "Amanda …"

"No, Orland." She jerks her thumb my direction. "This guy is going to try to make something horrible out of me, but the truth is I'm just fucking terrified, okay? I'm afraid for my fucking life. Living in a hotel room. Sleeping with a fucking gun. I fucking *hate* guns."

Twill sighs. "I bought her a gun. A little Bersa 380. Just in case."

"You're not worried she's going to shoot her ear off in the middle of the night?"

"Wasn't my idea," says Twill.

"I'm not an idiot," says Amanda.

"Right," I say. "Let's put a pin in that one. Where is the gun now?"

"In the car."

"The car? Which car?"

"My car. Under the driver's seat."

"So you lied."

"Yeah, I fucking lied." She pushes her face toward mine. A smile. Softer now. "Because I'm such a naughty girl."

"Mandy ..."

"You like naughty girls, Mack?"

I cut a look to Twill, just coming out of an extra slow blink.

"Oh, she's a peach, LT."

"I didn't know who you were," she says, back to normal. "I still don't." She looks across the table at Twill. "We don't, Orland. We don't know what the hell he wants. Who the fuck is he working for?"

"Okay, look." I take a cleansing breath. "This is a distraction we can't afford. The man on the phone mentioned numbers." It's the next obvious question. I try my best to sound befuddled. "What's all that about?"

Amanda and Twill look at each other. It's not something they consciously think about doing. They can't help it. It's the numbers that are connecting their brains. I can tell they both know exactly what I'm talking about. Question is whether they'll trust me enough to clue me in.

Twill looks back at me in silence. I know the expression. He's at a crossroads. We both are, sizing up the unknowns and weighing the options, juggling multiple alternate universes, none of which we see the same. In one universe, he's dirty and I'm clean, working a case and looking for answers preceding an arrest. In another universe, he's innocent and I'm dirty, working for the enemy, trying to frame him for something he didn't do, ready to leave him and his alleged niece dead in a hotel room if that's what it takes. The third option is that we're both dirty; he's trying to get away with murder and I'm just a clean-up hit man gunning for the original hit man, looking to assess the damage and extinguish a liability for the people that gave him the job. All three of those options make me someone who is looking to either put him in jail or put him in the ground.

The fourth possibility is maybe the least likely. Two guys, both innocent, looking for a way to trust each other despite every reason not to. Here I am asking them about numbers. It's the same thing other people are after. Bad people. I can feel Twill darkening as he thinks. I can feel him coalescing, condensing into an impenetrable ball of suspicion. He's at a crossroads in his story. He has to decide whether to consider me an enemy. I'm going to lose him unless I can loosen him up.

"You took a big risk hiring me," I say. "My history; my reputation. Probably corrupt and crazy as a loon to boot. Impossible to manage. Doesn't share. Doesn't trust. Won't take orders. Half in the bottle or dreaming about it most days. Stupid thing to do, really. When you think about it. When you think of how easily it can all come tumbling down around you and suddenly everybody who has any say in your life is asking what in the hell you were thinking, hiring me. Now I've got *your* job, and the OAG is taking a hard look at you for a change. Everybody's whispering. And here I've tricked you up into a hotel room with a gun and a woman you say is your niece. You've got to be wondering why you took the risk of bringing me on board. You've got to be wondering whether it was ever a good idea to trust me in the first place."

"I've already answered those questions, Mack," he says.

"Okay. Fair enough. But understand that I took my own risk in coming back to an organization that tarred and feathered me for something I never did and for being a man I never was. But I came back anyway. I came back because you made some promises and because you asked me to. That makes me a fool for trusting you. You know why?"

He keeps obstinately quiet. Two can play that game. I let the question hang until he answers it.

"Why?"

"Because the only person who would ever hire me under those circumstances is either a fool himself or someone who had a plan to use me as a fall guy for something bigger. I've never made you for a fool, LT. So I hope you'll understand when I say that's left me wondering if you've been using me from the beginning, paving the way for me to find that Russian doll and ruin the whole department with what was inside. That would make you and the monster you work for nothing short of diabolical."

"Monst ... You think *I* work for Big Man?" he asks incredulously.

"Who the hell is *Big Man*?" asks Amanda.

Twill ignores her, keeping his focus on me.

"Are you insane?"

"Maybe. Depends on who you ask. Fact is, LT, I tried to hide Suri from Big Man by sending her off to Bloomington in a trunk. You put Quentin Young on her tail and he tried to turn her into wallpaper. She's not so happy about that."

"You found her," he says, surprised. "You found Suri. Where is she?"

"That's something Big Man would dearly like to know. Isn't it?"

The question gets me an exasperated sigh.

"I'm not working for … You found her. That's all I was saying."

"She found me," I say. "She brought a friend to help her express her feelings. She blames me, see. She thinks I was working for the dark side. Fair enough, I guess, but it's just as fair for me to wonder the same about you."

"Quentin was a mistake," he blurts angrily. "I had no idea he …" Suspicion has taken a back seat to defensiveness. "You really think Big Man is pulling my strings?"

"Who the hell is Big …" Amanda tries again but Twill is busy defending himself.

"I wasn't … I wasn't …"

"Maybe you weren't and maybe you were. I was ready to give you the benefit of the doubt, LT. But the more I learn about you two, that hill keeps getting steeper. CPD wants you bad for Pete Chow. My guess is that leads them backward to Dennis and Carrie O'Toole."

He stares at me in silence like it's all too much to process. He swallows. His words are jumbled somewhere inside that long neck. This is the time not to let up.

"That sensation you're feeling around your chest? That's the mud getting deeper." I lean back, one foot on the table in front of me, keeping my eyes focused on his. "Now. Again. The man on the phone talked about numbers. What numbers?"

The words come unstuck, but his face is now red from the effort.

"We don't know what the hell he was talking about," he says. "It's gibberish. I don't have any fucking idea. Okay? Satisfied? Enough of this bullshit, Mack. We're out. We're done. Let's go, Mandy."

Twill tenses to stand, reaching. I push my foot down hard against the edge of the table, tipping it my way. The Glock slides away from him and drops to the floor at my feet. By the time Twill looks up, Sig is already out taking names. I let the table fall back to upright and step on the gun.

"Everybody keep your seat," I say. "We're not done."

Twill closes his eyes as his muscles go slack. Mandy, too, settles back down into her chair.

"To answer your question, LT, no, I'm not satisfied. Not by a long shot. Because I found the numbers you're pretending not to know anything about. I found them on *your* computer. I printed them out."

I let the bad news settle and pat my raincoat.

"I brought them with me. I might even know what some of them mean. So you'll need to factor that possibility in when you tell me what the hell is going on with you. In my experience, honest men make for bad liars. You might just be the worst liar I've ever met, Orland. Maybe that makes you an honest man. I'm risking everything, including doing time as an after-the-fact accessory to murder, trying to figure you out once and for all. But I'm fresh out of time, boss. I'm at the end. Understand? Lie to me again at your own risk. If it happens again, I'm taking you in and I'm sharing everything I know with CPD Homicide."

Outside, another siren rises and falls, scratching the glass from out in the rain. I reach down and pick up Twill's Glock. I eject the magazine and clear the chamber. Then I toss him the empty gun.

"Your move."

SIXTY

"Dennis gave her something."

Orland Twill speaks now like a man chastened. Any tone to suggest that he is, or once was, Ray's superior officer is all but gone. He's been backed into a corner; forced to make up his mind about who Ray is in the world. Forced to choose between alternate realities. So now he's chosen, and the words come unconflicted, as if from a man with very little left to lose.

Ray holsters his gun and listens. Tries to keep his eyes open and his mouth shut. Looks to me like he's struggling to do both.

"This is a week before he and Carrie died," says Twill. "Dennis asks Mandy to take his shirts to the dry cleaner. The Blue Lotus."

"They weren't just some dirty shirts," says Amanda.

"She can tell it all better than I can," sighs Twill without looking, apparently no longer able to muster the energy it will take to keep her quiet.

"Tell me about the shirts," says Ray, looking to her.

"They weren't dirty. I picked up Dennis' dry cleaning. Not all the time, but it wasn't uncommon. I did whatever I could to help him, especially when he was under a lot of stress." She splays five creamy, red-tipped fingers against her chest. "*I* loved him. Carrie hated him. Carrie used him for sport. You think she didn't have her own fuckbuddies on the side? She had more than one. Dennis said she used the Cayman house as a love shack. Dennis never used the Cayman house. Dennis had me. Just me." Her eyes well up and redden at the lids. Strands of hair are stuck to the side of her face. She pulls them free. "And I loved him. I did everything I could for him, including take in his fucking dry cleaning."

Ray moves his index finger in slow circle, coaxing her forward.

"Anyway." Amanda sniffs, pulling herself together. "This time the shirts he gave me were the same three I had just picked up for him a few days before. They were still hanging on the back of the office door where I'd put them. He stripped off the plastic and handed them to me and said he wanted them dry cleaned again."

"He wanted the clean shirts recleaned," says Ray, like he's testing his own hearing.

"Yeah. I didn't understand but I just did what he asked. He was in a really bad place at that point. Carrie's divorce action was breaking him. He loved her and it was just killing him. Two days earlier her attorneys had taken Dennis' deposition. It was … it was fucking brutal. He was barely functioning, so I didn't ask any questions."

"So you go to the Blue Lotus."

"I go to the Blue Lotus and give them the shirts. They give me a set of shirts back. Which was really weird because I didn't think Dennis had anything there to pick up. I bring the shirts back to the office and hang them on the back of Dennis' door. Dennis isn't there, but when I see him next, he asks me for the dry-cleaning ticket. I'd thrown it away because, you know, who cares, right? I paid, but it was only a few bucks, and I don't care about getting reimbursed. But he got all angry and we had to go rooting through the trash in my office to find it."

Amanda's eyes seem to lose their focus. Her fingertips submerge themselves inside her dirty blonde forest where they can worry and fidget in secret back behind her neck.

"He was irritated a lot with me at the end. We hadn't been, you know, *involved* for a while, but I think he blamed me for setting Carrie off on her rampage. Like it hadn't been his idea in the first place."

"The affair was Dennis' idea?" Ray asks.

Her eyes come back to the present. She looks uncomfortably at Twill next to her. Then she nods.

"He didn't have to ask twice."

"Okay, so you give him the ticket and what, he reimburses you?"

"No. He looked at it for a long time. I asked if anything was wrong, but he said no and tossed it on the desk. He excused himself to a meeting and I didn't see him again until that night."

"That night. You mean after work?"

"He called me late. Asked me to meet him at a hotel."

"A hotel. What hotel?"

"Residence Inn. Downtown. I asked why not just meet over at his place. I didn't get a good answer. He was leasing this place in South Loop. Carrie had kicked him out of his own goddamned house two months earlier. I'd offered him a spare room in my house, but I knew he wouldn't like how that looked in the divorce. So I helped him find a place that would work until he figured out a more permanent solution. He was hoping he might reconcile with Carrie. I knew there was no chance of that. Anyway, I was surprised to get the call from him at all. But at a cheap hotel? After ten? Something was up. But I got in the car and came over."

"You never should have done that," says Twill.

"We've pretty well covered that already," she says sharply. "Don't you think?"

Twill exhales through his nose, crosses his arms and stares up at the ceiling.

"You go to the hotel," says Ray. "What happens?"

"We kind of … He needed me. He felt alone. He needed someone to …"

"You did what comes naturally for two people looking to use each other. I get it."

"We weren't using each other. We …"

"Let me rephrase the question, Amanda," says Ray. "What happened that I give a shit about?"

"He gave her a flash drive," says Twill. "Two of them."

Still looking at Amanda, Ray points across the table, as if Twill's words are still hovering in the air.

"That," says Ray. "Flash drives. I care about that. Tell me."

"He handed me two flash drives. They looked identical except one was black and one was white. He told me he needed me to put the white drive into locker 717 at the We-Lock on South Spaulding out in La Villita. He told me the code was 4398. He wrote it on my palm so I wouldn't forget it."

She looks at her left palm and rubs it gently with her thumb.

"It's gone now," she says, clearly meaning *he's gone now.*

"What about the other drive?"

"He asked me to keep the black drive at my place. Someplace safe. I asked him what was on the drives, but he wouldn't tell me anything. He said they held information that Carrie and her attorneys wanted. The information did not belong to them. He wanted to keep it private."

"Why couldn't he put the drive in the locker himself?"

"I asked him that. He said Carrie's lawyers had him under surveillance. That's why he didn't want me coming to his place. He was pretty sure someone was watching it."

"So what'd you do?"

Twill spits out a disbelieving laugh and answers for her.

"She just did it. No more questions. No suspicion. She just did what this asshole asked. Nothing sketchy here. No, no."

"I loved him," she says softly. "He needed my help."

"And he sure loved you, didn't he?" says Twill. "He …"

Ray cuts him a sharp look.

"Don't make me put you in separate rooms. No disrespect, LT, but shut the fuck up and let her talk." He turns back to Amanda.

"What'd you do?"

"I went home and hid the black drive in my house."

"Come on," says Ray. "You didn't stick it in a computer? Open it up?"

"No. He told me not to. He told me it would log in my IP address. They'd know I'd seen it."

"They. Carrie's lawyers?"

"Yes. He said that would make everything worse. He made me promise."

"Where'd you hide it?"

"In a bag of coffee beans."

"Okay. Next."

"First thing the next morning I drove out to the We-Lock in La Villita. The code Dennis gave me opened locker 717. There was nothing inside. I put the drive in the locker, made sure it was locked and left." She looks up at Ray. "Well. I pretended to leave."

"Why is that?"

"There was a man there, standing at a locker at the end of the row. It seemed wrong, somehow. He was short and unshaven. Shoulder-length greasy hair. Long, dingy-green winter coat. He was fiddling with the locker combination, like he couldn't remember his code. We were the only two people in that unit of the facility, Unit D on the end, and I'm always on alert in those situations. He just didn't seem like he belonged there. So when I was done, I walked down the hall and turned the corner for the exit, but then I stopped and went back to look."

"And?"

"And the guy was at locker 717. I watched him open it and take the drive."

"What'd you do?"

"I hustled out of the building for my car. I heard him open the door behind me. I was, like, so terrified. I imagined him coming up behind me and … I don't know … hurting me. He just put out that kind of vibe. I pretended to take a phone call. I turned around as I reached my car and could see that he was nowhere near me. He was headed to the other side of the parking lot."

"Did you see what kind of car he got into?"

"Yes. A dirty gray Nissan."

"An older model Rogue," says Twill. "Wisconsin Plates. They came back to an Edith Michaels. I did some looking. Edith reported the car stolen two years ago."

"What happened next?" asks Ray.

"I drove past him on my way out. He was sitting in the car, engine off. He was bent into the back seat, working on something. I couldn't tell what. I drove up to the next block and waited. Five minutes later he drove past me. I followed him."

"You followed him," repeats Ray. "Because you were curious."

"Because I figured Dennis would want to know that someone had taken the drive. And, yeah, I was curious. You're damn right I was."

"Where'd he lead you?"

"All the way out past Stickney, near Midway Airport. A place called Lincoln Metalworks and Propane Supply. I kept my distance. I stopped more than a half a block away. I couldn't see much. He parked and got out of the car carrying a white propane tank, you know, like you hook up to a patio grill. He came back out empty-handed and was driving again in less than a minute. I lost him on the freeway. I came back home."

Ray turns to Twill. "I'm guessing you looked into the place."

"You guess right," says Twill. "When I heard this whole story, I went out to the We-Lock first. Tried locker 717. The code he gave her no longer works. My research shows that We-Lock is a Delaware corporation that franchises all over the US and Canada. The franchisee for the We-Lock in La Villita is XXL Enterprises, LLC."

No one else hears Ray's heart skip a beat. Just me.

"Same company that owned the Castle Hotel out in Aurora," says Ray. "And Windy Wharf Seafoods."

"Right," says Twill. "And the Blue Lotus Dry Cleaners."

"Your visit to the Lotus," says Ray. "I have the photo. You were researching."

Twill nods. "You thought I was what … laundering cash?"

"Associating with known criminals," says Ray. "Abetting a criminal enterprise."

"Other than you, who's concluded that the Blue Lotus was part of a criminal enterprise?"

"Same people that caught you coming out the front door."

"And who is that, exactly?"

"Her name's Frenchie Marie. That's what I call her anyway. Still don't know what she calls herself. She's not from around here. Maybe more on her later. I'm still on you and the Blue Lotus. You were researching."

"I went in and opened an account," says Twill. "I started using them just to see if I could learn anything."

"Did you?"

"I never bumped into Mayor Royce, if that's what you're asking," says Twill. "They use a lot of starch, but they get the stains out."

"And you never told me any of this? Even as you were shutting down my investigation into what the hell that place is all about?"

"Your investigation? It was my investigation being conducted at your insistence and for your own secret, twisted reasons. It was your fever dream and my name on the goddamned door."

"*My* fever dream?" Ray laughs just enough to cover the anger. "You got your picture taken coming out of the Lotus long before I ever came to you with concerns about that place."

"You were *under* investigation, Mack. OAG was looking at the whole department. How does it look if I'm sanctioning an off-the-books investigation by the guy who single-handedly brought the department to its knees?"

"You could have told me, LT."

"I didn't trust you, Mack. At that point you were nothing but trouble for me. I was done. I'm still done."

Ray chews the inside of his lip. He wants to argue. He pivots instead.

"We-Lock," says Ray. "More on that."

"XXL is the franchisee for eighteen other We-Locks in Illinois, Wisconsin and Michigan. I stopped searching, but you can bet there's more. I also drove out to Lincoln Metalworks and Propane Supply. I bought a tank of propane. Every tenth refill is free. Want to know who owns them?"

"XXL," says Ray.

"XXL."

"That's a lot of rotten eggs in one basket." Ray turns back to Amanda. "So I'm assuming you reported all of this back to Dennis?"

"I was planning to," she says unhappily. "I couldn't find him. Nobody at work knew where he was. He was a no-show the next day. I called him a lot. He didn't answer. I went out to his place in South Loop. I let myself in. He wasn't there. No sign of him. The next day the police found him in Carrie's driveway."

"How much of this have you told CPD?"

"None of it."

"None?"

"Nothing about the flash drives. I was afraid. The phone call threats really scared me. Orland called after the news about Dennis. I put him off, but then I called him back. We went for a drink. I didn't know what to do."

"You gave him the black flash drive?"

"Yes."

Ray turns to Twill.

"And you copied it to your work computer, along with photos of the dry-cleaning ticket she brought back for Dennis and the ticket you got for your own shirts."

"You've been digging," says Twill. "And in my back yard."

"Yeah. I'm halfway to China, LT." Ray jerks his head toward Amanda. "Why didn't you make any of this official?"

"Didn't feel safe," says Twill. "Didn't trust local law."

"You're starting to sound like me."

"God forbid," says Twill.

"What tipped you?"

"A few things all together. Kennedy at CPD Homicide stopped giving me the time of day. You were right that I never anticipated they'd open their murder book on the O'Tooles, but he went from giving a little information to giving me the finger in record time. I called up my IAD counterpart over there. Brice Koning. Good guy. I trust him. We go way back. I asked about Kennedy. I told him I was trying to get information on the O'Toole investigation. Brice turned into a clam. IAD over there clearly has a file on Kennedy. I didn't expect him to tell me anything confidential and he didn't. But I got the message: Stay clear of Kennedy and the O'Toole case."

"Okay. Anything else?"

"Yeah. I was being followed. Whoever it was is good. Too good to be some lowlife who likes sitting out in the rain on a bike. Different cars. Running patterns. Day and night. They were cops. At first I figured OAG was trying to close up a net. But then that didn't feel right either. Wendy called and told me there was a guy looking in our mailbox. She ran out to confront him, but he had a car waiting and was gone. She didn't recognize him. That's not a legitimate surveillance op, Mack. Certainly not the OAG boy scouts. The people who are on me are cops working off the books."

"You know, LT, when I say stuff like that, people call me paranoid. Crazy even. They tell me I'm low on sleep and high on anxiety. When's the last time you had a hot bath and a good night's sleep?"

"It's not like that," says Twill angrily.

"Maybe not," says Ray. "I'm still not convinced. Being followed wasn't enough to convince you to keep this from the police department for which you work."

"Worked," spits Twill. "You mean the police department that gave my job to *you*? Because no small part of my mistrust was OAG changing its investigation focus to *me* and then suddenly *you* ending up in *my* chair. The whole game seemed rigged. I didn't trust Chicago and I didn't trust Chandler."

"You actually think I wanted that job? I'm a disaster in your chair, LT. You had to know that was the Chief's call."

"The Chief's a good man. An honest cop. He brought me in. But he's too easy to manipulate. And his spine's too soft. I saw you with an agenda. You were carrying water for someone who wanted me out. Someone was angling to put you in control of Chandler IAD. That's big-time access for someone. You lied to Brewster and OAG so that they suddenly think I'm the problem and they start looking to hang the Russian doll fiasco around my neck."

"So your imagination made a run for the border," says Mack.

"Oh, I imagined a lot of things. I imagined the Attorney General made a phone call to the honorable Mayor of Chandler, or maybe directly to the Chief. The Chief folds like a cheap suit. He yanks me out by the short hairs and there you are, with a smile on your face, waiting in the wings with more years on the force than anyone else in IAD. So you end up in my chair."

"Quite a plot," says Ray. "I've got a half-written novel I'd like you to finish for me."

"You're saying none of that's true?" It's more of a challenge than a question.

"I'm saying the part about me carrying water and wanting your job isn't true. Also the part about the smiling."

"Seemed plausible enough to me," says Twill. "Still does, to tell you the truth. My point is that I wasn't trusting local law." He takes in an extra helping of air and lets it out. "I've been working with the feds."

"The Bureau?"

Twill nods. Amanda snorts in muted disgust.

"Trying to," says Twill.

"They're worthless," says Amanda.

"Slow," says Twill. "Maybe not worthless. I'm trying to convince them that they need to step in. It's a hard sell. They think it belongs with CPD Homicide. It does feel like they're slow rolling me, but I get that it's a big ask. They're being careful."

"You gave them the black drive?"

Twill nods.

"And?"

"If they can make heads or tails of whatever's on that thing, they haven't told me."

"So you're hauling your cookies over to that concrete monstrosity out on West Roosevelt and singing songs about corrupt local law enforcement? My name ever come up?"

Twill purses his lips and looks down at the table. He nods.

"Now and then. They're not impressed. Not yet."

Ray considers whether to let the next bit out into the room. He rolls it around in his head. Out it comes.

"You wouldn't happen to be working with an Agent Murray, would you? John Murray?"

Twill's eyes sharpen.

"He's been in the room," he says. "Yeah. How'd you know that?"

"The feds aren't coming to your rescue, LT. They aren't your friends."

"What the fuck are you telling me, Mack?"

"I'm telling you that your best hope right now is a washed-up homicide cop pretending to run IAD in your absence and who's *this close* to giving it all up for a Camel and a shot. That's me, in case you hadn't guessed, not the FBI."

"But …"

"Forget them. Understand me? Stop talking to the feds. They've got a leak."

"A leak? A fucking … A leak to who?"

"That's a story for another day. You've got just enough time on your meter to tell me what you're leaving out, Orland."

"Nothing. I'm not leaving out anything, goddamnit."

Ray is quiet for too many seconds. He leans forward in his chair, bringing his eyes closer to Twill's.

"I've been at this game too long, boss. You're leaving out the best part, aren't you? You keep steering around it like a pothole in the road. I'm not buying a word you're selling until you tell me the rest of it. You can either tell me now or I can read it later in the transcripts."

"What the hell are you…"

"Pete Chow, boss. I'm talking about dear, dead Pete. You need to start talking about him too."

SIXTY-ONE

"I did not kill Pete Chow," says Twill, trying to keep the pleading out of his voice. I lean back and look at him like I'm ready for a story.

"Convince me."

"Mandy's story," he says. "The guy watching her house. The threatening call about something Dennis had given her. It made me think Dennis didn't kill himself. Just a feeling."

"You mean a hunch, LT? A feeling unsupported by any evidence? Like the kind you always like to bust my balls about?"

Twill's face tightens, like he's a busy man with lots to do. For a second, I see my old boss.

"You want this or not?" he asks.

I gesture for him to continue.

"When the M.E. report issued, I got a copy and read through it. Something about it just didn't hang together. I'm not a murder cop, but …"

"The bat," I say. Twill looks up at me like I just guessed his weight.

"Yes," he says. "The bat."

"The bat?" Amanda's confused. I try to clear things up.

"Think baseball, not vampires. They found the murder weapon stuffed under a tarp in the back of Dennis' Tesla. Louisville Slugger."

She's still cloudy. "Yeah, okay?"

"If your plan is a little batting practice with your estranged wife before you kill yourself on the driveway, why try to hide the bat under a tarp?"

Amanda's busy thinking and blinking. I turn from her back to Twill.

"So you didn't like murder-suicide."

"No," he says. "I wanted Pete to clarify it."

"Why not go to the M.E. himself?"

"Because Pete did the actual forensics analysis. That's what I cared about. The M.E. is too far up the chain. I'd only met Pete twice before, maybe three minutes total. I knew the chances were slim that he'd open up to me, but I tried anyway. I made the trip up to his office. He essentially blew me off. He didn't think it was appropriate for me to be asking questions of him. Told me that all questions needed to be addressed to the Medical Examiner, not the Senior Forensics Tech. He all but threw me out of his office. Dead end."

"You say that like you don't quite believe it."

"It was the way he acted. He seemed afraid. Not just that he didn't *want* to talk, but that he was *afraid* to talk. He stopped talking every time someone in the hallway passed his office. The door was closed, but he still didn't like it. He wanted me to think he was just standing on procedure, but his nerves spun up way too fast for this to be about protocol."

"What'd you do?" I wave my hand at him like it's after a fly. "Never mind. I know exactly what you did. You went back to HQ, closed yourself up in your office and did some thinking. You asked yourself if there was anything out there that might make Pete Chow do something he didn't want to do, like turning a double into a single plus a suicide. Then you remembered all the press Andy Chow got when he scattered a bunch of cheerleaders all over an intersection. You did some research into Andy's hearing status. You even sent an email to Janice Kingfisher with the IPRB, trying to find out who else might have expressed interest in Andy's parole. Janice introduced you to a brick wall. I already know all of that, LT. The question I have is when you figured out that Pete's final forensics report had an earlier version."

Twill shakes his head to himself. Then he looks at me. I look in those eyes and I see a man who just might be more tired than I am. He's not too tired to show a little surprise at what I know. I like that in any man I'm trying to convince that I know more than I actually do.

"I found that out two days after I went to see Pete the first time. I kept reading the report and then one night I paid attention to that tiny footer on the last page." He shakes his head in disbelief. "V2. It was right there the whole time. Version 2."

"V2," I repeat. "May as well stand for visit two. Let's talk about that."

"Right. Yeah, I paid Pete a second visit. I went to his house."

"Standing under the eaves of his garage to stay out of the rain."

"How do you know that, Mack?" He's baffled. He looks to Amanda for some kind of help. Then he looks back to me. "How did you even know to be there?"

"I didn't and I wasn't. I have a source with a good camera and an eye for composition. He got you, Pete, and your Escalade, all in the same shot."

"This Marie person again?"

"Don't worry about that part just yet. I'm more interested in why you chose to bother the man at his house after dark."

"I wanted to have the discussion away from Pete's office. I thought maybe his work environment was getting in my way. Shutting him down. I wanted to put my concern squarely in front of him, in private, and get his reaction. I wanted to press him about the first version of the forensics report. I wanted him to know that if he was being pressured over threats about Andy, or himself, or hell, anything, I don't know, *anything*, that he could trust me. I asked him if cops were involved. I told him that my whole professional existence is about confidentially investigating cops who cross the line."

"How'd that sit?"

"He laughed."

"Not sure I've ever seen a laugh come out of Pete Chow. He laughed like it was funny?"

"No. Like it was preposterous. Like I was a shark promising to keep him safe inside my mouth. He told me that I'd forgotten who I was talking to. That he's spent his entire career around cops and that he doesn't trust any of them. Including me. The man was afraid, Mack. It wasn't that he didn't trust me. It was like he was afraid of me. *Me.* I told him that I didn't like the baseball bat under a tarp in the back of Dennis' Tesla and that made me suspect his conclusions."

"That move the needle at all?"

"No."

"So that's it?"

"I told him if he did not sit down and talk with me, in confidence, that I was going to sit down with the Chicago M.E. and propose that we have someone, maybe the Chandler M.E., conduct an independent examination of his forensics report. I was talking out of my ass at that point. I was grasping at anything."

"And, knowing Pete, he took it as a threat and dug in his heels."

"Yeah. It got testy. He didn't budge. But I came away more certain than ever that something was rotten and that cops were involved somehow. It validated my instinct not to go local with any of this. I think it was the way he laughed when I promised I could protect him."

"And you shared all of this with the feds?"

"They took a lot of notes," he says, nodding. "Said they'd get back to me. The feedback loop is long and slow with them. I kept following up. Daily. My contact over there said he was having trouble selling it. Not enough evidence to meet their internal standards for local compromise. They kept the door open. Told me to bring them whatever else I might find, but …"

Twill shrugs, half defeat, half anger. Then his eyes resharpen.

"You say they've got a leak. To whom? How do you know this?"

I shake my head.

"Not now. Stay on track. Pete Chow. Visit number three."

"Goddamnit, Mack …"

"Visit number three." I cock an eyebrow. "Boss."

He stares at me with eyes that used to belong to a man who could threaten my job. He wants to order me around. He wants to take me off a case or suspend me or just pound his big desk with his big fist. My eyes are bloodshot and weary, but they no longer belong to a subordinate, and he knows it. Eventually he loosens up the muscles in his face.

"I got a call. Pete said he needed to talk. He sounded upset. Scared upset. He asked me to come by his office around nine o'clock. So I did. The place was shut down except for security. I told the guard that I'm there to meet with Pete Chow. He tells me that Pete's not there. I asked if he knew where he was. The guard wouldn't say. He asks if he should leave a message. I declined. I left and called Pete's number. No answer. I went directly to Pete's house thinking either I misheard or that Pete misspoke. It never made sense that he wanted to meet at his office anyway."

"Not unless someone wants a reliable witness that you were looking around for Pete Chow the night he died."

"Christ," breathes Twill, closing his eyes.

"Keep going."

"I got to the house. It was dark. I go to knock on the door, but it's already partly open. There's a living room to the right of the entry. I walk in and there's a guy in a mask and gloves bent over an antique rolltop desk."

He gives me the same story he gave CPD, right down to the gun that doesn't fire and the mystery man's escape out the back. It all rings about as hollow now as the first time I read the report.

"I'm sure he was white," Twill adds. "I could see the skin around his eyes and I saw his wrist. Medium build and height. Not much else."

"So we're looking for a medium-sized guy with white wrists. How long can that take?"

"You weren't there," he says, exasperated. "It's all I got. It happened fast. And he could fight. The man had some moves. Wendy thinks he must have had MMA training."

"Wendy would know. She's trained a lot of cops. Not you, I guess."

"She's tried. I'm a desk cop. I've kicked myself a thousand times for not taking my gun in with me. It wasn't … I thought it was just going to be a conversation with Pete. And he was already on edge enough. I didn't want another confrontation with him. I didn't want him to … I wasn't … I'm not that kind of police. All I do is ask questions."

"Why'd you call it in to CPD?"

"Because it was my duty to do so."

"But you're afraid of local law. That's what set you on this path to start with."

"What choice did I have? I've just had the shit kicked out of me in a dead man's house. How suspicious do I look if I don't call it in? I hadn't thought about the security guard until you mentioned him, but that only proves the point. They'd have figured out I was there eventually. Hiding it only makes me look worse. And I hadn't done anything wrong. I called the fucking police and gave them an honest report."

"And now they're coming for you."

"What, you think I should have run? Not report it and find someplace to hide?"

"What have you been doing, LT, if not hiding?"

"Trying to get federal law enforcement assistance. Like I fucking said."

"Report said you saw no vehicles near the property that night. Pete's place is elevated and isolated from the surrounding neighborhood. How'd this guy get there? How'd he leave?"

"Must have had a car parked on a lower street and walked up. Or in the cul-de-sac. He went out the back then beat it on foot to wherever he parked."

"You say you got to the house and the door was open."

"Right. Not all the way. Cracked."

"CPD says they found signs of forced entry through a front window."

"Yeah."

"Okay, so who breaks a window to get in and then leaves the front door open as they clean up a crime scene and rummage around in a desk?"

"I don't know, Mack. Maybe before I showed up he, or they, had been in and out the front door after taking Pete away. I don't know. Sloppy, but not inconceivable."

"The driveway is fifty feet from the front door, LT. Who doesn't hear you drive up? Who doesn't hear you close the door of that goddamned behemoth you drive? You telling me the mask this guy was wearing kept him from hearing? Maybe he was deaf. Was he deaf, boss? This guy gets better and better. Hollywood would have given him one arm. Did he have both arms?"

"Damnit, Mack! I'm telling you what happened. You wanted the truth and I'm telling you the fucking truth."

"Then you've got a problem, LT, because this truth comes off with a little soap and water."

"I'm lying? You think I'm fucking lying?" He's starting to look like a thermometer in July. He kicks the volume up a notch. "I'm fucking making all this up?"

His hands grip the arms of his chair like he wants to break them. He fumes at me from across the tiny table.

Time to make a decision. He's done. It's all over unless I pivot.

So I do.

"No," I say, eventually. "I don't. I think you're telling me the only truth you can see from where you're sitting."

"Then maybe you should tell me what the fuck is actually going on. Let's start with this Frenchie person. Marie."

Twill's phone seconds the motion. I don't answer either of them. Twill stabs his hand inside his coat, then puts it to his ear.

"What's happening?" he asks. I watch his expression darken as his long face seems to fold in on itself. "Well. Shit. Call Earnie. He needs to be there. There's nothing to find. Relax. Honey? There's nothing to find. Me? Oh, I'm sitting in a fucking hotel room with Mandy and Mack playing a game of who do you believe. Ray Mackey. I don't know. Let me ask." He lowers the phone and looks at me. "It's Wendy. CPD's at my house with a search warrant. She wants to know if I should trust you."

The moment of truth elongates between us as Amanda looks on. Time to make a decision. Pick a direction. He's got to do the same. I give him a nod.

"Mack thinks he's on our side," he says into the phone, still looking at me. "Guess we'll see. Call Earnie. I'll call you back." Twill ends the call. "Thoughts?"

"Earnie Davidson?"

"Yeah."

"Good lawyer. My wallet was never that fat. He's dialed in?"

"Sixty percent," says Twill. "I reached out when I got the boot. He knows I'm talking to the feds. I think he should be at the house to supervise the search."

"Absolutely," I say. "You should be there too."

"That's the same as turning myself in," he says. "To fucking CPD."

"Yeah. It is. I doubt they've got an arrest warrant yet. But making them get one and then come find you is not going to help you any."

Twill and Amanda stare at each other. If she's got an opinion, she doesn't share it. I keep working on my own.

"Appearances matter, LT. You called them from Pete's house. You show up for the search of your house. You've contacted the feds. That's not a man with something to hide. Earnie can take it from there. No sense in looking like you're on the run. Don't make them hunt for you. This jig is up, boss. It's already bad enough as it is."

"Meaning?"

"Meaning, you're going to have to tell them where to find the Escalade. They're going to find Manhattan mud in the treads and they're going to find a murder weapon with your prints inside. I wouldn't say a word until you've told Earnie everything. But showing up to be counted will send a message."

"Earnie will want to talk with you too."

"Long as he doesn't charge me."

"What about Mandy?" he asks.

"Isn't that a good question," I say, looking at Amanda and back again. "For now, we'll be working together behind the scenes to find some answers."

"What?" she blurts. "Like hell. I don't trust him, Orland."

"I need her to cooperate, LT." I look at him hard. "You understand what I'm saying?"

Twill closes his eyes. Nods. Turns to Amanda.

"I want you to trust me, Mandy."

"I already do, Orland. It's him I ..."

"Then do everything he says. Everything. If you make it difficult for him, you make it difficult for me. And that's going to make it difficult for you. Understand? Promise me."

Amanda stares at him, mouth open. She gets ahold of herself soon enough. She looks at me like I'm a bum on her stoop asking to use the bathroom. Then she looks back at her uncle.

"Fine. Yeah, whatever. Fine."

I lean back and look at them. Twill and Amanda Ramada Tate, finally in hand. If I had a drink nearby, I'd propose a toast to small victories. This is the first time in a while that things are going the way they're supposed to.

That's when my phone rings.

SIXTY-TWO

Ray is not interested in another interruption. He pulls out his phone only to glower at it, ready to put it away again. He doesn't. The feeling in his gut won't let him.

"Not a good time," he says. Raj Malik sounds ready for that.

"Don't hang up. I'm parked outside the hotel."

"This again? Why are you …"

"Shut up for a second," he says. "Let me talk. I stayed on you from the parking garage. I wasn't the only one. Black Plymouth. MER912. That's Monster Elastic Rooster …"

"Raj."

"It's parked across the street in the same lot you parked in."

"How many inside?"

"Tinted windows, so it's hard to tell, but I'm pretty sure there was just one. Now there's three. Two other guys just rolled up in a blue, beat to hell Toyota, parked, and climbed in the back of the Plymouth. That's why I'm calling. I figured one guy is good for following. Three guys … that's for something else. There's also a guy outside the entrance of the hotel just looking at his phone. So that probably makes four."

"Any sign they're coming in?"

"Not yet."

"That might change. Call me. Stay in your car."

Ray ends the call. Twill and Amanda are both looking.

"We've got a situation," says Ray. "Someone's here to give you a ride."

"Me?" Twill tenses. "Who?"

"Three possibilities. It's either undercover CPD looking to roll you up while the boys with badges search your house. Or it's Big Man's goons, with badges or without, looking to shut you up before CPD proper gets a chance.

"Big Man?" Twill's voice is suddenly weary. "Ray …"

"Yes, Big Man," says Ray. "Isn't it always?"

"With you, yes. Or?"

"Or it's Frenchie Marie's foreign intelligence jarhead brigade looking to shake you for answers before you disappear beneath a dogpile of local prosecutors."

"Foreign intelligence? Are you shitting me?"

"You wish. How happy would CPD be if they had to extradite you from France before they could prosecute you?"

"France?"

"Luxemburg. Spain. Italy. Maybe it's the UK that wants you. I don't really know. Doesn't matter. Getting you out of the country was never really in the cards. You're too tall to fit in a suitcase. Plan B is to get some answers with a rubber hose and pair of pliers. They all know how to do that."

"They can't …"

"Sure they can. It's easy when no one knows they're here. Well. Except maybe their buddies at the Bureau, but they're way too busy looking the other way."

"What foreign intelligence service?"

"You haven't been listening."

Twill is shaking his head so hard it's in danger of coming off.

"I don't even …Why …"

"Because you're a steppingstone to Big Man. They think you're connected."

"Me?"

"They think so. They think they can convince you to give him up."

"Big Man? They think I'm going to deliver Big … If I could do that, I'd have done it a long time ago and taken the promotion. This is fucking absurd."

Ray leans back. Crosses his arms.

"Let me ask you an important question, LT."

Twill pinches his forehead with his fingers like he's trying to snuff out the candle of his own consciousness. It doesn't work. He looks at Ray. Waits.

"Can you tell me what spoofing is," asks Ray.

"Spoofing?"

"Spoofing."

"Spoofing?"

Twill looks to his niece for help. But Amanda's no help to anyone. Turns out she's allergic to the very sound of that word. *Spoofing.* Its effect is paralytic. Nothing moves except the rapid dilation of her irises. She doesn't even acknowledge the question.

Ray's watching Twill as intently as he's listening for the answer. He's looking for any reliable tell from a bad liar. All he gets is an honest man lost at sea.

"I have no fucking idea, Mack," says Twill. "Spoofing?"

"Good answer."

"What's it mean?"

"It means I'm in your corner to the very end, boss. We've got to figure out how to get you out of this hotel." Ray stands, scooping the clip and the bullet off the table. He hands them to Twill and walks to the window. "How'd you get here?"

"Rental," says Twill, reassembling his Glock. "I parked two blocks away. Followed a delivery guy in through the kitchen. I was careful. No one was on me. There was no way …"

"Save it. We were the ones with the tail, LT. Whoever it is was on Amanda's parking garage. They knew that the best way to find you was to follow her." Ray turns away from the rain-streaked glass and shoots a glance to Amanda. "Guess we should have taken Saul's Mercedes."

Amanda sniffs out an agreement with a single head nod. Ray pulls the number out of his pants pocket. He lights up his phone and dials. The voice at the other end is deep and to the point.

"What."

"Put her on," says Ray.

"You can talk to me."

"I can do all kinds of things I'm not actually going to do. Like stick a fork in my eye or start smoking e-cigarettes, both of which are more likely than me talking to you. Put her on."

"Look. That's not ever going to happen. I'll get her the message."

"Who am I talking to?"

"Delacorte."

"Delacorte. Okay, Agent Delacorte, you tell her I've got information on our boy and that if she wants me to share, she should probably think about doing her own telephone talking."

There's another deep syllable coming his way, but Ray cuts it in half and ends the call. Behind him, Twill is leaning his back against a wall trying to keep the room from spinning.

"What's happening, Mack? Who was that? I thought you said we needed out of the hotel."

"I'm working on that. We've got two things in our favor right now. Whoever it is doesn't know you're here and they don't know what room we're in."

"How do you know?"

"Because if they knew that, they wouldn't be sitting in the car. They'd be in the lobby or they'd be up here with us. They're watching the front. Maybe they've got someone on the back too, I don't know. But they weren't watching the kitchen. I'm guessing you got in clean. They're down there waiting for you to show up so they can box you in."

"Who'd you call?"

Ray's phone rings. He puts up a finger and looks at the number.

"Officer Santiago," he says. "What's shaking?"

"News to pass along."

"Let me guess. CPD is executing a search warrant on LT's house."

"Yeah. Shit man, how'd you know?"

"Just a feeling. Intuition."

"Bullshit."

"Okay, maybe I was sitting four feet away when he got the call from his wife."

"You found him?" Raffi lets his excitement slip. "You're with him? How is he?"

"Tall, tired and innocent."

"What can I do, boss?"

"Stop calling me that, for starters. Beyond that, stand by. Stay by a phone."

"You *do* understand cell phones, right?"

"Not really. Gotta go. This thing in my hand is vibrating."

Ray ends one call and picks up the next, pressing the flat of his hand against the cool glass. Nine stories down through the rain is a parking lot he wants to see but can't.

"You have a talent for making things difficult," says Marie.

"The nuns used to tell me the same thing. They eventually gave up."

"Information," she says flatly. Ray thinks he can smell the smoke through the phone.

"Right," he says. "So I figured the best way to get to Twill was to grab up the girlfriend. It took some work, but I convinced her that it was in her interest to play nice. Seems she has an aversion to public housing, or maybe it's just small places and bad food. Anyway, she took dictation and sent up the bat signal. We're at the Marker Westpoint Suites waiting for Twill to show."

"Well, that's good," says Marie. "Isn't it?"

"No. It's not good. Twill just called her. He's out in the rain someplace watching the hotel. He said there're two cars full of muscle down there that convinced him coming inside is a bad idea. Imagine my surprise."

"I see."

"So Amanda had to convince him that she's all alone up here and clueless. That she's not helping someone like me throw him a surprise party. She did her best to sell it, but he's spooked."

"He's waiting?"

"Doubt that. He's tall, not stupid. I'm guessing he's back in the wind. She told him to pick another time and place. He said he'd call. We're going to wait awhile. If he's still watching and sees me come out of this hotel then we'll never be able to use her again."

Silence. The sound of a lighter sending up a flame.

"So then this is you keeping me apprised?" Ray hears the skepticism in her voice. He ramps up the anger.

"No, this is me telling you to keep your amateur-hour goon squad as far away from me as possible. I don't know where you're from, exactly, but American law enforcement is big on trying to keep surveillance invisible. I'm working my ass off here trying to get you what you want but, to use your words, you have a talent for making things difficult. Your boys have been burned. Twill's got their faces and both cars. The guy at the entrance too."

A long silence.

"What are you asking, Detective?"

"I'm asking that you pull back your dogs and let me work. If I get him, I'll call. If you get him, you promised to call me so I could be there. Remember that promise? All the way back to this morning? Breakfast at Wendy's, Tiffany's freckled cousin?"

"I remember."

"And that's not all. I'm up here working my end of things, so how's that other thing coming?"

An extra beat. She's either trying to remember or working on her lie.

"I suppose you mean Marlo," she says. "I'm working on it."

"I'm getting close here, Marie. Are you for real or not?"

"You haven't called Agent Murray."

"It's been all of seven hours. And if you really thought I was going to march the FBI through a busy IAD office in the middle of the day, then I'm going to think you're not so smart after all."

"You haven't *called* him."

"I've been busy. I thought you'd approve of my priorities. You want me to grab up Twill or play games on his computer?"

Marie sighs. They both listen to the same silence. Watch the same rain.

"Does she have any idea where he's been?" she asks. "Where he might be going?"

"None," says Ray.

"You believe her? Is she listening to all this?"

"She's cuffed to the bathroom plumbing with the door closed. She's too scared right now to lie. I'm guessing Twill's highly mobile. I know one place he's *not* likely to be."

"Where?"

"His house. I got a tip that CPD geared up to execute on a search warrant. I'm guessing they're already over there, going through the closets. That means you're running out of time to stay ahead of this game. They're going find him, or he's going turn himself in. Then you can get in line for leftovers."

"What's your plan, Detective?"

"My plan? My plan is to order room service and watch Gary Cooper lose all his friends before the noon train shows up. Then I figure Amanda and I will spend some time driving in circles until we get another call. If you want this to work, Marie, you're going to do three things."

"Which three things am I going to do, Detective?"

"You're going to stay away from me until he's wrapped, bagged and ready to be picked up. Your boys are over-eager amateurs. Maybe they blend in better when they're eating croissants parked on the *Rue de Ravioli*, but not here."

"*Rue de Rivoli*," she says flawlessly.

"That was a test. You passed. They're fucking up your own operation, Marie. Keep them away from me. Understand?"

"And the second thing?"

"We spoke about a change of employment."

"Yes, well I have had my conversations about that. Someone from Chicago Homicide will reach out to start the discussion. It sounded like they can make some room, but that's all I can do. What's the third thing?"

"Thing number three is that you're going to get me the information we discussed."

"On your dearly departed Marlo, you mean. You really need to let her go, Raymond. Knowing anything about your love life is a bit outside my remit."

"You were the one with the photo."

"I needed your attention."

"You got it. You're running out of time, Marie."

She's got more to say. Ray ends the call anyway, turning from the window to face the others. They're staring at him in shades of astonishment and disbelief. Ray is used to that in people.

"Wrapped, bagged and ready to be picked up?" repeats Twill, appalled. "What in the ... Who's changing employment?"

Ray holds up a finger. Dials. Raj picks up in less than a full ring.

"Status," he says.

"Same," says Raj. "No change. They're just sitting there. Two in the front seat, one in back. Guy at the front door is still there. Nobody's moving. Everybody's smoking."

"Not everybody," says Ray. "Is their engine running?"

"Nope."

Ray sighs to himself. It's not a sigh. It's a leak. It's the sound of his optimism losing pressure. I know desperation when I hear it. Plan A is already dying on the vine, and Ray's alphabet only has a couple of letters. He's working through contingencies. Counting exits.

Train's coming, Ray.

But then Raj is in his ear, cutting through the silence.

"Wait ... They're leaving."

SIXTY-THREE

"Worthington?" Raffi's confusion comes through the phone loud and clear. "That case closed last year. What's that got to do with anything?"

Across the room, Twill is back on the phone with Wendy. He ends the call with her only to pick up a call from Earnie Davidson, Esquire, who is on the way to supervise the search of Twill's house.

"Maybe nothing," I tell Raffi. "Bring it anyway."

"I'm bringing the whole file?"

"Just the discovery file. I gotta go, Raffi. Thanks."

I disconnect and look over at Amanda sitting next to me, brooding in her chair like a cat stuck out in the rain.

"Can I have my keys back now?" she asks, combing her hair with her fingers.

"I don't like the way you drive." I take out the folded printer paper from my coat pocket. "But I might reconsider if you tell me what these numbers are."

She takes the sheaf and flips through several pages. Then she hands it back like she's too bored to continue.

"I have no idea," she says. "It's gibberish, like Orland said. You were the one who said you knew what the numbers meant."

"I said I thought I knew what *some* of them meant." I wag the papers at her. "But these forty-one pages are a still a mystery. They mean something to somebody." I bend a little and twist my head so I can find her eyes. "Don't they?"

Amanda doesn't answer.

"Guess I'm driving."

I take the lead out of the hotel room. Twill behind me. Amanda behind him. Raj assures me both cars are gone and that the man at the front door hitched a ride with the guys in the beat-up Toyota. That should make me feel better. It doesn't. We all pile into the elevator and head for the lobby.

"Kitchen?" I ask Twill.

"Lobby floor," he says. "To the left. End of the hall."

I nod but then think again. I hit the second-floor button just in time.

"What are you doing?"

"Nice chairs in that lobby," I say. "Good for watching elevators."

The doors slide open onto the second floor. We take a left and head for the window beneath the exit sign at the end of the hallway. I stop at the window for a look as Twill pushes through the door into the stairwell.

"Hang on," I say. Twill backtracks. We all gather at the second-floor window overlooking the street behind the hotel. I point. "I don't like that."

The car is a dove-gray Nissan, backed up against a building in the lot across the street. Engine running, exhaust climbing up the wet bricks behind. Looks like one guy behind the wheel and no one else.

"Think that's for me?" Twill asks.

"Could be. Hard to tell. Everybody else is gone. Might be nothing."

"Gee," says Amanda. "Wouldn't it be great if one of us had a camera, so that we could take a photo and enlarge it?"

Twill and I look at her. She pretends not to notice. Twill reaches for his phone.

"I'd do it myself," she says, "but someone confiscated my phone."

Phone, she says. Not *phones*. I reach into my coat pocket and hand back the phone that isn't a burner. She takes it, looking up at me. It would be the perfect time for some smartass remark about me not returning the burner too. She doesn't say anything. That tells me maybe Uncle Orland doesn't know everything about his niece. I'm guessing the burner knows more about her than he does.

Twill leans in, holding up his phone for us to see. He's got the photo of the driver enlarged. Grainy, but clear enough. Mid-forties. Nice haircut, this guy. Good shave. White shirt and blue tie playing shy inside his raincoat.

"I know this guy," Twill says. "This is FBI. This is … this is … you know. Agent Murray."

"You sure?"

"That's him. Why is the FBI dogging me, Mack? I'm the one hounding them. All they have to do is call me and I'll come running. You said they're not my friend. You said you know who Murray is."

"I don't know him, but I know someone who does. Who is your primary contact over there?"

"At the FBI? Agent Yarborough. Nicholas Yarborough."

"Nick? I know him."

Twill's eyes pop.

"You do? He never let on."

"He wouldn't. Good poker player, Nick. He hates me."

"Why does that not surprise me?"

I have to wait for a woman pushing a housekeeping cart to stop and disappear into a room three doors down.

"About ten years ago Chandler Homicide put the squeeze on one of Nick's informants. We were working a pair of murders and Nick was into a gun smuggling party. The snitch in question knew everybody. He could also read the writing on the wall. We pressed him and he bolted. Vanished into thin air. That left Nick and the Bureau high and dry. Things got ugly. I threatened to file a claim with OPR."

"Winfrey?" Amanda seems genuinely shocked.

"Not Oprah. O-P-R. The Office of Professional Responsibility. It's the FBI's version of internal affairs. Lanny Mandel has been top dog at OPR for donkey's years. I never actually went to see Lanny, but I dropped his name a couple of times just to get Nick's attention. Nick's not a bad guy. We were in each other's way." I look up to Twill. "Nick ever show you his belt?"

"His belt? Oh, the one on the wall?" Twill nods. "Yeah. Hard to miss."

Amanda's confused.

"His belt?"

I nod.

"Nick's a Texas boy. Spent his youth winning these big, silver rodeo competition belt buckles. He's got one on the wall of his office attached to a long, fat leather belt. Every time Nick sends someone up the river, he cuts a notch in that stupid belt."

"He never told me what it meant," say Twill.

"It means Nick likes to strut. Last time I saw him he looked like he might whip me with that belt." We all stare down at the car across the street. "You have his phone number?"

"Yarborough? Yeah." Twill starts tapping and scrolling. "It's here somewhere."

"Where'd you park your rental?"

Twill looks up.

"What? Oh, it's …" He looks out the window, then turns and points through the wall. "East. Next block over. Black Corolla."

"Keys." I hold out my hand. "You two stay up here. Call Yarborough and tell him you want to know why John Murray is playing your shadow. Let him know you're not happy. Don't tell him where you are and keep my name out of it."

Twill holds out his keys.

"Where the hell are you going?"
"To get acquainted."

SIXTY-FOUR

Ray takes the stairs down to first floor, exits the stairwell into the plushily carpeted main hallway and then slips down the smaller corridor that leads to a pair of dirty white swinging doors.

He pushes his way into a hissing cloud of steam that smells of seafood and charring meat. There's plenty of surprise to go around. He doesn't belong here. He walks with the confidence of a man who does this every day, nodding out a few *how y'doins* and a couple *good to see ya's*. He pats a sous chef on the shoulder as he corners away from the cooking line and heads for the large doubles waiting beneath an exit sign.

The kitchen spits him out into the rain on the east side of the building, around the corner from the rear entrance of the hotel. Ray pulls his coat closed and snaps up his collar.

The traffic on South Marker is irritated, full of horns and wet fantails that trouble the puddled lots and sidewalks. He moves in an erratic line, trying to keep the insides of his shoes dry. The sky above is an ugly, dripping rag dropped over the buildings. Dark gray wisps betray the wind off the lake as knobs of heavy cloud boil into the darkening afternoon.

And then there's me. I'm up here too. Ray doesn't ask for my perspective, but I give it to him anyway. He's old and hunched and wet, cowering from the rain. He doesn't like that angle. Hurts his pride. Every now and then he loses himself in the work. He forgets himself. That's when he starts to think that maybe he is as he ever was. I'm here to remind him that he isn't that guy anymore and never will be again. He doesn't like that much. He pumps a little more iron into his spine and picks up the pace.

Twill's rental is right where it's supposed to be. Ray slicks the water off his head and climbs in. Starts the car. Drives around the block so he can approach the back of the hotel from the north. He slows as he rounds the last corner.

The gray Nissan is still smoking up against the wall. Ray pulls into the lot and eases the Corolla to a stop so that the passenger door is only six inches in front of the Nissan's hood.

Corolla in front. Brick wall behind. He's just made his first FBI sandwich.

The two men look at each other through the glass. The agent in the Nissan looks angry and confused. He holds up his badge. Ray does the same.

Ray kills the engine and climbs out, dropping the keys in his pocket. He walks to the passenger side of the Nissan and waits patiently for the door to unlock. It takes a few seconds. But then it does.

"Detective Mackey," the man says as the door opens.

"Agent Murray," says Ray, climbing in and closing the door. "I'm told I owe you a phone call."

The man is not quite so perfect up close. The eyes have a little sag. Teeth are too small and not so straight. His chin comes to a point that could pick a lock, and his nostrils dilate obnoxiously with every breath. Maybe that's just a tell that the man's worked up. Maybe he's unnerved that Ray seems to know who he is.

"Funny way of making a phone call," he says.

Ray nods.

"Figured it'd be easier talking to you in person, being as you're already up my ass. Why are you here, Agent Murray?"

"You know why I'm here," he says. "I'm here for your boss. Former boss."

"You didn't get the word, apparently."

"And what word is that?"

"The word that you boys blend in like a herd of buffalo at a dance recital. Thought I was pretty clear with Marie."

"Who's Marie?" He's not playing dumb. The question is genuine.

"Marie is what I call the foreign intelligence agent pulling your strings. What do you call her?"

"Not Marie," he says. "And she's not pulling my strings. We're both doing our jobs. And you're in over your head, Detective. You're not in a position to see the bigger picture here. You need to cooperate and let us do those jobs."

"Gee," says Ray, "I thought I was cooperating. Do you want the man or don't you? Thanks to you guys, he's not coming anywhere near this hotel. Now I've got to start all over. You think I'm doing this for fun?"

"I don't know what you do for fun," says Murray. "And I don't care. I follow orders. That's all I do. Those orders include watching this hotel and, since we're talking, coordinating with you to search your lieutenant's computer. That's what cooperating means. That's how you help. Interfering with this operation is called obstruction of justice, not cooperating. You don't want that kind of trouble."

"No," says Ray. "You're right about that. I don't. I know the Feds take matters of operational integrity very seriously."

"We do."

Ray looks for a second like he might open the door and leave. He doesn't. He looks at John Murray instead.

"Then riddle me this, John: if I'm flirting with obstruction, what's in store for an FBI agent who betrays an on-going investigation by leaking confidential intel to persons outside the FBI? Foreign intelligence agents, for example."

"Not sure what you're insinuating, but …"

"I'm guessing that kind of thing is good for an immediate discharge, followed by a media shitstorm, followed by a federal indictment and the color orange."

"Listen …"

"No, you listen, Agent Murray. Orland Twill comes to the Bureau for help. He comes over with a story about murder and corruption and cooked forensics. He doesn't trust local law. The Bureau is not sure it wants in, but it opens a file and says they'll look into it. Marie finds a way to put you in the room. Why? Because her agency needs help too. A different kind of help. In fact, they want the *opposite* kind of help. They want to serve Twill up for lunch. Maybe he's guilty as sin and he deserves what he gets. But that doesn't really matter to Marie, does it? She'll do anything it takes to get Twill to cough up Big Man. That's who she really wants. She doesn't give a shit about Twill. She wants to take Big Man back across the pond as a trophy that maybe gets her a promotion and a free croissant. Marie's got her own belt on the wall. She's working on her own notches."

Agent Murray swallows. Didn't like the bit about the belt. He tries to cover with comical confusion.

"Big Man?"

"Why does everybody try to pretend they've never heard that name?" asks Ray. "Yeah, Big Man. He's the spoon in the soup. He makes your world go 'round, John, whether you want to admit it or not. Mine too. And Marie's. Point is, Marie has turned you into a foreign intelligence pipeline inside the FBI and you've been leaking like a sieve."

"You're out of your mind, Detective."

"You're not the first person to tell me that. So you're telling me Marie's got nothing to do with this … whatever this is. You're actually sitting out here on the clock for the FBI?"

"Are you deaf, stupid or both?"

Somewhere from the driver's seat a phone is vibrating. Murray doesn't react.

"Neither," says Ray. He points vaguely in the direction of the buzzing. "That's Nick Yarborough, calling to find out why, exactly, you are out here in the rain looking to surveil Orland Twill, and on whose authority. I'm betting he doesn't know that your instructions are to facilitate Twill's apprehension by … others."

For a moment, maybe two, there is only one heart beating in the car. Ray leans a little toward the driver's seat. He lowers his voice to something just above the sound of the buzzing.

"Bet he doesn't know you've been talking out of school."

Murray's phone stops. The silence lasts just long enough for whoever is calling to redial. Then it starts up again. The new buzz seems to carry a raw volt or two. The agent's nostrils dilate with every ring. He digs the phone out of his pocket and looks at the screen. I can't see the name. Neither can Ray. We don't need to. Nick Yarborough is all over the man's face.

There's a rule about talking to the FBI. Not a rule, a commandment. *Never lie to the FBI.* Just don't do it. Not even once. Not ever. But then, breaking commandments seems to be what Ray does best. Ask any of the nuns. Ask Marlo. Agent Murray is working on his blood pressure. The phone finally gets tired and stops its buzzing.

There's a fly on the dash. It disappears into a vent. Ray eases back into the seat and talks to the rain.

"I used to be homicide," he says. "Thirty years. Then I got this gig with IAD. I thought I'd hate it, and I was right. I don't like running around after other cops. It's a distraction. That's not the way this game is supposed to be played. There's us, and there's them. I don't want to chase us. I only want to chase them. But the price of bourbon and cat food being what it is, I didn't have much choice. So I took the job. I've been walking around thinking that I've sunk to about as low a station in life as a homicide detective can ever get. I … A … D. But I was wrong." Ray gives him a look across the car. "There is something worse than being IAD."

"I can't imagine," he says.

"Snitching for IAD," says Ray.

Murray screws up his face.

"You're snitching for yourself?"

"No. Not *my* IAD. The FBI's IAD. *Your* IAD."

"What …" Murray's eyes focus. "OPR? Fuck you."

"Imagine my predicament," says Ray. "I'm minding my business when I get pressed into service by an out-of-town agent who wants my good-for-nothing LT on a skewer for taking a walk on the dark side. Murder. Conspiracy. As bad as it gets. She wants me to betray the man who expects me to betray as many cops as I can on a daily basis. So maybe Twill's got that coming. Maybe I'm not gonna lose much sleep if he gets what he deserves. So I let her talk. She wants me to rake through my LT's hard drive, looking for God-knows-what. She's never too clear on that. Numbers. Some shit I still don't understand."

The fly has heard enough. It bounces manically against the window. Ray lets it out into the rain. Then he closes the window.

"If I cooperate, Marie says she has a way I can get out of the IAD shithole and start working bodies again. Don't ask me how she pulls that off, exactly, but she gets points for confidence. And she's shown me a thing or two about her reach with the law in this town."

"And if you don't cooperate?"

"If I don't cooperate, my LT is free to feed me to OAG for lunch. There's this kerfuffle about a Russian doll. Maybe you've heard."

"I have. Kerfuffle's not the word."

"It's worse than you know. But then here comes Marie. She pulls a couple of strings. Moves OAG's flashlight to show the guy in the shadows."

"Twill."

"Right. So I'm thinking maybe scratching her back might be worthwhile. Maybe I play that game. But then I get a tap on the shoulder from two guys who buy their suits and shoes from the same company store that you buy yours."

"FBI?"

Ray nods.

"Not from Chicago, these guys. They've both got decent tans. San Diego field office it turns out. Agents Fitzgerald and Gillespie."

Christ, Ray. Let's hope Agent Murray isn't into jazz.

"And what do they want?"

"They say they've got me cold consorting with a foreign agent trying to meddle in our justice system. Bad enough, right? The real kicker is that they think this foreign agent has some inside help."

Murray is silent. Listening. Thinking.

"I tell them I don't have any idea what they're talking about. They don't seem to believe that, and they paint a pretty bleak picture of my future. They want me to sign a cooperation agreement. I call their bluff that they've got any kind of case against me whatsoever. They do their best, but I've played this game long enough to know a weak hand when I hear it. So they back off a little. Tell me they're just looking for a little help. A little brothers-in-blue cooperation. They ask me to keep them apprised."

Ray looks over at Agent Murray looking back. He's framed perfectly against the rain-streaked window behind him. It's like the whole world is sweating, waiting for him to join in. Ray squints like something hurts. Shakes his head.

"Doesn't the Bureau train you guys on the finer points of interrogation?"

"Yes."

"Well, these boys need a refresher."

"Is that all?"

"No. See, Marie keeps pushing me for results. She wants me to turn my LT's computer upside down and shake it for loose change. I tell her I'm not so good with computers and I don't love the idea of getting caught wiping my ass with the Constitution. So, she gives me a search warrant signed by a federal judge and the number of an FBI computer whiz-kid to solve all my problems. That's you, by the way."

Ray looks at Murray. Could be an ice cream headache on his face. Could be he's starting to worry.

"So what's a disaffected cop with a dirty boss supposed to do? I snitch on Marie to the Feds, I lose my chance to get out clean. I'm right back in the shit with OAG, taking the ride for all of Twill's dirt. And if I *don't* snitch, the Feds come after me whenever they decide to make some kind of foreign interference case against Marie. They take their shot at me for obstruction and maybe they make it stick. You get what I'm saying?"

"Tough decision, is what you're saying."

"Right," says Ray. "Tough decision. Exactly. It takes me a whole bottle to think through that one. That's when I get a visit from some guy named Lenny. Lenny Mandel. FBI, Office of Professional Responsibility. OPR. I'm guessing you know him."

"Lanny," he says. The correction comes out a little dry and brittle. Murray swallows hard and repeats. "Lanny."

"Lanny. What kind of name is Lanny? Better question is when did I get to be so goddamned popular with the FBI? Anyway, Lenny ... *Lanny's* got a lot of questions about leaky pipes. He's obviously been trading notes with your San Diego counterparts, because he picks up right where they left off about me and Marie. Lenny wants to know if Marie has ever mentioned contacts within the Bureau. He tries to cozy up, you know, like all of us IAD cop-chasers have the same mission in life. But it's all happening too fast for my hangover to manage, so I play dumb. Could have dropped your name, but I'm still trying to figure which end is up on this thing. So I let it go. I leave him thinking we're on the same page and tell him I'll reach out if I hear anything."

Ray leans his head back against the seat rest and closes his eyes like he needs to gather his thoughts. What he'd like to do is go to sleep. Make Murray wait for a couple of hours. But he can feel Twill and Amanda looking at them from the window, wondering what they're sitting here talking about. Wondering if trusting Ray was a good idea. He opens his eyes and rubs his face. A mistake. He can still feel that four-fingered fist. Like Pinky's beating him all over again.

"And so now, Agent Murray, here I am, playing both ends against the middle, trying to deliver my LT to Marie just like she wants, as the Feds look over my shoulder hoping she's dumb enough to take the bait. Only there's way too much attention on this hotel for Twill to make an appearance. So now he's back in the wind and everybody comes away disappointed. Right?"

Murray shrugs.

"If you say so."

"No," says Ray. "Don't bullshit a bullshitter, John. I called Marie to complain that I don't work well in groups. She promptly told everyone to stand down. Everyone except you. Guess she wanted you to hang around just in case. We don't trust well in this business, do we? Always assuming the worst in each other."

"You a Pollyanna?"

"Hardly. I barely trust myself. Point is, I don't take Marie's word for it. I start looking out of every window I can. And sure enough, that's when I see you out here smoking a tailpipe. Now, I didn't know who the hell you are, but you look like an FBI recruitment poster, so I put in a call to the number I got from the San Diego suits and leave a message. Ten minutes gets me a call back from Lenny … *Lanny*. He tells me that no one from the FBI has any orders to keep Orland Twill under surveillance. But … and of this I am sure, Agent Murray … Lanny Mandel of OPR could not have been more interested."

Ray looks over at the guy in the driver's seat with eyes just a little wider. Murray tries his best not to react, but his best isn't good enough to keep those nostrils from flaring. Ray shakes his head at the story that just won't quit.

"Wait. It gets better. Marie is calling me while I'm on with Lenny … fuck, *Lanny*, so I tell Lanny to stand by and I take the call. Marie's all over me again about getting up with her man in the FBI to search Twill's computer. Agent John Murray. So I put two and two together and come up with it being you, Agent Murray, sitting out here in the rain. Could have been wrong, I guess. But I wasn't. It was you. Question is, who do I tell about this, if anyone?"

Murray's phone starts up again. His face twitches sharply. I pretend like neither of us care about the phone.

"I call Marie back. She's suddenly playing hard to get. So I call Lenny back. *Lanny. Lanny.* I'll never get that right. I call Lanny and tell him the car is gone and I don't have any intel except for a grainy photo I took of you from across the street. Lanny asks me to text it. So I do. He puts me on hold. Then he comes back on and asks if Marie has ever mentioned the name Nick Yarborough. I tell him no, but that I know Nick from way back as a stellar agent. I ask Lanny if it's Nick's office that has the leaky pipes. That's when Lanny gets squirrelly. Seems he doesn't want to answer my questions. We do the whole confidential investigation dance. That was pretty much the end. So I decided to come out and say hello. Now your phone can't stop vibrating."

Silence. It goes on for too long before Murray swallows.

"I hear you write fiction," says Murray, forcing an uncomfortable laugh. "How'r sales?"

"Rock bottom. But that just means I've got nowhere to fall. You, on the other hand, you're about to fall off a cliff, John, and it's a long way down. They're going to want to see who you've been talking to. I've been down that road. It's not fun. Does the FBI even need a subpoena to pull the phone records of one of their own?"

Murray tries his best for relaxed amusement. He manages to look a little sick. Ray keeps at it.

"You're looking a little green. For good reason. I get it. I do. All this has got to sit about as well as a bowl of chicken salad left out in the sun. You've got to be wondering about how you can safely get word to Marie. Let her know that her man in the Bureau just got burned. But here's the thing, Agent Murray, you need to be worrying about who's out there in the rain watching Marie. Or listening in. Can't rule that out."

The buzzing suddenly stops, like maybe John Murray's own phone has to think about that one for a second.

"What are you saying?" asks Murray.

"One cop to another, John, you might not want to know Marie right now. Or whatever it is you call her. I'd steer well clear. But, whatever you do, don't do it around me. Understand? Stay out of my way so I can do my job."

"Your job for who?"

"Still trying to figure that out."

"And Twill's computer?"

"I'll manage on my own. You're about to be too popular with the FBI for my comfort level."

"You're in way over your head, Detective," he says.

"No doubt. Tread very carefully, John. Nick Yarborough's going to get another notch in that belt of his. And it's gonna be easy."

Murray puts his pointy chin to work. "Get the fuck out of my car."

"Right." Ray opens the door and steps out into the rain. "Nice day for a walk."

He closes the door and makes his way past Twill's rented Corolla, locking it with a beep. He shambles off the lot and across the street toward the hotel. He can just start to make out Twill and Amanda marking his progress from the second-floor window. A black Dodge Intrepid turns the corner and plows through a small lake, just as Ray reaches the other side of the street. Raffi Santiago nods from behind the wheel, pulling into an open parking space.

Ray keeps walking like he doesn't know Raffi from Adam. At the corner of the building, just before he disappears from Murray's sight, he thinks about looking back. Just to check. He's a good eighty yards away and he can still feel that phone buzzing in Murray's pocket.

But he doesn't turn and look back. Doesn't need to. Murray's the meat in a brick and Corolla FBI sandwich left out in the rain. He's not going anywhere without a tow truck.

SIXTY-FIVE

Raffi meets the three of us around the side of the hotel. Twill folds himself into the passenger seat of the Intrepid and slides the seat back so his knees can come along too. I hold the door open and lower my head so I can look past Twill to Raffi.

"There's a party at his house. Get him there before it's over. Watch your mirrors."

"Got it," says Raffi. He grabs a file folder off the dash and hands it over Twill's lap to the window. "Here's the Worthington file you asked for. My old boss would have said that taking original IAD files out of the office is strictly prohibited."

"New sheriff in town," I say, taking the file. "Old boss is busy."

I open up the file and riffle through the pages of a dozen different documents until I find the one I want, tilting sideways to keep the rain off. I spend a few extra seconds on the last page, lingering over that feeling of being right for a change. Then I close the file and hand it back in to Raffi. Twill intercepts it.

"What the hell is this?" he asks, looking at the label. "Worthington?"

"Little research."

"Care to enlighten me as to how this – what might be the dumbest conduct-unbecoming-show-your-penis-to-the-wrong-person case I've ever seen – has anything to do with any of this?"

"Not really. No."

"Mack ..."

"There's no time, LT. Listen. Earnie needs to negotiate an opportunity for you two to go over to CPD and talk. Get out in front of it, LT. Don't wait for the arrest warrant. That's my take. But Earnie charges enough by the hour to know what he's doing. If he tells you to stand on your head, I'd do that too."

"Where are you going?"

"All the questions are nice and dry, LT. The answers are out there getting soggy. If I find anything interesting, I'll let you know. If I can't reach you directly, I'll reach out to Earnie."

Twill jerks his head behind him. "What about Murray?"

"He's gonna stay here and watch the rain for a while. Think about his future. He's going to think long and hard about whether I'm snitching for OPR."

"Are you?"

"Maybe. Day's not over."

"Have you?"

"LT."

"Damnit, Mack. I need to know what you know."

I squint and wipe the rain off my face.

"You sure about that? You're about to be in the question-answering business. Isn't that right, Raffi?"

"You're wasting your time, LT," says Raffi. "He's going to play it his way."

Twill looks up at me, flexing his jaw muscle. He wants to threaten my job. He can't. He gives up. Changes the subject.

"Mandy," he says. "She's headstrong. But she's a good kid, Mack."

"I'm sure she used to be, LT," I say. "Get going, Raffi. Don't stop for anyone. That's an order."

I close the door and slap the roof of the car. Raffi's Intrepid hisses away and around the corner. I look back at Amanda Ramada Tate leaning up against the hotel, trying to keep her cashmere dry. I dangle her keys in the rain and jerk my head in the general direction of the car that brought us here.

SIXTY-SIX

I feel around for the gun. It's the first thing on my to-do list as soon as she's in the passenger seat. The Bersa Thunder 380 is under the driver's seat just like she said. It's compact. A favorite concealed carry for decades. I pop the clip for a look. Fully loaded. I drop it in my coat pocket.

"You any good with guns?" I ask, climbing in and closing the door.

"No. But I'm excellent at being scared. Can I get my other phone back now?"

"You mean now that Uncle Orland isn't around to ask a lot of questions about why you've got a burner phone?"

"Uncle O knows all about it. It was his idea."

"I doubt that very much."

"Why didn't you tell him then?"

"He's got enough to worry about."

"Where are you taking me?"

"South Loop."

"Why?"

"Because if Dennis had a home away from home, then I want a tour."

I ease the car out of the lot and onto the street keeping my eye on Raj's cab. He stays where he is until I get all the way down the street to the corner. Just before I make the turn, I see his headlights come to life. Might be the first smile I've had all day. I fish out my phone and call him.

"Where we going?" he asks.

"South Loop. See if you can spot anyone on the road looking to tag along."

"Roger that."

"Also?"

"Yeah."

"Good work."

"Thanks, Mack."

The traffic is a nest of wet snakes feeding on the hope that smoother slithering is somewhere just up ahead. It isn't.

We drive in silence, mostly, the daylight around us prematurely failing. Amanda keeps her face to the glass. I can feel her gerbil wheel spinning. She's running through her options. Weighing risk against the likelihood of success. She wants out from under my thumb. Funny. All she needs to do is pour me a drink and find a Camel that can take me to bed. I keep that to myself.

"You like being a cop?" she asks.

I toss her a look and a shrug.

"Used to."

"What changed?"

"Me. The job. Everything."

"Retire. Do something else."

"There's an idea. Hadn't thought of that."

"Quality time with the wife."

"Don't have a wife."

"Girlfriend?"

"I've got a spoiled Persian cat with expensive taste in bourbon."

"There's a pussy joke in there someplace."

"I've heard them all."

"Bet it's tough being gay police."

"Stop it. You want to tell me the truth about Stan Papadopoulos?"

The question pushes her face back toward the window. I let it sit.

"Why didn't you tell Uncle O?" She asks it like she wants the guy in the Lincoln next to us to answer. "Back at the hotel."

"Uncle O is in neck-deep, which makes whatever's going on with you and Stan a distraction. Like I said, the man's got enough to worry about."

She faces forward with a heavy sigh. The wipers want to slap her around. She looks at me sideways, combing through her wet hair with her fingers. Clears her throat.

"Stan got me fired from the Merc," she says. "I wouldn't have left. Dennis and I were trying to, you know, knock it off. He wanted to do right by his marriage. He hated Carrie, but he also loved her. He wanted me as an assistant and a friend. Nothing else. I wanted to honor that. We talked a good game, but ... we were who we were. You know?"

I give it a slow nod and keep my mouth shut.

"So when Dennis left the Merc, he thought that was a chance for us to make a clean start. I knew better though. Me staying at the Merc and away from Dennis was the best way to keep our clothes on. Dennis kept asking me to come over to BSD. I declined. I kept what I had."

"A career."

"I'm just an assistant trader. I can't work on my own. So, with Dennis gone, Hillary set me up to work for Stan Papadopoulos. She didn't ask me first. Stan requested it, actually. He wanted an assistant. I consented." Amanda's hands have disappeared beneath the wet cashmere, worrying in secret. "So … fast forward a couple of months and then Stan and I …"

"Oh, come on. Cliché much?"

"He knew about me and Dennis. But Dennis was gone. We went to a couple of work functions. Innocent enough. Then …" she sighs. "You know."

"Yeah, I get it. You have a thing for married men who tell you what to do at work. You handle his laundry too?"

"Fuck you."

My triple D kicks in. The alter ego asshole in the back seat stares at the back of my head and remembers a certain St. Patrick's Day party with a pair of legs at the punch bowl that belonged to Ronni Lodge in the Records Department. It was the start of a week-long mistake that, so far, has lasted the rest of my life. I'm the married man in this memory. My other self gives me points for hypocrisy.

"Sorry," I say. "I'm no one to judge. Just trying to figure you out."

"Well, you can stop. I had a broken heart. Stan was a rebound. It happens every day. Not a good decision. I get it. I broke it off and it turned ugly. Stan ran to one of the corner offices – Hillary or Warren or one of the others – and made the case that I was a shitty assistant and that with Dennis gone I was just taking up space in the budget."

"So then you broke down and went to work for Dennis over at BSD."

Amanda nods.

"Didn't take us long to pick up where we left off. It might have made me happy if it hadn't made Dennis so unhappy. We couldn't help it. It felt good and terrible at the same time. Every time we vowed it was the last." Amanda shakes her head in time with the wipers. "Every fucking time. It never was the last time. Until it was."

"And Stan?"

Amanda nods.

"Right. Well. After Dennis died, Stan calls me up. Checking on me. Wants to apologize. Wants to make things right over dinner. Dennis was gone again, this time for good, and here comes Stan making another play. It just … It made my fucking blood boil. I think everything about Dennis had … I don't know … I was full of emotion. Dark emotion. I channeled it all into getting back at Stan Papadopoulos."

"And you did that how, exactly?"

"I called him up. Angry as hell. I didn't have to act. I told him that he got me fired and that I was going to get him fired. I told him I knew he'd been spoofing and that I was ready to talk to Hillary and Warren about it. That freaked him out. He was probably afraid of losing more than his job. I went off on him for like ten solid minutes. I think he shit his pants."

"How'd you end it?"

"With him begging. It was so fucking satisfying. He asked what it would take. I told him I wanted ten thousand dollars to keep quiet. I gave him two days to pull it together and to call me. I just wanted to scare him. Guess it worked because he called the next day. I told him to meet me at Blondie's out in Addison. It was one of Dennis' favorites. I wanted it to feel like Dennis was there with me."

"And Stan showed?"

"He showed."

"With the cash?"

"Yes."

"How'd it go down?"

"We sat in a booth. He had the money in a take-out bag. I told him to keep his fucking money. I told him I wanted him to know I was serious about going to Merc management if he ever contacted me again. I wanted him to leave me the fuck alone. Then I walked out. I haven't seen or heard from him since. Probably not the story he's telling. Is it?"

"Different planets," I say.

"He saying I actually took his money? He's such a fucking liar. It's my fault. I should have just left him alone. I was just so … I was coming apart. Grief, fear, and then rage. I wanted to hurt him. Fucking Stan. I'll let it drop. I'll let it go. I promise."

"You're going to do a little better than that," I say. She looks at me wide-eyed, trying to predict the future.

"What. The spoofing? You want me to go on the record about the spoofing, don't you? Testify against him. I'll do that. Hell yeah. Fucking Stan." We ride in silence for a block. Then she looks at me. "Better?"

The question comes at me with enough hope to sink a couple of battleships. Hope that heavy never belongs to the innocent. I let it go. Now's not the time for popping bubbles. I give her an encouraging nod.

"Better."

We finally make the Expressway. I give Raj a call.

"How we looking?"

"Impossible to say in this traffic, Mack."

"I figured."

My paranoia clears its throat. They're out there. Have to be.

"I'll keep at it," says Raj.

"Don't worry about it," I say. "I've got something else."

"What."

"Go back to the hotel. Behind the building you'll see an angry man in a gray Nissan pinned between a brick wall and black Corolla. I'm guessing he's still waiting for a tow truck to set him free. Let me know where he goes."

"On it. What else?"

"Don't tell Cleo I've put you on the clock. And if you do tell her, then give me a heads up. I want to know in advance how and why I die. And keep track of your mileage, Raj. This isn't for free."

SIXTY-SEVEN

He wants to leave her in the car. Do the thing himself. He's not keen on splitting his attention. Doesn't want to have to worry about keeping her alive if it turns out they're not alone.

Like she'd be any safer sitting in the car.

Doesn't matter. She's coming whether Ray likes it or not. She's already out, dodging raindrops on the walkway up to the front door. He has to hustle to keep up.

Dennis O'Toole's shelter from divorce is a squat, blue clapboard single-story with white trim, a pitched roof, a brick chimney and an attached garage, all holding down a soggy patch of lawn that needs mowing. The living room windows are large and dark, blinds pulled.

Lights glow yellow under the eaves. Somewhere a dog is barking in the rain. A car alarm howls up into the dusk after the sirens of Chicago. Ray waits as Amanda pokes the buttons on the keypad beneath the door handle. She starts to push. Ray puts a hand on her shoulder and pulls her back.

"Ladies second," he says, drawing Sig out into the twilit gloom. "Stay behind me."

Amanda steps aside. Ray pushes the door open with his foot. He stands sideways in the opening. Listening. He hits the switch on the foyer wall. The space in front of him explodes with light.

"Oh my God." Amanda's voice comes over his shoulder in a terrified whisper. "Oh ... my ..."

The explosion is neither entirely of light nor metaphoric. The place has been violently ripped apart. What was once a furnished living room to the left of the foyer is now a dry-walled canyon of debris. Toppled bookshelves. Disemboweled cushions. Broken backs. Fractured legs. Splintered frames and shattered glass. They step in and Ray closes the door, locking it behind. Amanda can't come to grips. Her fingertips try to keep the words in.

"Oh ... my ..."

I hover along behind as they move clockwise through the house, Ray in the lead. It's all the same. Room after room. Kitchen. Bedroom. Both bathrooms. Guest room. Study. The same. Every drawer. Every cupboard. Every closet. Every mattress. Every moving box, maybe two dozen in the garage, slit and emptied, contents strewn. They move as if through a battlefield, stepping carefully over the dead. Ray opens a back door to look out over a small back yard, dark and quiet. He closes the door and locks it.

He finds Amanda in the bedroom. She cries as she picks up a broken bottle of cologne.

"It's not him," says Ray, moving past over crunching glass. "It's just stuff."

"Easy for you to say," she sniffs.

I tell him the same thing. I show him all the boxes in his own garage. The master bedroom, perfectly preserved, where he still refuses to sleep. Marlo's hairbrushes. Her clothes. The photos of her parents. *Just stuff, Ray? Do tell.*

He kicks and picks through Dennis' things for half an hour. Amanda, tear-stained, ragged, has an armful of things she wants to take with her when they leave. Then she opens her arms and lets it all fall to the floor.

"Fuck it," she says. Hopeless. Disgusted. She sniffs again. "It's just stuff."

Ray is in the kitchen. Bags of flour, sugar and ground coffee have been dumped out on the counter.

"Someone's looking for a flash drive," he says. "This is all about data. Numbers. He had a laptop?"

"Dennis? Big-time geek. He knew computers. Hated them too, though. He was kind of paranoid about security. Anything can be hacked, he liked to say. It was like a broken record with him. Anything can be hacked. But yeah, he had a laptop. He kept it in a black, nylon satchel."

"I'm guessing CPD picked that up in the initial search."

"Dennis wasn't stupid," she says. "He was adamant that I not copy the flash drive to any computer. Like, not even open it."

"So if the laptop turned up clean, maybe that explains ..."

Ray gestures vaguely at the domestic demolition in every direction. He doesn't finish. He brushes flour from his hands instead. There's a bowl in the corner by the sink that managed to escape the carnage. He recognizes the cards inside. He grabs the stack.

"Odd thing to collect," he says. Amanda looks.

"Blondie's," she says. "He loved that place. *La Bamba Burger* with two slices of cheddar, large *Surfboard Fries*, and a *Big Dream* malt. Every time."

"I'm guessing he liked to play the lottery."

"They always drop two or three of those cards in the bag. Every time we came back, he'd have a winner to hand through the drive-thru window. It's about as easy to win something at Blondie's as falling out of a chair."

Amanda shakes her head. Ray can tell she's no longer standing in a dead man's house.

"It was those shakes he loved the best," she says. "*Big Dream* malted vanilla. Also strawberry. Somewhere in here …" she looks around the floor, pushing broken glass and cookware around with her foot until she excavates several cookbooks. "There." She taps her shoe to a red cover featuring a blender full of bananas. "He started making his own. He kind of lost his mind on those things. He joked that Blondie's was lacing their *Big Dreams* with crack."

"He wasn't wrong," says Ray, returning the cards to the bowl and opening cabinets. "I've had a couple of those … Hello …"

It's not Old Forester, but it's the same color. Barrell aged. Mostly full. He and the bottle stare at each other for a few extra-long beats. I quote him some Nietzsche to pass the time: *If you stare into the abyss, Ray, the abyss stares back at you.*

Ray has a few choice thoughts for the unsolicited opinion. But he leaves the bottle where it is. Closes the cabinet.

"This place is giving me the creeps, Mack," says Amanda. "I can't be here anymore." She steps forward, reaching past him to reopen the cabinet and grab the bottle. She turns to face him, her cashmere sucking raindrops from his coat. "If you take me back to the hotel, I have some unbroken glasses that might go nicely with this."

Hard to tell whether she's casting the booze as the seductive agent in this pitch to relocate, or her own flesh. Best bet is both. Either way, I'm ready with the Nietzsche all over again. Ray brushes me off.

"I'd rather go to your house," he says, one hand on each of her shoulders.

"Yeah?" She touches the tips of two fingers to the bruise beneath his eye. "That works too."

"Good." Ray uncups her shoulders and moves away, out of the kitchen. "Let's go see if you and Dennis have the same redecorator."

Amanda follows him to the living room, still holding the bottle, her other hand is back to her mouth.

"Oh my God. You don't think …"

"Sure I do. I think all the time. I'm even pretty good at it sometimes. If they were looking this hard here, what are the odds they gave your place a pass? Maybe they left you a chair so you can sit down and tell me the truth for once."

"What?" Fresh offense rising. "I … I *did* tell you the truth."

Ray talks as he shuffles through the detritus, stooping here and there to pick up scraps of Dennis O'Toole's life and drop them again.

"No. At best you shoveled bits of truth over the lie. I'm guessing Stan was every bit the pig you say he is. I'll bet getting even with him was way up on your to-do list. But the rest of it was about as real as your kitchen come-on back there."

"That … I wasn't … I was just suggesting …"

"Stop sputtering. I think you and Dennis were in this game together. Maybe you were the one playing hard to get and he lured you over to BSD by promising to cut you in."

"What game? That's not even …"

"Stop it. Dennis wasn't looking to stick with Carrie. That marriage was as dead as an interstate skunk. She was boxing up all the family money and looking to turn BSD upside down just to prove that Dennis was hip deep in the grift. She shouldn't have done that. That's what got her killed. Point is, that marriage was over a long time ago and you helped end it. Dennis wasn't looking for more of Carrie. He wanted you, Amanda Ramada Tate, his comely assistant, and you used that to maximum advantage."

Her eyes start a contest with her nostrils over who's angrier.

"I did *not* use *anything* …"

"Sure you did. Thanks to Saul Margolis, Dennis stumbled onto the recipe for a money milkshake, and you wanted in. So Dennis gets to feel the cashmere if he shows you a thing or two about how to pay for the future. Pretty heady stuff until the shit hits the fan and Dennis is asking you to pick up his dry cleaning and hide his flash drives. That's just before he and Carrie share an ugly headline in all the newspapers."

Ray picks up an oil of the Chicago skyline and then lets it drop to the floor again with a soft crunch.

"Then, suddenly, Dennis is gone. What's an assistant to do but pick up right where the boss left off."

"That's … Listen, my work for Dennis …"

"So you start with Stan because, why not, he's got it coming. Dennis had already hit Stan once. Maybe you and Dennis did that together. You both knew him. You both hated him. Made sense. Turned out to be easy. Stan rolled over and paid big. So, when Dennis goes to that malt shop in the sky, you decide to try it again. You get a burner phone and send out the demand. You put on your wig and drive Saul's blue Mercedes out to Blondie's to see if Stan is fool enough to pay out twice. Turns out the answer is yes. Stan comes and goes, leaving you a bag of cash under the table. You stroll in and pick it up, easy as you please. Good for you. That's some easy money. Couple of problems though."

Amanda feints for the front door, dropping the bottle onto a pile of couch stuffing.

"I want to leave now," she says.

"I'm sure you do. First problem is that when you drove out to Blondie's you never checked your rearview mirrors to see if you'd been followed. You were followed. By a guy who works for me. So I know what happened, Amanda. All the bullshit is entertaining to a point, but otherwise a waste of oxygen."

"Give me my keys. And my phone. Are you arresting me?"

"Second problem. The same people that wanted Dennis dead now want you dead too. The only thing keeping you alive is that these guys need to make sure they can account for every last byte of data that Dennis entrusted to your care."

Her mouth is open to speak, but the words are slow. Ray looks at her and points just to keep them in their place.

"Make no mistake, Amanda, these people would think nothing of torturing that information out of you. That was probably the plan. Couple of broken fingers gets them everything they need. But then you went and got a police lieutenant involved. They've got to assume that you've given Twill everything Dennis gave to you, and suddenly he's taking meetings with the FBI. Torturing you doesn't accomplish much. You might breathe a sigh of relief at that, but I wouldn't if I were you."

"Trust me, relieved is the last thing I am."

"No, the last thing you are is trustworthy, which is tied for last place with innocent. But feeling any sense of relief is still a bad idea. Like to know why?"

"No."

Ray shrugs. "Okay."

"Fine, goddamnit. Why?"

"Because you only torture people of value, Amanda. People without any value are just fleshy buckets of liability. They get a bullet to the head and left in the gutter for the street sweepers."

"You're just trying to scare me."

"Damn right. Being good and scared might just save your life."

"Who'd want to do that?" Her face is a tear-streaked scramble of fear and incomprehension. "To me? I mean I ... I ... Why?"

"Good question. There's a brigade of foreign keystone cops in town who think this is all about Big Man looking for some damage control."

"Big Man? Who ..."

"Yeah. Him."

"I don't …"

"Big Man. Think King Kong and the invisible man having a baby that comes out possessed with the spirit of Al Capone. He's had his fingers in every pie in this city for a long time, but now he's found a way to stick his thumb into foreign market economies and piss off powerful people with funny accents. They want to find him, put him in a big box and ship him back across the ocean so he can rot in some dungeon for jacking around the price of steel and pork bellies. Or maybe just find him and kill him and save the dungeon space for someone else."

"Great," she says, unconvincingly. "I wish them luck. Whoever they are. What's that got to do with me? Or Orland?"

"They're looking for Uncle O to flip on Big Man."

"But Orland's not involved in any of this," she says. "You believed him."

"Yeah, but they don't see it that way. They think you and Dennis reached out to Orland to help arrange a hit on Carrie."

Amanda reels in silence, threatening to join the rubble at her feet. Then the absurdity fades enough for her to find her balance.

"A hit? You mean …"

"Yeah, that's exactly what I mean. I'm guessing Carrie always knew Dennis was dirty. And that was probably okay with Carrie, money being what it is. But then you kept showing up as a lipstick stain on the collar of Dennis' marriage. Carrie finally snapped. You ever read her deposition?"

"No."

"It's a page turner. She was ready to shake Dennis and BSD to the ground and then call in the CFTC to sift through the wreckage. That stands for the Commodities Futures Trad …"

"I know what it stands for. They think I was involved in … in … And Dennis?"

"And Uncle O. Yeah. The three of you. That's the theory of out-of-town law enforcement. Carrie's lust for marital vengeance was threatening to leave Dennis without any money. Not good, especially if you're going to need criminal defense counsel."

"And why would he need that?"

Ray shoots her an eyeroll.

"Come on, Amanda. You still playing that game with me? You know why."

"Spoofing?"

"There you go. That's better. The theory is that Carrie was wise to both of Dennis' favorite extracurricular activities. You, for one. And spoofing, for the other. She and her lawyers were ready to start digging. Dennis was suddenly looking to stay solvent and out of federal prison. That's some powerful motivation. So Dennis sets you up to put the moves on a certain mob-connected police lieutenant, who just happens to know how to arrange a hit through a popular local dry cleaners."

"Put the moves … he's my fucking uncle!"

"Right. Pretty sick if it were true. I admit. I don't think the out-of-towners know Orland's your uncle. Hell, I didn't know until earlier today. The way you two have been sneaking around, it's not such a crazy thing to think."

"And they think …" An exasperated half-laugh. Hands on her hips. "Let me get this straight … they think Dennis sent me out to seduce Orland into arranging a hit on Carrie O'Toole."

"That's the theory. And then the hit goes sideways when the genius who got the assignment decides to make it look like a murder-suicide and ends up taking Dennis out in the process. No one told the hitman that Dennis was actually the client. Guess that's a downside of the anonymous-client business model."

"Dennis wasn't the client!" She's red in the face with anger, shouting at Ray's back as he kicks through a pile of magazines. "And I had nothing to do with Dennis getting killed. Neither did Orland. You can't possibly believe all of this."

Ray turns to look briefly at her before moving on.

"All of it? Of course not. I believe parts of it."

"Yeah? Well, which fucking parts?"

Ray stops and turns.

"Here's the part you need to believe. Dennis spent his last days on Earth shaking the trees for money. That takes knowing which trees to shake, and that made Dennis a dangerous man. Dennis showed you which trees to shake." Ray pats the sheaf of numbers in his pocket. "Or he gave you the information that might allow you to figure it out. That makes you a dangerous woman. A liability. Understand?"

"But I don't even know this … this … *Big Man.*"

"He knows you. Who'd you think you and Dennis were shaking down? I'm guessing you told yourselves they were all a bunch of shady traders who deserved what they got. Shit birds like Stan Papadopoulos who'd never be able to complain about the extortion. So you two kept shaking the trees. But you never stopped to think about the guy who owned the forest."

"What do you want from me? I mean … I mean … I don't even … I already said I would testify against Stan. What do you …"

"What I want, Amanda," Ray extracts the sheaf of folded paper from his raincoat, "is for you to tell me what these numbers mean."

"I told you I don't know!"

"Yeah. I heard you say that. I just don't believe it. Just like I don't believe that you never opened up the black flash drive that Dennis asked you to hide."

"I didn't!"

"Sure you did. Maybe not while Dennis was alive. But after he was gone? Come on, Amanda. You couldn't resist. You opened it up and got busy taking care of you. I'm willing to bet that the flash drive you gave to Twill – the one he copied onto his computer and then gave to the Feds – is missing some information. Names. Contact data. You kept all of that for yourself and left everyone else with a string of numbers nobody could ever hope to decipher. How'm I doing?"

"You're wrong."

"Am I?"

"Yes!"

"Couple of roads you need to think about here, Amanda. One road ends in me telling your uncle that I sat down with his naughty niece for a heart-to-heart. The story goes that you willingly, out of a selfless urge to make amends, came clean on everything, explaining the worst mistake of your life in the service of Dennis O'Toole, a man who manipulated you into a life of crime."

Amanda shakes her head slowly. Closes her eyes. Ray keeps at it.

"I seriously doubt that's how it really went down, but it's the story that makes you look the most sympathetic. Since you're the boss' niece, I guess I can stomach that if you can. That road leads to putting Stan Papadopoulos in jail, plus a plea agreement you can live with, and protection against anyone who might want you dead. The other road is shorter and forks at the end: prison or mortuary."

Amanda buries her face in her hands for a moment. Ray watches, letting it all sink in. He's close. He can feel it. He brings out his soft, avuncular voice to nudge her over.

"It's a lot all at once," he says. "I know. Let's just pull a thread, Amanda. See where it takes us." He wags the sheaf of paper. "Tell me about the numbers."

Amanda sighs heavily and puts her hands back on her hips. It's the wrong time for Ray's phone to ring, but it does anyway. He pockets the paper and answers.

"Mr. Mackey?" A woman's voice. Older. "My name is Francine Lucas. A mutual friend thinks it's a good idea that I talk with you about your late wife."

Ray imagines Marie in a back seat somewhere smoking and checking a box. She's running out of time, and she knows Ray is her best chance of getting her hooks into Twill. So Marie is either giving him what he wants or making it look that way. Either way, it's a meeting he wants to take.

"I'm glad you called," he says. "Now's not a good time. Can we meet in person? Tomorrow?"

"Of course," says Francine. "Call me at this number when it's convenient. I look forward to meeting you."

Ray disconnects. Marlo is suddenly in his head, smoking, leaning up against the doorway to their bedroom. White blouse. Cloud gray gaberdine pooling over bare feet. Her mother's pearls like dew on spider's silk.

Funny thing we do, she says. *Looking for answers we're better off not knowing. Playing hide and seek with the Devil. Who wants to win that game?* She turns and saunters off, trailing smoke and the sound of her voice. *That you, Ray?*

Then she's gone. All of her. He has to force himself back into the present. Amanda is at the window, leaning up against the sill, poking a finger beneath the blind. She looks back at him.

"Who was that?" she asks.

"Your conscience. You haven't been reachable lately, so it called me. Time for you to start being smart, Amanda."

She sighs and shakes her head slowly, looking back through the shade. Ray takes it as a good sign. A sign of resignation.

"If I talk to you … I mean I should have a lawyer present … but if I agree to talk to you …"

Ray is used to feeling a tremor in his chest, a small quaking, just before a case breaks open. He feels that now. He feels the end finally coming into reach. Hard, of course, to know what kind of end. Ray likes to be optimistic in such moments. I try to keep him real.

Amanda has stopped talking. Her mouth is open and flapping, but soundless. She extracts her finger from the shade and flattens herself against the wall, eyes wide.

Ray finally gets the picture. *That* kind of end.

SIXTY-EIGHT

"Amanda?"

The whisper I get back is harsh and ragged with fear. If I didn't know better, I'd swear her eyes were doing the talking.

"The bike. The bike. The fucking motorcycle. It's across the street."

"You sure," I ask, moving her way.

"It's the same bike. Fuck, fuck, fuck."

I move her away from the window and have a careful look for myself. At first, I don't see any motorcycle at all, just the white Sonata at the curb glowing wet under the streetlight.

But then I see it. Alone across the street. A little further to the right and it would have been beyond the window frame. The bike is all black. No brand names. No numbers. This thing all but disappears in the dark.

"You sure that's the one?" I ask. "You said you don't know your motorcycles."

"I can't tell you who makes the fucking thing," she whispers, "but I know it when I see it. And I wouldn't have missed it when we got here."

"Me neither," I say.

"Where is he?"

I let go of the shade and look at her.

"My guess is that he's coming in through the back. I want you to listen ..."

"The back?" She looks around wildly. "What ...what ..."

I'm on the verge of losing her to hysteria. I give her a good shake and lower my voice.

"Amanda. Listen. Amanda! Focus."

She swallows. Nods. I send my hands down into the pockets of my raincoat and pull out the car keys and the Bersa 380. She takes them like she doesn't know what they are. She looks at me like I'm leaving, abandoning her to her fate.

"You're leaving? Where are you going?"

I point to the back of the house.

"To make sure he feels welcome. He's not here for me, Amanda. Understand? Your life will change for the worse if you ever have to use that gun. But if you have to …"

She nods, jerkily, like someone else is working the muscles in her neck with a coat hanger.

"As soon as you hear him come in, I want you to slip out the front door. Don't bother closing it. Just get to the car. Lock the doors. Get the hell out of here. As soon as you hear him inside. Not before. Understand?"

She is frozen in fear. Listening.

"Amanda."

Another nod.

"Don't go home. Don't go to the hotel. Someplace public. Restaurant. Shopping mall. Stay around people. I'll call you." Her eyes are wide. Terrified. Listening. "Amanda!"

"Yes. People. Okay."

"Good. Stay focused. This is the other thing you need to hear. Listening?"

"Yes."

"When you get clear, you're going to think about disappearing. Hiding in some other city until this all blows over. That's a bad idea. It won't blow over, Amanda. Ever. They'll find you. If you're lucky, I'll find you first. If I have to come looking for you, I won't kill you, but I'll put you in jail. Working with me now is your best shot at a decent life. And Orland needs you to step up. Understand?"

Amanda's head quivers into a discernable nod.

"Use your words, Mandy."

"Yes," she says, looking at the gun in her hand. "I understand."

"Good." I nudge her in the shoulder. "Get near the front door. Talk to me about something. Anything. Keep it loud."

"What?"

"Tell me about Dennis. Go."

I give her another push toward the front door. It takes her a second, but then she moves.

"He was actually a really funny guy," she says awkwardly. I raise my hands toward the ceiling. She takes the hint and brings up the volume. "He loved to laugh. He had one of those faces, you know, like … like when he started laughing, you couldn't help but laugh with him."

I move the opposite direction, toward the kitchen, as quietly as I can. Once I'm there, I take the folded pages of numbers out of my pocket and put them in the oven for safekeeping. Then I yank Sig out of bed and point him into the hall that leads past the larger of the two bedrooms and toward the back door. Amanda keeps at it.

"The thing most people didn't know about Dennis was that he loved cooking. For an Irish guy, he really knew how to make Italian."

The back door has a frosted glass panel behind a pulled shade. If the back light were on, I'd get a glow that might get me a shadow. No such luck.

"Not that he ever followed a recipe. He'd start following every last measurement and then change up everything. He'd get a pen and edit the recipe as he went, like right in the book. He'd find a way to make it his. To make it better. And he was always right."

I crouch low up against the wall, eyes at the doorknob. I've kicked in a lot of doors in my life. Harder than it looks on television. This one's not going quickly or quietly. If he wants in, he's going to have to …

A dull thud shakes the door. The glass panel cracks and falls from behind the shade, tinkling to the floor. A black leather hand attached to a wet, black cotton arm snakes in beneath the shade and feels around against the door for the deadbolt. I wait until he's solved that problem and starts working on the knob.

"And it wasn't just Italian, either," says Amanda. "Don't get me started on his bangers and mash."

The door starts to swing. I grab the wrist before it disappears and yank at it hard, pulling the guy into the door as it opens. The door swings, slamming against the inside wall. The man attached to the arm swings in with it, coming to an abrupt stop with a loud thud and a grunt. I pull against his arm even harder, folding it against the door, trying to nose Sig into the hole I think belongs to the guy's ear. The black face mask makes that harder than it should be. Turns out that close is good enough to make the point. He stops struggling.

I listen for Amanda. She's no longer talking. I take that as a good sign.

"Let's have a look at you," I say, pushing my body hard against the man so that he pancakes his own arm between the inside of the door and the back wall. He grunts again in pain. In the distance, a car is revving up and fading fast. I pinch a bit of the facemask against Sig's handle, ready to pull. But I never get the chance.

SIXTY-NINE

Ray's not the man he was. He's lost his heft. His speed. His fists have gone soft. Maybe he couldn't have beaten this guy, even back then. There's something special going on here that makes that unlikely. But he'd have made it a fight. The once-upon-a-time Ray would have made it hurt.

Not today. Ray gets a finger in the eyehole of the mask and yanks it partly off the guy's face. But that's the only victory. If you can call it that. Ray's not going to live long enough to enjoy it.

The man hangs on to the door and uses his legs to walk up Ray's body and kick him hard in the face. It's ugly. Embarrassing. Ray flails backward into a small laundry room across the hall. He's still got Sig, but he's so off balance he's got no control over his own arms. The guy is all over Ray before he can get his bearings, a flurry of fists and hard rubber soles. Ray tries his best to aim, but the man is too close. Too skilled. Sig goes flying, hitting the wall and dropping behind the washing machine. Another hard foot-shot to the head is followed by six more hits by fists so fast he can only count them by the half-dozen.

Ray drops to the floor. Lights out. Almost. Still conscious but fading fast. I show him what I see through his own ears: Bruce Lee racking a round in a Glock-9 that he must have had tucked into his belt or a holster.

The only other sensory input worth a damn is what Ray can taste: the dirt from Dennis O'Toole's laundry room floor, and his own blood. It's a fitting final note. A note we both predicted more times than we can count.

No surprises here, Ray, I tell him. *You aren't half what you used to be.*

I can feel him smile a little; an eat-shit smirk he manages to give me from down in the dark beneath the pile of pain.

He's on the ladder. He's not waiting for the bullet. He's already climbing. Looking down at me as I'm looking down at him. He thinks he'll finally be free of me up in the big dream. Just him and Marlo, together again.

Maybe true, I think back at him. *Maybe not. There's always someone watching, Ray. Maybe that's me. Guess we'll see soon enough. Just a trigger pull away.*

Somehow, in the dwindling flicker of his consciousness, Ray gives me the finger and keeps climbing.

SEVENTY

Night breezes whisper.

Birds in the sycamore trees. Singing.

Ella. Alone and blue. Kiss me. Nightie-night.

Marlo takes another pull on her straw. She rotates on her stool. Licks the vanilla froth from her lower lip.

"It never empties," I say, looking down into my own frosted glass. Marlo shrugs.

"Never's a long time," she says. "There's a bottom to everything."

"Something Big Man taught you," I say. Then add, "I'm guessing. Or maybe Victor Roby."

Marlo smiles, amusedly. She stirs her shake. The straw is the same midnight blue as the Formica counter, which incorporates tiny silver flakes, scattered like chips of ice under a full moon. At the far end, Kyle Aubrey jerks a soda with one hand as he polishes the counter with another.

"You could just let it go, Ray," she says. "It doesn't matter. Not anymore. None of it matters."

"It matters to me," I say. "It matters so much it's killing me, Marlo."

"No. The Camels are killing you, Ray. And the booze."

"Maybe. But they'll never beat the round the Karate Kid just racked into that chamber. Meantime, before he twitches his index finger, I have to know, Marlo. I have to."

"I see. And did you tell me everything *I* needed to know, Ray? About that set of gams at the St. Patrick's Day punch bowl? Did you think I wouldn't care?"

"I thought it was too late. I didn't want …"

"Didn't want your tawdry confession to ruin my death?" She takes another pull on the straw. "Considerate to the end."

"You already knew about her," I say. "You could have told me."

"I could have. But it was your choice to either come clean, or not. You chose not. I'm choosing the same."

"I got into bed with a pair of legs and a sultry voice and a couple of eyes that made me momentarily weak in the knees. That's not Victor Roby. That's not Big Man. I'll own up to weakness. I'll own up to cowardice. But …"

"But you didn't," she says. "Did you, Ray? Own up."

"No," I say, staring down into my glass.

She reaches under my chin with the crook of a finger. Lifts. Smiles.

"If it's true, all of it, would you love me any less?"

"If it's true, Marlo, any of it, I'm not sure I could say I ever really knew you."

Marlo nods.

"Like I said, Ray. There's a bottom to everything. Love too, I guess."

She pulls the straw from her glass, white with ice cream. But it's not a straw. Too short. Five inches and narrow. There is no ice cream. It's white with an ochre tip. She puts it between my lips. Kyle Aubry is there, arm outstretched. I lean into the flame.

"Work to do, Detective," she says. Just her voice through the smoke. The stool is empty. Ella sings.

The stars fade. I linger on.

SEVENTY-ONE

His breath makes bubbles in the blood, inflating and popping and reinflating as the air leaves the nostril mashed against the laundry room linoleum.

Rising takes time. Too much pain, mostly in his chest. Heart attack, he thinks. Then, no. Not that. His biceps still work. He pushes himself up. Leans back against the dryer. Breathes in and out. Bleeds. Takes silent inventory. His nose is a faucet. He pinches it. Not broken. His tongue reports back two split lips. All teeth accounted for. He spits.

The problem is in his chest. Every breath hurts. Changing position is excruciating. He guesses he's got a couple of ribs that aren't what they used to be.

The only thing that doesn't hurt is listening. So he does a lot of that. Listens. The house around him is silent. The back door is still open. The rain is still falling like it's the first day of thirty-nine more. Puddles collecting in the hall. The sirens of Chicago birdsong, mourning in the dark.

He manages to stand, leaning against white boxy appliances. Smearing them red. He puts a roll of paper towels to good use. The room wants to spin. He fights that. Suddenly a new sound. Not a siren. He digs. Answers.

"Hey Mack."

"Raj."

"So Windy City Towing was hooking up the Corolla just as I got there. The guy in the Nissan stayed on the phone the whole time. When he was clear, he headed back downtown. I stayed on him. He went into a parking garage on Adams just up the street from the Rookery."

"Raj."

"I didn't follow him inside. I'm not making that mistake again. I parked and waited. He came out about ten minutes later with a silver Audi right behind him. Nice car. That garage had to be mostly empty, pretty dead anyway, so I figured the Audi was part of a meet up. Could be? Maybe? I got the plates, just in case. Elephant Ridiculous Mohamed seven one seven."

"Raj."

"They split up at the Ninety. Audi headed north, Nissan headed south. So I just kept on the main target. He pulled into the garage of a two-story house in Kenwood, off 46th and Woodlawn."

"Raj."

"I've got the address if you need it."

"Raj."

"So what's up with you, boss man?"

SEVENTY-TWO

It should take Raj at least forty-five minutes to make the trip. He promises to make it in thirty. I tell him it's not worth killing anyone. He makes one pitch for an ambulance but seems to know better. Smart kid. The sirens will hurt my headache.

Now that I'm up, it hurts just to think about lowering myself again. I stay upright. I shuffle slowly through the wreckage of Dennis O'Toole, moving like I'm headed to my ninety-eighth birthday party, pinching my nose with a bloody paper towel. In the kitchen I remember the papers I put in the oven. It hurts to pull open the door, but I manage. They're still there. I reach in and grab them. Put them back in my pocket.

I'm halfway through a slow three-quarter turn when I see Dennis' bowl full of Blondie's lottery cards. I grab the bowl and fan the cards out on the flour and coffee-dusted counter. There must be fifty of them. The top half of the stack is unused. The cards on the bottom half of the stack have all been filled out. I pick up a card for a better look.

Three games per card, four rows of bubbles for each game. That makes for twelve rows of bubbles, ten bubbles in each row, numbered zero through nine. Fill in one bubble on each row, hand it to the pimply-faced kid behind the counter wearing a white paper hat and then wait for him to tell you the good news. Easy enough.

Dennis has played all three games. One bubble blackened on each row, for a total of twelve. First row: 2. Second row: 5. Third row: 5. Rows four through six are all zeros. Seventh row: 1. Then an 8. Then a 7. For the last three rows he has selected 1, 9 and 2. At the bottom of the card is a circled, handwritten number: 62. I look at the next card. Same pattern, different numbers. The number in the circle is 25. I look through the others. Same thing. I start to see repeat sequences. A lot of 2-5-5's. Also 1-9-2's.

1-8-7.

0-0-0.

Half of this job is recognizing patterns. A man does a thing and then he does that same thing again. Maybe at the same time or in the same place or with the same person. That usually *means* something in this line of work. It helps narrow down the universe into something you can roll up and stick in your pocket. It's a good feeling. That makes you start looking for things you've seen before. Including numbers. Phone numbers. Addresses. License plates.

And now this. I feel the revelation in my rib cage.

I yank the printer pages out of my inside pocket. I push the thicker sheaf aside and focus on the thinner printout. I move my bloody finger over the undifferentiated string of numbers.

There. 255. And again. 187. And again. 000.

I pick a card at random, reading the numbers vertically. 2, 5, 5, 0, 0, 0, 1, 8, 7, 0, 9, 3. I hold the card up to the printout, looking at each of the number sequences that Kevin Canady highlighted for me in yellow.

And then, there it is. Like a kick in the head. I'd laugh if laughing didn't make me cry. Who ever thought IP addresses could be so emotional.

The numbers circled at the bottom of each card are still a mystery. I pick one at random. 62. I find that number here and there on the printouts – a six followed by a two – but if that's supposed to mean something, then I figure I've got a better chance of getting an answer from dearly departed Dennis O'Toole than figuring it out for myself.

I run my hands under the tap and find a clean paper towel. No sense in getting my blood on the evidence. I return the bloody printouts to my coat pocket, then blow away the flour and gather up the cards in a stack. I shuffle out of the kitchen, over a pile of cookbooks, kicking through broken porcelain and glass, one foot in front of the other until I'm through the living room and looking at the foyer.

The front door is still open to the wind, blowing a curtain of rain. I pocket the lottery cards and snag the bottle of bourbon from the couch cushion where Amanda had dropped it. Then I head for the door.

The street is empty. No Sonata. No motorcycle. Just a wet, yellow streetlight wondering where everybody went.

I lean up against the jamb, still pinching my nose with one hand and clutching the bourbon by the neck. It takes one slug to miss the Old Forester and a second slug to not care. I drink and wait and watch the rain, feeling the lottery cards in my pocket, wishing they were Camels. But they aren't Camels. They're puzzle pieces. Put them all together and they only make half a picture. The other half has to do with those circled numbers at the bottom of each card. According to

Amanda, Dennis was good with computers. Good enough to know not to trust them. He wanted an analog back-up just in case someone who knew how to work a delete key figured him out.

They figured him out alright. And then they deleted him.

I'm still leaning up against the door when Rajnish Malik's cab screeches to a stop out front. He comes running but stops sharply halfway up the walk when he sees me. I figure that's the power of human blood. As bad as I feel, I must look worse.

"Jesus …"

"Nah. Jesus is alibied up to his earlobes. This was someone else. Bruce Lee, maybe. You made good time. Run anyone over?"

"No. What the fuck happened?"

"Got my ass handed to me on a paper plate is what happened. I'm not sure you're going to make such a good detective after all."

Raj keeps coming until he's under the eave and out of the rain.

"No, I figured out that much. I mean …"

"Later. I need you to come in and move a washer and dryer."

After we rescue Sig from the laundry room, Raj takes me to Mercy Hospital because it's the closest. He wants to walk me in. He wants to wait. I send him on his way, promising to call him for a ride home.

I walk through the hissing double doors on my own steam. Busy night for Mercy. Everybody in the ER lobby is hurting for someone new and worse off to look at. That's me.

The blood puts the doughy guard by the entry on alert. He doesn't like Sig playing peek-a-boo from inside the flap of my raincoat. My badge and ID have to get involved. He settles down and lets me in.

My vitals blab to the intake nurse about my age and general ill health. Once that's established, I find a chair in the waiting room where I can sit down and hurt. I listen to other people's names as I wait my turn. I close my eyes, awash in the moaning misery around me. I try to calculate the odds that Amanda Ramada Tate is still alive and in the state of Illinois. The math makes my head hurt. I try to sleep instead. That almost works. *The Golden Girls* are too loud up in the corner, syndicated into eternity. Rose doesn't understand why Blanche is on Dorothy's last nerve.

I fish out my phone and call Amanda. No answer. I leave a message telling her to call, reminding her that running, trying to disappear, is a bad idea. I don't even convince myself. She probably should run. Disappear. I start to put the phone away, but it wants more attention. For a split second I assume it's her. Raphael Santiago pops that balloon in one syllable.

"Mack?"

"Raffi. What's doing?"

"Just wanted to let you know I delivered Twill to his house. No problems. His lawyer, Earnie, met us on the driveway. Place was crawling, man."

"I'll bet."

"No way I was getting inside. I hung around awhile. Earnie eventually came out to tell me they didn't need a chauffeur. Said he and LT had arranged a sit-down with CPD."

"Tonight, I'm guessing."

"As we speak. He said Twill told them where they can find his rig. Parked out at O'Hare."

"You don't say."

"You knew? Of course you knew. Earnie wanted me to be there to observe the search. So I headed out there and got the whole thing on video."

"They give you any trouble?"

"Nah. They were pretty accommodating. It was by the book. Lots of little evidence bags though."

"Could you see?"

"No. And they scraped all four tires."

"Checking for country mud."

"Right. I called Earnie and reported back. Is that *The Golden Girls* I'm hearing? Where are you, man?"

"New strip club for seniors. I need you to run a plate."

"Shoot."

"Elephant ... Jesus."

"Elephant Jesus?"

"Echo Romeo Michael seven one seven. Silver Audi."

"Got it. What's doin' with you?"

"Watching reruns. Just about to nod off."

Another three hours puts me in a test of wills with a man in blue scrubs.

"We're not a prison," he concedes.

"You got that right, doc. The food is better in prison. And you can get some sleep most nights. They might stab you in prison, but at least the shiv goes in quiet. They don't beep you to death."

"I'm saying ..."

"It's like a Chinese water torture for the ears."

"I'm saying we can't keep you against your will, but …"

The ER doc looks all of seventeen. He wants to admit me for observation. It's not the cracked ribs that concern him. Not much to do about those except try to not move any pianos or run any marathons. It's the concussion that bothers him. He wants to make sure my brain isn't going to swell itself out my ears. He doesn't have a visual aid for that issue, so he keeps pointing at the x-ray of my chest. Two fractured ribs and lots of soft tissue damage. I can't help but look around for Dr. Jha's shadow.

I tell him to wrap my chest and let me go. Turns out they don't wrap for rib fractures these days. Risk of pneumonia. He starts in again with the brain swelling concern. There's no sign of it now, but he says it could happen. I tell him the same is true about a meteor hitting the hospital.

Two-thirty in the morning brings a discharge against medical advice. They bludgeon me with warnings and hand me a prescription for the elephant on my chest. I make the call to Raj, but he's already outside waiting in the rain like he never left.

"Tell me you haven't been here the whole time," I say.

"I've been taking fares. I've been here maybe a half hour."

"You're a bad liar, Mr. Malik. Don't you sleep?"

"Between fares. How you doing?"

"Ever dropped a fork into a garbage disposal?"

"Got it. Where to?"

"Drugs. Home. Ask me any question about anything and I will shoot you in the ear."

It's pushing four a.m. before I'm home apologizing to Phil. She's facing the door when I walk in, perched on the back of the recliner with her tail stirring the air below. She curls it up and drops it in a rhythm that reminds me of someone drumming their fingers on a table, tired of waiting. Phil's never been one of those cats that comes running. It's my job to go to her. And I do. It's her job to pretend she's indifferent.

Raj wants to have a sleepover, just in case. I have to threaten to shoot him again to get him to go home. He does the things I can't before he leaves. Phil's food off the high shelf. Her bowl off the floor. I focus on the thing I can reach. I pour it into a short glass over a pile of ice. I toss a pain pill in my mouth and wash it down.

"You think that's a good idea?" Raj asks, scooping out the cat food with a spoon. I pull out Sig and set him on the counter where Raj can see him. Raj holds up both hands. "Okay. Okay. Just asking."

"Go home and get some sleep," I say. "Can you be back here about eleven?"

"Yes," he says. "Where are we going? To get your car?"

I start to shake my head, but that hurts too much. I turn away to wander out into the living room for the recliner, leaving Raj to clean up.

"Paula's a snitch these days," I say. "I need you to take me out to see a woman about a wife."

The house is quiet once Raj is gone. At first that feels like a blessing. Then it's too quiet. Too still. I feel like I might suffocate. Like I have a bag over my head. I make another call to Amanda. Nothing. I put the phone away. The stillness comes at me again. I should get up and put on some music; spin a little life into the room. Maybe Ruth Brown. Early Ella. But that would require getting up, which hurts too much to imagine. Plus, Phil is curled up on my lap. It's not in me to disappoint her. So I sit in the dark and feel the quiet thickening around me like an old burlap sack. The universe shrinks. Slows. Darkens.

I come awake fighting, thrashing in my chair, kicking at the chainsaw as it goes back in for bone. Phil is on the table, watching me with those ancient eyes. Marlo's eyes. My own eyes are streaming tears. My throat is dry and raw. My heart is trying to finish the job on my screaming ribs. My body is covered in sweat.

The clock on the shelf says 5:33. Phil meows. All I can do is pant back at her.

Standing up strikes me as a good idea. That's enough sleep for one week. The pain will keep me awake. I shuffle inelegantly into the kitchen and pop another pill, washing it back. Water this time. I brace myself against the counter and watch the tap hiss away into the dark hole in the sink. I try to remember who was working the chainsaw this time. I can't. Maybe Amanda Ramada Tate. Frenchie Marie. Agent John Murray. The ER doc. Everybody's a lumberjack.

I think about turning off the water. But I don't. Something about the constancy of the sound is reassuring. I let it run.

The book on the counter next to the blender is from Doris. *Soup and the Single Man.* Nothing cuts the grief of a widower like homemade wild mushroom and asparagus. French onion. Mulligatawny. She's got her favorites bookmarked with *Bucks* cocktail napkins. So, in the early days, trying to crawl out of the crater of Marlo's death, I'd given soup a try. Doris' punishment for her good intentions was to share my first bowl. Thereafter she started making the soup herself and bringing it to me. Every now and then my incompetence works out well.

I pull the book toward me and open it to the M's. *Mulligatawny*. Doris' loopy script fills one corner of the margin. *Great for a rainy day! Save this one!*

Then a winking smiley face.

I reach out sideways, flailing blindly at the faucet. I slap off the water without taking my eyes off the page.

Holy shit.

SEVENTY-THREE

Raj is early. Fine by me, because I was tired of waiting before it was even eight o'clock. I could have passed the time by sleeping, but I was afraid of never waking up.

By nine-thirty I'd made the call to Francine Lucas for a time and place. She picked up on the first ring. The call lasted fifteen seconds. I conclude that Francine has reached that age where everything in life except the absolute essentials is a waste of time.

"Don't be late," she'd said. "I'll have to move my bowels. Then there's bingo."

I spent the next hour sitting at the Smith-Corona with Phil trying to bang out another chapter in *The Russian Doll*. I'm up to the part about falling asleep outside Scooter's porn shop and losing my back windshield to a few carefully aimed bullets. Should be exciting stuff except that it's the falling asleep part that I find most intriguing. My chin hit my chest every ten minutes, and I woke up with Phil looking at me like she's trying to figure why she keeps me around. I'm guessing that by the time Raj pulled up, Phil was glad to have the place to herself again.

The air outside is sulking; heavy and wet but not actually raining. First time in a week. Raj sticks his hand out the window and looks skyward as I climb in.

"Not sure I remember what the sun looks like," he says.

"Fat, yellow guy. Spends all his time in Vegas and Hawaii."

I give him the address that Francine gave to me. He keys it into his phone and hits the gas.

"We need to make a stop first," I say. "Shouldn't take long."

"Where to?"

"The scene of my last ass-kicking."

"What?" Raj steers around an homage to Lake Michigan at the corner of my street. "You forget something?"

"Something like that."

I leave Raj in the car and haul my ribs up the walk to the front door. It takes me three times to key in the code that Amanda had the night before. I'm almost ready to go around back, but the door finally gives me a beep and welcomes me in. The place looks the same. No one has busted in and cleaned things up.

I make a broken beeline through the living room for the kitchen. I kick through the pile of flour-dusted cookware until I find what I'm looking for. I bend down for it but my chest doesn't like that idea, so I get my knees involved. That's no picnic either, but I manage to get the thing – red and covered in bananas – out from under a frying pan and stand again. I drop it on the counter with a slap.

Milkshake Masterpieces – 201 Recipes to Change Your Life.

Emerging from the pile of bananas is an icy glass blender full of something frothy and chocolate.

I pull the stack of lottery cards out of my pocket and pick one out at random. The filled-in bubbles spell out an IP Address of 255 000 187 093. The number circled at the bottom of the card is 48. I open the book to page 48.

The Kahlua Mocha Milkshake is in a tall sundae glass that sits on a white counter among scattered coffee beans. A brown and white striped straw is emerging from a cloud of whipped cream littered with chocolate shavings. Beneath the photo is a recipe, followed by a square of blank lines beneath the heading: *Make Your Own Magic.* Dennis O'Toole has used a black pen to write down his own idea of a magic Kahlua Mocha Milkshake. It doesn't sound particularly appetizing.

Nigel Whitscombe, Pinskeep Securities, London.

Following that is some contact information. Phone. Email. Brokerage address. Home address. Family members. Everything a guy might need to reach out and tap Nigel Whitscombe on the shoulder with a life-changing proposition.

I turn the page. Peppermint Pattie Paradise. Dennis has noted that, for his taste, the most important ingredient in this shake is Juliette Moreau at Françoise Aubert SAS International Trading. Paris. Husband Henri. Daughter Anne. Father Marc Villeneuve, Councilman for the 9th Arrondissement.

Page 52. Vanilla Valhalla. Kamin Chopra. Zerodha Broking, New Delhi. Kamin's got five different phone numbers. His wife, Saira, has three.

Page 88. Strawberry Fields Forever. Yvonne Williams. NYMEX. Manhattan. Divorced. Single mom to two kids at East Side Middle.

Page 106. Peachy-Perfect Parfait. Constantine Papadopoulos. Chicago MERC. One wife, three kids and a mistress.

I fan the pages in front of my face. The breeze smells like money.

SEVENTY-FOUR

Francine Lucas is in the Legacy Horizon Senior Living theater, right where she said she'd be. Dead center of the room. If the theater was a turntable, she'd be sitting on the spindle.

Not that it matters. She's the only one in here. The lights are on and the screen up front is ablaze with a silent slide show of Chicago in the summer. A sprawl of hardwoods towering over a bike trail in Big Marsh Park dissolves to a bucket of roses on a sun-splashed corner of Uptown. Makes sense. It's as close to a sunny day as either of us will ever get today.

I make my way down the aisle, taking off my coat with painful difficulty and flicking away beads of water. She looks sideways at me as I make it to her row.

"Detective Mackey."

"Mrs. Lucas. Thank you for meeting me."

"Just as well. I don't like telephones. Trouble finding me?"

"None. You made it easy."

"Guess you wouldn't be a very good detective, would you?"

She has a strong, thin voice and a full head of coiffed hair that frames her wrinkled face like a white raisin nestled in a ball of cotton. Large pink plastic glasses on an Italian nose with another pair, smaller and black, hanging from a string of blue glass beads around her neck. She's in a pink, felted wool jacket to match the glasses. The theater rows are just wide enough for the walker standing at the ready on the other side of her. I saunter forward and drop my coat over the back of a faux velvet seat.

"That *would* make me a bad detective," I say. "But I've got to tell you, ma'am, some days I wonder if I could even find myself in a mirror."

"I have those days too," she says. "One thing is for sure though."

"What's that?"

"Call me ma'am again and the next time you see yourself in a mirror will not be a pleasant experience."

"It's already unpleasant enough as it is."

"Then call me Francine."

She sticks up a hand for me to shake and I follow orders.

"Understood. Call me Ray."

"Sit already, Ray. My neck is starting to hurt."

On the screen, seven laughing kids and a corgi are all on the same playground slide in Roseland. I sit with a groan that comes out too loud.

"Hurts that much to sit down, maybe you should be living here too," she says.

"Maybe I should. Nice place, from what I can see. It's even got its own theater."

"I never come for the movies. I come for the quiet." She points at the screen. The Chicago skyline from Lake Michigan in the middle of summer, sun exploding from ten thousand windows. "This is how I see our city now. It all costs a pretty penny. But it's comfortable. They do keep track of you though."

"Oh?"

She shows me what I thought was part of her necklace. It isn't. It's a black plastic rectangle on a cord.

"Someone knows where I am twenty-four-seven."

"Our lives are not so different, Francine."

"I fall, they come running."

"Where can I get one of those?"

She laughs a little. "You want mine? Your face looks like you might need it more than I do."

"Frightening, I know."

"Our mutual friend warned me you look a little rough."

"Did she now? Yeah, well, Frenchie Marie is nothing if not a keen observer."

"Frenchie Marie?"

"It's what I call her."

"You must know her well."

"Seems like forever. How long have you known her?"

"I don't know her at all. Just the one phone call. She told me Marlo Kline was your wife. That you are having some trouble … what," Francine leans toward me and smiles, "… remembering her, I guess. She thought I could help. Widow to widower."

"I see." I lean back, adjusting my ribs to the seat, looking at the screen. Pigeons in a park cluster beneath an old hand in a bag.

"She wanted to know if it was okay for you to call me."

"Thanks for stepping up," I say.

"Oh, I told her I wasn't interested. Practically hung up on her. But then …" She breaks off and loses herself for some seconds looking at a rainbow over Humboldt Park. Then she looks back at me. "I know what it's like to lose a spouse. And I liked Marlo. She was important to me. I decided I owed it to *her* to talk to you. So the next day I called your employer. Got your number. That wasn't easy. I kept at it until I wore them down."

"I'm grateful to you, Francine. Thank you."

"Not sure I can be of much help. I didn't know her well. But what would you like to know?"

The question nearly swamps the boat. *What would I like to know?* I want to know everything.

"How did you know her? What was your relationship?"

"We became acquainted after my husband died. I needed a private detective."

"So your relationship with Marlo was professional."

"Yes."

"Exclusively?"

"Yes. I was a client to her. Nothing more. I felt like she was more than just a detective to me."

"What was she to you?"

"My last hope for the truth. Someone who listened when no one else would. She was everything I needed her to be at exactly the right time."

"What was your husband's name?"

Francine looks at me with dark brown eyes remarkably clear for someone her age. They guard the threshold of history, those eyes, assessing whether I'm worthy. They disappear in a slow blink. Francine takes in a breath and gives me a nod.

"Dominic," she says. "Dominic Lucas. Everyone called him Lucky."

Never been hit by a train before. Now I know what that feels like.

SEVENTY-FIVE

Ray doesn't answer. He can't. All he can manage is to stare back at the widow Lucas and to try and calculate just what it means that she was once Marlo's client. She is patient, watching him. In his periphery, the screen dissolves from something reddish to something bluish. That's as much as he cares to discern.

"Lucky Lucas?" It's almost a whisper. "Your husband was …"

"You know of him then."

"Yeah," says Ray with a slow nod. "I do."

"Tell me what you know. I don't want to bore you."

"There's literally no chance of that."

"Indulge me."

"Okay. I know that once upon a time your husband was a force to be reckoned with in this city. I know he was a tough prosecutor before he went into politics. Good reputation. Threw himself at the drug problem in the seventies and made a difference. Took down Smiley Whatshisname…"

"Farrar."

"Smiley Farrar," he says, pointing at her. "That's it. Smiley Ferrar and his South Shore heroine fiefdom. That was a big win." Francine nods with a remembering smile.

"It was."

"And I know that when Lucky went into politics, he grabbed the 42nd Ward by the neck and never let it go. He knew how to build a coalition. Knew how to make half a loaf feel like a full meal. Held the 42nd for four terms, unopposed, and was ready to go again, but …"

Ray breaks off. He looks up at the screen. A paper lantern parade through Chinatown, faces glowing. Francine finishes for him.

"But he died," she says.

"Yeah," Ray's turn to nod. "He died. A year and change before the primary."

"How. How did he die, Detective?"

"Well, my understanding is that he fell off the side of his cabin cruiser while it was docked in Belmont Harbor. Hit his head on the pier. Drowned."

They watch the screen together in silence.

"Your memory is accurate," she says at last, "but incomplete. You left out the part about him being drunk, as he often was when he spent time on the boat. That's something else Lucky was known for. He was a drinker."

"Yes," says Ray. "The finding was that he was intoxicated at the time he drowned." He squares himself to her as best he can. "Francine, sorry … are you saying that you hired Marlo to investigate the death of your husband?"

She nods slowly.

"No one would listen to me. The police conducted their investigation. Reached their conclusions. I was shouting into the wind."

"What, exactly, were you shouting?"

"That his death was not an accident. That Lucky was murdered."

"Murdered by whom?"

"Bubba Jones. Or someone hired by his campaign. Wasn't my idea to call a private detective. I was in a grieving freefall. Lucky was gone and I was alone. Well," she casts Ray a look, "I *felt* alone. I was surrounded by people. Lucky had lots of friends, or what passes for friends in politics, but none of them were my friends particularly. I felt like I'd fallen into a well and no one could reach me."

Francine shakes out a rueful laugh.

"What," says Ray.

"Makes me think of Senator Kahn's wife. Nancy. Poor woman. What she must be feeling now. I met her once at a fundraiser for the Shedd Aquarium. Nice enough woman. A little aloof. Like she didn't want to be there. I could relate. There was a politician's wife, surrounded by smiling, gladhanding people, none of them actual friends. She just wanted to go home. I thought of calling her last week when I heard the news about her husband. I wanted to tell her that I know how she's feeling. It was a foolish impulse that I'm glad I resisted."

"Why? Sounds like a compassionate impulse to me."

"Nancy Kahn is getting a thousand of those calls, from people she doesn't really know or care about. That just makes the hole deeper."

"You had it worse, I'd think. Bob Kahn had cancer three different times. I suspect his wife was always wondering when that shoe would finally drop."

Francine slowly shakes her head.

"Death of a spouse is a singular experience, Detective. There is no preparing for it. Senator Kahn beat cancer three times, and then, one day out of the blue, he didn't. We all like to think the people we love the most are immortal. I don't have to tell you that."

"No," says Ray. "You don't."

"I was no different. Lucky was dead and I was alone. I felt like I was the only one holding those last moments of his life in my hands. No one would believe me that his life was taken by force. Not even the police. That's when your wife, your future wife, called."

"Wait. She … Marlo reached out to you first?"

Francine nods again.

"Asked if she could come by and talk. Said she didn't want to talk on the phone. Wouldn't tell me why she wanted to see me except that it was about Lucky. It really put me off. I wasn't interested. I hung up on her."

"I take it that wasn't the end."

"She called back. Told me she thought Lucky's death wasn't an accident. That got my attention."

"Because you believed the same."

Francine nods.

"Me and me alone. Until Marlo called."

"What made you think Lucky was murdered?"

"That's not a short story."

Ray nods, cutting her a look.

"Most of the stories in my business are short on candor," he says.

"Oh, it's all true," says Francine.

"Then that's all I care about."

"I thought this was about Marlo," she says.

"Lucky first."

Francine sighs, looking at a shot of two cops leaning against a black-and-white, eating ice cream cones. Willis Tower rises in the background, a gleaming tentpole holding up an infinite blue tarp.

"Where to start," she says. "Lucky and I were not a happy couple when all of this happened. We were effectively estranged for the last two months of his life. He spent a lot of his time living at his office and on that damned boat. Drinking too much, which was always true, but … it had gotten worse. We were both angry. We dealt with anger differently. I cried and yelled a lot. Lucky drank."

"What caused the anger?"

"I don't know about your marriage, Ray, but when you're married as long as Lucky and I had been married, you feel pretty certain that you know everything there is to know about your spouse. Surprises are rare and can be, well," she looks, eyebrows raised, "unsettling."

A pang in Ray's old and battered heart. Unsettling surprises. He wants to tell her he knows exactly what she means. He wants to open himself up. He doesn't. Up on the screen a black and yellow clown can't get out of an invisible box.

"I take it you learned something about Lucky you didn't know."

"Didn't know he had a second daughter," she says. "We already had one of those. Lianne. Smart. Successful. Married to a good-for-nothing jackass who just happens to be the linoleum king of Boca Raton. Lianne sells commercial real estate and sends me something from Hallmark every Christmas and Easter. Silly me, but I thought she was the only daughter in the mix. Turned out, to my surprise, Lucky'd gone off and had one of his own."

"That does qualify as a surprise," says Ray. "Tell me about her."

"Kaylee. Twenty-three at the time. Single mom of a seven-year-old. Rose. Lucky's granddaughter. I found out Kaylee had popped up on Lucky's radar a couple of years earlier."

"Money or love?"

"Kaylee? Please. She wanted money. Lucky had no idea she existed. Or so he said. I didn't believe him when I first learned about her, but I think that was probably the truth. He'd crossed paths with some strumpet in Vegas on one of his junkets for the city council. She stayed in Vegas, whoever she was, just like the saying goes. Kept little Kaylee to herself."

"But then Kaylee grew up and learned how to use a phone."

Francine nods.

"Lucky sent her some money. A lot of money that first year. He tried to keep it quiet."

"From you."

"From everyone. But, yes, from me. He said she disappeared for a while. He figured she'd moved on. But she popped up again a little over a year before what would have been Lucky's fourth term."

"What was the ask?"

"Said her mom had died and she wanted twenty thousand dollars to help get into a new house. Lucky balked. He couldn't keep that kind of money secret, even if we had it to spare. And we didn't. So he drew the line. Told her she needs to live her own life." Francine grips Ray by the wrist and squeezes, old eyes full of anguish. "His own daughter he says this to. Can you imagine? His own daughter. And granddaughter. I don't care who she is or what she's up to. Maybe you don't give her the cash, but maybe you try to connect with your own kid. And your own granddaughter. We could have afforded her a little help. But *live your own life?* That's not the man I married. Well. I thought. I was wrong."

Francine shakes her head, still angry all these years later.

"Anyway, next thing Lucky knows, couple, three weeks later, he gets a visit from the competition."

"Frederick Jones," says Ray, "Bubba."

"The same." She looks. "You know your local politics."

"I've got a nose for all the bad smells. Helps keep my shoes clean."

"Well. Lucky and Bubba go for a drink. Those two hated each other but pretended otherwise. Bubba was always either the loudest critic in the room or the constituent that needed some kind of government assistance for his Gold Coast car dealerships. Bubba was always joking about coming to take the 42nd away from Lucky. Wasn't a joke, turned out. Anyway, Bubba takes Lucky for a drink. Tells him that he's running for Lucky's seat and, also, that he knows all about Kaylee and Rose."

"So Kaylee found herself a sympathetic ear."

"Right. And she filled it with stories about how she was the product of a non-consensual encounter in a Las Vegas limo."

"Non-consensual. Actual rape?"

"Yes. Not that I believe it – Lucky swore nothing like that ever happened – but, yes. She told Bubba she'd been reaching out to Lucky for help to raise her daughter, Lucky's granddaughter, but that Lucky wanted to pretend they didn't exist."

"And so Bubba thinks he has an issue to run on."

"That's the threat. But what Bubba really wants is a truce. You see, Bubba's half-brother …"

"Of course," Ray interrupts with an eyeroll. "Convicted for sexually assaulting a postal employee in the back of a mail truck. You don't talk about my family history of sexual assault and I won't talk about yours."

"That's it."

"Did they shake on it?"

She gives Ray a dismissive look.

"Lucky was always too stubborn and proud for something like that. A deal with Bubba Jones? Not in a million years. He gave Bubba what for and stormed out. Came home, drank his courage up and told me all about Kaylee and Rose and what was happening with Bubba. He didn't earn any honesty points."

"He thought it was all coming out. He was trying to get ahead of it."

"Yes. We fought for a week. He took up semi-permanent residence on the boat. I barely saw him. Then one day he was dead."

"How'd you hear?"

"Belmont harbormaster found him floating late morning. Called the police. They fished him out and called me. My sister and I drove out to the morgue." She looks at Ray with eyes less clear than before. "Did you see your wife's body after she passed?"

The question hits Ray in the chest, only from the inside. It knocks him backward a few years. Marlo on the hospital bed, her hand, suddenly alien in its flat, lifeless pallor, in his. Ray nods.

"Yes."

"Didn't look like her, did it?"

"No," he says. "It didn't. Not really."

"The spark is everything."

The words feel like the closing of a door behind her, sealing them inside a dark room where nothing exists but an absence. A blackness where once had been light. Ray blinks. Nods.

"The spark is everything," he agrees. "I don't mean to make you relive that, Francine. I'm sorry."

She waves her hand in the air, dismissing the memory.

"The police did their investigation. Officer came out to the house and interviewed me. Told me it looked like Lucky was drunk and fell off the side of the boat, hit his head on the corner of the dock and drowned. I accepted that. I accepted it completely. I wasn't thinking of anything else at the time."

"But that changed?"

"Two, three days later I screwed up the courage to go out to the boat. It looked a mess. Lucky had been living there pretty much around the clock. The man could not pick up his clothes or wash his dishes to save his life. Other than that, it looked pretty much as it always had. But I then I noticed the owl on the shelf."

"The owl?"

Francine holds her wrinkled, liver-spotted hands four inches apart.

"Plastic barn owl about so big. He had three of them. One in his office at work, one in his office at home and one on the boat. Little recorders inside. He showed me how they work once. There was a big bribery scandal in the 39th Ward during Lucky's second term. Guy named Marcus Henry. You remember him?"

"Vaguely. Maybe."

"Suffice it to say, Marcus would have kept his job if he could have proven his version of a certain conversation. Lucky learned the lesson."

"Okay. I take it the owl on the boat had a story to tell."

"Lucky had a visitor the night he died. He must have become concerned and switched on the owl. There was about five, six minutes of sound and then a lot of silence."

"What'd you hear?"

"Recording quality was pretty bad, but I could hear Lucky arguing with another man about whether he should be running for another term. The other man kept referring to Lucky's daughter and saying she was an issue. Heard the word limousine once or twice too."

"An issue?"

"Yes. An issue in the election. He kept repeating that Lucky had his head up you know where and that his daughter was an issue the voters would have to confront. She was going to ruin Lucky's legacy in the 42nd."

"What was Lucky saying?"

"Lucky was drunk and angry. Those two things often went together. He denied that he had a daughter. He said he would be making a report to the FBI and ordered him off the boat. I'll spare you the expletives. He was worked up. Then there were sounds of something physical happening. A scuffle. A fight. Grunting. Struggling. I could hear a glass break. Then there was just …" Francine shakes her head. "Nothing. Dead air."

"Did you share that with the police?"

"You kidding? I called them as soon as I got home. They sent someone out for another interview. He took me back out to the marina so I could show him where the owl had been. I also showed him the other thing I found too."

"Which was?"

"Only three crystal tumblers that belonged to a set of four. I bought those tumblers for Lucky myself. Anniversary present."

"Any signs of broken glass?"

"None that I found. Police said they didn't find any broken glass in their investigation. I concluded the guy must have cleaned up before he left. Problem is the owl didn't seem to hear any kind of cleaning up."

"Okay. And about that owl, you recognized Bubba's voice?"

"I'd never met Bubba Jones. Seen him several times, but … It was either him or someone from his campaign. Had to be."

"What did the police … was it CPD?"

"Yes. CPD."

"What did CPD have to say?"

"They said they'd look into it and reconsider their finding. It took them ten days. The evidence was inconclusive, they said. They stuck to the accidental death report."

"And the owl recording?"

"They said analysis of the recording revealed Lucky, highly intoxicated, ranting to himself about the election and his daughter."

"To himself."

"Yes. I couldn't believe what they were telling me. There were two voices on that recording." She holds up two fingers so Ray can count. *'Two.* I fought with them until they hated me. I demanded the recording be returned. All I got back was a transcript that was different than what I remembered. It read like Lucky was rambling on to himself. That's when I knew the fix was in."

"The police."

"Yes."

"Why?"

"Best guess is they had something to gain from Bubba making the council. He's got cops in the family. Meanwhile, Lucky was big on police reform. He took them to task. Or maybe it was just plain money. Bubba had more money than we ever did, and he would have known just who to pay. I don't know the how or why. But police were in on this thing. Had to be. I know what I heard on that recording."

"Did they even follow up with Bubba?"

"I demanded that they investigate Bubba Jones and his people. They assured me that they did that already and that there was no evidence Bubba ever paid a visit to the boat. I told them to investigate the daughter. Kaylee. They said they did that."

"And?"

"No evidence. Most they found was that she had made contact with Bubba's people to help his campaign and they were not interested because she sounded like a crank. I knew that was wrong too because Lucky told me about Bubba taking him for a drink and proposing a truce. Like I told you. I tried to tell the police, but they'd made up their mind. They were done."

"Were there any other suspects?" Ray asks. "Did Lucky have enemies you knew of?"

"Sure, Lucky had enemies. This is Chicago brass knuckle politics. All kinds of people hated Lucky. But none that I knew of who would actually, you know, kill him. He had a gambling problem once upon a time. Horses. Practically lived out at the Hawthorne track. He got in over his head. There were some rough characters in that mess. Not Bank of America, you understand."

"I get it."

"But Lucky paid what he owed. He found the money."

"Where'd he find it?"

"Bank of America, among other places. Our savings. We were teetering. We put the house in Lianne's name. She was barely in college at the time."

"Did Lucky pay back any of the original debt in ways other than cash?"

Francine looks at Ray with a new and uncomfortable seriousness.

"You mean did he pay out in political favors?"

"Sorry to ask," he says. "This isn't an interrogation. You don't have to answer. The cop in me doesn't know his place sometimes. Well, ever."

"There were rumors," she says, looking back at the screen. Fireworks raining red and blue light over the city. "Lucky assured me there was nothing to them. I believed him. I guess I still do. He had his problems, obviously. But I believe he valued his integrity as an alderman."

Ray leaves his thoughts about unicorns and honest politicians for another time.

"Okay. So CPD reaches its conclusion about Lucky's death. What happened next?"

"I was despondent. Angry. Deeply depressed. Grieving Lucky. Feeling like I'd failed him. I blamed myself, if you can believe that. I spent several weeks not wanting to get out of bed. Lianne pried herself free of the good life and came back to visit for a few weeks. She thought I was losing my mind. And I was. She wanted me to just accept that Lucky died from Jack Daniels and stupidity."

"You tell her about … about her surprise half-sister."

Francine nods.

"She was angry on my behalf about Kaylee. Really angry. She wasn't interested in pursuing any kind of justice for Lucky and wanted me to stop chasing phantom killers. All of which made me feel worse. That's about the time your future wife called."

Francine closes her eyes in a long blink and shakes her head.

"Marlo Kline. She was a lifeline in the dark. Like she had extra lifeforce inside of her to spare. Hope. Fight. Resolve. She made me feel so much better about myself." Francine looks at Ray with a sad smile. "She was something. No offense to my Lucky, God rest his soul, but I wish I'd had a spouse like Marlo. You're a lucky man, Ray. She's gone too soon and you're still a lucky man."

"Thank you," he says, trying to believe his next words and failing. "I am a lucky man."

"I hung up on her that first time, like I said. She didn't give me a chance to hang up the second time she called. She just said, *Mrs. Lucas, I don't think your husband's death was an accident.* Everything changed with those words. I invited her over. We talked for two hours in the middle of the night. It was raining hard then, like it is now. I made tea. She let me cry and vent. She was very kind. She said she wanted permission to investigate Lucky's death. I hired her on the spot."

"Hang on. I'm confused. What the hell'd Marlo know about any of it?"

"I asked her that, obviously. She said she had an informant, wouldn't tell me who. Information that someone was blackmailing Lucky to keep him out of the race. She wanted permission to look into it for me. I was … delighted is the wrong word." Francine looks at Ray. "Enthusiastic, I guess."

"And Lianne?"

"Not so much. She thought Marlo was scamming me out of my money. Wanted me to send her packing. We had several fights over Marlo. I can be very stubborn, Mack," she says almost apologetically.

"You?" Ray says. "I find that hard to believe." He gives her a smile in exchange for a self-deprecating laugh.

"I held my ground," she says with a nod. "She wasn't wrong to think I was losing my grip on reality. I developed an anxiety condition. Started hearing things."

"What kind of things?"

"People out in the bushes at night. I started to worry that whoever killed Lucky was looking to kill me because I was determined to make a stink. Lianne is not the most comforting person. She'd tell me it was nothing and then go up to bed. That left me awake and afraid. I called Marlo a couple of those nights. She was kind enough to come over and keep me company. Lianne hated that. She appointed herself Marlo's supervisor. Tried to keep her close. I suppose I should have appreciated her protective instincts. I didn't."

"How'd Marlo react?"

"Like a pro. She leaned into it. Welcomed it. Kept Lianne apprised. Accepted Lianne's invitations to lunch as if they weren't just opportunities for Lianne to convince her to drop the case for the sake of my peace of mind. But Marlo never gave in to the pressure. Lianne eventually gave up and went back home. She was convinced all of it would all come to nothing. She was right."

"What can you tell me about Marlo's investigation?"

"I gave her the police reports and all my correspondence with them. Gave her full access to the boat and to Lucky's office. All his papers. She tracked down Kaylee and interviewed her. Living in Bakersfield working for a pool cleaning outfit. Daughter Rose, in the third grade. That was then. Rose has her own kids now. Twins. Graduating this year."

"You're in touch?"

She shakes her head.

"The internet is a wonderful, terrible thing," she says.

"Cyber snooping, are we?"

"None of them know I exist. And you're one to talk about snooping, Detective."

Ray raises his hands.

"No judgment here. What did Marlo learn from Kaylee?"

"Basically the same story Kaylee gave the police. She was angry at Lucky for not giving her the money. She contacted Bubba Jones' campaign. Long telephone call. She wanted ten thousand dollars to go public. They brushed her off. Told her that was not the kind of campaign they were running. Liars. Bubba turned right around and used her story to his advantage. Tried to."

"What else with Kaylee?"

"She gave up. Went back to cleaning pools and raising her kid. The only thing new Marlo got out of her was that she had embellished the part about the rape. She thought that would be irresistible to Bubba. So she made it up."

"Must have felt good to put that part to rest."

"It did. Infidelity I can forgive. Keeping the secret I can forgive. And have. Lucky was no rapist."

"What else?"

"Not much. If Bubba or his people were on that boat, there was no way to prove it. Marlo spent some weeks looking into all the other campaigns. And there were a lot of them. Once Lucky was out of the running, seemed like everybody jumped into the pool. I felt like she was wasting her time. It was Bubba if it was anyone."

"What'd she find?"

"Nothing. They all came up clean."

"What about the Royce campaign?"

"Same. Nothing."

A bride is tossing her bouquet from the Centennial Wheel at Pier Park.

"Did she investigate the police angle?"

"We talked about it. Filing a claim. Going to some agency. Felt like throwing good money after bad."

"So what'd you do?"

"Pulled the plug." Francine wags her finger at the screen – girls in apple-green kayaks paddle the Chicago River through canyons of glass and steel – but seeing something else. Remembering. "There was a campaign worker. What was his name? Blake. Blake Wilhower. Hiltower. Wilhaven. Blake Wilhaven, I think. He was working for the Howard campaign. You know Trent Howard?"

"No."

"Always running for something. Never elected. Anyway, he jumped into the race for the 42nd. Had this campaign worker, Blake Wilhaven. I think that was his name. My brain … Someone shot him in the head while he was sitting in his car outside the Howard campaign headquarters. Marlo wanted to look into that. Nothing came of it."

"She say why she wanted to look into it?"

"I asked. She said she wondered whether two dead bodies in the race for the 42nd Ward was really a coincidence. But it went nowhere. Just another drug crime. That's when I said enough was enough. I didn't have the money to keep at it. It was time to move on with my life. Marlo said she'd keep snooping around for free, but nothing …" Francine shrugs. "You know, nothing came of it. Royce got elected, of course. He was very kind. He invited me to the dedication of the fountain out at Lurie Garden. Got a proclamation out of the city council honoring Lucky. I endorsed Royce fairly early on and I think the right man got the job. I'm not sure what I'd have done if Bubba had won. We'd probably be having this conversation at the prison for angry widows."

"And Marlo? Was that it between you two?"

Francine nods.

"For the most part. She checked in on me a couple of times. She had another case out of the country for quite a while. South America someplace. Venezuela, I think. Caracas? She brought me a necklace from a marketplace." Francine smiles apologetically. "Sweet, but I'm not much for leather and beads."

"Did you talk about the case when she came back?"

"She wanted to know if I was still pushing for answers. If I'd hired someone else. I hadn't. She offered to keep snooping around. I declined. That was kind of it. Not sure I saw her again after that. Truth is, Mack, I didn't know she had died until your friend called. Frenchie. Who again?"

"Marie."

"Odd name. Is Mattia French for Marie or something?"

Ray comes to attention like she's poked him with something sharp.

"What?"

"She told me her name was Mattia Lewis. I'm just curious about how she gets to Frenchie …"

"Wait. Stop. The person who called you was Mattia Lewis?" Ray neglects to hide his surprise, which turns out to be contagious. Francine pulls back, widening her eyes.

"I thought we were talking about the same person."

"Tia Lewis? Mattia?"

"That's what she said."

Ray leans back in his seat and stares up at the screen. Lightning forks above the city like Willis Tower and the Tribune Tower are part of a science experiment. He grabs for his coat, still draped over the next seat. He pulls out the printed photograph, unfolding it as he hands it over.

"What's this?" she asks.

"Recognize anyone in this photo?"

She trades the pink glasses for the black pair hanging from her neck. Then she pulls the paper up close to her face, as if wanting to sniff all of the figures sitting around that ballroom table.

"Sam Royce," she says. "Recognize him. And that's her," she taps the woman whose hand is beneath that of Victor Roby. "That's Marlo. Isn't it?"

Ray doesn't confirm or deny. Francine keeps tapping.

"When she came back from Venezuela her hair was shorter, but that's her alright."

"Marlo ever tell you about any associations she had with members of the Royce campaign?"

"Associations? No. I think she said she … she *talked* to them. Like she talked to the other campaigns. I mean … *associations* …" She squints again at the photo. Then she stops breathing. Ray notices.

"Francine?"

She pulls the page even closer to her face.

"He's the … that's the … He's the one who took my statement. Twice. That's him."

She turns the photo to Ray, pointing at the man he expects will be the late officer Tony Rickens, in a too-tight tuxedo at the far side of the table, speaking into the ear of the newly minted alderman, Samual T. Royce.

But that's not where the pearlescent pink nail of Francine's index finger is touching. She's pointing into a small cluster of people standing about ten feet behind Victor Roby. Specifically, at a man drinking from a champagne flute. Not much left in that glass, the way his back is bowed, like he might not know whether he's drinking bubbly from a flute or blowing air into a sax. Eyes closed. Elbow pointing out toward the table. *That man*, says the fingertip.

It's a man he'd never noticed, never recognized, in all the times he's looked at this photo. He'd seen him without *seeing* him, hiding in plain sight. He'd always focused on the table. Ray takes the photo back. Squints. Brushes a finger over the man's face.

He was a lot younger when this photo was taken. That's one thing. Age is nature's disguise. Not to mention all of this dark, wavy hair.

But time sure hasn't made him any shorter.

Christ, Ray. What kind of detective misses the tallest guy in the room?

SEVENTY-SIX

I leave Francine Lucas with my head still spinning. The pain in my chest is the only thing that seems to slow it down.

Raj is at the curb where I left him. He wants to play twenty questions. I tell him to play by himself and drive.

"Where am I going?" he asks.

"I don't care. Just do it quietly."

The white plastic bag on the seat next to me is from Bodega Bay Chicago, sitting on top of Dennis O'Toole's *Milkshake Masterpieces – 201 Recipes to Change Your Life*. Raj sees me looking.

"It's a Reuban," he says.

"You slipped off for a sandwich?"

"I figured I had time. Man's got to eat. That one's yours."

"Maybe later. Thanks."

"You gonna tell me what's up with the milkshake book?"

"No. I'm going to sit here quietly and look at the rain."

Raj reaches for a pocket.

"Mind if I smoke?"

I hold out my hand.

"Give me one of those things."

Raj lights up and then knocks out one for me. He offers up a flame, but I wave him off before I can think about it. I put the Camel where it belongs and look out at the rain like I promised, sheets of it, drowning a city that's been holding its breath for weeks. They say the Colorado River is turning into a dry scar. Arizona. Texas. Dying for a drink. Chicago is stuck in a car wash that never quits. Hardly seems fair.

Marlo liked to say that the world is about as fair as it is flat. She got that right. I've thrown that bit of wisdom around more times than I can count. I've wanted to carve it above my doorway just so I remember. Now those words sound like a rationalization; words to justify an effort to get a mob-connected politician elected alderman. *Fair? Of course not. The world's about as fair as it is flat, Ray. Now quit your whining and marry me.*

I pull out the photo I'd just finished showing Francine. It's new to me all over again. I was always so focused on the banquet table. Marlo. Victor. Royce. Rickens. But two inches to the left … there he is, drinking bubbly like it's New Year's Eve and the woman at the microphone is starting in about old acquaintance being forgot. How do you forget an old acquaintance it turns out you never really knew in the first place?

I rotate the page in the wet, gray light. What the hell were you doing with these guys, Marlo? I want to believe you weren't hired by a campaign to work a widow out of a murder accusation and into an endorsement. But that's getting harder to believe by the day. Private detectives get hired and then start asking questions. That's the way the world works. A PI who shows up asking questions already has a client. So who were you working for when you reached out to poor Francine?

Raj can't hear my questions, so he asks one of his own.

"You really want me to drive in circles?"

"Yes."

I fold up the photo and put it back in my pocket. The smoke I smell is from Raj's Camel, not the unlit stick in my mouth. It almost works if I don't think about it. Problem is not thinking about it. I put the cigarette on the dash and pull out my phone. Ten pokes gets me the voice I want.

"Gotta a feeling I should have let this one ring through," says Santiago.

"You should listen to those finely-honed instincts, Raffi. One day they might save your life."

"Or at least my productivity. I'm guessing you need a favor."

"A favor? Well, since you asked. I need whatever you can get me on the murder of a guy named Blake Wilhaven or Wilhower."

"Whose case?"

"CPD. That's why I'm calling you, Raffi. You're the one with the connection over there."

"Yeah, well she's the only one I've got and you're gonna wear her out, Mack. She's got her own job to do. And you're asking for public informa …"

"That takes too long. I need it yesterday."

"Of course you do," he says with a sigh. "Date of this murder?"

"I don't know exactly. Within a few months of the date that Sam Royce was first elected Alderman of the 42nd Ward."

"Aww, Mack." I can hear Santiago shaking his head. "Jesus H. That's some ice-cold shit, man."

"I'd have asked you for it right after Blake Wilhaven took a bullet to the head, but you were still chasing girls on the playground. I'd have paid closer attention myself, but I didn't know I'd ever give a shit. Turns out I do."

"You have an address?"

"No. It happened outside the campaign headquarters of a candidate named Trent Howard. Wilhaven, if that's his name, was in his car at the curb. My source remembers it as a drug hit."

"Who's your source, or is that more information that I'm better off not knowing?"

"Good question. Maybe use those finely-honed detective instincts of yours, Raffi. Thanks for this. I owe you one, buddy."

"One? Need to brush up on your counting skills, Mack. I'll get you a calculator."

The phone goes quiet. I tuck it away. Raj is burning holes in my face with his eyes.

"Does the murder of that Wilhaven guy have anything to do with your book of milkshakes?"

I give him a look.

"None of your business. Why are we driving in circles?"

"Because you …"

"Let's try a straight line for a change. Two triple one West Roosevelt."

Raj's eyebrows get excited.

"The FBI? You're meeting with the FBI?"

I look back out at the slop, still too much in my head to have a conversation. Raj doesn't need me anyway.

"That's the address for the FBI, Mack. I know this fucking city, man. Why are you meeting with the Feds? Is this a terrorism case you're working? What's happening with the FBI? Is this about the milkshakes? Come on, man."

SEVENTY-SEVEN

Nick Yarborough makes me wait in the lobby for twenty minutes before sending someone down to escort me up. The kid is young and serious. Agent Stern. He walks too fast for my ribs and has to wait for me to catch up. He knows how to wear a suit, but he needs a facial relaxant.

"Bad day?" I ask as we step onto the elevator.

"Great day," he says grimly. "You?"

"Spectacular. Today's already a week long and I haven't had lunch."

He nods at the Bodega Bay Chicago bag hanging from my finger.

"Looks like you brought it with you," he says.

"Just in case," I say. "Who wants to starve to death waiting to talk to the FBI? Am I right? I always try to bring a little something. CIA is different. ATF too. Eating lunch near those guys is a good way to lose an arm. Uncle Sam doesn't feed those savages."

I don't expect a smile, and he doesn't disappoint. The doors slide open and he leads me up glossy hallways to a windowless conference room. He holds the door open and gestures inside. I follow instructions and sit at a slick wood table big enough for ten slick wooden men.

"Something to drink?" he asks, preparing to leave me alone.

"God, yes."

The man himself doesn't arrive for another ten minutes. Agent Yarborough is the same muscle in a suit he's always been. Broad shoulders swinging long arms. Wide-set, heavy-lidded eyes above a boxer's nose and a square jawline that comes with a jet-lagged shadow that thinks it's five o'clock before ten in the morning. He's still hanging on to most of his hair, black, cut close and orderly. His tie is standard issue black, and his shirt sleeves are rolled up over hairy forearms. Nick closes the door and extends a hand.

"It's been a minute, Mack," he says. The Texan twang is still disarming. "You look like you've been working a rodeo from the wrong side of the bull."

I stand with a wince and a grunt, shaking his hand across the table.

"Joke's on the bull," I say. "I left him with a bad case of overconfidence. Speaking of rodeos, you run out of belt yet?"

"Belt?"

"You know, that strap of leather on your office wall."

"Oh. That. Nah, I guess there's still room for a few more notches before I hang things up."

"Hang things up? Retirement? You?" I try my best to dummy up some disappointment. "Say it ain't so."

"Young man's game, Mack. Two, three years."

"Don't be silly, Nick. It only gets better." I spread my arms. "Look at me."

"I am looking at you. I might retire this afternoon." Yarborough looks at his watch. "I'm busy, Mack. I almost don't have the time to wonder why you're here."

I give him a smile and a headshake, lowering myself slowly back into the chair.

"I may suck at rodeos, Nick, but I know bullshit when I smell it. You know exactly why I'm here."

"Yeah?" Nick sits heavily. "Remind me."

"You've got a plumbing problem. One of your investigations has suddenly gone soggy and you're worried about getting that tie wet. I'm the guy on your list of people to call that you keep avoiding."

"That so?"

"Yeah. And I get that. I do. I've got a reputation full of question marks. Nobody seems to know what side I'm on. You're working an investigation for a guy who thinks I'm a big part of the problem. That means somewhere in one of these offices my mug is up on a corkboard with a thumbtack stuck through my forehead. You don't want to talk to me until you've figured out more of the puzzle. But you can't because you don't have all the pieces. I got tired of waiting. So I came to you."

We look at each other for a few seconds. I watch Nick Yarborough get a little older.

"You're here about Orland Twill," he says calmly.

"There you go. See, that wasn't so hard."

"You here looking to help him or hurt him?"

"Neither. I'm here to give you some of those missing pieces so you can do your job. But there's a problem."

"Which is."

"Which is that I don't know how long it will take this conversation to hit bad-guy radio."

Yarborough leans back and crosses his arms.

"Are you accusing me of something, Mack?"

"I don't know enough yet to make accusations. But I'm here, aren't I? I'm taking a risk, Nick. That's what I'm telling you."

"And just how can I put you at ease?"

"John Murray still showing up for work?"

"Haven't seen him."

"Tallish. Handsome from a distance. Up close he looks like a leaky faucet with a nice haircut."

"Today, Mack. Haven't seen him today."

"Maybe because he's hiding. Or maybe he's home brooding, suspended pending investigation. Either way I'm guessing Agent Murray's in a dark room someplace thinking things through."

"What kind of things?"

"Big picture things. Career things. Public housing options. John's just been busted leaking investigation details to a foreign intelligence service. More than leaking. He's been taking assignments."

"That's not his story."

"I'm shocked. Who'd have guessed that? But the fact remains. And thanks for confirming that he's on suspension."

Irritation. Like I'm an itch he can't scratch.

"I'm not going to talk about John Murray, Mack. Okay? I can't do that." The words hang around like they mean something. Then Nick's expression changes from no to yes in a single blink. "But I can listen."

"I'm sure you can. I need some assurance here, Nick."

"What can I do, Mack? You want me to pinky swear? I'm the goddamned FBI."

"So is John Murray. Or, was." We play the staring game for a few seconds. All he wants me to see is boredom and irritation. But that's the very least of what's on his face. The man has trust issues. Gives us something in common. "Tell me this, Nick."

"What."

"If a man is arrested for spoofing, what crime has he committed?"

Nick Yarborough screws up his face like I've started barking.

"Spoofing?"

"Yeah."

"Spoofing?"

"You need your hearing checked. Yeah, spoofing."

"What the fuck is spoofing? It's a scam … it's a … it's a …"

"It's a federal crime, Nick. A crime on the list of things the DOJ supposedly cares a lot about. I'm guessing you've heard of the CFTC?"

"Futures trading? Look, Mack, the FBI's a big organization. That's not what I do, okay? That's too white collar for me. I suck at math. Drugs. Human trafficking. Terrorism. Even government corruption. But the pissing and moaning about the price of pork bellies? Come on, man. Maybe you'd like to take a stroll down to the third floor. Ask for Ivan Lessimer or Andrea Schilling. I'll call ahead and ask them to open up a file. If this is about commodities futures, then I've got better things to do."

He's either genuinely disinterested or he's got a black belt in bluffing. It's as much assurance as I'm ever going to get.

"Congratulations," I say. "You ready for the listening part?"

Nick looks at his watch. He sighs and opens his hands above the table. That's my invitation.

"There's a woman in town from parts unknown. She keeps company with several jar-headed hard cases that never utter a word but that walk and carry themselves like Secret Service on vacation. They'd be right at home in this building. At first I figured she was from the Bureau. I got that one wrong."

"Name?"

"She lets me call her Marie, but I think that's because she didn't like me calling her Frenchie."

"Why Frenchie?"

"Because her French is flawless. Turns out she's got a thing for languages. She can speak all of them. Turns accents on and off like light switches."

"Okay."

"The suits pulling Marie's strings want to put the squeeze on Orland Twill. They think I'm the guy to deliver him to the juicer. With a little help from G-Man John Murray."

Nick has more than a few questions. I do my best to give him the basics. We have an actual conversation for a few minutes. I can't tell if he's waiting for me to drop Big Man's name. But I don't disappoint.

"Hold on," he says, pinching the bridge of his nose to hold back a headache. "Big Man."

"Yeah."

"I've heard this about you, Mack."

"I'm sure."

"So let me just …" Nick holds out his hands as if to keep me at bay. "Let me …" He leans back in his chair and closes his eyes for several beats. "Some foreign intelligence service, you don't know who, sends over Marie, not her real name, to find ..." Nick laughs a little, "... Big Man, aka José Beggemon, a law enforcement wet dream fairy tale, and to take him off the board."

"Right."

"Because he, Big Man, mastermind of an organization I can't fucking pronounce ..."

"*La Pourriture.* The Rot."

"The Rot. Great. Big Man and The Rot. Sounds like a bad grunge band."

"Is there any other kind?"

"Ask my stepson. So Big Man and The Rot have momentum on an international spoofing syndicate that's making a lot of very wealthy, foreign-government-connected commodities investors very angry."

"You're a quick study, Nick. I don't care what people say."

"And this Marie woman thinks that the key to finding Big Man is grabbing up Orland Twill."

"Yes."

"Because she believes Twill is an active lieutenant in the Chicago chapter of The Rot ..."

"Yes ..."

"And who was, she believes, instrumental in the murder of," Nick pulls out three fingers one at a time, "Dennis O'Toole, Carrie O'Toole and, most recently, Pete Chow."

"Correct," I say with a nod. "But Marie doesn't care about the murders so much as the spoofing and the money. People die all the time. Money lasts forever. The murders just get her Twill's full attention so he'll be in a cooperative mood. Problem is, Marie can't seem to get Twill in a room to have the conversation. He dumped his tail at the airport and hasn't been going to work or sleeping in his own bed. She thinks I'll have better luck."

"And have you?"

"Had better luck? Depends on who you ask. My face and ribs have pretty strong opinions on that subject."

"You've seen him."

"Yes."

"Twill did this to you?"

"No."

"You were with him when he called me about Murray."

"Yes."

"Does he know you're here talking to me?"

"No."

"And the O'Tooles were murdered why, again?"

"My opinion?"

"Who else?"

"Dennis was murdered because he knew how to identify all of Big Man's spoofers and was making a lucrative hobby out of blackmailing them. Carrie was murdered because she made no secret of knowing that Dennis was dealing dirt and was prepared to prove it in a court of spoiled matrimony, which made her another liability."

"And Pete Chow?"

"Over a barrel. Pete's only chance of getting his brother Andy out of prison alive was to dummy up the forensics on the O'Toole killings to make it look like murder-suicide rather than a double homicide."

"And … and …" Nick's face wants a name.

"Marie."

"Marie. Marie believes this is all Twill's doing."

"She thinks Twill helped put the O'Toole murders in motion."

"Why?"

"Because someone asked him to."

"Who?"

"A woman who worked closely with Dennis as a brokerage assistant. That was her job whenever she wasn't sleeping with him and managing his dry cleaning."

"Amanda Tate," says Nick with authority.

"Right. Twill's niece."

"I'm aware."

"Then you're ahead of Marie on that one. Not sure she gets the family connection yet. She assumes a more typical, hotel room variety of persuasion at work here. Anyway, Marie thinks Dennis and Amanda wanted Carrie out of the picture. Divorce was getting ugly. Carrie was looking to blow the whistle on Dennis and take away all his money. Dennis is afraid his wife is going to send him to prison. So he wants to pull her plug, stay out of jail and keep the family fortune to himself. That sounds good to Amanda, so she reaches out to Twill with both breasts. Twill puts the hit in motion through the dry cleaners."

"The dry cleaners. I don't …"

"The Blue Lotus. A Big Man front for every sin known to man. That's another conversation. Point is, Marie has photos of Twill going into hotels with Amanda and coming out of the Blue Lotus, so she adds two plus two and comes up with Twill using a Big Man connection to put the hit on Carrie O'Toole. The hitter decides to cover his tracks with a murder-suicide story, so he ends up whacking Dennis to make that happen, not understanding that Dennis was the one wanting Carrie killed in the first place. Pretty big oops."

"So, Marie thinks …"

"Hang on. Let me finish. Murder-suicide becomes the story: Dennis is distraught about the divorce and snaps. Takes a bat to Carrie's head and then shoots himself in the driveway. To sell that story, Big Man gets Twill to pressure Pete Chow into cooking the forensics. That works for a while, but then Pete starts losing sleep at night and Twill has to shut him up before he comes to his senses."

"All of that is Marie's world view," says Nick.

"Yeah."

"Okay. And Twill is involved in the spoofing how?"

"Not at all. Twill knows as much about spoofing as you do."

"Okay, so Marie thinks the bodies alone give her the leverage she needs over Twill. Get him to flip on Big Man. Rat him out. Bait some kind of trap. Take Big Man in. Go back to France or wherever. Get a medal."

"Right."

"And she doesn't work with local or federal law enforcement because …"

"Because the plan is not to take Big Man in. The plan is to take Big Man out. Foreign assassination on US soil. Pretty big ask, don't you think?"

"She's told you this?"

"Of course not. That would make her stupid. Marie's a long way from stupid."

"So you're just speculating."

"That's one word for it. Deducing is another."

"Even if you're right, she's got to find Big Man first. If he even fucking exists in the first place. She needs information. Coordination with local or federal law enforcement would seem a good idea, even if she lies about her true purpose. She can't just breeze into town and …"

"Marie says she *has* been coordinating. Informally."

"What?"

"She says the Bureau is helping to cross t's and dot i's but that you've got some conflicting investigation that keeps you in the shadows."

Nick pulls in his chin, taken aback.

"That's not true."

"You sure about that?"

He doesn't appreciate the cocked eyebrow.

"Yes, I'm sure. I'd know."

"If it was true, would you tell me? Would you tell me if there really is cooperation going on?"

"No. I wouldn't. You don't exactly rate for classified information."

"Unlike John Murray."

Nick leans into the table.

"The Bureau is not involved, Mack. So, I ask again, why doesn't this woman, this agency, work directly with local or federal law enforcement?"

I lean back and give him my best shrug.

"Take your pick. Because she doesn't like paperwork and she doesn't trust anyone but her own people. Or because the founders gave Twill some legal rights to play with. Lawyers are inconvenient and have a way of gumming up the works. Or because Marie knows she'll be stuck at the back of the line until America is good and done talking about the bodies. I'm guessing Marie's idea of a good time is to come in under the radar, grab up Twill, talk about all the trouble he's in, threaten to toss him to the wolves unless he flips on the boss, get what she needs, and then toss him to the wolves anyway."

Nick frowns to himself. Thinking. Scratching his chin. I keep at it.

"Besides, why buy the cow when you can get the milk for free? Marie actually *has* been coordinating with local and federal law enforcement, Nick. Maybe you just weren't aware. Ask John Murray. My guess is John has opened up doors for Marie all over town just to help get things done. Ever notice how local law enforcement scrambles to get out of the way when the Feds show up at the door?"

"No." The word comes with some extra attitude.

"Come on. You're just remembering the exceptions. You're remembering me and Stretch. Long time ago. That was exceptional."

"You're exceptional alright, Mack." He's angry all over again. "We lost a good source all because you wouldn't get out of the goddamned way."

"Let that go, Nick. That's ancient history. Focus. All it takes to get Orland Twill suspended pending investigation is the FBI taking a couple quiet meetings with the Chandler Mayor's office, or the Chandler Chief of Police or Dan Brewster and his boys over at the OAG. Your man John Murray worked with Marie to take the OAG's focus off of me and put it onto Orland. That puts me in Twill's office with the authority to grant access to his well-protected IAD computer. Marie hooks me up with a fake subpoena and a phone number for tech-savvy Agent Murray. All she wants is a peek behind all the passwords."

"Fake subpoena?"

I dig through my pockets until I find the piece of paper I need, damp and folded three times over. I flatten it out. Nick pulls the subpoena across the table with a finger.

"Looks like a valid subpoena to me," he says.

"Yeah, well, yesterday I had my partner pull an IAD file for me to look at. Cop named Worthington pulled his pecker out one too many times and got caught. He wanted to fight us rather than go quietly. Judge Selkirk authorized the unsealing of some court records we needed." I reach across and tap the signature on the would-be subpoena. "That's not how the good judge signs his name."

"So this is a fake. A good one."

"Yes."

"All to get into Twill's computer," Yarborough mutters to himself.

"Yeah. Quietly. No fuss. Just an invitation from me as the acting head of the Chandler IAD." I point at the paper in his hands. "This was all about putting me at ease enough to unlock the door and let them in."

"Pretty convenient," Nick says. "Twill out on his ass and you being the acting head of IAD."

"Simple, really. Doesn't take a genius to predict a suspension in Twill's future once the FBI starts whispering to the right people that the hammer is about to fall."

"Whispering to whom?"

"I'm guessing Murray took a meeting with the Chandler Mayor's office. The mayor taps Chief Loudermilk on the shoulder. Then I get the tap, because nobody particularly cares if I get dirty in the coming shit storm. Twill and I accuse each other to death and then they bring in someone competent who actually wants the job."

"Meanwhile, unbeknownst to your chain of command, you're in the position to grant quiet access to an FBI search of Twill's computer."

"Right."

"But you'd obviously clear any search with your command." Nick gives me a look. "Right?"

"Would I? Maybe not if the price is right."

The sigh comes out weighing a ton, full of understanding. Nick nods his head.

"Marie's buying your silence," he says. "How much?"

"I told her I'm looking for a job with CPD homicide."

"Are you?"

"Beats IAD. She's busy pulling strings."

"And that gets her a quiet invitation upstairs."

"She thinks so."

"And she's looking for what, exactly?"

"Come on. Looking for a bunch of numbers that nobody can make any sense of, at least not without more information. Don't look so confused. We're past the bullshit, Nick. I know you've got the files. Twill gave you a copy when he came in for help and got ratted out instead."

Nick's eyes harden.

"Not by me, goddamnit."

"I'll have to take your word for that, Nick. Because it's either that or I have to take my concerns over to Lanny Mandel and OPR."

Nick's one of those guys who goes cold and hard when he gets angry. I watch his jaw tighten the pressure on his molars.

"You do what you have to do, Mack. You want his fucking phone number?"

"Settle down. I've had enough of IAD cops for a lifetime, Lanny included. Here's a history lesson instead. Orland Twill comes in here with a story that's a hard sell for the Bureau. It's a bit off-menu for you boys. Not enough domestic terrorism for your taste. No exploding buildings or White Supremacist plots. But it's got an interesting local corruption angle. A respected police lieutenant is getting squeezed out of his job and into a career-ending OAG investigation for no good reason. He tells you he's being made to take the fall for corruption within the Chandler PD. He tells you he's losing his job so someone with mob connections can take over."

"Who?"

"Me."

"You're telling me you're connected?"

"No. I'm not telling you that. Orland Twill is telling you that. Or at least he was. We've worked through all of that."

"So you really have talked to Twill."

"I have. He tossed me the ball so he could go turn himself into CPD before they picked him up for Pete Chow's murder. I told him he should try to get ahead of that train. He's lawyered up with Earnie Davidson."

"Does he know you're here telling me all of this?"

"No. I already told you that. He has no idea. You look confused."

"I am confused."

"I'll bet you are. Twill came in here couple days ago and put me at the center of all his problems. I'm a scheming, corrupt bastard with an eye for power and influence in the Chandler PD, looking to step on Twill's career for a leg up. Orland and I are past all that now. You've got some unlearning to do."

"He now thinks you're a great guy, does he?"

"Point is he's moved on."

"Moved on to what?"

"To being investigated for the murder of Pete Chow. But we're getting ahead of ourselves, here. I'm not done. Twill tells you, probably sitting in this very room, that he's being followed around Chicago. He doesn't know who's following him or why, but he knows a police tail when he feels it. He figures it's no coincidence that he's got a niece suddenly getting death threats from someone on a black motorcycle. Turns out somebody wants something Dennis O'Toole gave to Amanda right before he died. Twill tells you a long story about two flash drives, one that Amanda takes out to La Villita and puts in a locker, and one that she stuffs inside a bag of coffee for safe keeping. Twill thinks his niece doesn't have long to live and he thinks the police have his back only because that's where they want to stick the knife. So he gets Amanda to dig the flash drive out of the coffee and, after buying her a gun and a hotel room, he brings the whole story over here to you. How'm I doing?"

"I'm listening."

"Twill lays it all out. Explains why he thinks the fix is in on his career and why he doesn't feel safe consulting local police. My name comes up a lot. You're not convinced. Dubious even. But it's unusual enough that you tell Twill you'll open a file and look into it. Since then, you've had a tail up on me just to see how I'm spending my time. I'm guessing that was Agent Murray. How convenient to John Murray that you and Marie were both asking him to follow the same guy. At least Marie had the common sense to put a bug under my car. Now I'm taking taxis everywhere."

I pause, giving him a chance to tell me I've got it all wrong. He doesn't. I keep at it.

"While John was out on the road, you've been here looking at the numbers on that flash drive hard enough to make your eyes bleed. You can't make heads or tails, so you zip them off to the FBI egg-head number-crunchers and now they've all got a bad case of the shoulder shrugs too. Let me know if you're bored, Nick. I know you already know all of this."

"Still listening."

"Here's what you don't know. Agent Murray, meanwhile, has been keeping Marie informed of your progress, playing my shadow and waiting for me to invite him in for a look at Twill's computer. He's pilfered a copy of the numbers that

Twill gave to you and he's delivered them to Marie. Only she can't make any more sense of them than you can. Marie figures Twill has only given the FBI half a loaf. She knows there's something out there she doesn't have yet. She wants anything else incriminating that she can use to get Twill's attention."

"I don't understand," Nick says. "Marie thinks Twill is so dirty, but then why does she think he came to the FBI and handed over the flash drive?" Nick's face flushes. "I mean, assuming that's what happened."

I give him another shrug.

"Beats me. I'll be sure to ask her next time I see her. Maybe she thinks Twill was just laying down his cover story in advance, turning in meaningless information while bolstering his credibility."

"In advance of what?"

"Killing Pete Chow."

Nick closes his eyes and takes a breath.

"Why again?"

"Because Pete was cracking. Losing his resolve. Preparing to come clean about dummying up the forensics on the O'Toole killing. Preparing to revert back to his initial finding. Double homicide."

"And you know this how?"

"One of the last things Pete did on planet earth was to send me a message asking to talk. I'd pushed Pete pretty hard about the O'Toole report and he was sticking to his guns. But then he sent me an email attaching a copy of his original forensics work-up. V1. Version one."

"And version one concluded what, double homicide?"

"Double homicide."

"You've got that in writing?"

"I do."

"Where?"

"Someplace safe. Now that Pete's dead, you're the only person who knows." I give Nick a smile I want him to remember. "If someone comes looking, Nick, I'm gonna know who to blame."

"You've turned paranoid, Mack."

"I find it keeps me alive. You'll get the original forensics report when I'm ready. Not before. But that's not quite all. Pete had more he wanted to tell me. The message said he wanted to talk. I never got the chance. He said *it's not the brothers; it's the boss.* That means something to me."

"It's not the brothers … I'm … what the hell does that mean?"

"Goes back to an old case Pete and I worked ages ago. You remember the Cicero Four case?"

Nick shakes his head, then stops.

"Bombing?"

"Bombing."

"Yeah. We had a piece of that, I think. Remind me."

"Three brothers and a cousin conspire to plant a bomb in the boss's car. Boss gets wise just in time and lobs the thing out into space before it detonates. It comes down into the bed of a passing pickup. Boom. Truck explodes and plows into a park bench where two of the brothers were watching the fun. So, three dead: the pickup driver and two of the conspiring brothers. Looks like the bomb-throwing boss is going down for a triple until Pete runs the forensics and figures out it was actually the brothers to blame, not the boss. I fought him tooth and nail, but Pete turned out to be right. It was the brothers, not the boss. He liked to remind me of that every chance he got. For decades. *It was the brothers, Mack, not the boss.* Then I get the message from him that I'm talking about, a day after I pressed Pete about the O'Toole forensics and a day before Pete gets a bullet in the head and a ride out to a Manhattan irrigation ditch. The message was the reverse. It's *not* the brothers, it *is* the boss."

"Meaning …"

"Meaning Pete was ready to reverse his finding on the "O'Tooles. Double homicide, not murder-suicide. And it meant he thought the boss was to blame."

"What boss?"

"My boss."

"Twill."

"Yes."

"You're saying Pete Chow was implicating Orland Twill in the death of Dennis and Carrie O'Toole?"

"Well, that's certainly the world Frenchie Marie lives in. Twill set up the hit on the O'Tooles and then he killed Pete to keep him from cleaning up the forensics."

"And when you received Pete's email, that's what it said to you?"

"When I received Pete's email, that's exactly what it said to me."

"So then you *are* here to implicate Twill."

"Like I said, Nick, I'm here to give you the information you need to do your job. You've only got part of what was originally on that flash drive. It won't make any sense without the rest of it."

"And I suppose that somehow you've got the rest of it?"

I pull the Bodega Bay Chicago bag up from the chair next to me and put in on the table front and center. Nick looks at it, warily confused.

"The rest of it is a sandwich?"

"Don't be silly. The rest of it is all about milkshakes."

SEVENTY-EIGHT

It's another hour before Ray reemerges back out into the sluice. He glances skyward and pulls up his collar. He holds the empty Bodega Bay bag above his head to keep off the worst of the weather. Or maybe just so no one thinks he's with the FBI. Not a good look. He's afraid of water, this guy.

It takes him fifty steps before he stops thinking about Nick Yarborough and starts in again with Francine Lucas and the photo that doesn't quit giving up secrets. He sees Marlo sitting at the table, her hand under Victor Roby's. She turns back and looks at Ray, like he was the guy who took the picture. He imagines a smile. It feels like a knife.

He walks half a block in the rain to find Raj parked at the curb, right where he's supposed to be. He opens the door and tosses the sopping wet bag in the back seat. Then he climbs in.

"You left the book and the papers," says Raj eagerly.

Ray seals himself into the front seat with a groan. He slicks the water from his head and looks at Raj. "You noticed that, did you?"

Raj lights up a new Camel.

"Yeah. I noticed that. Is the FBI going to help?"

"Help with what, exactly?"

"With whatever you asked them to help with?"

Ray sizes him up. He's thinking as much about that smoldering Camel as Raj. "And just what have you deduced that thing is?"

"You haven't told me dick about this case, man."

"Deduced, Raj. Deduced."

"Deduced." Raj smokes, considering the question. "Well, I have *deduced* that you want them to help clear your boss, who is in a shit ton of trouble for something you don't think he did. And I have deduced that the names and other information in the book of milkshakes is about some kind of extortion racket."

"So, you looked."

"Yeah, I looked. I deduced you didn't care, or you'd have put the book out of reach."

"I'll remember that," says Ray. "Anything else?"

"Yeah. Those two guys that you met up with at Blondies. I figure they're involved."

"Involved how?"

"I think the guy with the beard, you know, Whitey-Whiteish in the Lexus was, like, maybe he's a victim of the extortion. Like he did something bad, and someone is squeezing him for it. And the big Samoan dude was a bodyguard. Or maybe not a bodyguard, but muscle, you know, someone who can squeeze back better than Whitey can." Raj cracks the window and blows out a long white, jet. "They thought *you* were the squeezer. Because that's what you wanted them to think. And then there's the dirty blond in the cashmere."

Ray's eyebrows laugh a little.

"What about her?"

"She's the one I followed out to Blondies that day. She picked up a bag of something Whitey-Whiteish left behind. I told you then that it looked like a drop. A pay off. And I still think that's what it was. Extortion money. I think *she's* the squeezer. And now I know who she is."

"Oh yeah?"

Raj mugs a self-satisfied expression.

"Yeah. See, I can drive and listen at the same time. I've been doing both right under your nose. Her name is Amanda Tate. She works at BSD Securities. The guy we picked up from his mom's house on West Blackshire Loop and drove to your office is Kevin Canady. Also known as Blue Shoe, which is a kind of drink but I'm thinking it's also a kind of mob name. Am I right? That's right, isn't it? Blue Shoe. Come on, Mack." He waggles the cigarette. "I'll give you a Camel."

"Want me to take you in for bribing a police officer?"

"You want to walk home in the rain?"

"What else?"

"Uh, let's see. Kevin was paid to break into Amanda's house and search her computers. He works for Whitehorse, I.T., which has the account to service the computers at BSD Securities. So these people, whoever they are, also wanted Kevin to search or sabotage the BSD computers. They're looking for something that they either want to steal or destroy or both. Like maybe Amanda has been using incriminating information to blackmail people. People like Mr. Lexus Whitey-Whiteish. So I'm thinking Amanda isn't feeling so safe. Amanda has a relationship with your boss. A cop. A lieutenant. Could be romantic, but I don't think so. I'm thinking …"

"Wait. Hang on." Ray pokes Raj in the arm. "Why isn't it romantic?"

"I caught a glimpse of a goodbye hug outside the Westpoint, before your boss got in the other car."

"A glimpse of a hug?"

"Yeah. You know. I had the angle on the front and the side of the hotel." Raj sticks the Camel between his lips and reaches past Ray to open the glove compartment. He taps a small pair of binoculars with this finger, then snaps the door closed again. "Anyway, that hug seemed more, I don't know, paternal. He doesn't look like the type to have a girlfriend that young."

Ray's gut reacts to that one. He can't help but remember his pretend pizza date with Nadia, fully under her spell despite the twenty years between them. Wasn't really a date. It was business. But the whole restaurant had seemed to think it was a date. He did too for a few minutes. And that had felt good. He had remembered that feeling. Missed it. He thinks of the novel he has barely started writing. *The Russian Doll.* He wonders whether he'll write Detective McMannis as a man who would pursue the comely Polina if she let him, despite her age. He wonders if he will give Jack McMannis the stones to try.

"He doesn't look like the type?" asks Ray. "And what type does that look like, exactly?"

"I don't know. Not like him. It's a feeling, mostly. But your boss has got that posture, you know?"

"Don't I. It keeps him tall."

"He looks like a married-forever kind of guy. He's got the ring. He's set. Amanda's like a daughter. A niece or something. Daughter of a friend maybe. Am I right? I'm right, aren't I?"

"You about done?"

"Not even close."

Raj shakes his head and turns in his seat to face Ray squarely, his enthusiasm like a kind of inner light that glows out of his eyes and his teeth and the nose of that Camel.

"So Amanda's been using some kind of dangerous information to extort money out of people and now she's in way over her head. She went to her tall, excellent-posture cop friend for help, and he stepped up. Or he tried to anyway. Something went sideways. And now he's going down for something bad unless you can help him. So now you're going to the FBI for help because your boss has enemies. Cop enemies. He doesn't know who his friends are any more. You've just spent almost two hours talking to the Feds and giving them papers full of numbers and a milkshake book full of handwritten information about people who live, like, all over the world, man. And you left all of that stuff with whoever it is you just met with in there. So I'm guessing the Feds are officially, like, looking into it."

Raj spreads his arms, a prelude to a congratulatory bow.

"Deduce that, motherfucker," he says. "I'll give you a second or two to find the words to express your admiration."

Truth is, there are no words to be found. Ray is speechless, which makes this a rare moment in the life of a man who is almost never at a loss for language. Doesn't last long. The moment is so brief, in fact, that Raj does not even recognize the pregnancy of the pause. But I do. Then it passes.

"Rajnish Malik," Ray says, sounding impressed. "As I live and breathe. Who knew you had such an active imagination? You ever thought of writing books?"

It doesn't land. Raj isn't listening. He's back in his own head. Back in the story. Back in the case.

"Oh, and you got the milkshake book from the house where you were almost karate chopped to death. So I think whoever used to live in that house is dead. Right? Because he was keeping tabs on all of the people in that book." Raj snaps his fingers and points at Ray. "Blackmailing them! The dead guy from that house was working with Amanda Tate. They were like a team. He was squeezer number one and she's squeezer number two. Squeezer one is dead because someone was looking for the information in that book and now they're after Amanda Tate, squeezer number two. I don't know how the super old murder of this Wilhaven guy fits into any of this, but I'm working on it." Raj smiles. "You find those words yet, boss?"

"Only one," says Ray.

"Yeah?"

"Drive."

SEVENTY-NINE

Raj drops me off at the entrance to the parking garage. I tell him to circle before swatting the door closed. The traffic around the financial district is thickening. I'm betting he only makes two laps before I'm back in the cab.

I take the elevator to level four and have a look around. Amanda's white Sonata is right where it's supposed to be. Saul Margolis' midnight blue Mercedes is not. I fish out my phone and make a call to the people who sign her paycheck.

"Amanda is not in," says the receptionist.

"When do you expect her back?"

"I couldn't tell you."

"Have you seen her at all today?"

"No, sir. Can I leave a message for her to contact you?"

"Sure. Let her know her conscience called. She knows the number but let me give it to you anyway."

I spell out the number and end the call. I head back outside just in time to catch Raj making the turn east onto Madison. I meet him in the middle of the street and climb in, closing the door on a chorus of wet horns.

"That was fast," he says, accelerating. "Let me guess. The white Sonata is there, but the blue Mercedes is missing."

I give him a look as I'm dialing Nick Yarborough.

"Nick. Mack. Miss me yet?"

"Kinda busy, Mack."

"Amanda Tate."

"What about her?"

"If you want her, and you do, you're going to need to pick her up. She's in a blue Mercedes-CL. Illinois plate, Kimo Lima Edward 7-1-3. My guess is that she's got a new yen for travel."

"Thought you said she'd make contact."

"She will. But I think it's gonna be long distance."

"I'll get the word out."

I end things with Nick to find Raj beaming my direction.

"What's with you?" I ask.

"I was right," he says. "I knew it."

"You know, you're getting pretty cocky about all this, if you ask me."

"Just sayin', Mack."

"And I'm just sayin' that cocky gets you killed, Raj."

"Roger that," he says, bringing his grin back under control. "Where to?"

"Maybe you should tell me, Sherlock."

The grin is suddenly back with a vengeance.

"Amanda's house."

The house is right where I left it, only a little wetter. Amanda's driveway is empty, and I don't see anything at the curb that gives me heartburn. I tell Raj to keep his speed up and to take a tour of the block anyway.

"What are you looking for?" asks Raj.

"I never have any idea until I find it. Someone parked. Someone idling. Black motorcycles."

"Black motorcycles?"

"Yeah. My midlife crisis is running late. I'm in the market for a black bike. You see one of those, let me know."

We come full circle. I point through the windshield at the curb about six houses away from where I'm headed.

"Right here. You stick out like a sore yellow thumb but nothing we can do about that now." I wake up Sig and rack a fresh round into the chamber. Then I nose him back into the holster. "Keep your phone in your hand and your eyes on the house. If anyone so much as slows down to take an interest, call me. If there's trouble, stay clear. No heroics. 9-1-1 is your new favorite number. Got it?"

Raj's heart is busy inflating his eyes.

"Raj?"

"Yeah, got it," he says, swallowing. "Fuck, man."

"Welcome to the life."

I'm back under the rain for the half-block hobble to Amanda's. The ER doc is in my head insisting that I limit my activity as much as possible. Then Dr. Jha is suddenly in there too, shaking his head with that kind of disappointed futility on his face that should be reserved for parents and teachers. Now they're both doing it; looking at x-rays and shaking their heads.

Three houses to go. The sky is a seething dirty sock that belongs on the freeway. I try to think about the next time that I'll be dry on the outside and wet on the inside. Tonight can't come soon enough. If I could make the world spin a little faster, I would.

I walk up the driveway like I own the place, heading straight through the side gate and into the back yard. I look into all the same windows I did when Kevin "Blue Shoe" Canady was snooping his way through Amanda's desktop. Best I can tell, no one is home except a bunch of gutted sofa cushions and mostly empty drawers. I try the back door. It doesn't give me any trouble, so I let myself in.

I stand amid the wreckage of Amanda's kitchenette and listen to the air molecules for a few moments. All I hear is rain and the ache of my own bones. I keep my head on a swivel. Whoever redecorated Dennis' place had a two-house contract. Everything that used to be in a cupboard or drawer is now on the floor. Everything that used to have any sort of integrity is now a million-piece memory, which I guess makes Amanda Tate's house a perfect microcosm of the entire city.

I shuffle through the rooms, stepping on paintings and books, pillows and mirrors, makeup and broken bottles of wine. The small, walk-in closet is a mountain of clothes looking for hangers. I lean into the small office where Kevin Canady had once hacked his way into Amanda's computer. The monitor is bent and shattered on the floor underneath the computer itself. Someone opened up the back of the thing and ripped out all the thinking guts, leaving the metal shell among the wreckage of paper, glass, and splintered wooden shelving. That's a lot of extra time for someone who could just as easily throw the whole damn thing in the trunk. Unless you're on a motorcycle.

I leave the computer carcass on the floor and exit the office. Down the hall is the door to the garage. I make the trip and open it.

Saul Margolis' midnight blue Mercedes gleams in the flickering fluorescents from beneath toppled towers of metal shelving. Of all the things that have tumbled down on top of the car and bounced off again onto the floor, a jumbo-size package of paper towels and a hard-shell yellow suitcase have managed to hold their position on the hood. There's enough space between them for me to see Amanda Ramada Tate in the front seat looking back at me, comfy in her cashmere.

Well. Not actually looking back. And maybe not so comfortable. Necks don't usually bend that way. I pull out my phone and poke at it.

"Nick. Mack. Miss me yet?"

EIGHTY

I call in the body that used to be Amanda Ramada Tate to CPD and wait. They arrive in waves of black and white, blue and red.

I have to tell the same story three times to three different teams with badges and notepads. I tell them I'm with Chandler IAD following up on a witness who stopped answering her phone. I knocked on the front door and then started looking in windows. Back door was open. I followed the mess from room to room until I got to the garage. That's when I got my phone involved.

They want to know more about the IAD case that's brought me out in the rain. I give them a sad smile and shake my head, explaining the departmental confidentiality protocol for IAD cases. I shrug my shoulders like a man whose hands are tied. I get a bunch of knitted brows and upside-down smiles. They know it's the same in their department, but they don't like it anyway.

Detective Aikens is younger than I am but older than all the others. He's got all the same questions and a pair of tired eyes that keep disappearing behind lenses that like to steam up in humid weather. He has to take off the glasses and dry them off on his sleeve every couple of minutes. We pause and watch the EMTs finally get Amanda out of her demolished garage and into the ambulance.

"When was the last time you saw her?" he asks, reperching the specs.

"Yesterday."

"And what was that about?"

"Business. The case I'm working."

"The one you can't say anything about."

"The same."

He looks up from his pad. The glasses are still mostly clear from the last wipe. The eyes behind the lenses may be tired, but they've seen a thing or two.

"You do know that the IAD confidentiality bullshit isn't going to hold in a murder investigation."

I shrug.

"Here's hoping you're right. The world wouldn't make much sense if it did. Look, you make your requests, and I'll work the approvals. Won't be easy. My LT never met a rule he didn't love. And he's been hard to corner recently. But I'll make the pitch."

He nods and moves on.

"How'd Amanda look? Last time you saw her."

I point to the ambulance.

"Better than that," I say.

"Any reason to think her life was in danger?"

In my head, Amanda is bolting out the front door of Dennis O'Toole's demolished house as I take a beating in the laundry room.

"I worked homicide for thirty years before I turned IAD. Everybody's life was always in danger. I miss that. Most exciting thing that ever happens in an IAD file is someone's feelings getting hurt. Wounded pride. Broken rules. Riding a desk to retirement is easy on the bones, but sometimes I'd kill just to see someone in danger of getting killed. Know what I mean?"

Detective Aikens gives up a soft laugh with a hard look in his eyes.

"Maybe you shouldn't have gone over to the dark side," he says, clicking his pen.

"Maybe you shouldn't always state the obvious."

He wants to know why I took a taxi to a murder scene. I tell him my car came down with some sort of bug that makes it unsafe to drive. I don't think he really understands what I mean.

It's a good ninety minutes before I hobble my way back to Raj. I close the door with a groan. He's full of wide-eyed questions. Most of me wants to sleep. My ribs aren't sleepy. Neither is my phone. I give Raj a look and put the thing to my ear.

"This Ray Mackey?"

"Last I checked."

"Sergeant Kennedy. CPD Homicide. Got a minute?"

"Let's say I do. What's on your mind, Sergeant?"

"Word is you might be looking to improve your work life. Start chasing bad guys again. Any truth to that?"

I venture a sideways glance at Raj. He's busy splitting his attention between watching the cops boil out of Amanda's home and trying to eavesdrop on my conversation. I think about asking Sergeant Kennedy where he got his information, but I don't see the sense in wasting my breath. Frenchie Marie is making good on her end of the bargain. Pretty good bet that she'll be popping up soon to collect on my end of that bargain.

"What self-respecting cop doesn't want to chase the bad guys?" I ask.

Kennedy laughs in a way that tells me he doesn't like anything about this phone call.

"So you've saved some self-respect, have you?"

"I keep some hidden in my sock where no one will look. You saying you've got space over there?"

"No. I don't have space. But I can make some. Someone will have to go. You're not going to be very popular."

"I'm used to that. I can't start right away. Things are sensitive right now. I can't leave my chief hanging until he gets someone in my chair."

"Chandler PD is fucked up, you know that?"

"Is that a real question?"

"No. I can't take you on immediately anyway."

"Need me to interview?"

"Let's just say you're pre-vetted. Reach out when you're clear to transfer. Give me a couple of weeks to rearrange some chairs before you start yapping about it. Chicago's a small city."

I end the call with Kennedy wondering who Frenchie or her fake federal friends poked to make that happen. How far up the Chicago PD chain of command did the poking start? How many pokes did it take to get down to Kennedy? Or did it start with Kennedy? I tell Raj to take me back to the station, punching Raffi's number into the phone as the car eases away from the curb and swings around in the opposite direction.

"Mack."

"Raffi. Earnie Davidson give you his number?"

"Yeah, I got it somewhere."

"Call him. Tell him I need to talk to Twill. In person. Give him my number."

"What's going on? I mean other than me being hired as your answering service?"

"I'm headed in. We can talk when I get there."

I end the call as Raj stops for a red. He swivels his head my way like a Pakistani owl. I can tell he's still processing my call with Sergeant Kennedy.

"You're leaving Chandler PD?" he asks. "You're quitting? Where are you going? Are you keeping a badge? Private security?"

I give him a look that says he's wasting his time. *Deduce* is now his new favorite word. He tries to broaden the inquiry and work backwards.

"If you could do anything you wanted," he asks, eyes narrowing, "what would that look like?"

"It'd look like me sleeping on the way to the office."

Raj takes the hint unhappily and we ride in silence, a smokey yellow capsule burrowing a tunnel through the rain. I keep my eyes closed, like maybe I was telling Raj the truth. Like I've finally surrendered to being unconscious. But wanting to sleep isn't even half the battle. Needing to sleep counts for even less. Sleep is a fawn in the forest. It knows better than to venture out on wobbly legs and curl up next to me. Not with the broken sticks for bones in my chest. Not with the chainsaws in my head.

The city passes beneath me to the rhythm of Raj's wipers. The cracks and the potholes in the road sound up through the tires in jagged couplets that feel for all the world like the heartbeat of some poor schmuck hooked up to life support; some guy who doesn't know what exactly landed him in the hospital except maybe an allergy to that moment when the future turns into the present. So the guy, the patient, the life-allergic schmuck, keeps looking backward into the past, hoping for the solace of the familiar. Joke's on him. The past doesn't look like it used to. Someone has graffitied the walls and rearranged all the furniture. There is no going back.

"When do I pick you up?" asks Raj as he pulls the cab up to the front steps. I empty my wallet on top of the front cupholders between the seats and shake my head.

"Time I started driving myself for a change."

"But won't whoever you're … *evading* … find you?"

"It's time they did. I'll call you if I need you. Go spend some quality time with Cleo before she trades you in. Take her out to dinner. It's on me."

Raj picks up the meager collection of presidents between us, fans the bills, and then rolls them up and slides them into his shirt pocket. He doesn't say anything. He doesn't have to.

"You took me every place except the bank," I say. "I'm good for it. Meantime, take her to Blondies. Buy her a *Big Dream*."

EIGHTY-ONE

He's a miracle of balance, this guy. Micro-muscle flexes in each leg, his torso, his back, shoulders, counteracting gravity as he holds Little Ray and aims for the aqua-blue urine cake over the drain. Question is how long it lasts; whether sleep will finally take him where he stands, here and now, nudging him forward into the white tiled wall in the lobby men's room of the Chandler Police Department, splitting his head open on the plumbing. He doesn't need his eyes open to aim. But it helps to stay conscious.

"The elusive Raymond Mackey."

Eyes open. Posture tightening. Dilation. Inflation. The sound of his name releases the right amount of adrenaline and the last of the piss. Ray shakes, tucks, zips. Looks over his shoulder.

"Chief," he says, turning as Warren Loudermilk unzips and assumes the position at the neighboring urinal. "Slumming in the first-floor john?"

Chief Loudermilk laughs. He's wearing his dress blues beneath a navy trench, hat tucked under his arm. His snowy coif has been neatly brushed into silver and the cowcatcher beneath his nose has been combed and clipped into a perfect follicular triangle. Nothing about him is wet, which means he stopped in to take care of business on his way out the door.

"You think it's beneath me to piss with the rank and file?" asks Loudermilk.

"First floor is beneath everyone, Chief." Ray washes up and yanks a paper towel free. That small act is like a bat to the ribs. "You've already got the man-of-the-people reputation. You don't need to come looking for it in here. Not all dressed up."

The Chief shrugs. Shakes. Zips.

"I dust off the dress blues for funerals, press conferences, and academy graduation day. Care to guess?"

"Who died?"

"You're good. Delmont Williams. Cancer finally kicked his ass. Best fire chief Chandler ever had. Bar none."

"Cancer is having a good run of it this month."

"Senator Kahn? Poor bastard. He was a good man too. Could always count on Bob to at least try to do the right thing by people. Unlike just about everybody else in Washington. But damn if Bob didn't get cancer like I get a case of the sniffles. Three times. It loved the guy. Finally caught up to him. Del too, damn it. Crying shame. You know him?"

Ray nods.

"Del? Yeah. Hard not to know Del. I liked him. Not sure it was so mutual. He was a good man."

"They want me to say a thing or two." Chief Loudermilk washes his hands and leans into the mirror, brushing his mustache with a finger. He clears his throat. "People are looking for you Ray. They're looking for you in my office, which means they can't find you in yours."

"Who, exactly?"

"The people you're supposed to be leading into battle."

"You mean the people I'm supposed to be babysitting until I'm replaced."

The Chief turns and leans against the sink. He holds his hat with both hands down against his waist.

"Look. Ray. I get that Acting Director of IAD is not your cup of tea. I get that you never asked for it. But I'm asking you to step up. I'm asking you to do the job. I'm asking you to make a show of it. Those people up there are working hard to keep the wheels on the IAD wagon. They need someone with approval authority to keep the paperwork moving. For now, that someone is you."

"Chief ..."

Loudermilk holds up a hand. The hand gestures at the general wreckage of Ray's face.

"I don't know where you've been, or what you do all day. Looks like you've been in quite a scrape. Maybe you fell down the stairs. We can talk about that if you want, but otherwise I don't want to know and I'm not going to ask. Wherever you've been, whatever you've been up to, you need to be here." The Chief points resolutely at the floor, like he means the lobby men's room. "You need to be here working. Understand?"

"Yes, sir." It comes out with a tired sigh.

"I don't know what you've heard, and I'm not about to talk out of school, but Orland Twill is now in a shitload of trouble. Which means even more attention for Chandler IAD, as if the OAG investigation into your Russian doll ..." Loudermilk searches silently for the word.

"Debacle," suggests Ray. "Catastrophe? Nightmare? Fuck-up?"

"You're too hard on yourself, Ray. I was going to say misadventure. A mistake, yes. You were played, no question. You were used. And now we're all paying the price. Dan Brewster and OAG are all over me like a second skin for an interview. I've been playing hard to get, but he'll corner me eventually. I'm running out of excuses. Delmont's funeral got me off the hook today. Guess the poor bastard died for something after all."

"Sorry, Chief."

"Don't be," he says, his voice like a pat on the back. "OAG will work itself out, Mack. It's all going to blow over. I'm convinced it was an honest mistake on your part. Forgive yourself and move on. Point is, IAD is now under more scrutiny than ever. I need the unit to be functional. Understood?"

"Yes sir."

"Good. Now," the snowy caterpillars above his eyes arch their backs. "If you can see your way clear to making that happen, then once I get Twill's replacement locked down, I'll lean on Bill Wexler to see if he can make room for you in Homicide."

An empty beat bounces around the bathroom tile. The Chief obviously wants the offer to have an impact. He gets his wish.

"You'd do that?" Rays asks.

"Can't make any hard promises. I'm not forcing anyone on Bill that he doesn't want, but it helps that Stretch Martin put in his papers last week."

Surprise works some magic into Ray's eye muscles. It's not what he was expecting. Ray has dropped in to visit his old partner once a week ever since Stretch had taken a bullet to the cheek. Their talks have mostly been upbeat: Stretch managing the pain; adjusting to the new look in the mirror; getting back in the game once he has fully healed. They'd tiptoed around the psychological damage. Ray had known that would be an issue. Thirty plus years on the force, first time catching a bullet. That'll get any man to thinking how much time he has left. But Stretch had never mentioned turning in his badge.

"Stretch is out?" Ray asks. The Chief nods. Points, in warning.

"Not for publication, but yeah. Getting his face shot off in that salvage yard changed his retirement timeline. His wife is probably driving that bus. I don't blame her. But that leaves Bill Wexler short a homicide cop. Sounds like Stretch has been singing your praises. Thinks you saved his life out there. He thinks you've been getting a raw deal around here ever since they kicked you to the curb for playing on the wrong team."

"He's not wrong."

"I agree. Like I told you before, had you come to me directly, I'd have shut that nonsense down and kept a good homicide cop on the team." Loudermilk shrugs. "But here we are, Ray. What's done is done. Wexler listens to Stretch. And maybe a little encouragement from me convinces Bill to give you a second chance. I can try. That work for you?"

Ray nods, saying nothing.

"Good. But understand, Ray … that's exactly what I'm asking you to do now. I need you to *try*. Think you can do that?"

"I can try," he says. Chief Loudermilk gives him an avuncular, if dubious, smile.

"You can try trying?"

A patrol officer pushes into to the room with a sour look on his face, a pool of water on the crown of his hat, and squishing shoes. He's young and wet. Ray guesses he's been on the force less than a year. He stops abruptly when he sees none other than the Chief of Police, arms crossed, leaning up against the sink.

"Officer Nash," says Loudermilk. Everyone in the room knows it's a credit to the Chief that he knows the man's name.

"Sir."

"Tough day in the slop?"

"Yes, sir. I mean no, sir." He takes off his hat and shakes it. "Just water, sir."

"You've been out photographing intersections."

"No one in this city knows how to drive, sir."

Loudermilk stands, crossing the room and gripping the young officer's wet shoulder.

"Not on the recruitment poster, I know. But it's all important."

"Yes, sir."

"You're a credit to the badge, Nash. How about a break? Spend the next couple of hours driving an old man to and from a funeral?"

The kid laughs like he just found five bucks on the sidewalk.

"Thank you, sir."

The Chief flicks a hand in the general direction of the urinals.

"Do your thing. I'll be outside." He puts on his hat and nods Ray's direction on his way to the exit. "Try your best to try, Detective."

"I'll try to do that, Chief."

The IAD office is boasting one-hundred percent attendance. Everyone is where he or she is supposed to be, at a desk working files or phones or both. Almost everyone. Ray is *not* where he is supposed to be. Everyone knows it.

Stephanie Nellis is just setting down the phone when he enters.

"Can I help you?" she asks, deadpan, flipping a silky brown tendril over her shoulder. "Do you have an appointment?"

Ray finds the playful insolence refreshing. He gives her more of a smile than his energy can afford.

"Yeah. I'm in the market for a vacant office full of neglected files. You got one of those around?"

She looks up at him like she's mentally sorting through inventory.

"Just one," she says pointing. "All the way in the back. Past the angry mob. Let me know if you need help." She grabs a brown accordion file from her desk and hands it up for him to take. The pink sticky note on the front says *Mackey Holding.* "Everything that's come in for you since you've been gone. In case you get bored."

He takes the file and makes his way to the center of the office. He stands and waits as if for a bus, coat draped over his arm. Mark Forge is on a call that won't end. Everyone else gives Ray the attention he wants. Carolyn Schumer leans back in her chair and yanks at a licorice whip. Glen Sugarman crosses his arms, cufflinks glinting in the fluorescent wash. Raffi Santiago crosses his legs and works a fresh stick of gum out of its wrapper. Steph stands and makes her way to the copier where she can hear.

"Sorry I've been …" He searches for the word that might do some justice to his absence. He can't find it. "… away. Away and out of reach. I know I've got some digging out to do. If what you need is not already on my desk …" He breaks off. Closes his eyes. Starts again. "If what you need is not already on LT's desk, bring it in and I'll work it into the batting order. Okay?"

He looks from one to the other until he has connected with all of them, even Mark Forge who is dividing his attention between Ray and whoever he has on the other end of the phone. In the back, Glen Sugarman is rising from his chair, gathering files as he negotiates his pinstripe suitcoat off the back of the chair. Glen wants the kind of attention that might take the entire afternoon. Santiago is closer.

"Me first, boss," Raffi says, standing.

"You'd better run."

EIGHTY-TWO

Twill's desk sits just as Kevin Canady and I had left it. The computer looks no worse for the violation. The chair behind the desk is another story: papers and files, crisscrossed and flagged with all manner of neon strips – *"IMPORTANT" "READ & SIGN" "TIME SENSITIVE"* – just so I can't sit down without a pang of urgency.

I sling my coat over the back of the chair as Raffi enters, dropping the accordion file on top of the stack and relocating the entire pile from the chair to the desk so I can sit down and stop my ribs from screaming. Lifting the stack doesn't help. The pain escapes in a groan I can't control.

"What the hell happened to you?" asks Raffi.

"Door," I gasp, just as Glen Sugarman makes it to the center of the bullpen with a handful of files. I can see him stop and turn, doughy shoulders slumping, as Raffi grabs the knob and swings the door closed.

"Mack?"

I sit and breathe for a second.

"I took a martial arts immersion course. Learned every move in the book in about ninety seconds. Have a seat."

Raffi sits, but he's not done.

"Seriously, Mack, are you okay?"

"Couple fractured ribs and a bruised ego. A headache that won't quit. Can't breathe out of my nose so well. I'll live. You said you've got information."

"Three things," he says after an uncertain pause. "First, my CPD source says the forensics from LT's SUV are hairy. They got a gun with LT's prints. Nine-millimeter Makarov. Soviet era."

"Okay. Unusual. What else?"

"They got Pete's blood. They got a match on the mud in the tires. Traced it to the farm ditch near Manhattan where they found Pete. Pete has broken ribs and a broken arm. Sounds like a pretty tight case." Raffi shakes his head in disbelief. "I can't even ... do you really think ..."

"Have they charged him?"

"No. She said they're talking with him for now. He showed up on his own and made himself available. That must have helped. Sounds like not everybody over there is on the same page about whether to pull the trigger and charge him or keep talking. The brass is involved. That's all she knows."

"Okay. What's thing number two?"

He hands me a few sheets of paper stapled on one corner.

"Blake Edward Wilhaven," he says. "Forty-five calibers to the temple outside the campaign headquarters for Trent Howard. *Your* source is batting a thousand. *My* source declined to provide anything more than what's available through public channels."

"Did you lean on her?"

"No, I did not *lean* on her," he says, offended. "I said thank you very much and promised to leave her the hell alone."

"I hope that wasn't a hard promise," I say, flipping through the pages. "So this is the official summary? Can we get any reports? Witness statements? Ballistics? Evidence …"

"Mack." I glance up. Raffi's eyes have lost their humor. "Submit a request. This is what you get for now."

"Right. Okay. And the shooter?"

"At large. And probably in a retirement home by now. What is it with you and ancient murders?"

"Drug related?"

"Looks that way. Multiple unnamed informants tied Wilhaven to gangland supply. Residue in the trunk. A hot piece under the driver's seat that he obviously never had time to reach."

"Informants," I read.

"Yeah."

I look up.

"The case is based on informants?"

"Yeah."

"Who?" I rattle the sheets at him, irritated. "What informants?"

"Come on, man." Raffi gestures at the report. "This is what you get."

"Okay. What's thing three?"

"Uh, yeah. Everybody's favorite dry cleaner burned down last night."

The jolt hurts my ribs.

"What?"

"Three in the morning. No findings. Too soon. But no real question it was arson. I understand there's not much left."

"Suspects? Leads?"

"Come on. The news is twelve hours old. I don't know. Nothing yet. And I work at Chander IAD, not Chicago Fire. We'll read about it in the newspaper. Maybe someone figured we were getting too close."

"Maybe."

"I understand it was a good job too. Nothing left. Whatever The Blue Lotus was, it is no more. Guess we'll never know."

I must make some kind of face.

"What," he says. "You mean you know what it was?"

"It was Costco for criminals, Raffi. A clearing house for the Big Man felony market. Leave your shirts and pick up a ticket with coded instructions on how to claim your heroin or your guns or your girls. Or your flash drives. Very convenient. Everything but a drive thru."

"What? How do you even know this?" Raffi gestures in amazed frustration. "What is ... what is ..."

I wave him off.

"It's more story than we have time for. I'll fill you in later."

"Later?" His voice is rocketing past irritation toward anger.

I shift in my seat. A pen on the edge of the desk decides to end it all and heads for the floor. My reflexes want to catch it before it lands. It's a painful mistake that comes with undignified noise. Raffi's tone collapses back into concern.

"Have you been to a hospital, Mack?"

"Yeah," I say clutching my side. "Good times."

"Who did this to you?"

I take a few seconds to straighten myself and open my eyes again.

"The guy who took down LT in Pete Chow's house. He had the same skill set. Amanda and I were kicking through the remains of Dennis O'Toole's place. Kung Fu showed up unannounced."

"Dennis O'Toole? You mean the ..."

"Yeah, him."

"The murder-suicide case?"

"Murder-murder."

"Murder-murder? I thought ..."

"You and everybody else."

"How's Amanda?"

"Dead."

"*Dead?* Like ..."

"Like Twill is now down one niece. Broken neck and a ruptured throat sporting a mean set of knuckle prints. She had two broken fingers, which means they had a conversation of sorts before he stuffed her back in the car. Hard to know whether she interrupted him tearing her place apart or he interrupted her getting her suitcase out of the garage. Either way I need to tell LT. You get through to Earnie Davidson?"

"Yeah. He said he'd call you. How …" Santiago closes his eyes. "Wait. Go back a second. This thing with LT is connected to the O'Toole thing?"

I nod.

"Yeah."

"How?"

"That's a pretty big sandwich, Raffi."

Raffi huffs out an objection.

"Yeah? Big fucking surprise. You've been starving me for long enough, Mack. I'm getting sick of being your man Friday and never getting a scrap of … of *anything*."

"I think you mean, *girl* Friday, and that's a pretty old reference from someone so young. When's the last time you watched Cary Grant and Rosalind Russell have a drink?"

Santiago's eyes go hard. The fine Chicano features tighten. The dancer's body tenses. He leans forward in his chair, jaw set. I've never seen the man angry before. It's not comfortable.

"When's the last time you read Daniel Defoe?" he asks. "Friday was Robinson Crusoe's native manservant. I look like a manservant to you, Mack?"

I start to raise my hands, a prelude to some sort of self-defense I can't articulate. He doesn't give me the chance.

"I've killed two men for you. That's two suspensions and two investigations with a million hard-ass questions each. I didn't save your ass twice so you could treat me like the fucking hired help. I'm fed up with the *knowing-less-is-better-for-you* crap. You want my help, then you're going to tell me what the fuck is going on. *Boss*."

The accusation lands squarely inside my chest, kicking at places already tender. We stare at each other across the desk for an eternity of seconds until I finally manage a nod.

"You're right," I say. "You're not a manservant, Raphael. As cops go, as partners go, you're as good as they come. I mean that. You *have* saved my worthless ass twice and you've deserved better from me. I'm sorry. I am."

"I don't need the flattery or the apology, Mack. I just need you to let me the fuck in. Talk to me."

We sit in silence. Then I take a careful breath and give him as complete a version as I can. I leave some out: my growing concerns about Marlo; job offers to jump ship at IAD and accept an offer to resume a career in homicide at either CPD or, more recently, here; and all of my rank conjecture about this case that might confirm for Raffi that I've lost my marbles. So the story is shorter than it could be. A lot shorter. Twenty minutes has his eyes spinning and his mouth full of questions.

"So then it's all about the spoofing? Big Man's spoofing ring. All of it? The O'Tooles, Pete Chow, LT, this foreign agent, what's her name, Marie, and her goons?"

"Looks that way to me. Lot of money, Raf. Lot of power."

"And you think it's all José Beggemon. Again?"

"That's not a real name. You do know that, right?"

"Is Big Man any better?" he asks. "You want to go with Sasquatch?"

"Big Man doesn't pretend to be a real name, Raffi. Points for honesty."

Raffi laughs in disbelief, shaking his head.

"What is it with you and this guy?"

"Beats me. Marie thinks he's obsessed."

"With you?"

I nod.

"I'm thinking maybe it's mutual," he says.

"I'm beginning to wonder that myself."

"We're right back to you walking out of Deke's Salvage Yard."

"Meaning?"

"Meaning why aren't you dead, Mack?"

"Bad luck."

"Seriously. Kung Fu had you beat. He had the shot. He didn't take it."

I give him a slow nod.

"He had instructions," I say. "Big Man needs me."

"Needs you for what?"

"Don't know, Raffi. Next time someone doesn't kill me I'll try to ask."

Santiago leans his head back and stares up at the ceiling.

"This is a lot to process, man."

"Sorry, partner. You asked."

"So we've got to find mister martial arts."

"That'll be easier than you think."

Raffi looks up.

"What?"

"I got his mask part of the way off. Looks exactly like the cop patrolling Pete Chow's place the morning after. He ran me off when I dropped by for a look."

"You sure about this?"

"Near-death pain sharpens my memory. I'm sure. He's a CPD cop with a black motorcycle in his garage. The number on his police cruiser is 0705. Think your contact at CPD will run that down for you?"

Raffi winces a little.

"She's getting skittish. Looking over her shoulder is hurting her neck."

"You feel like trying?"

"Of course. Just sayin' it's getting sticky. I kind of promised. What else?"

"You sure?"

"Yeah, man. Don't go weird on me. I'm all in. I just needed to be informed for once."

"You'll regret that."

"Don't I know it," he sighs. "What else?"

I reach behind me for my coat, which feels like I'm ripping something inside. Raffi stands quickly to help

"Sit down. I'm an idiot, not an invalid. Don't baby me."

He sits. I search the pockets of my coat until I find the burner phone. I toss it across the desk and Raffi plucks it out of the air with one hand.

"Amanda Tate's burner. She doesn't need it anymore. Get it to someone who can download the data and get it back to you without a lot of noise. I'd do it myself, but …"

"But everybody here hates you. You can't get a favor to save your life."

"You don't have to sugar coat it. Use the bogus IAD file Twill set up for Quentin Young. That'll keep things confidential for a while."

Raffi turns the phone over and over in his hand.

"What are you expecting to find?"

"Several calls to Constantine Papadopoulos. I'm guessing we'll find calls to a few other spoofers working on a straight line between here and some east coast airport. Amanda would have wanted to fill her suitcase with money before disappearing."

"Disappearing where?"

"Doesn't matter. Anywhere she could lay low. Let the dust settle. Sketch out plans to hopscotch her way around the world, making new enemies and scooping up cash. Who'd have guessed."

"Guessed what?"

"Between the two of them it was the cashmere sweater that had all the brains. I told her not to run. Going back home was …" I stop, letting the thought land unfinished, remembering Amanda slumped in the front seat of Saul Margolis' midnight blue Mercedes. Santiago is waiting. I wave him away. "No point in insulting the dead. Get going, Raf. I want to find this guy."

"What are you gonna do, now?"

I lay a hand on the stack of files in front of me.

"My job. I guess. Wait for Earnie Davidson to set up a meeting with LT." I nod at the office beyond the door. "Listen to you-know-who until my ears bleed."

Raffi stands and spins away from the chair for the door. He pulls it open to reveal Glen Sugarman in a chair ten feet away, doughy brown fingers interlaced over a lap full of files. Raffi gives me a soft smile and a sharp wink.

"Next."

EIGHTY-THREE

Glen Sugarman sits heavily in a cloud of sweet cologne, holding up the files so Ray can see them.

Ray wants to close his eyes. I can feel the ache all the way up here against the ceiling. He wants to lay his head on the desk. I show him what that would look like to poor, patient Glen. He doesn't care. He wants it anyway.

He keeps his eyes open. Points to an unoccupied rectangle of desk between them. Glen sets the files down slowly, his large brass cufflinks knocking against the wood.

"Done all I can do on these, LT," he says, splaying his fingers over the stack.

Ray shakes his head.

"I'm not your LT."

"Okay. Apologies. I've done all I can do on these, Mack." He reaches forward and fans the files out across the desk. "Three are stage two. The rest are stage one. You have to review and sign off before I can push them forward. I'm out all next week for my procedure, so it kind of needs to be soon or ..."

"Your procedure?"

"Yeah," says Glen, hesitating, gauging whether Ray is serious. "I was out of leave time?" Ray squints, still not understanding. Glen keeps at it. "You signed the override? In the doorway? On my back?"

"I'm messing with you Glen," Ray lies. "I remember. How you feeling?"

"Hurts when I cough."

"Hurts when you cough," Ray repeats. "That sounds terrible."

"Doc wants to remove an obstruction. They call it a fatty growth." Glen lifts his left arm and thrusts a meaty finger into the emerging tent of his pinstripe suitcoat. "They're going in here. Right through the armpit. Orthoscopic. Should take about an hour. Maybe even longer."

Ray furrows his brow in concern, fatigue receding.

"An hour?"

"Or longer. Or longer."

"And you're out all week?"

"Just to be safe," says Glen. "If something goes wrong … I mean I told you about it, Mack. You signed the override."

"Right. I remember the part about me signing the override, Glen."

"Doc says I should rest. Post-op, I mean. He said a week would be good. I worked my caseload up to a stopping point." He waits for Ray to comment. The silence must make him uncomfortable. "You know. To accommodate the absence. Next week."

This is the part where Ray is supposed to take an extra breath and count to ten. The clock up on Twill's bookshelf is keeping track. He makes it all the way to four.

"You worked the substitute teacher for some extra recess time is what you did, Glen."

"No, man. This shit's real, Mack. I …"

"This is some real shit is what you mean. You saw your chance and you took it, Glen. You want to slide your load to my desk while you put your feet up."

"No, no, man. You want to talk to my doctor?" Glen Sugarman, his face now an animated show of irritation and disappointment, jabs his hand into various pockets for a phone he knows isn't there. "I'll … I'll get you his fucking number, man. I will. You can talk to …"

Ray leans forward, ignoring the splitting pain in his chest.

"You wouldn't be planning on going someplace next week, would you Glen? Someplace sunny and dry? Someplace you won't feel like coughing? Vegas? L.A.? You've got people in L.A., don't you? A brother. You got a line on some Lakers tickets, Glen?"

Someone has turned down the sound on Glen Sugarman. His mouth is open but he's not putting out any words. Behind him comes a sharp knock on the door. Whoever it is doesn't wait for an invitation.

"Incoming," says Steph through the rapidly opening door, her face an alarmed apology. "I tried to put him in the conference …"

She doesn't get the chance to finish. A hand from above and behind her shoulder pushes the door open the rest of the way. Glen Sugarman rotates backward in his chair for a look.

Matt Wendig is a bulldog dressed in standard business attire better sized for a pug. The barrel chest is stress-testing buttons not quite concealed beneath the blue striped tie that lies left of center over his belly and stops three inches short of his beltloops. His face is tense and florid, impaled on the thick, pink stalk of his neck with something disturbingly like foreskin that brims over the edge of his too-tight collar like a collapsing, well-yeasted pastry. His barber keeps things short on the sides but leaves enough hair up top for the chestnut dye to really take hold.

"Lieutenant," says Ray, far too casually. "Maybe we can choose a time when I'm …"

"Fuck that. I'm tired of chasing you, Mackey." He pushes past Steph into the office. "We're doing this right here and now." He turns to Glen and points. "You. Go get yourself a cup of coffee. This won't take but a minute."

Glen looks across the desk at Ray and starts to rise.

"Stay where you are," says Ray, extending a hand Glen's direction but never taking his eyes off of Wendig. "This isn't a good time, Lieutenant. Steph here will pencil you in for some time later today."

"Sure," Steph starts, but the lieutenant cuts her off.

"We've tried that already. You're never fucking here. This happens now."

Ray gives him a slow blink.

"This must be the part where you get red in the face about me wanting to schedule face time with your rank and file so I can ask questions about Detective Coopersmith."

"It is. You've got half my department pointing fingers at the other half as they wait for the shoe to drop. I can't get a fucking thing done and I'm sick of the bullshit." Wendig takes another look down at Glen Sugarman. "Son, I believe I asked you to step out."

Glen rises. Ray follows suit, the muscles tightening around his eyes as he stands, the only visible indication of the pain in his chest.

"Sit down, Glen," says Ray. "Doctor wants you to rest. Don't complicate the procedure before it starts."

Wendig, confused, watches Glen slowly lower himself back down into the chair. Steph, still filling the open doorway, crosses her arms. Behind her, the Chandler IAD staff is all ears.

"Procedure," says Wendig, pulling in his chin. Glen points vaguely at his own chest.

"It's a fatty …"

"The procedure is not the point," Ray interjects. "The point is that Glen here has waited a long time for this meeting and that you need to wait your turn."

The lieutenant is not prepared for the full-frontal insubordination. It's not a language he often hears, so the translation takes an extra beat or two.

"I don't have to wait for shit," he says. "This is a goddamned police department and I out rank both of you."

"You're right about that. Ordinarily that might be something you should raise with the Chief of Police. But I'm guessing you already have, and he told you to go back to work and let IAD do its job. Not what you wanted to hear. So, you waited until the Chief left the building to say a few words about Delmont Williams and watch six firemen lower him into the ground. Once he was gone you came down here to kick the dog and do a lot of barking."

Wendig's hypertension has him by the throat. His eyes want out of their sockets. His jaw works in silence for a handful of seconds, then he takes two steps forward. It looks like he wants to take a third, but Twill's desk gets in the way. When his voice comes, it sounds like it's coming up from someplace under the floor.

"Whoever rearranged your face deserves a medal," he says. "It was no surprise to me when you were kicked out of this department the first time. You should be in prison. That's where traitors belong. Prison. How exactly you managed to worm your way back in here is a mystery for the fucking ages. If you think anyone in this building has any respect at all for you, the Chief included, you're twice as crazy as everyone thinks you are. But make no mistake, Detective, I have a department to run and I'm goddamned going to run it without you in the way."

Any number of ways for Ray to respond to a superior officer in these circumstances. Glen and Steph have opted not to breathe until he decides. The rest of the office is quiet except for two phones that are left to go unanswered. Ray sorts through his options until he finds the one most likely to trigger the aneurism: polite, professional condescension. He gives Wendig a smile.

"Yes, sir. Well, I certainly get that you don't appreciate what must feel to you like inter-departmental meddling. And I'm sorry about that, Lieutenant. I am. But that's the job. I haven't met anyone yet who likes it, including me," he jerks his head sideways, "including Detective Sugarman here, but it's still the job. IAD performs a vital function in this police department." Ray points a finger over Wendig's shoulder at all of the eyeballs. "Everyone in this office is working their asses off for the greater good. They do the job whether people like them for it or not. Me included. Now …" Ray puts his hands on his hips and sizes up the man across the desk. "IAD has questions for your department. Lots of them. Important ones. Like who in your shop knew that Ryan Coopersmith was spending his weekends slinging horse out in Wicker Park. Keeping quiet about fellow officers engaging in felonious conduct is a violation of this department's Code of Conduct. Pretty sure you know that already. Maybe that's why you're down here raising a stink. You can bet we're going to follow the silence in your department, Lieutenant. We're gonna see just how high up it goes. We can set up an interview with you any time it's convenient."

The electric charge in the room changes. Just a little. Just for a second. It's a flicker that registers in the eyes of Matt Wendig. Ray sees it. I'm guessing Steph and Glen Sugarman pick up on it too. Uncertainty. Apprehension. Then it's gone again as Wendig's entire face tightens like someone with a wrench has given the bolt in the back of his neck a couple of clockwise turns.

"Fuck you, Mackey," he says, aiming for calm and menacingly confident. "This isn't over."

"We're counting on it, Lieutenant," says Ray. "Thanks for dropping by to get things started."

They all watch him storm out back the way he came.

"Jesus," says Steph, looking down at Glen and then back to Ray. "Now what?"

"Each of you need to write up a statement of that exchange. Exactly as it happened. Don't do me any favors. Just preserve it for posterity. Steph, I want pink sheets prepared for every officer working the property division under Wendig in the past eighteen months."

"Got it, boss. On your desk?"

"Only the sheet for Wendig." Ray points sideways. "Get the rest to Glen. He can decide the interview order and start taking statements week after next. When he's back from leave."

"Me?" Glen asks in a rising panic as Steph exits. "You're giving this case to me?"

Ray's phone seems almost as upset as Glen.

"Don't exercise yourself before your procedure," says Ray, holding up a finger. He opens the phone and puts it to his ear. "Mackey. Yeah, hi Earnie. I've been waiting. When and where? Can do. See you then."

Ray snaps the phone closed.

"You're making *me* run the Coopersmith case?" whines Glen. "You're punishing me. You're …"

"It's the job," says Ray as Steph Nellis reappears in the doorway. "This is what we do. Steph?"

"There is a Chelsea Wolfe here to see you?"

"Wolfe. Wolfe?"

"Says someone named Nick referred her. Says you'll know."

"Ah. Right. Send her in. Hold my calls and no visitors. Glen, I'm gonna need that chair."

EIGHTY-FOUR

I don't know Chelsea Wolfe from Eve, but she's fully dressed in a smart blue suit beneath a wet, black raincoat and carrying a briefcase instead of an apple, so there's a start. Asian. Plump. Sleek black hair tucked behind her ears, curling just above her shoulders. She's in two-inch heels and still staring me in the chin. She's got a freckle pattern on the left side of her face that vaguely resembles a crescent moon. I close the door behind her and shake the hand she's offering.

"Agent Wolfe," I say. "Thanks for coming."

"Chelsea," she says. "I'm not an agent."

"I thought Nick Yarborough …"

She hands me a card. *Chelsea Wolfe. Carter Wolfe Contracting.*

"The Bureau always uses its own," she says. Then she smiles. "Except when they don't."

Chelsea Wolfe's eyes slip away from my face and saunter around the office. Her shoes don't take long to follow. I watch as she circumnavigates the desk, lingering at parts of the shelving, books, the clock, the photos of Orland and Wendy, stopping at Twill's computer, then moving on with special interest at the ceiling and the top of the door.

"So tell me, Chelsea," I ask, when she's come full circle, "who's hiring you for this gig?"

"You are," she says. "Or maybe the City of Chandler. Your choice."

"All right. But you're keeping Nick informed."

"Did I say that?"

"No, you didn't."

"Good. I didn't think so. That wouldn't be like me."

"You've been briefed?"

"I have."

"What do you need from me?"

"A signature."

"How long will it take?"

"Depends on how long your name is."

That one gets her a smile.

"Oh, I like you," I say.

"Nick said we could find each other in a big, crowded room. This one is disappointingly small and mostly empty."

"How long?"

Chelsea pooches her lips, darting her eyes around the space.

"Twenty, thirty minutes."

She moves to the desk and places the briefcase on top of the files Glen Sugarman left behind for me to read. She opens the case and removes a three-page contract for me to sign.

"Initial the lower corner of every page and sign on the last," she says. "Shoot me an email and I'll send you back a copy."

I hunch over the desk, find a pen, and do as I'm told. In the open briefcase next to me is a collection of opaque, factory-sealed plastic bags that must contain the tools of Chelsea's trade.

Her Asian heritage and doughy features are disguising her age. She's older than she looks. I give her another once-over as I hand her the agreement.

"I'm guessing there was once a time when your first name *was* Agent," I say. "You soaked yourself in the locker room culture over at the Bureau until it threatened to become toxic. You finally got fed up and took your training and skillset off to market. Made some real money for a change. You're good at what you do, and you didn't burn any bridges, so the black suits keep ringing your phone.

Chelsea gives me a look, half sad, half amused. The freckled moon on her cheek slips into a sideways smile.

"Where can I hang my coat?"

EIGHTY-FIVE

Earnie Davidson works in a firm with too many names on the door. But his name comes first so maybe that's all that matters.

The receptionist is younger than my raincoat. She parks me in a well-appointed alcove and asks if I'd like something to drink while I wait. I think about telling her the truth, but I'm not exactly thirsty for disappointment.

She's a willowy type with long arms that she plants one at a time into the sleeves of a fuchsia-pink raincoat, sashing it tightly at the waist. She pulls a thick tail of black hair out from inside her collar and lets it fall against her pink shoulders, simultaneously stooping to snag a black purse from under her desk. Three male lawyer-types file out of the office in a line, each bidding her some version of a good night. Turns out her name is something that shortens conveniently to Luce. I gesture vaguely from the couch in the corner at the exodus.

"Looks like the ship is sinking, Lucy."

She grabs the door just before it closes and turns to me. Her face is angular, eyes a sharp mineral green.

"Lucinda," she says, tucking a playful scold inside a flinty voice. "Closing time. This ship floats just fine. Besides, do I look like a rat to you?"

"Far from it. But I hope you know how to swim just the same."

"Earnie knows you're here," she says. "He'll come out to get you."

"That sounds a little menacing. And expensive."

My phone rings as Lucinda slips out the door with a wave. Nick Yarborough doesn't have much time to talk so I do the listening, learning things I didn't know. When he finally gives me the chance, I tell him about my twenty-eight minutes with Chelsea Wolfe.

"She knows what she's doing," he says.

"Yeah, I got that. I'm glad somebody does."

"Any contact with you know who?"

"Not yet."

"Maybe you should reach out," says Nick.

"Works better the other way. Won't be long. Marie's time is running out."

"Where are you?"

"Earnie's lobby, getting stoned on the smell of money. What kind of chumps spend entire careers working for the government?"

"I told you, Mack, I'm getting out. You should too. At some point enough is enough. You gotta get down off the bull, or up off the ground in your case, and go have a life while you still can. Ah hell … my wife's callin'. I gotta git. Keep in touch."

I want to tell him not to take those wife calls for granted. I want to tell him that any one of those calls could be his very last. And then what are you? You're just a lonely hump holding an empty phone in one hand and an empty glass in the other. Your only hope of any call from someone who gives a damn is the last call from the bartender who threatened to cut you off an hour ago because he doesn't want you to kill yourself on the drive home. Once you're safely home, even the bartender stops caring. Kill yourself all you want. That's what I want to tell bull rider Nick with the notched belt on the wall and the wife and kid at home. Don't take that wife call for granted.

I close the phone instead. The office around me is quiet except for a woman's voice on a phone down the hall, muffled and full of rising intonations. Whoever she is, she's got a lot of questions. Makes me think of Marlo and all of my own questions.

I open the phone again and look for Marlo's fingerprints in my recent calls list: *Unknown Caller. Number Blocked.* But there are no new fingerprints. I knew that already. I poke in some numbers.

"Hi there," I say when she answers. "Probably not expecting this call."

"No," says Tia Lewis. "I wasn't. I'm just headed out."

"You and everybody else. I'll be upstairs at The Gwen at eight o'clock and I'd like you to be there too. I'll be in a drink-buying mood."

"Upstairs at The Gwen," she tuts. "A bit upscale for you, isn't it?"

"More than a bit. But when it comes to a woman like you, a guy like me has to reach a little. More than a little."

"A woman like me."

"Someone who spends all her time in high society. Lots of fancy friends with glassy smiles and pockets full of money."

"Maybe you've got me confused with someone else."

"Don't think so."

"I don't think I can be there."

"I've got a hundred-dollar bill that says you're wrong."

"How do I collect?"

"Meet me at The Gwen at eight, that's how. I'll have Ben Franklin with me."

"But then I lose the bet."

"You're no dummy, are you? I'll be waiting."

"What makes you think I won't stand you up?"

"Because you want to understand Marlo as much as I do."

EIGHTY-SIX

Earnie Davidson has his sleeves rolled up. He's got a watch worth more than my house on one wrist and a cheap blue Chicago Marathon rubber band on the other. He's older than I am but looks half my age. His body is a lean, taught temple wrapped in Egyptian cotton and tied off with silk. The tie, loosened but not sloppily so, is on the cyan side of azure, setting off the gray eyes and the head full of well-trimmed silver hair. Other than that, we could be brothers.

Earnie leans forward in his seat, still fussing with the cell phone on the conference table next to a yellow legal pad. I sit opposite in silence, leaving it to him to appease the gods of technology that have never known I even exist except for sport.

"I'm not usually the one who sets this up and makes it work," he mutters, presumably to me. "Luce could do this with her eyes closed."

The room is just the right size for so many empty chairs. At the head of the table is a rolling cart that supports a large computer monitor, a black empty rectangle that reflects the rest of the long ovular table and the empty room behind me. At Earnie's back, a long bank of windows looks down twenty-three stories at the last of the wet gray daylight sliding down the glass and steel and circling away into the Chicago drains. Squares of amber, hundreds of them, thousands, are just beginning to glow to life, above and below, from the buildings that stretch away into the gloom. I talk to the top of Earnie's silver head.

"I'm guessing when Lucinda closes those eyes, the whole world goes dark."

"Noticed that, did you," he says without looking up from his phone.

"Hard not to."

"I assure you," says Earnie like he wants me to believe whatever he's about to say, "she's twice as competent as she is attractive."

"Then she needs to run for President."

"First year Harvard Law. She works reception when she's in town. Okay. Here we go."

The monitor at the head of the table switches from black to the home screen of Earnie's phone. It's a photo of him crossing a marathon finish line looking better than I do now. Seconds later, Orland Twill is staring out into the room.

"Can you hear me, Orland?" asks Earnie.

"Loud and clear," he says. "Hey, Mack. Jesus. You look like hell."

"Thanks, LT. You're looking larger and thinner. Didn't think that was possible."

"What the hell happened?"

"One of your old friends taught me a new handshake."

"The same guy?"

"Pretty sure, yeah."

"Where?"

"A hallway and a laundry room."

"Where, Mack?"

"Dennis O'Toole's home away from home."

"Please tell me you got him."

"Well, I'm betting his hands are sore. Does that count?"

"No."

"I thought you'd be here in the flesh, LT. Where exactly are you?"

"Don't answer that, Orland," says Earnie. "No offense, Mack."

"None taken. Guess, we're all still working on the trust game. I get it."

"I don't want him taking any chances. Orland, is anyone in the room with you?"

"No. Wendy is out procuring any kind of food that doesn't come in a cellophane bag."

"I'm assuming *CPD* knows where you are?" I ask.

"Of course," says Earnie. "His other choice is a cell following arrest. Didn't have a lot of choice."

"So, no arrest yet."

"Not yet," says Earnie. "We're talking. It's been one long hypothetical-laced proffer session. Lot of arguing on their side about what happens next. For now, Orland has been forthcoming. CPD is getting a lot of free information, and they want to keep it coming. The fact that Orland dialed in the FBI before any of the shit hit the fan has bought him some credibility and some time outside of a cell. There is definitely a contingent over there that wants to bring down the hammer; arrest him and get the party started. But so far, they're proceeding carefully."

"Earnie's modesty is showing, Mack," says Twill. "He mortgaged his reputation and that of his entire firm to keep them from pulling the trigger."

"I knew you were in good hands," I say.

"Okay, that's enough of that," says Earnie, looking at me. "I don't have all night so let's get to it. We'd like to hear where you are in your investigation, obviously, but first … Orland received a communication that we are hoping you can decipher."

"What kind of communication?"

"From Mandy," says Orland. "I surrendered my phone to CPD when I turned myself in. I just got it back this afternoon. There was a text from her waiting for me. You got it, Earnie?"

Earnie looks at the phone on the table like it might bite him.

"I don't have the printout and don't want to touch this thing and have you disappear. I can keep you out of jail, but I can't be trusted not to fuck up a video conference. Just hold up your phone so we can see it."

Orland fiddles with his phone and then holds it up to the camera. A green text bubble fills the monitor screen.

> *Hey. I found the thing I know nothing about. Also some things inside that thing. Giving to a friend for safe keeping. I'm okay. Don't worry. More later.*

It's a text from the dead. Either cell phone subscriptions now perpetuate into the afterlife or Amanda was able to fire off a message before someone put a fist into her throat and a hairpin kink in her neck. I've got ample confusion about what the hell the text means, but I've got twice as much regret about the news I have to break to her uncle.

"Got it?" asks Twill.

"Yeah," I say. "Got it."

"I've tried calling," he says, "but she's not answering and so I guess I *am* getting worried. Can you make any sense of this? Do you know where she is? Did she go with you to O'Toole's place?"

I'm not sure about Twill, but judging by the deepening furrows in Earnie's forehead, Earnie certainly knows something is wrong. Too many years as a courtroom telepath, reading the minds of jurors and witnesses. Or maybe it's the way I close my eyes and flatten my palms against the conference table as I let all of the air hiss out of my lungs.

EIGHTY-SEVEN

Earnie and I have to wait for Twill to cycle through a stages of grief preview before we can make any headway. He hits anger and denial pretty hard, skips bargaining and acceptance altogether, and schedules depression for later. He goes back to anger for seconds, raging at me for letting it happen. I take it on the chin. We both know it's not fair, but maybe it feels good to have someone who's still alive that he can blame.

"You say you told her not to run, Mack," says Twill, accusingly. "Run from who? You? You act like she's guilty of something other than being a victim."

"That's a long story, LT."

The hi-def monitor puts some more pomegranate into Twill's cheeks. Turns out the speaker works fine too.

"Well, I goddamned want to hear it!" he shouts. "She never trusted you. Never. I trusted you to look out after her. She didn't want that. She was afraid of you. Of course she was. You abducted her at fucking gunpoint. I'm wondering if it was a mistake for me not to listen to her."

"I handed her a gun, LT. I got my ass kicked so she could get out of Dennis O'Toole's house. You think *I* killed her?" The question wants to be sharp. I try my best to keep it flat.

"Did you?" he asks. "You're awfully curious about where I am right now. You want to know why we're not meeting in person? *You.* That's why. Am I next?"

I can feel my own anger rising. My heart wants out of my chest, picking fights with my fractured ribs. I let my temperature drop before answering.

"Maybe. Yeah, that's a real possibility, LT. You just might be next. But not by me. I think you know that. I think you both do. You need to be a lot more concerned about CPD."

Twill laughs, and not in a funny way.

"Oh, well that's just great. That's perfect. You were the one who advised turning myself in to CPD in the first place. Get in front of it, you said."

"It was your best option. I'm betting Earnie here agrees. And so far, so good. Doesn't mean there aren't any risks."

"Risks? Listen, Mack …"

"We need to stay focused, Orland," Earnie says, cutting him off. He can see this meeting spiraling before it starts. He keeps his attention on me. "I want …"

"Earnie …" Twill starts.

"Orland. Take a breath." Firm. In charge. He turns to me. "Mack, I want to know if Amanda gave you anything."

I take his cue and give it a couple of beats. Then I shake my head.

"She gave me plenty of lip and a lot of dirty looks," I say. "LT's right. She didn't like me much. Or trust me."

"Then who's the friend she's referring to in that text?"

"No idea. Wasn't me. Last we spoke I was threatening to put her in jail. I was trying to save her life, sure, but I wasn't painting a very rosy picture about her future. She didn't like that much. She did get all dewy-eyed for a minute. She wanted to whisper about things someplace quiet over drinks and a couple of pillows. Not the first time the idea of jail made me look more attractive."

Twill shouts through the television.

"Jail for what, Mack? What is it you think she did?"

I let the question settle into the thickening silence. If Twill could reach through the screen and pull me across the table by my tie, he would. Earnie knows a helpless situation when he sees it. He leans back in his chair and lowers his hands to his lap, resigned, waiting. Outside, the darkening world has receded, secreting itself behind our window reflection, as if to listen in on my answer unseen. Nothing for me to do but jump.

"LT, I'm sorry for how all of this is gonna land, especially now that she's gone. I don't know what kind of relationship you had with Amanda. But her side of that relationship was not particularly honest."

"Stop worrying about how it's going to fucking land, Mack," says Twill. "I'm listening. So talk."

So I do. It's ugly, just like I promised, and the story plays out over Twill's face like a bad smell. He keeps interrupting to stop the stench, but that only keeps it coming. Pretty clear that, in his estimation, Dennis O'Toole was beneath his niece. He doesn't like me confirming that she was on top.

"I already knew they were involved," he interrupts angrily. "That's not news. Dennis sounds like a shit to me, but so what? Mandy is … *was* … a grown woman."

"Carrie O'Toole seemed to take exception," I say.

"Carrie O'Toole was one to talk, from what I hear. Doesn't matter. We don't put people in prison for adultery."

It's a complicated silence that fills the room. Maybe each of us takes his own detour into the past to wince in shame and think out a prayer of gratitude that we don't put people in prison for adultery. Or maybe they're both thinking about me. Maybe not. But I'm sure thinking about me. Somewhere out in the ether I can feel Marlo smile a little, just enough to hurt.

"I don't care much about the adultery," I say, "except that's what seems to have set everything into motion. Maybe Carrie was a piece of work. Or maybe that's a pretty convenient judgment coming from the woman riding Carrie's husband into the sunset. Doesn't matter. I'm more concerned about the extortion."

"What on earth are you talking about?" Twill's question comes out hostile with a squeeze of uncertainty.

"I'm talking about spoofing."

Twill closes his eyes in anger.

"If you give me one more fucking riddle, Mack … What in Christ's name is spoofing?"

I look at Earnie. I can tell the word isn't new to him. He gestures at me anyway. His hand tells me it's my show. I look back at Twill.

"Let's say you want to make a killing selling bourbon to thirsty humps like me. You know how to make the juice, but the input costs are problem. You know a guy who knows a guy who puts you in touch with someone who just happens to work for some futures exchange buying and selling commodities. You take him out for a drink and the two of you hatch a plan. It'll cost you up front, but it's gonna be well worth it in the end."

Earnie flips the page over on his legal pad and gives it a headline. *Spoofing Scheme.* Twill looks tired and irritated. I keep at it.

"So you pay the fee and toast the future. Next day your new friend gets busy placing offers to sell a shit-ton of corn, barley, rye, and wheat. He does it again. And again. The offer volume builds. All the double-breasted sheep that make the futures markets go round and round look at their computer screens and take note. What's going on with the corn, barley, rye and wheat, they ask. Somebody knows something I don't. What if we're looking at a glut in the market for the raw ingredients that go into making a good Old Fashioned? Wheat everywhere. Rye everywhere. Prices might drop. A trend starts. Prices do drop. The trend accelerates. Prices drop more. And then, when the price is right where you want it, your new friend places a set of orders to *purchase* all the corn, barley, rye, and wheat you can afford. Then he turns around and cancels all the bogus offers to *sell* those same ingredients before those contracts can be executed."

Earnie clears his throat.

"It's a classic way of manipulating the futures markets," he says. "Spoofers basically create a false picture of supply and demand and then, when the market responds to that false picture, the spoofer cashes in."

"It works in reverse too," I say. "Let's say you're in the business of selling heavy metals to arms dealers. You own a big pile of lead that you want to unload at the highest price possible. You have your spoofing friend place a lot of orders to purchase lead. The order volume accumulates. The chart line for lead on screens around the world starts to rotate upward. All the double-breasted sheep take notice. What's going on with lead? Everyone wants lead. Maybe I want lead too before it gets too expensive. A trend starts. Prices rise. The trend accelerates. The market value of lead goes up even more. When the numbers are high enough, you start selling off your pile of lead at the elevated market price. Your spoofer friend pushes a button and cancels all of those orders to purchase lead before those contracts can be executed."

"They fake a market demand so the price will rise," says Twill. "I get it, professor. What the fuck does any of this have to do with … with anything I care about? Dennis was a spoofer, is that what you're saying?"

"Dennis was a cog in a widespread, and by that I mean a cross-continental, spoofing syndicate. Dennis was just a worker bee. One of dozens, maybe hundreds of commodities traders in brokerages all over the world. His job was to place an order to buy or sell some commodity – gold, silver, wheat, bitcoins, pork bellies, crude oil, whatever he was told – and to then withdraw the order whenever he was told to withdraw it. In isolation, Dennis' impact on global markets was limited at best, but in combination …"

"In combination with whom?" Twill asks.

I look at Earnie. He's busy scribbling.

"You're not getting it, LT," I say. "Imagine Dennis O'Toole sitting at his trading desk at the Merc wearing a hat with a bright red lightbulb on top."

"Mack …"

"Indulge me. Hat. Bright red lightbulb. With me?"

"Christ. Yes."

"He places an order to trade whatever. Aluminum. Sorghum. And the light goes on. On cue, he rescinds the order before it can be executed. The light goes off. Okay?"

"Yes."

"Now. Let's go up about three miles into space and look down at our little blue marble of a planet. You can see Dennis' lightbulb turn on and turn off again.

As the world turns, you can see dozens of other red lightbulbs doing the same thing. On, off. On, off. You see them flicker like that in brokerage after brokerage, only one lightbulb per shop, maybe two or three lightbulbs in the larger brokerages. But it's enough. The market registers a surge of interest in barley futures; price goes up. Or the market shows a trend that buyers around the world have decided to get out of the barley business. Price goes down. This kind of coordinated spoofing is enough to influence the markets. Disrupt them. Control them. Milk them."

Silence. I can see each of them imagining blinking lights from space.

"A network," says Earnie more to himself than to me.

"Yeah," I say. "A network. See, it turns out it's not so easy to identify spoofing and prosecute the spoofers. Success in that area has really only come in the modern age of HFT."

"Which is what?" asks Twill.

"High frequency trading. Another acronym the world doesn't need. Imagine hundreds of thousands of orders and cancellations executed in, like, mere fractions of a second." I pinch my thumb and forefinger together to make the point. "I'll say that again: hundreds of thousands of trades in a fraction of a second. High frequency trading allows a single trader or a small handful of conspirators to make serious market impact, and serious profit, on a single spoofing gambit. Those spoofs are a little easier for law enforcement to go after because they stick out like a sore thumb. Gives you a chance to spot, isolate, and focus on algorithmic anomalies. Great big Matterhorn spikes on a graph. Okay? But the spoofing we're dealing with is a different game."

"Coordination across brokerages," says Earnie, amazement creeping into his tone. "The trades are smaller. It's diffuse. It's all about the aggregation."

"That's the theory," I say, glancing at the monitor. Twill is still struggling.

"You mean …"

"I mean if you put all of those red lightbulbs into one building, one brokerage organization, and you gave them the order to spoof up the price of wheat, the scam would be easy to spot. The Justice Department would have the subpoenas out before lunch."

"Okay …"

"But if, instead, you're able to coordinate the buying and selling of dozens or hundreds of otherwise unrelated commodities traders around the world …"

"You become invisible," says Earnie. "You disappear into the market."

"Exactly. To the Justice Department algorithms, your stealth organization of red lightbulb-hatted crooks looks like the market itself and nothing more. And you don't need monstrous orders to accomplish the same result. Moderate orders will do. It's a trading volume that, on an individual basis, no one gets very excited about. But even a moderate trading volume multiplied dozens or hundreds of times by dozens or hundreds of traders around the world gets you the same result with only a small fraction of the risk."

"But how do you get dozens or hundreds of commodities traders around the world buckled into that kind of cooperative harness," asks Earnie.

"One at a time. Carrots and sticks. Lots of patience."

"Then who's telling all these traders what to do? Who's at the top?"

Twill knows the answer before Earnie has finished asking the question. He closes his eyes. It comes out as a whisper.

"Goddamnit."

"Yeah," I say, looking up at the monitor. "Him."

"Perfect," says Twill. "José Beggemon. Always fucking Big Man. The boogie man in the budget."

"Brilliant, if you really think about it," I say. "He's created his own organization by co-opting individuals in other organizations. One here. One there. Two over there." I point up at the ceiling. "Go back up into space and take another look down at all of those red lights. But see them as one connected entity. That's Big Man's spoofing syndicate."

"Sounds to me like you admire him," says Twill, wanting it to sound like an accusation.

"I admire the patience," I say. "The ambition. Most days I feel pretty proud of myself getting my shoes on. But this guy … It's what he's always done best, LT. He turns people. He corrupts organizations one person at a time. He goes to school on this individual, that individual. Finds out what makes them tick. Starts pushing buttons. Plays with carrots and sticks. Waits. He introduces one fungal spore of black mold and waits. He is the rot. *La Pourriture.*"

"Who's your source for all this?" Earnie asks.

"I got some helpful background from another spoofer. A guy who used to work at the Chicago Mercantile Exchange with Dennis and got fired around the same time. I got him to open up and spill some beans."

"And he just, what …" Twill snorts out a laugh, "agreed to incriminate himself?"

"Cystic fibrosis is turning out the lights on this guy. He's only got a few months before he goes to that giant volleyball tournament in the sky."

Earnie is confused.

"Volleyball."

"Favorite sport. Go figure. Point is, he wanted to do something good on the way out. He cares what his kids think about him, so I told him I'd keep his name out of it. Consider him deep background. He doesn't know anything about the top. He was recruited by a guy who knew how to make his gambling debt disappear. He got his trading orders electronically just like normal. He didn't ask questions. He opened an investment account for his kids. It kept getting fatter on its own."

"And you're saying this guy and Dennis O'Toole both got fired from CME for spoofing," Twill asks.

"Hard to say. Sounds to me like CME was suspicious and cut three people loose without putting too fine a point on the reasons. One of the three, a guy named Simon Feeks, died of cancer. The guy who opened up to me has CF. Like I say, he's on his way out. And then there's Dennis O'Toole. He took a bullet on his wife's driveway."

"Okay," says Twill, "but Amanda was just an assistant at CME. She couldn't spoof anybody because she couldn't actually trade anything."

"You're wrong about that, LT. Amanda figured out she could trade herself."

Twill's jaw tightens and flexes before he opens his mouth.

"Fuck you. That's … that's …"

"Let him talk, Orland," says Earnie, looking at his watch. "Let's have it, Mack."

"Dennis was a man possessed. Something about Amanda scratched every itch. He was never able to just turn the page and move on. He might have been the only person who thought they were a secret. His wife testified she saw it happening for years. The people at CME saw it too. Dennis managed to put an end to it for a while, but Amanda, ever the dutiful cashmere assistant, was always conveniently nearby. When Carrie finally showed signs of calling it quits, Dennis showed signs of remembering his vows. Getting fired from CME scared him. Made him look clear-eyed at a future without his wife and all of her family money. Maybe that's not fair. I didn't know the guy. Maybe he loved her. Sounds like he tried at the end. Leaving CME put some distance between him and Amanda. Maybe that helped him try."

"Sounds like it didn't take," says Earnie. I shake my head and shrug.

"Few months. Then Amanda invited herself to join Dennis over at BSD Financial."

"She invited herself. Her idea?"

"Yeah. At the time she was playing the cashmere assistant to another Merc trader named Constantine Papadopoulos. Everyone calls him Stan. More on him later. Amanda eventually breaks things off with Stan and he shows her the door. She makes the call to Dennis at BSD and whatever marital resolve Dennis had pancakes in two seconds. He finds her a desk. Amanda is suddenly back under foot, just like old times. That was the ball game."

"Go back," says Earnie. "After leaving CME, how long did it take Dennis to land a job at BSD Financial?"

"Not long. BSD yanked him off the street before he could finish his drink and reorganize his life. He was talking about moving to Boston, closer to Carrie's family. Getting a reserved parking space at one of the big six accounting firms. Rebooting the marriage. Too bad. He'd still be alive."

"Do you know who at BSD snatched him up?" asks Earnie, working his pen across the pad. "I used to know a guy over there."

"A partner named Saul Margolis."

"Previous connection?"

"Don't know. Maybe they knew each other. It's a small city. The salient point is that Saul Margolis was another of Big Man's red lightbulbs. I figure once word reached Big Man that Dennis was in the wind, Big Man put the word out to Saul to do whatever it took to bring Dennis on board with BSD and to lock him down. Hook him back into the system and keep the payoffs coming. Problem is Big Man never counted on Saul Margolis having a mind of his own."

Earnie looks up from his pad.

"And you've actually talked to Saul?"

"Yeah. Once on the phone about his car. It's a slick-looking blue Mercedes that Amanda liked to drive when she wanted to be alone and stop being a blonde. Saul's officially on semi-retirement in Isreal, which means he's someplace that's actually nowhere near Isreal so he can keep Big Man guessing."

"He's hiding," says Twill.

"Yeah. Saul's afraid of the kind of permanent retirement that comes with a loud noise he'll never actually hear."

"I thought Saul was doing Big Man's bidding," says Earnie. "A spoofer. Getting Dennis on board."

"He was. But Saul is one of those guys who likes solving puzzles. Turns out in his spare time at BSD, Saul was sleuthing out Big Man's spoofing syndicate. Putting names and employers to those red lightbulbs. Who knows, maybe it wasn't all that hard to figure out who else was playing the game. Look for trading patterns. Get some good data sources. Reverse-engineer commodity orders similar to the ones you've been instructed to make. Maybe it just took paying attention. Keeping track." I point to Earnie's pad, now full of indecipherable scribbles. "Keeping notes."

"Why?" Twill asks. "I mean, what's the ..."

"Don't know. Security maybe. Idle curiosity. Blackmail. Whatever the reason, I'm guessing Saul was proud of what he'd managed to figure out. He bonded with Dennis and eventually couldn't help giving him a peek behind the curtain. Maybe they had a deal. A partnership."

"Then Saul got spooked?"

I give Earnie an affirming nod.

"Right. Saul turned invisible about the time Dennis' world started to wobble. Carrie O'Toole decided she wanted a lot of lawyers in her life. In coming over to BSD, Amanda might have snapped whatever last straw was holding that marriage together. Carrie had family money behind her. Dennis did not. So maybe Dennis started feeling insecure about the future all over again. He took Saul Margolis' hobby and went pro."

Earnie sets down his pen.

"Meaning?"

"Meaning Dennis started shaking down his fellow spoofers. Not so sophisticated either. Give me a bag of money or you go to prison. That kind of thing."

A sound of anguished exasperation slips out of the monitor.

"And you're suggesting that Dennis and Amanda were doing this together."

"No, LT. I'm not suggesting that. I'm telling you flat out that's what was happening. Bonnie and Clyde without the Tommy guns. Amanda was no dummy. I'm guessing something about the spoofing slipped out in the pillow talk while they were both still at the Merc. He was getting some extra spending money, and she was doing the spending. Once she left the Merc and went to work for BSD, the two of them became partners in extortion. Dennis showed her the ropes by going after Stan Papadopoulos. Dennis and Amanda both hated the guy. I've met him a couple of times and believe me, I get it. Anyway, it turned out a little easier than taking candy from a baby. Stan paid big. Then, once Dennis was in the morgue, Amanda ventured out on her own. First thing she did was put on a wig, hop in Saul's Mercedes, and hit Stan up a second time."

"He paid *again*?" Twill's angry edge has given way to astonishment.

"Like she'd pulled three cherries on a slot machine."

"Okay, back up," says Earnie. "So Dennis ends up dead because he got caught shaking down this spoofing network."

I wince. The pain in my chest doesn't know when to stop. Earnie thinks I'm disagreeing. He's not wrong.

"It's not so simple," I say.

"Why not?"

"It starts with Amanda. The O'Toole marriage was already teetering, but, if you believe Carrie's deposition testimony, Amanda gave it a big shove. Once Carrie decided she was done, she came at Dennis with a vengeance. She knew Dennis was involved in shady trading at the Merc and she knew that when he moved over to BSD he'd just picked up where he left off."

"Carrie was in on the spoofing, or she just knew about it?"

"Not sure what kind of details Carrie had," I say. "When it comes to husbands, most wives could teach Sherlock a thing or two. Maybe Carrie knew a lot. Maybe just strong suspicions. But she wasn't counting any dirty money herself."

"And you know this because …"

"Because the divorce action she started was set to pull everything out into the sunlight. You don't do that if you're only going to implicate yourself as a knowing accessory."

"Okay, so Dennis sees her coming," anticipates Earnie. I nod.

"Like she's all four horsemen of the apocalypse wrapped into one angry wife. The depositions in the divorce action didn't leave much for the imagination. She was coming for Dennis and, since Saul had made Dennis a BSD principal, she was coming for the firm too. She was going to ruin his career. Bankrupt him. Send him to prison. What's a guy to do? Dennis buys enough antacid to fill a bathtub and sends up a flare to Big Man."

"How?" says Twill. "They're old friends? They go have fucking coffee?"

I shake my head.

"Nah. Dennis wouldn't know Big Man from Adam. No one knows Big Man. That's how he rolls."

"So?"

"So Dennis sent some shirts to the dry cleaner and waited for instructions."

"You lost me," says Earnie.

"The Blue Lotus Dry Cleaners. LT has some familiarity. It's a big pile of ashes now."

"What?" Twill's face gets closer to the screen. His eyes are intense and bloodshot with fatigue, stress, and residual rage.

"Yeah. Santiago tells me it burned to the ground last night. Arson."

"Suspects? Leads?"

"Not that I know of. CPD's not exactly ringing my phone."

"Someone want to fill me in here?" Earnie asks, looking from me to the screen and back again.

"The Blue Lotus Dry Cleaners is a Big Man front," I say to Earnie.

"A front for what?"

"Anything and everything, as long as it's illegal."

"Okay … And how did that work, exactly?"

"I only know pieces. Somehow you get cleared to use the system. So they know you. Trust you enough to make you worth the risk. To anyone else," I reach over into the neighboring chair and rummage through my coat pockets until I find the photo of Twill. I unfold it and hold it up to the screen, then hand it across the table to Earnie. "To anyone else, like LT here in a spiffy Cubs hat, it's just a place to take your dirty clothes and get photographed."

"You took this photo?" Earnie asks.

"No. Frenchie Marie's people took the photo. She gave it to me to convince me that my boss is up to his eyeballs in Big Man mischief."

"Okay, one thing at a time," says Earnie.

"Let me explain something," says Twill. "I don't know anything about …"

Earnie holds up a hand, cutting him off.

"Stop, Orland. Stop. I don't want you to explain anything. Not now. We talked about this. You have an attorney-client privilege and I want to protect it. If I had my way, you wouldn't be in this conversation at all." Earnie refocuses on me. "The dry cleaner."

"Right. Well, let's say your thing is drugs. Maybe you're looking to buy. Maybe you're looking to sell. You've been vetted. You're in the club. You go to the Blue Lotus with bag full of laundry. They pull up your account. They know who you are. They know to look for a mark on a sleeve or maybe a missing button just to verify this isn't about a ring around the collar. You leave the shirts and get a ticket. The ticket is coded with the combination for a locker at one of several storage facilities owned by XXL Enterprises. They're all over the place. Big orangish eyesores. So you hustle out to the designated locker and put in your request along with some upfront cash for the service. The next day or two, you go back to pick up the shirts. The guy behind the counter hands them over neatly folded in a box or on hangers wrapped in a plastic bag with a ticket. The ticket is coded with information for another combination locker. Inside the locker are instructions on when and where the deal goes down. Or maybe just a place and time to meet a contact who can work the details. Point is, Big Man is open for business, wholesale and retail. He's making a killing, and I mean that both ways."

I look from one to the other. They're both trying to make sense of it. It looks painful, so I add a little more.

"Look, it's just a communication system, and it works for anything, not just drugs. Sex trafficking. Human smuggling. Bribery. Contract killings. It's a clearinghouse for criminality. Big Man is a broker. He gets a cut of all of it up front, even if he's not directly involved in whatever deal is going down. Also helps him keep his finger on the pulse. He gets to know who's doing what with, or to, whom."

"Risky," says Twill. "Lots of opportunity for that to go sideways."

"Sure, but look at the bigger picture. He's trading volume here. The upside is huge. And he's containing some of the risk by laundering, sorry, most of the communications. Maybe a particular deal goes bad, but the crime laundry operation is still raking it in. And even if, worst case scenario, the laundry gets busted, I'll bet you my next drink that Big Man has the same operation running through dozens of other businesses. All it takes is a coded receipt. Marie tells me he's doing the same thing in Europe."

"Marie," spits Twill. "Will you tell us who this fucking Marie …"

"No," says Earnie. "One thing at a time."

Silence. Earnie has his head in his hands, elbows on the table, staring at the photo of Twill in a red cap coming out of the Blue Lotus. Twill is leaning back and staring at the ceiling of whatever room he's in. They're trying to assimilate. I can sympathize. I wait. Earnie is the first to come up for air.

"So Dennis sees Carrie coming for him. He reaches out to Big Man for help. He goes to the dry cleaner. He's already approved? He's in the club?"

"He's a spoofer. He's in. He sends in some shirts."

"What's he want?" Twill asks. "Carrie dead?"

"Maybe. But I doubt that. I think he just wanted to know what to do about the coming shit storm. He wanted a way out."

"So he sends in some shirts," coaxes Earnie.

"He sends in some shirts. He gets a ticket. He drives across town, puts his worries into the designated locker and goes back to his miserable ulcerated life and waits a day or two. When Big Man's instructions are starched and hung and ready to be picked up, Dennis is too busy drowning, so he sends Amanda to run the errand. She comes back with clean shirts and a new ticket, which she throws away because she doesn't yet understand that it's not about the shirts. It's all about the ticket. He makes her dig it out of the trash. He follows the ticket out to a storage facility out in La Villita. He opens the locker and finds a flash drive waiting."

"Instructions," says Earnie.

"Instructions."

"To do what?"

"Best guess? To copy BSD Financial trading information. Particular commodity trades over some designated time period. Something to cover all spoofing trades by Dennis O'Toole and Saul Margolis and whoever else at BSD is or has been in Big Man's pocket. Maybe more. Maybe all BSD confidential client and trading data."

"Why?"

"Hard to say."

"That's never stopped you before," says Twill.

"*Touché*. It is pretty clear that Big Man was planning to sabotage BSD's network. I think he wanted to get a copy of everything he thought had any value before he wrecked it."

Earnie sets down his pen again and pinches the bridge of his nose right between the eyes.

"How … how do you …"

"Because I talked to the guy Big Man was grooming to do the job. Guy named Kevin Canady, aka Blue Shoe."

"Blue Shoe?"

"It's a bad mocktail. Hawaiian Punch, white cranberry juice and Seven-Up. It's also a gang name. No alcohol in the mix means Kevin was still a trainee in the Big Man ranks. Earning his stripes."

"How?"

"Kevin was a senior tech at an outfit called Whitehorse I.T. Services. Whitehorse has the contract to service BSD's computer network. I arrested Kevin for breaking into Amanda's house and searching all her hard drives."

"What?" says Twill from atop the rolling cart at the end of the table. "He broke into her house?"

"Well. Not exactly. He had a key. Big Man wanted to make it easy."

"And he was looking for what?" asks Earnie.

"Something he couldn't find. Same thing that a guy on a black motorcycle eventually started demanding of Amanda in the middle of the night. I assume you know that part of the story."

"I do, yes," says Earnie, scratching his head. "So this Kevin person was looking for something Dennis gave to Amanda before he died."

"Right."

"He's looking for sensitive trading data copied from BSD's network."

"Right."

Earnie crosses his arms over his chest and closes his eyes tight, like he's engaged in some internal struggle to keep his own unruly thoughts in order.

"And presumably, the plan was, once the sensitive data had been copied and preserved, they send this Kevin person …"

"Canady."

"They send Kevin Canady to BSD on a routine Whitehorse I.T. service call so he can corrupt their network and prevent anyone from accessing that same data."

"Or to make it very difficult. They were going to offer Blue Shoe a choice: either do the job and get a bunch of money, or don't do the job and get ratted out for whatever else Big Man had on him, like breaking into Amanda's place. Kevin already has a couple of strikes against him. One more puts him away and his daughter grows up without him. He'd have done just about anything to stay out of jail. I took away Big Man's leverage by arresting him ahead of time."

"Okay," says Earnie. "So, Kevin is in the system and the BSD network is safe."

"No, I released Kevin without any charges."

"Wait," says Twill. "What?"

"Long story. I traded Kevin's freedom for something I needed."

"Like what?" Irritation and confusion are battling for control over Twill's face.

"You really don't want to know that, LT. The point is that BSD's network is still safe."

"How? Why?"

"Because the FBI sent over a preservation of evidence order this afternoon. Now it's an unlawful obstruction of justice for anyone to poke a BSD delete key or to do any other tinkering."

Twill spits out a stupefied laugh.

"You've been working with the FBI?"

"Yeah. Everything in BSD's network should be safe."

"You told me that the FBI was compromised. They had a leak."

"It was. They did. I plugged the leak and connected with Nick Yarborough. He's all in. Seems to be anyway. Nick called me while I was waiting for this meeting and gave me the news about BSD."

Earnie holds up his hands.

"Okay, both of you … just … shut the fuck up a second. This is like wrestling a goddamned octopus." We all sit in silence again for a good ten seconds. Earnie picks up the thread. "Dennis copies the BSD data. As Big Man instructs. He takes it out to La Villita …"

"No. Dennis is full-on paranoid at this point. He thinks Carrie's lawyers have him under surveillance. So he gives the flash drive to Amanda. She takes it out to La Villita. She puts it in the locker. Before she leaves, she sees someone open the locker and take the drive."

"Right, right," says Earnie. "She follows him out to the propane tank place. Lincoln Metalworks. Owned by XXL. I've heard this part."

"According to Nick, the FBI has been snooping around Lincoln Metalworks on a drug case for months. Their investigation stems from a bust in Deming, New Mexico, eighteen months ago. Found three kilos in a truck of propane tanks, some with tops that screw off. They traced the tanks back to Lincoln Metalworks."

Earnie opens his mouth to speak, but I hold up a finger.

"Point is, it occurs to me that this is how Big Man moves some of his contraband, including whatever his runners take from those lockers. That flash drive went from Dennis O'Toole, to Amanda, to a La Villita locker, to a runner who knows nothing about anything, into a screw-top propane tank, then to Lincoln Metalworks, then to wherever Big Man orders his deliveries."

"But we know what was on that flash drive, right?" Earnie's voice sounds hopeful, almost desperately so. "Because we have the second flash drive. We have the copy Dennis made and gave to Amanda to hide. She gave it to Orland. Orland made a copy. He gave it to the FBI. He gave it to me. We know what's on the drive, lots of numbers, we just don't know what it means. Right? Tell me I'm right."

"Okay. You're right."

"Am I?"

"No."

"Shit. I knew you were going to say that. Why?"

"Because I don't believe the second drive was really a copy of the first. That was misdirection."

"A lie, you mean," says Twill.

"Yes. A lie."

"Whose lie? Dennis or Amanda?"

"Both. Dennis lied to Amanda. Amanda lied to you. The second drive contained the data that Dennis wanted to safeguard the most. It was all of Saul Margolis' research. It was the who's and where's of Big Man's spoofing network."

"It was gibberish," says Twill. "Like he said, it was pages and pages of numbers. I couldn't make heads or tails of it. I showed it to Nick. He was clueless too."

"He's not clueless anymore."

"Oh yeah? Why?"

"Because I explained to him what it all meant."

"You?" Twill's voice is heavy with incredulity. "You, the luddite with the dinosaur flip phone who doesn't know one end of a computer from the other."

"Yeah. Me."

"Well, what the fuck does it mean?"

I hold up a couple of fingers.

"Two files on that drive. One contains a list of IP addresses floating in a sea of random numbers. These IP addresses correspond to individual computers and brokerages at which Big Man's spoofers are placing commodities orders. It's a numerical key to the whole network."

"And the other file?" asks Earnie.

"That one stumped me. Turns out I was reading it the wrong way. Like I said, Nick called while I was waiting in your lobby. He got an analysis back from the Bureau computer geeks. Forty-one pages of numbers. Nonsense if you read left to right. But if you read the numbers vertically you get a five-digit trader ID number, followed by a nine-digit transaction number, followed by a brokerage ID number, and a date, a time, a commodity code, and so on. Repeat for forty-one pages. Nick says the key turned out to be reading the columns, not the rows, and getting the right font type and font size so it all lines up. Keys to the kingdom."

"Jesus," says Twill. "No wonder they want it."

"There's more," I say. "Nick says there was a third file on the drive. Deleted, but nothing is ever really deleted, is it? The boys in black resurrected the dead."

"What was it? More numbers?"

"Lots of letters mixed in this time. A list of names and contact information of commodities traders."

"The spoofers," says Earnie.

"All over the world. Where they work. Information about their families. Possible leverage. The motherload, and all in readable English. Makes me think Saul was working the extortion angle even before Dennis came on board. Maybe that's the one flaw in Big Man's big scheme. The corruption eventually gets corrupted."

Earnie's not in the mood to philosophize.

"And Nick said this file had been deleted from the drive?"

"That's the only file Amanda really needed," I say with a nod. "Dennis gave her a flash drive and told her to hide it. If everything else somehow got confiscated or destroyed, he wanted a backup. She said he was skittish that way. He distrusted the security of digital information. He also had a back-up for the back-up."

"Which was what?"

"He encoded a subset of the IP addresses into a stack of lottery cards and then cross-referenced those with handwritten notes of spoofer names and contact information that he put into the margins of a milkshake recipe book."

"Okay," says Earnie. "Well, that's some kind of paranoid."

"Maybe. Maybe not. He's dead, isn't he?"

Earnie's eyes concede the point.

"Well, if Amanda had the book …" starts Twill.

"She didn't. I don't think Dennis fully trusted her. He misled her about what was on the drive, but she figured it out. She probably couldn't make any more sense out of the numbers than we could. But the list of names she understood. So she copies the list of spoofers, deletes that file from the drive, and hands the drive over to Uncle O here, figuring no one would be able to make heads or tails of the numbers."

"Why?" asks Earnie. "Why turn it over at all?"

"Because I was all over her," says Twill, defeated. "She was getting death threats to not tell anyone what Dennis had given her. She was pretending not to know. I could tell she was lying. She was terrified. I kept pushing until she told me the whole thing about Dennis giving her the flash drives. Even then she didn't want to give it to me. It got ugly. Shouting and tears. The whole works. Eventually I wore her down. She dug the drive out of a canister of fucking coffee beans." Twill laughs cruelly at himself. "I guess it was all a show. She saw me coming. She'd already deleted the file. She worked me like a pro."

"Happens to the best of us, boss," I say. Twill's got his eyes closed, but maybe he can see me anyway. Maybe in his mind's eye he can see me holding a Russian doll. Twill's head bobs in a slow nod.

"Right," he says. "I'm sorry, Mack."

"Don't be, LT. I mean that."

Twill sighs.

"So her plan was to leave me to twist in the wind with CPD up my ass and disappear with a list of white-collar criminals she could extort for a living."

I'm quiet for too long, which is probably answer enough. Eventually I clear my throat.

"She sent you a text," I say. "Maybe she had information. A plan to help. That's a pretty cagey message she sent. She knows anybody could be looking at your phone. Seems like she was trying to do something right for a change. So she must have cared, LT."

"You're trying too hard, Mack," says Twill.

"No. That's really how I see it. She'd have gotten in touch. Long distance. Someplace warm and dry. She went home to pack a stupid suitcase. Broad daylight. Probably thought that made it safe. Turns out her garage was plenty dark."

"Christ," mutters Twill, rubbing his face with his hands. He's come full circle, back to imagining Amanda's lifeless, broken body. "You think it was the same guy who killed Pete?"

"I do, LT. Same skill set."

"How's that?" Earnie asks. "Sounds to me like Amanda got a fist through the neck. Pete got two bullets to the head."

"Yeah, but Pete got bullets only because they needed evidence to plant in LT's car. Ask CPD the right questions, Earnie. If they're in the mood to be honest, they'll tell you Pete had a broken arm and some broken ribs. Not the cause of death, but it is a signature."

"How do you know this?" Earnie asks sternly.

"A guy I know actually has some friends, unlike me. One of those friends owes him a favor."

"A leak," says Twill. "CPD has a leak."

"The good kind, for once," I say.

Earnie makes a note on his pad and circles it.

"I'll talk to CPD about Pete's body," he says. "And I'll see if I can learn what they know about Amanda. If we can get a lead on Amanda's murder, maybe we can learn something helpful about Pete's murder. If I can convince CPD that the two murders are connected, maybe that gives Orland some breathing room."

"From your lips to God's ear, Earnie," sighs Twill.

"That makes you and me the lucky ones, LT," I say. "This guy could have ended either of us just as easily."

Twill ponders that one for a few seconds. Then he nods.

"Why are we alive, Mack?"

"Because this guy had instructions to pull his punches," I say. "We're useful. When Big Man's done with us, we'll know it."

"Great. Terrific. Well maybe we can keep his murder count to two."

"Four," I say. "You're forgetting Dennis and Carrie O'Toole."

"What?"

"Same guy, LT." I hold up four fingers. "Dennis, Carrie, Pete, Amanda. He killed all of them."

"Is that fact or gut speculation?"

"Gut."

"That's what I figured. Well, let's work one murder at a time, shall we? Let's find this motherfucker."

"That should be easy enough," I say.

"What?" Twill leans in. His eyes are the size of fists. Earnie is paying some fresh attention too. "Why?"

"Because I know who he is."

EIGHTY-EIGHT

Ray thinks of himself as man beyond ego. It's not a compliment.

His self-satisfaction these days is a rowboat. Modest as far as boats go. He never imagines a yacht. A cruise ship. A speed boat. No. Just a wooden skiff. Scarred. Chipped. Peeling paint. One oarlock busted, the other missing entirely. But it floats. It might hold him up in the world, if only he were still in it. He can recognize the shape of the hull from below, framed against a dreary, watery daylight, as he sinks to new depths.

So, he's a man beyond ego in the sense that his ego is beyond him. He can't reach it anymore. He's given up trying. The age. The addictions. The loss. The pain. The creeping incapacity. He's let go of the rope. Given up.

Mostly. There's still the occasional moment that delivers the old spark. A visceral memory of competence that makes him feel something like pride.

This moment is one of those. He's saved the best for last.

Earnie has his mouth open, but Twill beats him to it.

"What do you mean you know who it is? You mean like …"

"Yeah," says Ray too casually.

I'm not the only one who sees him basking. But I'm the only one who knows it's compensatory. I'm the only one who knows it's just a moment.

"Don't have a name yet," he says, "but that won't take long."

"Well?" Twill asks, irritation skyrocketing.

"Our kung fu wonder is CPD," says Ray. "I hooked his mask and got a peek underneath before he fractured my ribs. It's the same guy I saw in a police cruiser patrolling Pete's house the morning after he went a couple of rounds with you."

"Asian?" Earnie interjects.

"Kung fu is a discipline, Earnie. It doesn't have a race. This guy's as white as David Carradine wrapped in a bed sheet. LT wanted me to find a guy with white wrists. I found one. He's got a face to match."

"You sure it's the same guy?" asks Twill with a new excitement.

"Like I said, same skill set. Hell, I'm betting it's the same mask. I got the number off the cruiser. Santiago is working through his CPD favor list to track it down."

"I can work the question from my end," says Earnie. "We're meeting with CPD every damn day. I can just ask…"

Ray holds up a hand.

"Please don't. This needs to be done quietly. I don't know who you're talking to, Earnie, and I don't know who they're talking to. Too many people listening in for my peace of mind. We'll get there. And when we do, we're gonna find a black motorcycle in the garage plus a truck with Manhattan mud in the treads. Course, if the guy is half as smart as he is tough, he'll have washed the truck down two or three times by now. Still, we can hope."

"And you really think he's good for all four?" asks Twill.

"Think about it," says Ray, holding up a finger. "One: Pete Chow. Kung Fu beats the crap out of you in Pete's house when the hallway floor is still wet with Pete's blood. When Pete called you up on the phone and asked for a meeting, I'm guessing he was in the hall on his knees with a gun to his head. He asks you to meet him at his office. So you do. He's not there, but …"

"But security is there," says Earnie. "A reliable witness that Orland was looking for Pete the night he died. CPD likes that little fact."

"I'll bet," says Ray. "It's made to order. LT eventually makes his way to Pete's place. By the time he gets there, Pete has two extra holes in his head. His body is in a bag and the bag is in the cargo hold of a truck safely parked on some nearby street."

"A truck. Why a truck?"

"Because this is not the job for a motorcycle. Our man knew he was going to drop Pete's body in Illinois farm country saturated with two weeks of solid rain. So it's a rig. He owns it, rented it, or stole it."

"And what … he's just that confident I'm gonna show up?"

"He was listening to the call, LT. He was a gun barrel away from the receiver. Pete asked for a meeting and you said you were coming. Once Pete is dead and in the truck, the Karate Kid is back up at the house with a mask over his head and gloves on his hands, waiting for you to show. He kicks in the front window to make it look like a burglary. He empties the gun that killed poor Pete and sticks it in his belt where you're sure to find it on a pat down. Once you show up and put your prints all over the murder weapon, he kicks your ass but good …"

"And takes the gun back," says Twill.

"Right. Mixed martial arts, you said."

"Yeah," says Twill, like he's reliving the beating. "The man had skills. Once I had the gun, he just kind of exploded. Fast. Solid. Very sure of himself."

"Been there," says Ray.

"But I could have brought my own piece," he says.

"Could have. But you're IAD. IAD doesn't like guns. Calculated risk that paid off. You left it in your truck. Doesn't really matter whether you were armed. This guy was not worried about taking you down one way or the other."

"True."

"So the guy leaves you clutching your gut and begging for air and drives his rig out to Manhattan where he dumps Pete's body in a ditch. He saves a bunch of mud for your tires and just enough of Pete's blood to give CPD forensics something to talk about when they open up your Escalade."

"Christ," whispers Twill. Ray holds up a couple of fingers.

"Two. Amanda Ramada Tate. Broken neck. Blunt force trauma to the larynx. Same skill set. Not a day earlier, a guy comes through Dennis O'Toole's back door and chops my rib cage into kindling. He could have killed me easily enough. I was staring up into the business end of a Glock that could have gotten the job done. But it didn't get the job done. He never pulled the trigger. Because *I* wasn't the job. *Amanda* was the job, and she got away. She was home free as long as she didn't go home. She went back anyway for a suitcase and a fist to the throat."

Earnie is taking furious notes. Twill is staring into space. Ray adds two more fingers to the two that are still in the air.

"Three and four. Dennis and Carrie O'Toole. The guy who tore through me to get to Amanda was riding a black motorcycle. Amanda recognized it as the same bike she'd seen outside her place. That puts the odds at somewhere north of one hundred percent that the Karate Kid was the guy who made the threatening phone call to Amanda. A painful death if she shared what Dennis had given to her before he died."

"Why even make that call?" asks Twill. "Why not just kill her then?"

"Because Big Man has this guy on a leash. Amanda was suddenly in league with you, a police lieutenant. Kill her and maybe no one knows what she has told you or given to you about his spoofing syndicate. Big Man's got his foot on the brake until he can assess the damage and figure out how to work you into the frame. Meantime, all our boy can do is sit on his bike and make threatening phone calls."

Earnie circles something illegible on his pad and sets his pen down.

"Your point is that this martial arts guy is a straight line back to the O'Tooles."

"Right," says Ray. "The whole reason for killing Pete in the first place was to keep him from correcting the forensics on the O'Toole murders. Big Man wanted his boy to keep the murder-suicide cover in place."

Earnie snaps his rubber Chicago Marathon wristband, frowning.

"So he took out Dennis and Carrie ..."

"Because Big Man told him to," says Ray.

"Spoofing."

"Yeah. Spoofing. Dennis and Carrie were both threats that Big Man needed to put down. I'm betting the spoofing network has been his hobby for decades. He's proud of it. He loves the idea that he's managed to reduce sovereign governments to such impotent rage that they have to resort to sending hit squads across the ocean to shake all the bushes in Chicago."

"You mean this Frenchie person," says Twill. "Marie."

"I don't know her name. But yeah."

"So Big Man knows about her?"

Ray nods.

"Big Man's been playing Frenchie Marie the whole time, which maybe makes Marie not even half as smart as she thinks she is."

"Playing her how?" asks Twill.

"Big Man has his sources. He knows he's shaking up commodities markets. He's pissing off some very big money, all of it connected to the government-favors market."

"How do you know that?"

"Because I've been alive too long, walking around with my eyes open. All concentrations of wealth derive from concentrations of power and vice-versa. Show me a man with a mountain of money and I'll show you a Christmas card list that reads like a register put together by a bureau of elections."

"So you're thinking big European money has called in the favor. Take Big Man off the board if you want the campaign money to keep flowing."

"Yeah, and I'm betting that whatever government sent Frenchie Marie our way has a mole at the water cooler with Big Man's number on speed dial. He knows they're over here looking for him. So what's a criminal mastermind to do?"

"Out with it, Mack," says Twill. "I'm tired of guessing."

"He's part magician, this guy. So he settles on classic misdirection. He puts it out on the street that Orland Twill, a lieutenant with the storied Chandler Police Department, is in the pocket. That he arranged to have the O'Tooles killed. That he intimidated Pete Chow into dummying up the forensics. That he killed Pete to keep him from changing the story to double homicide. Marie steps off a plane in the Windy City and starts sniffing the breeze. She picks up the scent. She sets up shop outside the Blue Lotus and pays attention for a while. Sure enough, out comes LT with a Cubs cap and a bunch of clean shirts."

"Wait," says Earnie. "You're saying Big Man outed his own laundry operation?"

"Sure. I'm guessing he knew that after my Russian doll misadventure, LT had Santiago parked outside the Lotus for a week taking down license plates. Jig was up at that point. He sanitized the Lotus back into a regular dry cleaner and shifted the criminal operation to some other front we know nothing about. At that point the Blue Lotus became strictly theater. Good for a helpful photo-op. A way to sting the stingers, both from here and abroad. Along comes LT in a Cubs cap, right on cue. Frenchie Marie is off and running in the wrong direction, just like Big Man wants."

"You think he torched the Lotus?" asks Earnie.

"That's my guess. Encourage Marie to bite that hook even harder. Make it look like the law is getting too close. Add some credibility to the photos and the rumors and rake in a little insurance money while he's at it."

"So Marie thinks I'm in league with fucking José Beggemon." Twill speaks under his breath, more to himself that to either Ray or Earnie. "Guess everybody wants me dead."

"Cheer up, LT. Marie wants you alive. She's after Big Man and she's betting you'll flip on daddy. Big Man has wanted you alive too, otherwise you'd be dead already. Just ask Amanda. Big Man needs a patsy and you're made to order. But, listen, that's a temporary stay of execution. Once CPD has enough evidence that you offed Pete, it's going to be inconvenient to have you alive trying to prove your innocence. That's when Big Man wants you dead. I'm guessing we're already there."

"Okay, so Big Man wants me dead, and Marie wants me guilty. But how could she think I'm guilty of anything, let alone working for Big Man …"

"Not so far-fetched from her perspective," says Ray. "Marie showed up in Chicago and put her ear to the ground. That's what she heard. So she puts a car on you. Sees you sneaking around outside your wedding vows with a young, hot-looking blonde. Amanda Ramada Tate. Turns out Amanda just happens to be the assistant to Dennis O'Toole, a commodities trader who Frenchie Marie already suspects of spoofing and, not-for-nothing, who recently killed his wife before shooting himself in the head, or so the story goes. So now Marie is really tuned into the Orland Twill show. She's all over you like a cheap suit, boss. She follows you out to Pete's office. She asks herself why this dirty cop is taking a meeting with the guy who prepared the primary forensic analysis on the O'Toole murder-suicide. Starting to make some sense?"

Ray waits a few beats for an answer. Neither Twill nor Earnie says anything. But they both give him a slow, shell-shocked nod. Ray keeps at it.

"Now, maybe Marie is getting played for a chump by Big Man, but she's no dummy. She never believed the murder-suicide story. I don't know her training, but she knows a double homicide meant to shut people up when she sees one. When she sees you take a meeting with Pete, she does the math: one plus one equals you putting pressure on the Medical Examiner's office to keep the story just the way you like it."

"Murder-suicide," says Twill.

"Right. So Marie puts a guy with a camera and a pack of cigarettes up in an empty house with a good view of Pete Chow's driveway. Tells him to wait. Eventually you show up with a lot of questions and an angry index finger. Looks like you were giving Pete what for with a side of ultimatum."

"I wasn't," says Twill.

Ray looks at Twill, trapped inside the monitor, for a second or two longer than is necessary.

"I know that, LT," he says. "Earnie here knows that. Big Man definitely knows that. But Marie's camera says different."

"I just wanted him to admit the double homicide. That's all I wanted. Now that Pete's gone, we're stuck with the murder-suicide report."

"I wouldn't be so sure," says Ray.

Twill hollows out a laugh and fills it with derision.

"The M.E. is not going to reopen this case, Mack."

"He will if we show him Pete's original report."

"What?"

"Double homicide, right there in black and white."

"You have the original report?"

"I do."

"You do? Really?"

Ray looks across the table at Earnie.

"Does the sound work on this thing?"

"How?" Twill asks.

"Pete sent it to me."

"What? Why?"

"I asked him to."

"So did I, goddamnit. Why you?"

"Hard to say. Maybe because I kept my index fingers to myself. Maybe because Pete thought you put the O'Tooles to bed and that he was next."

"Why would he think that?"

"He turned out to be right."

"Not about *me*. Why would he think *I* would do that?"

"Hard to say now that he's not around to answer questions. I'm guessing someone helped him think that."

"So you're just guessing."

"No. Pete sent me a note telling me it's not the brothers, it's the boss. You're the boss, LT. That's all I need."

"I don't know what that fucking means, Mack."

"It means Pete was afraid of you and so he sent me the report."

"Where is it?"

"Safe."

"Can we see it?" Earnie asks.

"No. Too many cooks in your kitchen, Earnie. If it makes you feel any better, I said the same thing to the FBI."

"Does Marie have it?" asks Twill.

"Of course not. But she doesn't need it. Like I said, she knows a double homicide when she sees one. And she thinks you're the man that made it all happen, LT. Every bread crumb she picks up confirms her belief. She just doesn't understand that Big Man is the one dropping the crumbs."

"Breadcrumbs ..."

"Yeah. You pay Pete a couple of not-so-friendly visits. Then Pete turns up dead. Then it turns out you were looking for Pete the night he died. You were at his house. Your prints are on the gun. Pete's blood is in your car. Long story short, Marie is convinced you're working for Big Man. Killing people, or helping to kill people, to protect his global spoofing interests. So, Marie decides it's in the interest of her minders and their foreign investors to pressure you into a proposition."

"A proposition," Earnie repeats. "Which is what?"

"Deliver Big Man and maybe she loses any and all evidence she has of your association with this whole sordid mess. The photos. The word on the street. And whatever she can convince me to pull off of your computer that connects you to Pete, or to Dennis, or the Blue Lotus, or to the spoofing. She'll promise to stay her hand, destroy all evidence, if you deliver Big Man. That's my guess."

Twill dismisses the idea with a swat at the camera.

"If she really thinks I had some hand in killing anyone, she's not about to just destroy ..."

"She doesn't care about the bodies, LT. She doesn't care about you or your murdering ways. Murder is a local concern and Marie's not from around here. She only cares about all of the angry money in the commodities markets. She only cares about Big Man. When Marie thinks about you, the only thing in her head is what might motivate you to turn over your big, bad, spoofing boss. You being a murderer on the run actually helps solve that problem. That's your motivation to talk turkey. I'm sure she was prepared to treat Amanda like a poker chip too, just in case you might be motivated to bargain over the freedom of your lover."

"My lover," says Twill, disgusted.

"Pretty sure Marie has no idea Amanda was your niece."

Earnie gestures over the table.

"But now Orland's turned himself in, and Amanda is … well, so …"

"So, yeah, Marie's lost most of her leverage. But she's still got a hand to play if she can get in a room with you. That's why she keeps bothering me. She's hoping I can deliver."

"Deliver what? Me?"

"You."

"How?"

"Convince you to listen. Let her make her pitch."

"What pitch can she possibly make now?"

"Best guess? Powerful people on both sides of the pond want Big Man off the board. Her powerful people will talk to our powerful people. They'll convince each other that maybe you going away for murder is not the best use of time and resources. You agree to deliver Big Man, and she'll make some phone calls to get that conversation started."

"That's a short conversation," says Twill. "I don't know anything."

"She doesn't know that."

The weariness is suddenly back in Twill's voice.

"I know that look, Mack. I've learned to hate that look. What are you planning to do?"

"Me?" Innocent. Nonchalant. Ray looks at his watch and rolls back his chair, wincing at the pain of that effort. "I'm going to take Ben Franklin someplace swanky and quiet for a dark, gold bath with a couple of ice cubes. Then I'm going home to fall asleep underneath my cat." Ray manages his best to stand and grab up his coat, slinging it over his arm. "And then I'm going to help Frenchie Marie every way I can."

EIGHTY-NINE

Upstairs at The Gwen. The bartender takes a glance. Looks away.

Nobody recognizes me. Could be because I look like I do, and because I walk like the arthritis is now one joint away from claiming a full-body victory. Could be they're all pretending to not know me just to avoid the *what's the news?* and *how you been?* conversation. Or maybe it's because I've only been in the place once before when I was dozen years younger than I am now. Doesn't matter. I'm glad to feel anonymous.

The tables are squat and dark, nestled into low-lit assemblages of plush, plum-colored chairs. The place is half-full. Couples and singles. No big parties except a foursome up at the bar. Mary Lou Williams is on the piano, working out *Little Joe from Chicago*, circa 1939. I head for a table near the windows. I pull up a plum and sit.

The place has changed since I was here last, but I can't say exactly how. It hasn't lost any of its high-flying swanky cred. It's dark and glossy and well-lacquered with just the right amount of crystal and glass to keep the light from getting bored. Not surprising. The Gwen itself, the hotel beneath me holding the bar up in the air, is nothing to sneeze at unless you're allergic to 1930's art deco, Gwen Lux sculptures, or the ghosts of Prohibition. Before it was The Gwen, it was the Conrad. Before that it was *Le Méridien*. Three names I could never afford. The facade is a historic landmark. The architect ripped the face off the old McGraw-Hill Publishing building and sewed it on to a brand-new hotel, Hannibal Lecter style.

I'm not an architecture buff. But Marlo was. She knew the history of every building in Chicago. The Rookery. Rockefeller Chapel. The Opera House. St. Jane. The Frederick Robie House. The Gwen. They were like family to her. Brothers and sisters and uncles and cousins. They all had personalities and complicated histories full of secrets. Last time I was here at The Gwen was with Marlo. The crack about Hannibal Lecter earned me a scowl and a sharp yank of my tie. Like I'd disparaged a member of her family at the Thanksgiving table.

We were out on the rooftop around a fire table with Doris and Buck for a cool, clear night of cocktails and chocolate fondu. Doris and Buck were celebrating their first year married. We were there to toast the last twelve months and pick up the tab. We all got good and drunk and laughed about things that had no business being funny. Doris had eventually grabbed one of Buck's fingers and led him away, down to their room for the night. That left us alone by the fire.

"I'd have liked to have been an architect," Marlo had said, curling up on the long, cushioned bench and pulling my arm around her shoulders. She'd nuzzled her face into my neck, right under my jaw line where it fit perfectly, like two pieces of a jigsaw puzzle. Buildings towered above us in all directions, fracturing moonlight.

"One more joke about steel erections and I'm booking a room."

"No, Ray, seriously."

"Okay, then. Architecture." I'd watched the blades of orange flume stab out of the hole in the center of the table, pricking at the twinkle-lit night. My drink was on the table, hopelessly out of reach. I'd stroked her hair. "The appeal being …"

"The integrity of it," she'd said. "You make your mark in stone and steel and glass. Two stories high or a hundred. That's your declaration. That's who you are. No bullshit. No lying. No hiding. No excuses or games. A hundred thousand tons of granite. This is who I am. Deal with it."

"If you're suggesting that you lack integrity, I'm here to tell you you've got it in spades, honey. I'm still not sure where you manage to put it all."

"Sneaking around taking pictures for Rushmore American Insurance? I don't think so."

"Someone's got to hold people like Victor Roby accountable. If not you, then who?"

That had made her laugh. Not in a good way.

"Victor Roby? Accountable? Victor's gonna skate, Ray. Prosecution's full of holes. He'll beat the arson rap. Then Rushmore will bring an action for fraud. Maybe he'll pay out a few bucks. Who cares? I mean really. The man torches his own warehouses and files a claim. Not sure I should care about that as much as I have. I'd rather design buildings."

"I'm guessing Henry planted this seed," I said. "He strikes me as a wannabe architect. Maybe it was his posture."

"My father planted a lot of seeds. That's what farmers do. The thing he and Cora did best was raise children. My mother and kids …" Marlo had shaken her head with a laugh. "She loved them. Collected them. They fostered for years.

Jimmy and I always had to make room for one or two others at the table. In the bathroom. Around the tree. They'd be under foot for a few months and then they'd be gone. The house would feel empty by comparison. Just me and Jimmy. Then here'd come another one."

"Well, hell's bells, Marlo, there's your yen for architecture," I'd said.

"What?"

"You grew up wanting a bigger house."

"Aren't you clever?"

"Yes. Also explains Jimmy."

"I'm afraid to ask."

"Hard to get attention in a house like that. His best bet was to misbehave. Ditch the personal accountability and develop a nose for trouble. Start shaking down the neighbors."

"You're too hard on Jimmy, Ray. He's just trying to figure things out. He's smart, enterprising …"

"Oh, Jimmy's enterprising all right. I'll give you that. His whole life's an enterprise."

"He'd do anything for me."

"Guess, we've got that in common. That and a fondness for my money."

"Our money. If you're so smart, why didn't I turn out the same way? You think I didn't want my parents' attention as much as Jimmy?"

"You were cut from different cloth, sweetheart. No, scratch that. You were chiseled from a block of granite. Reliable as rock. A hundred million tons of integrity. You're the very stuff of your precious buildings. All you need is a brass plaque and an awning. And a doorman to keep the riffraff away. That'd be me."

"The doorman?"

"Well I'm not the riffraff, honey."

"Jury's still out on that, Ray. Feels to me like you're still angling for a hotel room. And there's a fly in your ointment, by the way."

"Oh?"

"Stone makes for bad marriage material. Too unforgiving."

"So then you think I'll need forgiving. Maybe I should feel offended."

Marlo had stretched her hand up past my arm, blindly, finding my face with her palm.

"It's inevitable, darling," she'd said.

"Forgiveness for what, exactly?"

"For not knowing me like you think you do."

The server is young and blonde and wearing a tiny sign. The word *Mercy* has been etched into the fake brass. I'm guessing that's a name, not a mission. Either way she's exactly what I need. Mercy turns out to be full of quiet enthusiasm. She recommends a drink called a *Chicago Picasso*. I know it's named after the sculpture in Daley Plaza, but I have to wonder if the recommendation is inspired by my battered face. She says it's an old-fashioned style drink with sherry, two types of whiskey, and a little smoke.

I tell her I'll settle for three fingers of Old Forester with a couple of cubes to open up the bourbon. She leaves the drink menu and swishes away like she's not disappointed. She's back in a flash with a smile and the only thing I need more than an hour of sleep. Another ten minutes and I'm ready for another. Mercy brings that too. I want to thank her parents for not naming her Temperance, but she's gone again with a tray full of drinks that don't belong to me. Another few minutes and I'm ready to flag her down for a pillow. I don't get the chance.

"First Torali at the Ritz, now Upstairs at The Gwen."

Tia Lewis drops her coat unceremoniously over the back of a chair, like it's a wet towel she no longer needs. She pulls an errant wisp of mahogany hair behind an ear with a blood red nail and slips into the chair across from me. She's in a black silk blouse and a simple gold pendant in the shape of a leaf that likes her olive-complected décolletage. For a woman roughly my age, she's managed to weather the years better than I have.

"Our thing seems to be expensive rooftop bars that we look at through rain-streaked windows," she says. "You just might be higher brow than you let on."

"Didn't know two drinks are enough to make it a thing," I say. "Maybe our thing is me getting a nosebleed so you can feel at home."

"Afraid my home is a lot closer to Mother Earth," she says.

"So then we're a couple of lowbrow fish out of water. Bottom feeders drinking up in the clouds."

Mercy breezes by with a chilled glass of pale yellow and sets it on the table in front of Tia. She cocks an eyebrow.

"You've anticipated me."

"I've been here twenty minutes with nothing to read but the wine list. They have three different *Chenin Blancs* in this joint. I told Mercy to save the most expensive bottle for you."

Tia sips, giving a slight nod of approval.

"And why would you do something like that?"

"Because the last time we met I was paying attention. You told me that if you want big doners to loosen up and give, you don't meet them in the soup line at the homeless shelter."

She smiles, glancing around the room. Then back at me.

"That what I am, Mack? A big doner?"

"You are to me."

"Because."

"Because you've got the rest of the story."

"Do I?"

"I think so. That's worth a nosebleed and an expensive drink. I'll even pay you the hundred bucks I don't owe you."

"Thanks, no," she says. "I make charity cases my business. But I'm not one of them."

I can feel a crack in her confidence. Her nervousness is poking through. It's not that she wants to be here. She doesn't. But she couldn't help herself. Her next drink is more than a sip.

"What is it you want to know?"

I knock the cubes around in my glass. My eyes make sure hers don't go anywhere.

"Had an interesting chat with Francine Lucas."

Something inflates Tia's eyes a little. I've had a good drink do that to me on occasion, but I'm guessing it's the sound of Francine's name.

"Did you?" she asks.

"Yeah. She took me to a movie and told me a story or two. That surprise you?"

"A little," says Tia, recovering. "She hung up on me. I assumed that was the end of it. I must have piqued her curiosity. She tracked you down? Called you at work?"

"You could have just told me. Why didn't you?"

She blanches. Defensive.

"She didn't want to talk to you. If I'd have told you about her, you'd have tracked her down. Called her up. Invaded her privacy."

"You're right. I would have. You were a journalist. Tracking people down and invading their privacy is in your blood. So what's the real reason?"

Tia drinks, pretending an interest in two women at a table across the bar. A long sigh brings her back.

"Shame, I think," she says without looking. "I don't like who I was back then."

"Back then. You mean a couple of days ago, in a different swanky bar, drinking a different *Chenin Blanc?*"

"No." She doesn't appreciate the sarcasm. "Back in the days of Marlo Kline. I was …" Tia doesn't finish. She takes another big drink instead. Mercy is making another pass. I catch her eye and give a nod Tia's direction.

"Just you and me here, Teelew," I say.

"Don't call me that."

"Why not?"

Tia takes the wine down to almost nothing and looks at me hard.

"Because it's not your name to say. That's why."

"You think you're the only one carrying around a big bag of shame when it comes to Marlo?"

I can see her eyes drop their guard, just a little. Mercy swoops in to trade Tia's empty for a full. Tia barely notices.

"Don't know if I'm the only one or not, Mack. But it sure seems like I'm the only one talking."

It's my turn to drink, so I do. The burn feels like a confession.

"You told Marlo she was making a mistake marrying a cop. You told her I'd end up cheating on her."

"Yes," she says. "I did."

"Well, you were right about that. Just the once and at the very end, but there it is anyway, like a roach in an almost empty bowl of soup. I was afraid that her knowing about it would kill us both. Turns out I was only half-right."

"You didn't kill her, Mack," says Tia.

Her hand finds mine and gives it a squeeze. My Triple-D must like what it feels, kicking in to give me a bird's-eye view of the table.

What must Marlo think of this scene? Ray and Teelew out for a drink, twisted into knots over her like a couple of wet shoelaces. The husband baring his soul, confessing his sins, just to leverage some drop of truth out of the lover. I look at the hands in front of me like they belong to other people. I don't want Tia's hand to be hers and she doesn't want my hand to be mine. But neither of us tries to break the connection. It's as close as either of us is ever going to get to what we need.

"You didn't kill her," she repeats, eyes intense with empathy. "Cancer did that."

"I've tried that logic," I say. "Never works."

"So then you told her? About … you know …"

"No." I say the word down into my drink. "Why stop at betrayal when you can add a cowardly lie of omission? I kept it to myself. I kissed her goodbye, and she bowed out. Took the secret with her."

"What secret?"

"The secret was that there was no secret. She knew everything about me. Marlo always knew everything. Turns out I didn't know anything. She left me with an anvil of guilt and a bag full of questions. They both just keep getting heavier."

Tia nods slowly, saying nothing.

"She didn't want me to know she knew. I figured that out after she was gone."

"Maybe it didn't matter to her," she says. "Maybe she knew you'd beat yourself to death." Tia gestures across the table at the carnage holding a half-empty drink. Her other hand gives mine another squeeze. "That what you're doing, Mack? Finding ways to beat yourself to death?"

"Maybe. Maybe I'm just trying to figure out who I married." I break contact and empty my glass. "Your turn, Teelew."

Tia leans back in her chair, both hands now cupping the base of her wine glass like it's a crystal flower growing out of the table. I rattle my cubes at Mercy. I wait.

"I was obsessive," she says eventually. "Jealous. Angry. The newspaper business was bad for me in a lot of ways. Marlo was bad for me in a lot of ways. I had a substance problem."

"What flavor? More than the weed, I take it."

"All flavors. I'm not going to talk about that."

"Okay."

"I think I couldn't stand myself without her. Every time she came into my life …" Tia considers the glass and then drinks. "Hope is a terrible thing, Mack."

"I understand."

"Do you?" she asks, disbelieving.

"Yes." I don't blink so that my eyes alone might be convincing enough. Last thing I want is a dialectic on the vagaries of hope. Mercy's too busy and there's not enough bourbon in the world to drown that subject. Fortunately, Tia seems ready to let it go.

"Well. Every time Marlo left it made me worse than the time before. After she came to see me, that last round, it was pretty clear that she was just breezing through. She was like a bird singing on my windowsill that I couldn't catch. A bird that didn't want to be caught."

I nod affirmingly, half to her and half to the new glass of Forester.

"I asked her to lunch. She left first. I followed her. All day. I followed her all goddamned day. Like a lunatic. Like some kind of predator. I followed her until she went home. So then I knew where she lived. I had asked, but she was evasive, so I'd let it go. I'd wanted to show her that I was relaxed about us. Well. The *possibility* of us. Like knowing where she lived was not all that important to me."

"So you followed her instead."

Tia smirks at herself.

"Pathetic, but true. And not good. Seeing where she laid her head just took me deeper. I camped out in my car a couple of nights half a block away, just so I could see who came and went."

"So who came and went?"

"Lots of people. The building was five stories high and half a block long. Every person that walked through those doors I imagined was there to see her. I wanted to catch her coming out with someone, you know, arm-in-arm. That never happened."

"But you kept at it."

"Yes."

"And you ended up in the bushes outside the home of Francine Lucas. Under the moon."

She closes her eyes, absorbing the blow.

"This isn't easy for me."

"I never thought it would be," I say. "I don't show my adultery card to just anyone."

Up at the bar someone laughs like he's biting at the air. The joke must have been cruelly ironic, the way everyone looks away and shakes their head. Mary Lou Williams keeps scattering piano keys across the lounge. Beyond the windows is a twinkle-lit deluge, like Upstairs at The Gwen has been tucked into a cliffside waterfall. Tia takes a sip of courage.

"Marlo met a woman for lunch. There were several lunches. She was young. Beautiful. The legs, the hair, the eyes. Expensive clothing. The whole package. I assumed the worst. I was devastated. I think I *wanted* to be devastated. I think I was looking for pain. I self-medicated into oblivion. But I kept following. And this woman kept turning up." Tia looks up from the table. "How do you know about the bushes?"

"You scared Francine near to death. She thought whoever killed Lucky was out to pull her plug for not believing in accidents."

"You're saying Lucky wasn't an accident?"

"Not according to Francine."

"I didn't even … I saw an older woman. I didn't know who she was at the time. I did some research …"

"You did some research and found out the house belonged to a Lianne Lucas."

"Yes," she says, looking a little stunned.

"Lucky had a gambling thing. He and Francine transferred title to their long-legged, whole-package daughter for safe keeping."

"At the time I had no idea that Lucas meant Lucky Lucas. That took me a couple years to figure out. Then I learned who Lianne Lucas was. I felt so stupid. So ashamed."

"Because then you realized then that Marlo was working, not dating."

Tia nods. Then shakes her head.

"Bit of both, I guess. I decided Marlo had seduced the daughter so she could get close to the mother. Francine."

"And why did you think she was trying to get close to Francine?"

"Like I said, I didn't know about Francine at the time."

"But over the years some pieces started to fall into place. You figured out who was who. Mother and daughter. You decide Marlo was working the daughter to get in good with the mom. Not true, by the way."

Tia leans in, starving for whatever morsel I can offer.

"No?"

"Not according to Francine. She says Lianne hated the very idea of Marlo. Thought Marlo was working Francine's grief. Says Lianne was keeping a close eye on Marlo to make sure she didn't take advantage. She was trying to push Marlo out. You ever see any actual signs of … of …"

The words are angular and clunky. I can't get them out of my throat. It's not the question that scares me. Not any more than a man is afraid of leaping off the top of a building. Leaping is nothing to fear. It's the landing.

Tia smiles. I can see her humiliation has a mean streak and doesn't like to drink alone.

"Did I ever see any signs of a sexual relationship?" she asks.

"Yes," I say. "That."

"So you're thinking that a romance with me might just have been anomalous. Sowing some wild oats. But if she also pursued Lianne Lucas, then maybe …"

"Did you or didn't you see anything like that?"

I know what I sound like. So does the couple sitting at the nearest table. Tia's face registers the change in tone.

"I don't know," she says. "No, I guess. Maybe I just interpreted things in the worst possible light. I'm not confident in anything I concluded back then."

"Okay, but years later you're still putting together the puzzle. And you conclude that Marlo was trying to get in good with Francine. I want to know why."

She looks at me with old hurt in her eyes and a side of anger for the guy making her rip off the scab.

"Years later? After everything? I concluded that Marlo used me, straight up. I was a tool. Okay? A fucking tool."

"A tool for what purpose?"

"I don't know," she lies.

"Sure you do, Tia. You think Marlo was working for the Royce campaign. Shoulder to shoulder with Victor Roby. Trying to get Royce elected to Lucky's seat. She seduces Lianne to get close to the grieving widow. Charms Francine into endorsing Royce. Meanwhile she sweettalks you into some helpful publicity. She even wrote the articles for you just to make it easy. A good one about Royce and a damaging one about Bubba Jones. She stole your business cards to infiltrate the Jones campaign and dig around for helpful dirt. Am I close?"

"Close enough," she says sadly, anger at me fading. She looks up with fresh hope. "Was I wrong? I hope so. I honestly do, Mack. I don't want to think that of her."

"Francine tells me Marlo showed up believing Lucky was murdered."

"I thought it was an accident. He fell over ..."

"That's not what Francine believed."

"Okay, but as far as the state of Illinois is concerned?"

"Accident," I say.

"Did Francine have any idea who did it?"

"Bubba Jones. Or someone in his camp. Francine says Bubba was trying to blackmail Lucky over a secret daughter who wanted some inconvenient attention. A meeting on Lucky's boat got pushy. Lucky goes over the rail, ass over tea kettle. Francine says she found evidence, but CPD couldn't be bothered. She thinks CPD was doing Bubba Jones a favor."

"Bubba had cops in the family, I think," she says, trying to remember. "And a cop-friendly platform. Lucky was all about police reform that last term. Bubba must have needed a campaign counterweight for his half-brother assaulting the postal worker in the mail truck. Some insurance against that skeleton in the closet."

I shrug and drink. "That's the theory."

"What evidence did Francine have?"

"Audio recording of a muffled conversation leading up to a struggle. CPD buried it, according to her. Few months later, Marlo shows up singing the song Francine wanted to hear. Francine hired her on the spot. Lianne smelled fraud and wanted Marlo gone. When that didn't happen, she settled for watching Marlo like a hawk. Holding her close, yes," I pause, giving Tia a look, "but maybe not in the way you were afraid."

"You hope," she says with a half-smile, then lets it go. "Did Marlo find anything?"

"She struck out. Case closed. Left for Caracas on a case for another client."

"The client with a missing nephew Marlo smuggled back in a bag of coffee beans."

"Right."

"What do you think?"

"I think that's not literally true," I say.

"Not the bag of beans. Do you think Lucky was murdered?"

"I think he was threatened. I think things got out of control and he got a stiff shove over a short railing. Gravity did the rest. A year later and Marlo is smuggling some kid out of Caracas two steps ahead of the banana mafia while you're back at the Trib putting a nice spit-polish on her Sam Royce puff-piece." I lean forward, rolling the tumbler between my palms. "Look. Enough bullshit, Teelew. The thing you're not telling me is that you knew Marlo was carrying water for Royce all along."

"I didn't. I didn't know." Anger now, sharp and hot. Eyes smoldering in their shame.

"Yeah? You don't make it at the *Chicago Tribune* without good instincts, Tia. You knew and you published the piece anyway. You were in love and you published it like she wanted you to, and you waited for her to come back and knock on your door."

"I didn't know. I … I *suspected*. I didn't know. The election was over. I told you. The *Trib*'s election coverage had changed. Pre-election coverage of the candidates turned into post-election coverage of the winners. What I published was after the fact and didn't make a bit of difference. Royce won the 42nd Ward without any help from me."

"I don't care about newspaper ethics, Tia. What I care about is what made you … I'll use your word, *suspect* … what made you suspect Marlo was working for Royce?"

Tia's shoulders sag, resistance leaving her body. She talks to the table more than to me.

"Like I said, I followed her everywhere for a while. I bankrupted my sick leave to do it. She spent a lot of time at Royce's headquarters. Lot of meetings with Victor Roby. Their favorite was a place out in River North around Grand and Dearborn. A bistro café called The Cellar."

My brain paints a picture my stomach doesn't like. Marlo and Victor Roby. How many times had she spoken of Victor as an enemy? Her efforts to assist a failed prosecution for insurance fraud and the arson of his own warehouses. Her hours of surveillance with me riding shotgun to keep her company as she leveled her massive telephoto out the car window at Victor's living room like a sniper's rifle. Turns out there's a friendlier backstory she never bothered to share. I try to keep my tone level.

"Anything else?"

"One meeting at Royce's house, with a lot of other people."

"Who?"

"I don't know. Campaign staff."

Tia looks at me, setting her glass slowly on the table. Too slowly. Her eyes stop blinking. Her breath hitches.

"Wait. Hang on." She points accusingly. "You don't think it was Bubba's people who did the shoving, do you? You think it was Royce. You think … Jesus. You think Marlo was covering up for Sam Royce. Containing a threat. Finding out what Francine knew. Keeping her pointed toward Bubba Jones and … and *away* from Royce."

She doesn't need me for this part. I drink and listen and watch the rain smear the city lights behind her.

"You think Marlo was hired for damage control. And that I was just an added bonus. In a runoff between Royce and Bubba Jones, she … she … what … she told Royce she could get the *Chicago Tribune* to put its thumb on the scale? She knew there had to be an interview to substantiate the article, so she interviewed Bubba's campaign as me. Gave them my business card. Impersonated me."

"And worst of all?" I ask.

"Worst of all." Tia laughs at herself. "Worst of all, she knew I'd fucking publish it. She knew I'd publish both of them, or some version of them. Had the *Trib* not changed its coverage strategy, I'd have published the hit job on Bubba too." She looks at me with suddenly tired eyes; wet and angry and sad. "Because I'd have done anything for her. And she fucking knew that."

"Her meetings with Royce's people; why didn't you tell me that at Torali?"

"Because I don't want any of this to be true. Because she's dead and that's not who I want to remember. And neither do you." Tia finds my hand again for another squeeze. "I didn't see the point of humiliating myself just so I could tarnish your memory of her. I allowed myself to assume that she'd changed in the intervening years. Or that maybe I'd gotten everything wrong and there was some other explanation. I didn't know for certain. That was good enough for me to pack it all away. And not tell you. I'm sorry."

She leaves her wine glass alone so that both hands can hold mine. The sensation is light, warm and smooth. Her eyes are back to soft brown and pleading as she leans into the table. The gold leaf on its chain swings clear of her blouse, flinging perfume molecules into my glass. My amygdala goes ticklish. I leave my hands where they are.

"I really am, Mack. I know what it is to love her. I didn't want to hurt you. I hated you for so many years. I hated your name."

"You've got a lot of good company."

"I want us to keep talking, Mack. This has opened up a lot inside me. A lot of old feelings, good and bad. Let's continue this. Come to my place. It's not far." My hands get another squeeze. "You and I are connected through her. Through Marlo. We can help each other. We can talk. Or not."

It would take a blind man not to see the loneliness in Tia's eyes. The desperation. The hurt. She's a broken-hearted almost-recovered addict in freefall and I'm the one who gave her the push. She needs someone soft to land on. My ribs are already broken.

"I'm not a lesbian, Tia," I say, as if to apologize.

"Neither was Marlo."

NINETY

Poor Ray. Never much for surprises. He likes the control. Or the illusion of it.

He'd never expected a few drinks to turn into a date. Ray never expects a date anytime, anywhere, full stop. He may be crazy, but he still lives on planet Earth, and on planet Earth the odds are much better that Abe Lincoln will push open his lid, grab his stovepipe, and take Abigail out for another night at the theater.

Nevertheless. Look at him. Bedtime. Standing under the granite eaves of The Gwen, shoulder to shoulder with a willing woman his age, watching the rain pound North Rush Street as the valet retrieves her car and the evening gears itself up for something he can't possibly handle with two fractured ribs and a broken heart.

Think about this, Ray.

Tia Lewis thinks the mutual connection to Marlo is going to make this easier. It won't. It makes it harder. It puts Marlo in the room to watch. It gives her a front row seat and a bag of popcorn. It bookends her passing with the carnal spectacle of the man she married surrendering himself to sexual gratification with women he did not marry. It ends badly. He knows it and I know it. And Tia will certainly know it soon enough. A conflicted heart tends to muck up the hydraulics. Not to mention the two cracked ribs that make even simple standing and sitting a fresh exercise in agony. Just how does he think this is supposed to work?

And yet. Here he stands. Waiting. Opening his wallet to find the valet's tip, just to have it ready. Tia is quiet and still next to him except for the occasional shifting of weight that brings her shoulder into contact with his arm. Hard to know what exactly she's thinking. I'm guessing relief and fear are both on the list.

"Here we are," says Tia, pointing.

Ray follows her finger up the street to a blinking black Audi, waiting its turn for a hole in the traffic. The Gwen's valet parking is under reconstruction, requiring off-site accommodation somewhere on the next block. The Audi makes its move, screeching forward into its lane and splashing its way toward The Gwen.

It slows to a stop at the entrance, cuing up behind a beat-up, muddy-green Pontiac. Both cars take their turn coming in out of the rain.

The Pontiac is like an old friend, its turn signal an orange wink. Ray watches with an equal measure of bemusement and relief. The man emerging from behind the wheel is as familiar as the car itself. It's the military, government-issue posture; the shoulders that long for a suit, making the ratty denim shirt look like a costume. It's the same Easter Island head that Ray is used to seeing from behind. The man walks around the front of the car, headlights splashing up against his legs, and opens the door to the back seat.

"Your car, Mr. Mackey," he says without any hint of expression, ironic or otherwise.

Ray bends at the waist just enough to see inside. Frenchie Marie is busy lighting a cigarette. There's a man in the passenger seat he's never seen before. Middle Eastern. Deep set eyes. Short black beard.

Ray straightens and turns to Tia, handing her the folded bills for the valet who is now dripping at attention by the light-beaded Audi.

"Raincheck," he says apologetically. "This is a conversation I need to have."

"I don't understand," she says, her face arranging itself around the sudden disappointment. "Is this work? Were they waiting for you?"

"Yes and yes. Go home, Tia. Be kind to yourself. Resist your demons."

"Will you call me?"

He gives her a third yes. But this one's a flyer. He has no idea. A long shot, if you ask me. Too many of his own demons are in the way. That, and I'm not sure he has what it takes to make that phone call. I've seen Ray chase certain death into the darkness a hundred times. Without hesitation. Without near enough bullets in his clip. But I've never seen him shake in his shoes waiting for a valet.

His heart ratchets down a notch. He turns away from Tia for the comfort of more familiar territory, stepping off the curb for the ratty Pontiac and its sweetly burning interior.

NINETY-ONE

"Don't remember calling an Uber."

The car accelerates through the rain beneath a stoplight just losing its yellow. Marie's dress is a lacey, pale buttercream, shoes to match, glowing beneath a dark overcoat. She gives me the hint of a smile and lets out some smoke.

"Attractive," she says. "Age appropriate. Are you dating now?"

"I'm lacking courage and stupidity."

Marie makes a face and shrugs.

"Looked promising enough to me. Sorry to interrupt."

"I don't think you are." The urge to pat my pockets for a Camel is distracting. "Where are you taking me?"

"To work, Detective Mackey. It's time to work. I have done my part. It is time for you to do yours."

"You mean ransack my boss' office?"

"He's not your boss. Not anymore. He's done. It's your office now."

"How convenient for you."

"And ransacking is hardly the word. So dramatic. We're collecting evidence of criminal conduct."

"Even so, this is not the time. I need more of a heads up than this."

Marie shakes her head. The on-coming headlights catch her earrings.

"You've had more than enough notice. And I've got a search warrant that's not getting any younger."

"A couple of days. Forty-eight hours. Your warrant will still be good."

"Tonight, Detective. Now."

"We had a deal, I thought."

"We did. And I've performed."

"How's that, exactly?" It's a stupid question that looks like I'm stalling for time. Marie indulges me with a dutiful patience.

"You said you wanted contact with one Courtney Briggs. AKA Suri. Have you not received such contact?"

"Yeah, and then some. Lots of contact to the face."

"No accounting for friends. You said you wanted to work homicide again. Have you not received offers?"

"A couple, actually. Yeah."

"I worked hard for those, Raymond. I owe people favors. I don't like owing favors. It's your turn now."

"Hang on. There's still the other bit."

Marie pulls on the cigarette. Exhales through the crack in the window.

"Marlo?" she asks. "The photograph?"

"Stop playing."

She considers the burning paper stick between her fingers.

"I found a man you can speak with. He seems to know a thing or two about that photograph. And about your late wife. He will meet you tomorrow morning. Eleven o'clock."

"So you owe yet another favor."

"No, fortunately. Just money for him. He came pretty cheap in the scheme of things. I've paid him, so now he owes me. I cannot guarantee he'll satisfy your curiosity. But then, other than to say you're wasting your time trying to understand the dead, I don't really care about whatever it is you need to learn about the late Marlo Mackey. That's your business, not mine. As long as it earns your cooperation."

"Guess we'll see," I say. She doesn't seem to like my conditional tone.

"Tonight, Detective. We do this now."

"I'm not ready to do this now."

"There's nothing to be ready for," she says. "Nothing for you to do. Let us in. Witness the execution of a search warrant. Or you can wait out in the car if you like."

I crack my window and let in some water, watching Chicago slip by in the rain. The cars, the buildings, the umbrellaed pedestrians like dark, wet dandelions growing out of the streetcorners, all whoosh by like they're leaving town in a hurry. Like they know something I don't. I think of Marlo at the table, her hand beneath Victor Roby's. I think of my hand beneath Tia's, her lips in a replay without any sound. *We can talk. Or not.*

"Eleven o'clock where?" I ask without looking.

"He likes Chinese," says Marie. "I gave him the address of the place on 107th. Best Kung Pao in the city. Not that you would know. The last time you were there you refused to eat anything."

The car swerves to avoid a cardboard box in the road and finds a pothole in my rib cage. I grit my teeth to suppress the groan. I turn away from the window and look at her.

"Midnight abductions mess with my appetite. I'm not meeting him on your turf. I want a private conversation."

She thinks this is mildly amusing.

"You think I'll be in the next room with my ear to the wall? I have other things to do, Detective."

"Then it shouldn't matter."

"I don't really care where you meet him. I don't care if you meet him at all. Like I said, your marriage doesn't interest me. I'm just trying to be accommodating. My patience is wearing thin."

She crushes the butt against the headrest in front of her and drops it in the small pile of others at her shoes.

"Collecting butts?" I ask.

"Throwing them out the window is against the law in this country. One must be respectful. Where do I send this person?"

My brain grapples. Public, but not crowded. Not inside. Not at first.

"*The Bean,*" I say.

"*The Bean?*"

"Yeah. You know, the big silver legume in Millenium Park. I'll meet him there and we can go to a place of my choosing. Something tells me you'll follow us wherever we go, but you won't be able to set up in advance. That'll have to do."

"A bit cloak and dagger, don't you think?" She looks at me, waiting for an explanation. I don't give her one. "Suit yourself. But this makes us even."

"What's his name?" I ask.

"You don't get a name. Not from me. I promised. He seems skittish about the police. Maybe your easy charm and powers of persuasion will put him at ease."

"How will I know him?"

Marie shrugs.

"Wear a red carnation. How many people do you expect to see standing out in the rain at *The Bean?*" She shakes her head a little and smokes. "He'll be disappointed about the Kung Pao."

"If he's real, if he knows something, I'll make it up to him."

"And if he doesn't know what you want him to know about Marlo?" she asks. "You'll hold that against me, I suppose."

"Let's just say this little ride we're taking tonight is premature. This time tomorrow would be much better."

"You don't trust me," she says with mock disappointment.

"You want me to trust you? I don't even know your real name."

"I'm beginning to like the sound of Marie," she says.

"I don't know which language it is your bosses speak."

"Does that matter to you?"

"Not particularly fond of Russian at the moment."

Marie laughs. It is surprisingly genuine. Uncomplicated.

"I'll bet," she says. "You really think Russia sent me? You think Russia is upset at the idea of spoofing in the futures market?"

"Could be. They've got their own investments to protect. And I'm guessing Russian is one of your languages."

"Good guess. But don't you think it more likely the Russians are the ones bankrolling Big Man's mischief? An economy that cannot deliver to its own people, let alone fuel aspirations for a hegemonic world order? The ability to effectively manipulate commodities markets could surely come in handy. Munitions alone …"

"That what your intel says?"

"Our intel?" Marie snorts out a soft, smokey laugh. "Our intel. My, oh my, Detective. Our intel is not mine to share and none of your business. You're missing a security clearance or two. You want me to lose my job?"

"You're seriously telling me this is all about tweaking a geopolitical balance of power? That you've been tasked by some western democracy, or democracies, to let some of the air out of Vladimir Putin's tires?"

"I'm not telling you anything, Detective. You insinuated that I'm a Russian operative. I'm suggesting that that is a particularly ludicrous supposition. The only thing I am actually trying to tell you is that I am done waiting for you to deliver on your promise."

Two blocks ahead a cluster of flashing lights surround a firetruck on South DeLuce. Chicago's finest are out in the rain redirecting traffic.

"Find another way," says Marie calmly. Her man at the wheel reroutes.

"What if you're wrong about Twill?" I ask.

"We're not wrong about Twill."

"What if you are? What if he's not the pipeline to Big Man that you think he is?"

"Then we keep at it. We keep pulling threads until we have him."

"Until you kill him, you mean."

I let the accusation float in the smoke like a glowing flake of heat-borne ash, looking for a reaction. She gives me nothing.

"Because those *are* your orders, right? To put Big Man down. To root out *La Pourriture* once and for all."

"Must we?" she asks with a hint of exasperation. "You've made that particular stab in the dark before, Detective."

"Come on, Marie. The due process machine is Big Man's briar patch. You're not risking that. That's why you're riding around in the rain in this shitty Pontiac, pulling strings and whispering in people's ears, and not holding joint press conferences with the Justice Department."

Marie slips her hand into a black purse. Somewhere in there is a nine-millimeter she's nudging out of the way with a bejeweled finger. She extracts another cigarette and a lighter. Her way of communicating boredom and indulgence. I want to ask if she's got one to spare. I don't. I keep at it.

"Maybe the stars and stripes want Big Man dead as much as you do, which makes someone like you too convenient to resist. Uncle Sam leaves the back door unlocked so you and your ex-military hit squad can come and go as you please. Eventually Big Man shows up in a ditch, you get a promotion, and everybody on this side of the pond shoulder shrugs their way past any questions."

I have to wait for the exhale, but she gets there.

"Let's assume," she says, "strictly for the sake of argument, that what you say is true. Are you saying you'd object, Detective? That you'd like to keep José Beggemon alive? After what he has done to this city? Your city. The murders. The graft. The human trafficking. The public corruption. After what he has done to you? Ruining your reputation. Your career. Turning your friends and colleagues against you. Using you as a tool for his own objectives. His own amusement. I mean let's be honest here, Raymond, he's having a bit of cruel fun with you."

Another in a thousand street corners. Two men fighting, yanking an overburdened grocery cart in different directions, produce a splash of angry sound that comes and goes in a sloppy hiss. I keep my eyes on the wet, blue skin of the road, maybe to pretend at my own boredom and indulgence. But my ears are all too interested.

"We believe you are innocent," she says comfortably. "Well, innocent is a relative term, I suppose. No one is innocent. We believe you are innocent of the illicit, criminal collaboration of which you are so routinely accused. Let's put it that way. But make no mistake, you have helped Big Man immeasurably. Unwittingly, yes, or so we are prepared to assume, but you have helped him just the same. He's out of your league. You're a mouse in a cage to him. And you think that won't continue? You think if someone finally identifies him, puts handcuffs on him, feeds him into your hallowed justice system, that he will face punishment in the slightest? You think there is any accountability to be had on that road? Do you think he will not laugh in your credulous American faces?"

I turn to look at her.

"This face look credulous to you, Marie?"

She studies me through the smoke. I let her take a good long look.

"I don't know what he sees in you, Detective. But it's something. Isn't it? Even you must admit. Maybe you're such an easy mark he can't resist. Maybe you're such a difficult mark he likes the challenge. I don't know. My question is whether you think he'll ever leave you alone."

She turns away for the window, giving me a chance to answer her question. I can't. I don't. She fills the silence.

"You say our effort is to root out and sanitize the world of *La Pourriture* once and for all. *For all*, Detective. *For all* knows no flags or borders. *For all* includes everyone in this country too. It even includes you. Wouldn't we all be better off, on both sides of the pond as you put it, to be free of him?"

"Can I take that as an admission that you and your friends aren't over here to take Big Man into custody?"

"I admit nothing of the kind. Besides, we've got to find him first. *N'est-ce pas?* That's the immediate goal. And your old lieutenant, properly motivated to keep himself out of prison, is going to help us do that."

"If you think for one …"

Marie holds up a hand, cigarette glowing in my face like a hot taunt.

"No. No. I'm done, Detective. I'm not accountable to you. We do this now, or there is no meeting tomorrow about Marlo. And those job offers dry up. Understand? I'm tired of playing."

I figure I've made my point. I'm reluctant. I'm not ready. She's caught me by surprise. I try my best to sound disappointed.

"I take it Agent Murray is waiting for us someplace?"

"Agent Murray had an unexpected conflict." Marie gestures at the passenger seat in front of her. "Meet Agent Bashar. Felix, Ray Mackey."

The man in the passenger seat sticks up a hand without rotating.

"Convenient. The Bureau must have an agent vending machine someplace. Let's see a badge."

"How about we dispense with the theater," says Marie. "You don't need to see his credentials."

"Why not?"

"Because you don't really care about crossing the t's in your Fourth Amendment. It's a nice show, but you don't care. You're getting what you want out of this relationship. You want Big Man gone and I'm going to do that for you. You want to go back to solving bodies, a fresh start in a new department, and I'm going to do that for you. You want answers about dearly departed Marlo. I'm doing that bit too. So let's stop pretending you care about the legalities. You know we can fake a badge if ever we need to."

"Who is we?" I ask. Marie and I connect eyes over the back seat, the smoke between us washing briefly in a halogen tide.

"You know, Detective, at some point persistence ceases to be a virtue and becomes simply irritating."

"I walk that line every day. Today's no different."

"You should focus on tomorrow. Tomorrow the world changes."

"Yeah? What happens tomorrow?"

"Tomorrow, we pull our strings at CPD. I get a private audience with your old lieutenant. I show him what we have. I show him the evidence of his guilt. His ugly connection with Big Man's network. I describe the road he is on. Show him where he is headed."

Marie takes another pull on the cigarette. She blows a thin, blue stream out into the rain.

"And then I give him a choice. If he tells us what we need to know, and if we can verify what he tells us, then he will rapidly discover he has powerful friends on both sides of the Atlantic who can deliver him from the prosecution that's about to flatten him. He will learn that the world cares more about stopping José Beggemon that it does about the sins of Orland Twill. He will need to move, of course. Sell the house. Change his identity. But we are all very good at that kind of thing in this business. We know how to make people disappear. Meanwhile, you get to turn the page. Solving homicides and learning what's new with your dead wife. And all of that happens with, or without, Agent Bashar handing over his credentials."

"With," I say with some finality. Marie laughs out a cloud.

"You're an odd, tedious bird, Detective," she says. "Felix."

Felix Bashar, or whatever his name is, slips a hand into his coat pocket and hands his ID over the seat. The car is dark and full of smoke, but I can tell this thing's about as real as the subpoena. I'm guessing that having lost John Murray, Marie has been forced to fake FBI involvement just to keep me in the harness. I do my best to seem satisfied and hand it back.

"How long will this take?" I ask.

"Not long," says Felix. "Thirty minutes. Less."

"What do you need from me?"

"Access. Building, office, computer. Log-in credentials will help. The more I'm forced to hack my way in, the longer it will take."

"Can't you just seize the thing? Throw the computer in the trunk?"

"Unnecessary," says Felix, like he doesn't intend to say anything more.

I leave Felix alone and refocus on Marie.

"None of this shit is legal," I say. "Or you'd turn on all the lights. You'd walk through the front door in the middle of the day, flashing badges. Flinging subpoenas and confiscating computers."

Marie taps the cigarette against the headrest. She shrugs.

"Turn on the lights, the roaches scatter. Everybody loses. My country. Your country. Global commodity markets. You. Orland Twill certainly loses. If I can't convince him to cooperate tomorrow, he's getting a life sentence. And maybe that's the greatest travesty against justice that you and I should be losing sleep over. Twill *should* go to prison. After what he's done? If you're half the murder cop you think you are, then you agree."

"I do agree. But I'm not convinced that you believe your own words."

"You think I don't care about the bodies. That's not true. I won't pretend I'm less concerned about turmoil in the futures markets, but I can care about more than one thing at a time. I do care about the bodies. But Big Man makes Orland Twill look like a Cub Scout in the dead body department. Get rid of Big Man and we're netting big in the positive. I'll trade Twill for Beggemon any day of the week and sleep just fine at night. And I think everyone else will too. Even you."

Marie studies me in a moment of silence, trying to gauge whether she's getting through. I don't give her anything to work with except an expression that can't get past the word sleep. She picks up the thread and keeps at it.

"Only one person wins if we do this with all the lights on, Detective. And we're all a little tired of that. I know I am. Aren't you? The people I report to sure are. Maybe if your Justice Department was not so ..."

She has to search for the right words. It takes her another cycle of drag and release.

"Camera shy," she says at last. "American justice doesn't want to be in this particular frame. If it did, maybe then we could go in, badges blazing, and get the job done. Joint press conferences, as you say. But that's not the reality. We have to keep the lights off if we want any federal assistance. We wish we did not have to contend with such complications. They are not complications of our making.

We have to live with them just the same. You need to trust that we know what we're doing. Do that, and we both get what we want."

We ride in silence. Felix Bashar knocks the driver softly with the back of his hand. Points. The driver nods and changes lanes, making a left and lining up for the last two miles of road that will deliver us to the Chandler Police Department. Marie's words are still in my head.

Do that, and we both get what we want.

"Reminds me of a case," I say to the window. "God. What. Maybe fifteen years ago. Triple homicide. Gangland bullshit. My partner at the time, Stretch Martin, was on extended medical leave. Appendicitis, I think. Something. Anyway, Stretch is out, and I have to partner with this knucklehead from CPD. Derek Fezz, aka Fizzy. First two bodies were in CPD's jurisdiction. Third body to drop belonged to Chandler. So Fizzy and I are joined at the hip and neither of us likes it much. He's got maybe two years on me, but he makes like each of those years is good for ten. A font of wisdom, Fizzy. We didn't get along so well."

"Big surprise," says Marie.

"One day we're looking for a junkie witness to murder number three. We're crawling around inside the hull of this old scow moored up at the Canal Street Marina. It's the middle of August. Smells like we're crawling around the Devil's rectum. I'm holding the flashlight. Fizzy pushes up one end of a filthy mattress and, surprise, there's our guy, hiding out with a couple of rats. The rats take off; they're fine. Better than fine. They're healthy. Our witness, not so much. He's been dead for a week and change. The needle is still stuck in his arm. I play the light around, trying to hold onto my lunch. There are two rolls of cash near his head, down where the sagging mattress is still touching the floor. Two."

"Convenient."

"Like it was made to order. So Fizzy tells me to go call it in. Tells me to go out to the pier and double-check the slip number so the EMT's know how to find us. The chance at a lung full of fresh air is tempting, but I tell him I don't need to check the slip number. So Fizzy, still holding up that stinking, soggy, shit-stained mattress, looks at me standing there with the light and he can tell that I'm not blind and I'm not stupid. He knows I've seen the cash and that I'm not leaving him alone. He thinks my objection is that I'm afraid he's going to take both rolls, rather than giving me half of the find. We don't have any discussion about it, but I can tell that's what he's thinking. You know why he thinks that?"

"He thinks you're dirty. He's heard rumors. Unfounded, of course."

"You're way off, Marie. Fizzy didn't know anything about me and this is long before any rumors. Guess again."

"I'm not in a guessing mood. Is there a point to any of this?"

"Fizzy thinks what he thinks because it's exactly what he would be thinking if the roles were reversed. *I don't want to leave you alone, because you're gonna make off with my share of free drug money.*"

"Are you trying to tell me something, Detective?"

"Me? No. But if I were, it'd probably be that if you really want to know a person, Marie, then pay attention to what they assume about you."

"I see. Well, how profound. Am I making inappropriate assumptions about your motivations? Have I hurt your feelings? Do you feel misunderstood? Manipulated?"

I look at her without response. Her tone is mocking, but her features are black iron hard. Then she softens her mouth into a sympathetic smile.

"You get to be human, Raymond. It's no crime to want a better life. You haven't asked me for cash or to kill your enemies."

"Isn't that exactly what you're doing? Killing my enemy?"

"Big Man's fate is his own. The salient point is that you never asked. Did you?"

"No. I didn't."

The car pulls up to the curb across the street from the building in which I make a second home. The driver cuts the engine. The rain kicks it up a notch. Marie looks at me expectantly.

"Well, don't hold us in suspense. Finish your little story. You bagged the money as evidence and sent Detective Fizzy home with something to think about."

"Fizzy? Yeah, Fizzy left with plenty to think about. That's true. He tried to reach the cash with one hand while he was still holding up the mattress with the other. He was half as smart as he was greedy. Lost his footing and fell flat on top of the corpse. Mattress came down on top of him like a piece of moldy bread on a death sandwich. For all his trouble, Fizzy got no cash and a hypodermic stuck in his temple. After that came the case of hepatitis that nearly killed him. So, yeah. Plenty to think about."

I open the door into the rain. Felix Bashar does the same. I give Marie a look before stepping out.

"Coming?" I ask as innocently as I can. I can tell the invitation takes her by surprise. She recovers quickly enough.

"Pass, thanks. I'm every bit the luddite you are. You and I were made for a different age, Detective."

I jerk my head in the direction of the white stone building lurking in the rain.

"Pretty sure I can lay my hands on some bottom drawer bourbon. Couple of clean glasses from the break room. We can get acquainted while Felix does his thing. I told you a story, maybe you can tell me one."

"I don't drink on duty," she says, coaxing another flame from her lighter. "And I'm always on duty. Alcohol is carcinogenic, in case you haven't heard."

"Never made you as a teetotaler, Marie."

"Oh, I'm full of surprises. Alcohol is an addiction made for the low-born brute who's either too stupid or too stubborn to rise above his circumstances and make something of himself."

"I know some powerful, wealthy, high-born lushes who'd beg to differ."

"Let them beg. Booze is a drug like any other: an indulgence made for a weakness of character. Any voluntary dulling of one's senses is an invitation to predation. Show me a man with a drink in his hand and I'll show you a human tool looking to be used against his own better interests."

"I think I should feel insulted."

"I'm glad we can agree on something," says Marie.

"Temperance in Chicago has already been tried. Maybe you should brush up on your American history."

"I don't need American history. My grandfather was a liquor wholesaler. He gave the business to my father. My brothers inherited when he died. Together they ruined more lives than your Al Capone ever dreamed. I never touch the stuff."

"Sad story. What country again?"

Marie puts the cigarette to her lips and gives me a shoulder.

"Stay out of Agent Bashar's way, Detective. And you'll need to find your own transportation back to the hotel."

Felix is out now, door closed, heading around the back of the car. Could easily be a gun in his hand. But it's not. In a succession of clicks, an umbrella telescopes up into the dark, wet air and floats above my open door like a black parachute.

"Since when have you ever been good for a round trip, Frenchie?"

"*Bonsoir,* Raymond." She gives me the briefest of smiles before looking away. "See you when I see you."

NINETY-TWO

Barney is manning the security desk, per the norm. He's a beat cop from way back who retired himself into a quieter after-hours gig here in the HQ lobby. A lonely job, but he's not so alone. He's got both eyebrows with him, thick, bone-white shrubs that want to swallow his ruddy forehead and start laying claim to his scalp. Barney and I always got along. We've got good music and old movies in common. He's never acknowledged the ugliness that got me the boot, so I don't know what he believes about me. Whatever it is, he's always had the decency to keep it to himself.

Barney turns down a radio somewhere beneath the desk playing *Blues Before Sunrise.* He and the shrubs give me a nod as I walk Felix Bashar up for the ID check and sign-in. Felix shows his credentials, prints and signs his name. On the line next to his name, he prints the initials of his employer in all caps. FBI. He catches me looking over his shoulder as he signs. I pretend my interest is purely sartorial.

"The Bureau issue the black suit and tie when you join up or is it a peer pressure thing?"

Barney laughs to himself as he hands Felix a lanyard. Felix doesn't crack a smile, which makes him more authentically FBI than his badge. We head across the empty lobby for the elevators.

"You do any work with Nick?" I ask as I hit the button and the doors close.

"Nick?" he asks. "Yarborough?"

"Yeah."

He shakes his head.

"I'm in computer crimes. Nick's got his own little fiefdom up on the eighth floor. His parking space was five slots away from mine. We mostly saw each other coming and going. I'm in the Springfield office now, so it's been a while. You and Nick tight?"

"Not really, no."

"Didn't think so." He says it like he's talking to the crack between the doors. "You maybe want to stop testing me so I can do my job and we can both go home sooner rather than later?"

"You sound a little nervous for an elevator ride, Felix."

"You're confusing nervousness with irritation, Detective Mackey. Bet that happens a lot with you."

The elevator spits us out and we walk the hall in silence. I use my key to access the empty IAD office, glowing a dim, spectral blue from lonely desktop electronics and the sodium vapor parking lights refracting through the rain-streaked windows.

"Lights on or off?" I ask.

"It was just a metaphor," says Felix wearily. "She didn't literally mean lights off."

I shrug and hit the switches on the wall, pointing through the silent explosion of light to Twill's office. Felix nods and heads that direction. As he walks, he hands me the folded subpoena from his coat pocket.

"Sign this. You'll see a blank for any necessary system and computer usernames and passwords on the second page. Fill that out and initial." He pauses in Twill's doorway and snaps on the lights, surveying the room. "Any locking file cabinets or drawers?"

"One against the back wall," I say, pointing.

"Keys?"

"Combination."

"Put it on the sheet with the passwords."

"Okay. What else?"

"Give me the codes. Have a seat. Read a book. Let me work."

I write the sign-in credentials and the combination code he needs on a scrap of paper and hand it over. He tries to take it, but I don't let go so easily.

"What?" he asks with a sigh.

"Nothing. I want to remember the moment that sends me to prison."

"Jesus Christ." Felix snaps the paper from my fingers. "You're not going to prison."

"Can I get that in writing?"

"What do you think a subpoena is, Einstein? Stop talking, will you?"

I take a seat on the visitor side of the desk so I can fill out the rest of the paperwork. I have to make space by separating two stacks of paper. On the left are the case files I'm supposed to review for Glen Sugarman in advance of his procedure to remove a fatty obstruction. The irony alone gives that stack some extra heft.

On the right is the stack of colorfully flagged files and loose documents that had originally been deposited in my chair by my fellow IAD officers looking for a supervisor's review and approval (*"IMPORTANT" "READ & SIGN" "TIME SENSITIVE"*). On top is the accordion file of material Steph Nellis had collected in my absence and handed to me with a pink sticky note: *"MACKEY HOLDING"*.

I pick up Steph's accordion file like I'm a butcher guestimating a pound of meat. I drop it again and try to push all of it aside without standing. The pain in my ribs comes out my mouth. Felix Bashar looks up from Twill's keyboard, more in irritation than concern. I grimace an apology and slump back in my chair, eyeing the stacks of paper on the desk. They look back at me resentful and accusing.

Who can blame them? I'd promised everyone I was back to help. I'd promised to dig in. I'd fire me in a hot second.

Felix works from behind the business side of Twill's monitor with a quiet intensity that begs to not be interrupted. His eyes are bright, golden-hazel finches darting left and right as he reads, pecking briefly at seeds of interest before moving on. Every now and then he shakes his head in disappointment and furrows his brow and then, just as quickly resets his expression to something sharply anticipatory. The pattern repeats itself over and over until he suddenly stiffens into a new attention.

"Find something?" I ask.

"Quiet."

"Just seems like maybe …"

"Seriously. Shut up, Mack."

Felix pats himself down until he finds and extracts what looks like a small cigarette lighter. It's not a lighter. Maybe I just want it to be a lighter. He uncaps the flash drive and bends below the desk. When he comes back up, his face is more relaxed.

"Almost done," he says, sounding suddenly concerned about my patience.

He's not lying about being almost done. Ten minutes more on the computer, followed by a search of Twill's desk, shelving and filing cabinet, and I'm up by the door with my finger on the light switch. The clock nestled among Twill's photos of marital bliss says it's one-thirty in the morning.

"You going to tell me what you found?" I ask, turning off the light. "Can I get a copy?"

"No and no," says Felix not turning around, striding across the empty office for the exit. "You're not authorized. The less you know the better."

"The less I know, the more I want to know. Not sure that's better for anyone." I snap off the office lights, pull the front office door closed behind us and make sure it's locked. "How about I give you some guesses and you paw at the ground like Mr. Ed. Once for no, twice for yes."

He takes the suggestion about like I expect. So I keep it up. By the time he checks out with Barney and hands back the lanyard, Felix has some color in his cheeks. Outside, he keeps his umbrella to himself.

"Tell Marie I've done my part," I say. "I expect her to do hers."

Felix doesn't respond. I watch him cross the parking lot and the street beyond, pushing through curtains of rain for the waiting car without so much as a backward glance.

I catch a cab back to The Gwen. I think of calling Raj for the ride but something in me finds an ounce of compassion for a good kid too eager to please. I say let him get his sleep. He can have mine while he's at it. I'm not using it.

Paula is right where I left her: at the curb on North Rush Street with a good view of the Nordstrom manikins, still supervising the rain with fashionable disapproval. I pay the cabbie and climb out like it doesn't hurt. I open up Paula and climb in in with a groan, giving it some volume this time. It feels good not to have to suppress the pain for a change. I pull Sig out of the holster and set it in the passenger seat, feeling better for not having the extra weight hanging near my battered chest.

Outside, a man in rags with a long, soggy beard and hollow eyes shuffles past my window, talking to himself. He shouts something ugly and flips a finger at the manikins without breaking stride. They watch him pass, unmoved.

I pull out my phone and poke in Agent Yarborough's number. Nick doesn't sound happy to hear from me. I don't take it personally.

"It's two in the fucking morning, Mack."

"Explains why I'm so tired. Thought I was just getting old."

"Just a minute." I can hear him getting out of bed. Going someplace where he doesn't need to whisper. "What do you want?"

"I promised to keep you updated."

"Okay. So?"

"Contact made. The deed is done."

"No shit?" Nick suddenly sounds more awake. "What can you tell me? Was Marie there?"

"She was busy not being stupid. It was just me and a guy named Felix Bashar, an agent of yours. Ring any bells?"

"Bashar? Felix Bashar? Uh, yeah. He worked out on Roosevelt until about nine months ago. Computer crimes. He's in the Springfield office now. He did the hacking?"

"Not really hacking if someone gives you all the passwords and dusts off the welcome mat."

"You know what I mean. Bashar, huh?"

"He had a badge and a gun and a stick up his ass. So, yeah, could have been him. His credentials looked suspicious to me, but what do I know? If it really was Bashar, then the Bureau's got another rogue agent getting paid by some foreign government to do dirt on American soil. Although I guess that's not the most disturbing possibility."

"What's worse?"

"That you're actually the one in the dark, Nick. That Central Justice has an understanding with said foreign power to take care of José Beggemon and they decided not to tell you about it."

"What? Come on."

"Yeah, well, Marie assures me there's coordination, Nick. Covert. But still. First John Murray, now Bashar."

"The US Government. Complicit in a foreign hit job. On our soil. That's what you're saying."

"Marie's not openly conceding to an execution plot as such. She keeps tipping her hat to due process, but she's less convincing on that score. I just figured that if Bashar's for real like Murray was for real, then you should know about him sooner than later."

"You got that right. I'm on it. I'll text you a photo of Bashar."

"My phone isn't that smart."

"What?"

"No texting."

"Email?"

"No. But I can pick it up at home on my laptop."

"You need an upgrade, Mack."

"Me or my phone?"

"Both," he says. "I'll let you know what I find. And I'll reach out to Chelsea Wolfe. Let her know the rat took the cheese. If I know Chelsea, she's already plugged in and tracking."

NINETY-THREE

Rounding the corner into the neighborhood gets me to thinking about Phil. As usual.

Something about that last turn always seems to spark a telepathic connection. Phil feels me coming and sends back a jolt of anticipation that I read like a buzzing in my brain. Somehow, between all of the rain and the dark between us, I can feel her. She's on the back of the chair in the living room, eyes on the window, stirring the air with her tail, looking for the sudden wash of headlights over the glass. I'm guessing those lights have a smell to her: tuna and good fingertip bourbon.

I need to send a gift to Judith Kravitz. Can't figure out how much she likes me as a neighbor, but she loves Phil. Judith uses her key to come by and take Phil for a few hours in the middle of the day. Not sure what they do over there. Watch bad television and moon over old photographs of Judith's late husband would be my guess. Phil gets all the pulled chicken she can eat, and Judith gets in on that deep, full body thrumming that Phil uses to solve all the world's problems.

One of them is hungry and bored and the other is lonely. Who am I to tinker with perfection? If something ever happens to me, Phil lands on her feet and Judith gets more permanent companionship.

Maybe that makes me the best neighbor ever.

Or maybe that gives Judith the key to my house and a motive to kill me in my sleep. I don't need another reason to stay awake, but now I have one anyway.

Six houses from the one I own I spot a car at the curb with a couple of shapes inside that make my ribs hurt. Probably nothing but my own paranoia, but I'm not in a betting mood. I maintain my speed until I hit my driveway and turn in. I push the button on the visor, but the garage door stays where it is, punishing me for not changing the batteries in the remote. I grab Sig off the seat next to me and check the clip. Then I climb out into the rain. The walk to the front door is maybe ten steps. It seems like thirty. If it wasn't for all the rain on my back, I'm pretty sure I could feel the eyeballs.

I open up to find Phil right where I thought she'd be. I get a meow and a swish of tail.

"I know," I say, closing the door. "Long story. I'll tell you later."

I leave the lights off and the door unlocked. I step into the hall just long enough to hit the switch at the bottom of the stairs. I don't need to see the stairs, but the same switch also turns on the lights in the upstairs hallway and will set a glow in the upper front window. It's two-thirty in the morning and I come home and go straight up to bed. That's what I'd think if I was out there parked at the curb, smoking and waiting and listening to the rain, and I see the upstairs light. How are they supposed to know I gave up sleeping?

Phil is at my ankles. I try to give her head a scratch, but it hurts too much to bend. I exit the hall and cross the living room, slowly lowering myself into the high back chair on the far side of the sofa. That puts the recliner squarely between me and the front door. Gives me a second or two to refine my aim before they know where I am. Not that I think it will come to that, but you can't be too careful. My ribs can't take any fight that involves much more than a trigger pull, so that's what I'm preparing for.

My gut tells me they'll try the front door before breaking in through the back. What's it to them? They know I can't go anywhere. They might even knock.

Phil takes a seat on my lap. She wants her nip. We both do. I massage her head with the hand that isn't holding a gun. Then I shoo her away. She meows discontentedly.

"Sorry, sweetheart," I say. "First things first. We've got company."

NINETY-FOUR

Phil looks up at me from her perch on the fireplace mantel. Like she knows I'm up here against the ceiling, even if she can't see me. Like maybe I could find a way to detach myself and dip into Ray's cache of Old Forester and float down to give her a few drops.

Doesn't work that way. If I was capable of fetching and dispensing booze, Ray would've put me to work himself. I'm nobody's barkeep. I'm just here to judge. Bear witness. Remember.

Phil looks away, back down across the living room at Ray, who sits facing the door, gun hand in his lap, Sig's barrel knocking a slow rhythm between his leg and the side of the chair like he's keeping time with the second hand of the watch strapped to his wrist. Bulova. Silver plated. Vintage. Minimalist. Just the essentials. An anniversary gift from Marlo, back when she was alive, and Ray was a real man. Back when he had a gold pin for fidelity and a body that could get things done the way he wanted them done.

Christ, Ray. Look at you now. Hiding behind the recliner. Hoping for the best. At least you're comfortable. Get in a few long blinks. You don't need to see. Let your ears carry the load for a while. You'll know when it's time.

Whenever Ray is feeling his age, or as is increasingly the case, whenever he is feeling more than his age, he checks his brain and his gut for solace. Sure, the body is gone, but he can still think. He can still figure things out that others can't. He can still stay one step ahead. Intuition, sharp as ever.

Is what he tells himself.

Truth is, all of that is slipping too. How can it not? The booze. The loneliness. The stress. Chronic lack of sleep. Triple D getting worse along with the paranoia. How could it be that his mental and intuitive faculties are not also slipping away? Bleeding out.

And he knows it. That's the sad thing. If he's really honest? He knows.

Even now. He porpoises back up for a conscious breath. Opens his eyes. He's realizing that he's put so much attention into preparing for the shapes outside in the parked car, that he never took a second to wonder whether someone was already waiting for him inside the house. Never checked the back door. Never canvassed for signs of entry. Never looked upstairs. He has chosen to sit in a chair with his back to the kitchen and, behind the kitchen, the cellar, which makes for a nice dark place to hide until Ray is in bed asleep.

That's the possibility now dawning in those eyes with a sharp shock of adrenaline. Sig has stopped knocking against the chair, like a watch that has suddenly run out of time. Ray's famous intuition shows up a bit late, whisper panting that someone else is in the room. The hairs on the back of his neck refine that a bit. The someone is behind the chair.

He wants to spin out of his seat and fall away from the threat, pulling Sig up and out into position as gravity does its thing. Firing at whoever it is that he can now feel along his spine. But his ribs aren't up for the pain. Doesn't matter; he's just not that fast anymore.

He gets in a shoulder twitch. His gun hand rockets Sig upward as if on its way toward fulfilling some well-considered plan. But there is no plan, considered or otherwise. Ray's rocketing hand is but a flailing, desperate, desultory defense to a flailing, desperate, desultory life.

No plan. Just Ray with a garrote around his neck and a large, quiet man behind the chair, going to work on him like the boss is watching.

NINETY-FIVE

Hard not to wonder if this is a dream. *The* dream. Again.

I'm in my chair. Waiting for the front door to open. Only it doesn't open. I can't keep my lids up. I drift off into the nightmare that has been waiting for me all day, just like every other day. A large man choking me to death in my living room; dragging me around by the neck like a sack of dirty laundry. Next he'll drop me on my face and grind a heavy knee into my back so I can't go anywhere. Then someone will hand him a chainsaw and tell him to take off my legs. I usually get to see who that second person is. Usually someone I know. *Thought* I knew. Stretch Martin. Twill. Marlo. Big Man in one of a thousand masks. That's when I wake up screaming. Every time.

So. Part of me wonders. Part of me hangs in there, waiting for the big reveal and the shrieking chainsaw and the raw, full-throated scream that scares the cat and brings me back into the waking world.

But the rest of me knows better. My nightmares have never known the waking intensity of fractured ribs. This is no dream.

The pain in my chest is beyond excruciating. Whoever this is has more than enough muscle in his arms to get the job done. He hauls me backward across the room, pulling hard on the rope around my neck, ramming his knee repeatedly into my spine so that maybe I'll stop flailing and cooperate in my own strangulation. My foot catches the fireplace poker set, which comes crashing to the floor. I scream every profanity I can think of at this guy, but he doesn't offend easily. In my periphery I catch a flash of white; Phil leaping for cover.

Maybe I *should* cooperate. Maybe this is the part where I finally get off this ride. Climb up into the big dream and pull up a cloud. Get some decent sleep for a change. Look up Marlo and talk about old times. Laugh and share a milkshake and forgive each other. Beats hanging around this place by the neck.

My flailing shin catches the table lamp, sending it to the floor in pieces.

I shouldn't be able to shout profanities. I shouldn't have any fresh air in my lungs at all. My inconvenient flailing should have stopped seconds ago. I should be as limp as dish rag.

Truth is, I can't cooperate in my strangulation. Even if I wanted to.

He's got a couple of problems, this guy. First, he's using a slick nylon cord for a garrote. The kind you get at any hardware store for tying a tarp to the back of a pickup so junk doesn't fly out all over the road on the way to the dump. Not a bungee cord. Bungee cord would have been much better. Just a piece of nylon rope. I'm guessing he tested it with bare hands right there in the middle of aisle nine. It wants to slip. Especially in cotton gloves. He has to keep adjusting his grip. A piece of old electrical cord would have been a lot smarter.

Bigger problem is that in the half-second before he slipped the cord over my neck, my reflexes sent my gun hand up in the air and Sig got in the way. Now he's got the steel barrel of a nine-millimeter handgun lodged against my head, between my chin and my clavicle, keeping his slick nylon cord from touching the right side of my throat. Won't take long for him to solve that problem. Couple more knee-shots to the spine should do it. But at least I get a chance to tell him what I think of him.

He starts alternating between kneeing me in the back and pulling the rope in different directions, trying to remove the obstruction. I do my best to flail at his face with my left hand and hold on to Sig with my right. The tip of Sig's barrel is digging beneath my right orbital bone and it's all I can do to keep it there. Problem is that my index finger is inside the trigger guard where it belongs. The trick is to squeeze four fingers around Sig's handle to keep the barrel digging into my face and the garrote away from my neck, and yet *not* squeeze my index finger, as he swings me backward around my living room, lest I blow my own brains out.

If this guy were only half as smart as he is strong, he'd have let go of the nylon and squeezed my hand before dragging me out of the chair. The suicide story writes itself.

I keep flailing. My chest is raw, liquid pain, but I can still breathe. My left hand wants an eye, but the man with the rope keeps turning his face away. Best I can manage is an ear. I grab and twist like it's a doorknob. It gets me a scream in my ear and another knee to the spine. The flat of my foot finds the fireplace wall. I give it a hard shove that sends us both over backwards onto the coffee table and then the floor, both of us on our backs, me on top of him, looking at my smoke-stained ceiling.

Sig has come loose with the impact, skittering out of my hand, finally bringing the nylon cord tight around my throat. I swat blindly at the floor, feeling for Sig's profile. Nothing. No choice but to give up on the gun. I need both hands to try to dig the rope out of my neck. I try to burrow beneath it with my fingertips, but it's too tight, like trying to pry a tree root out of the ground. I can feel the man's body beneath me tightening like a single-purpose muscle, the flexor or extensor in the foreleg of a thoroughbred, sensing the home stretch and digging deep for the finish line.

I can feel the grip of a gun digging into my back. The man brought his own piece to the party, just in case the rope didn't work. But unless his navel or my spine can pull a trigger, it's useless to both of us. Neither of us can take our hands off the rope.

In my field of vision, pricks of brilliance popcorn into view at random, here, there, then multiple places at once, coalescing and expanding, melting like home-movie celluloid over a hot bulb, until my brain is a single explosion of white that starts to cool and dim to blackness along the edges.

And then I am rising.

The pressure against my trachea falls away as if a shank of nylon is no longer sufficient to hold me to the planet and this life. The split-second divides itself *ad infinitum*. I feel myself floating toward my own ceiling, the big dream just beyond. Beckoning.

Marlo, I think to myself. *Marlo. Marlo.*

NINETY-SIX

The split-second passes.

Oxygen. A violence of hacking and drool as I regain some slim percentage of my wits. I am not rising on my own. I am rising because the man beneath me is rising. And not happily. I fall from his body to the floor, and yet he continues to rise, screaming as he goes. Then choking. I find the strength to turn over and push myself backward on all fours until the fireplace stops me. I sit up in a fit of coughing and gasping, both hands at my throat. For once, the actual choking sound in the room is not my own.

"Quiet," says Pinky calmly. "We all weary o' yo' noise, little man."

All nine of Pinky's fat fingers are wrapped around the neck of a man I've never seen before. Not as beefy as I had imagined given his strength, but he's too tall and too brown to be my kung fu friend. He's dressed tone-on-tone, black cargos and a t-shirt to match. Black cotton gloves. He likes to disappear when the lights are off. His hair is pulled back in a tight knot. Both of his feet are now six inches off the ground, hands pulling at Pinky's tree trunk wrists and making no difference whatsoever. His legs kick. His face makes a gurgling sound, the inside of his mouth is fleshy beet-red, and his eyes are like freshly washed turnips. He's getting a first-hand lesson on how to strangle someone.

"Alive, Pinky," I croak. "Alive would be better."

But white flesh mountain does not take orders from me. Pinky stiffens his prodigious arms, stretching the coconut palms on his sopping, dingy yellow, short-sleeved Hawaiian shirt over his mammoth gut, like maybe the palms are bending under hurricane-force winds, lodging the polyester fronds somewhere inside the sweat-ripened folds of Pinky's armpits. Pinky's feet are large, padded and bare, each slopping over the edges of well-worn flip-flops. He looks like a monster grub on vacation. Pinky knees the guy somewhere near the gut. The Glock in the man's waistband clatters to the floor.

The man hanging from Pinky's arms begins to shake and thrash.

"Pink!"

Suri's voice, firm and confident. I can see her silhouette in the doorway, blue, dimly lit rain plunging behind her like she's just stepping out of Niagara Falls.

Pinky lowers the man to his feet, holds him upright almost gently with his left hand as he brings his massive right fist to the left side of the man's head. The punch sends him flying. He lands mostly behind the sofa with a thud. Then stillness. He's either dead or dreaming.

My right hand finds Sig with two fingers. I pull it closer. I point it at Pinky.

"I was sitting here," I rasp, as if through kerosine, "waiting for you." The pain comes in colossal waves that crash over and over and over inside my chest. I can't help the tears. I don't try. "What took you so fucking long?"

"Thought we'd let you get settled," says Suri. "Didn't know you had company. We'd have come in sooner. You don't need the gun, Mack. Want me to call you an ambulance?"

Pinky makes a move to pick up the Glock on the floor. Sig leaps forward at the end of my arm like an angry dog on a leash.

"Stop," I say. "Just … just … No offense. I know you just. Saved. My life. Thanks. For that." I have to breathe before I can finish. "But I still haven't. Recovered. From your last. Beating. And I. Can't take another one. So believe me, Pinky. I will kill you where you stand. And not feel. Too bad about it."

Pinky raises both hands and then lets them drop, taking his arms down like a couple of freshly cut sequoias. He stays put. We look at each other until Suri is standing between us. The green vines and pink flowers are still climbing up her neck like before, but the wig is new. Shoulder-length, straight and jet black with threads of silver. Jeans, tennis shoes, and a ratty, pumpkin-colored Windy City Cruises t-shirt. Her face, wet with rain, has had some fresh attention. Suri may have kicked the heroin, but she's back on cosmetics. This is the sex worker I used to know and love. She smells like Macy's, first floor. She gives the Glock a shove my way with her foot.

"Easy big guy," she says, lowering herself so she can look me level in the eyes. "Put the gun down. We're here to help."

NINETY-SEVEN

The guy behind the couch wants to play dead. The cough gives him away.

"You know who he is?" Suri asks, helping me off the floor to the recliner. The job is difficult enough to change her question. "What's wrong with you, Mack? Did he do this to you?"

"No," I croak. "I came pre-broken."

"Hospital?"

"No. I don't know. I need to lie still. Vicodin. Kitchen sink."

Suri looks up and points. Pinky moves for the kitchen.

"I don't know the guy," I say, trying to breathe in a way that doesn't hurt. Failing. "I don't know him."

Pinky returns. Suri reaches. She takes the cap off a cold bottle of water and hands it to me. Dispenses a pill. I do the rest. God, the pain.

"Fuck," I whisper.

"What do you want us to do with him?"

I think about it through the pain for a few seconds.

"The cellar. Door is in the kitchen. Switch is on the wall. There's a big steel support beam down there. And a plastic-coated cable bicycle lock. Bubble gum colored. Can't miss it. Worked like a charm before. I think his neck size is about the same as the last guy. Combo is 1131."

Suri glances up at Pinky and nods. He doesn't need any further instruction. He stoops behind the couch and grabs the guy by one ankle, dragging him away. There are fifteen steps down to the cellar. Suri and I listen to my would-be strangler count every one of them.

"Someone doesn't like you," she says, raking my hair back in place before sitting on my coffee table, her knees almost touching mine.

"That's a long list. Why are you here, Suri? Thought you disappeared."

"That's the plan," she says. "But I'm still doing your job, Mack."

"Meaning?"

Suri relocates from the table to the couch. Phil doesn't miss the chance for a new lap.

"Meaning you told me about the mayor," she says.

"Suri."

"I couldn't let go. I wanted something to tie him to that fucking dry cleaner."

"Let him go. It's not worth it. He's out of politics. We missed him."

"Shut up and listen, Mack."

Suri flips her fake hair behind her shoulders and leans in, fixing me with those eyes.

"I've been watching the place. Pinky and me and Butch, one of Pinky's friends. Pinky and Butch trade off keeping me mobile. Two nights ago, we see this guy coming out of the Lotus. We call him plug. We've …"

"Plug. Like a fire plug?"

"Butt plug. Pinky's name. He's only got four. He rotates. What name you get depends on factors I still haven't quite figured out. Hunger might be the biggest factor. Anyway, this guy's a plug. We've …"

"What are the other three?"

"Three what?"

"Names."

Suri smiles indulgently. Sighs. She pets Phil in long, smooth strokes.

"Asshole, needle dick, tool," she says. "Most people fall into those categories. Hole, plug, needle or tool. So, we've …"

"Which one am I?"

"What?"

"Just curious."

"Pinky only gives you a name if you don't have one of your own."

I give Suri the same look I always gave her over coffee and cigarettes when she had information about some creep I wanted to interrogate and that she didn't want to give up. I never had to force her, threaten her. All I needed was the look. All these years, she still knows how to read my face.

"Tool," she says. "Okay? You're a tool, Mack. Don't feel bad. Most people are tools. We're all being worked by someone. Now." Impatience, moving to irritation. "You about ready to move on from this?"

I close my eyes, wanting to sleep. "Please."

"We've seen this particular plug before. He comes and goes but never has anything to pick up or drop off. I was tired of writing him off and hanging around for something better that never came."

"You follow him."

"We follow him. He drives an Audi."

In my head I see Rajnish Malik watching Agent John Murray pull out of a parking garage with a silver Audi close behind.

"Let me guess. Silver."

"You know the car?"

"I think so. Keep going."

"He leads us all over town. This and that. Nothing interesting."

"Worth a try," I say.

"Nothing interesting until he parks downtown and walks his way into 121 North LaSalle."

Eyes open. "City Hall."

"Easy as you fucking please."

"You're saying the plug is Mayor Royce?"

"No. I have two eyes and a brain. It wasn't Royce."

"So then what do you have, Suri?" I don't mean it to sound petulant, but I think it might anyway. I've got a hot burning sensation on the left side of my neck where the nylon cord was trying to saw its way in for a slice of my Adam's apple.

"More than a coincidence is what I have," she says.

"Not much more."

"You want to let me finish?"

I close my eyes again and take another drink of water. The cold feels good in my throat but turns to instant pain when it reaches my chest. I keep the sips small to avoid coughing. I lay my head back and listen.

"We sit on the car, waiting for him to come back. Plug shows up three hours later. By then Pinky had to go to his audition and I'm in Butch's car."

"Wait." Eyes open. I look at her with a little extra pain in my face. "Wait. Hang on a second."

"He's got the acting bug," she says, lifting her shoulders. "So?"

"Pinky?" I point in the general direction of the cellar. "That Pinky?"

"Yeah. Big into Shakespeare. He's not half bad, Mack. Who knows; maybe one day you knew him when."

"You're shitting me."

"Yeah, I am," says Suri with a little topspin. "You won't let me finish a sentence so I'm shitting you. Okay? Pinky's niece is the one with the audition. Price of borrowing his sister's car is to get Shayna out to Lake View Arts. Can I fucking finish or do you have more judging to do?"

I reclose my eyes, leaning my head back against the seat.

"Plug leads us to this coffee dive out in Edgewater. He's in there fifteen or twenty, then he comes out. Climbs into a black Navigator just pulling up to the curb. Okay? Fucking Navigator. Clean. Nice."

"Yeah. Okay."

"So he's behind tinted windows for another ten. Then he's out again. Back in his Audi and gone."

"You get the plates? Any photos to go with this story?"

"I've got 'em." Suri pulls a phone out of her back pocket. She scrolls as she talks. "I had a feeling Royce was the one in that fucking Lincoln, so we let Plug go and followed the Navigator. We made it as far as Park West before Butch ran out of gas."

"Of course."

"Butch's neighborhood has a siphoning problem, so he started the day low." Suri hands me the phone. "Scroll left. Anyway, Pinky picked me up and we came out here. I figured I'd show you a photo and maybe you could give Plug a real name."

I'm looking at a dozen grainy shots of a man in a rainy parking lot. One of the shots gets the corner of the building I recognize as the Blue Lotus. The man could be anybody. Medium build. Dark clothes. Collar pulled high; hat pulled low. Could be anybody who doesn't like to get wet. I keep scrolling. A shot of the man approaching a silver Audi. Climbing inside, one hand on the door.

"You get the plate on the Audi?"

"Later," says Suri. "Keep going."

Next, a dusky photo of the street corner outside *Shot in the Dark Coffee*, which I assume is in Edgewater. The door is closing behind Plug's backside. The next photo is of Plug emerging, stepping out into the rain, both hands on his collar. In the foreground is the behemoth hood and half a tinted window of a black Lincoln Navigator waiting at the curb.

I don't care so much about the Lincoln or even who is inside. Not now. I can't get past the face of Alexi Novak looking over the hood.

Stoli. Jesus Christ. It's Stoli. Suri is scouring my face.

"You know him," she declares. "Who is it?"

"Alexi Novak."

"Okay, so? Who is he? Russian?"

"Parents came over from Belarus. His brother, Jovah, decorated cop working for CPD until his mother, Ivah, shot him in the back for getting a little too close to the truth. Long story there. Alexi helped cover up the murder. Then he killed Ivah. Had her killed. Overdose in the old-folks home. Nice family. Alexi's the last man standing under the family tree. He's a Big Man lieutenant. Goes by the name Stoli." I look up at Suri. "Ever heard that name in your circles? Stoli?"

Suri looks through me for a second or two. She tightens her lips. Nods.

"Yeah," she says, head down, like she's talking to Phil. "More than once. Stoli. Girls called him Boots. Something about his leg. Likes to choke and be choked. Pays well. Very well, actually. Good manners."

"A well-mannered choker. Imagine that. He shops the corners?"

"Girls that know him work the clubs, so I'm guessing he does too. I never laid eyes on the man."

"Well, you have now." I waggle her phone. "He's a plug. Drugs. Prostitution. Human trafficking."

A scream of profanity stabs its way out of my cellar. We both look.

"If Pinky kills that guy," I start.

"He won't," says Suri. "He won't. So you've met him? Stoli. Alexi."

"No. But I met the bottom of his boot once." I point to the floor. "Right there. Stepped on my face and told a guy bigger than Pinky to take my legs off with a chainsaw. I had a bag over my head at the time. I didn't know who it was. I figured it out."

I look at Suri. Courtney. Horror plays across a face that is somehow, in spite of it all – the stepfather nightmare, the years of addiction, the abuse, the stripping, the hooking, the daily razor scrape of living alone on the streets of Chicago – somehow, is still beautiful. Innocent, even. Imagine that. How can that face be innocent? But it is. That face. All she can do is slowly shake it at me.

"Mack …" she manages.

"Not that I can prove any of that, mind you," I say. Then, almost forgetting, "And you're gonna love the best part."

"There's a best part?"

"Alexi's a long-time friend of one Samuel T. Royce. He works in the office of the soon-to-be former mayor of the great city of Chicago."

"Jesus," she whispers, eyes wide. "That really *is* the best part. That's more than a fucking coincidence, Mack. Right? I mean, seriously."

"You're not going to get Royce, kid. Get that idea out of your head."

Anger now, barely controlled.

"Plug … Stoli is … is fucking working for Royce. Okay? Pretty fucking clear if you ask me. And the man who beat me to within an inch of my life? Stuffed me in a trunk and took me out to a landfill to die? What's his name? Rickens? Fucking Rickens? Remember him, Mack?"

"Yeah, Suri, I do. Look …"

"Well Rickens was fucking working for Royce. And the fucks who tailed me to Bloomington and plastered Carl all over the wall of a shitty hotel? They worked for Royce."

"I get that you want that to be true, Suri, but you're way ahead of any evidence."

I sound like Twill, and that nearly kills me. Doesn't matter. She's not hearing. She's not listening. She keeps coming, pointing blindly behind her.

"The guy you have chained up down in your fucking cellar right now? The one who almost strangled you to death? Working for Royce."

"No."

"Wanna bet?"

"Big Man, Suri. They all work, or worked, for Big Man. Not Royce, except in seemingly legitimate ways. Rickens worked security. Alexi Novak is an adviser. Some kind of liaison on labor issues. Union stuff. Now ..." I hold up a finger to keep her from cutting me off. "Would not surprise me if Royce is in Big Man's pocket. Okay? Can I prove that? Not in a million years. And neither can you."

Suri leans in again. Whispers.

"Did it ever fucking occur to you, Mack, brilliant detective friend of mine, that Samual Royce *is* Big Man."

NINETY-EIGHT

Has it occurred to him? Of course it's occurred to him. Countless times.

But always in a paranoid, drunken stupor. Never in the daylit hours. Never while holding a cup of coffee and thinking rationally. The mayor as Big Man has a certain grandiose, comic book appeal. Nothing else. Nothing that comes with any actual evidence. He can imagine it. Sure he can. But Ray can imagine a lot of things. He can imagine that he's still the man he used to be. He can imagine not needing a drink to get him through the day.

But now she's got him imagining Samuel T. Royce all over again. Not that Ray concedes anything to her. No. Ray's too stubborn to concede that someone else might be right about anything. Certainly not this.

But what if it were true? What if the single most effective crime boss to afflict the Upper Midwest since Al Capone not only managed to stay invisible, but also had the audacity to run for mayor? And then won? Is it so outlandish to suggest that hiding in the glare of the very brightest spotlight lessens, rather than increases, the chances of discovery? Look at what happens when Royce's name turns up on a list of dirty money: every corner of Illinois Justice circled the wagons and shut down the inquiry. Sure, the list turned out to be a fake. But still, he thinks. It's possible. Maybe.

Ray arranges his face in a way to demonstrate that he's dismissing the idea out of hand.

"Stop it," he says. "Forget him, Suri. Cut yourself free of this. All of it. Let Pinky be the only white whale in your life. Don't play Captain Ahab chasing after Royce. That's not going to end well."

"What are you …" She lifts both hands at him like she's trying to talk sense to a pile of filthy laundry. "I don't even know …"

"Let it go is what I'm telling you. Live your life. Go someplace warm and dry. Meet someone nice under a palm tree. Have a puppy. Buy a kid. Other way around, maybe. Be happy. You've earned happy, Courtney. This is not happy. This is ugly and dangerous. I'm glad you came back, but only so you could save my wrinkled ass and I could live long enough to tell you that you shouldn't have come back. You've somehow managed to put it all behind you. You've beat back every demon with a grip on your ankle. I don't know how, but you did, and you're still pulling in oxygen. Don't die face down in this dirty puddle. Cash in your chips and go. Stay ahead of this. Someone besides Pinky needs to live through all this to tell your story. I wouldn't bet on that being me."

Suri's brow wrinkles.

"What does that mean, Mack? What are you saying?"

"I'm falling apart, kid. Any day now someone will hoist me up on cinder blocks and strip me for parts. My saving grace is that there's not much left to strip that's worth a damn. You're younger. Stronger. You've got the instincts of a survivor, but those instincts don't count for anything if you don't use them. You've got to get the hell out, Courtney. And you need to do it yesterday."

She wants to fight him. She blusters and argues her point in inarticulate fits and starts. He's not hearing it. Rising now, pushing himself up from the lounger on his own steam, face imploding in pain. She stands with him, evicting Phil. She puts one hand on each of his shoulders, no longer arguing, only concern.

"What can I do?" she asks. He hands back her phone. Points to a pen on the table.

"Write down the plate numbers for the Lincoln and the Audi. Let's go downstairs and see what we can learn."

They take the stairs together, side-by-side, Suri holding him by the shoulders. The pain in his chest is better for the pill in his bloodstream, but the fear of making a wrong move is as sharp as ever. So he moves with caution. Like an old man.

Pinky is sitting on the bottom stair in the wan glow of a single caged bulb, his bald, grublike, tropical themed, polyester-stretched enormity blocking their final arrival. Beyond Pinky's shoulder Ray can see his attacker standing, hands behind his back, chained by the neck to an iron beam with Marlo's pink bicycle lock.

Suri gives Pinky a gentle kick in the back. Pinky stands and turns, handing Ray a cell phone.

"Cargo pocket," he says, moving to the corner of the cellar, next to a stack of boxes full of old tax paperwork that Ray is too lazy to haul upstairs and out to the trash. Or too weak. "Locked. Want I should beat his ass for the password, boss?"

"Boss?" Ray looks at the phone in his hand and then back up at Pinky. "Thought I was a tool."

Pinky cuts a glance at Suri, the accordion flesh folds of his neck pancaking and re-expanding over the tropical sunrise of his collar. Suri shrugs him an apology.

"All bosses be tools," he says to Ray. "Shit ain't personal, man."

"And this guy?" Ray hitches his chin in the direction of the iron pillar.

"Him a needle dick, boss. Ain't nothin'. Cryin' an' screamin' like a bitch."

Ray separates himself from Suri. Takes the last step to the floor on his own and walks slowly across the dusty cement, stopping within ten feet of the man who had nearly given custody of Phil to Judith Kravitz. He can see now that Pinky has repurposed the nylon garrote to tie the man's hands.

"English?" says Ray quietly. Half of the man's face is slick with blood that is starting to dry and cake around one nostril. His eyes are like boiled eggs, white and large with fear. The left socket is already swelling, the skin reddening its way to purple. The neck hole of his black t-shirt is stretched large enough for three necks.

"Fuck you, mutherfucker," he says hoarsely.

Ray nods. "That works. Who sent you?"

The man spits ropes of bloody phlegm and screams, revealing large, white, blood-limned teeth. The tendons in his neck flare out to his shoulders like schooner rigging as his face shoves a rictus smile out into the room, presumably meant to haunt Ray's dreams. He'll have to get in line.

Movement, suddenly, from behind. Pinky pushes past Ray with surprising speed and slaps the man hard in the left cheek with the doughy frying pan of his open palm. The contact is hard enough to knock out another wet scream and to spin the man's face counterclockwise around the beam, from twelve o'clock to just past three and back again.

Pinky stands so close to the man that Ray has almost lost all sight of him. He wipes his bloody hand on the man's shirt then sweeps one massive leg sideways at the man's ankles, bringing him to the ground in a slow, jerking drop as the plastic sheath of the bicycle lock tries to hold his neck to the beam. Pinky sweeps his leg again and yanks at the neck hole of his shirt until the man is sitting flat on the concrete, cringing, squirming, waiting for whatever is coming next.

Pinky turns and moves back toward the stairs, resuming his post against the wall.

"Boss," he says.

Ray nods dispassionately and looks down at the man on the floor. Then he focuses on the phone in his hand, bringing it aglow with a finger tap. The screensaver is a photo of a tattoo. A skeleton in a swastika-emblazoned helmet, jaw unhinged, boney torso emerging from the hatch of a tank, one hand clutching a serrated knife, the other a bottle. The light brown skin tone behind the tattoo seems to be a match for the guy in front of him.

"This your tat?" Ray asks. He gives the guy ten seconds of silence. Doubles it. "Okay. Well, want me to ask my friend here to get those clothes off so we can find out?"

Pinky takes a step.

"No," he says, eyes full of pain and hate and more than a little fear. "It's mine."

"Guess the Illinois Nazis are loosening up their purity test. Membership must be down."

Ray takes two steps closer and holds the phone up to the man's face. It unlocks with a click.

"Damn," Pinky whispers to himself.

Ray navigates to the texting app. He scrolls and reads at random, just to get a sense of the man.

"Tank?" he says eventually. "People call you Tank? That what the tattoo's about? The tank?"

"Fuck you."

"You keep saying that. You must like getting slapped." Pinky shifts his weight. Ray waves him off. He keeps scrolling until he finds a texting thread he likes. It's the most recent thread of the bunch. And the shortest. Only two bubbles. The first consists of Ray's address, followed by a terse *tonight*. The second bubble is shorter still: *Roger that. Tanq out.*

A click. A thought that registers as a sound inside his head. He hears it. So do I. *Click*. Pieces snapping together. Tumblers aligning, releasing the lock. *Click*. It's a wildly intuitive leap, to be sure. But Ray can see the other side of the leap. He sees the landing. He's pleased with himself in advance. Maybe he should be. Sometimes this part of him still works like a pro.

"There it is," he says to himself. Suri is suddenly behind him, looking over his shoulder. Ray uses his index finger to peck out a response.

Done. Messy tho. Wanted to bargain. He knew some things. Tanq out.

Ray looks up. Tank is now all wide-eyed attention, wondering what Ray just typed and to whom.

"Here's what I think, Tank. I think the tattoo is not about you being a Nazi. You're no Nazi, are you? Little tan for that. I think the tat's all about the tank. I think you got loaded one night after beating up old ladies and stealing purses and you went to some dime-a-dozen ink artist who gave you an off-the-rack image of a Nazi skeleton that you liked. But you couldn't give a shit for the swastika. It was all about the tank. And the bottle in that bony hand. What's the skeleton drinking, Tank?"

Tank looks away, then back again, trying to look irritated by nonsense.

"I'm guessing it's gin," says Ray. "I'm guessing that's your favorite."

"Fuck you, man," he says. "Fuck you too, fat boy. Slap me again and you'll wish you hadn't."

Ray holds out a hand at Pinky, keeping him in position.

"I get how badly you want to change the subject," says Ray. "I do. You'll change it even if it hurts. But right now? I want to focus on why you spell Tank with a Q. Ten bucks it's short for Tanqueray."

He lets it sit for a second. The man tries to hold the look. He can't.

"You got yourself a name, don't you? You're in the club."

"What fuckin' club? Out'chu mind, mutherfucker."

"Come on. You know what club. I just sent them a text. We'll see what they have to say." Ray glances at the phone. "Nothing yet. We'll see."

Tank looks back, face tense, nose still bleeding.

"Tank-with-a-Q. Mr. Tanqueray. Guess you could have called yourself Ray. Good thing you didn't, because then we'd have to kill you."

"Who'd you fucking text?"

"Come on. You know who. You look worried, Tank. You should be worried. I'd be worried. They're gonna think everything went great tonight. But that's not exactly true, is it? Because you blew it big time. Should have left the rope at home. You fucked up. And now they'll think you lied about it. Now you're going up for attempted first degree murder of a police officer. That's going to put you in pre-trial detention like a chicken in a cage full of foxes."

Ray waits. Gives the image a chance to set itself before continuing.

"How long you think Big Man's gonna let you keep breathing? He'll make it hurt, Tank. You know he will. He likes to send messages to everyone watching. And there's no better message than pain. Is there? You know that. You'll remember this cellar like a long, lost dream. You'll call out for my big friend here like he's your mother."

Ray stays quiet for a good minute, looking at the phone like a response is imminent. Then he looks down at the bloody mess at his feet.

"But you're luckier than you think," he says. "Turns out you tried to kill me at just the right time. No way you'd know this, Tank, but you've actually got a way out of this mess."

Ray holds up a corrective finger.

"Well. Not *out*, out. You're going to pay some kind of price for trying to strangle me in my home. But I can improve your odds of blowing out another birthday candle. If you want me to explain more, just sit there and bleed on yourself. If not, I'm more than happy to save my breath and call the cops so they can get on with the last and shortest phase of your life."

Ray looks at the phone again, then down at Tank. He's quiet. Focused.

"Right. Okay, well there's a woman I know. She's from out of town. Not sure how long she's staying, but she's in town now. Works for people with a hard-on for Big Man like nobody's business. She's ready to make a deal with anyone who can help deliver the prize, Tank."

"Lying mutherfucker. Fuck you."

"Yeah, okay. Your choice. I don't care much. I'd prefer to do it your way. I would. Lot less for me to worry about discipline-wise. I can do this by the book, turn you in, go about my day."

Ray lapses into silence, like he's rethinking everything. He's not rethinking anything. He's letting Tank's worry build. Letting Tank think about the way out he may just have prematurely dismissed.

"But here's the thing," he says. "Unlike me or any other corner of the Illinois Justice System, the agency this woman works for does not care anything about who you are or what you've done, including strangle me. They only want Big Man. Understand what I'm saying? She'll make any deal she needs to make. Believe me when I tell you that if you've got some information, she's got the connections to make a conversation worth your while."

"Lyin' ratfuck shithead mutherfucker."

Ray lifts his hands like he's under arrest.

"Hey, like I said, I'm not hard-selling anything. I'd just as soon see you bleed out in pre-trial detention with a toothbrush shiv in your eyeball. The thought of seeing you get any kind of break – a free pass out of the country, witness protection, community service for nearly choking me out – it hurts my soul. It does, Tank. Believe me. A little old-fashioned vengeance would keep me going for a while. But I owe this gal a favor. You're probably my last chance to make good. So maybe think on that, while we wait for a …"

The phone in his hand vibrates, focusing everybody's attention like a lightning rod. Ray holds up a finger. Looks.

Stop typing. Idiot. 9:00. Same place.

Ray looks backward at Suri, raising his eyebrows.

"Didn't take long," she says, reading over his shoulder.

Ray looks down at Tank. Waggles the phone.

"They want to meet," he says. "Same place. Tell me where that is, I'll set you up with my friend. You two can bargain for your future and I won't have shit to say about it. That's the best deal you're gonna get, Tanqueray. Just shake your head and I'll call the cops. Lie to me about the location of this meet and I will throw you to the fucking wolves."

Climbing the stairs is like climbing Everest. Suri takes the water from him. Sets it on the table. She gets him on the couch. Adjusts the cushion under his head. Ray points at the plastic bottle.

"Glass. Ice. Bourbon."

"I can do two out of three," she says.

"What good is a drink without a glass? There's a bucket in the garage."

"You want to beat your addictions, Mack? There's no time like the present. Take it from me."

"I'll beat my addictions on a day when I haven't been beaten. Or strangled. Could be a while."

"Doesn't it bother you that you need a drink in your hand so badly. Even at a time like this?"

"Sure it does. But it bothers me even more that I don't have a drink in my hand, especially at a time like this."

"The booze isn't your friend, Mack."

"I'm holding my enemies close."

"You know how your addictions kill you, Mack? They make you stupid. They devour your instinct for self-preservation. Take it from me."

"When your high horse is done taking a shit in my living room, maybe you could trot into the kitchen and make yourself useful?"

"No, no," she says. "Fuck you, Mack. I don't need the attitude."

"Good. Then maybe you know how I feel."

Suri glowers for a second. Shakes her head. Sighs. Leaves him for the kitchen and returns with a tumbler sloshing two fingers of amber and as many cubes. She hands him the glass. Ray has already adjusted the cushion under his head so he can drink. She sits on the edge of the sofa and watches his face change, anguish melting like frost in the sun. Phil has found her way between Ray's ankles. Suri administers long, languid strokes. Ray puts a drop on his finger and holds it out to Phil. She takes it with enthusiasm and a silent kitty sneeze.

"Jesus," says Suri. "That's fucked up."

"Right? I'm trying to keep her from smoking."

"You should be up in bed," she says. "I can get you there."

"You say that to all the guys. I'm afraid I'll never wake up. Couch is better. I just need a couple of hours. Don't worry if I wake up screaming. It happens. Meantime, make yourself at home. Did Phil eat?"

"Pink fed her. I think he's in love," she whispers. "Sweetest thing."

"Long as he doesn't eat her," says Ray, closing his eyes.

"Be nice. What's the plan, Mack?"

"Plan is for you to keep an eye on things while I sleep. Cut Needle Dick's hands free. He's not getting out of his collar. Give him a bottle of water."

"You want him to stay hydrated? He nearly killed you."

"I know. I was there."

"Okay. Then?"

"Then I'm going to work and you're going to get on with your life."

"You are not going to that meeting," she warns.

"We'll see. And never you mind. You're retired."

"How about I go instead. Report back."

"How about you get that idea out of your head."

"This woman you told him about. This the Frenchie chick you told me about last time?"

"The same," says Ray.

"She's hunting Big Man."

"Yeah."

"Feds?"

"Feds are involved. She's shy about the details."

"You really gonna call her? Turn your strangler friend over?"

"Still thinking about that one."

Suri places her hand over his.

"I'm worried about you, Mack," she says, looking like she means it.

"I've been strangled and beaten before."

"Not talking about that. I'm talk …"

It's too close to home. He's not going there. So he interrupts.

"Why'd you burn down the dry cleaner?"

"What?" Suri sits up straight on the edge of the sofa like she's been slapped. Removes her hand from his. They look at each other in the dark. Ray lets her work her way through the options until there aren't any options left. She clears her throat. "How'd you know?"

"If there's one person on planet Earth who'd know the Blue Lotus had burned to the ground, it'd be you, Suri. You'd have told me about it already. You'd want me to know that the dry cleaner is a pile of ashes. But you kept that to yourself." Ray takes another drink. Closes his eyes again for a long blink. Sleep is a train, slowing into the station. "Let's have it."

Suri sighs. Rubs her face. Looks at him.

"Tired of looking at that place," she says. "After we followed Plug … and then ran out of gas trying to follow the Navigator … Pinky picked me up. We went back to the Lotus. Sat there for hours. For fucking nothing. Like always. I wanted to hurt them, Mack. I didn't know how. I felt Rickens beating me all over again, pulling me out of that trunk by the hair. I remembered Carl's face, across that hotel room, looking at me, terrified, before he just fucking exploded in front of me. I wanted to hurt them. The mayor. Big Man. I decided it was time to leave this place. This fucking city. You told me they were using the cleaners to do their dirt. I decided that building was important to them. So …"

"So you said goodbye," says Ray, closing his eyes. They stay closed this time.

"Yeah," she says. "I said goodbye. Once you've killed a couple of people, arson seems like not such a big thing. Felt good, watching that place burn. Pinky had nothing to do with it. Leave him out of it. What are you going to do about it?"

Ray laughs softly, as much as the pain will let him.

"You're under arrest. You've got a shit-ton of rights. Something about silence."

"I was going to leave. That night. Just disappear for good. But I wanted to come see you. I wanted to show you Plug's picture. Alexi's picture. Stoli. And some license plates. I wanted to tell you I was sorry. About last time. I'm sorry I doubted you, Mack." He feels her lift his hand to her cheek. "You're a good man."

NINETY-NINE

She lets me sleep for more than a couple of hours. Dreamtime makes it feel like ten. I died at least twice. If I woke up screaming, I don't remember it. I can see the beginnings of alleged daylight through the slats in my blinds. The sun, wherever it is, sounds like rain. It's the smell of butter in the eggs that brings me fully awake.

"Breakfast in bed," I say as Suri sits me up. The pain in my chest is bad, but not like earlier. It's my throat that wants the most attention. "I could get used to this. Maybe we should get married."

"You haven't tasted the eggs yet," she says. The wig is off. She's a bald beauty again. The tumbler is gone. She hands me a bottle of water. "Plus, how'd it look for you to marry an arsonist?"

I reach for the plate of scrambled eggs on the table. Swallowing is a chore, but I manage.

"How's our boy?" I ask.

"Hydrated."

"And Pinky?"

"Bathroom. He's been walking around with Phil on his shoulder. I think she likes it."

"She likes perches. Confirms her superiority complex. The eggs are delicious. About that marriage."

"I'd love to see you marry again, Mack," she says, far too seriously. I finish the eggs and put down the plate. "It'd be good for you."

"Time for you guys to go," I say like I can't hear.

"Why?"

"Because I'm going to call someone to come take out my trash and it'd be better if you were someplace else. Hawaii, maybe. Mexico."

"Who's taking out the trash? What are you going to do?"

"Take a long hot shower. Go to work."

"Let me at least get you upstairs. I'll wait for you to take a shower."

I stand from the couch like I'm lifting a bus.

"I'm okay. The meds will kick in." I put a hand on each of her shoulders, marveling at how someone so slight can be so mighty. So impervious. So incorruptible. "You need to go, Suri. Don't tell me where. The less I know the better. Send me a postcard from someplace you aren't."

The hug lasts a long time. I drink in the press of humanity against my own. I realize I'm starving, and not for food.

Pinky is waiting by the door when we separate, Phil luxuriating in his enormous arms. Suri stoops for the couch. Puts her wig back on. Combs her fingers through the black and silver. She holds my face in her hands and kisses me sweetly on the lips.

"Don't look back," I say.

And she doesn't.

ONE HUNDRED

Paula and I sit in a large dirty puddle near the corner of West Hightower and Cleveland. Another car hisses past. I watch it disappear like a water-skier behind a muddy fantail.

I slide the window down an inch. The air smells like wet grease and wood smoke. My chest feels better, as long as I don't move much and I keep the seatbelt off. My head and my neck are still upset. They seem to think a Camel would help. If they could call a lawyer, they would.

Ruth Brown is on the oldies station serving up allusions to washed-up love like she's slinging over-easy eggs and reheated hash. Rain is a bringdown, she sings. Well, ain't that the truth.

Skillets is in a two-story bread box made of dirty white bricks. It sits across a street that looks more like a rusty cheese grater for all of the potholes. I'm on the far side of a mostly empty parking lot that once belonged to a Circuit City before the circuits ran out of juice. I've got an unobstructed view of the entrance and the dozen or so spaces of dedicated diner parking. I don't have enough cover for comfort. I feel exposed without something – a van, a dumpster – encroaching the line of sight for my benefit. But I am at maximum distance. So there's that. And the rain works a little like a dirty curtain. Guess it'll have to do.

I take a look at Tank's phone, just to make sure there hasn't been a change of plans. Nothing.

I've set up a good half-hour early. About right since I don't know who I'm meeting. I figure he'll know me. I'll know him by a face that looks surprised at a dead man dropping in for breakfast. Just the same, better to show up early and get a feel for things.

Fifteen minutes of rain on the roof. New arrivals show up mostly in pairs, all unlikely. Seniors. Women holding purses at the sky like some kind of offering. A couple of punks. Nope.

But there are also three different singles. All men. All candidates. One in particular; pretty big, this guy. A little swagger to that gait. Doesn't seem to care much about the rain. What he cares about most is who or what is behind him. He keeps looking, even as he yanks open the door and steps inside. Looks like a plug to me. He's my best guess so far.

I wait another couple of minutes. No one else shows. It's one of those three. Has to be. He's inside waiting. I figure it's safe enough to make the call before I go in. I pocket Tank's phone and pull out mine. One ring is all it takes.

"What."

"Agent Delacorte? That you? How you been, brother?"

"What do you want?"

"Put her on."

Silence. I'm waiting for Delacorte to refuse and for us to do the whole who-gets-to-speak-to-whom dance again. But then she's on the phone.

"Detective."

"Marie. Got a present for you."

"I like presents."

"This one is chained up to a beam down in my cellar. He tried to ration my oxygen last night."

"Sorry to hear," she says. "Sounds like you came out okay."

"Glad to know you care."

"Who is it?"

"One of Big Man's boys."

"How do you know?"

"Just how many people do you think want to kill me?"

"How should I know? Maybe a lot."

"Turns out this one's got himself a liquor name. Tanqueray."

"Ah," she says, understanding. "I see. The tell-tale taxonomy."

"Yeah. Figured you'd like a chance to ask him about his friends."

"You figured right," says Marie with a smokey laugh. "And to what do I owe this sudden generosity?"

"Honestly? I don't want the paperwork. It's another investigation up my ass. Another six million questions about what I'm into and who I know and why they want to hurt me. I don't have the time or the patience. You can have him if you get him out of my house. Process him however you want. Take him to Paris. Lock him up in the Louvre. Put him to work cleaning French toilets. I told him that if he plays ball, you'll cut him a sweet deal."

"Did you? Well, you over-promised, Detective."

"Maybe. But Tanqueray doesn't know that."

"I could turn him loose. That's a pretty sweet deal."

"Man tried to kill me, Marie."

"You think I want the paperwork?" she asks, irritated.

"What I think is that you want to get close to Big Man and you don't care about much else, including murder, attempted murder and paperwork. Use him as bait. Wire him up and make him a snitch. Beat him with a rubber hose. Whatever works best for you."

"We'll see what he knows. I suppose I should thank you."

"We're even, Marie. No matter what happens with Twill or the guy in my cellar, I want that job at CPD. And I want the meeting we talked about." I look at my watch. "That's in two hours and change."

"Your rendezvous at *The Bean* is still on," she says. "I offer no assurances about what the man can tell you about the dead. And as for the job offer, it's already in your pocket. That too is now out of my hands. I've done my part."

"Come on, Marie. You could undo all of it if you wanted to."

"We have an understanding, Detective. It's done."

"My backdoor is unlocked. Tanqueray was strapped. His piece is on the counter behind the coffee maker. Get rid of that too while you're at it. Leave the cat alone. Lock up when you leave. Don't give my neighbors anything to talk about."

I disconnect. Refocus. A father and son hop out of a white pickup and run for the front door. My watch gives me ten more minutes before I'm due inside. I poke in another few numbers.

"Nick. Mack. Got a minute?"

He does. I give him the short version, leaving out where I am and why. Last thing I want is a carful of Feds showing up for breakfast. Nick is cautious. Skeptical even. But what I'm asking of him isn't such a big lift, and the payoff could be huge. It's a gift, really. I'm full of gifts today.

"Who else knows?" he asks.

"Nobody. Let me know how it goes."

"Of course. You okay?"

"I'll live. For a little while anyway. Working on a painkiller addiction to go with all the others."

"You get the photo of Bashar I sent?"

"Not yet. I'll check my email at work."

"Get yourself a real phone. Please. Where are you?"

"Just headed into breakfast. Then to HQ to earn my paycheck."

"And to check your email."

"And to check my email. Anything from Chelsea Wolfe?"

"Not yet. Gotta go, Mack. You've complicated my day."

I disconnect. Drop the phone in my pocket. Crank the ignition. Sig is in the passenger seat. I check the magazine, rack in a fresh round and slip him nose first into the shoulder harness just a little too hard. The pain stabs upward, lancing from my chest through my recently strangled throat and directly into my brain.

It takes a couple of deep breaths to recover. When I reopen my eyes, I can see the guy I'm here to meet. He's not going in; he's coming out. And in a hurry, beelining for his car, pulling on the bill of his baseball hat. Maybe it's the rain. Maybe not. Turns out he was inside the whole time.

Guess I'm not the only one who likes to set up early.

He augers himself into something sleek, gray and tinted and speeds off in the rain. Suppose I could follow him. I look at my watch. I don't really see the point. I've got another meeting this morning that I don't intend to miss.

Besides, I know where he's going.

ONE HUNDRED ONE

My head feels swimmy. Maybe the weather has finally waterlogged my brain. Maybe Suri's eggs needed reinforcements. Or maybe the world is finally starting to make some sense. I'm drowning in a puddle of ugly truth.

I push my way into IAD knowing I don't have much time before I need to leave again. I brace myself for the simmering resentment and the onslaught of administrative need. Turns out I've forgotten how I look. All I get is a room full of wide-eyed stares. Steph Nellis manages to make a sound in the shape of a letter.

"Oh …"

Her beautiful head swivels in horrified astonishment. I make a crooked line around the desks for Twill's office. Raphael Santiago is on the phone. I tap him twice on the shoulder without slowing. I leave the door open. By the time I've made it to the chair behind the desk, Raffi is closing it again.

"Mack …" He lowers himself slowly into a chair, watching me like I might suddenly burst into flame. He slides the two stacks of files – the Glen Sugarman stack and the *everybody else* stack – sideways so he can see me. "What the fuck happened?"

It's the obvious question. I hold up a finger, moving to the bookshelf behind the desk. I pluck the tiny black, dime-sized microphone out from behind the photo of Wendy Twill. I work my way counterclockwise around the office, removing spyware from nooks and crannies. Six devices total. They all fit in the palm of my hand. I drop them all onto a sheet of notepaper and wad it up into a ball. I toss it to Raffi, who is watching me, spellbound. I put my finger to my lips, then point to the paper ball.

"Put that in my bottom desk drawer, would you? I need to sit."

He's got plenty of questions, but he knows better than to ask them. Raffi's up and moving and out the door before I can fully lower myself into Twill's chair. By the time he is back, door closed and seated, I'm breathing a little easier.

"Thanks," I say. "If we're going to talk about this, I'd rather be alone."

"What the fuck is going on, Mack? What happened to you?"

I give him the longest answer I can, knowing that Raffi is done with not being read in. Still, I leave out a healthy twenty percent, including my morning outside *Skillets*. One swimmy head is better than two.

I may have swamped the boat anyway. Raffi sits across the desk in silence, staring at me, slowly shaking his head.

"In your cellar," he says eventually.

"Yeah."

"He's still there?"

"Yeah. Unless he picked that bicycle lock."

"And Suri …"

"In the wind. I hope."

"And you say Marie's working for Big Man?"

"Seems so," I nod.

"Not a foreign agent, then."

"No." I give him a look. "You want to rub that in, go right ahead."

"Not trying to rub anything in, Mack."

"She may be from out of town," I say, "but Marie's all about helping Big Man protect himself."

"How long have you known?"

"Not long enough. Since a breakfast meeting this morning that never happened."

"So wait." Santiago closes his eyes like he's downloading from the ether. Then he opens them again. "Big Man knows his spoofing operation is in trouble. He gets someone, your kung fu guy, to rub out Dennis and Carrie O'Toole. He extorts Pete Chow into an official murder-suicide report by the Medical Examiner. Then he gets rid of Chow to prevent him from changing the forensics back to double homicide. And he puts … he puts Marie in play not only to help set up LT for the murder, but to …" he points at the monitor in front of me, "to work you to empty LT's computer."

"That's the gist. Yeah."

"Because Big Man thinks Amanda gave LT some kind of information she got from Dennis. Something that gives away the game on the whole spoofing thing."

I look at my watch and give him another nod. "Names. I.P. addresses."

"And then you … you … I can't even … you actually fucking do *this*? You bring in a guy – a fucking *Big Man* guy – and let him just …" Raffi gestures at me in Twill's chair. "… just sit there … and … and …"

"Empty LT's computer? Yeah. I did that."

"Why in the …"

"I told Marie I wanted to work bodies again. Get out of Chandler IAD and into the fellowship of CPD Homicide. Marie whispered in Big Man's ear, and he made it happen. I got the offer. I can leap whenever the dust settles."

It takes a minute. Raffi looks at me uncomprehending.

"You're leaving?" He laughs in open disbelief. "You're never going to make it to CPD Homicide, Mack. You *do* get that, right? I mean ..." he gestures generally at Twill's computer, "this here sends you to fucking prison."

"You're half right. I'm not going to CPD. Or prison."

"Why?"

"Because Chelsea made sure that LT's actual directory was locked away out of sight. Same with the department's internal network. Big Man got to see and take only what we wanted him to see and take. A virtual directory, she called it. It's all voodoo to me."

"Chelsea? Who the hell is Chelsea?"

"Ex-Bureau. Nick Yarborough sent her over. She wired the office for sight and sound."

"Those were bugs," he says, jerking his thumb in the general direction of my cubical.

"Yeah. She also booby trapped the computer. The fake files downloaded from LT's computer can be traced upon uploading to any internet-connected device. Nothing yet. We'll see."

"Jesus." Raffi looks around the office for any other signs of surveillance. "You're working for the Feds."

"I'm not working for anyone. *With* is a better word. Nick does for me; I do for him."

"You do for him? What are you doing for him, exactly?"

"Helping him find some leaks," I say, reminded that I need to look for an email from Nick attaching a photo of Felix Bashar. I could do that on Twill's computer, but maybe I want to keep my fingers off the keys until someone can dust them for prints.

"Leaks," repeats Raffi. "FBI leaks?"

"Yeah. That and handing him a chance to bust up an international spoofing ring. Way above Nick's paygrade. That'll put another notch in his bull-riding belt before he retires."

"And what's he doing for you, I mean, aside from keeping you from going to prison for the computer thing?"

"Guess we'll see. He's got a couple of cars outside my house, waiting for Marie to show up and take Big Man's trash out of my cellar."

"How do you know she's coming?"

"Because I called and asked her to."

"But she'll just turn the guy loose, Mack. He's …"

"You've already forgotten about the Feds? Tank's not going anywhere fun. Look, Raffi, this could go on all day. I know you want it all, but I'm on short time here. I need some help."

Raffi sits and stares through me. He's still processing.

"Raffi."

A knock on the door and Steph Nellis steps in. In her hand is a folder with a familiar yellow sticker on the front: *MACKEY HOLDING*. It reaches the desk before the rest of her, like a dog pulling her across the office.

"Sorry to interrupt," says Steph. "I wanted to make sure you have this. I meant to have it on your desk. Didn't expect you so early."

She doesn't mean it as a dig, but her face registers the risk. She's looking at me like she's trying not to look at me. It's either the swelling on the side of my face or the rope burns on my neck that has her attention.

"I didn't mean …" she starts.

"Forget it. Thanks, Steph. I haven't even read the first holding file yet."

I lean forward and reach for it, still perched atop Glen Sugarman's pre-fatty-obstruction-removal procedure workload. The pain in my chest has other ideas. I must make a face. Steph nearly lunges for the first file and combines it with the second, handing me both with a pained smile.

"Which file is angrier," I ask.

"It's a horserace," she says. "There are messages from Lt. Wendig about the Coopersmith investigation in both files. He's pretty hot."

"I can't wait. Thanks."

Steph takes her leave and closes the door. I hand Raffi a slip of paper from my shirt pocket with Suri's handwriting.

"More plates," he says.

"Top one is a silver Audi. Bottom is a black Navigator. Tell me what comes back."

"Okay. What else?"

"Where are we on finding Kung Fu?"

"Not where we'd like to be. I asked my CPD source to find out who was driving cruiser 0705. She said it's complicated. That cruiser is a floater, not regularly assigned. Depends on the schedule."

"I gave you the date."

"Yeah, but it's a different set of records and she's getting squirrelly about … You know."

"Squirrelly about being a rat. I figured your charm would overcome all that."

"You figured wrong. I'll try again. I'm not optimistic."

"Keep at it. Face-to-face, maybe. Take her out." I give him a wink. "Get those lips involved."

Raffi resists a laugh.

"Fuck you. Get the lips involved. Fuckin' pimp is what you are."

"Next thing: Amanda Tate's phone. Anything?"

"I burned a favor in forensics. He'll get to it, but I can't ask twice. He's home with the flu."

I don't hide the disappointment. "It's like everybody's got their own goddamned life."

"Tell me about it. I followed up with Chicago Fire about the Blue Lotus. They confirm arson, but no details. They didn't appreciate the call."

I carefully push myself up from the desk, the *Mackey Holding* files still in my hand. Raffi watches, my pain all over his face. Suri is in my head.

I was so tired of looking at that place. What are you going to do about it?

"Let the dry-cleaner thing go," I say. "Waste of time."

Santiago furrows his brow in confusion. I try to shrug with a convincing lack of concern. Nothing to see here. Move along.

"Until they do their thing and file a report. Let it go."

ONE HUNDRED TWO

Didn't take long to get used to Twill's office. My old cubicle makes me feel like I'm squatting in the corner of an old ice tray. I'm not eating much so I know I haven't gained any weight. It feels like it anyway. I don't fit here anymore.

Case files I've never seen before have taken over the desk. Urgently polite sticky notes proliferate. I look at the two *Mackey Holding* files in my hand, not quite sure why I bothered to bring them, and plop them down on top of the others. I can feel the eyes of my temporary subordinates stealing glances, wondering what I'm doing out among the commoners. Wondering what train hit me on the way to the office. Waiting for me to fall over dead.

Marlo is still up on the shelf where I left her. Everything about her is the same – the eyes, the lips, the politely impatient expression, the hair in the breeze – everything except maybe the quality of her soul and whether I ever really knew her at all. I think of the Marlo meeting I have so persistently demanded from Marie and that I'd now be a fool to keep. I look at my watch, calculating the time I have left. Not long.

I roll out the keyboard. The monitor glows to life. I pull up my email screen and look for new messages. Dozens of those. Hundreds. Jesus. I narrow my focus to new messages from Nick Yarborough attaching photos of FBI agents named Felix Bashar. There's only one of those.

I open it up. No words of greeting from Nick. Just the attachment. The Felix Bashar in the photo looks nothing like the Felix Bashar who put his fingers all over Twill's keyboard. Funny thing is that the real Felix looks nothing like an FBI agent, while the fake Felix needs to get out of the crime business and get into the movies. Probably too late for that.

I bang out a reply to Nick, sharing the good news and assuring him that fake Felix got his photo taken on our lobby security cameras and left his prints on Twill's keyboard. Worth a shot, but I'm guessing fake Felix got the part in the first place because he's not in the system.

I push back the keyboard and sit, looking at the piles of paper. The thought of standing hurts. I reach for the two *Mackey Holding* files instead. I open the one that I've ignored the longest. On top is the memo from Lt. Matthew Wendig to Chief Loudermilk about my investigation into Ryan Coopersmith. It's long and too hot to touch. He's copied me as a courtesy. He could have just emailed it. But Wendig wants it on paper. Something that will have to go into a physical file. Something I can't simply delete. The only word I catch before flipping past it is *insubordinate*.

Behind Wendig's memo is a plain white envelope, unaddressed except for my last name and *CONFIDENTIAL*, written in blue block letters. I tear it open. Inside is a slip of paper. A cumulus logo and web address for some digital storage outfit called Data Cloud. I flip it over. On the back, in the same blue pen, is a username, *Naughty_Niece*.

Beneath that is a password: *Blondies_Big_Dream#C6114*.

Revelation is buried in an unbidden slide show playing in my head. Amanda dead in the front seat of Saul Margolis' midnight blue Mercedes, bludgeoned into the next life. Amanda in Dennis O'Toole's demolished home, dropping a bottle of bourbon onto the extruded foam of a couch cushion, arguing for her freedom, peeking behind the blinds out into the darkness. Amanda outside the Marker Westpoint Suites, cashmere soaking up the rain. Amanda's cryptic text to her uncle Orland: *I found the thing I know nothing about. Also some things inside that thing. Giving to a friend for safe keeping.*

A friend? With Twill in custody, Amanda didn't trust who might be looking at his phone. That makes *me* the goddamned friend. Not a friend of hers, a friend of *his*. I'm the … I'm an idiot is what I am.

I'm on the Data Cloud website in under twenty seconds, pecking in the sign-in credentials with two fingers. But I'm pecking too fast to get it right. Two strikes and I get a lock-out warning. I take a breath. Try again.

There is only one file associated with the *Naughty_Niece* account. That file contains only two images. I double click on the first.

The icon inflates into a photo of the thing Amanda admitted she knew nothing about. A motorcycle – Suzuki, all black, no plate – parked at a curb in the rain, the only light source from someplace above and behind. A streetlight. There is no visual context from which to identify which curb. Which streetlight. Doesn't matter. I know anyway.

I'd given her gun back. And the car keys. I'd told her to wait for the motorcycle man to come in through the back of the house and to then just get the hell out. Just get in the car, lock the doors, and go. *He's not here for me, Amanda. Understand?*

Even if she did understand, she still managed to make some extra time for stupidity. As I was getting my ass handed to me in Dennis O'Toole's laundry room, Mandy was across the street snapping photos in the rain.

I double click the second image. The motorcycle seat is open, up on its hinge. Inside is an Illinois license plate, partially beneath some kind of black cable, a glasses case, and scraps of paper. Upside-down and backwards, I can make out a *C6*, with the remainder of the plate obscured. I look again at the password I used to sign in: C6114. Check.

I enlarge the photo, trying to make something of the scraps of paper sandwiched between the curls of black cable and the license plate – magnetic, I'm assuming; easy to take on and off as necessary. The scraps are paperclipped. The top piece is blank. No, not blank, just facing away. All of the good parts are on the other side. But I know the dimensions of that scrap of paper like I know the silhouette of an Old Forester bottle in the dark. It's a dry-cleaning ticket.

The paper beneath the ticket is a letter-sized sheet of paper, folded into quarters. Only a portion of the visible one-quarter-sheet is available for inspection. An image. Part of a shape. Light and shadow. I enlarge the photo, but that only makes it worse. I scale it back. Nothing I can define. A fraction of an image in poor lighting.

I'm ready to give up; to find Raffi and give him another plate to run. My brain shifts into strategy mode: running the motorcycle plate, getting a name and address, and putting Kung Fu into custody. I don't trust Chicago PD to cuff one of their own. It will need to be Chandler PD that makes the arrest. No, not Chandler either.

A tendril or two of my subconscious refuses to let go of the image on my screen. I look again. A background, smooth and pale. A foreground of geometry, a dark and sloping angle inclining up to a murky, broad horizontal bar. A shaky, dark cellphone snapshot of a folded photo inside the seat compartment of a Suzuki. At night. In the rain. No way.

I move my cursor up to close the image.

Stop. Not a horizontal bar. A branch. My blood runs cold.

Oh God oh God oh God.

I yank my phone out of my pocket and jab in the numbers. *Pick up pick up pick up.* Two rings. Three. *Damnit.* Four. *Pick …*

"Hey handsome."

"Doris. Thank God. Where are you?"

"On my hands and knees cleaning up dog puke, if you can believe it. Barkley got into the …"

"Stop talking, Doris. Listen to me. You are in danger."

"What?"

"I … Let me ask you something. It's been a while since I've been to your house. That giant bird feeder that Buck made for you. Looks like a pyramid?"

"Yeah? So? Ray …"

"Is it still hanging out in front of the house?"

"The birdfeeder?"

"Yes. The birdfeeder."

"Uh, yeah. What …"

"I want you to get out of the house, Doris. Don't do anything else. Just get out. Leave the dog puke. Do it now."

"And go where?"

"Anywhere you don't usually go. Stay away from the bar."

"I have to open today. Kyle has a thing."

"Then the bar stays closed. And don't run your usual errands. Something different. Think."

Silence. Dead air.

"Doris?"

"I've got a friend laid up at St. Johns with a broken back."

"Springfield. Perfect. Go for a drive. Make it a long visit. Anything feels weird or off call 911 or drive to a police station. Don't go home until I personally tell you it is safe to do that. Understand?"

"Ray …"

"Doris. Do you understand?"

"Yes, Ray, I fucking understand. Okay? Except that I don't understand anything. The goddamned birdfeeder? What the hell is going on?"

I take a breath. Try to find calm.

"Look. Okay. I'm sorry. I'm … it's been a rough twenty-four hours. I'm …"

"Are you okay?"

"I'm fine. People looking to get to me may try to use you to do it. Maybe I'm wrong. I hope I'm wrong. But I'm not taking the chance. Tell me you're headed for the car."

"Yes. I'm getting my keys. You're really scaring me, Ray."

"I'm trying to scare you, Doris. Get that adrenaline up. Get going."

ONE HUNDRED THREE

I stare out vacantly at the office around me, seeing nothing. Reordering the known world. Shuffling priorities. My monitor glows from the back of the desk. I look at my watch.

Okay. Calm down.

I yank my keyboard forward and get to work, hooking into the law enforcement portal to the Illinois DMV database and entering my credentials. I enter the motorcycle license plate number. Three seconds, maybe four. I get a list of one. Double-click.

And there he is. Five-eleven. Brown and blue. Thirty-three. Oval, hairless face with a thin, lipless slit for a mouth and a chin that wants to be someplace else. I'd recognize that mug anywhere. And I just happen to know that below the mugshot is an average-sized frame hung heavy with muscle and a couple of brick-hard hands plugged into some greased-lightning reflexes.

I'm scribbling on the back of Amanda's envelope just as Santiago is draping an arm over the cubicle.

"Wanna play good news, bad news?" he asks.

"Good news," I say without looking up.

"I've got data on those two plates you gave me. The Audi is registered ..."

"Alexi Novak," I say, still not looking. "AKA Stoli."

"I really hate it when you do that," he says. "You can run your own plates next time and I'll focus on real police work."

"Sorry, Raf. I'm not myself."

"I really think you might be."

"What else?"

"The black Navigator," he says. "You tell me, genius."

"The Mayor of Chicago."

"Wrong. A three-time loser named Clinton Duffy. Assault. Home invasion. Possession with intent. He just cleared an eight-year stretch. Out for the past eleven months. Riding in style."

"Big Man Muscle."

"That was my thought," says Raffi. "The man is six-one. Two hundred thirty. System puts his pillow on East 59th."

"Washington Park. That's not where he lives."

"Because?"

"How long you think a Lincoln Navigator lasts parked at the curb on East 59th? Big Man's putting him up. He's got a garage. Let's have the bad news."

"Bad news is about Kung Fu's cruiser. My CPD source is sending my calls straight to voicemail. Three times now. I think she's done, Mack."

"We don't need her."

"What?"

I hand the envelope to Raffi.

"What's this?"

"Kung Fu's name and address."

"What? This is the guy? Edward Lee Little?"

I nod, looking at my watch.

"*Officer* Edward Lee Little," I say, pushing myself up out of the chair with a groan.

"How'd …"

"Amanda Tate. Turns out she dropped by this office with a link to some bad photographs before she went home to get killed."

Santiago extracts the Data Cloud logo from the envelope and flips it over. Then he looks at me.

"We got him?"

"We know who he is," I caution. "You haven't got him yet."

I make my way across the bullpen for Twill's office. Raffi follows. He stops in the doorway, watching as I circle the desk and grab up my coat.

"*I* haven't got him yet?" he asks. "What are you saying?"

"Real police work, Raphael. Go get a warrant. Reach out to Naperville PD. Put together a team. Get out there and bring him in."

"Naperville. Why Naperville?"

"It's a Naperville address, right?"

"Yeah, but it's not their case, Mack. It's not their collar."

"You're right. It's our case. And it's your collar."

"My collar?"

"Yeah. You're wasting your talents, kid. You wanted in? This is in."

"Mack, I'm Chandler IAD. I'm not … I'm not …"

"Sure you are, Raffi. Don't sell yourself short. Call Stretch Martin. He's still on medical leave but call him anyway. Chief said he's turned in his papers, but I'm guessing he's secretly itching to turn off the TV and do some police work. He's originally from Naperville. He knows absolutely everyone that matters in that department. Stretch is looking to prove he doesn't hate me. Tell him I said to hold this one close. Not Chicago. Not Chandler. Got it? Naperville."

"Yeah," he says, oozing uncertainty. "Naperville. Edward Little, mysterious assassin."

"Talented maybe. I'll give him that. And tough. But not so mysterious. I'm guessing that name of his got him some early attention. Little Eddie Little had a tough adolescence, kids being what they are. Decided early on he needed some muscle and some skills to even the score and hold his head up wherever the big kids enforced the pecking order. When he wasn't busy pulling the legs off ladybugs, he worked his way through the karate fashion belts then slid sideways into mixed martial arts. Maybe college or maybe not. Maybe he skips the books and throws in with the police academy straight away. Gets himself a gun and a shield and a license to be a prick with something to prove. The psych profile almost writes itself. I'll bet Big Man saw this kid coming a mile away. Signed him up early."

My phone rings. I open the line while I'm still talking. "Or maybe I'm all wet. Just lock him up."

"Lock who up?" asks Raj Malik in my ear.

"Raj?"

"Hey, Mack. Gotta minute for your favorite cabbie?"

"No, actually."

"Been doing some amateur sleuthing. I think you might want …"

"Sorry, Raj. Can't do this now. Gotta go."

I kill the call. Santiago hasn't stopped looking.

"What charge?" He asks. "Murder?"

"No," I correct. "Attempted murder and assault of a police officer. Two police officers. Me and LT. I can ID him. That'll do for now. We can charge the murders later. Right now, you need to get this plug off the street."

"Plug?"

"Forget it. Check the house. Get an APB out on the bike. Put Naperville on the phone with Chicago with a request that they bring in cruiser 0705 and make Officer Little available for questioning. Stake out the CPD parking lot. Whatever it takes. Just get him off the street. Call Ernie Davidson. Tell him what's going on."

Putting my coat on is harder than taking it off. Santiago waits until I'm done grimacing.

"Where are you going?"

I grab Twill's umbrella from the brass stand in the corner. Then I head for the door.

"Off to see a man about a woman I used to know."

ONE HUNDRED FOUR

Ray stops, surveys the venue. His choice. He hadn't had long to think about it, but Marie had let him choose. So here he is.

No place for someone to hide. Just a large, flat two-tiered plaza with a single, one-hundred-something ton, polished metal legume in the center. No bushes or boulders or buildings behind which one might loiter unobserved. Just *The Bean*.

Cloud Gate they named it. Like that was ever going to stick.

It's silver. Like a blob of liquid mercury. Bulbous and arched, thirty-three feet high, sixty-six feet long, warping Millennium Park and the towering sentinels that align Michigan Avenue to the west and Randolph to the north, like soldiers at attention before a funhouse mirror.

The Chicago sky, seething its dark, wet uniformity, will not be mocked from below. Neither will I. But nothing and nobody at ground level gets a pass.

It's public, Grainger Plaza, but not crowded. No large clots of people, amoebas to unwittingly absorb and seclude malign actors. Not today, anyway, in the pouring rain. Less than two dozen today. Mostly pairs. A couple of trios. One foursome. Two pre-teen brothers pose under *The Bean*'s middle arch, out of the rain, jumping, irresistibly slapping the mirrored sides of the thing as parents wrangle umbrellas and cellphones. A trio of young women walk the perimeter, single file, umbrellas aloft – black, pink, black – left hands flat against *The Bean*, slicking away the water as they gaze at their reflections, transfixed, as if holding hands with themselves in a Salvador Dali dream.

And then there's Ray. Alone. Off in the northwest corner of the plaza. Observing from beneath Twill's dripping black umbrella. Trying to convince himself that what he's doing here is rational. Non-suicidal. That's a hard sell if you ask me.

But he does his best. Tells himself that he's in control of how this will all play out. Takes false comfort in Sig's painful weight against his rib cage. And the Glock 9 tucked into the small of his back.

He'd kept himself busy on the ride over. Three calls, all good. Mostly.

First, Doris, on his way out of the building and back into the rain.

"Doris. Are …"

"I'm fine, Mack. I'm fine."

"Where are you?"

"On the road. Headed to Springfield. It's you I'm worried about. I'm just calling to make sure you're okay."

"Me? Never better."

"Now I'm really worried. Who's after you?"

"Other way around. I'm after him. The nets are closing as we speak. You just worry about keeping your eyes on the road. I'm fine."

"I love you, Ray," she'd said, stopping him dead in his tracks halfway down the stairs. "You know that. You're important to me. You have to take care of yourself. The job isn't worth it. Nothing is worth it."

"I'm okay, Doris. Really. Let's have a drink tonight. Catch up."

"I'd like that. Where?"

"Let's see how things go. Hopefully Bucks. If not, maybe some swanky Springfield hotel watering hole."

"Perish the thought," she'd said. "You're saying I should find a hotel?"

"We'll see. Not with a little luck."

Then the call from Stretch Martin, as he had navigated the never-ending detour between 134th and Spalding, equally reassuring. Invigorating, even. Stretch had wanted more details, suspicious that Santiago had left something out. He hadn't. Stretch still wanted more. Wanted everything. All Ray could do was hit the highlights. His old partner, his more recent enemy, now sidelined from the force and forever scarred by a bullet that had sliced open his face in Deke's Salvage Yard, had listened without interruption.

"Christ," Stretch had said when he was done. "What is this fucking world coming to, Mack? Back in the day … when we were beating the streets … at least you fucking knew who …"

"There's no going back, Stretch. We are where we are. Understand?"

He had understood, just as Ray suspected he would. Ray had also been right about Stretch wanting off the couch and back in the game. And about Stretch wanting to make things right again between them. Wanting to erase five years of hating Ray for, he'd believed, selling out to street scum like Cosmo Green and to the relentless corruption machine that controls them. Stretch had said he'd jump in with both feet. He'd take his unsightly scar straight to the Naperville PD and light a fire.

"Let Santiago lead on this, Stretch. He's good. He needs the boost. Wexler could do worse than bringing him into homicide. Keep an eye on him."

"Will do, Mack. Watch yourself."

"Always do, Stretch. Thanks."

Finally, the call from Nick Yarborough, mostly while Ray was sitting in a parking garage on the periphery of Millennium Park. That had been another big shot in the arm: the FBI had picked up four of Marie's boys outside his house, plus Tanqueray-Tank from the cellar. All in custody.

"What about Marie?" Ray had asked.

"No sign of her," said Nick. "And her boys aren't talking."

"Not surprised. It'd have been stupid of her to be there. Still, it's a big setback for her, Nick. She'll be in Dutch with Big Man for fucking this up. She's got a demotion coming. Now they'll wonder how long we were on to them and whether they can trust what fake Felix pulled off of Twill's computer. Anything on that yet?"

"All's quiet," Nick had said. "Maybe they're just slow to upload the data."

"Maybe. Or maybe they can smell a shit sandwich when they get one. I dragged my feet on the computer thing like it was the last thing I wanted to do, but maybe Marie saw through it. Stupid she ain't."

"Guess we'll see," said Nick before getting back to his day. Marie's lack of stupidity was ringing in Ray's ears as he'd left the parking garage and opened his umbrella. No, he'd thought, Marie was not stupid.

Unlike Ray. Because here he stands. Under an umbrella in the pouring rain on a lonely corner of Grainger Plaza. Slightly hunched to take some strain off of his ribs. Watching *The Bean.* Waiting. But for what, exactly? Waiting for inevitability to tap him on the shoulder. Or shoot him in the head.

Because it's hard to fathom what he thinks he's doing here. They'd tried to kill him. Now that Twill's computer has been pillaged, Ray has clearly outlived his value and, true to form, they had tried to put him down. What was it he had told Amanda? In Big Man's world, people without any value are just fleshy buckets of liability. You get a bullet to the head and left in the gutter for the street sweepers. He'd imparted that wisdom to persuade Amanda not to be an idiot. Good advice in hope of avoiding a violent, stupid death. A wasted effort, turns out.

But Ray could teach Amanda Tate a thing or two about stupid. Because now they'd tried to kill *him,* and they had failed. He was alive, and upon his contacting Marie to offer up Tanqueray Tank for questioning, they *knew* he was alive. Alive and, as far as Marie was concerned, clueless as to her true allegiance. Why else would he have called her and offered up the man who had tried to strangle him?

Never inform someone who tries to kill you that you're still alive. If that's not carved in stone someplace, it should be. Ray has now disregarded that common sense for the sake of a gambit. A low percentage flyer. A couple of cars full of FBI windbreakers waiting at the corner of his street to see who shows up.

Worth it? Maybe. Maybe. But there's always a downside cost. Isn't there, Ray? Now that the trap has been sprung, now that four of Big Man's boys plus Tanqueray Tank have been placed into custody, Big Man and Marie know the jig is up.

They know … that *you* know, Ray. And they know – and here is the salient part as you stand out here in the rain waiting – they know exactly where to find you to finish the job.

Why? Because they know you'll show up for this pointless meeting. They know you can't help yourself. Just ask Suri. She gets it. She told you this morning: *Know how your addictions kill you, Mack? They make you stupid. They devour your instinct for self-preservation.*

You're an addict, Ray. A junkie. You'll do anything for a hit. I'm not talking about the booze. Or the Camels. You're hooked into a dead woman. That's worse than crank or skag. You can't let her go. You'll do anything for another hit of Marlo. Anything. Even this.

Ray tries his best to tune me out. He suddenly gets a little help from across the plaza. His entire body stiffens when he sees him. He watches. Tracks. No question about it. One man. Sixties. Maybe late sixties. A little hunched at the shoulders. Black umbrella, long brown raincoat, floppy brown hat over a nest of white hair. Casual gait. Avoiding *The Bean* like it's radioactive. Staying outside the camera sprays. Walking the perimeter.

Ray switches umbrella hands and plots an intercept course that catches the man's attention. They meet at the back of the plaza.

"You seem to share my lack of interest," says the man with a smile, nodding sideways at the main attraction. His face is long and narrow and deeply lined. Lots of character, someone has surely said.

"Beans give me gas," says Ray. "Except coffee beans. What say we get out of the rain."

A smile. A nod.

"I'm parked off of Randolph," he says, starting to turn. "Not far."

Ray doesn't budge, even as the man's shoulders threaten to turn.

"Problem?" asks the man.

"I'm about as interested in getting in a car with you as you are in getting in a car with me. So let's keep this public." Ray points over the man's head. "There's a coffee shop right across Michigan. Donuts to die for."

"You don't understand," he says, face bending into something sad, apologetic. "I'm not the person you want to talk to. I'm the person who takes you to that person."

Ray cocks an eyebrow, bringing up the hint of a disbelieving smile.

"I look like a turnip to you?"

"So my guy spooks easily." A shrug. "These are his terms for talking."

"Right," says Ray. "Tell Marie it was nice doing business with her."

"Marie? I don't know a Marie any more than I know this Marlo chick, okay? But look. If this is no good for you, that suits me just fine. I got other things to do that don't involve standing out in the fucking rain." He gives Ray a curt smile and little salute. "Have a better one."

The man turns his back and takes a step away toward *The Bean*. Ray should let him go. He almost does. He calls out instead.

"Where'd you hear the name Marlo?"

The man turns. Steps back into the puddle he'd just left.

"I'm an errand boy, Mr. Mackey." The lines on his face move like they have some role in making the sound come out of his mouth. "You want to learn something about Marlo, let me take you to the man who sent me out into the weather to bring you back."

"And how do I know this man knows anything at all about Marlo?"

"Because this man knows everything about everything, Detective. He's the biggest man of them all."

That gets the guy a couple of empty beats as he watches Ray's reaction. The lines around his mouth move. A smile stretches out in the silence.

"Bullshit," says Ray.

"You're not convinced." The man gives half a nod. "Let me show you a photo."

He switches umbrella hands, reaching into his coat pocket. Ray tenses, ready to reach for Sig. The man extracts a cellphone. Scrolls. Stiff arms it beneath Ray's umbrella so he can see.

He expects to see a face. A Big Man imposter. But it's not a Big Man imposter. It's not even a face. It's a Shell station, streaming water over the roof like a trawler in heavy seas.

Ray is confused. He thinks it must be the wrong photo. Then he sees the car. The blue Corolla with a sharp dent above the left rear, hooked up to the pump.

He jabs his hand into his coat and yanks Sig out into the weather.

"You're wasting time," says the man with that same sad tone.

"Shut it," says Ray, needing an extra hand. He drops the umbrella to the pavement so he can pull out his own phone. "And keep your hands out where I can see them."

He dials. Waits. Soaks in the rain, heart hammering in his battered chest. One ring. Two. *Come on*, he thinks, willing her to pick up. *Come on.*

The voice lacks Doris' feminine lilt. It's old. Soft with phlegm.

"Ray," says the voice. "Good to talk to you. At last, right? Like we've known each other for years."

The man in front of him extends his own umbrella over Ray's head. Ray tightens his grip on Sig. He pushes it out at the man's chest.

"Who is this?"

The voice coughs. A smoker.

"Come on. You want to know about Marlo? I'm good for whatever you want to know. But I'm not waiting all day. Understand what I'm telling you, Ray? You don't have long."

ONE HUNDRED FIVE

We walk under our umbrellas, shoulder to shoulder, like a couple of old classmates seeing the sights. I keep a grip on Sig, stuffed down into my coat pocket, but ready for anything. My new friend doesn't seem to care much.

He wasn't lying about the ride. He's got a good spot just off Randolph. Dirty white Tacoma with an oval CHI sticker on the back window. I think about memorizing the plate number but then decide I don't care enough. He collapses his umbrella and tosses it in the bed. I do the same and climb in.

"Seatbelt," he says to me with a wink. "It'll ding us to death."

I let go of Sig and strap in. The twisting sets off an inferno of pain in my chest. The guy next to me pretends not to notice. He fires up the truck and off we go. The rain comes down harder, like it wants inside to get out of the weather.

I ask him about his boss and how being a criminal conspirator is working out for him. He wants to talk about the rain. Last time we got this much rain. How long it will take to dry out from all the rain. What all the rain does to the ball fields.

I opt for silence and try to figure out where we're going. The possibilities narrow as we ride. We muddle through town to the 90, then head east. He blows past Chinatown and keeps at it.

Then I get it. Really not that mysterious when I think about it. I know exactly where we're going.

No surprise that all the ragged potholes of 107th Street are right where I left them. Same with the hole-in-the-wall Chinese joint where, once upon a time, Frenchie Marie offered me a plate of Kung Pao and a story about Amanda Ramada Tate and her boyfriend Orland Twill. Should have known this is where I'd end up. Full circle.

The street looks worse during the day. So does the restaurant. Same Chinese characters that I can't translate. Same dirty-curtained sidewalk windows. But the flickering neon is dark and dead. Something about the gloom at night that really brought the place to life and made you want to go inside at gunpoint. My escort gives me a genial nod.

"This is where we part company," he says. "I hate Chinese."

I open the door and step out into the rain to look around. Just up the street is a gleaming black Navigator, tinted windows streaked with rain. I imagine Carter Duffy at the wheel making a phone call to someone inside the restaurant. *They're here*, he's saying. Right on cue, the door to the restaurant pushes open. I close the door to the Tacoma and step across the sidewalk. In I go.

The door closes hard behind me. I'm dizzy at the smell of leftovers.

"What happened to the mask?" I ask.

Little Eddie Little isn't in a talking mood. He makes me turn around in the entryway and pushes me up against the door, jabbing a Beretta into my spine for the pat down. He finds Sig and the Glock and keeps going, worried that I'm strapped down to my ankles. When he's satisfied, he spins me back around. The sudden torque hurts so much that I groan.

"Still hurts I guess," says Eddie without a smile.

Rage, instant and hot, filling me like I'm a driver's side airbag. I want to grab his neck and ram his face into the glass-framed menu on the wall. I don't. I can't. I smile instead.

"Just the rain," I say. "Brings out the arthritis. You'll see one day, Eddie. Unless you run out of birthdays early."

Eddie blanches a little at the sound of his own name. Then he nods and steps aside, gesturing me past him into the restaurant. I take the hint as he turns the key in the lock behind me.

The place looks and sounds exactly like a closed Chinese restaurant. No hissing from the kitchen. No silky, pajama-clad hostess. The dragon-emblazed podium and front counter, dark and empty. The plastic pagoda fountain, dry. Window light only, nothing electric. No breathy flute or plinky, contemplative music. Just the sound of an old man, somewhere yet unseen, clearing his throat. Eddie Little gives me a nudge.

At the back of the dining room, up against a water-stained wall, are three red vinyl banquettes. Rectangular tables. Red tablecloths. Glass tops. In the middle banquette sits Doris, looking disheveled and frightened in her raincoat, blue to match her eyes and her dented Carolla, with a long smear beneath her nose, red to match the tablecloth.

Next to her – right next to her, shoulder to shoulder – is Alexi Novak. Stoli. His raincoat is draped over the back of the banquette. He's in a navy sport coat and a dark tie. I'm guessing the mayor's office has a dress code. His hair is a short silvery white. I remember from the photographs on his mother's etagere what he looked like as a child. Cute kid. That was before all the murdering. All the Big

Man mayhem. Before he and the man called Hell showed up in my living room and started all my chainsaw nightmares. He's not so cute anymore.

Alexi gives me a little wave with his gun hand. I can't tell from here what he's holding but I'm guessing it gets the job done.

My eyes find Doris' eyes, wide and wild like a couple of savage blue animals. I try to impart calm. *Everything will be okay.* She knows better. I have to tear my gaze away. It crosses a small sea of empty square tables to a lone square table at the window, squatting in the dingy shade of a dingy curtain.

The man is not as big as I had always imagined. He's looking at me. Cigarette in his mouth. Black raincoat on and open. The raincoat is dry. He's been waiting a bit.

"Raymond," says Victor Roby. "Sit, sit. Rest your bones."

ONE HUNDRED SIX

"Drink?" asks Victor, taking a drag. He owns a couple hundred gray hairs clinging for dear life to a white, mottled scalp. Large nose. Couple of dark eyes that look like they've seen a thing or two, sizing me up from beneath a heavy, protrudent brow. He cocks a furry gray caterpillar. "Water? Green tea?"

In my mind, the little square table beneath the half-curtained window has become the large round table in the folded paper photo. The table in the hotel ballroom celebrating Sam Royce's first big win. Only it's like everyone else has excused themselves and walked out of that photo. Royce. Rickens. Marlo. Just Victor now. Looking up, facing me. I want to smash his face with a bat. I don't have a bat.

"Trying to cut back on the green tea," I say on cautious approach.

Victor reaches down into his pocket and extracts a pack of Camels and a red plastic lighter. Puts them on the table. Slides them across with a liver-spotted hand. He's got a gold ring the size of a small football. Same hand that was on Marlo's hand. I want to grab that hand and …

"What's this? My last meal?"

"Never know," says Victor. "Sit already."

I sit. Push the Camels aside. Hands on the table, I tip my head sideways toward the awkward couple in the booth on the other side of the restaurant.

"I'm here. Okay? You don't need her. Let her go. Tell her I'm a dead man if she calls anyone. She won't risk it. Just let her leave."

Victor smokes.

"You're a hard man to control, Ray," he says. "She helps with that."

I open my mouth to make another pitch, but Victor isn't having it. He holds up his cigarette hand with a slight shake of his head and something like a smile.

"No," he says. "She stays."

He retracts the hand back to his face. Another drag. He lets it go, smoke climbing the curtain to the window above like it wants out. He settles back into his chair.

"Now. Marlo Kline Mackey. Dearly departed. How can she rest in peace, Ray, if you keep rattling her memory?"

I don't know how to respond to that, so I don't. A small, ornately carved mirror on the wall in front of me catches Eddie Little in the reflection. He's sitting on the stool at the hostess station in front of the door, Baretta on the counter, scrolling through his phone.

To my right, all the way in the back shadows, Alexi clears his throat. I look and wish I hadn't. The sight of Doris, transfixed in a state of terror, threatens to rattle me off my game. Something I can't afford. She can't afford it either.

I turn away, wondering how Stretch and Santiago are making out. I was too late on Eddie Little's APB. I needed it yesterday. I kick myself for not finding Amanda's note earlier. All I had to do was open a file and an envelope. I look down, realizing my hand had found the lighter on its own, turning it end over end in my palm like a talisman.

"I understand," Victor says, stabbing the butt into the windowsill, "that there are things you want to know. So. Here I sit."

"Did she work for you?" I ask.

"Did she work for me?" Victor spreads all five fingers over his chest. "For me? No."

"For your organization."

"For my organization," he repeats contemplatively.

I'm full up on bullshit. I drop the lighter and reach down into a pocket like something inside is biting me. Across the room I can feel Alexi come to attention. Tensing. Ready to stand on his something less than two legs and take aim. I pull out the folded page and open up the photograph, slapping it on the table.

"For Sam Royce," I say. "Back in the day."

Victor picks up the photo with a wistful smile. A long, deep sigh.

"Where has the time gone?"

"Did she work for you?"

He gives it a beat or two, not in a hurry to answer.

"Complicated question." His eyes keep their nostalgic glaze. Remembering. "I miss Marlo. She was … I do miss her."

"Yeah, well she hated you."

Victor puckers. Nods.

"Eventually. Maybe. I like to think I had the respect of a worthy adversary. Less about actual hate and more about Marlo never liking to lose. She was something."

We stare at each other, listening to the rain slide down the window. I wait. A spray of traffic. Nothing comes.

"You going to make me ask every question here, Victor?"

He smiles, sniffing out a laugh. I cut a quick glance toward Doris. Alexi's gun is spinning quietly on the glass.

"Let me tell you a story."

"I'm listening."

"Good." He reaches for the Camels and lights another one up. Looks at me through the haze. Holds out the pack. "I don't like smoking alone."

I shake one out and set the thing on fire. Dr. Jha is in my head with his John Lennon glasses and his rubbery accent and his little pointing stick and my x-rays. I set him on fire too. The nicotine burns like hot honey. My last cigarette, I think. I want to close my eyes. I don't.

"Young man," says Victor, "who worked for our organization. Tom Collins. Good lookin' kid."

"Tom Collins," I say, blowing smoke. "You people should have gone with snack food names. Pretzel and Corn Nut. It's enough to put me off the booze for good."

Victor smiles. "We call you Old Forester."

"Yeah, well I don't work for you."

A shrug.

"We both know that hasn't been true. But maybe it helps you to say it. Anyway. Tom Collins. Everyone called him Gimlet, just because he hated it. Smart. Talented. But lost. Confused. Fucked up. I'll just say it. Kid was a mess. Wife, two years in the ground from a hit and run. Gimlet needed some structure. Someone in his life who a gave a shit. He gets himself recruited. Wanted to be a numbers guy. The organization needs a good numbers guy. So he gets to work on the books. Investments, taxes, capital portfolios, the works. Under close control, you understand. He's young. He's learning. Our other numbers guys are watching him like a bunch of hawks. Ready to tear his throat out at the first sign. Once you see our books, you either perform or you die. Understand? But Gimlet was good. Impresses every fuckin' body. Best numbers guy we've ever had." Victor's hand arcs up over the table. "Rises like a fucking comet."

Smoke. His and mine, holding the light together.

"Fast forward. Five years. Six. New Year's Eve at one of the usual hangs. Lots of us. Lots of clients. Lots of women. Understand? That's how we did things back then. Now we're more careful. Smarter. But back in the day?" Victor shakes his head, answering his own question. "So, Gimlet ends up sharing a drink with a five-alarm fire named June. Beautiful girl, this kid. Sandy brown hair. Thousand-watt smile. Legs that go all the way to the floor. You with me?"

Victor looks at me like he wants some kind of affirmation among red-blooded men. I don't give him any.

"June could've knocked poor Gimlet over with a pinky finger. The kid falls hard. They get involved. Can't keep their hands off each other. Risky, because she's a company asset. She belongs to the organization. Okay? That's the way it works. But they're both so goddamned sweet everybody kind of lets it slide, you know? Even Hardcore pretended not to see, and Hardcore was responsible for managing June's time and talent, so ..."

"What, pimps and hookers don't get drink names?"

Victor waves the question away like so much smoke.

"There's a whole protocol. Don't worry yourself. Point is, they're so adorable that even Hardcore lets it go. Then one day, June up and disappears. Gone. Poof. Everybody waits. She doesn't show. That left a June-shaped hole on Hardcore's balance sheet. She was an earner."

Victor looks at the Camel, flicking away the ash.

"Gimlet gets pressed to within an inch of his life. I mean Hardcore really rattles the kid's cage, looking for his bread and butter. But Gimlet knows fuck all about it. Zip. No fucking idea. Better: he's upset. Out late every night, scouring all the corners looking for her. He's a numbers guy, not a corners guy. But he's out there anyway. Desperate. He gets up in Hardcore's face demanding he go out and rattle all the Johns to get some answers." Victor laughs. Points. "Gimlet even wants to go to *you people*, the cops, and do a missing persons thing. Can you imagine? Anyway. No luck. June stays missing and the world keeps turning."

"I'm getting old here, Victor," I say, trying my best to sell what I can't.

"In a hurry to die, are you? Listen, I was the first one here, okay? Waitin' on everybody else. Sittin' at this fuckin' table looking out the window waiting for them to bring in the blonde bait and for you to make up your fucking mind. Show some fucking respect."

Victor stares at me, anger just beneath the surface, not blinking. I smoke and keep my face the way I like it. Across the room, I can feel Doris' heart hammering its way out of her chest. I wait. Victor dials it back.

"Okay. Here's the thing. Turns out Gimlet's talents were not limited to numbers. Kid knew how to lie like nobody's business. You don't fuck with Hardcore when he's having a bad day. There's half a graveyard can tell you that. But Gimlet? Kid never flinched. I figure it was the love that made him so goddamn credible. He knew exactly where June was the whole time. Holed up in Knox

County eatin' for two, is where she was. Galesburg. Gimlet was the one who got her out. Put her up. Supported her. Love made that punk fucking fearless."

"Eating for two. So it's his kid?"

"Nah. Some John's. But at first Gimlet thought it was his bun in the oven. That got him going. I don't think he completely trusted that June wasn't lying. Lying to him. Lying to herself. She couldn't have known for sure either. She was on the fence about what to do. Does she? Doesn't she? The ol' fetus deletus is a lot easier if it's not Gimlet's kid."

Victor smokes. I look away, taking inventory. Eddie in the mirror, still on the stool, squinting, unpinching his fingers to enlarge something on his phone. Alexi, both hands on the table, turning his gun in slow circles on the glass. Doris, sniffing, one hand up, wiping her eye.

"She's fine," says Victor. "You worry too much, Ray. Nothing happens to anybody until I'm done talking. You want me to stop?"

I fill my lungs again, feeling my ribs. I show him my palms.

"Good," he says. "Real choice for June was what to do next, once her close brush with motherhood had passed. Go back to work for Hardcore – beg, plead for forgiveness, take a beating, all that crap – or keep running. Well, turned out she was done with the life. She wants to keep running. Disappear. Start up her own nail salon in Toronto. And Gimlet, that stupid lying love-struck fuck, he decides that sounds like a great fuckin' idea to him. They'll disappear together. Just as soon as he figures out how he can finance the transition from numbers guy to boyfriend on the run and cut himself loose. Okay? Great with numbers, dumb as a fucking tree stump that kid.

"Money was the problem. Ain't it always. Gimlet comes back to the hive, like nothing in his life is different. He cooks our books and takes what he's due. Every two, three days he's back out to fuckin' Galesburg to pay the bills. And he keeps it up like that, back and forth, back and forth, like nobody is gonna start scratchin' their head about it. He makes it a whole year. Can you believe that? A fuckin' year."

Victor smokes. I watch him, the guy Marlo tried to put away, the guy who covered Marlo's hand with his own. I want a Louisville Slugger for his head more than ever. Still no bats around.

"Well," he says. "Long story short, somewhere around month ten or eleven, the little hairs on the back of Hardcore's thick black neck start to stand up. He puts a tail on Gimlet. One trip is all it takes. There's June, sucking down gin fizzies in a crappy hotel bar. She lasted about another three weeks. Then she really disappeared. For good. Hardcore made it hurt."

"And Gimlet?"

"If Hardcore'd had his way…" Victor shakes his head. Then he smiles. "But Hardcore did not have his way. He never asked permission to do June the way he did. He paid a price. And he did not get to have his way with Gimlet. Why, you ask." Victor leans forward, elbow on the table, Camel coiling smoke. "Because ours is a merciful organization, Detective. We believe in second chances. And smart decision-making. Gimlet stayed in the harness. He worked our numbers like his life depended on it. Because it did. And that decision, that bit of mercy, has saved us a lot of money over the years."

"Marlo," I say, her name in a floating blue cloud, suspended in the smokey light. "What does any of this have to do with Marlo?"

"I'm telling you this story, Ray, because I told the same story to your future wife the last time I saw her. Long time ago. Well. Not the last time I saw her. Last time I saw her she was outside my house with a camera the size of a canon taking pictures of me for the prosecution. Trying to send me up the river for arson. You know that whole thing?"

It's not actually a question. I nod anyway. It gets me a smile.

"I know you do, because I saw you too. Riding shotgun. Keeping your wife company like a good husband should. Take your husband to work day. Anyway. Last time I actually *talked* to Marlo was years before. That's when I told her the story. We were having lunch together at Jimmy Flat's. You know the place? Flat's Deli? On Van Buren by the park? Gone for ten fucking years now and I still miss it. Best corned beef in the city. Anyway, it's just the two of us. Me and Marlo …" He stops. Finger in the air. Smile on his smash-worthy face. "Only she wasn't Marlo back then." Eyebrows up. "She was Mattia Lewis, ace reporter for the *Trib*. Okay? Okay. So it's me and make believe Tia talking over a beer and couple of sandwiches you could kill for. She's pushing me for details about Sam Royce. Like always. What he's like as a candidate for the 42nd … what he might do as an alderman … his relationship with the unions, the police, blah, blah, that kind of thing just like normal. Okay?"

He wants to make sure I'm keeping up. It's a silly concern. I feel like I'm at the table with them, corned beef untouched, looking for Marlo's eyes. I smoke and wait.

"Okay," he says. "So she tells me this rumor she's heard. Rumor was, get this, rumor was that poor, dearly departed dumbfuck Lucky Lucas had a secret daughter. Okay? And that before Lucky took a swan dive onto the pier, he was getting squeezed. Rumor was, she says, that Sam Royce was doing the squeezing.

Rumor was that Lucky wouldn't play ball and ended up with some fingerprints on his back."

Victor pulls the pack of Camels his way like maybe he wants to light up a second stick before he's done with the one in his hand. He pokes his finger around in the pack. Smokes the one he's got. Slides the pack back to my side of the table.

"So Marlo … Tia … wants to know if I have any comment about this rumor. I tell her I know shit about any of it. Told her Lucky dying was a loss to the whole city. He was the fucking king of the 42nd Ward, that guy. A legend. Sam thought the same thing. A legend. A lost legend. First thing Sam did once he got elected was to pressure the city into a proclamation and a fountain honoring Lucky fuckin' Lucas."

"Come on," I say. "Payback for an endorsement by the grieving widow. Marlo work that one for you?"

"Oh." That smile again. His uppers are as real as dime store pearls. I'd like to knock them down his throat. "Someone's been doing his homework. Okay, you got me. Backscratching in politics. We're all shocked, I know. Still. Sam didn't have to do anything for the widow Lucas. He was in. He won. He was broken up about Lucky. He did a good thing by Francine."

I want to argue the point. Victor has his hand in the air.

"Don't get lost in the weeds, Ray. Marlo-Tia wants to know if I thought the story of Lucky having a secret kid was true. I told her fuck if I knew. But that reminded me of Gimlet and Lucy and so I told her that whole story that I just told you. Well. Same basic story. Told her I was reading a book about a bunch of wise guys. Far as she knew I was just a political campaign manager who liked mob stories. Anyway, I told her the story and you know what she asks me?"

"How could I?"

"Because she asked the same question you are now. She asked what any of it had to do with Lucky Lucas, just like you're asking what any of it has to do with Marlo. She didn't see the relevance, is what I'm sayin'."

"What'd you tell her?"

"That she'd have to figure that out on her own. She never did." Victor smokes, sizing me up in a narrowed-eyed silence. "I wonder if you'll do any better."

"Look. Victor. My whole body hurts. I'm full up on riddles. I want some answers and then I want to put this behind me. I want to take my friend and go and never look back."

"Just like that," he says with a disbelieving smile.

"Just like that."

"Okay," he says. "I like a man with purpose. Fire away."

"What'd she do for you? No bullshit. Give me the worst."

"The worst? What are you afraid of, Detective? You worried you didn't know who you married? That she falsified her resume when she applied for the job of beloved? God forbid she once consorted with bad people. Helped them do bad things." Victor raises both hands in mock alarm. "God fuckin' forbid. You ever tell her you had a cheating heart?"

"Fuck you."

"Fuck me? Shame on you, Raymond. You think anything I could tell you today about Marlo changes who she really was to you? What kind of fucked up betrayal is that? Fucking someone else? Adultery? Bad enough. That's one thing. But turning your back on what she gave to you, and only to you? Allowing *me* to tell you whether what she gave of herself was good enough? Was genuine? Allowing *me* to tell you that? Shame on you. I'm no boy scout, okay? Hand to God, I've done a lot to be sorry for. But I've never done that. My wife? God rest her soul, what she gave to me in the short time I had her? I'll take that to the grave, and I could give a fuck what she did before she met me. Shame on you."

The insult is as hard and brutal as any fist, landing in my chest amid all the other fractured bones. All the worse for its sincerity. Its truth. All I can do is stare at him. He splits the curtain with a finger. Looks out the window. Smokes. Looks back. Shrugs.

"She covered the campaign. Interviewed everybody. Went to the rallies. Promised us a piece in the *Trib* and then failed to deliver. Well. She delivered late. Post-election. Great piece, but totally useless. We didn't care because we won anyway."

"And that's it?"

Victor makes a face. Looks at his Camel.

"She also cozied up to the other campaigns. It was a fuckin' dog fight, that race. She wanted to stay tight with us, so she opened the lid a little, let us know what was doing with the other campaigns. Especially Bubba Jones."

"She spied for you."

"Spied. Come on. We talked. She'd, you know, share. Didn't amount to much."

"She came to you as Tia Lewis?"

"Yeah."

"And you knew that was a cover?"

"Of course."

"How?"

Victor stubs out his second, only half spent. Opens his hands.

"Good campaign manager makes it his business to know."

"Why'd you think she was there?"

"She was investigating. It's what detectives do."

"Investigating what?"

"How Lucky Lucas stopped breathing."

"And you didn't bust her? Throw her out?"

"No. I brought her in. Got a great late article out of her. She was something."

"And the candidate was aware?"

"The candidate doesn't have to know everything. Better that he doesn't."

"Right. The rumors that Lucky had a secret daughter: Marlo ever say where those rumors came from?"

"Did *she* tell me where they came from? No."

"Do you *know* where they came from?"

"Yeah. They came from me."

"You?"

"Me. Yours fucking truly. You hard of hearing or understanding?"

"Understanding." I mash my Camel into the sill. "What are you saying?"

"I'm saying I knew who she was, but she didn't know who I was."

"She didn't know Big Man was serving as the campaign manager for an upstart politician?"

Victor laughs. The sound detours into a phlegmy cough before becoming a laugh again. He grabs the pack of Camels. Sticks his finger into the hole. Sets the pack down again.

"Well, who would ever think that?" he asks.

"You tipped Marlo off about Lucky's kid. You drew her in."

"You think I knew she'd show up playing reporter? Come on."

"Then why?"

"I thought she needed to know. What she did with the information was … well. It was unexpected."

"Then where'd *you* learn Lucky's secret?"

"Some kid we pinched from Bubba's camp." Victor makes a face. "Pinched. He left Bubba and came over to Sam. No one was really in the race back then. There was no race. No campaigns. It was still Lucky's seat and he was probably going to go again and everybody else was expecting to keep their day jobs for another term."

Victor knocks out another Camel and offers me the pack.

"You trying to kill me?" I ask. He puts the pack on the table and slides it my way.

"Anyway, this kid had some relationship with Bubba and picked up this tidbit that Lucky had a secret. He parts company with Bubba and walks the tidbit over to Sam Royce. Everyone knew Sam wanted Lucky's seat. The kid was shopping for a job with the next alderman, whoever that was going to be. But Sam was as pure as the driven fucking snow back then. He wants nothing to do with it. He sends the kid packing. I forget his name."

"Blake Wilhaven," I say. Victor snaps his fingers. Points.

"That's it. He ended up with some other campaign, I think."

"He ended up in his car with a bullet in his head."

"That's right. Yeah. Drugs or something. This fuckin' city."

"You've been puppeteering Royce from the very beginning. Grooming him. That much I get. And I'm willing to bet you had a hand in bumping Lucky off that boat to clear the way for Royce's future. Makes sense. What I don't get is why you clued in Marlo."

"Seems a stupid move to you."

"Yeah."

Victor smokes. Looks over the top of the dirty curtain, out the window at the rain. Shrugs.

"It was stupid," he says. "Selfish. I was enamored with the poetry of it all. I wasn't thinking about the risk."

"The risk?"

"Yeah," he says. "That scared me a little. I could have given her a lot. But once she actually showed up? Like, standing there in the fucking doorway with a bullshit name and a bullshit business card? I changed my mind on the spot. Gave her nothing. Too much risk."

"The risk to Royce or to you? Your criminal empire."

"The risk to her," he says taking a steep drag, then emptying his lungs. "The risk to Marlo."

"I still don't understand."

"Of course you don't. And I still don't like smoking alone."

Victor picks up the pack of Camels. Holds it out. I take it and knock out a cigarette. Only it's not a cigarette. It's a rolled-up piece of paper. I take it down to my lap and unroll it. The penmanship is messy, but I can read it.

Taped up against the table. Easy does it.

I put the slip in my pocket. I pull out a Camel and put it where it belongs. I lean in. Victor gives me a light as I brush the fingertips of my right hand along the underside of the table. I know a Glock 9 when I feel one.

"Why?" I ask. Victor shrugs.

"I'm eighty-two. Lucky I made it this far." He tips his head across the restaurant. "You're not the only one on their to-do list."

"Aren't you the boss?"

"What gave you that idea?"

"Everything. The guy who brought me said you're the biggest man there is."

"Got you in the car, didn't it?"

Victor watches me slog through everything he's told me. Reweighing all of it. He smiles a little.

"Something on your mind?"

"Yeah," I say. "Gimlet and June. Let me ask you something."

"Shoot."

"How do you know the kid really went out with the trash?"

Victor nods a little, puckering his lips.

"You're maybe not so dumb after all."

ONE HUNDRED SEVEN

Ray smokes as he asks his questions. Leaning back in the chair, legs crossed. He's trying to affect a casual look. You'd never know the fervent work going on under the table, above the hem of the tablecloth. Fervent and careful. Wouldn't want the hardware clattering to the floor.

His attention is too divided to be safe. The gun strapped up under the table, slowly peeling away the duct tape corners with his thumb and forefinger as his ribs scream at him about his posture. Doris and Alexi in the back booth, Ray wanting to look, wanting to reassure her somehow, not liking the feeling of her so afraid, forcing himself to block her out. Little Eddie Little, no longer on the stool, no longer in the mirror, now somewhere generally behind him, pacing. Add to that a splitting headache, working a cigarette and playing twenty questions with Victor Roby. It's too much all at once. Concentrating on everything means he's not really concentrating enough on anything. Certainly not any kind of plan.

Between them sits the photo of Marlo and Victor and all the others at the Sam's-the-man banquet table. Victor absently rotates the photo with two fingers as he talks, smoking and telling back-in-the-day stories that Ray has to decode while he does everything else.

The photo stops turning. Victor keeps talking. He taps the man in the crowd, off to the side, drinking his champagne like he's playing a sax. Ray looks at Victor. Nods. The photo resumes its lazy spin.

He should have taken off his coat. He's too hot. Or maybe it's just too much bottled up adrenaline. Either way his hand is sweaty. His fingers keep losing the tape and he has to find the right corner all over again. The tape gives way when he is not suspecting, pulling away under the weight, separating from the table. He loses contact, the Glock swinging free like a metal flap on a hinge, banging against his hand. He's got a second and change, maybe less, before the whole thing drops. Victor's monologue hitches on the drama he can see rapidly unfolding in Ray's widening eyes.

It's a blind, panicked grab. Ray catches the piece by the tip of the barrel and a flange of tape. A long blink tells Victor all he needs to know.

"You okay, Detective? You seem …"

"I'm good," says Ray, stripping tape from metal.

"Probably time to wrap up. You look tired. You need some rest. Know what you should do maybe?" Victor takes a last pull on the Camel. Stubs it out against the wall and leaves it on the sill. He looks at Ray. "Don't go back to work. Don't go home." He nods in Doris' direction. "Take your friend over there to some hotel. Do what comes natural. You should try The Bradford in Old Town. Great place. I been there. Nice beds. Top floor has a great view of Lincoln Park. About a block away from the Chicago History Museum. Stay a couple of days. Go read up on Al Capone. Don't tell your boss." Victor looks at his watch, then back. "Think about it, Raymond. That could be happening right now. Very soon anyway."

Ray's gears are spinning so fast they're stripping. The translation snaps into place, word and meaning colliding like a couple of taxis around a blind corner. He thinks about his phone. No one took his phone. His beleaguered brain thinks it can make out the shape of it in the inside pocket of his suitcoat. He wants the phone. Victor is still saying words at his face. They're all meaningless now.

"Barrister's Ball might have been fun if it weren't so late in the month. Ever been to that? Down at the Wharf? Entertainment is always top notch, but you have to like lawyers and really bad food. That's already come and gone though. Next year maybe. You okay, Ray? You seem, I don't know, like you need some sleep."

"The Bradford," says Ray softly, thinking, not seeing.

"Yeah. That's right. Just a suggestion. Okay. Here's how this is gonna work, Detective." Victor's voice has some extra volume. "I'm gonna scoot on out of here. Let you and Blondie and the boys finish up. Okay? Good luck to you. Be sure to lock up when you leave. Any questions?"

Ray can feel Eddie Little over his right shoulder. Eddie's been waiting for the wrap-up. Indulging the conversation.

Across the room, Alexi is stutter-sliding out of the banquette, pulling Doris by the sleeve. The right leg with the heavy boot makes its first appearance from beneath the tablecloth. *Take off his legs* Alexi had said, handing off the chainsaw, as that same boot had mashed the weave of an oily burlap bag into Ray's bloody face.

Ray looks up at Victor, now in the process of standing, pushing up.

"Why?" he asks again. "And don't tell me it's because you're eighty-two. Why me?"

"Not about you, Ray. I don't care about you. No offense."

"Victor. Why? You know what I'm asking."

"Because love never fucking quits," he says. "Choke it. Drown it. Beat it bloody. Make it crawl through the shit for half a century. It just keeps on and on, like it's never been touched. It keeps on like you're worthy of it. Like you've never stopped being worthy."

He looks down at Ray hard, emotion barely contained, like a man with a lot more to say. But he keeps the last of it short.

"That, and because a Tom Collins is not a fucking gimlet."

"And Big Man?" Ray asks.

Victor drops his liver spotted hooks into the pockets of his raincoat.

"Maybe, Ray, you should consider that Big Man is neither."

"What? Neither?"

"See you 'round Ray." Victor may be eighty-two, but he moves like he's not a day older than eighty-one and a half. "I'll be in the car, boys," he says, shuffling out of sight. Ray can hear Eddie Little work the key in the lock. The door opens to the sound of rain. And then he's gone.

"Nice chat?" asks Alexi, pulling Doris alongside.

"Alexi," says Ray, exhaling, looking him up and down, trying to ignore the sight of Doris. Banishing Victor from his thoughts. "How's City Hall treating you?"

"Let's go," says Alexi. Eddie shuffles up along Doris' other side. They look down at him like he's a dog who's wet the floor.

"You two go on ahead," says Ray. "We'll catch a cab."

"A cab?" Alexi shakes his head. "No. There's a back room right here I want to show you. Nice and dry. Let's go."

Ray looks up at him, trying to think. Trying to find calm. The pain in his chest is waning. Then it's gone entirely. Nothing hurts now. His face. His neck. His head. Pain is a luxury for the living. It checks out whenever death enters the room.

"You know what Ivah told me, Alexi? Before you murdered her? She said you were a good boy. Better than your brother, Jovah. She loved you best of all. You made her proud, Alexi. Imagine that."

It's an act of desperation, invoking your killer's mother. Inviting her into his head as a witness. Clogs the gears a little. Slows the roll.

It's good for a moment of shock. A little anger in the eyes. Not much else. A little smile, maybe.

"You sound afraid, Ray," says Alexi. "You afraid? I've seen you afraid before. I've heard you cry and beg. I've seen you piss yourself. We going to do that again? In front of your girlfriend here?" Doris makes a sound as he squeezes her arm. Part whimper, part moan. "Maybe you should be a man this time."

"Okay." One last drag. Ray stubs out the butt, dropping it next to Victor's. "I've got a proposition for you. For both of you."

Alexi whisper laughs. Shakes his head. Ray keeps at it.

"We've got your phones. Houses. Cars. Both of you. Victor too, poor old schmuck. Feds have been on you for weeks. Point is, the rain out there is about to turn to shit. I'm the only one with an umbrella big enough to keep that suit clean."

Alexi laughs, looking past Doris at Eddie. He gives Doris a sideways push, handing her over, letting go of her right arm as Eddie squeezes her left. Alexi closes the distance. Sits in Victor's chair. Points the gun.

"They want Royce," says Ray, not flinching. Making bullshit promises like there's no tomorrow. There might not be. "They want Big Man. They'll cut any deal you offer. Full immunity. Relocation."

"We found Nadia," Alexi says quietly, just above a whisper. "San Francisco. And **Mila Kozlova**. The girl too. Danica. Cute kid. Not anymore. Sad. But it was quick. Painless. You know why? I'll tell you why, Ray. Because they never tried to bargain with bullshit. They never cried. They never pissed themselves. The woman and the girl took it like real men. Unlike you." He knocks out all three syllables softly against the table with the butt of the Glock. "Un … like … you. So you're not going to get the quick and painless version." He tilts his head sideways. "Neither is she."

The sound is sudden. Loud, piercing. As if Alexi's entire body is ringing. Or maybe it's just the adrenaline surging through Ray's body on an Indie 500 loop, no place to go, nothing to do except sharpen every sense; amplify every stimulus.

Still. It seems like he's ringing. Alexi must think so too, given the full-body jolt, the reflexive tightening of his grip on the Glock as he glances down at the pocket full of noise. He gets the phone halfway out. It's Ray's only chance. Everybody in the room knows it, consciously or not. Now or never.

He swats at the Glock, trying to angle away as it explodes at face level. Below the table Ray twitches his finger, firing blindly twice. Alexi rockets backward, tipping over onto the floor with a scream. The Glock goes with him, still firing.

Ray launches himself up from his chair, turning the table on top of the man, then following it down, left shoulder first so that he can pin Alexi and take away his aim. Makes sense. Problem is that Alexi is not Ray's biggest problem.

Eddie. The thought is a scream inside Ray's head as he smashes down on top of Alexi. *Doris.*

The scream in Ray's head is not the only scream he hears. Beneath him, Alexi is screaming.

Doris is screaming. Eddie is screaming.

Ray swings Victor's Glock toward the only two people left standing. The right side of Eddie's face is covered in blood, one hand around Doris' neck, trying to gain some purchase with the other. No Baretta in sight. Doris is flailing at him. Thrashing. Screaming. Ray shouts.

"Doris! Drop! Drop! Go heavy!"

And she does, unlocking her knees. Gravity pulls her free, slipping her out of Eddie's wet red hands. It's all Ray can do to stay on top of Alexi, still screaming, wriggling to get free of the table.

He keeps his focus. He's got a clear shot. He takes it.

Eddie spins away like a top, clutching his shoulder. The table beneath Ray tilts, rolling him sideways against the upturned legs, as Alexi's Glock emerges, firing blind, hoping for the best.

Alexi's hand. It's the only clear shot Ray has. He takes it.

ONE HUNDRED EIGHT

Hard to focus with all the screaming. Sounds like everybody is still alive. Good to know. My Triple-D kicks in, sharp and clear, like it's tapping a vein of adrenaline to give me an extra-sensory view of myself, sitting on the overturned table, Alexi flailing beneath me, sounds of agony from Doris' direction. The smell of violence fucking everywhere.

I scoot my way across the underside of the table, keeping my weight on Alexi. His hand is gushing, no longer holding the Glock. I reach. Grab up the bloody gun. Now I have two. I crane my head around behind me. I can't see her.

"Doris!"

"Ray! I'm here. Are you …"

"The gun. The gun. Get the gun, Doris. Where is it?"

"I have it," she says, crying now. "Jesus. Are you okay?"

I work on standing rather than answering. I feel old again. Everything hurts. My chest is broken. I'm finally off the table but I can't get off the floor. I push myself away, scooting backward on my butt towards Doris. She's standing, half red and sticky, holding Eddie's Baretta with two shaky hands, pointing it in the direction of the hostess podium. Eddie is propped up, breathing heavily, applying pressure to his shoulder. His right eye is missing, the socket is black, seeping mottled gore.

I keep scooting on the floor, one gun in each hand, until I have an angle on both Alexi, still half under the table, and Eddie at the podium. At Doris' blood-spattered shoe is a white ballpoint pen with gold lettering. *Chicago Tour* is all I can make out. The rest is a red mess.

"Are you injured?" I ask.

"No. My neck hurts, but …"

"Okay." I nod Eddie's direction. "Get on the other side of him. All the way to the far wall. Steer a wide berth. Keep the gun pointed."

"Why? What am I doing?"

"If he shoots at me, I want you to put him down. Understand?"

"But I've got his gun," she whispers. I whisper back.

"He's still got the two guns he took off of me when I showed up."

Doris starts to shake. Her neck, arm, hair and hands are covered in Eddie's blood. The moment has caught up with her. She's overloading. She wants out of her own body. I go loud and stern.

"Doris!"

She jolts. Nods. Starts across the restaurant. Slow at first, then almost a run. Eddie's got one eye closed and the other eye missing in action. I wait until she's in position against the wall.

"Edward," I say in a loud voice, still keeping part of my focus and one gun on Alexi who hasn't stopped whimpering. "I know you can hear me. I want you to slide both guns out into the middle of the room. Do that and I'll get you something to staunch the bleeding. If I have to shoot you again to get your attention, you better believe I'll do it."

I give him thirty seconds. His eye stays closed. He breathes in and out, shallow and ragged. Nothing else. I pull the trigger, putting a bullet in the top of the podium. Eddie jerks to life, good eye popping open. Doris twitches too, gun shaking. Eddie's luckier than he knows. He reaches a hand behind his back.

"Easy does it, Ed," I say.

First comes the Glock. Then Sig, spinning to a stop in the middle of the room. Eddie closes his eye again. Back to his breathing exercises.

"And your phone," I say. "Wouldn't want you making any calls. Let's go."

He reaches into his pocket. Throws his phone. It clatters away under a table. I gesture for Doris and point at the guns.

"Bring those. Add yours to the pile. Then go to the kitchen and see if you can find a couple of clean rags or towels."

"You were serious?" Incredulous. Offended. "I say let him fucking suffer."

"Ever spent life in prison, Doris? Eddie's a cop. It's not going to be pretty. Death is better. Go."

To my right, Alexi finds whatever it takes to slide himself out from under the table. He's got one good hand clutching the pulpy mess that used to be his left knee. The other hand isn't so good anymore. The bleeding is bad. Doris is halfway to the kitchen.

"Doris." She turns. I'm working on my shoelaces. "I need a cord or a cable or a rope."

She's back in under a minute. She throws two towels angrily at Eddie's face and brings me an electrical cord.

"I had to chop it off the back of a blender."

"It'll do." I hand her one of the shoelaces and point at Eddie who has wadded up one towel against his shoulder and the other against his eye. "Ankles only. Tie the tightest knots you can. Make it hurt."

"Are you okay, Ray?"

"First things first. Get busy."

I swap the Glock into the pile of hardware and reclaim Sig, keeping Doris covered as she kneels carefully at Eddie's feet. She works fast. The man's in shock. Whatever he apprehends with his one eye, he's more focused on breathing and plugging the hole in his shoulder.

Once Doris is clear I scoot my way over to Alexi. Between here and there is his phone, upside down on the floor. I slip it into a pocket and keep scooting. I pull up alongside and have a look at the knee. It used to be the thing that made his longest leg bend. Not anymore. Not ever again. I thread the electrical cord around his thigh and pull it tight. Everything moves. He screams in pain. Then I use the second shoelace to tie off his arm above his bleeding hand. More screaming.

"You're not crying, are you, Stoli? What would Ivah say?" I place the ends of the electrical cord into his sticky good hand. "Twist. Keep it tight. Unless you want to bleed out, in which case, be my guest. And you've got a new nickname by the way. Everyone calls you Plug, now. It's got nothing to do with that electrical cord."

I push against my laceless shoes, sliding back across the floor to the collection of guns. The pain in my chest is excruciating. Doris is at my side on her hands and knees.

"What can I do?"

I ignore the question, rummaging through my pockets for my phone. Santiago picks up on the first ring, speaking before I can make a sound.

"Mack. Stretch and I are headed out to Edward Little's place. Warrant in hand. We …"

"Stop talking, Raffi. Pull over. Put me on speaker."

"Pull over?"

"Do it."

It takes a minute. "Okay. What."

"Twill is hiding out at the Bradford Hotel while he is negotiating with CPD. Top floor. I don't know the room. Big Man is going to take him out. Could be happening now. If not now, it's imminent. They won't kill him there, but they're coming to take him someplace quiet. I don't know who to trust at CPD. Call Nick Yarborough. Tell him to send as many windbreakers as he can spare. Get LT out of there right now. Call Ernie Davidson. Tell him to get in touch with his client. Let him know what's happening."

"Where are …" starts Raffi. Stretch cuts him off.

"On it," says Stretch. I hear the siren cut on as Stretch barks orders. "Turn around. The Bradford's in Old Town. Go, go. Punch it. Mack? Still there?"

"Next," I say. "I'm having Chinese with Alexi Novak and Eddie Little. They're both losing their appetite fast. It's a little hole-in-the-wall on 107th just south of Delaware. I need a couple of ambulances. Make that three ambulances. I also need a full back up. There's a black Navigator parked up the street. Carter Duffy is behind the wheel. Unless he took off when all the shooting started, he's on his way in to see who's still breathing."

"Mack, are you hurt? Are you okay?"

"I've been better, Raffi. Gotta go."

I cut the call and unfold myself, dropping my shoulders to the floor. Going down hurts. I hear my own scream in my head, I just don't know if it made it out of my mouth. I don't want to move. The Triple-D kicks in again. I look dead, sprawled like this. Gun hand out to the side by my hip. I can't tell if this is me looking down from the perspective of a stress-aggravated dissociative disorder, or if this is me looking down as I climb the ladder up into the Big Dream, ready to leave everything behind. Heart punctured by a fractured rib. Bleeding internally like nobody's business. I can't tell if I'm watching or dying.

Doris is a one-woman swarm.

"Mack. Oh God. What's happening? Is it your heart? What can I do?"

"Take four tables," I say like I'm talking to the ceiling. "Turn them on edge. Arrange them in a semicircle. Then prop me up so I can aim."

"Let's just hide in the kitchen."

"I can't move. And I'm not about to let these assholes out of my sight. Can you do that?"

Doris chokes back a sob. Nods. Gets to work.

"I was halfway to Springfield," she says. "They got me at a fucking Shell station."

"I saw the photo," I say.

"I'm so sorry."

"Apologize again and I'll shoot you myself. This is all on me, Doris. I'll be apologizing to you for the rest of my life, however long that turns out to be. Maybe another ten minutes."

"I should have …"

"Stop. Nothing you could do. You sure as hell know how to work a pen is all I can say."

"It was all I had. Either that or a paperclip or a hair scrunchie," she says, dragging the second table into position. Then she stops. Looks at me. "That phone rang, Mack, and I just … I saw you moving and it was like … now or never."

Makes me wonder. I fish around for Alexi's phone. I tap the screen and hand it up to her.

"Do me a favor. Hold this in front of shitbird's face over there and bring it back."

It takes a couple of tries, Alexi screaming up at her, contorting his face, but she gets there. She hands it back, phone now open, and starts working on table number three. I open up the call list on Alexi's phone and find the most recent call.

And there it is. Funny how surprised we can be at the things we already know. I can't help but laugh.

"What?" Doris pauses. "What could possibly be funny?"

"Nothing." It's suddenly the best I've felt in weeks.

Doris pulls the last table into place. She helps me up off my back, slowly pulling me up by the shoulders. I hook my arm over the edge of a table. I grab up Sig off the floor and check the magazine.

"What now?" she asks.

I grab a Glock from the pile and rack a fresh round into the chamber. Hand it to her.

"Get down here with me on the floor. Back-to-back. Keep as low as you can. You cover the front door. I'll cover everything behind the kitchen." I wait until she's down on the floor with me. I look into those oceanic eyes like I'm cliff diving. "Breathe before you shoot. He makes a big target. Aim for the chest, sweetheart."

ONE HUNDRED NINE

"They pulled the fire alarm. People everywhere. Herding out into the rain."

Stretch Martin's scar is still angry. It bisects the left side of his face from his chin up to his ear. It looks like it might be hot to the touch. I still can't look at it without seeing Stretch's entire cheek flopping open at Deke's Salvage Yard. Wind blowing. Bullets flying. His eyes finding mine in the dark. He should be dead. We both should be dead.

"CFD ladder truck is trying to get close, but no way that's happening because ComEd's got two utility trucks all cattywampus working on the overhead powerlines. People are running for their cars to get out of the rain. Total cluster."

But the man behind the hot, angry scar, my old partner, seems calm, relaxed, one shoulder pressed against the window to my hospital room, arms crossed, telling me how things went down at the Bradford. Just like old times. He's working on a beard to go with the mustache. It's patchy; sparse in all the wrong places. Still a long way to go before it can hide the past.

"I'd called it in to Naperville as well as the Feds so now they're all starting to show up. Absolute circus. We get the room number, top floor, like you said. Fucking elevators are shut down. We climb the stairs, going the wrong way, pulling ourselves up through gobs of people going down. Fire alarm's going off, the whole thing. Get up there. Twill and his wife both there and accounted for. I'd called the lawyer, whatshisname, Davidson. He'd called Twill and told him not to open that door for anyone. And they don't. Not even to us at first. We have to convince him through the peep hole. Twill keeps asking for you. Santiago had to convince him I didn't have a gun to his head. Your LT is a little low on trust."

"Can you blame him?"

"No. Just sayin'. Anyway. Finally, they let us in. Place is clean. Everybody's okay. We leave a Naperville hump with them and head back out into the hallway. Close the door."

Stretch points his finger across the hospital room. I know better than to look. His head's still in the hotel.

"Santiago spots these two guys. Coming out of the stairwell. They're all the way at the end of the fucking hall. I'm lookin' through two dozen people. Something about 'em, Santiago says. So we stop. And they keep coming until one of them sees us, and then they stop too. And the four of us are at opposite ends of the hall staring at each other, trying to get a better sense of things through all the people. They could've been anybody. Which makes them dumbasses, because all they had to do was pick a fucking door and pretend to be looking for a cardkey. But no. Guy on the left sticks his hand in his coat, pulls out a piece. Fuck. So now it's on. I yank my weapon and start yelling and everybody in that hallway goes berserk. I'm afraid this guy's gonna test his luck. No way for us to shoot back without killing the tourists. I mean this guy's drawing down and doesn't care who he hits, right? Guy next to him loses his nerve. Grabs the other guy's arm and runs. They're both headed back for the exit. Santiago bolts. I'm right behind at first, but the kid is too fast. He's a fuckin' cheetah. He's gone. We chase those motherfuckers down twenty-five flights, screaming for people to get out of the way. I'm worried they're gonna duck off onto some other floor but I can see Santiago tearing through the people below me so I figure he knows what's he's doing and I keep going down. Twenty-five fucking floors, Mack. All the way to the parking garage. By the time I get down there I can hear that it's on. Two rounds, people screaming, running. Goddamned fire alarm. All that. And I come through the door. Gun out. Ready for anything, okay?"

Stretch points to the floor like there's something under my hospital bed. I don't look.

"Santiago is flat on the fucking concrete, out in the open, both hands on his gun, head up, aiming toward the end of the garage. Kid's not even breathing hard. I'm over here behind a concrete pillar about to lose a lung or two. It's like he's just getting out of bed. I follow his aim. Each of these shitheads has himself a car for a shield. Four hundred feet away, two o'clock and ten o'clock. They've each taken one turn, popping up to take a shot, but they can't hit for shit. People screaming. Fucking fire alarm. Jesus. Feds are running in through the main exit across the garage. I'm just about to let the kid know I'm there. One of the guys pops up and sends over another bullet. And *bam*. Santiago squeezes the trigger once. The guy at two o'clock goes down with a hole in his right shoulder. Now the guy at ten o'clock pops up like some fucking video game. *Bam*. He goes down too."

"Left shoulder?"

"Fucking right *shin*," says Stretch, eyes widening for emphasis.

"Serious?"

"As a heart attack. The kid found the motherfucker's shin underneath the goddamned bumper of a Dodge minivan four hundred fucking feet away. Both alive. Each in the ER cuffed to a goddamned gurney."

I laugh in appreciation until the pain in my chest takes away the humor.

"So this is what I want to know, Mack," says Stretch. I wait. Watch him refold his tree branch arms back over his chest. "I ask you: what in the name of all that is sacred and holy is that boy doing in IAD?"

"Wasting his talents," I say. "Waiting for someone to invite him to the party."

Whatever Stretch wants to say next never makes it out. My phone wants attention. I point. Stretch stands and reaches for it between the plastic juice cup and the plate of uneaten scrambled eggs. Hands it to me. I look at the number.

"Speak of the devil," I say.

"Mack."

"Raffi." I put the phone on speaker. "Stretch here was just telling me about you lying down on the job."

"Don't say lying down. I've been up two days straight."

"Go home," I say.

"Shit to do, Mack. Chief's got me riding a desk with a suspension pending ticket. But, yeah, I might bug out early."

"You IAD pansies," says Stretch. "Homicide starts its day with a bowl of nails for breakfast and a hundred one-handed pushups. Give me a couple of days on a good case and I'll whip you into shape."

"Excellent," says Raffi. "Let's start with some sprint work and running stairs."

Stretch makes a face like he's been shot. I can hear Raffi smiling.

"How do you feel, boss?" he asks.

"With my fingers. What's happening?"

"First, the ballistics on Carter Duffy. Two nines to the back of the head. Point blank. Never saw it coming. Still looking for prints in the Navigator, but the word is everything in the back seat was wiped clean."

"No surprises there," I say.

"Victor Roby?" asks Stretch.

"No question. His instructions were to go wait in the car. He knew it was going to be a short ride. He was one step ahead of everybody the whole time. Left me a gun under the table, wished me luck, took care of Carter, and now he's in the wind. What you want to bet he took the first cab to the airport?"

"Why'd he do this, Mack?" asks Raffi. "What turned him?"

"Victor likes a good Tom Collins. Big Man's people kept calling him Gimlet. I'm guessing that was just the tip of the iceberg."

"You know, I'm getting really good at figuring out when you don't want to talk about something, Mack."

"One of these days we'll go out for a drink, Raffi."

"Yeah, yeah. You want the rest?"

"I'm all ears and broken ribs."

"Wanted to give you the preliminaries from our tossing Edward Little's place."

"Let's have it."

"From the boots in the garage? Traces of mud that match the mud in LT's tires."

"Manhattan farmland," I say raising my eyebrows at Stretch.

"Naperville forensics says it could come from all kinds of places, but Manhattan farmland is on that list. Same thing with residue inside a bucket we found in Little's garage. I'm thinking he dumped Pete Chow's body and brought back some mud to throw on LT's tires."

"Makes sense. What else? Tell me there's more than mud."

"Ammunition mixed in with a coffee can full of nails and screws. Care to guess?"

The only thing I know for sure is what I want the answer to be.

"Nine by eighteen-millimeter cartridges. Too short for your average nine-millimeter, but just right for a Soviet-era Makarov."

"Figured you'd get that right," says Raffi. I look up at Stretch.

"Gun that killed Pete Chow."

Stretch nods.

"We need to check the gun shows," he says. "Antiques dealers."

"Already on that," says Raffi. "We're generating a list. It's going to take some manhours to go through it."

"Count me in," says Stretch. "Beats watching *Judge Judy*."

"Anything else?" I ask.

"A shit-ton of karate and MMA awards. Rental paperwork for a storage locker in La Villita."

"We-Lock Storage?" I ask. I can hear Raffi smiling.

"Yep."

"Large enough for a black Suzuki?"

"Yep. We've got the bike, Mack."

"Not many good days in this business," I say to Stretch. "But this might be one of them."

Silence on the phone. He's waiting. A dark-skinned nurse in blue scrubs bustles in with a plastic syringe and a face full of efficiency. I try waving her off.

"Need anotha draw," she says, Jamaica in every syllable.

"I gave at the office. Couple of times."

"Look at you, po-po making funny. Hilarious. Les go."

"Can we do it later?" I ask holding up the phone. "Police business."

She stands bedside, tying off my arm with latex tubing like I haven't said anything. Shaking her head.

"Cops and firemen," she says. "See a needle. Always terrify."

"I'm not terri …"

"You wan' outta dis place, baby?"

"Desperately."

She slips the needle into the vein. The syringe fills with blood. She gives me a wink and a smile.

"Then you got to ride the bobsled 'til it stop."

She removes the needle and applies a bandage. She unties the latex with a snap, turns in her scrubby white sneakers and leaves with a backward wave.

"Sorry I wasn't there for that," says Raffi through the phone as the door clicks.

Stretch stops laughing into his hand.

"Mack is thinking about staying another night," he says.

"I'm thinking the same thing," says Raffi. "Might shoot myself in the foot and come on over."

"That's not at all what I'm thinking," I say. "I'm thinking you're not done, Raf. I'm thinking you're holding something back. You're saving the best for last. I can feel it."

"Not sure what you're talking about, Mack. Look, I gotta go. Feel better, man."

"Raffi! If you make me get out of this fucking hospital bed and hunt you down …"

"The less you know the better, Mack," he says. "Maybe later. We'll go get a drink sometime."

"Funny," I say, looking at Stretch. He's laughing. "You about done?"

"Okay," says Raffi. "There is one more thing we found."

"Let's have it."

"Blue Cubs baseball hat. Two small spots on the bill."

"Blood?"
"Blood."
"Pete Chow?"
"Carrie O'Toole."

ONE HUNDRED TEN

It turns into a longer call. A nurse and two orderlies later, I move Stretch over to the door so he can flash his badge and limit the interruptions. They want to hear all about my date with Victor Roby and the boys. I navigate carefully around the things I'm not ready to talk about.

"He said he killed Nadia."

"Victor?" asks Raffi.

"Alexi," I correct. "Said he got all three of them: Nadia, Danica and Mila Kozlova. Said he found them in San Francisco."

"Risky thing to tell a cop," says Stretch. "What do you think?"

"I think Alexi knew I was going to be dead in a couple of minutes. I think he wanted to stick a knife in me and twist it while I was still alive. I had a thing or two to say about his mother, so he wanted it to be my turn. He picked the right words, but I don't think they were true. Hope not, anyway. I told Nadia to disappear someplace on the east coast. I don't see her going to San Francisco. Just the same, Raffi, reach out to SFPD. Give them some descriptions."

"On it," he says.

"Either of you know anything about a Barrister's Ball?"

"Barrister's Ball?" asks Stretch. "What's that?"

"Something Victor said. He said I was too late for the Barrister's Ball. Down at the wharf. Said it was too late in the month and that I'd have to really like lawyers and bad food."

"Got me," says Santiago. "I'll put it on my list and poke around when I can."

The door swings open into Stretch's shoulder. He's ready with the badge and the usual brush off, but Nick Yarborough isn't having it.

"Hell if this ain't a party," Nick says, filling the small room with big Texan charm. He shakes Stretch's hand like they don't hate each other. "Sounds like y'all had some fun out at the Bradford yesterday."

"Word gets around, I guess," says Stretch as I end the call from Raffi.

"It does indeed. Our boys came back full of stories. Everybody's talkin'. Sounds like your boy knows how to shoot. Sorry I missed it."

"Thanks for picking up the phone," says Stretch.

"Happy to help," says Nick, then flicking a finger my way. "Mind if I have a minute or two with Sleeping Beauty over there? Won't take long. I've got somewhere to be."

"Be my guest," says Stretch, letting him pass. "More the merrier."

"I need the room," says Nick flatly, not turning back.

The pause is so pregnant it's showing. Stretch gives me a wave and bows out, taking his scar and his dislike for Nick Yarborough with him. Nick walks over to the radiator against the window and sits. I wait as he takes a silent inventory.

"You look like hell," he concludes. "What's the damage?"

"Couple of ribs that graduated from cracked to broken. I'm supposed to be glad they didn't pop any balloons."

"Shit boy, where I'm from they call that a good day at the rodeo. They keeping you here for that?"

"They keep promising it'll only be a few more hours. So maybe by Christmas. What do you know?"

"Chelsea Wolfe."

"Yeah."

"She reached out last night. Said she got a ping."

"A ping."

"Means her network got a poke in the ribs from whoever finally plugged in that flash drive."

"I know what a ping is. Does it mean we have an address?"

"We do. Sulphur, Oklahoma. Little speck on the map about eighty-something miles south of Oklahoma City."

"Can we send someone in?"

"Did that already. Two arrests. Three-bedroom rattrap with a cellar full of blow, five computers and a dedicated server. All of that is now getting logged and processed. It'll all be on a plane to us tomorrow. Meantime, our guys did a little on-site cyber snooping."

"And?"

"Lot of connections on that server, big and small. I'm talking global, Mack. Brokerages. Exchanges. Banks. Government offices."

"Those are all pretty big," I say.

"On the small end they found laundromats, dry cleaners, video rentals, auto repair, it's a long list. Bookstores. Car rentals. Fucking pizza delivery joints. And it's all over the place. Your Frenchie Marie friend told you the truth. This is Big Man's criminal commerce business model. By the way, the Blue Lotus is now a pile of ashes. You hear that?"

I nod. "I heard."

"My guess is Big Man found out Marie was talking out of church. He had the place torched 'cause he knew you'd come looking. Probably had her do the torching just to rub her face in the mistake. Marie should be looking over her shoulder. Only question is why she gave the Lotus up to you in the first place."

I think about correcting his misimpressions. Arson is arson, after all, and I am still a sworn police officer, at least for the time being. But then I think of Suri getting pulled out of Rickens' trunk by the hair. **I think of her watching Carl paint the walls red in Bloomington.** *I wanted to hurt them, Mack. I didn't know how.*

"Said it yourself," I say. "The brilliance of this model is its stability. One outlet burns down, gets compromised, there are dozens of others within driving distance that can do the same thing. These places probably flicker on and off like fireflies. Marie told me the truth about one small speck of the network, the Blue Lotus, because it enhanced her credibility with me. It was a gamble, but she won that bet."

"Is that you beating yourself up?"

"No. I've got a lot of other people to do that for me."

"Let yourself off the hook, Mack. You did good here. This is a win. A big one."

"What happens next?"

"Our geeks are gonna tear through that server and send the raw data up the food chain. Investigation plans will develop from there. I suspect this is where you and I lose control of this whole thing. The spoofing network is global. There's gonna be a lot of cooks in this kitchen. I'll keep you in the loop best I can, but don't hold your breath."

"I appreciate that, Nick. You really stepped up on this. I'm going to forget everything I once thought about you."

I extend a hand. He takes it and we shake.

"Likewise," he says.

"What's the latest on the guys you picked up at my house?"

"Marie's boys still ain't talking. Same lawyer for all of them."

I let out a soft laugh.

"Mickey Shaw."

"The one and only."

"Big surprise," I say. "What about Tanqueray Tank? Him too?"

"Not yet. He hasn't lawyered up. He wants a deal. Says you promised him full immunity, relocation, new identity … that true?"

"Maybe."

"Jesus H, Mack. I can't sell any of that."

"You should try. We need to keep Tank on the hook, Nick. He can put a finger on a face. You're going to want him to testify."

"What face are we talkin' about?"

I tell him all about me texting on Tank's phone and my visit to *Skillets*. Nick chews his lip in silence for a while. Then he nods. "Okay," he says. "I'll try. You better be sure, Mack. Once you pull the pin out of that grenade …"

"I'll call you when I need you."

"And I'll be there. But you could think about sitting on this a bit. Let the dust settle a little. Why the hurry? We could just book him. Give Tank lots of time to think about his future."

"Tank is ready to talk right now. How long you think that's gonna last? One conversation with Mickey Shaw turns him from a small fish into a big clam. Get him the best deal you can and start dangling."

Nick points.

"He put those marks on your neck, Mack. He tried to strangle you."

"Yeah, I was there. He's a small fish, Nick. Let's use him. Open him up and keep him talking."

Nick sighs.

"Okay. Eddie Little is two floors down. I'll swing by his room and see if he's up to chatting."

"Tell him I said hello. Tell him not to sweat the eye-patch. Halloween will be here soon enough. He won't be the only pirate in prison."

"I'll call you in the morning. Let you know how it went." Nick shakes his head. "You're really going to do this, aren't you?"

I give him a shrug.

"Gotta ride the bobsled 'til it stop."

ONE HUNDRED ELEVEN

"Morning, Jeannie," I say over the top of her monitor. "Boss around?"

Eugenia Fredericks is headed for the Smithsonian. One day. Not in the flesh. Just her likeness. One of those hyper-realistic mannequins dressed just so in a classic, loose knit Eugenia Fredericks sweater – yellow, navy, sky blue, Kelly green on St. Patrick's Day, lime, or reliably pink if it's between May and August – little doily collar flaps peeking out. Reading glasses on a chain of colored glass around her neck. A head of moppy gray hair framing an expression made of wrinkled iron. Hard, thin lips that do not bend up or down. Black almond eyes. Not actually black. They're more of an intense hazel. They just feel black when she looks at you.

Her desk is remarkably clean except for the single stack of papers in front of her. She affixes a red plastic flag to the top page and flips it over.

"Detective Mackey," she says, not looking up. "He's in a meeting. It'll be a while."

The Eugenia Fredericks mannequin is no doubt destined for some exhibit on American police department administration. A few wardrobe adjustments and she could work well in the American Women's Prison Library exhibit.

"I know he's in a meeting," I say. "I'm supposed to be *in* that meeting. I just don't know where the meeting is."

Eugenia inclines her face, taking in the horror show on top of my shoulders. If she has any thoughts about my appearance, she does not share them nor even hint at what those thoughts might be.

"No one told me," she says, adding some new wrinkles to her forehead.

"No one told me either until …" I look at my watch, "until about ninety minutes ago. I tried to get them to have the meeting at my place so I could stay in bed, but Dan Brewster didn't like that idea much. Something about being beneath the dignity of the OAG. So now I'm late for said meeting because I've been down in the IAD conference room waiting for everyone to show up. No one has. So my finely honed detective instinct tells me that I got the wrong conference room. Thought I'd try yours."

It hurts to stand for more than a few minutes. Every other breath comes with a stab in the chest and the voice of my ER doc suggesting I stay off my feet as much as possible. He wants me to lie down. If I can't lie down, he wants me to sit down. Anywhere will do as long as it's not behind the wheel of a car. Suits me. I want to sit down. I want to lie down. But I resist the urge. I smile and wait for Eugenia Fredricks to think things through.

The slit beneath her nose opens to deliver a verdict, but then those black hazel eyes focus on something behind me. Two guys, suits, ties, bumble-thumping their way through the door, each holding a stack of two banker's boxes full of documents. Eugenia's eyes seem to know what the boxes are all about. She stands, pointing past me.

"Follow me," she says.

"Me?" I ask, knowing better.

"No, not you." Her pointing arm directs me down the hall to the conference room. "You go that way. You two come with me."

The seventh-floor conference room is more than a little improvement over the room IAD uses to sort out who has done what to whom. Tall-back, toffee-colored leather chairs surround a table that is large and oval and polished to a rich glossy brown. I don't know my woods, but I know real wood when I see it. Pretty sure the table downstairs is made of something else. The south wall is all glass, broken into three massive panes, streaked with rain and looking out over the puddle of greater Chandler. On the west wall, above a sideboard with a set of glasses and a pitcher, is a framed print of a lakeside Chicago skyline painted on a day that today does not resemble.

Centered on the east wall are four portraits framed behind non-reflective glass: the President of the United States, the Governor of Illinois, the Mayor of Chandler, and the Chief of the Chandler Police Department, Warren K. Loudermilk, Jr. They're all looking down at me with expressions of integrity and general disapproval. Three of those guys aren't actually in the room.

"Detective Mackey," says the Chief from the head of the table.

Dan Brewster and Connor Knobb have both swiveled their chairs around to see who is coming in the door. Connor, closest to me, still has his suitcoat on. Brewster, a seat closer to the Chief, has his sleeves rolled up. His chin is just as square and cleft as the last time we met. His hair is twice as shellacked.

"Unless there is some kind of emergency," the Chief continues, white mustache brushing the words on their way out, "you are in the wrong place at the wrong time."

"I can fit most of my life into that sentence," I say, closing the door behind me. I walk around the table and pull out a chair, my back to the windows. They all look at me in stupefied silence. I sit like it's not excruciating. "Dan," I say with a nod. "Connor."

"This is a private meeting, Detective," says the Chief. "Whatever *this* is," he gestures in a languid swipe at my bruised face and ligature marks, "we can address it later. Set up a time with Jeannie." The polite smile on his face is less credible than the one in the photo above his left shoulder.

"Jeannie's busy with boxes," I say. "This won't take long. I thought maybe I should drop in and correct Brewster's record."

"Officer," says the Chief. It's a one-word sentence. His face is changing color. "You will remove yourself from this room. Immediately. That's an order. Do you understand?"

"Probably should do this in a separate meeting, Mack," says Brewster directly across from me. "I can come down and see you after we're done."

"Doesn't work so well," I say. "I'm about to be fired, in case you didn't pick up on that. Who knows where I'll be when you're done up here. In a trunk maybe. Besides, if we do a separate meeting, Chief here doesn't get to be a part of it, which would be a shame."

"I'm not going to repeat myself," says Loudermilk, preparing to repeat himself. I don't give him the chance.

"This is your meeting, Dan. It's OAG's investigation, not his. You want me to leave, I'll leave. But if your instincts are telling you that this is the moment your case breaks open and starts whistling Dixie, then maybe you should take a few minutes and listen while I'm still around to talk."

"This is rank insubordination," declares the Chief.

"You're right," I say, not looking. "Dan?"

Brewster looks sideways at Connor Knobb, whose jaw is now slightly ajar. Brewster looks back at me. Opens his hands over his yellow notepad.

"Okay, Mack," he says. "Let's have it."

"I will not tolerate this," shouts Loudermilk, pointing. "You are suspended pending further discipline. You will leave this room …"

"Chief. Chief!" Brewster holds up a hand, knowing what he needs to do. "This is an investigation conducted by the Office of the Attorney General of the State of Illinois. It may be your conference room, but that is merely my accommodation to you; it is still my meeting. You may leave and we can reschedule. Or you can evict us, and we can reschedule so Detective Mackey can enlighten us at some other venue. Or you can sit quietly and not interrupt. It is your choice. I cannot imagine how it is not in your interest to stick around and hear what the man has to say. But I can tell you, Chief, that your unwillingness to let him speak only whets my appetite."

Loudermilk looks like he might throw the pen in his hand at Brewster's face. He sets it on the pad in front of him. Folds his arms over his chest with an angry huff. Brewster turns to me.

"Detective, I'm not here to protect your career or your freedom. Get that? What you say in this room can and will be used against you. Waste my time and you will wish you hadn't."

"I'm guessing you're here talking about that email," I say, pointing to the single sheet of paper on the table halfway between the Chief and Brewster. "The one from the Chief to Lieutenant Twill, supposedly authorizing my investigation into the whereabouts of a certain Russian doll."

Brewster looks at the page. Pulls it toward him with a finger.

"Supposedly?"

"The email's about as real as a six-dollar bill," I say. "I'd never seen it before our last interview. I assumed it was genuine. I assumed it was something Lieutenant Twill wanted to keep buried. My union rep, Fisher Freed, said he'd found it on his desk. Maybe he did, or maybe someone typed it up and slipped it in his briefcase so he could release it into your investigation."

"*Not* authentic, then," says Brewster. Connor Knobb starts scribbling on his notepad.

"Twill never briefed the Chief on my investigation until after I'd found the doll and brought back the flash drive implicating Judge Jolie and Mayor Royce. Twill knew I was off the leash, but he didn't know much about what I was doing. He tried his best to reel me in without getting the brass involved. I'm guessing that's exactly what he told you when you interviewed him."

Brewster closes his eyes in a long blink, centering himself.

"Okay. You're saying … you're saying that you were investigating the Russian doll thing without any informed authority … and that Chief Loudermilk was not in the loop. Twill was covering for you."

"Correct."

"Okay, but Chief Loudermilk has just authenticated this email, Detective. Just now." Brewster taps the page in front of him. "Like, fifteen minutes ago. He says he typed it himself. He says he knew everything in advance. If what you say is true, why would he do that? He covering for you too?"

"Yes."

"You're saying he's lying."

"Yes and no."

"Detective."

"He's lying about that email. That's a fake. He's telling you the truth about knowing everything in advance."

"Everything. The doll investigation?"

"Yeah."

"He knew about your doll investigation in advance."

"Yeah."

"How? From Twill?"

"No. I'm sure part of Twill wanted to be a good soldier and read in the Chief, but he didn't. Like I said, Twill had my back."

"Then what is the Chief's source of information about your investigation into the Russian doll?"

"His handler."

"Excuse me?"

"His handler. His Big Man connect."

Silence. Then a half-sad, half-exasperated, head-shaking sigh from the Chief. Connor has stopped scribbling. Brewster pinches his eyes with a thumb and forefinger.

"Big Man," says Brewster.

"Yeah. José Beggemon. The Boogie Man himself."

"You're here, accusing the Chief of the Chandler Police Department of working for organized crime."

"I'm here telling you that he was the inside man."

Silence. I take a breath deep enough to hurt my ribs. I wish I had a Camel in the room.

"Look. I got worked by a good-lookin' Russian to conduct an off-the-books investigation into a missing doll that Big Man wanted to be found. Like I said, turned out that Twill, knowing nothing, gave me all the slack I needed. Nevertheless, the Chief was here to make sure I got the job done without getting fired. So far so good?"

Silence. Just a distant siren cutting through the wet, gray morning seven stories below.

"Good. So I find the doll and bring back a list of payouts that stinks up our department for the next decade and blows up the court system, among other things. I should have been fired for that. I had no idea what I'd done, but I should have been fired anyway. I wasn't fired. Twill fired me, but then the Chief unfired me. Know why?"

"Why?" asks Brewster.

"Because the Chief, here, is a cop's chief. A champion of the rank and file. Understanding. Big on second chances. All that. I didn't get fired. Hell, I got promoted. As this department's reputation with the court system crumbles to dust and all of our cases go to the back of the line, I get promoted. Head of fucking IAD. Why? Because the Chief of Police is all about forgiveness. Unless your name is Orland Twill. That'll get you a knife in that back."

"I'm not …" Brewster closes his eyes. Shakes his head. "You lost me."

"Come on, Brewster. You started this investigation with me in the crosshairs. Mack-the-mole. The mob's wrecking ball. Then suddenly here's this email in the mix. An email indicating that Twill had fully briefed the Chief of Police on everything I was doing, something Twill had never shared with you in your investigation. Makes it look like I'm in the clear and Twill's got something to hide."

"And what's he hiding?"

"He's not actually hiding anything. But suddenly here's this fake email. Makes it look like Twill had explicit authority from the Chief of Police to let me hunt all over Chicago for a Russian doll. If the email was real, why wouldn't Twill say something about it when the OAG kicks in the door and starts asking questions? Most natural response in the world, right? *Don't look at me, I briefed the Chief and the Chief gave his blessing. Right here in this email.*"

The Chief is huffing in disgust next to me. Brewster's brow is furrowed and ready for planting. I wait until it looks like he wants more.

"Twill doesn't even mention the email, and for good reason: it didn't actually exist until someone dummied it up. But now OAG has it. And what does OAG think about it? I don't know. Sure looks like Twill was trying to keep it hidden. Like maybe Twill did not have my back after all. Makes it look like Twill was playing hide the ball so he could bury me. Like he wanted you to think I was out there all on my own, no authority from anybody. Makes Twill look like he wanted you to lock me up as a rogue operator doing the mob's bidding, poisoning the department with bad information. Right? Why else would Twill sit on information that, were it true, gives both of us some cover, clearly showing I had approval from the Chief of Police?"

They all stare at me. Connor's mouth is still slightly open. Adenoids maybe. I keep at it before anyone can think of something to say.

"So the OAG investigation pivots to what Twill knew and when he knew it. Why is he trying to sink poor Mackey? Is someone out there working Twill to receive the Russian doll flash drive and then set poor sap Mackey up for the fall?

Next thing I know I'm summoned to an after-hours one-on-one with the Chief. He's decided Twill can't be trusted to run IAD. He wants me to sub in while they look for a replacement. Think about that for a second. Me? Who on this earth thinks I should run IAD for more than a couple of heartbeats?"

I take turns looking at everyone in the room. No one disagrees.

"Doesn't make any sense, does it? Not unless Chief wants me in place for something else."

"Something else," repeats Brewster. "Like what?"

"*Like what* is a long story that we're gonna save for another day. It's still too soon and it's not for me to open that bag. I'm sure OAG will be dialed in soon enough. But when it happens, you should get in line for that investigation, Brewster. It's a barn-burner. Let's just say that the plan was to put me in Twill's office so I could prop the door open for others."

"Others," says Brewster. "People working for Big Man, I'm guessing."

"Sounds less crazy when you say it. The idea was to get what they needed and then sit back and watch me disappear under a new avalanche of old accusations."

"Mack-the-mole," says Brewster.

"The same. I'm thinking about writing an illustrated children's book."

Loudermilk clears his throat. Leans forward against the table. His mustache looks like a snowy cowcatcher on an incoming train.

"Sounds to me like you've given free access to someone you shouldn't have," says Loudermilk. "You've compromised some kind of confidential information, maybe the entire department, and now you're trying to get ahead of it. You're trying to somehow pin it on me."

"There it is," I say to Brewster, nodding sideways. "That's the play right there. Mack-the-mole up to his old tricks. It just came out earlier than he expected."

We all sit in silence, watching Dan Brewster come to grips with an investigation he no longer recognizes.

"You want us to believe that Chief Loudermilk is taking his instruction from … from …"

"You can say the name. You said it just a second ago. It gets easier every time. It's a name that means nothing and everything at the same time. No one, someone, and everyone. Help him out, Connor."

Connor's mouth opens the rest of the way. It's empty.

"From the mob," says Brewster. "Taking his instruction from the mob."

"Well. Close enough."

"And how does that happen, exactly? Since when?"

"Since a very long time ago," I say, reaching into my coat pocket. "Long before anyone called him Chief. We're talking pre-mustache here."

I pull out the folded sheet of paper and flatten it out against the table. I use an index finger to help identify the faces.

"That's a young Sam Royce, celebrating his first political victory as alderman of the 42nd Ward. Over his shoulder is Officer Tony Rickens, CPD Homicide, deceased. You know the story on Tony. Murder times a hundred. Trafficking. Racketeering."

"I know about Rickens," says Brewster.

"Right. Dead in a landfill. Six bullets and a nail. If this photo had been taken today, the guy standing in Rickens' shoes would be Alexi Novak, aka Stoli, long-time friend of Royce. Brother of slain CPD Officer Joe Novak. Jovah. You remember that?"

"I do," says Brewster. "I was with the DA's office back then."

"Okay, well Jovah's kid brother Alexi, is an assistant to the mayor. He was just taken into custody at a Chinese joint with a bullet to the knee and another bullet to the hand. Alexi's a Big Man lieutenant. Abduction. Murder. Attempted murder. Human trafficking. Alexi's the kind of guy that kills his own mother. Then again, she was the kind of mother that kills her own son. Families, right? Point is, she knew too much about why Jovah was murdered and how Alexi and his Big Man associates covered it up."

Brewster is confused. I'm looking for wisps of smoke to start curling out of his ears.

"I thought Jovah Novak was murdered by, uh, whatshisname," he says. "Little hairy guy. Bishop. Wayne Bishop. He confessed."

"You've got a lot of unlearning to do, Brewster. Don't worry about that. In fact, forget Alexi. Let's stay focused." My pointer finger skips over Marlo and taps the guy next to her. "Next is Victor Roby. Royce's first campaign manager and a numbers guy for Big Man going way back. Also an arsonist. Alleged arsonist, I should say. He burned down his own warehouses for the insurance and then managed to beat the rap. Paid a civil settlement to Rushmore American and kept walking. He's my new best friend. Long story."

My finger makes a leap away from the banquet table, out into the crowd. It lands on the guy waiting for that last drop of champagne to slide out of a flute that might as well be a saxophone.

"And this tall, thirsty, handsome devil is Officer Warren K. Loudermilk, Jr., of the Chicago Police Department, enjoying the victory of his candidate, Samuel Royce."

I tap the photo twice more, just like Victor had done, only without the smoldering Camel or a gun beneath the table. Brewster reaches. Pulls the photo closer. Connor leans over into Brewster to get a better look. The Chief tries to stretch himself imperceptibly taller so he can see while pretending not to have any actual interest.

"Give me a fucking break," says Chief, slumping back into his chair.

"Quiet, Chief. Please," says Brewster. "And this is somehow … what … implicating?"

"Being a supporter of Sam Royce?" I ask. "No. Just a point of reference. See, the 42nd Ward should not have been a seat for Royce or anyone else to win. Dominic Lucas had that seat locked up for another term. Lucky they called him. But then Lucky turned unlucky and died. Fell off his yacht, smacking his noggin on the pier and drowned. The easy explanation was that Lucky liked to drink and misplaced his center of gravity somewhere near the railing."

"But?"

"But I don't like easy explanations."

"You've got a better one?"

"Lucky went over the railing during an argument with someone who wanted him out of the race ahead of time. Someone who knew that Lucky had a secret daughter out in Las Vegas claiming she was the product of a back seat rape. That turns out to be not so true, by the way. His secret kid was not so secretly desperate for money and looking for some attention from her well-known daddy. I digress. Point is, Lucky didn't like the idea of knuckling under to blackmail and that's what sent him over the railing. What Lucky's pushy visitor didn't realize was that Lucky had the kind of alcoholism that comes with a touch of paranoia."

"Meaning?"

"Meaning there was a listening device on the boat. It was active."

"I don't understand. You're accusing Chief Loudermilk of this?"

"Of being the pusher? No, no. Come on. The pusher was Sam Royce."

"Mayor Sam Royce."

"Is there a different one? But back then he was just an ambitious criminal defense lawyer looking for a race he could win."

"This is …" Chief is shaking his head, pretending to laugh, trying to find the right words. "This is …"

"Crazy," I say. "I know. It's what I do best. Royce wasn't there to murder anyone, mind you. He was there to try to talk Lucky out of embarrassing himself in the campaign and risking a baby mama rape investigation. I'm guessing Royce figured that logic would be pretty easy for Lucky to follow. He was wrong. Lucky wasn't swinging at that pitch. In fact, Sam Royce wasn't the first person to make that pitch. Another candidate-in-waiting, a car dealer from River North named Fredrick Bubba Jones had tried it already. Bubbah made the pitch over drinks in broad daylight. Lucky told him where to put the idea of him dropping out of the race. So then it's Royce's turn. He makes his own pitch after dark on Lucky's boat. Lucky's an angry drunk. Royce defends himself. Lucky's luck runs out."

"An accident."

"My guess."

"Where does the Chief come in?"

"He comes in as a green CPD Homicide dick. Interviewing widows and hiding evidence. Cleaning up broken glass from the deck of Lucky's yacht. Making sure the recording of Lucky's last moments never saw the light of day. Keeping Sam Royce out of the spotlight." I point at the photo in Brewster's hand. "Clearing a path to victory. Officer Loudermilk's name is all over the investigation report."

"This is such a load of horseshit, I can't even …" Chief Loudermilk doesn't finish.

"His name is also all over the investigation into the murder of a guy named Blake Wilhaven. He was somebody's campaign worker who caught a bullet to the head in a car full of guns and drugs that weren't actually his. I don't know whose campaign worker he was or how to connect those dots because it was all too long ago. But my guess is that the only thing Wilhaven was dealing was information about Lucky's secret daughter and that he died from an overdose of knowledge."

"You're alleging that Chief …" Brewster corrects himself to the proper timeline. "That *Officer* Loudermilk was batting cleanup. That he was a fixer."

"Right. Lucky, then Wilhaven. Wet cleanup on aisle corruption."

"And why would he do such a thing?" asks Brewster. "The Chief, I mean. If any of this is true."

"Have to ask him," I say, jerking my head towards the Chief. "Big Man is a pro in the incentives game. I'm guessing money. Professional advancement. Maybe some mistake on the Chief's resume got erased. The salient point is that once Officer Loudermilk stepped across the line, there was no going back. Not ever. Big Man has had the Chief and Royce by the balls ever since. It all goes back to the race for the 42nd Ward."

"You're delusional, Mack," says the Chief, then turning to Brewster. "You need to read this clown's psych profile. Last place he belongs is on a police force."

"And yet," I say, "you made sure I got the job and kept it. Plus a promotion."

"Not my …" The words are escapees. They slip beneath the snowy mustache and exit his reddening face as a shout. No other words make it.

"Not your what?" I ask. "Not your idea? Not your decision? You're the Chief of Police. That's why they call you Chief. Whose decision was it to keep me on the force if not yours? Don't answer. Maybe keep that to yourself for now. Talking is not in your best interests."

The table is quiet except for Connor's scribbling and page flipping. Brewster knows that any investigator's best friend is silence. He waits for more. I don't disappoint.

"Hey. Who am I to judge? It's not like either one of them has paid any kind of a price over the years. It's not like they weren't rewarded. Look at them now. By any stretch, the Chief's career advancement to the big chair here on the seventh floor has been meteoric. And Royce? He's closing the books on a long and illustrious political career as a very popular mayor. He's out without a scratch. Lot of golfing in his future. Funny thing is the mayor's name was on that list of payoffs I pulled out of the Russian doll. That should have been the thing that brought him down."

"The list was phony," says Brewster. "OAG is closing that book."

"The list was just phony enough to inoculate the mayor from further inquiry. Judge Jolie went nuclear, and for good reason. OAG decided not to humiliate itself all over again going after the mayor. Good thing, too. The deposits would all have turned out to be fake. Just like with Jolie. So why do it again? I get that. But so does Big Man. Aside from all the chaos, insulating Royce from future scrutiny was the whole point."

Brewster is shaking his head like I've offered him creamed spinach.

"I'm not interested in the mayor, Detective. Ship has sailed. Okay? And you're losing credibility points. Let's keep the focus on Chief Loudermilk. Are you really here suggesting that I investigate the death of Dominic Lucas decades after the fact?"

"What, too busy?"

"Too smart."

"Yeah, you are," I say after a second or two of suspense, "No, I'm not asking that. Your remit is to figure out what happened with the Russian doll investigation. I get that. I'm just providing some context."

"Context. Okay. Context is good. I like context. You have any context from this century you care to share? I asked you not to waste my time."

"Word on the street is that if you're still walking around breathing in oxygen, it's because Big Man still has some use for you. Either now or maybe you've still got some potential off into the future. But once your usefulness is gone?" I shrug, pointing to the ligature marks on my throat. "There goes the oxygen."

"Someone tried to kill you," says Brewster. "Big Man, I'm guessing."

"I gave them what they wanted. Then I ran out of usefulness."

"Probably should report that to the police. What's it got to do with me?"

"I ferried a flash drive full of poison into this department. You need to figure out if that was just me being Mack-the-mole, a rogue asshole working for the dark side, or if I was just a dupe and someone on the inside was pulling my strings. Most recently, you seem to be of a mind to chase Orland Twill up a tree. Especially now that Pete Chow is dead and every dog in town wants a piece of that action. LT can't catch a fucking break. Now he's got a murder rap to beat. I know that none of us are supposed to know that yet, very hush-hush and all that as CPD tries to figure things out. But all of us know it anyway. And I'm here to tell you Twill's not their guy and he's also not your guy."

"You think Twill has been set up. Framed for Pete Chow. Why?"

"You know anything about spoofing?"

"Spoofing?"

"Spoofing."

"What the hell is spoofing?"

"Trust me, Brewster, you don't have the time."

"Or the interest, suddenly. I have nothing to do with whatever other investigation is underway involving Orland Twill. Or spoofing, whatever the fuck that is. My only investigation, is *this* investigation."

"Brewster," I point at the email, "last time we met you looked at me with that email in your hand and asked me if I smelled what you smelled. Well, I did, and I still do, and if you don't anymore, then its only because you've normalized the stench. And that's when you should quit your job."

Brewster looks at the email like he's reading it all over again. He's not. I keep at it.

"Pretty tidy, don't you think? Chief promotes me to temporary head of IAD a day before CPD pinches Twill for plugging Pete Chow? Almost like he knew there'd be a good reason to keep me around. Turns out there was. I took a turn in the big chair and kept the door unlocked, just like Chief and his handlers wanted me too. I granted access. That's when my usefulness ran out and made me a big bag of liability. Time to rescind my brand-new promotion. Send me up into the big dream with a reinvigorated reputation as a mole. Poor corrupt Mack; ran with a bad crowd and paid the ultimate price in his own living room."

Brewster gives me a long and serious stare.

"Are you suggesting, Detective, that the Chief of the Chandler Police Department, the man sitting right here, set you up to grant confidential access to criminal elements and then went to your home and tried to kill you? Are you … I mean …”

“Settle down, Brewster. Of course not. Can you imagine two old farts like me and Chief wrestling around on my floor? Taking pee breaks every fifteen minutes? A guy could sell tickets to that kind of death match and retire a wealthy man.”

“Then what are you saying?”

“I’m saying that the Chief was Big Man’s point person to make sure I couldn’t tell any stories about my adventures as head of IAD. Big Man supplied the soldier to get the job done. Guy named Tanqueray, aka Tank. Chief’s job was to coordinate the hit. Tank’s job was to bring a Glock and a shank of rope.”

Loudermilk is shaking with apoplexy.

“This is … this is all a bullshit, fantasy fucking fever dream! I’m not sitting still for any of this!”

Brewster turns to him sternly.

“You are free to leave, Chief. Next time you interrupt, I will insist on it.” They play the staring game for a few seconds before Brewster turns back to me. “Doesn’t make sense to me, Mack. Why does Big Man need the Chief of Police to do this? If I’m Big Man, I take care of that with my own people. Keep the Chief’s hands clean.”

“If you’re Big Man, Brewster, dirty hands are what makes a Chief of Police *your* Chief of Police. The Chief of Police *is* your people. And if we’re talking about Chief Laudermilk, that strategy has worked for decades. And, not for nothin’? The higher up the puppet, the harder it is to convince anybody he’s got strings. Look at the mayor.”

“Forget the mayor.”

“See how that works?”

“Any actual evidence to go with this story?”

“Oh, sure,” I say with a confidence that I hope sounds more convincing outside my head than it does on the inside. “Plenty. Tanqueray Tank is in a cell right now singing for his supper. He and Chief liked to meet for breakfast at a grease festival called *Skillets*. Last meeting was a bust. Chief showed up for a post-strangulation debrief but Tank was tied up in my cellar, thinking about his future. I showed up instead. Chief seemed in a hurry to leave. We’ve got all the texts.”

The Chief’s color has changed from red to something just a little pinker than his mustache.

“Looking a little pale, Chief,” I say.

“You … none of that is true. You can’t prove …”

"I don't have to. That's not my job. The Bureau is already working hard on that. They've got a couple of blue windbreakers down in the lobby right now waiting for us to finish up."

The Chief's eyes dilate in the shock of a new reality.

"I know," I say. "But you should count yourself lucky. They wanted to wait in your office. Actually, they didn't want to wait at all, but I convinced them that they might want another hour to pull the subpoenas together."

"You invited the FBI ..."

"They didn't need an invitation, Chief. You know how it is; the Feds are never as accommodating as OAG investigators like Brewster, here. I'm guessing they're gonna want to use their own conference room. They're also going to want a peek at your phone records. I'm guessing they find Pete Chow's number in there someplace."

"And that would be significant how?" asks Brewster.

"Pete sent me a message before he checked out. He said it was the boss, not the brothers. Don't try to make sense of that. It'll break your brain. Goes back to an old case Pete and I worked once, the Cicero Four. I'll tell you about it the next time we're both holding glasses."

"Bombing case, right?"

"That's it. Point is, Pete telling me it was the boss, I always thought he was implicating Twill, my boss. Twill was pushing Pete hard for the original forensics work on the O'Toole murders. Poor Pete knew he was in trouble for taking a double homicide and smudging it into a murder-suicide."

"O'Toole?" Brewster is confused. "I thought ..."

"Of course you did, along with everybody else. But you thought wrong, Brewster. It was a double, not a single. Big Man had Pete over a barrel and Twill figured it out. Twill was applying pressure and poor Pete didn't know who to trust. He was worried about a set up. He was worried Big Man had sent Twill over just to see if Pete had the spine to stand firm against some pressure. Just a hunch, but I think Pete wanted to come in out of the rain. He knew better than to trust Chicago PD, so he's thinking maybe Chandler PD. The Chief of Police. Twill's boss. My boss' boss."

I look over at Chief Loudermilk. His face is starting to look a little slack. I'm sure there's a murderous rage in there someplace. He doesn't have the energy.

"He reached out hoping you'd wave him in," I say. "But that's not what you did, Chief, was it? You tipped your hand when you slammed the door in Pete's face. That left Pete out in the rain and me as the only person left in the world of law enforcement he could trust. So Pete tossed the ball to me knowing you'd likely picked up the phone and told your handler that the jig was up. He was right about that, wasn't he? The bad guys put a bullet into Pete and dumped his body in a Manhattan ditch. Then they put Twill in the frame and sat back to watch the fun."

"Any idea who killed him?" asks Brewster. "Who actually pulled the trigger?"

"Yeah. I have an exact idea."

The Chief finds enough juice to snort out a little more contempt.

"You going to accuse me again?"

"No. You've already got more than you can handle. The trigger man is another cop. Irony is this guy's so good with his hands, he never needed a gun in the first place. He only needed the gun to catch Twill's fingerprints. He's in a hospital now with a guard on the door, a patch on his right eye … and your name on his lips."

"You're fired," says Chief Loudermilk, quiet but stern. "And that's only the start."

"I have no doubt," I say. "IFOP is standing by, ready to make a splash the papers will love."

I push myself up from the table, biting down on the surge of new pain. I hold out my hand for the photo. Brewster takes a last look and passes it up.

"We need to continue this," he says. "I've got questions, Mack. Lots."

"Get in line, Brewster. Sometimes a man can watch his future unfurl before him and it's as clear and certain as anything he knows about his own past. Mine's nothing but questions."

ONE HUNDRED TWELVE

The banker's box is either half full or half empty. Point is it's not full. I'm not sure if that's good or bad. You'd think it's fair to judge a man by what he accumulates in a career. What he takes with him when he leaves.

Most of the paper relates to the collection of files I might need when the boys from OAG, FBI, CIA, FTC, and God knows who else, start machine gunning questions at my face. Bits and pieces of files I've snagged and stuffed away, just in case. The forensics on the bloodbath in Bloomington. Unrecognizable after-photos of Carl. Quentin Young. A file of scraps relating to the Russian doll investigation: Nadia and Danika, Mila Kozlova, Steven King, Randy "Mouth" Sweet, Billy Wise, Ivah Novak. Burkhart Lang, aka Hell. I also toss in the stuff I received from CPD about the O'Toole investigation. The scant pages from Raffi about the Wilhaven murder. Couple dozen lottery cards from Blondie's that Dennis O'Toole filled out as low-tech codes for high-tech addresses. Nearly fifty pages of numbers in which to disguise the IP addresses of futures traders around the world, all of whom will one day soon get a knock on the door from someone with a lot of questions.

And then there's this. A sheaf of paper attached to an email from the late Pete Chow. The original forensics analysis on the O'Toole murders. Version 1. Double homicide.

And this: a wadded-up piece of paper with a collection of surveillance hardware inside. I toss that in the box too.

Still doesn't amount to much. Half a box. I grab Marlo's photo from the shelf at the top of the cubicle. I hold her in my hand for a few beats. I know I have words. I just don't know what they are.

Everything ends, Mack, she thinks up at me. *This was never your bag anyway.*

And she's right, of course. As always. She's right. IAD was always just a means to an end. Something to keep me close to the game as I looked for Suri and tried to connect the dots between the mayor and his dry cleaner. I want to tell Marlo that my problem is not in wanting to stay. I already know IAD isn't my bag. My problem is not having any bag at all anymore. Or maybe just an empty bag with a hole in it.

I look down at the photo, brushing Marlo's face with my thumb. I don't need to tell her anything. She already knows everything.

I slip her in the box just as Steph Nellis glides to a silent stop next to the cubicle.

"I can't believe you're leaving," she says. "It's, like, so sudden."

"Spoken like someone who's never been canned. It's usually pretty sudden. Think of it this way: I'm leaving just as suddenly as I showed up."

"Guess that's true," she says. "Will you come back to visit at least?"

"Never know, Steph. Maybe I'll file a complaint against Lt. Wendig just so I can stop in and see how everybody's doing."

"I like that idea," she snickers. "Who should we assign your case to? Raphael?"

I could give her a preview of coming attractions. I could tell her my guess is that Raffi will be upstairs working bodies within six weeks. I resist. Better to let that one play out on its own.

"No," I say. "I like Raffi too much to wish me on him like that. Give me to Glen Sugarman. Let's make it interesting."

She laughs. The sound is delightful. I get what Raffi sees in her. I'd have to be blind not to.

"The IFOP called," she says. "I'm supposed to tell you that they got your message and will assign you a rep. They will be reaching out to the Chief or his delegate sometime next week. You're supposed to call them back when you can."

I stand up from my chair with the usual grimace and groans.

"You okay?"

"No. But I will be."

"Can I help?"

"I need to get this box down to the parking lot. Problem is I can't lift the damn thing without it ruining my day. Care to walk me out?"

It's a slow walk, but it's as fast as I can manage. Steph holds the box with one hand and holds open the door to the office with the other. I can feel the IAD staff behind me. They're all wondering if I'll stop and take a last look. Steph too. Even me. I wonder too. It's an open question until that last step out into the hall.

Marlo, from behind, from down inside the box in Steph's arms: *It was never your bag, baby. Keep walking.*

Raj is more than just a little impressed with my escort. He helps me into the passenger seat and closes the door, lingering out in the rain long enough to see Steph disappear back inside the station.

"Damn," he says once he's back behind the wheel.

"Easy, cowboy."

"Just sayin'. No wonder you work so hard. She a cop?"

"Part of the team," I say. I give him a sideways look. "How's Cleopatra?"

"Alright, alright. I still got eyes, don't I?"

"Not for long if Cleo sees where those eyes are spending their time."

"You're no fun, man. Where to?"

"Lunch. I'm buying. Surprise me."

He drives with confidence. I'd have guessed he's up for visiting Cleo at Sonny's, just a few minutes away. Turns out I'm wrong. He's heading the opposite direction.

"That box your office hottie just put in my back seat," he says.

"What about it?"

"That's either homework or someone in this cab just quit, or was just fired. Pretty sure that's not me."

"Nothing's forever, Raj. Get used to that early and you'll have a happier life."

"Want to talk about it?"

"Gee, what do your budding detective instincts tell you?"

If he's got an answer, my phone doesn't want to hear it. I look at the screen but don't recognize the number.

"Detective Mackey. Chelsea Wolfe. Good time?"

"I take them wherever I can find them," I say. Next to me Raj ducks us under a yellow turning red, fantailing water left and right. He lights up a Camel and hands it over. God bless this kid. "Nick tells me we got a good ping."

"Sounds like it," says Chelsea. "I wasn't guessing Sulphur, Oklahoma. You?"

"If I was chasing the Devil, that might be the first place I'd look."

"Are you? Chasing the Devil?"

"Feels like it sometimes, yeah. That was good work, Chelsea."

"Glad you think so. I'm calling to collect. I need my equipment out of your office."

"You might have to wait on the equipment. My office is a crime scene. Also, it's not my office anymore. Never was, really. I'm officially ex-police."

"Sorry to hear," she says. "Officially retired, then?"

"Looks that way."

"Congratulations."

"Thanks, I think. I took most of your equipment with me. I'll get it to Nick to get back to you."

"Your retirement makes me curious about getting paid. If you're not there …"

"I'd send the bill to City of Chandler Procurement Services. While you're at it, why don't you shoot a copy to the Chandler Chief of Police, Warren K. Loudermilk, Jr. Put a smiley face on it."

Chelsea chuckles.

"Because why not, right?"

"It'll keep him from missing me."

"Tall guy? Big ass mustache?"

"That's him. Why?"

"I kept the video feed running for a day. In my experience, you never know, and once you've got everything set up and running …"

"You may as well keep it up and running. What'd you get?"

"About 11:30 in the evening, the day after the main event, your Chief walks into the office and takes a seat at the desk. Kept the lights off. He signed onto the computer with the admin password and started clicking around in our fake directory. Not sure what he was looking for, but he didn't try to delete anything. Then he rummaged through the drawers for a bit. Then he just sat there in the dark. Twenty-eight minutes, stroking that mustache like it was a cat curled up under his nose. Then he left."

"Interesting. All that in your report?"

"It is if you want it to be," says Chelsea.

"I do. Copy to me and a copy to Nick. No one else."

"Will do. Good working with you, Mack. Call me any time."

I end the call and crack the window, blowing smoke and thinking about the Chief, sitting at Twill's desk in the dark. Question is why? Because he'd finally committed to a sit-down with Brewster, that's why. I'm guessing he wanted to make double-sure the phony authorization email to Twill was tucked into an in-box where it should be if it were real. He wants to give Brewster the authorization to crawl through Twill's email. He wants to look like a man with nothing to hide.

Then it took him twenty-eight minutes to sit in Twill's chair and take stock of his life; wonder how one thing has led, so inexorably, to another. Welcome to the club, Chief.

Raj hits the freeway, headed west. The sun should be out in front of us, slowly cannonballing into the Pacific. It isn't. At least not that I can see. Nothing in front of us but dirty wet sheets that someone has hung out in the rain between the buildings.

Suddenly I get it. I know where Raj is taking me. I can't help but smile as I blow a little more gray out into the city. It's all about the Big Dream.

We place our orders at the counter and head for a booth. Frankie Vali serenades half a dozen diners with *Tell it to the Rain*. Raj drops his wet coat on the seat and then helps me get my coat off my shoulders. He hovers as I sit and slide in. I feel like his goddamned great-grandfather.

"So," he says, a prelude to an agenda if I've ever heard one. "Ex-police. What are you gonna do now, Mack?" There's an odd flake of hope buried in that tone.

"Each lunch," I say.

"And tomorrow?"

"Nurse a hangover."

"All day?"

"Maybe. How many days are you planning on covering here?"

"Couple of things I've been meaning to tell you."

"Okay."

"I've been doing some poking around."

Raj shifts himself in the booth like he needs to get comfortable, waiting for me to express some curiosity. I'm curious enough, but I keep it to myself. Eventually he jumps.

"The other day in the car? The day I took you out to the FBI building? With the milkshake book? You were talking on the phone with your partner about this guy, Blake Wilhaven."

A kid from the counter shows up with a tray. She's freckled and scrubby clean in a ponytail, black tennis shoes, and a red and white Blondie's apron. *Home of the Big Dream*, it says in a whipped cream script.

She unloads two *La Bamba Burgers*, a large order of *Yakety-Yak Surfboard Fries*, and two *Big Dream* shakes. Then she's gone again.

"Eavesdropping," I say, plunging a surfboard into the ketchup. "Nice. Isn't that against cab driver ethics?"

"There are no cab driver ethics," he says, chewing. "We aren't bartenders."

"God, ain't that a crying shame."

I have to wait for the swallow and the *Big Dream* chaser before he continues.

"So. Wilhaven. First, I did some basic print media searches. I had to go back a couple of decades. The *Trib* covered the murder in a single paragraph. Drug related. Gang affiliations suspected. Chicago police. Blah, blah, no leads. Okay? The campaign manager for a guy named Trent Howard acknowledged that Wilhaven was an employee but denied knowing anything else. You with me?"

"I'm here as long as the food holds out."

"From there I dug into public records and social media. That got me the brother: Gary Wilhaven. Lives out in Oak Brook. Works as a district manager for Krispy Kreme. So I go pay him a visit."

"You what?" So much for acting uninterested.

"Just wanted to talk. And, you know, coffee and a doughnut and a smoke. Gary tells me …"

"Wait. Gary tells you? *You?* You dress up like Wyatt Earp again?"

"No."

"So you're what, a curious cabbie? Why does he tell you anything?"

"He might have …" Raj winces. "He might have had a misimpression that I'm writing a book about unsolved murders."

"Great. That's great. You know, Raj, a lot of people out there don't like being asked about murder. A lot of people might take that kind of thing personally."

"I'm fine. You want to know what he told me, or …"

I eat. He takes advantage.

"Gary tells me his kid brother Blake was never into drugs. No way the drug gang thing tracks. Says the family never got any answers but he said Blake and his ex-wife hated each other and he always wondered if she put a hit out on him. He thought there was some life insurance. So I'm thinking, what? I'm thinking I want to talk to the ex, right?"

The shit-eating grin is almost more than I can take.

"So you do," I say after a deep pull on my straw.

"So I fucking do. Sharise Bonet. It's a quick trip to a cute little mailbox out in Palatine. Get this: Sharise Bonet's a cake designer. A cake designer, Mack. The brother's a manager for Krispy Kreme and the ex-wife designs fucking cakes. I want to know how much Blake Wilhaven weighed when he took that bullet."

He's looking for a laugh. I'm fresh out.

"Anyway, turns out the brother was right. No love lost between Blake and his ex, but Sharise agreed that Blake was not into drugs or gangs. Says to me that he was big into politics at the time they split. He was working for a guy named Bubba Jones, who was running for alderman of the 42nd. Sharise said Bubba's campaign fired him and he went to work for? Drumroll? You're never gonna believe this, man."

"Sam Royce," I say. "The mayor before he was a mayor."

Raj looks suddenly crestfallen. I feel like I've kicked a dog for panting.

"You knew? Ah, man. Shit, Mack. Here I am, carrying on …"

"What else?"

Raj eats. I wait.

"Sharise said Blake worked for Royce and then they fired him too. Then he went to work for Trent Howard's campaign. That's when he got popped. I asked her what she thought about it. She said she didn't really know, but that if she had to guess she'd said it had to do with some secret that Blake kept bragging about. Something he thought everybody was going to want. She asked him about it once and then stopped caring. She thinks the secret, whatever it was, got him shot."

"She tell the police?"

"Police never interviewed her. Did you know about the secret?"

"No," I lie. "Wouldn't be much of a secret if I did."

I size him up from across the table, sucking another cloud or two out the dream.

"Lot of work you put into a single eavesdrop, Raj. You've really got the detective bug, don't you?"

Raj's smile lights up like someone has plugged him into a wall socket.

"Yeah, Mack. I do. I really do. And that's the other thing I wanted to tell you."

"You're pregnant."

"What? No. I applied for a PI license. Yesterday. I'm so pumped I can't sleep at night. Look, Mack … I was thinking maybe … you being out of a job …"

"You can't be serious," I say.

"I am! I am! We could go into business together. Mackey and Malik. M&M Investigations. You'd be the first M."

"You'd tell everybody you're the first M."

"Yeah, of course. But you'd know better."

"I do know better."

"Don't say no. Just …"

"No. There. I said it. Sorry."

"Just think on it awhile, man. You could teach me everything you know, and I'll do anything you need. I'm a fast learner and eager as fuck. I'd be like an intern."

"An intern with his name on the door. Who's gonna capitalize this business? Me?"

"Me," says Raj like he was waiting for the question. "I told you my dad taught me how to save. His sister taught me how to inherit."

"Excuse me?"

"It's not huge, Mack. But it's enough. It would get us a head start."

I can't look into his face for another second. The eyes, the smile. They're blinding. I focus on the burger. Shake my head. He lets me eat in silence. I wipe my mouth and do some more damage to my milkshake.

"Okay, first? Head starts? They come at the beginning, kid. I'm at the end. I've had my ride on the roller coaster bobsled and I'm not getting back in line. Second? I don't know how much money you're talking about, and I don't want to know, but you should put it in the bank. Invest it. Figure out what you want to do …"

"I know what I want to do. I just told you what I want to do. It's been invested for eight years. It went in at four hundred thousand. It's more now. I haven't touched it. I've been waiting. My dad …"

His words circle my brain, looking for a place to land where they might be understood. No luck. I try my best to ignore them.

"Proud, hard-working Pakistani cab driver taught you how to save, yeah, you told me. Christ but you're full of surprises, aren't you? What's Cleo got to say about this little plan you've been cooking up?"

The smile across the table fades. It's his turn to hit the fat red straw.

"Ah," I say. "She doesn't know, does she? You haven't told her. You know she'll hate it."

"She won't if you help me convince her. She worships you, Mack."

"Stop it."

"It's true. You know you're the only one she lets call her Isis? I tried it once. Didn't go over so well."

"It's not her name, Raj. She's cutting me some slack in case it's dementia."

"She'd go for it if she knew you were involved. She trusts you."

"She'll squash me like a bug under a heel, Raj. Then she'll come after you. You'll die before you get a single client."

I can feel the weight of his disappointment in my own chest. It hurts like it's my disappointment.

"Look, I know you've got stars in your eyes. Stars are generally good. But you're talking about the PI business, Raj. Those stars? They're the shooting kind. Understand? They're using live rounds. There are maybe a thousand reasons this is a bad idea. Let's just take me out of the equation right now, okay? I'm out and that's final. Okay?"

"Okay," he deflates.

"Now. If you really want to move forward with this, maybe I can talk to some good PI's I know. Serious. Ethical. Good relationships. I can tell them you're looking for a way into the game. I'll sing your praises. Start from the bottom and work your way into the business. See how it sits. Keep your money dry until you're ready to hang out your own shingle. Meantime, I'll sit in the shadows. You can tell me about your cases, and I'll throw in my two cents for free. You have to handle Isis. I'm old, not stupid. How does that sound?"

"You sure you won't consider …"

"What. Working for an agency owned by my intern? Pass."

"It wouldn't be like that," he says. "Think about it."

"No, you think about it. I've made you the best offer I can."

My phone rings out the excuse I need to end the conversation. Raj plows a sour look into the last of his *La Bamba Burger*. I answer the call.

Orland Twill sounds tired. Santiago has called and brought him up to speed. He wants to know if it's too early for a drink. I wait a beat before answering. Like maybe I'm consulting my watch.

ONE HUNDRED THIRTEEN

The guy outside room 1721 looks at me like I'm the last cigarette in the box. He's got nothing to do but sit and stare at an empty hallway, waiting to switch places with his buddy in the lobby, who's easier to make than a penguin in the desert. And then here I come. Someone to frisk.

This morning I was police. Now I'm not. I don't want to feel that loss, but I do anyway. I approach slowly, dangling Sig from one finger.

"Name?" he asks, taking the gun and turning me around.

The guy is built like a brick fireplace. I'm guessing his first name used to be Officer. Then he traded in his badge and a box of excessive force demerits for the code to the men's room at some private security firm.

"Mackey, Raymond. It's all on the badge," I say, realizing I should have left the badge on somebody's desk. "I called ahead for a reservation."

He kicks my legs apart. I raise my hands as much as I can without triggering enough pain to make a scene. He pats me down, then radios the guy in the lobby. He gets his 10-4 then gives the door a couple of knuckles. Twill opens up with a drink in his hand. Like he's expecting me. He takes a sip of what I thought was mine.

"Detective."

"The Four Seasons," I say, looking around as I lower myself carefully into a plush blue rocker. "I like your taste in safe houses. Mind if I stay the night?"

Twill hangs my coat on a hook, then sits across from me on the couch, setting his drink on the table. Wendy appears from behind with two fingers of bourbon in a lowball. She hands it to me and sits next to her husband. Behind them are a lot of windows I can't see because all of the blinds are pulled. I'm guessing he's not here for the view.

"Safe house is tomorrow," says Twill. "Both of us."

He's as lanky as ever, but those shoulders of his are slumped. He seems tired. Wendy looks better, less stressed, not as old, twice as Asian, two feet shorter.

"CPD is really rattled after the shit show at the Bradford," he says. "They say they'll put us up until they finish sorting out whether they want to charge me and lock me up for murder. Meantime," Twill puts a foot up on the table and lifts a pant leg to reveal a pallid foreleg and a dark, black ankle monitor. "Fashion accessories."

"Too sexy," I say.

"And once we're in their housing, it'll be totally CPD's show. No visitors. No calls except to and from Earnie. It's just their way of putting me in a cell for safekeeping. That's why I wanted to see you tonight."

"Who's paying for the B-Team outside?" I ask, pointing my glass at the door.

"Same person paying for this hotel," says Twill. "Me. Best I could do on short notice. We should be okay for the night."

I look over at Wendy.

"Edward Little," I say. "Awfully good with his hands and feet."

Wendy closes her eyes with a long sigh and a nod.

"I know him," she says.

"I figured."

"I taught him. Years ago. Good student. Talented. Then he wanted to join the MMA program as an instructor. I tried it for a week, then sent him packing. No patience. Much too aggressive. I should have known, Mack."

"Come on," I say. "No way you could have known. Don't go down that road, Wendy." I look back at Twill. "Where do things stand?"

"You tell me, Mack," he says. "What do we need to know?"

I spend the next twenty minutes trading the bourbon for everything I know. Almost everything I know. They sit there and take it all in without interruption, absorbing like a couple of sponges. When I'm done, Wendy stands and reaches for my glass.

"If you insist," I say, handing it to her. Twill rubs his face with both hands.

"Amanda," he says. "Mandy. Mandy. Mandy. Christ. First time I've been glad my brother is not alive." He looks at me with tired eyes. "I don't mean that. But this would have destroyed Walter."

"She tried, Orland," I say. "Real guts taking those photos. Getting them to me. She was smart enough to know that you don't have much privacy these days. That's why she went through me. She was loyal to you in the end."

"Nice try," says Twill. "She lied to me six ways from Sunday. Betrayed everything I stand for. Everything her father stood for."

"She'd have reached out eventually, once she was clear of Chicago."

"You mean once she was on the road, extorting commodities traders around the globe."

I can't finesse the truth into something more comfortable. I don't try.

"She had a second phone. I asked Santiago to burn a favor. We pulled the records. You don't need all the details. There's enough on that call list to have put her away for a while. Would have been ugly. She found Dennis and then lost her way."

"Stupid …" Twill shakes his head. Whatever he wants to call his dead niece, he doesn't finish.

"She shouldn't have gone home," I say. "She paid for that. She put up a fight, but she was no match for Eddie Little. Any luck, maybe they find some of his DNA under her nails. As it is, between the blood, the mud, and the ammunition, we have enough of a forensics case to tie Eddie to the murder of both of the O'Tooles and to Pete Chow. I can make him for assaulting me at Dennis' place. What about you?"

Twill shakes his head.

"He was wearing a mask."

"He's MMA trained. You could testify to his skill set. Hell, so can Wendy."

"Yeah," Twill laughs rubbing the side of his face with his palm. "I can do that."

"That helps. And then there's Earnie Davidson. With what we've got, he'll be able to take you out of the frame and put Eddie Little in your place faster than you can say reasonable doubt. And CPD knows it. A little extra luck and maybe Eddie cuts a deal and saves you the time and money. Any way you slice it, boss, CPD's case against you is losing steam as we speak. It'll take time. Everything does. But the wheels are grinding in the right direction. I'm guessing you never see an arraignment."

Wendy closes her eyes and sighs herself back into the sofa cushion. Fresh hope. Twill finds her hand and gives it a private squeeze.

"I don't know how to process Chief Loudermilk," says Twill. "That's not even real."

"It's real. Once you get clear of this circus, there's another one waiting. I'll be there too. It'll be ugly, LT. Chief'll go down swinging. If we're lucky, the Feds will go first; soften him up for the state. He's got a lot of stories to tell if someone can find the right buttons to push. That makes him the one who needs a safe house."

"I just …" Twill laughs to himself, looking at his wife, then back at me. "Big Man? Fucking Big Man?"

"Yeah." I nod into my glass. "Ever since Warren Loudermilk was beating the streets for CPD and Sam Royce was looking to be alderman for the 42nd. Lucky splits his noggin after as stupid scuffle and, whammo, two opportunities at the same time, like two seeds that Big Man planted in bloody soil and has been nurturing ever since. And look what those two seeds grew. Goddamned oaks, LT. A chief of police and a mayor."

Twill shakes his head, mixing the sadness, disappointment and utter disbelief in his head like a bad drink.

"Then the Russian doll comes along. With the Chief in place, Big Man can roll that ball any direction that works best in the moment. Pick any target that works. First I figured that was me. Just like old times, Mack-the-mole. But it turns out you were the target. You get pushed out of the job so you can play the patsy for Pete Chow's murder, and I get to sit in your chair so I can oversee the ransacking of your computer for any evidence of spoofery."

"Spoofery?" asks Wendy.

"Don't." Twill holds up a hand. "Later. I promise."

"Once that's done, Big Man gives the order and I'm as good as dead and so are you. My Sig Saur saved me by getting between my neck and a rope. Victor Roby saved you by spilling the beans to me. And just in time."

"Why?" asks Twill. "Why does a guy like Roby just suddenly up and flip like that? After so many years."

"Love," I say.

"Love?"

"Love. I asked the same *why* question of Victor while I was sitting there trying to pull the tape off the gun. And that was his answer. Love. Said it was because love never quits. You can do whatever you want to it – beat it, burn it, choke it, bury it – but it keeps on like you're worthy of it. Like you've never stopped being worthy."

"Any idea what that means?" asks Twill.

"Not a clue," I lie. "Victor was talking in code for most of that conversation. I got what he was telling me about you at the Bradford. Some of the other stuff he said, not so much. Does the Barrister's Ball ring any bells?"

"The Barrister's Ball?" Twill looks at Wendy. She shakes her head.

"Victor said I was too late for the Barrister's Ball. Down at the wharf? Said it was nothing but lawyers and bad food but somehow it was too bad I had missed it."

"Got me," shrugs Twill. "Someone should be able to run that down."

"Raphael Santiago," I nod. "As soon as he gets some well-earned sleep. And speaking of, I think our boy might be making the move to Wexler's shop."

"Homicide?"

"Stretch Martin has him under his wing. He's good for it, LT."

Twill nods in silence, his weary brain dismantling the IAD machine he'd spent so much time building. He leans forward, elbows to knees.

"I'm not sure how to say what I need to say, Mack. Other than Earnie and the Chicago Police Department, you're the only one who knows where I am. That's because you're the only one I trust." Twill extends a hand my way. "I'm sorry it took me so long to get here. I'm sorry for the things I said to you. I'm sorry I ever doubted you. Thank you."

It's an awkward, satisfying shake.

"What are you going to do?" I ask. "When all of the dust settles?"

"Assuming I'm fully exonerated? No idea."

"The City of Chandler is going to owe you one hell of an apology. And it's going to need a new Chief."

Twill makes a smirking sound. Then silence, his and hers, as the thinking starts.

"Something to mull over," I say. "In all of your spare time."

"I'm going to teach his skinny white ass some self-defense," says Wendy. It hurts to laugh. It feels wonderful.

"What about you?" asks Twill. "You going to fight this?"

"IFOP is spinning up. We'll see what the department wants to do. If I know Mayor Houston, he's not going to let Loudermilk call the shots in my case. Chief's about to get some leave time so he can interview lawyers."

"He can't have mine."

"And we're a day or two away from the media losing its collective shit. This'll be ugly, Orland. For everybody."

"I'm in your corner, Mack," says Twill.

I struggle up to my feet. Hand him my glass.

"First priority is to fix my ribs and learn how to sleep again. Harder than you might think. After that, it's anybody's guess."

"Can you drive okay like this?" asks Wendy.

"My doctors don't seem to think so. My ride is a cab down at the curb; a fresh-faced Pakistani kid, smoking cigarettes and trying to decide which questions will irritate me the most."

"I have a question of my own," says Wendy, retrieving my coat. I can tell it's the thing on her mind that has wanted into the conversation from the beginning. "Big Man. Do you think he'll try again? Is he still coming for Orland?"

"Hard to say. The bungle at the Bradford has put a lot of law enforcement light on this whole thing, state and federal. Big Man is anything but stupid. Just the same, I'd assume the worst for a while. Keep your guard up."

She takes one sleeve; Twill takes the other. They ease the coat up over my shoulders. I do my best not to groan.

"Just lock me in a room with this asshole," says Wendy. "I'll break him into lots of little men."

"Maybe he already is," says Twill. "Lots of little men. We think of him as one guy, like we think of Shakespeare as one guy. Historians think Shakespeare could have been several guys. Maybe Big Man is an urban myth that refers to a syndicate. An association. A multi-headed serpent. What do you think?"

"Multi-headed serpent? I think you get points for conflating Shakespeare and Homer."

"Seriously, Mack. I've been wondering."

I shake my head.

"Big Man? No, Big Man is singular, LT. Neither an association, nor a syndicate, nor a multi-headed serpent. Just one head."

Like magic I'm back at the table with Victor. Those eyes through the smoke, telling me things his lips would not. That nearly invisible smile. I look at Twill.

"Reminds me of another thing Victor said that stumped me for a while. We'd been talking about how a Tom Collins is not a gimlet. I ask him about Big Man. Victor says maybe I should consider that Big Man is neither."

"Neither?" asks Twill. "Neither a Tom Collins nor a gimlet? What the hell does that mean?"

"That's what I wanted to know. Never got the chance to ask because that's when Victor left to put a couple of bullets in Carter Duffy's head, and all the fun started. But then later at the hospital the doc gave me a slug of morphine and a lot of quiet time to work things through. Sometimes I do my best thinking in the middle of a half-conscious haze. That's when it all came together."

"Care to enlighten us?" asks Twill.

"Victor wasn't referring to the drinks. He was telling me that I should consider that Big Man was neither big, nor a man."

"What?"

"He was telling me, LT, that Big Man is an old, well-dressed, teetotaling black woman who knows the word for rot in every language. Hates liquor. Loves cigarettes and Kung Pao. And winning. She loves winning like nobody's business."

ONE HUNDRED FOURTEEN

The elevator ride down is crowded with tourists complaining about the weather. The starchy ginger with a monogrammed purse that costs more than my car has a freckly kid by the elbow. He's got an open mouth and a finger up his nose. She wants to know what happened to my face.

"Bad yenta allergy," I say.

Her face looks like I'm speaking Chinese.

"That's like what, lentils? Couscous?"

"Something like that, only much worse when it's airborne in closed spaces."

The phone call from my pocket is unexpected but a nice way to get me to the ground floor without further inquiry. I look at the screen and recognize the number. There's a reason for that.

"Calling to remind me of my manners?" I ask.

"Awfully hasty exit," says Tia Lewis. "I was ready to take it personally, but then I decided you're secretly shy."

"A quality unbecoming."

"Hardly. I like shy men."

"Funny, I thought you liked women."

"I like all kinds."

"But you hate cops."

"I'm coming around on that. I'm thinking about a drink. You?"

"Me? I'm always thinking about a drink. I just had two drinks and I'm thinking harder than ever."

"How about we share? I'll come to you this time."

"My neighborhood's a little closer to the ground than yours."

"This again. Try me."

I give her directions and disconnect the call with those two words still clinking around in my head like a couple of ice cubes. *Try me.* She's not after a new bar. The butterflies flapping around in my gut agree.

I stand under the hotel entrance watching the rain pound the cement. Doesn't take Raj long to pull his cab up alongside. He leaps out and runs around to grab the door and help me in. The valet and the door man watch in silence. I can feel Sig sitting heavy in the holster. Maybe a bullet or two through the valet stand would stop all the staring.

"Okay, Mack," Raj says after we're both finally in and I'm fumbling with the seatbelt. He reaches over to help. I swat his hand.

"I can manage."

"I'm thinking you were in there having a drink with the FBI." He snaps his fingers like he's trying to remember. "Agent … what was his name again?"

"Nice try, Sherlock. Let's go."

"I'm right, aren't I?"

I point out the window. Raj puts the car in gear.

"Where to now?"

"Bucks. 73rd and Warner. That's the end of the line. I'm meeting someone there who'll take me home."

Raj makes a face. I don't give him a chance to make any words.

"Whatever that expression means, keep it to yourself."

"You still thinking about my offer?" he asks, lighting up, pulling away.

My brain knows exactly where to find the tenderness, like a tongue knows its way to an abscessed tooth: my cab driver has more money than I do. A lot more.

"No," I say. I leave it at that.

Kyle is at the bar bent over a book as I shuffle in. Slow night. Three singles and a double, all at tables. Diana Krall hovers in the air, covering Patsy Cline's *Crazy*. All the money waves like it's glad to see me.

"Hey Mack," he says. I can tell by the way he doesn't react to the bruising or the ligature marks that he's already been briefed. He and Doris have been talking. I'm guessing he's all up to speed on our shootout at the Kung Pao Corral.

"Kyle," I say with a nod, coming to a stop at the bar. "Reading on the job?"

He looks down at the book, then holds it up. *Moby Dick*.

"Spoiler alert," I say. "Doesn't go well."

"I'm aware. Comparative Lit. I'm reading like three books at the same time. *Moby. Wuthering Heights. The Picture of Dorian Gray*."

"I think your professor might be obsessed with obsession."

"Ah, right, but here's the question, Mack: obsession over hate, obsession over love, obsession over self. The same? Different? Discuss."

I point up at the ceiling like Patsy and Diana have all the answers.

"It all leads to crazy, Kyle. If you don't know that already, you will. And you're not gonna learn it in a book."

"A man of obsessions, are you?"

"My obsession is sitting in a dark booth with a cold drink."

"I can make that happen," he says, hitching his chin at the far corner. "I'll bring it to you."

"Good man. While you're at it, bring me your best *Chenin Blanc.*"

"Excuse me?"

"Not for me, kid. Where's Doris?"

"Haven't seen her."

I nod and shuffle through the bar to the back. I think of taking off my coat. The idea is about as appealing as dropping to the floor and rattling off fifty pushups. Something I could have done once upon a time. The dropping to the floor part is still easy enough, but not the rest.

I decide to keep the trench coat on. Who knows how long I'll be here. Just ask the butterflies. This could be a one-drink proposition.

I slide in. Kyle is at the table with the drinks before the pain is gone from my face.

"I'm not supposed to bring it up," he says. "I know you're hurting. Let me know if I can do something, Mack."

"You just did," I say, raising my glass in grateful salute.

I put the Old Forester to work as Kyle turns and heads for the bar. He's only halfway home when the front door opens. Tia Lewis steps in out of the rain, shaking an umbrella that she leans against the wall. She's a vision in wet black with a molten interior that the coat keeps trying to hide.

It doesn't take her but a second to spot me and head my direction, shedding her coat along the way. The dress is a soft pleated blood-orange with a form-fitting bodice. The carnelian pendant around her neck is capped in silver to match the earrings.

She stops at the table and takes me in, starting at my face and neck. She doesn't get much farther than the shoulders. I watch her absorb the violence and then find a place to put it. I can see she doesn't want to be the next person in my day to ask for an explanation. Big points for that.

"Don't worry," I say. "It feels much worse than it looks."

"Can I assume this is all mine?" she asks, tossing her coat and sliding in. For a split second the butterflies and I think she's referring to me. Then I get it.

"Well *I'm* sure not going to drink it."

She takes a sip, looking around, nodding with pretended approval.

"Bucks. Clean. Quiet. Tucked away." She half nods then looks up. "There's money on the ceiling."

"I hadn't noticed," I say. "Sorry about the other night."

"Don't be. Looked like ..." she lingers on my face. "... serious business. Everything work out?"

"More or less. How have you been getting on?"

"Better than you from the look of things."

We dance around each other for a while. News and weather in a shallow banter. She tucks her silky dark hair behind her ears and closes her lids over liquid brown eyes in a half-serious, half-flirty game of peekaboo. She smells divine. Flowers in the rain. Almost helps her mask the desperation. No hiding that. But it's not me she wants. Not really. It's the dead woman next to me. Guess we have that in common.

"I'm glad you called," I say after Kyle has dropped off a second round.

"Me too," she says, not understanding. Her smile sheds the last of its clothing. "I had a good feeling."

"I have more information," I say. "About Marlo."

I wait for her smile to pick up its clothes and slink off into her wine glass to recompose itself.

"Okay. What do you know?"

"She went to work for the Royce campaign, undercover, posing as you, on behalf of a client."

"The widow Lucas."

"Kind of. Francine was not the one who started it. Marlo showed up at Francine's door already on the hunt. She had information in her back pocket that Lucky's death was not the accident everyone thought it was. She wanted to investigate what she thought was a murder. Francine was her first stop. Turned out Francine was already on board. She gave Marlo the grand tour; opened all the cupboards and drawers."

"You're saying she used Francine," says Tia.

"Too harsh. Marlo and Francine wanted the same thing."

"Answers."

"Right."

"Then you don't believe Marlo was actually ..." Tia doesn't finish.

"Working for Royce to cover up a murder and get him elected? No."

Tia closes her eyes in a silent prayer of gratitude. It doesn't last long.

"So then it was Royce?"

"Murder? Doubt it."

"He's innocent?"

"Mmm, don't really believe that either. Maybe not premeditated murder, but Royce was on the boat and Marlo knew it."

"How?" she asks. "Who told her that?"

I take a sip.

"Victor Roby told her that."

"What?" Tia's eyes want out of their sockets.

"Hang onto your glass. It gets better."

I walk her through the basics. A young, mobbed-up number cruncher in love with a soon-to-be pregnant, soon-to-be hunted, soon-to-be dead sex worker. A life of keeping tabs on an adopted kid who may or may not be *his* kid and nurturing a slow-simmering revenge fantasy. The big chance he's looking for comes with playing the campaign manager for a mark, Sam Royce, wanting to nudge Lucky Lucas out of the running for the 42nd Ward. The kid, meanwhile, one-half of the infamous muckraking duo, Teelew and Makline, is fresh out of college. She scraps a career in journalism to hang out a shingle as a PI. Her first case is a doozy.

"Jesus Christ," whispers Tia. "I didn't even know she was adopted."

"Who did? Not me. Maybe not her." I drink. Tia waits. "I'd have thought she'd have told me; all the conversations we had about her parents. I went to Henry's funeral. Is it possible she didn't know the truth staring her in the face? She told me Henry and Cora were big into collecting foster kids. Like it was all Cora lived for."

"And Jimmy," says Tia.

"Yeah. Jimmy was different in every way. I used to joke that *he* was adopted. Marlo always scoffed. Turns out I was close. Which makes Marlo either clueless or … Hell, maybe she did know. Marlo had her secrets."

"Okay, but Victor Roby? The sperm donor is … is fucking …"

She doesn't finish the thought. I drink and squint.

"Maybe. He seems to doubt that now. Point is, Victor thought of Marlo as his daughter, whatever the DNA might have to say about it."

"And so he tips Marlo off … what, anonymously?"

"Of course."

"You're saying Victor tipped her off that Lucky was murdered and that Sam Royce had something to do with it."

"Right. So Marlo swings by Francine's place and picks up a client. Then she swings by your place and picks up some business cards. Then she infiltrates the Royce campaign."

"How did Victor know she was going to do all that?"

"He didn't. His plan was to keep feeding her anonymous tips until she connected all the dots and told someone with a badge. She was trying her luck as a PI, and this was a leg up. A good start. Meanwhile, Victor's idea of a good time was that the dominos start falling, hopefully crushing Royce and his would-be puppet masters."

"The mob, you mean. And you know who these people are."

"Yeah. But the less you know about that the better."

"But …" Tia shakes her head at the incomprehensible. "But nothing happened. Royce got elected."

"Victor pulled the plug on the whole idea."

"Why?"

"Because suddenly there's Marlo at the door, flesh and blood, maybe *his* flesh and blood, pretending to be you. Victor knows better, but he doesn't let on. He lets her into the campaign, just like she wants. He could have given her the whole story right then and there. But he can't."

"Why?"

"Too dangerous. To tell her was to kill her with information. Victor saw the future and blinked. He couldn't do it. He realized she'd die like her mother. Then they'd come for him. So he played along but told her nothing. Got her to do a little digging in the Bubba Jones camp as the price for continued access to Sam Royce. So she played reporter with Bubba too and shared what she learned. Victor toyed with her. Frustrated her. Just to keep his tracks covered."

"And Victor, he just … what, he just told you all of this?"

"More or less."

"Why?"

"Last chance to balance the books."

"Where is he now?"

"God knows. The guy is what, eighty-two, eighty-three, and on the run?"

"Why is he on the run? For telling you all of this? They know?"

"Long story. Point is Victor's odds aren't good. You need to understand something, Tia."

"What?"

"The minute you share any of what I'm telling you is the minute you pop up on a list of people who need to die. Understand? They'll make it hurt just to get a better sense of what you know and who you've told."

Her face drains of some of its color. She swallows.

"And then they'll come for you," she says.

I point limply at my own face.

"I'm already on that list. Somewhere near the top, I suspect."

"Why are you telling me this, Mack?"

"Because I know you loved her. What you think about Marlo matters."

"Never seemed to matter much to Marlo," she sulks.

"It matters to me. She wasn't working for Royce."

"She used me, Mack. She used my feelings against me. She knew I'd publish some version of her article. Why'd she even want that?"

"Not sure. Best guess? She'd hit a brick wall with the Royce campaign. She'd come up empty, but she wasn't convinced. She wanted to keep that door open for the future. Preserve her options. She liked her cover. It gave her access to the inner circle. She'd promised them an article."

"And she wanted to keep the promise." Tia shakes her head. "Jesus. And she knew I'd get it published. Because she knew I'd do anything for her approval. That's pretty shitty, Mack."

"I won't argue, Tia. She was a force of nature. Single-minded when she knew what she wanted. I'm guessing she told herself she was doing you a favor. It was an article you were going to have to write anyway, and you were under the gun as it was."

"Not the point," says Tia, sharply.

"Not the point. I agree. Neither is the fact that Marlo was young and impetuous and less mature than she would eventually become."

"So, what, she just files the case away for later, lets me publish an article I edited but never wrote, based on interviews I never conducted, and then runs off to … to fucking Caracas? To smuggle some kid back in a bag of coffee beans?"

I nod.

"Victor set that up too. Waited until Marlo'd done enough digging into the campaign and seemed frustrated at coming up dry. The kid in trouble in Caracas was actually in trouble with Victor's employer. A few whispers in the right ears and the kid's uncle is suddenly asking Marlo for help. She couldn't resist. Off she goes. Venezuela or bust."

"And when she got back, the world kept turning."

"Just like Victor knew it would. It shook her loose. She moved on."

"She got played," says Tia. I shrug.

"Saved the kid's ass. But, yeah. She did what Victor knew she would do. Just like you did what Marlo knew you'd do."

"Well. It's still shitty."

"No argument."

In my head Marlo is leaning back in her chair, rooftop at The Gwen, drink in hand, smiling at me through the tabletop fire.

Stone makes for bad marriage material, she'd said. *Too unforgiving.*

So then you think I'll need forgiving. Maybe I should feel offended.

It's inevitable, darling.

Forgiveness for what, exactly?

For not knowing me like you think you do.

Tia is lost in thought, no doubt replaying her own conversations. A voice across the bar snags my attention. I look. Doris is talking with Kyle, keys in hand, dressed for the rain. She looks my way. Dangles the keys. I nod and empty my drink.

"I've spent a lot of years unfairly depriving Marlo of her full humanity," I say. "You have too. I get to be the worst version of myself whenever I'm having an off day, which is usually. People get to shake their heads and think what they will. Maybe they hate me. Maybe they forgive me. I'm guessing it was the same for you when you were in the barrel looking for your next hit of whatever. Or crouching in the bushes outside Francine's house." I give that point a second or two to find its way home. "She was who she was, Teelew, not who I, or you, want her to be."

"And love her anyway, you're saying."

I nod.

"Like Victor told me last time I saw him: love keeps on like you're worthy of it. Like you've never stopped being worthy. It works that way for Marlo too."

Tia places her hand on mine.

"I see why she said yes to you, of all people. You're not so bad for a cop. I never would have guessed."

"I'm retired," I say. "Again."

"You are? Since when?"

"Few hours ago."

The smile is back.

"Can I take you someplace to celebrate? Your place?"

Calling it my place is just Tia being diplomatic. She means *Marlo's* place.

"Thanks. Been a long day." I glance over at Doris. "And I've already got a ride home."

ONE HUNDRED FIFTEEN

I am many things.

Mostly depending on Ray's state of consciousness. I am a deep scratch across his existence, a fissure that he can feel in his psyche, like he might feel a secret notch on the underside of a table with his finger. A discomfiting break in the continuity of himself, the man in the mirror. Raymond Mackey.

Sometimes he thinks of me as a personal haunting. The kind of company Scrooge gets on Christmas Eve. I am his punishment for not being the man he used to be. The man he imagines he might have been. I am here to make sure he doesn't forget. I am here to forestall any sort of forgiveness that he might otherwise be inclined to bestow upon himself for his own benefit, either consciously or in any of the backhanded ways that one's sense of guilt can be diluted and allowed to wane. The distraction of the now, for example, or self-sacrifice masked as bravery, or the convenience of memory lapse. Or even the erosion of mental acuity. Ironic, I know.

Sometimes he thinks of me as an invisible functionary, an ethereal bureaucrat, sent from beyond the veil to catalogue and report back his shortcomings. His missteps. Measuring his suffering. Gauging his contrition. His self-awareness. His worth.

Sometimes, when the bottle is mostly empty, I am her. I am Marlo. A more compassionate kind of haunting. Checking in on Phil. Checking in on him. Caring. Still caring. Not forgetting him. Knowing him.

And sometimes I am none of those things. I am simply *other*. I am company in the dark. Someone who sees everything. Understands everything. Tells him the brutal truth. Infuriating. Irritating. Intrusive. Refusing to leave. Always there, thick and thin. Hovering. Hovering.

Mother penguin from St. Evangeline's — may she and her stinging ruler and her empty black eyes rest in peace — might have encouraged Ray to think of me as God, or as a divine emissary, looking after his soul.

Ray does not think of me as God. He is neither religious nor schizophrenic. Not yet anyway. But he has wondered, if I am Heaven sent, whether he stands a snowball's chance of making the cut. This he asked once from the floor of the kitchen next to empty bottle number two. I told him the jury was still out. And then, suddenly, so was he. *Out.* Tumbling into dream. In our relationship, that counts as leaving. Ray knows how to leave when he wants. When he needs to. I'm always here when he comes back. Waiting.

Tonight he is not yet so drunk. He can still pretend I am not here. And so he does. Whenever I show him the view from my lofty vantage point above the turntable and the too dry fern, he finds the strength to push me away. To keep me out of his head like I'm a bad pop refrain he picked up in a grocery store. He can do it, but it takes distraction. It takes a better song.

It helps that he is in such good and welcome company. Phil on his lap, pinning him to his recliner, thrumming rhythmically from deep within her animal softness.

And Billie, speaking of better songs. The *Lady in Satin.* She is here too, up in the air with me. She sings about being a fool to want the man she wants, stirring the mood like a broth.

Ray closes his eyes. Drinks. He sets the tumbler on the floor carefully, so as not to wake Phil. She lifts her head anyway. Ray dips an index finger into the glass. Phil takes the drop of Forester with a sneeze and a sharp shake of her head.

"Well, yeah," he says, thumbing her head. "It's a man's drink. What would you think if I started drinking milk?"

"I'd think you'd made a positive change in your life," says Doris, appearing from the hall. She's wrapped in his terrycloth robe, toweling damp hair.

"Eavesdropper," says Ray. "How'd you get to be so quiet? Phil's part human and you're part cat."

"I've only got eight lives left."

She sits on the couch, curling her naked feet beneath a pillow. She sets her phone on the table and holds out a hand in his direction. He lifts the tumbler from the floor and passes it. Doris takes a drink. Hands it back.

"You're sure this isn't intruding?" she asks.

"Stop."

"Just, maybe a couple of nights. I can't sleep alone in my house. I'm really kind of ... I don't know, Ray. Freaked out. Paranoid? Vigilant? I mean, that kind of violence ... That kind of horror ... I'm not cut out for it. I'm not sure how you keep it all together." She combs her fingers through her wet hair. "Please tell me this gets better."

Across the room is the chair in which Ray was recently almost strangled to death. Somewhere beneath him is the place where Alexi Novak stood on his back as a man called Hell fired up a chainsaw and launched a never-ending nightmare that won't let him go. He's sitting in the chair in which Pinky tenderized his head. He relives all of it in an instant. He wonders if he'll ever sleep again.

"It gets better," he lies. "Live a normal life. Get back into your routines. It'll fade. Meantime, stay as long as you like. I'd take Barkley too, but Phil's got a say in this." He strokes the length of Phil's body. She stretches. Curls. "It's her house more than mine."

"Barkley is fine with the neighbors," says Doris. "He's over there most of the time anyway. Their kids love him."

"What'd you tell them?"

"That I'm staying with a sick friend."

"You could've lied," he says. Doris scoffs.

"Ray. Come on. You're not sick, are you? Beaten up. Swollen. Bruised. Strangled. Broken."

"Unemployed."

"Unemployed. Half-drunk. I'm not looking at a sick man."

He wants to tell her that's only because she doesn't have x-ray eyes. He wants to tell her that Dr. Jha would beg to disagree. He wants to tell her about a shadow on his lung. Instead, he lifts the tumbler to his lips. Drinks. Sets down the glass. Looks at her. The humor hasn't held. She's suddenly serious again.

"I thought I was going to die, Ray. I thought you were dying of a heart attack and that I was going to be there alone and that …"

"Hey," he says. She's staring into empty space with time-travelling eyes. "Doris. Look at me. Look at me." She does. She wipes an eye with the heel of her hand. "Breathe in and out, Honey. You're alive. You're okay." She nods, taking instruction. "You were a trooper." She nods. "You and that pen saved both of us."

"If I hadn't stopped for gas …"

"If you hadn't stopped for gas, they'd have picked you up someplace else. And if they hadn't picked you up someplace else, I'd have been there all alone. Two against one. End of story. You evened up the odds."

He offers up the drink again. She waves it away.

"It's a lot to process, Ray. I'm not like you." She sniffs. "I need some help, I think. I'm going to call Dr. Warren in the morning."

"Who?"

A silly ruse. Ray knows the name. He remembers Sam almost every time he closes his eyes. *The dream you keep having every night is trying to express something important. You need to understand what it means. We all need to better understand what scares us.* Guilt, I offer. Advancing age. Uselessness. Ray pushes me away.

"Who?" Doris offers an incredulous expression. "Samantha? Dr. Warren?"

"Oh. Her. I forgot about her. That was ten days ago."

"Well, I'm going to ask her for help. If you don't mind."

"Why would I mind?"

"Because you're seeing her."

"The shrink?"

"Shrink. She's a psychologist."

"Six of one-half," says Ray. "I saw her. I'm all fixed up."

Doris laughs softly to herself. "Ray."

"Don't, Doris. It wasn't for me."

She knows better than to push.

"How are you sleeping?"

"Don't know," he says. "Haven't had time. I'm out of practice."

"Are you still writing? How's the book coming? The one about the doll."

"Ditto. Been a little busy. I'm barely into the thing. And now I'm already thinking about the next one." Ray lolls his head sideways to look at her. "Want to be in a book, Doris?"

"No, thank you."

"Too late. You don't want to be a dame? I'll give you a heart of gold."

"Can you make me younger and thinner? And fearless. I'd want to be gritty and fearless. And rich."

"I'll see what I can do," he says.

"Does it have a title, at least?"

"Still kicking that around. *The Big Spoof*, maybe. You know anything about spoofing?"

"Spoofing? Sounds dirty to me."

"It is dirty. Don't ask." Ray extracts a lighter from the side pouch of the recliner. "Mind if I send a Camel to bed?"

"Depends on whether you want me to leave." Doris leans forward, stretching her fingertips to brush the top of his head. "Do you want me to leave, Ray?"

"It is my house," he says.

"True." She leans back into the cushion. "And your house is hosting my lungs. But I could go back to my place. Alone. Afraid. Blow my cover story with the neighbors."

"Stop. Christ. Okay." He drops the lighter back in the pouch. "You and your clean air."

"Good. Since I get to stay, I have a question."

"Of course you do."

"Back at the restaurant. That guy's phone. Alexi."

"What about it?"

"So I hold the phone up to Alexi's face. It opens. I hand the thing to you. You poke around for a second. I think you were looking for who had called him. But then you laugh and put the phone away. I keep playing the afternoon over and over. All the blood and violence and fear, thinking I'm about to die, and then I get to the part of that little laugh of yours. I'm ... baffled."

It's an opportunity, I tell him. He thinks it over, time slowing.

He could let her in. He could tell her about his phone. Not just his phone. Other phones, apparently. Alexi's phone. Any phone. The call in the train yard just before Deno Porter squeezed a bullet into his temple. The call on the cellar stairs in Steven King's house, just before the wheelman started working that automatic like a firehose. The call to Raffi waiting with Nadia and Danika and Mila Kozlova outside Deke's Autobody just as the bullets were starting to rip. And that call to Alexi, just before the tipping point at the Kung Pao Corral. The call that launched a Chicago Tourism Board promotional pen from Doris' coat pocket into Little Eddie Little's right eye.

Always the same signature. *Unknown Caller. Number Blocked.* Her signature. Marlo.

He ponders the moment hanging in front of him. It's an opportunity.

If he told anyone, it would be Doris. He could explain. With her, he could try. But he doesn't know how he would even start that sentence. *Do you believe in an afterlife, Doris? Have you ever thought that Buck is sending you messages?* He wonders if he would feel less lonely just for having tried. Just for having put his own words in the air for someone else to hear.

Maybe. Or would he just feel that much crazier?

Because, when he really thinks about it, without the help of Old Forester or the encouragement of his empty house, the very idea is full-on insane. So, he worries, is that what he'd see in Doris' eyes? Concern for his sanity? Hearing his own words in the air, he'd have to prove his sanity, not just to Doris, but to himself. He'd have to show her he doesn't believe it. He'd have to show himself. He'd be forced to choose between sanity and Marlo.

So. He worries. He worries that sanity may be a sacrifice he is simply not strong enough to bear. Ray opts for crazy.

"Ray?" she prods. "Who called?"

"Unknown caller." He clears his throat. "Number blocked. All of that effort for nothing. Typical. It felt funny at the time. Pain has an odd sense of humor."

She looks at him for a second or two of silence. She knows him well enough to know when he's shining her on. If he had to guess, he'd guess that she's making a mental note to come back to it another time. She'll work on him until he gives it up. The Dr. Warren thing, too. Doris'll keep pushing.

"This woman tonight," she says, pivoting. "At the bar."

"Tia Lewis."

"Is it a serious thing, you two?"

"Serious? It's not even a thing."

"Does she know that? Because she …"

"Pretty sure she knows," he says. "I'm guessing she wants to know the same about you."

"Me?"

"Yeah, you with the dirty blonde locks and the car keys in one pocket and the liquor license in the other."

"What'd you tell her?"

"She never asked."

"What would you have told her?"

"That you're dating tall, dark, handsome and employed. How's that going?"

"Barry?" She sighs, tugging at a blonde strand. "A nice distraction. Clock's ticking, though. He's a little too … squared away. A little too perfect."

"Ah. Perfection. A quality I like in people I hate."

"He's not someone to hate."

"You're not trying, Doris. Put your back into it. I'll help. I've got lots of new time on my hands."

"You going to fight the dismissal? Sounds to me like your Chief has given you a pretty good hand to play. Can't imagine anyone over there is going to want those kinds of headlines."

"Don't know yet," he says, taking another drink. "Maybe. Maybe bargain my way back into a pension. Something tells me you've got an opinion on this, Doris."

"My opinion? I'd like to see that whole building as a pile of rubble. The way they've treated you? They owe you, Ray."

"Maybe. Then what?"

"Another department. Chicago PD. Would they hire you?"

"They already said they would."

"You applied?"

"Sort of."

"Well, there you go."

"It wasn't a sincere invitation. Which is okay, because it wasn't a sincere application."

"I'm confused."

"How about you hire me as a relief bartender."

"You? I'd be bankrupt in a month."

"I could work from home. Research and development."

"Sorry, no. The less booze in your life the better. And you're going to need to find something to keep you out of the house. Out and engaged."

"What would you think if I joined a PI firm?" he asks, surprised at his own question.

"PI. Private investigator? Are you interested in that? What firm?"

"I know a guy who's putting one together. Wants to put my name on the door."

"Your name," she coos. "My."

"At least the first letter," he says. "I'm just kicking it around."

Doris smiles.

"I like this idea," she says, not knowing nearly enough. "Raymond Mackey, Private Eye. Following in Marlo's footsteps."

"Always," says Ray.

"You're going to need a fedora. You realize that."

"Stop. Just an idea. Probably a bad one."

Doris' phone pings and buzzes against the table. She stretches. Looks. She sighs and sets her thumbs to typing.

"Kyle," she says under her breath. "He says we're a case short of whiskey."

"It wasn't me."

"Need to get on that first thing. It's like the world doesn't get that I almost died." The message whooshes away. She keeps scrolling. She laughs to herself. "Boy. Knew *he* wouldn't stay out for long."

"Who? Kyle?"

"Mayor Royce."

Ray comes to attention. Sets his drink on the floor. Extends his hand too eagerly toward Doris, compressing his ribs.

"Ow! Damnit." His entire face puckers in pain. "Mind if I see that?"

Doris extends the phone, then pulls it back.

"I'm exhausted," she says. "I'm going up to bed. Which bed would that be, Ray?"

It's not that he didn't know the question was coming. He'd been trying to answer it for hours.

"You dames really know how to make an exit," he says, buying time. Doris swings her feet to the floor, scooting forward to the edge of the couch. She places one hand on his arm.

"Let me tell you something before you answer," she says.

"Okay." It's the shampoo he smells. Or the conditioner. Not his. She's in the air now.

"I love you, Ray," she says. "How do I know that? I know that because I cannot imagine a world without you in it. You're among the dearest friends I have. When I was in that awful restaurant holding a gun on one-eyed Eddie, I wasn't thinking about tall, dark, and handsome Barry Wilder or whether I'd ever see him again. He never entered my mind. Not once. I was worried about you. I was worried that something was going to happen to you. I was worried that if I survived, I would be left with a world without you in it. And the very thought felt like a bullet to the heart, Ray."

He wants to speak. He wants to deflect. A joke. A quip. A self-deprecating barb. Anything. He's got nothing. He sits. Waits.

"So," she continues. "Is this going somewhere? I have no idea. Maybe this is the way we're supposed to be here for each other. Or maybe we keep going. I'll never stop loving Buck. Missing Buck. Wanting Buck. There's a hole in my heart that fits him perfectly. That's never going to heal. I don't want it to heal. And I have no interest in unseating Marlo. I couldn't if I tried. We both know that. Maybe that limits us. Or maybe it makes us perfect for each other. I don't know. I honestly don't. Time will tell. I guess. I hope. We'll see. But I know this much." She squeezes his arm. "You have to take care of yourself, Ray. You have to care enough to try. To see where this goes."

Silence. Only Phil's deeply contented vibrations. Across the room the needle has ascended the next wax speedbump, climbing out of the groove that holds the waning orchestral strains of *You Don't Know What Love Is*, riding high and quiet before slipping down into the next song. Even the rain outside seems to have stopped.

"Take the room with the made-up bed," he says. "No one's slept on it for over five years. I'm guessing it still works."

I can tell the significance isn't lost on Doris. So can he.

"You sure that's okay with you?" she asks.

He looks. Musters a smile.

"Sleep well, Doris."

Ray reextends his hand, picking up where he left off. She places her phone in his palm. Lingers. Leans in, kissing him on the mouth, gently palming his battered face. Then she stands and heads for the hall. He listens to her retreat. Climbing the stairs. Walking the hall above him. The small creaks and groans of a house occupied in the middle of the night. Once again.

He looks at the screen in his hand.

Developing Story: Royce to Fill Big Shoes.

Chicago Mayor Samuel Royce has been tapped by Governor Alyssia Young to finish out the term of Illinois Senator Robert Kahn. Senator Kahn's death at age seventy-nine last week in Washington marked the end of a long and distinguished political career and left a hole in Illinois' congressional delegation that is now Governor Young's legal responsibility to fill.

Speaking on condition of anonymity, sources close to the Governor's office indicate that Governor Young has selected Royce for the job. Neither the Governor, nor Mayor Royce, who has recently said that he is retiring as Chicago's mayor, could be reached for comment.

Senator Kahn died after attending the Barrister's Ball at the Anthem, a popular music venue and convention center on Wharf Street in the Southwest Waterfront area of Washington, D.C. The annual event is hosted by Georgetown Law School, the senator's *alma mater*, celebrating new graduates. The cause of Kahn's death remains unknown, pending release of an official autopsy. A three-time survivor of cancer, Senator Kahn reported only last month that he had received a clean bill of health, with no signs of illness.

A long-time champion of campaign finance reform, immigration reform, and environmental causes, Senator Kahn was also the longest serving member of the Senate Committee on Agriculture, Nutrition and Forestry which, among other things, oversees the Commodity Futures Trading Commission, a hotbed of controversy during Kahn's term.

Ray can't finish. He tosses the phone onto the couch. He leans his head back, lowering his lids with a long sigh that dissolves into Phil's purring. He breathes, waiting for her words to find him.

My father was a criminal. I had two brothers who were criminals.

And you took the road less travelled?

I've got a nose for crime, Detective. I put it to productive use.

He imagines her, Frenchie Marie, Big Man by yet another name. She's smoking a foreign cigarette, looking out the back seat window of a car that doesn't look anything like a moss-green, beat-to-hell Plymouth. She's watching the rain-slick city slip past her and away as she heads for a private airstrip someplace, pilot waiting.

He imagines her as a child, born into a poor, rural crime family. Mother dead, father and brothers consumed in criminality, with no time or interest in raising a girl. So, he imagines, she is raised in convenient surrogacy, teachers by day, a school system that keeps her young brain engaged and developing, and by night, maybe a chicken ranch, or whatever one calls a brothel in her part of the world, where she is mothered by women trafficked from different countries, the air thick with acrid-sweet perfumes and mother tongues, languages she must work to understand.

On the occasions on which she is home, or what passes for it, she is pressed into domestic service. Abused. Violated. Ignored. Dismissed. She knows things, of course. That's a potential problem. So they keep her quiet with threats, slathering fear on top of the abuse. Horrific warnings. The hungry undead. The boogieman eats little girls who tell.

My father used to tell me that the Devil would come get me if I told.

Drinkers, these men in her life. The brothel. The family.

My grandfather was a liquor wholesaler. He gave the business to my father. My brothers inherited when he died.

Abuse always came with fumy breath. The family business was wholesale liquor. That and the brothel sideline and the trafficking to feed the brothel. He imagines a color-coded taxonomy of spirits framed and hanging on the dining room wall like a family tree. Ray doesn't know. Not really. Not much. But he can stitch together fragments and snippets. His intuition knows how to sew. And he can imagine. He can imagine that young Frenchie Marie developed a healthy contempt for booze and drunken thugs. Men easy to manipulate. Common. Fungible. Disposable. Good for soldiers. Good for pawns.

Such raw beginnings might have fueled a life meant for law enforcement. That's what she had wanted him to believe, anyway; that hers was the road not taken in her family. A lie, of course. She took the same road her father and brothers had travelled. She widened it. Paved it. Turned it into the Autobahn. They underestimated her at every turn. She was too smart. Too ambitious. She grew up. Kept going to school. Kept getting smarter. And, one-by-one, she put them away. With a smile, he assumes.

Devil was busy, I guess.

Then she took over. She devoured the boogieman of her nightmares. And then she became him. José Beggemon. Big Man.

Ray opens his eyes. Not something he particularly wants to do. He wants to sleep. He needs to sleep. What he doesn't need is the dream. He can feel it waiting for him, lurking just behind the veil, chainsaw idling. Dead-of-night screaming is probably the last thing Doris needs. At least one of them should get some sleep. He thinks about sleeping out in the car.

That makes him think about the other thing he needs. But he can't have that either. Not here, anyway.

He grabs what he needs from the side pouch of the chair, then lifts Phil off his lap, holding her as he works on standing upright. It takes time, the pain in his chest awakening, refreshing itself. I show him what it all looks like from my perspective. He hates me for it, just like always.

He sets Phil back down in the chair and steps carefully over the empty tumbler on the floor. He could have picked it up. Put it on the table. But that would require stooping. So he keeps moving.

He stops halfway to the door so he can listen. Billie is slipping into another melancholic groove. *I get along without you very well,* she sings. But no one is buying it. Certainly not Ray. It's not a song meant to be believed. He's not really listening to Billie anyway; he's listening *through* her, up through the floorboards. He's listening for the sound of the woman sleeping in Marlo's bed.

A creak. A window sliding open in its frame. An old, achingly familiar groan of bedsprings that he feels inside his broken chest. *I get along without you very well. Except sometimes.* Ray keeps moving.

He slips out the front door quietly, closing it behind him with a soft click. He leans up against the house under the eave and puts the Camel where it belongs. The flame is the tiny white spark that Ray understands in the infinite universe that he doesn't. He takes a drag. Holds it. Blows a long trail out over the yard, the smoke curling in on itself, then billowing out in the direction of the sidewalk and the dark street beyond.

All to the sound of dripping.

Not rain. Dripping.

He looks up, just as I take my position somewhere above the roofline, halfway between the house and the elm. There are clouds, enormous dark individuals, drifting, lumbering away from each other, limned in silver by a moon he cannot yet see.

He pushes off from the house, tracing the narrow walk to the driveway, and then down the driveway to the street. He puts the Camel between his lips and pats himself down. Finds his phone. He flips it open and scrolls until he finds the most recent … what. The most recent touch. Let's call it that. A touch. The most recent poke in the chest. Because why not?

Unknown Caller. Number Blocked.

Ray takes a drag. Blows his smoke. The damp pavement brightens in an ever-widening silver sheen.

He hits redial. Pokes back. Holds the phone to his ear.

Because why not?

He shambles along Maltese Road, slowly, just behind the pain in his chest, arcing through a neighborhood long asleep and dreaming. I keep floating along behind like a balloon tied to his belt loop.

Nice night for a walk. Just the three of us.

An Assurance from the Author

Dear Readers and Listeners:

Whatever may be lacking in the depth of my creativity or intelligence (please hold your fire), I can assure you that there is nothing artificial about it. Indeed, I want you to know that artificial intelligence has played no part in any aspect of either the writing or the audible performance of this book, both of which are the exclusive product of red-blooded human effort. That we live in an age in which such assurance has become necessary in the realm of the creative and performing arts is, well, I will let you choose the adjective. We live in interesting times.

For Your Consideration

Independent writers and publishers, deprived of the reach and resources of their gold-plated, establishment relations (by a difference that requires astronomical telescopes and laser technology to calculate), live and die by the reviews of their readers, or the lack of such reviews. The same astronomical tools and laser technology is necessary to measure the depth of gratitude the author feels for those who, having now finished this novel, are willing to leave a review on Amazon to either encourage other readers or warn them away. It takes just a moment, and you will have made a tremendous, even if incremental, difference in the lives of those who read independently published books and those who write them. Also, Heaven. You'll go to Heaven. Eventually. Thank you.

ABOUT THE AUTHOR

Owen Thomas has written seven books: **The Lion Trees** (which has garnered over sixteen international book awards, including the Amazon Kindle Book Award, the Eric Hoffer Book Award, the Book and Author Book of the Year, the Beverly Hills International Book Award and, most recently, a finalist in the 2020 Book Excellence Awards); **Mother Blues** (a novel of music and mystery set in post-Hurricane Harvey Texas); **Message in a Bullet: A Raymond Mackey Mystery** (the first in a series of detective novels); **The Russian Doll: A Raymond Mackey Mystery** (the second book in that series); **The Big Dream: A Raymond Mackey Mystery** (the third book in that series); **Signs of Passing** (a book of interconnected short stories, and winner of fourteen book awards, including the 2014 Pacific Book Awards for Short Fiction, also named one of the 100 Most Notable Books of 2015 by Shelf Unbound Magazine); and **This is the Dream** (a collection of stories and novellas that explore that perplexing liminal distance between who we are and what we want). Owen lives and writes twelve hundred feet up the side of a volcano on an island in the middle of the Pacific Ocean. You can reach Owen through his author website at www.owenthomasliterary.com.